THE SPIKATUR CYCLE

The Dray Prescot Series

THE SPIKATUR CYCLE

Kenneth Bulmer

writing as
Alan Burt Akers

Published by
Bladud Books

First published in 2010 by Bladud Books

Originally published separately by Daw Books, Inc., as:
Beasts of Antares (1980)
Rebel of Antares (1980)
Legions of Antares (1981)
Allies of Antares (1981)

This first omnibus edition published in 2010 by
Bladud Books, an imprint of Mushroom Publishing,
Bath, BA1 4EB, United Kingdom

www.bladudbooks.com

ISBN 978-1-84319-847-5

Contents

Beasts of Antares

The Spikatur Cycle

Beasts of Antares is the first volume of the Spikatur Cycle chronicling the history of Dray Prescot on the marvelous and horrific world of Kregen four hundred light-years away under the red and green fires of the Suns of Scorpio. Reared in the inhumanly harsh conditions of Nelson's Navy, he has been transported to Kregen through the agencies of the Savanti and the Star Lords. Dray Prescot is a man above middle height, with brown hair and level brown eyes, brooding and dominating, with enormously broad shoulders and superbly powerful physique. There is about him an abrasive honesty and an indomitable courage. He moves like a savage hunting cat, quiet and deadly. The portrait he presents of himself is enigmatic and attractive.

The people of the island empire of Vallia, cruelly oppressed by invaders, call on Prescot to shoulder the burden of leading them to liberty. This he has vowed to do to the best of his ability, and then thankfully relinquish the imperium, for there are other tasks set to his hands on the unforgiving and rewarding world of Kregan.

The Spikatur Cycle brings Prescot closer to the realization of many of his dreams and each book is arranged to be read as complete in itself. He is determined to do what he feels is laid upon him; but he finds it is not so easy, particularly when the Empress Delia and his comrades are determined to keep him out of trouble. But—he is Dray Prescot, Lord of Strombor and Krozair of Zy, and that canny old leem hunter will not be prevented from buckling up the brave old scarlet breechclout and with a sword in his fist hurtling off beneath the Moons of Kregen into fresh headlong adventure.

Alan Burt Akers

One

At the Sign of the Headless Zorcaman

Naghan Raerdu was a most entertaining character. He had a remarkable penchant for laughing so much the tears squeezed out of his closed eyes and no one took much notice of what else he was doing. His face expressed habitual surprise that people never took him seriously, and his body, short, stout, robust, supported on thick waddling legs, conveyed an impression of undirected manic energy. He was apim, a member of Homo sapiens, with brown Vallian hair and eyes and a blobby chunk of gristle for a nose. He'd been a soldier in the Phalanx, rising from brumbyte to Relianchun. With his bright popping eyes, his highly colored cheeks, his glistening mouth from which a glass was seldom absent, he looked quite unlike what he was.

Naghan Raerdu had turned into a first-class spy.

His jolly red-faced exterior concealed the mentality more often associated with the gray, inconspicuous secret agent. And he liked to laugh.

He finished laughing now as he said, "This fellow Chuktar Mevek—leastways, that's what he calls himself—means what he says. In a matter this important he will deal only with the emperor."

"It's a trap." Turko spoke in a dismissive way, perhaps a little warm at having to state the obvious. He stretched his arms in which the sinuous muscles spoke eloquently of the enormous man-crushing power of him. He had the wrestler's trick of emphasizing statements by physical movements. Since his elevation to the nobility he had flowered wonderfully and yet he remained a good comrade. Naghan Raerdu's spying mission had been into Falinur, near the center of Vallia, Kov Turko's new province.

"I think not, kov." Raerdu spoke up stoutly. He was often called Naghan the Barrel for obvious reasons. "I took soundings." He laid a chubby finger alongside that blob of gristle that passed for a nose.

"A trap," repeated Turko. He half turned away, and his profile showed, keen as an eagle's. "That unhanged villain Layco Jhansi wants to lure the emperor into his clutches by this story, and then—chop."

"With respect, kov, this Mevek has suffered and has no love for Layco Jhansi."

"He told you this?" Nath Karidge, that tearaway cavalry commander spoke up. He happened to be here because a new task was to be set to his capable hands. Now his reckless face was thoughtful in the shadows under the trees. "Or—you saw for yourself?"

"Both, and yet it was the way Mevek spoke that impressed me. I have seen men's faces when they talk like that. I was Relianchun in the First Phalanx at the Battle of Sicce's Gates, and, after we were beat... That was a bad time for Vallia." Naghan the Barrel did not laugh. "It is my view that Mevek speaks honestly and can do what he promises."

The problem was a knotty one. Around the heap of tumbled ruins that had once been a pretty village, up here in the north of the province of Vindelka, the trees grew vigorously, thrusting their roots into crevices and completing the work of destruction. The streaming mingled radiance of the Suns of Scorpio fell in a muted, wavering undersea vision of green and russet gold. A short way off the animals snorted and stamped their hooves, tossing their manes. The cavalry escort waited beyond the line of trees. By the slanting rays from the twin suns the day was waning. Night would soon be here. A decision had to be made before the twin suns, Zim and Genodras, sank beneath the horizon and the first moon of Kregen, the Maiden with the Many Smiles, swam roseate and shining into the night sky.

Naghan the Barrel cocked his red face up and squinted at the position of the suns.

"Chuktar Mevek will wait for you, majister, at the Sign of the Headless Zorcaman until the hour of midnight."

His golden beard glinting in that dappled light, his four arms and tail hand relaxed, Korero the Shield coughed one of his dry little coughs. A magnificent golden Kildoi, a marvel with his shields, an adept of Disciplines, Korero was, like Turko, a valued comrade.

"Mevek may speak the truth," said Korero, "but the risk is not worth taking."

"I agree," said Turko. "You'd be running your head into a noose."

With a flick of his pelisse, furred and smothered in gold lace, Nath Karidge added, "Majister, the danger is too great."

In that uncertain light they all stared at me. The scent of evening hung sweetly on the air, and insects buzzed. The zorcas snorted and stamped their hooves. Overhead the trees bowered us in shadow.

I stared back at them.

"Three of you," I said. "Three right-roaring rapscallion hellions. Since when has a little danger, a few risks, bothered you?"

They each found it necessary to make immediate and finicky adjustments to their clothes or harness or weapons. I did not add, as in justice I ought, that if anyone trembled at risks taken and dangers dared, it was me. Korero the Shield, with four arms and a tail hand and an enormous competence

4

in the midst of battle, with a dry humor and practical outlook; Turko the Shield who was now Kov Turko of Falinur, a Khamorro, a feared man who could break the strongest opponent, a man with a gently sarcastic manner; these two were good comrades, trusted friends, and right tearaways. And Chuktar Nath Karidge, the beau sabreur, a cavalryman—no, a light cavalryman—who swore on Lasal the Vakka and had no great expectations of living beyond the next charge, he was here because I wanted him to put his talents to good use. And, all three, all three reckless daredevils, all cautioned me gravely, with long faces, direfully warning me of risks and dangers.

By Vox! It was enough to make a fellow laugh.

"With your permission, majister, I will have to take back an answer soon. Mevek is somewhat touchy in these matters." Naghan the Barrel laughed his wheezing, tear-splattering laugh. "I fancy it is how he has kept his head on his shoulders for so long fighting his guerrilla actions against Layco Jhansi's mercenaries."

"Risks," said Korero. He pulled his golden beard. "I do not hold with them."

"Nor me," said Turko.

They spoke seriously. I considered. Yes, it was true that both Korero and Turko were among the more sober headed of my boon companions. They were not as foolhardy as most, not as ready to jump in without a thought. Both had carried shields at my back in battle. Perhaps that was why they were less reckless, or perhaps their function as shield bearers to the Emperor of Vallia had made them more cautious. All the same, the humor of the situation remained.

"You say this Chuktar Mevek will deal only with me directly?"

"Yes, majister. And, in addition, he was firm on the point. We can take no more than three companions to the Sign of the Headless Zorcaman."

"Five of us," said Turko. "And I daresay he'll have a little army waiting."

"As much as any man may," said Naghan the Barrel, and he spoke more strongly. "Chuktar Mevek has my trust."

Nath Karidge put his fist onto the hilt of his sword. He carried a curved sword of a pattern of his own design, specially made for him. He looked at me. "If we go, majister, at least let me bring on my two half-squadrons in support."

"Would that not be breaking faith?"

He stirred the dust with his cavalryman's boot.

"Aye. But, by Lasal the Vakka, when you treat with rogues you must watch your back."

The others nodded. There was no need for them to amplify. This view was one commonly held among my comrades concerning certain eventualities and certain people. What Karidge had said merely cloaked a deeper meaning.

5

There was no need to amplify, yet Turko said, "Honor is a precious commodity. Yet honor cannot stand in the way of our proper duty."

I refused to allow myself to think about this at the moment. Later on I pondered the implications deeply, as you shall hear; but, right now, the decision must be taken.

And, really—and as they knew only too well—there was only one conclusion I could come to.

I said, "We go. We go now. Rather—with Naghan I go."

At once, speaking all over each other, they were baying out their outrage. I calmed them.

"If you wish to accompany, you will be most welcome. But, if you think the risks too great, why, then—"

In mercy I couldn't go on. Their faces expressed the utmost consternation and chagrin and downright fury.

They knew—I trusted they knew—that I merely baited them.

In the language spoken over most of Paz, the Kregish language which had, I surmised, been imposed on the people, there are many fine terms of abuse and contempt, many resounding oaths, many expressions of love and fidelity. Some have a reasonably exact counterpart in the languages of Earth; some are purely Kregan. To call a fellow a fambly is to express your opinion of him in gentle, friendly terms, and yet you also let him know you are giving him a little stick. When, half under my breath and turning toward the zorcas, I said, "Famblys!" these men of mine knew exactly what I meant. Mind you, the oafish of two worlds might misunderstand, that seems obvious. To call a man a fambly is not the same as calling him an onker, or a hulu, or any other of the colorful names available in the Kregish tongue.

"I shall station my two half-squadrons—" began Karidge.

"No. I judge Chuktar Mevek will scout the approaches. Anything like a follow-up cavalry force—and he'll be off."

"Quidang, majister!"

Yet, as he spoke, Karidge indicated that he might bellow out "Quidang!"—a standard acknowledgment of an order—but he didn't like the idea at all. He was a cavalryman. It was hard for him to grasp any idea that anything at all valuable could be accomplished without the exciting jingle of harness and the onrushing stamp of hooves.

We mounted up and Karidge gave orders to the cavalry to await our return, and we set off as the suns declined. Up ahead lay a rich and fruitful land between the generous arms of a loop in the Great River, She of the Fecundity. This part of Vallia was blessed with richness; the land sent forth its goodness in thickly growing crops, in trees heavy with fruit, in grasslands where cattle grazed and grew fat. Westward on the outskirts of the semi-desert Ochre Limits the land yielded many rich minerals. This land was called Vinnur's Garden. It lay between Falinur to the north and Vindelka to the south. It was coveted by and laid claim to by both provinces. Just who was the rightful claimant no one now could say. I had partially solved the squabble by an arbitrary parallel dividing Vinnur's garden in half. The locals didn't much like the solution, but had to acknowledge there was not much else to do. Falinur had been the kovnate province of Seg Segutorio until he had relinquished it and I had appointed Turko. Vindelka was the kovnate province of Vomanus, half-brother to Delia. Both were blade comrades. Neither would press his claim against the other.

Some of the annoyance felt by the southern Falinurese against Seg for not actively advancing their claims had led, coupled with his attempts to put down slavery, to the people throwing in their lot with Layco Jhansi. Jhansi had been the old emperor's chief minister, and he had betrayed him. The plot to kill the emperor had misfired, Jhansi had fled to the safety of his own province, Vennar, to the west of Falinur, and in the Time of Troubles he had waxed strong. He had troubles on his northern borders, but just lately he had attempted to invade southward into the imperial province of Orvendel, having subjugated Vindelka. We had bested his army at the Battle of Ovalia and had subsequently campaigned successfully northward to liberate Vindelka. My projected trip to Hyrklana had perforce been postponed yet again...

So, now my spy Naghan the Barrel brought word that the people of Falinur were grown tired of Layco Jhansi.

The time was ripe to strike the blow that would free the province. All the island empire of Vallia had been in turmoil, invaded by mercenaries and reiving barbarians and by the iron legions of our rival empire, Hamal. We had won back most of the south and the midlands, and the northeast stood for us. But there was still much to do. If Turko could take over in Falinur that would be another good step forward to the final liberation of all Vallia.

The twin suns sank as we trotted past fields rich with crops. Very few lights showed from farmhouses or villages; these people had grown to live with waves of invasion. The miracle was the land was in such good heart. We moved on, silently.

Just what we were trotting so silently into did not bear thinking of. I looked ahead at the dark squat figure of Naghan, who clamped his short legs around his zorca and hunched down with your typical infantryman's handling of a mount. After the disastrous Battle at Sicce's Gates, where the Phalanx had been upset by the clansmen, Naghan had been cut off. He had lived off the country, saved his life, kept his spirits and had kept out of the way of our enemies. In the fullness of time he had reported back. His story had interested me, and on meeting him I realized that here was a man of parts, resourceful, hardy, and like a chameleon able to survive in places where no one would expect him to last a couple of heartbeats.

He had proved ready to take employment with me, as a spy, a secret agent—the name did not matter overmuch. The interesting aspect of this was that Naghan Vanki, the emperor's chief spymaster, did not know of Naghan the Barrel or the other agents recruited in similar ways. A small corps of intelligence men was being built up, quite distinct from the large-scale organization controlled by Vanki and which served Vallia to the best of its ability in dark times and in good.

We halted on the brow of a hill where the road, dim and barely visible before the rise of the Maiden with the Many Smiles, trended down toward the shadowy and misshapen lumps of darkness that indicated a village. Not a light showed.

"Chuktar Mevek risks much in coming this far south to meet you, majister." Naghan the Barrel wiped his face with his neckerchief, a gaudy article of red and lilac and green with brown spots. That kind of neckerchief the Kregans call a flamanch, and very useful it is, too. Usually it is fastened at the front by a brooch or a pin or a nolp, and now, having wiped his face, Naghan slid his nolp up and down as he spoke. "We are in good time. And his men have us under observation already."

Not one of us showed the least surprise or consternation. We were old campaigners. If Mevek had not scouted the approaches and kept a lookout we would have been far more concerned.

"All the same," said Turko, following on that line of thought. "It means we may have some difficulty if we have to pull out quickly."

Although we had only Naghan's assertions to guide us in this enterprise, we felt we were not going in entirely blind.

I, for one, felt confidence in Naghan Raerdu the Barrel, and his opinion was that this Chuktar Mevek would hold to his word, even if we did not reach agreement. If Naghan was wrong, why then it could easily be a quick scramble to get free...

I nudged my zorca.

"No sense in hanging about."

We rode slowly down the path which glimmered into smokey grayness as the first moon lifted. The Maiden with the Many Smiles shone bleakly, it seemed to me, cutting a pallid sickle in the sky. Soon she would take on her usual pinkish hue and the shadows would warm to a russet fuzz. We rode on.

This little village was called Infinon of the Crossroads, and the inn with the sign of the Headless Zorcaman squatted in one angle of the cross. The other houses were fast shuttered. The stillness and the ghostly moonlight were broken as men rode out with a clatter, casting bars of shadow across the road, to surround us. A few quick words between their leader and Naghan and we went on, riding up to the inn and dismounting.

A warm fug of ale fumes and cooking and sweat met us as we entered.

The place presented the appearance one would expect from a small village in a prosperous countryside, and the ale would be good.

The floor was swept clean. That floor was made from sawn planks, not beaten earth. Pots glittered. The enormous fireplace gaped black and empty, save for a brass jar filled with dried flowers. The men who escorted us and the others who awaited our coming wore ragged clothing of a raffish, free-flowing kind. They were much burdened with weapons. Almost all were apims. They sat about on the settles and benches, and I surmised they would keep quiet as their chief spoke. If there was trouble—I gave them a glance that appeared casual and which totted them up and assessed them.

Twenty. Twenty ruffians, guerilleros, as ready to slit your throat as to greet you with a pleasant Lahal.

One of them, a fellow who wore a gaudy sash of a color I took to be plum, so dirty and festooned with gold lace was it, walked forward. His face looked like an old boot. His hair was lank. But he smiled.

"Llahal, koters," he said, giving us the name of gentlemen of Vallia. "The Chuktar will be here in but five murs."

Karidge would have started hotly demanding to know why the emperor should be kept waiting, but I silenced him. I looked about, saw a long lanky lout with his feet on a bench. Walking over, I pushed his legs off, so that his heavy Vallian boots crashed to the floor, and sat on the bench. I took off my wide-brimmed hat, placed it on the table, and said, "I will wait five murs."

As a mur is shorter than a terrestrial minute, the ball was, as they say, in Mevek's court.

The long lanky lout glowered, but he said nothing and straightened himself up. The eyes of the others in the taproom—by Krun! You could feel them, like a pack of drills.

My companions remained standing. The fellow with the unmentionable sash and the face like an old boot swallowed.

"I am Vanderini the Dagger. I will fetch the Chuktar—"

He went out through a rear door in something of a hurry.

Karidge chuckled nastily. A chuckle can express many profound emotions.

Turko and Korero looked as though offensive smells were obfuscating the pleasures of life. Naghan the Barrel let one of his wheezing laughs shake him up, the tears pouring from his eyes. He clapped his belly.

"I am parched. Will no one fetch a stoup, for the sweet sake of Mother Dikkana, who brought forth the saint who gave us ale?"

Someone laughed—that was easy to do with Naghan the Barrel—and tankards were forthcoming. I sipped.

Four and a half murs, all that took. On the fifth, as the calibrated clepsydra on its shelf above the mantelpiece showed, Chuktar Mevek walked into the taproom.

To sum him up in a single glance would be easy, and probably completely wrong.

This Mevek, who called himself a Chuktar, the equivalent of a brigadier general, was quite clearly hard as nails, hard-bitten, hard as old leather. He was strongly built, with a flat, impassive face in which his brown Vallian eyes were deeply set. He looked like his men, save that he wore more ornamentation. Yet I judged that to have accomplished what he had, in raising so many people willing to stand against Layco Jhansi and his mercenaries, he had a spark, a charisma, a touch of that genius Kregans call the yrium. He looked at me carefully. He reminded me by that stare, by his impassivity, of a wild animal in the moments before it leaps.

Then: "Llahal, majister. I will not give you the full incline as all emperors are due. I hear you have banished such flummery."

"You are right. Llahal."

"They say the kov who ran off is a friend of yours."

"You are right and wrong."

He merely lifted one dark eyebrow.

"Kov Seg Segutorio is a friend of mine. He did not run off."

"He was not here when—"

"I have heard this before. It is unworthy of you if you wish to prove your friendship. Kov Seg Segutorio was about business for the empire—for the old emperor—and those to whom he confided the care of Falinur failed him. He did not fail them."

"You fight for your friends—"

I broke in. "This wastes time. The past is dead." Well, that is not strictly true... "What do you wish to tell me?"

Now he did not exactly lose that coolness, but he reached out and fingered one of the many loops of precious gems encircling his neck and depending on his harness. His eyebrows drew down.

"Perhaps it is you, majister, who has somewhat to tell me."

I stood up.

"Shilly-shallying, Mevek, is for those who have all the time in the world. I do not. There are mercenaries, reiving rasts, cramphs from Hamal, abroad in Vallia. The people called me to be their emperor and free them from tyranny. That I will do, although I did not seek the task. If you can help me win back Falinur, all well and good. If you are powerless, then we have nothing to say to each other."

He digested that. Then, as I had suspected he would, he picked out the item that touched him most nearly.

"Powerless? Me? Oh, no, majister, I am not powerless."

"Do not think these men here can stop me from leaving." And here I put on a little of the bravado I detest and which, sometimes, serves well. Sometimes it is a disaster. "I do not think you could stop me if you had twice as many men."

10

He wiggled those eyebrows of his again, and I came to the conclusion that, impassive as his flat face was, those eyebrows were weather indicators to his state of mind.

"I have been told you are Jak the Drang."

"Yes."

"Then I believe you."

I nodded. "Then we understand each other." I pulled my riding cloak off and tossed it on the table. I sat down. "I do not think you are powerless. Now, let us Rank our Deldars and see what we can agree."

At that familiar opening challenge from the famous game of Jikaida, Mevek, nodding in his turn, visibly relaxed. We had sparred. His amour propre had been maintained. Now we could get down to cases.

His story followed the lines I expected. When Jhansi's mercenary troops deteriorated in quality with the hiring of more and more of them from dubious sources, the country folk began to suffer. That was a normal risk run by any commander who hired mercenaries. The defeats in the south were almost matched by unhappy encounters with the Racters in the north.

The Racters, once the most powerful political party in Vallia, were now penned in the far northwest where a concentration of their estates gave them a base. Jhansi fought them and the battle did not go well.

"What you are saying is now that Jhansi's fortunes are at a low ebb, you wish to change sides."

His eyebrows flared.

"No, majister, not so. Many of us have opposed the Kov of Vennar from the moment he crossed our borders."

"As I am the emperor, you may understand that Layco Jhansi is no longer the Kov of Vennar. His province lies under an interdict. His head is forfeit to the empire. He is a traitor."

"Just so. But he still runs his kovnate, whether he is kov or not, and he still sends his damned mercenaries to keep us down."

I said, "You have intelligence of the battles we have won? You know our armies have cleared Vindelka?"

"Aye."

"Then you must realize that the time will soon come when we will march north, through this very spot, and go on into Falinur and west into Vennar, and Layco Jhansi will swing very high indeed."

In a low tone, almost surly, he said, "You will need my help."

"I welcome your help, Mevek. As to needing it—that may be a different matter."

Vanderini the Dabber, he with the sash and the face like an old boot, stepped up. That face wore a scowl.

"By Vox! But this new emperor has a stiff neck! If I did not hate Jhansi so much, why—"

"There will be a place for you, Vanderini," I told him, without a smile. "In the new Falinur after we have liberated the province. At least—" And here I judged the time had come to apprise these desperadoes of their new lord. "At least, if the new kov I have appointed listens and approves of you."

They swung to glare at me on this.

"New kov?" growled out Mevek. "What new kov?"

"Kov Seg Segutorio is about vital business for the empire. He has relinquished Falinur. Your new lord is appointed. He is Kov Turko, whom you will obey in all things."

Now, as you know, the rights and the law on Kregen regarding titles and property and inheritance are not quite the same as on this Earth. Necessarily, they must differ.

Mevek hoisted his eyebrows. I began to suspect that he was well aware of his eyebrows, and used them on purpose, to fool credulous folk into thinking they could read his mind.

"If this Kov Turko proves himself—"

"He will."

"Then we will give him the welcome that is his due. But I recall the old kov, Naghan Furtway, and his nephew Jenbar. They had little love for the emperor. Their seed still grows here."

Perhaps this was the root cause of the disaffection in Falinur. The past is not dead, its tendrils twine and choke the new bright growths...

"You know Naghan Furtway proved a traitor and fled overseas. He is allied with the Empress Thyllis of Hamal, and that mad woman seeks only evil for Vallia. You know."

"I know."

"So that Kov Turko will bring a new light and spirit to Falinur. You will see."

Now, all this time Turko had been standing there silently. I could see him. His face, that handsome Khamorro face, remained impassive. But the muscles in his arms roped and jumped. He would wait just so long for me to fiddle around like this and then, why, then Turko the Shield would start to show these hardy, near-bandit guerrillas that he was their new kov and they'd better get to like it...

Korero the Shield stroked his beard with his upper left hand in a most judicious way. He had kept his two lower arms well inside his cloak, and his tail with its powerful grasping hand was tucked up out of the way, so that he did not look like a diff but could pass as an apim like us. Now he smiled.

"It seems to me we are all agreed, but we cannot reconcile ourselves." His voice carried that tinge of mockery he knows so well how to intimate; goads to infuriate his listeners.

Mevek almost bit.

"Agree! Of course we agree that Jhansi must be put down, but as for this new kov—" And then he caught himself, and that dull, impassive look settled again on his features.

"Good," I said brightly. "When do you think the Kov of Falinur should show himself to the people? I do not think he is a man to wait until after the victory."

"Indeed, no," put in Korero.

Turko said nothing.

Mevek said, "If he is the kov for us he will lead us in battle. I have Freedom Fighters, in hiding. We lack weapons of quality, but we fight. Send for this new Kov Turko and bid him join us—if he dares!"

Turko opened his mouth. I lifted my hand.

"We will send weapons. Our armies will march north. They will be commanded by Kov Turko of Falinur. You will send word to your people. They will rise. Together, we will sweep Jhansi and his mercenaries back to Vennar. Then..."

I had overlooked a point. Not all the Falinurese felt the same fierce detestation of Jhansi shared by the men in that room.

As Turko looked at me, his head up, his handsome face verging on a scowl—for I sensed he was not completely sure of what I was about—I went on in a heavy voice, for what I had to say did not please me.

"When we beat Jhansi's men at Ovalia, they were led by a damned Hamalese, a Kapt Hangrol, and by Jhansi's toady, Malervo Norgoth."

"Hangrol has gone back to Hamal—"

"Poor devil," I said, whereat they looked at me strangely. They did not know the kind of punishment the Empress Thyllis handed out to people who failed her.

"And Tarek Malervo Norgoth skulks somewhere in Vennar. He is out of favor, serve the rast up stewed black."

"We were attacked by hordes of screaming savages—yet they were once ordinary citizens of Vallia. This is sorcery." I did not miss the flicker of fear in many faces. "This displeases me. Can you contain this? Can you handle these misguided fanatics? Will you succumb to the sorcery of Rovard the Murvish?"

This did not go down at all well.

Many were the protestations, many the oaths, many the knotty fists thumped on tables. But these men had felt the breath of fear. Rovard the Murvish, an initiate in the Brotherhood of the Sorcerers of Murcroinim, an adept of real powers, had almost trapped me in a web of sorcery. Jhansi had a trenchant tool in this sorcerer.

At last Mevek said over the hubbub, "We have seen the misguided men this wizard has spelled. Yes, they fight like crazy animals. But, they may be killed."

This, then, was the nub of my displeasure.

We talked for a space, with Turko growing more and more tense and showing every symptom of blowing up, quite unlike his usual distant mockery of me. I inquired about various people whose welfare in Falinur obsessed me, including Lol Polisto and his wife Thelda and their child, and learned he was known in this part by reputation; but his guerrilla deeds took place dwaburs away across the hills. The problem of the men under the thrall of thaumaturgy, fighting like maniacs for Jhansi, would have to be faced. When we fought and met them in battle, they would, as Mevek had so crudely said, be slain if we were to free the country.

"At the least," I said, "you can always smell Rovard the Murvish a bowshot off."

They ventured hesitant laughs at this. Sorcerers, to the ordinary man, are no joking matter.

A man wearing a fur cap poked his head in the doorway and said, "Nath says there are men skulking about to the north of the village."

My first thought was that I'd misjudged it badly when I'd tallied Mevek's band at twenty. He still had outposts.

Mevek jumped up at once.

"That will be that damned rast Macsadu and his foul masichieri." Masichieri are very low-class mercenaries, barely better than bandits. "He has been scouring the countryside for us. Well, we owe him, and tonight he'll bite off more than he can chew."

Vanderini walked quickly to the door, drawing his sword. The others followed, their weapons making a fine show.

Mevek eyed me, "It is best, majister, if you remain here where you will be safe. Macsadu does not know I have more men than usual, more than he expects."

"No," I said in a mild voice. "I do not skulk—"

"You are the emperor!" Now Mevek looked astonished, and his eyebrows formed a black bar. "Emperors do not—"

"Jak the Drang does," I said.

He nodded, convinced at once. He jerked his head at Turko. "The stylor had best hide when the fighting begins."

Because Turko bore no weapons, Mevek had judged him to be a stylor, outside the scope of fighting men, a stylor being a man who can read and write and as a scribe carries pen and ink and paper instead of sword and spear.

Now Turko's mouth opened in earnest.

I said, "This Macsadu. I hear he is a by-blow of Jhansi's."

"Aye. A vicious man-hunter. He slew his own mother when Jhansi tired of her. Now he extorts taxes and tortures for pleasure. We have a score to settle."

Turko got out, "I'll be at your side in the fight, Mevek, and judge how you conduct yourself."

The guerrilla chief gave Turko a puzzled look, started to say something, changed his mind, said, "Please yourself, stylor. If you are chopped, do not blame me."

Nath Karidge drew that curved sword of his. "It appears to me, Mevek, that you have been lax in your scouting and have sucked us into a trap. You had no business arranging this meeting if you were being followed."

Very quickly I stopped the argument. Outside the inn the sudden sounds of combat flowered in the night. Perhaps Mevek had made a mistake; we were in for a fight and that was that.

Somewhat surlily, Mevek said, "I have enough men to thrash that cramph Macsadu, do not fear—"

Vanderini catapulted through the doorway. His old boot of a face bore a huge bloody gash. He was yelling. He twisted and slammed the door, shoving the bar across.

"Scores and scores of the bastards! They've tricked us!"

The noise outside faded and then increased. The door bulged. The bar broke. In a smashing welter of splinters fierce armed men thrust through. Their weapons glimmered darkly with blood.

"You stupid onker!" yelled Karidge.

He fairly hurled himself forward, shouting, "Into them before they deploy!"

Korero threw back his enveloping cloak. His four arms raked up and his tail hand curved. Steel glittered.

With a whooping rush the mercenaries charged.

In the next instant a confused and murderous struggle began across the cleanly swept floor of the taproom in the Sign of the Headless Zorcaman.

Two

Of the Disobedience of Nath Karidge

The windows exploded in fountains of splintered wood and patterned glass and struggling men collapsed inward to sprawl, still fighting, over the tables and settles. The guerrillas and the mercenaries hunting them fought madly across the floor.

Korero's glittering figure swirled like a lightning bolt of destruction.

Nath Karidge, characteristically the first to get in among his foemen, swung his curved sword with precision and gusto.

Naghan the Barrel whipped a stout clanxer, a straight cut and thruster of Vallia, into his adversary and then stiff-armed it about in a horizontal slash that dislodged the Adam's apple of the next.

Vanderini, swearing horribly and the blood running down his face, cut back into the pressing mass.

Chuktar Mevek, a sword and a dagger swirling, fought madly, as though working out a private grudge eating away his soul.

And I, Dray Prescot, I fought too, seeing that these miserable masichieri sought to kill me and I didn't have the time to die, not right now, with all I had still to do waiting to be done.

A screaming wretch flew over the battling throng. He turned a complete cartwheel as he whistled though the air. He departed from the taproom through the only window so far unbroken. Wearing the windowpanes like a collar, he vanished.

So I knew Turko the Khamorro was in action.

The fight, for all its shortness, was exceedingly ferocious.

One of the problems with low-class mercenaries is their rapid loss of interest if the day goes against them.

Not for me to judge any man in what he does, unless that happens to be against the well-being of Vallia and he is hauled up before me in my capacity as emperor. I did not condemn, nor even cavil, as the mercenaries, seeing that we were not to be easily plucked, lost interest. By ones and twos, and then a half dozen at a time, they ran out of the shattered doorway. A few hardy souls left were either cut down or persuaded to depart. I noticed that Mevek far preferred to cut them down than let them escape. He had his reasons, I did not doubt.

Some of these dubious fighting men were not apims, not Homo sapiens, being diffs of various races. A Rapa with his wattled neck and vulture head and waving tufts of feathers pressed me and I cut him a little, so that he shrieked and, turning, ran off. A Fristle, his cat face a bristle, spat at Korero, whose arm—one of his arms, the speed made it difficult to see exactly which one of the assemblage—raked out and biffed the Fristle through the gaping window. Korero used the hilt of his sword.

A Brokelsh, coarsely furred and coarse of manner, sought to drive his spear through Mevek's guts. Mevek was, at the time, hotly engaged with a fellow who tried to bring a cleaver down from the crown of Mevek's head to the junction of his collarbone.

Mevek dealt with the cleaver fellow just in time, and swung about. He saw what happened.

Turko hove up, twitched the Brokelsh's spear away, upended him, twirled him as a maid twirls a feather duster in all the old plays and heaved him over the heads of the rest of us out the window. Then, without pausing, Turko slid a long thrust of a sword in the grip of the next mercenary who had delusions of grandeur. The Khamorro grip fastened on the screaming wight and he was twitched up, up and away.

Turko, perfectly balanced, breathing easily, not in the slightest discommoded, looked about for the next one.

Mevek stared at Turko.

The fight was dying. A few more quick flurries, the shriek of a fool who hadn't the sense to duck, and the masichieri departed.

But the battle was not over yet, and we had not escaped scot free. A number of Mevek's men sprawled on the floor in their own blood, wounded, dead and dying.

"It seems," said Mevek, breathing hard and his eyebrows twitching uneasily, "that I owe you my life. And I do not know your name." Turko smiled.

A commotion outside drew our attention to the open doorway, and once again we grasped our swords ready to beat off a fresh attack. Introductions could wait. Crossing to the door, I peered out cautiously.

The Maiden with the Many Smiles illuminated the crossroads. The shuttered houses remained dark and mysterious. The folk of this village of Infinon of the Crossroads wanted nothing to do with the night's nefarious doings.

The stink of spilled blood and the tang of dust obliterated the smell of the flowers of the white shansili trailing on its trellis over the door.

A group of riders astride totrixes were bringing their clumsy six-footed steeds up in a rush, and the moon glinted from their lance tips and harness. These were the fellows come to finish the job the masichieri had failed to do. I did not doubt that Jhansi's illegitimate son, Macsadu the Kroks, rode at their head.

"They mean to finish us off once and for all," growled Mevek at my shoulder.

"Aye," panted Vanderini, shoving up with his sword crusted with blood. "But we'll—"

"Yes, you old wart," said Mevek, by which I judged there was a comradeship between them.

"We can but fight," I said. "We would never reach our zorcas in time."

"And if we could," said Karidge, stepping out and, surprising me, looking in the opposite direction, "I do not think, majister, you would gallop off."

"I would, Nath, and thankful to be able."

His reckless face looked shocked as he swung back.

"But, majister—"

"I have work to do for Vallia, Nath, work such that it would ill betide me to get killed before it is done."

"Ye-es," he said. The doubt was alive in him. "I see."

"No, Nath, you do not see now. But, I think, you will see one day. And, if we get out of this scrape in one piece, soon."

17

"Where is this marvel who makes men fly?" bellowed Mevek. "By Vox! I would have him stand at my side in the fight."

"I am here, Chuktar Mevek," said Turko, in his silky tones.

"How you manage it, and without naked steel in your fists, passes me. But, by all the names, you are a marvel."

"Men have said that before, Mevek," I said. "I am glad to see you share their opinion."

The totrix riders were now almost on us. They rode knee to knee, in a jingling, ominous trot, and it behooved us to duck back into the inn before they speared us where we stood.

Again Nath Karidge looked away at the crossroads. The intensity of his stance, the piercing stare, gave me to think. So, when the first shafts arched and the steel birds struck in among the totrix riders, I was not surprised.

Zorcamen rode swiftly from the shifting shadows. They bore on in a close, disciplined mass. Archers in front, loosing with the fluent rapidity of experts, lancers following on, they galloped along the road.

The archers fanned out, still shooting, using their nimble zorcas with superb skill. As the zorcabows opened out, so the lancers bored on through in a solid bone-crushing charge. The lance heads with their red and white pennons all came down. The steel heads glimmered cruelly in that wavering light.

When the half-squadron hit, they plunged in like a fist into a tub of butter. In a twinkling the individual combats broke out as the melee swirled along between the shuttered houses. Caught utterly by surprise, thrown into confusion, the totrix men gave no thought to fighting—only to flight.

A trumpet pealed the recall. As one, the lancers disengaged. The archers shot until their targets flitted into the shadows and were lost.

Karidge yelled in his strong voice: "No pursuit, Jiktar Tromo! Form up, emperor's guard!"

With drilled precision the two half-squadrons swung back and formed at the door of the Sign of the Headless Zorcaman.

"Well—by all the names!" declared Mevek.

His men huddled, gaping at the red and yellow uniforms, the feathers, the furred pelisses. Yes, zorcamen, archers and lancers, make a fine show, by Krun!

Nath Karidge was staring at me in great uncertainty.

Mevek, however, voiced the mutual thoughts first.

"So you brought a bodyguard, emperor, after all."

"It was necessary," said Karidge, very firmly, brooking no argument, no recrimination. "The emperor did not order the bodyguard. I did so on my own responsibility." He looked down, and then up, defiantly. "I disobeyed your orders, majister, and now I accept that I will be sent as a simple trooper, to pay for my crime."

"You assume I would send you to a cavalry regiment?"

He suddenly looked aghast.

"But—majister—"

Karidge was a zorcaman first, last and all the time.

"I am minded to send you to the Phalanx, to be a brumbyte." I said brumbyte deliberately, and not soldier, for I wished Karidge to understand the situation.

"Majister..." He spoke in a weak, strangled voice.

"I shall speak to you, Chuktar Karidge, about this later. For now, I thank you for your two half-squadrons. They judged it nicely. Jiktar Tromo? Send him to me later on."

"Quidang, majister!"

Then it was a matter of clearing up and finalizing what was understood between the guerrillas and myself. I heard Karidge saying to Korero, "In the Phalanx—I admire them, of course—but to trail a pike as a brumbyte! One of your muscled fellows with a vosk-skull helmet and a damned great pike and the view of the fellow in front's backside! By Vox! I couldn't bear it!"

"Cheer up, Nath," Korero advised him. "The emperor has a funny way with him at times."

"Aye!"

Keeping a straight face, I walked over to Turko and Mevek who were arguing about payment for the damage to the inn.

"These folk have been badly treated," Mevek was saying, his flat face now filled with passion. "I shall pay for the damage. And then—" and he laughed "—I shall find a damned convoy of Jhansi's and take from it what he owes."

"I feel I have a better claim," said Turko.

"You are then a rich man, you who save my life and refuse to tell me the name of the man to whom I owe it?"

"No, I suppose, if all goes well, I could be rich one day. But wealth does not interest me for itself. It is what may be done with riches—like paying for this damage."

I said, "Let Mevek pay and take the gold from Jhansi. I like the sound of that."

There, you see!" burst out Mevek. His impassivity had quite deserted him. "The emperor speaks sense."

"I shall return to Vondium now, Mevek. You call yourself a Chuktar?"

The note of interrogation prompted him to a long, circumstantial story about once having served in a mercenary army raised somewhere in Pandahem, and he was a Chuktar by that right as well as being the leader of his guerrilla band.

"Then Chuktar it is, Mevek. An ord Chuktar, I would say." Ord—Kregish for eight—meant he had only two more steps to go before becoming a Kapt.

"Thank you, majister—"

"And now you serve the new Kov of Falinur, Kov Turko?"

He squinted up at me.

"What has passed cannot alter my decision—"

Turning to Turko the Shield, I said, "Kov, I would like to introduce to you Ord-Chuktar Mevek, a fine fellow and one whom you must watch. Mevek, you have the honor of being presented to Kov Turko of Falinur."

Well...

I suppose to a tired old cynic this was all childish stuff. I am tired, right enough, even though I recognize tiredness as a mortal sin, and I am cynical enough betimes; yet I viewed this confrontation with a quiet relish. The sight of Mevek's eyebrows was reward enough.

Turko maintained a marvelous composure, and yet I knew well enough that superior Khamorro was thoroughly enjoying himself. And, with all this fun and games, we had made a significant breakthrough in relations with some of the people of Falinur. Oh, there were many of them who would side with Jhansi, and detest their new kov. But we had to be patient, and do the right things—the right things in our eyes, of course—and eventually demonstrate that we were not bloodsuckers, not slavers, and were seeking the good of all the folk of Falinur.

That was just about impossible, given the tenacious clinging to slavery of many of the masters of Falinur. But I felt strongly that Turko would succeed. He was going to bring a different technique to Falinur from the mild methods of Seg. I might deplore this. But, as the surgeons say, you cannot amputate without losing a little blood.

We left Chuktar Mevek with promises that we would soon return with the army of liberation. At least, Kov Turko would lead that army; I planned to travel to Hyrklana. With the cavalry escort fore and aft, we rode back south as She of the Veils, the fourth moon of Kregen, rose to follow the Maiden with the Many Smiles between the stars.

Three

In Which Nath Nazabhan, Kapt of the Phalanx, is at Last Named

"A sorcerer was reported sniffing around one of the university buildings."

"Ortyg Voinderam has absconded with the Lady Fransha, and her father, the Lord of Mavindeul, having recovered from a fit occasioned by his paroxysm of rage, vows vengeance, and his agents have been seen in Drak's City."

"Filemon, the shoe contractor, has defaulted on payment for a thousand hides."

"An outbreak of horn rot is reported in the zorcas of Thoth Valaha."

"It is reported that an idol of Mev-ira-Halviren opened its eyes and spoke, since when a multitude of the credulous flock to the temple of this outmoded religion, and the priests wax fat."

"A Hamalese spy has been apprehended in Delphond and is being brought to Vondium in chains."

"It is reliably reported that..."

"The latest situation appreciations show that..."

"What are your orders concerning..."

And so on and so on...

The motives of anyone who takes on the job of putting a country back together again after seasons of unrest and destruction surely need very close scrutiny.

While the process of reconstruction is going on there is little time if any for introspection. It is all work, work and more work, from long before the twin Suns of Scorpio rise to long after they set. All the same, despite the constant crushing work load, doubts must creep in. Self-analysis is probably engendered by the pressures and fatigue. And then, as they say in Balintol, you'll forget which hand to use and stand there, motionless, like a cartwheel.

Enevon Ob-Eye, my chief stylor, had recruited a large and growing bureau to handle the paperwork.

Every death warrant was seen by me, personally, and in many cases with discussions with the magistrates concerned to delve deeper into the matter, the sentences were commuted to lesser punishments. This damned Hamalese spy, for instance...

"Hang him," said Nath Nazabhan, the fierceness of his words matched by the anger he felt against the enemies of his country. "Hang him from the highest branch in all Vondium."

I sipped the wine, for it was evening and the lights had been brought in and the curtains closed. My small workroom with the books and charts, the arms rack, enclosed us. The wine was superb—Vela's Tears from Valka—and I swallowed down, keeping Nath waiting before replying.

Then: "Nath. It is high time this vexed question of your name was settled."

"You will not hang this Hamalese spy?"

"Probably not. If you ask him which he prefers, to be hanged by us or sent back to the Empress Thyllis, what do you think he will reply?"

Nath's face creased. "So we hang him?" He could see the funny side of that. "Because it is more tender?"

"He might be won over. At least, we must make the attempt. Naghan Vanki will earn his keep as the chief spymaster in this."

"I am privileged to command the Phalanx. We are the most powerful fighting force Vallia possesses. I leave spies and darkness of that kind to Vanki's faceless minions."

"And, Nath, that is the problem. Your father's rank of Nazab gives you the right to call yourself Nazabhan. We have talked on this. You are the Kapt of the Phalanx. I have warned you often enough that the Phalanx is vulnerable—"

"And have we not overturned all who came against us?"

"Yes, yes. We have done well together. And you keep shying away from this business of your name."

Enevon Ob-Eye rustled papers at the side of my desk where he had brought in the latest reports. A small folding stool allowed him to sit down to the job. His own offices were large and crammed with people and files and papers.

"If I may speak for Nath, majis? He wishes to remain in the Imperial service, with your blessing, as a Justicar governing a province or city. He has no ambitions to be ennobled in the main ranks of the peerage—at least—" and here Enevon squinted his one eye up— "that is how I read the situation."

"That is so, Enevon." Nath spoke crisply.

I said, "You know that at any time you wish you may be appointed Justicar to govern the city or province of your choice. The imperial provinces around Vondium are in our hands once more, and arrangements can be made that will not unduly upset the incumbents." Nath Nazabhan was a good comrade, a fine man, who led the Phalanx and who was devoted to that immense cutting instrument of war, as the brumbytes within the ranks were devoted to him. So, I added, "You'd have to leave the Phalanx, of course."

"That, I am not prepared to do."

Enevon closed his eye. I leaned back and sipped the wine.

"So, as you are set in your ways, Nath, and it is necessary that you be rewarded—"

"It is not necessary, majister!"

"Oh, but, Nath, it is."

Nath, as a superb example of the splendid young fighting men who had fought shoulder to shoulder to liberate Vallia and stave off the attacks of the predators feasting on the prostrate empire, a blade comrade, a man of unquestioned loyalty, Nath must be seen to shine in that galaxy of gallants who had stepped forth to save Vallia in her Time of Troubles.

"You remember the Battle of Kochwold, Nath?"

"Who can ever forget it?"

"We had three Phalanxes there. It was a famous victory."

"Aye."

"It appears to me that Nath na Kochwold has a ring."*

"Majister?"

Enevon rustled more papers and pulled out a large sheet much embellished with fine writing and scrollwork. He placed this down before me and then fussed in his meticulous way with the sealing equipment. I looked steadily at Nath.

"Kyr Nath! No more shilly-shallying. Your rank will be formally announced when the lists are promulgated. You are Nath na Kochwold." Then, and I hoped in no testy way, I added, "There are so many Naths on Kregen you have to accept the needle in this." And I signed and sealed the patent.

Nath opened his mouth, shut it, opened it again and his lower jaw moved sideways before he spoke.

"And I keep the Phalanx?"

I nodded.

"Then, majister, I thank you. By Vox! I shall have no difficulty in remembering my name!"

The feeling of relief I experienced in having pushed that problem to a solution lasted for some time as we worked on. But, inevitably, more problems came crowding in and the proverbial light at the end of the tunnel remained obscured. Mind you, to call rewarding Nath—or anyone of the people who labored so hard for Vallia—a problem is to be foolish. It was just Nath's insistence on remaining with the Phalanx that prevented my using him in a wider capacity for which he was perfectly suited.

Plans for Turko to march northward to Falinur pushed ahead. An army had to be collected. It had to be equipped and fed. And, at the same time, the rest of the territories regained in the island had to be protected.

Two new plants for processing the bumper crop of mergem we had been blessed with this season had just reached completion. Mergem, a

---

* na: The word "na" in Kregish for "of" carries connotations of higher rank than the other common word for "of"—"ti"—and is used more of provinces and cities rather than towns or estates. A.B.A.

leguminous plant, when dried may be stored for long periods and then reconstituted. It is rich in protein, vitamins and minerals, with trace elements—although at the time I knew nothing of them, by Vox!—and has seen many a beleaguered city safely through a siege. With little persuasion from me, the Presidio, to whom I was delegating more and more responsibility, had ordered the planting of vast areas of mergem. These two new processing facilities would give an even larger return than the traditional methods of grinding and drying in the suns light. Now we could use not only the pods, but the stalks as well.

And, as all good Kregans know, you can flavor your reconstituted mergem with all manner of tasty fruit juices.

Delia burst into my room as I shoved the mergem file away. She looked marvelous, rosy of face, brilliant of eye, quivering with passion.

"Dray! You sit here! What are you about? Why haven't you done something?"

I stood up. I think—I am not sure—Enevon killed a smile. I searched for meaning, and for words.

"Come on, Dray! We can't just do nothing! We must hurry!"

"Yes," I said. And I tried to put a snap, a ring of decision into my voice. "We must act!"

"At once!"

"Of course..."

Now my Delia is the most wonderful person in two worlds. That goes without saying, although I have said it, will say it and continue to say it. But, all the same—what in the frozen wastes of the Ice Floes of Sicce was she talking about now? By Zim-Zair! It was enough to make a plain old fellow like me jump up and down on his hat.

And here came Jilian, recovered of her wounds, roaring into my little study, shouting that we must hurry. Jilian with her black leathers and her pale face with those dark brilliant eyes brought a heady wash of action wherever she went. Jilian, with her whip and her claw.

"Don't just stand there, Jak!" she called.

Delia said, "Oh, you have to take a two-handed sword to stir him up when he gets like this. Come on, Dray!"

I swallowed. Venturing all, I said in a voice that was little more than a husky croak, "Where to?"

Both women—both gorgeously beautiful women—stared at me as though I was bereft of my senses.

"Well, I don't know!" said Jilian.

"I've no idea," said Delia. "But we must hurry!"

Now I shut my mouth most firmly. I put both hands flat on the desk. I closed my eyes.

Enevon coughed. "I think, majis, this matter touches the business of Ortyg Voinderam—"

"An imbecile I'll sink my claw into if—" began Jilian.

Now I grasped what was going on—well, some of it. Ortyg Voinderam had eloped with the Lady Fransha, and Delia as Empress of Vallia no doubt knew far more about the affair than anyone could guess. From this knowledge I judged that young Idiot Voinderam had not obtained an opinion from the empress. Delia would not interfere in matters of the heart. But, as she was the empress, these were matters that were of concern to her.

After all, in the mating of noble houses coalitions formed and business was transacted and heads could be parted from shoulders.

I ventured again, attempting to sound as though I was fully apprised of the situation. "So no one knows where Ortyg has gone?"

"Where he has taken poor Fransha!"

"Now, Jilian," I said in my reasonable voice. "Perhaps she went willingly. Perhaps they are in love—"

"Of course they're in love! That's why she went! And that's why we have to get her back!"

I shook my head. I reached for the glass of Vela's Tears. I sipped the strong red wine that comes from Southern Valka. I was all at sea again. These women...!

A kind of brain wave occurred to me then, and I spoke up with a firmer voice. "Call all the members of both households. Call all our chamberlains. Contact Naghan Vanki. Order a fast voller. Saddle a dozen zorcas and two dozen totrixes. Have the Emperor's Sword Watch stand to arms—No." I felt I'd gone far enough. I didn't want the Emperor's Sword Watch given unnecessary burdens, turned out of barracks at all hours, their training program interrupted. "No, cancel that last order."

Delia saw through all that nonsense on the instant.

"You may think it all very funny, Dray. But it is serious. Ortyg and Fransha are passionately in love and the match is generally regarded with great favor—"

"Well, why—?"

"Because if they run off like this the families will never agree, old Larghos of Mavindeul, Fransha's father, will turn against Ortyg Voinderam and make his daughter wed that Fridil Goss. Then you know what will happen."

I did. My old antagonist, Natyzha Famphreon, with the wizened face and lush body would rub her hands with glee when she heard the news. She was a leading member of the Racter party, once the most powerful political force in Vallia, able to dictate to the emperors, and now sadly fallen away and confined to their locus of discontent in the northwest. After Turko had regained Falinur we had to deal with Layco Jhansi who fought the damned Racters to the north of him. Many men expressed the pious hope that they'd kill each other off before we had to march against them.

I looked down at the cluttered desk. A paper protruded from a file—a thin file, just opened—and on the paper two names were written out fairly. Weg Wegashtorio. Nath Karidge. The next file concerned the state of our airboats. We could buy none from Hamal, seeing Hamal was at this time our mortal enemy. We could not manufacture airboats ourselves, only our flying sailing ships. Embassies had gone down south into the Dawn Lands in the hope of buying fliers. I had to go to Hyrklana not just to find our friends; making deals to buy fliers was also on the agenda there. I sighed.

All these pressing problems of empire, and I was being entwined in the passions of lovers. A world might shiver and shake and empires totter and fall, but two foolish young people in love must take precedence.

Well, there is a justice in that, I suppose...

The other three people in my study were well aware of the network of agents—spies—I had set up distinct from the empire's chief spymaster, Naghan Vanki, and his organization. Enevon had been an active participant in our plans.

So now Delia could burst out hotly, "We have worked hard up there in Mavindeul. The stromnate is ready to declare for us if they are guaranteed support. And old Larghos has no love for Natyzha, despite he holds his stromnate at her hands."

A strom, the equivalent of an Earthly count, has certain powers. We had promised to make Larghos, Strom of Mavindeul, a strom in his own right with his own province if he threw in with us. The marriage of his daughter Fransha was a part of this, for young Ortyg Voinderam was the son of the Vad of Khovala, and Khovala's southwestern border marched with that of Mavindeul. If everyone agreed, Mavindeul would rise, Khovala would march and we would send troops across the Great River to join in the attack from the imperial province of Thermin, whose governor just happened to be the father of Nath of Kochwold. It all fit perfectly.

And now passions could not wait, and the couple had eloped.

Enevon coughed. "If the Lady Fransha is married off to Fridil Goss, a puppet of Natyzha Famphreon's, Mavindeul will not dare declare for us, for they will get no support from Khovala."

"I suppose," I said in a vague way, "Khovala will not support, anyway, seeing their vad's son has the girl he wants?"

"It will not rest with them. Mavindeul holds the key."

A vad is the rank of nobility below a kov, which roughly equates with a duke, and a vad is very high on the tree of rank and power and prestige. Old Antar Voinderam wasn't going to stick his neck out for nothing, and nothing would be all he would get if he tried to march against Natyzha Famphreon without the support of Mavindeul. Rather—he would get something—a great many dead soldiers in his forces.

The situation was perfectly simple. It was not at all complicated. After all, this was just the kind of problem your real emperor would tackle and solve twice a day before breakfast.

But—I wasn't a real emperor—at least, not in my own eyes. I was just plain Dray Prescot, tackling a colossal task with all the wits and cunning I may be blessed with. The sooner I could wrap up this business of liberating the Empire of Vallia and hand the lot over to my son Drak in working order, the better.

By Zair, yes!

And together with that, there was no denying the fascination of handling these problems. How did you perform the balancing act necessary to gain your ends? How did you please everybody? Well, that can't be done, of course. There is a pull, a dark tide in men, that urges them to meddle with the lives and destinies of other people. We felt that we were acting for the right reasons in attempting to free Vallia from the hordes of mercenaries and slavers who had descended on the islands in the Time of Troubles. We believed that these people gathered together under the new flag of Vallia. The moment I suspected the tiniest suggestion of corrupting power—I'd be off, by Vox, off and away and out of it.

It is not necessarily true that absolute power corrupts; it does do so, lamentably, but it is not a rule that it must.

Anyway—how many men-in history have possessed real, true, genuine absolute power? Perhaps it is having only the illusion of absolute power that corrupts. I did know that the passions of young lovers were, if not more important than, at least certainly as important as, the devious political maneuvers we were forced to in our struggle to clean up the mess in Vallia.

Rather heavily, I said, "Send everyone suitable to try to trace Ortyg and Fransha. We can hope they have left a trail. I'll go and see Antar Voinderam if he is still at his villa here. And I shall try to catch Fransha's father, Larghos, before he departs."

I closed the next file on the desk. It concerned the Opaz-forsaken zorca horn rot, a frightful business.

"I don't like the idea of Larghos sending to Drak's City to hire assassins."

Four

Concerning the Power of Phu-Si-Yantong

"See to it, Vanki," I said to the empire's chief spymaster.

"Yes, majister."

His flat and chilling voice was just the same after all this time. His face, pale, composed, held that containment of himself, that inscrutable knowingness, that perhaps he did not realize revealed so much. This was a man who lived in the shadows and was of the darkness. And in contact with people in the everyday run of rubbing elbows they would regard him and know that this man lived within himself. He had proved a master of his trade. Also, and for this I forgave him much, including his part in dumping me under a thorn ivy bush in the Hostile Territories, he was devoted to Delia.

Anyone who tries to run a country, even a ramshackle kind of place as Vallia then was, cannot do it all alone.

You have to learn to delegate.

"And remember, the welfare and happiness of Ortyg and Fransha are more important than a possible advantage on the fringe of Racterland."

Naghan Vanki still wore his trim black and silver clothes, cut in the latest fashion and inconspicuous. Black and white are the Racter colors. He moved his hand over the papers on his desk, the same kind of damned papers that cluttered my desk.

"Once I thought the Racters held the chief hope for the country. Events have altered my appreciation."

With a quick look at his clepsydra—the time was flying by!—I turned to leave. "If Mavindeul does not throw in with us and rise, we'll soon be in a position to attack the Racters from the south, anyway, as soon as Kov Turko has cleared his Falinur."

"My sources inform me that Antar Voinderam will not risk an attack on the dowager Kovneva of Falkerdrin until he is assured of success." Had Naghan Vanki been in the habit of smiling, or of allowing any expression on that chilling face of his, now he might have smiled. Old Natyzha Famphreon, the dowager Kovneva of Falkerdrin, was a holy terror. No one—but no one—could ever be assured of success against her until she was battened down and on her way to the Ice Floes of Sicce.

"We'll do our best to accommodate him." I opened the door, and then thought that Vanki might profit from a little jolt. "You know there is zorca horn rot in Thoth Valaha. We are going to be short of saddle animals if we're not careful. I want a full report of our negotiations with the countries in the Dawn Lands we have approached to purchase airboats."

Vanki said, just a little quickly, "We continue to try in the Dawn Lands, majister." Then he halted himself, about to say something and checking himself. Oddly, I had the clear impression that he knew something, had thought I knew, and had suddenly realized that I did not know.

"Yes?"

He was very smooth. "I will have the report on your desk before the suns rise."

It would have been childish of me to have said, "In triplicate!" as I almost did. We were operating on a level a little above that kind of pettiness.

"We desperately need vollers," I said. Vanki, like most Vallians, called airboats fliers. Voller was the Havilfarese name, coming from the places where they were built. "And we need saddle and draught animals. I shall be going to Hyrklana as soon as I can shed some of this work load. Not that we will get much joy out of fat Queen Fahia. But we must have transport!"

He saw that I was seized by the urgency of this problem. It was vital to the continuing struggle.

"Much of the mergem crop has been planted where the forests were cut down for the sailing ships of the sky."

"We'll just have to forage wider for lumber."

"Yes, majister."

About to burst out, as the old intemperate Dray Prescot would certainly have done, I held my tongue. Spymasters may become two-edged weapons. If that happened Vallia would be in for much bloodshed before we righted the ship of state, so to speak. He watched me with that calm stare as I went out. Our parting remberees were polite, that was all.

But, for all that, Naghan Vanki was an invaluable servant to Vallia.

The urgency of everything was enough to drive a man wild with baffled impatience.

Both Antar Voinderam, Ortyg's father, and Larghos Eventer, Fransha's father, had left the city before I could contact them. Messengers were on their trail. After seeing Vanki, there was one more man I would see, perhaps in this case as in so many others, the most important man of all.

Riding back through the nighted streets of Vondium, passing ruins still sprawled in ugly decay but bright with wild flowers, grim and yet glowing reminders of the Time of Troubles, I relished the scent of moon blooms. She of the Veils sailed the sky above. Her fuzzy golden and rosy glow illuminated buildings and avenues, glimmered molten on the still waters of the canals. Truly, even half in ruins, Vondium was still the beautiful city, proud in her beauty.

At my back rode the duty squadron of the Sword Watch.

Formed out of loyalty to the emperor, formed at the beginning by my blade comrades without my knowledge to protect me against the cunning and viciousness of assassins, the Emperor's Sword Watch kept guard. This was a squadron from 2ESW, for 1ESW was away up north with my son Drak. With him, also, was the Emperor's Yellow Jackets, 1EYJ, helping to finalize our campaigns up there against the clansmen. With them were Seg Segutorio and Inch, and I hungered to see my blade comrades again and talk and carouse and sing and generally forget that I was supposed to be a puissant emperor.

The two second moons of Kregen, the Twins eternally orbiting each other, lifted over the serrated rooftops, and the night brightened with a confusing crisscross pattern of pinkish shadows.

On such a night assassins might stalk abroad. I would have to go and see the Hyr Stikitche in Drak's City, the haunt of thieves and vagabonds and assassins, and see what he would tell me of Larghos Eventer's doings. Not damned much, for old Nath the Knife, the Aleygyn of the Stikitches, was touchy concerning the honor of assassins.

All the same, he had sent many of his fine young men to serve with 1EYJ, and they had fought passing well.

These thoughts as we hurried along brought up the business interrupted by this passionate elopement. The stray thought did occur to me of that horrendous time when Delia had, by mischance, been abducted. "Shades of the Lady Merle and Vangar Riurik," I said to myself. Well, that affair had turned out all right in the end, and I hoped that this one would as well.

Despite the urgency of our ride, the beauty of moons-drenched Vondium, half in ruins, could not fail to stir me. If working for mere artifacts of brick and stone is not simple foolishness, it was in my mind to believe we did right to struggle for the well-being of this city.

New schools had not only to be equipped and staffed and funded, they had to be built...

A flurry of alarm shook a patrol of the Sword Watch forward, their zorcas running with upflung horns as they passed me, grim-faced men surging up to ride knee-to-knee in a compact body around Shadow, my beautiful black zorca. The staccato crack of hooves, the creak of leather and clink of harness, were punctuated by brief shouts, of interrogation and answer, as the forward patrol sorted out the pother.

Jiktar Rodan had the command of the duty squadron this night. His iron-hard face beneath the brim of his helmet looked like a mere mask, carved as one with the helmet itself.

Shadow slackened speed. Rodan rode level with me. Swords glimmered in the light of the moons. Up ahead the shouts lifted.

A zorcaman came hurdling back, pelisse and feathers and plumes flying. He bellowed it out.

"A party of drunks, Jik! Shall we round 'em up?"

Rodan looked annoyed. He had quite clearly mentally braced himself to meet a savage attack upon the person of the emperor he was sworn to preserve with his own life if necessary, and all it was was a parcel of drunks. Yes, one could sympathize with Jiktar Rodan.

He started to say, "Round 'em up—" and no doubt would have gone on to order them thrown into the nearest dungeon and forgotten.

I said, "Who are they?"

The zorcaman bellowed, "Citizens, majister!"

"Then let them fall into the gutter and sleep quietly, we have urgent business ahead of us tonight."

"Quidang, majister!"

Jiktar Rodan looked across at me before he fell back into his position at the head of the duty squadron. He took a breath. We had seen action together. He had taken wounds.

"Yes, I know, Rodan. I am too soft with them."

"Yes, majister." These old hands, training up the youngster, soldiers who had served with me for seasons, know how and when to take liberties with the emperor—not that they were regarded as liberties by me. We all did our jobs for Vallia and that was what counted. He went on, shaking his head, "We need to put a little backbone into them, by Vox!"

I forbore to ask if he meant his youngsters or the party of drunken citizens.

Certainly, the reaction of the duty squadron had been prompt and sharp, and had there been real trouble ahead then these lads of 2ESW would have nipped it in the bud.

Ortyg Voinderam, who had run off with his Lady Fransha because he couldn't wait for the legal bokkertu to be concluded, might benefit by a season or two of being trained up by crusty old vikatus like Jiktar Rodan. Vikatu the Dodger, the archetype of the old soldier, the old sweat, can teach lessons to civilians as well as the swods in the ranks...

When I dismounted in a convenient inner courtyard of the imperial palace—convenient because it hadn't been burned down or knocked to pieces—Rosala, one of Delia's handmaids, was talking to a soldier in the half-shadows of an archway.

I heard her say in a teasing voice, "And here is the emperor now, you famous jurukker, and I must fly!"

She danced across the flags toward me.

Delia knows how to look after her people. Rosala called the soldier a jurukker, that is to say guardsman, and I, perforce, had accepted this nomenclature. I will not belabor the point about my ambivalent attitudes to bodyguards and the like. They have their uses. And the men forming a juruk—a guard—are the important part of the structure for me.

"Majis!" said Rosala, pert, half laughing. "The empress bid me tell you she has gone with the Lady Jilian. She hopes to be back late tomorrow."

Throwing Shadow's reins to the groom who hurried up, and with a pat for the zorca's gleaming black neck and a word or two for the groom, Yando the Limp, for he had taken a wound at the Battle of Kochwold, I went into the palace. Rosala lingered.

"Do not suborn that soldier from his duty, Rosala..."

She knew I teased her.

"Majister!" Her eyes, her lips, her hair, all looked magnificent in the light of the moons. "He stands guard like a famous juruk, like the best soldier in the Sword Watch. Do you think he would desert his post for me?"

I did not answer. Truth to tell, as I went into the palace in search of Khe-Hi-Bjanching, I realized that any soldier with any sense—anyone without commitments—would desert his post for a girl like Rosala. But she was handmaid to the Empress of Vallia. She was, besides being a girl of remarkable beauty, a girl of immense common sense. She knew the dangers thronging around an imperial palace on Kregen.

And the news she brought that Delia had gone off meant, I judged, that Delia and Jilian were going their own way about finding the Lady Fransha.

Now I am well aware that I am a crusty old curmudgeon who takes delight in foolish notions that appall the more sober-minded, plain Dray Prescot with the weight of an empire in ruins hanging on my shoulders. Yet, I think, and I truly believe, that I was genuinely more concerned for the safety and happiness of Ortyg and Fransha than I was for the political maneuverings surrounding their match. So, as I found Khe-Hi-Bjanching wide awake in the chambers given over to the Wizard of Loh, I felt the leap of gratitude to him and hope that all might yet be well.

"Majister," he greeted me. "I have been trying—but so far my powers fail me."

All my sudden hope vanished like thistledown.

The chamber was illuminated in the mellow glow of samphron oil lamps and was filled with comfortable furnishings. There was nothing of the tawdry bric-a-brac of the common sorcerer here. Wizards of Loh, the most famed and feared thaumaturges of Kregen, as far as I then knew, needed no gimcrack trappings of skulls and bats blood and reptile inner parts and pickled dragons.

"You have been into lupu, Khe-Hi?"

"Yes. I sent my powers out and found nothing. It was strange. Ortyg Voinderam is no sorcerer of any kind, surely?"

"No. Not as far as I know."

I felt the chill. If another sorcerer were at work here, preventing Bjanching from discovering the whereabouts of the runaways by means of his kharrna which gave him the power of observing events at a distance, then that other wizard might be the wizard...

Bjanching saw all that on my face.

"If Phu-Si-Yantong is interfering here..."

"Sink me!" I burst out. "I'll have that devil's tripes one of these fine days. He is a maniac and although I have searched for some I have failed to find goodness in him yet."

"I do not know anyone who would say he was capable of an ounce of goodness—"

"Well," I grumped, "I suppose he must have some redeeming features. If we could discover what they were perhaps we might talk to him—" I looked at Bjanching. "Have you contacted Deb-Lu-Quienyin?"

"I was about to do that when you arrived, majister."

Deb-Lu-Quienyin, with whom I had been through a fraught time or two, had remained with Drak and my friends in the north where I fancied he would be of inestimable value to them. He was just about the most powerful Wizard of Loh there was—always excepting that crazed power-mad devil Phu-Si-Yantong.

Even though I had spent much time in company with Quienyin and Bjanching, and had seen Wizards of Loh performing their mysteries, I, like anyone else on Kregen, could never fully feel at ease as they set about their arcane rituals.

Khe-Hi-Bjanching wore a severe robe of a lustrous black. No runes or magical symbols sullied his vestments, and the pallor of his face and the fiery red Lohvian hair seemed, by contrast, all the more striking. As a young—or relatively young—Wizard of Loh, Bjanching might have been excused displays of thaumaturgical fashion. He disdained them. He was able to exert his power and go into lupu—that strange, half-trance state in which his kharrna extended and gave him pictures of people and events many miles away—without fuss and without many of the physical preparations of other Wizards of Loh I had known.

Waiting as Khe-Hi-Bjanching prepared himself, calmed his whole body and psyche, began to infiltrate the tendrils of his power into those arcane other worlds no mortal might tread with impunity, I found my sense of screaming impatience easing. This would take time, and time I did not have, yet I could wait quietly.

Bjanching's eyes rolled up until, in the moment before he placed his palms over them, his eyes glared forth sightlessly in white blankness. The waiting was mercifully short. The Wizard of Loh's breathing lengthened and drew out, softer and softer, shallower and shallower, until it seemed he did not breathe at all. The chambers gave no sound. We were two primeval spirits, isolated in the great mysteries.

Then—Bjanching lowered his hands.

He stared at me, and in his face that knowing look told me he had broken through.

I leaned forward eagerly. "Quienyin?"

No answer.

"San?" I gave the Wizard of Loh the honorific of dominie, or sage, and I breathed in a deep draught of the close air.

"Majister—" The voice was Bjanching's. "San Quienyin is there, on the periphery, and he is trying to make contact with me. But..."

I put my teeth into my lip.

For a long space the two wizards sought to reach each other through that timeless, formless, unknowable hinterland of the occult. Sweat began to roll down Bjanching's face. Abruptly, he jumped up, his black gown swirling. He took three faltering steps, beginning to spin around in that dervish-like whirling by which some wizards summon their powers. Instead of going on with the rituals that had been unnecessary for him for so long, he tottered and collapsed into his high-backed chair.

He looked at me, and that look of knowingness had fled.

"What is it?" I asked.

"Majister—Quienyin and I were separated, as by a barrier of enormous force. This is new. We must work and investigate and—"

"Yes, yes. Tell me!"

"We cannot discern a single thing concerning the whereabouts of Voinderam and the Lady Fransha."

"Now the devil take it!" I said, and I swore.

"But, majister—do you not see?"

"I see, San, I see very well. Phu-Si-Yantong—"

"Yes! That arch devil has interdicted our powers, and that means he has achieved a recrudescence of power taking him into an altogether new plane. I think, majister, I believe, we are in for a fight passing anything that has gone before."

"And it's a fight you must win, or all Vallia is doomed."

Five

On the Day of Opaz the Deliverer

Emder's long, competent fingers deftly pulled the leather straps of my fancy sword belt into the correct position so that I might haul the buckles tight. Quietly-spoken, Emder, an invaluable man who acted as a valet as a mere part of his many functions. His neatness was of that unfussy kind an untidy person does not take as an affront.

"Now the mazilla, majis."

He lifted the enormous collar ready to wrap it around the back of my neck. Now these ornate collars of Vallia, these mazillas, I had had trouble with before. They are stiff with gold wire, heavy with bullion, ablaze with gems. They poke up from your shoulders and enclose your head like a glittering oyster shell.

Emder leaned sideways and took a look at my face. He sighed.

"Today is the Day of Opaz the Deliverer. I know the processions will go on from suns rise to suns set—"

"And the damned speeches, and the ceremonies and all the rest of it. By the Black Chunkrah!" I said, most feelingly, using a hallowed clansman's oath. "I ought to be well out of it."

Emder pursed up his lips and gentled the huge collar down onto my shoulders. Mind you, the thing did give a weird kind of comfort, for it would take a monstrous blow of a sword to cut through that expensive protection. That was how they'd started in the first place, back in the days when Vallia was a motley collection of little nations all struggling for preeminence.

Well, by Vox, we weren't far off getting back to those ancient days now!

Emder began closing the fastenings.

"The people expect to see their emperor on this day, majis. And, as well, it is the day we keep in remembrance of the Battle of Voxyri—"

"That anniversary I'll keep, and with pleasure." The Battle of Voxyri had taken place outside Vondium and inside the city after we'd broken in. It had taken place on the Day of Opaz the Deliverer. That battle had given us back Vondium, the capital of Vallia, and had seen me enthroned and crowned as emperor—for what that was worth.

Then, and I own somewhat petulantly, I said, "And the empress has not returned?"

"Rosala waits in patience, majis, and Floria with her."

I'd left Bjanching beginning the work he and Deb-Lu-Quienyin must tackle to attempt to thwart this new and horrifying power of the arch maniac, Phu-Si-Yantong. I'd completely forgotten about the celebrations arranged for today. And, all the time the processions wended about the city and the bedecked narrow boats glided along the canals, and the bands played and the people cheered, all the time wizards would be struggling and battling, one against the other, on planes far removed from the gorgeous and barbaric splendor of the Day of Opaz the Deliverer...

"The empress didn't forget about the punishments I'm going to have to endure today." I wrenched a buckle tight and the mazilla swayed. My robes glittered. I felt a fool. "She took good care to see she wasn't here to share my discomforts."

"Majis!"

"All right, all right. I'm just in a foul mood."

"Yes, majis."

Good old Emder! A comrade, a friend, and a fellow to make sure the last button was sewed on the last shirt, the boots were polished to mirrors, the swords all held edges.

There was nothing else for it. I had to do my duty this day. This was all a part of being emperor, just as much as worrying over zorca horn rot and the supply of corn and the new gold mines, and payment of the troops and education for the youngsters. And—all the rest of that...

I will not go into details of the lavishness of the Day. The twin suns shone, Zim and Genodras, blazing down out of a clear sky. The waters of the canals scintillated in light. The houses were festooned with flags and bunting and draped curtains and streamers. The people shouted. The processions wound in and out, and the priests went through their rituals, earnestly and with dedication, and sweating more than a little.

The bands played. Contingents of various regiments marched. The people pranced through the avenues and crowded the narrow boats so that the canals became solid walkways.

Chanting lines of folk weaved in and out, all repeating over and over those ancient litanies, chief of which resounded all day among the half-ruined houses.

"OO-lie O-paz ... OO-lie O-paz..." Over and over, rising and falling, Oolie Opaz, on and on and on.

Surrounded by dignitaries and nobles and functionaries, I went as prescribed from place to place within the city. How different this was, by Vox, from those earlier times! Now I was surrounded by comrades, men and women who had fought with me shoulder to shoulder against our common foes. Now I had no fear, not now, not on this Day, of the poisoned frown, the disgusted look, the turning away in contempt.

The Second Sword Watch were there, inconspicuous, but there, ready in case a more deadly threat manifested itself.

Messengers in relays kept me informed on the progress of Bjanching. He had not gained clear contact with Quienyin. The two Wizards of Loh continued to investigate the extent and force of this new power wielded by Phu-Si-Yantong.

Vallia is a civilized country of Kregen, with wild enough parts here and there, as I well knew. But all the same, these processions, the brilliance of jewels and feathers, the caparisoned animals, the uproar with the banging of drums and gongs and the fierce blowing of trumpets, the smells and the scents, the sheer vitality of it all, this was a splendid and barbaric spectacle.

But the luster of the Day was dimmed for me until almost halfway through, just as we were approaching the hour of mid.

"I am parched!" quoth Nath na Kochwold—who remembered his name with the utmost clarity—and he smiled. "I look forward to the meal they have prepared with almost as much pleasure as I look forward to the march past. By Vox! What we have left of the Phalanx is a poor remnant. But they will march with a swing."

"They will, Nath, they will."

We alighted from the narrow boat and burst into the light of the suns and the roaring welcome of the crowds. Above us lifted the bulk of the Temple of Opaz the Judge. Glistening, impressive, floating among the clouds, it seemed, that vision of spire and dome. I looked up. The manifestation of Opaz in the guise of Judge was traditionally linked with midday, the balancing point between night and night. Here the priests would have prepared a mouth-watering repast to tide us over the next part of the Day's events. We were all sharp set.

The marble steps glistened with gold-veined whiteness. Crimson drapes stained the marble with the semblance of blood. Ranked lines of men held back the pressing crowds. The color, the excitement and the heady energy of the celebrations filled everyone with the passionate conviction that it was divine to be alive on such a day as this.

Pausing for a moment to speak to one of the swods guarding the marble stairs, I was aware of his hard, tanned face, the direct look of his brown Vallian eyes. He was a spearman of the Fifteenth Regiment, trim in leather and crimson, his shield with its proud devices angled just so, his stout spear precisely vertical, its steel head polished to a starry glitter.

"Lahal, Kalei." I noticed the absence of rank badges. "You were a Deldar when we fought together."

"Aye, majister. But I got into a fight with a poor fellow out of the Phalanx. They stripped one Deldar rank from me for every tooth he lost."

"Then—" I said, remembering. "Then he lost seven teeth." Kalei's hard face showed pleasure.

"I will make ob-Deldar again in three of the months of the Maiden with the Many Smiles."

"When you reach shebov-Deldar again send me a message. I will make you a zan-Deldar at once."*

His pleasure increased. I was not being magnanimous. I was not pandering to the men in the ranks. A kampeon is a veteran, a soldier who has received recognition, a man who has won renown in the army. Kalei was a kampeon. Such men are valuable, as precious as gold to an army, for from their experience and war wisdom comes the training of the youngsters. Kalei was too valuable to spend his life carrying a spear as a swod in the ranks.

And, at the same time, he had to be subject to the same iron discipline,

---

* ob: one. shebov: seven. zan: ten.

what the swods call mazingle, as the men he trained up. There was no question of my instantly restoring his rank as a Deldar. That would undermine discipline.

Kalei knew that.

He saluted, an enormous bashing of his spear against his shield, and I nodded and walked on up the marble stairs.

"Rembeere, Kalei!"

"Rembeere, majister!" And then, unexpectedly, he added in his stentorian Deldar's bellow, "May Vox of the Cunning Sword go with you always, majister!"

The soldier near the foot of the wide sweep of marble steps moved. In neat precision they opened ranks. Their weapons and harness glittered. A sedan chair borne by eight Womoxes swayed up the steps from a narrow boat moored next to the boat in which we had arrived. The chair was sumptuous. It was splendid. Crimson velvet curtains and drapes of cloth of gold concealed the occupant. Tassels of bullion glittered. Feathers waved. The rear Womoxes, massive, bull-headed men from the island of Womox off the west coast of Vallia, raised their carved and gilt-encrusted carrying poles so that the sedan chair remained level.

I turned to look back down the steps.

The chair was altogether more ornate, more regal, than the usual run of gherimcals, for the normal gherimcal of Kregen serves functional needs of carrying people about. This palanquin concentrated glory and splendor within itself.

At the side of the gherimcal walked Rosala and Fiona. So I knew.

I walked back down the steps, leaving the dignitaries and the waiting priests above me. I did not run. I do not know how I did not run.

I lifted the cloth-of-gold curtains.

Delia said, "We found not a single sign of them, and I'm late for the Day of Opaz the Deliverer—what a way for an empress to carry on!"

And I, Dray Prescot, laughed.

Neither Delia nor I cared a fig for being empress or emperor. We just wanted to get the job done.

"Whatever you do, my heart," I said, "the people of Vallia love you."

So we went up together to the Temple of Opaz the Judge.

Delia looked superb. She was radiant. She wore a simple sheer gown all of white, with those two special brooches, and a cape of scarlet and gold, crimson and silver, in an artful blend that combined sumptuousness with good taste in a miraculous fashion. Her brown hair was dressed high, threaded with gold and gems, and those outrageous tints of chestnut lent the perfect touch of natural beauty. Like us all, she carried arms, a rapier and a dagger swinging from jeweled lockets on a narrow gem-encrusted belt over her hips.

"And I am famished," she said as we walked up.

"Jilian?"

"She continues the search. But the trail has gone cold, I think."

When the people saw Delia they went wild.

Fantastic cheering and roaring, shrill cries calling down the blessings of Opaz upon her, a bedlam of love and good wishes broke in an inferno of joy to the clear skies over Vondium.

Delia smiled. The whole world brightened. She looked wonderful. With an incredibly graceful gesture, she lifted her hand, bowing to the people left and right and then walking on, her head high, proud, superb, radiant—Delia—Delia of Delphond, Delia of the Blue Mountains.

And I, Dray Prescot, was privileged to walk along at her side. Yes, it wasn't all bad, being Emperor of Vallia!

The rest of the day passed in something of a blur. All the necessary rituals were gone through with proper deference. Whenever I was called on to give a speech outside the customary rote observances, it was very easy to remind the citizens of Vondium of the perils through which we had just passed, and to harp on the dangers we still faced.

"We of Vallia believe! Our children clamor to be heard. We cannot let their justifiable ambitions go unheeded. The land calls for purification. From all over the continents and islands of Paz our oppressors have flooded in. We have fought them. We have driven them back from Vondium, the proud city, and from many of the provinces."

Standing on an obelisk, or at the summit of steps, or upon some balcony banked with flowers, I would say the same words, or almost the same, telling these people that we had come a very long way, and that there was a very long way still to go.

"The iron legions of Hamal have invaded us. The slavers, aragorn, slavemasters have taken away our loved ones, our fathers and mothers, our husbands and wives, our children, brothers and sisters, taken away to be chained in slavery. The flutsmen wing in our skies, pillaging and slaying. The masichieri march against us with rapine in their hearts—no! No, my friends. I am wrong! These masichieri, all the rest of the scum, they have no hearts that beat in human breasts."

The crowds would yell at this, raging, knowing the awful tragedies that had overtaken us, knowing what we had to do to bring Vallia once more into the light of Opaz.

While I was, as you will see, preaching to the converted, I was uneasily aware that since our successes the hard edge to our purpose might fall away.

After all, many and many a mile separated the hated foe-men now from the citizens of Vondium. Despite the ruins everywhere thrusting their harsh reminders upon us, it was deceptively easy to feel the victory had been won. The sounds of the drums were muffled by distance. Yet Vondium remained the heart of Vallia. Nothing less than total dedication could be required...

Delia looked sharply at me as I walked back from the balcony where the last speech had been vociferously received.

"Dray?"

"I was thinking, even as I spoke—we must do this, Vondium must fight on, nothing less than total dedication can be—" I looked at her, seeing her beauty and the wary look on that face I know so well. "Can be tolerated, permitted?"

"You said required."

"Yes. We run perilously close to deep waters."

"Come away and drink a glass of wine. The suns decline. They have a fine Tardalvoh here which will curl your toes."

We were due to dine this season with the Bankers Guild. Each season on the Day, various authorities took it in turns to host the emperor and empress. The Bankers Guild, formed by a number of Companies of Friends to further their own ends, would surpass all efforts at entertainment. Well, I will not bore you with details of what we ate, the golden plates and all that high living. After the feast, the reckoning.

We had changed from the foolish sumptuous clothes of the day to evening attire, with the smaller nikmazillas that are so becoming a part of Vallian costume. Turko and Nath and a few other nobles were talking in a corner when the portly form of Nomile Ristemer rolled up.

"Majister! May I present my son, Mileon Ristemer, of whom I am inordinately proud. He has but just returned home to offer his sword in your service."

I nodded and shook hands in the Vallian fashion.

Old Nomile Ristemer was one of the elite of the banking fraternity of Vondium, immensely rich before the Time of Troubles, still a very wealthy man. His interests extended to many parts of Kregen. He was stout, chunky, with short legs and a strut to his walk. His face was not quite doughy and he had a swab nose. His brain was like a cold chisel. He was nothing like Casmas the Deldy of Ruathytu, right out of his class altogether.

His son, Mileon, partook of that chunky appearance, but he had kept himself in shape and looked what he was, a tough, experienced mercenary. When a mercenary achieves enough distinction, his comrades may see fit to elect him to the august company of brethren who wear the silver mortilhead on its silk ribbon at their throats. He is then a paktun. Of course, the word paktun is more often than not used of any mercenary, as I have said. The silver mortilhead, the pakmort, showed a discreet glitter at Mileon Ristemer's throat.

"You will, I trust, majister, find room and service for my son."

Constantly I was being approached in this way, and I dealt with the applicants as they deserved and in as just a way as I could contrive. Mileon Ristemer looked likely. His father was not a noble but had been given the title of Kyr, a kind of honorific, by the old emperor. The son was plain Koter Ristemer.*

"I shall be glad to have the honor to serve you, majister. I shall not require pay. I have one or two ideas that, I believe, will prove of great value in future campaigns—"

"Where have you seen service, Koter Ristemer?"

"In various countries of Havilfar, and in Loh."

"I am interested in any new schemes. Make an appointment with my chief stylor, Kyr Enevon. I trust we can serve the interests of Vallia together."

Mileon visibly drew himself up, his shoulders going back. Maybe he hadn't been used to dealing with raspy, down-to-earth characters like me before when taking service as a paktun.

"Quidang, majister!"

He rattled that out, and the word, the tone, the very vehemence of that soldier reply, sounded strange in the golden, refined world of the Bankers Guild.

I nodded. I fancied Mileon Ristemer would shape up.

Three or four other young hopefuls were introduced to me in the course of the evening, and if I mention Mileon alone at the moment it is not because the others did not serve Vallia well, but that Mileon's scheme— well, all in good time you will hear about that, by Zair!

We fell into a conversation about the army Turko would need to bring Falinur back in to our kind of civilization. He well knew my face was turned against hiring mercenaries. My son Drak had hired paktuns and had won battles with them. There were mercenaries in the army that had marched into the southwest under the command of Vodun Alloran, the Kov of Kaldi. He had taken the Fifth Army down there and had won victories and was now attempting to consolidate what he had conquered. But more than one of my comrades now grasped the essentials of the policy of using Vallians to fight Vallian battles.

The dancing began and there was singing and laughter and much drinking of toasts.

Standing a little back from the main throng, a glass in my hand, talking quietly to Strom Vinsanzo, a small and somewhat wizened man who knew how to make one golden talen equal two in a season or so, I could see Mileon Ristemer laughing with his partner in the dance. The pakmort glittered at his throat.

---

* "Kyr" is conferred by the emperor, "Tyr" by a high ranking noble. Koter is Vallian for Mister, equating with the Havilfarese Horter. A.B.A.

Vodun Alloran, the Kov of Kaldi, returning to his native Vallia as a successful paktun and wishing to fight to regain his kovnate, did not wear his pakmort. That would be, he had said, too flamboyant. Watching Mileon, straight-backed, limber, most gallant with his partner, I wondered afresh.

And it was perfectly clear that old Nomile Ristemer was enraptured by this soldier son of his, proud and strutting, unable to stop prating about Mileon and the return of the warrior son so dear to his heart. I knew just how he felt. I had to turn away from Strom Vinsanzo with a small word of apology.

Delia, with a graceful gesture and her sweet smile, disengaged herself from the group chattering about her. She walked across to me quickly.

"Dray! You look—"

"Aye. I look the ugly old savage I am."

"Agreed. And the specific?"

"Look at Mileon, there, and old Nomile! I was thinking of Drak, and Zeg, and Jaidur, and—"

"Our three sons make their marks on the world."

"They do. By Zair, but I am proud of them, all of them!"

"I have been thinking that you ought to know what I've been up to in that direction since you went away."

We kept our voices low and we walked together along the terrace, past the serried columns, and the dancers took no notice of us, as was proper.

"And, too," I went on, and I know my voice was troubled, "I am thinking of our daughters. You know the wild she-cat Dayra has become, with her whip and her claw and her black leathers. Jilian, who is much the same, refuses to help because of her vows—"

"And so she should!"

"Aye. You Sisters of the Rose have more secrets than an army of bungling men." I could feel Delia's hand on my arm, a reassuring and invigorating feeling, and that firm hand did not tremble by so much as a spider's eyelash. "And there is Velia and Didi, and they will soon grow big enough to bring more headaches—"

"And Lela?"

I sighed. "Lela. I have not seen her since I came back from my long banishment on Earth. I—it is damned hard, my love, damned hard, when a crusty old father feels his eldest daughter refuses to come to see him—"

"She does not refuse!" Delia's tones were sharp, a rebuke.

"I know, I know. She is busy with the Sisters of the Rose. But you girls of the SoR work her too hard."

"Now if Jilian Sweet-tooth had been our daughter—"

I stopped. "So that is her name!"

"No. Sweet-tooth is what we call her."

"She is ready enough to talk about her banje shop, but not anything about the things we really want to know—no. About the things I really want to know."

"I do not press for your secrets of the Krozairs of Zy."

This was familiar territory. We were a partnership, a twinned one, Delia and I. And we each had our own inner lives, and mostly we shared everything. But there remained these spaces between us that were not empty, distant, repellent but were spaces filled with the light of love.

Then, and Delia astonished me profoundly, she went on to say that she had arranged for our daughters to visit the River Zelph, in far Aphrasöe, and there bathe in the sacred pool of baptism. I turned her to face me. I looked down into her gorgeous face and I saw the love and the pride in our children there, and the defiance—and a little hint of furtiveness?

"Furtive you should be, Delia of Delphond! By Zim-Zair! You take our girls there, all those perils—the mortal danger—why—why—"

"Yes! And this explains where I and the girls have been. Your explanations of where you have been involve your funny little world with only one tiny yellow sun, and one silver moon, and only apims to flesh the world with color and not a single diff anywhere in sight! I think your story far stranger than mine!"

"But the dangers—"

I could feel myself shaking. We had bathed in the sacred pool of baptism, and were thereby assured of a thousand years of life, and our wounds would heal with miraculous swiftness. But the Savanti nal Aphrasöe guarded the pool. There were monsters. I had gone through some parlous times there. And now Delia was calmly telling me...!

Well, when I'd calmed down, I saw the rightness of it. Truth to tell, it solved a problem that had been bothering me.

"But that does not explain where Lela is gone to now," I said.

"No. I hope she will not be much longer. She is devoted, to Vallia, to the SoR, to her family—" said Delia.

"Ha!"

"—and to the work entrusted to her."

"Do you know what that work is?"

"No."

"And how many eligible young bachelors has she turned down this season? I believe I could form a regiment from them!"

Delia laughed. "I believe you could! Lela has her heart set on no man yet. There is time."

And, thinking of young men who were in love with my daughters, I felt the wrenching pang strike me that Barty Vessler was dead, struck down by a vicious cowardly blow from Kov Colun Mogper. Well, my lad Jaidur was after that rast, and after his accomplice, Zankov, too... What a tangle it all was! And yet, as always and now with more force than ever, I believed there was a pattern, a grand design, woven by the Savanti who had brought me to Kregen in the first place, or by the Star Lords who brought me here to work for them or hurled me back to Earth on a whim or for the defiance I showed them out of stupid stubbornness.

"It is an unholy thing in a man's life," I said, turning and resuming our promenade along the terrace, "when he does not recognize his children and they do not recognize him."

"But you know them all now, my heart, all, save—"

"Lela."

"She will come home soon, I feel sure. But—"

I saw Naghan Vanki walk out of the overheated room where the dancing and the perfumes and the feathers coiled among the laughter and the music. He looked swiftly along the terrace, turned, saw us, and started at once to walk down. He wore an elegant Vallian evening dress, of dark green and in impeccable taste. Black and silver leaves formed an entwined border. His rapier and dagger swung. His mazilla was the formal black velvet, smooth and fashionable.

"Majister!"

"But what, Delia? Vanki!"

"I have not heard from her in too long..."

"Get Khe-Hi or Deb-Lu to suss her out in lupu! By Zair! If she is in danger—"

"No, no! I have arranged all that. If she were dead I would know."

"Majister! News has come in." Naghan Vanki halted before us. His pallid face was as tight as a knuckled fist. "My people report they are on the track of Voinderam and Fransha."

"Who?" I said.

Delia looked at me.

Vanki's face expressed nothing.

Then I said, "I see. This is good news. Tell me where they are and I'll be off at once."

Although Naghan Vanki was the empire's chief spymaster, there were few people in the land aware of that fact. Among the gathered nobility and gentility and bankers here at Bankers Guild, there were, I suppose, not above half a dozen who knew.

So the people, attracted by the intrusion, could leave off dancing and a little crowd gather at a discreet distance along the terrace. Much protocol was relaxed on the Day of Opaz the Deliverer once the formal celebrations were over.

"But, majister—" said Vanki.

"You—" Delia shook her head.

Some of my people walked across. Many of them you know, many have not been mentioned so far. But they were friends, a goodly number

44

ennobled by me. They were concerned for my welfare. I said, "I will go after the runaway lovers and see what they say for themselves. After all, no one condemns them for their actions."

Trylon Marovius puffed his cheeks dubiously.

"You are the emperor, majister. It is not meet you should go haring about. Send men—I will go for you willingly."

"Yes," quoth others, and a whole crowd joined in. "I will go. And I! Me, too!"

They were all well-meaning, anxious, concerned lest their emperor should go chasing off into dangers on the trail of two runaways. I suppose my old beakhead of a face began to draw down into the ferocious expression that, so I am told—tartly—can stop a charging dinosaur in its tracks.

Delia's warning voice reached me. "Dray..."

"Sink me!" I burst out. "Am I not the emperor! Cannot I go and risk a danger or two?"

They didn't like that. Lord Pernalsh shook his head. He was taller than I, broader, a veritable man-mountain.

"Not while I live, majister!"

A chorus of affirmation followed. Vanki whispered close to my ear, his breath fluttering, "My people will handle this." He was not there when I turned to answer. In his customary way he had blended into the background when the crowd arrived. A spymaster he was, Naghan Vanki in his black and silver, and a damned slippery fellow with it.

Delia was making covert signs and the gathered people began to drift away. Something of the sense of petulant frustration that had shaken the old emperor, Delia's father, was going to rub off on me pretty quick, by Vox! I felt caged. I felt as those savagely noble wild animals, caged and chained for the arena, must feel as they are whipped and prodded behind the iron bars.

I, Dray Prescot, puissant emperor, was caged up.

We stood alone.

"It seems to me—" I started to try to express my feelings of being shut off, caged away from the hurly-burly of Kregen.

Delia was sharp with me.

"The trouble with you, Dray Prescot, is that you are feeling sorry for yourself!"

Six

Sword for Delia

The Lord Farris flew in with more problems. As commander-in-chief of the Vallian Air Service, Farris was entitled to fly about in an airboat. But we were desperately short of fliers. A fresh source of supply for the powered airboats had to be found. I greeted Farris warmly, for his dedicated loyalty to Delia always warmed me, and we got down to the latest series of headaches.

Anyway, I'd had the last laugh on that crowd at the dance at the Bankers Guild. The people sent off after the news reported that the eloping couple—whom they found in an inn enjoying themselves—were not Voinderam and Fransha.

So, I could afford a nasty laugh at their expense.

Farris sat down across from me in my little study and sipped his wine, for it was evening.

"It is these slaves we have freed," he said. "They have received their plots of land and their allotments of seeds and implements and animals, and they work hard enough—although if they work as hard now as they did when they were slaves and were whipped for nothing, I cannot truthfully say."

I waited for him to go on.

"They must be protected. The farms on the borders mainly, of course." He saw my expression. Both of us detested the idea that within the island of Vallia there should be borders between us and our enemies. All Vallia was one country, or should be. "The flutsmen drop down from the sky and raid and burn and kill. We have had incursions over ten dwaburs into what we regard as Vallian soil—"

"It is all Vallian soil!"

"Aye. But these damned raiders don't understand that yet. And the truth is, the troops we have on the ground cannot be everywhere. The sailing fliers are subject to the winds. And my force—" He spread his free hand.

"There is one clear answer. The freedmen must be able to defend themselves."

"They fight well enough, given the chance, for it is their homes and wives and children who suffer."

"Right. I shall see to that. Is there any news out of the Dawn Lands on vollers?"

"Nothing. Anyway, down there in Havilfar they are a strange lot. You might stand a better chance in Hyrklana."

"If I ever get away." I told him what had happened at the Bankers Guild.

And Farris laughed. I glared at him reproachfully, whereat he laughed the harder.

"I remember when we picked you up in the Hostile Territories," he said. "My Val! If I'd been told then that you would be the emperor who has my undying loyalty, why—" He stopped himself. His shrewd brown Vallian eyes appraised me. He nodded. "Yes, I think I half-understood it, even then."

"And Naghan Vanki was with you—"

Then a messenger announced himself to say that Filbarrka nal Filbarrka had arrived.

"Send him in! By Vox, he will be a sight for sore eyes."

When Filbarrka came in he was just the same. Bouncing, roseate of face, twitching his fingers together, he brought a breath of the clean air of his zorca plains into my study. Filbarrka of the best zorca country in Kregen, he was a man who had organized the zorcabows and the lancers that had so materially contributed to the rout of the ferocious clansmen of Segesthes in the Battle of Kochwold and subsequently.

"What brings you to Vondium, nazab?" I asked.

"That confounded horn rot in Thoth Valaha. They seem to think I can work a magic cure-all for them."

"Can you?"

"Yes, majister."

I sat back. Trust Filbarrka nal Filbarrka!

"So I just looked in to see if you were still here."

"And right welcome you are. We need more zorcas. If we cannot obtain sufficient, what do you say to forming a few regiments of men mounted on marlques, or on freymuls?"

"The poor man's zorca!" Filbarrka bounced up and down and his fingers performed prodigies of entwining. "They are pleasant enough, but—"

"Quite. But we are poor men, are we not?"

"My stock is down, granted, majister. But the colts come along well, some beautiful little—"

He went on enthusiastically, for Filbarrka and zorcas lived together. As the governor of the blue-grass sections of Delia's province of the Blue Mountains, Filbarrka rated the rank of nazab. I valued his wisdom. When, in the course of our conversation he heard of Farris's problems with the freed slaves, he perked up. It was very quickly done.

"Let me at them! I have ideas—"

Well, Filbarrka was a fellow who never lacked for ideas!

As the conversation wended on in the way these rambling discussions do, and I ruefully reflected that this was not the way to clear my desk, I was also forcibly brought up short by the fact that Filbarrka was supposed, when I contacted him, to provide zorcas for Nath Karidge. Instead, here we were reasonably and carefully discussing ways and means of mounting freed slaves on a wild miscellany of saddle animals, and trying to train them up to look out for themselves...

Somehow or other, I had given the job of creating a second-line cavalry force to Filbarrka. He was enthusiastic. He is always enthusiastic. "The trouble will be a lack of maneuvering skills, an inability to get up in the morning and carry out long marches, and a certain liability to panic at the unexpected. But we'll polish 'em up. I'll bring in some of my lads—you know what they are like—and we'll start off with maces and round shields. We'll add darts and lances as these fellows improve. Some of the quilted cloth you produce here in Vondium will be capital for protection, with bronze arm and shoulder bars. We'll keep it simple to start with."

Farris smiled and lifted his wine.

"You convince me, Filbarrka. No doubt of that."

We thrashed that out to Filbarrka's satisfaction. He would be based in Vondium to begin with. Then I said, "I was going to ask you if you could supply five or six hundred prime zorcas."

He lowered his wine. "Five or six hundred? That sounds like a new regiment and remounts—"

"Yes."

Farris, rather incautiously, I thought, said, "We can buy zorcas overseas—"

"Oh, yes," said Filbarrka. "There are other zorcas in the world, of course. And, there are other mountains besides the Blue Mountains."

We took his point.

"All the same," I said, "we will buy saddle animals from Segesthes. We have to. But—and I own to being selfish here—for this new regiment I would like to have the best. The Jiktar is to be Nath Karidge."

"But he is a Chuktar." They both looked surprised. I did not think they knew of my threat to stuff poor Nath Karidge into a Phalanx.

"He remains a Chuktar, with a step. But this regiment will be a cavalry reserve, the basis for a much larger force, when we can find the zorcas and the right men."

In the end we sorted it all out and I pulled that thin file from under the stack of other files, and wrote down the reassuring fact that soon six hundred zorcas would be taken on strength. I was looking forward to telling Nath Karidge.

Turko and Korero came in and my little study began to fill up. These men had all campaigned together and were comrades in arms, and so I pushed the papers across my desk, put my feet up and let the evening roll. We were joined by other comrades and adjourned to a larger chamber. Pretty soon we started singing. It was a good night.

A good night, yes—but not the way an emperor should carry on when he has a ramshackle empire to run. No, by Krun!

Delia's remark that I was feeling sorry for myself carried a deal of truth. Well, if Delia says something, it usually is true and if it is uncomfortable into the bargain, then that means you must spruce up and see about setting matters right.

Nath Karidge did not join us that night as we sang the old songs. As always, or almost always for the exceptions proved the rule, I started up "The Bowmen of Loh." We all sang lustily.

"I suppose Seg will give command of his Second Army over to someone and return to us," said Turko as the last refrain died away.

Seg Segutorio, the master bowman, the best Bowman of Loh on Kregen in my estimation, was sorely missed.

"Aye," I said. "And as soon as Inch sorts out his Black Mountains—" And then I frowned.

This nonsense with Voinderam and Fransha had put back our plans, and Inch would have to battle on alone in his Black Mountains for a space. Turko spoke up. j

"The quicker I can march north and sort out Layco Jhansi the quicker I will be able to hook left and reach Inch."

"They make little progress in the Blue Mountains," said Filbarrka. "That great rascal Korf Aighos told me there are winged devils in great numbers in the mountains, barring off the Blue from the Black."

We all digested that unwillingly.

Then someone started up that silly song, "The Milkmaid's Pail," and we all joined in and, for some of us, drove back the shadows.

Now while these raucous parties we held on Kregen were not your Viking-type carouse, nor yet your Hussar or Lancer shindig, they were vociferous and splendidly barbaric. A couple of aides got into a paddy over a little shishi who had jilted one of them. The cause of the quarrel was not altogether clear. The occasion was turned to jest and merriment as we escorted the wrathful pair to the nearest guardroom where we would find a couple of wooden swords. With the rudis they would settle the matter, get the black humors out, and then with clearer heads—that might be ringing with all the Bells of Beng Kishi—try to solve the problem.

With the wooden swords solemnly carried on a red velvet cushion, we trooped out into a practice yard. The guards on duty smirked with pleasure at the thought of young bloods knocking hell out of each other. We had an audience as we went out under the Moons of Kregen. The stone walls bore the marks of fires. One side of the courtyard was a mass of rubble where the stables of the state carriages had been destroyed.

We were making a din. Yet I saw a man half in the shadows. He carried a long pike. He was going through the manual of drill as taught to a brumbyte in the files. At our noise he turned and dropped the pike. It clanged on the cobbles.

The Maiden with the Many Smiles shone in fuzzy pink glory upon the face of Nath Karidge.

"Nath!" those devils with me chorused, filled with glee.

Karidge just stood there. He wore a brumbyte's kit, a soldier's harness that held a bronze-studded leather coat, a vosk-skull helmet, and he slanted the brumbyte's shield, the crimson flower, in the approved position.

"Majister!"

These frolicsome men with me couldn't understand why Chuktar Nath Karidge, the reckless cavalry commander, should attire himself like this and go through the manual of drill with pike and shield.

I knew.

"Let the two hotheads at each other with their wooden swords," I said. "Let the strict code of the Hyr Jikordur apply." At this there were gales of laughter, for the Jikordur specifies the code of conduct and the rituals of combat in duels—often to the death.

The rowdy part set about arranging the duel in strict conformity with the Hyr Jikordur and I went across to Karidge. I knew why he had dressed like this and was going through the manual of arms of a pike-wielding brumbyte. Karidge regarded me stonily as I approached.

"I see you prepare yourself, Nath." I was very easy with him. "That is as it should be."

"Majister!"

"And, too, that is why I have picked you for your next assignment."

He licked his lips. The vosk-skull helmet shadowed his face, but the glory of the Moons of Kregen spilled down and set that hard, reckless face stark against the bronze fittings.

"I think your wife will approve."

"She was most wroth. She told me that, much as she admires all sections of the Phalanx, she could not really credit being married to a man not in jutman's uniform."

I nodded. If, sometimes, I refer to any of the riders of Kregen as horsemen, forgive me. Jutman is the word, for there are most marvelously varied bunches of saddle animals, and one does not always detail zorcaman or totrixman or voveman.

I told Nath Karidge what I wanted. As I spoke so his features loosened, and then tautened. He smiled. The sparkle grew. His enthusiasm seized him up as a giant winged monster of Kregen's skies snatches up its prey.

"I shall serve to the death, majister—"

"Aye, Nath. Aye, I know that. And it grieves me, as well as affording me intense pride in you. The empress—"

"I shall begin at once."

"You may select your officers and troopers from whatever regiments of the cavalry arm you wish. I do not restrict you in any way. You are to form a regiment of the best, the smartest, the toughest—in short, Nath, you will create a cavalry regiment that is just simply the finest in all the world."

"And this regiment will be the empress's personal bodyguard!"

"Just so. You are herewith promoted instantly to ord-Chuktar. The regiment will be known as EDLG, the Empress's Devoted Life Guard." I gestured in a way I tried to make nonchalant, to hide the guilt I felt at the next words I would say, guilt at the expense of the rest of the army. "Your officers will be a rank higher than customary. Jiktars will command the squadrons. I want the best, the finest, the—"

"Yes, majister."

On a sudden, Nath Karidge's voice sounded soft.

I swallowed.

"This is a thing I should have done seasons ago."

"I can only say that the honor you do me—" He did not go on. I do not think he could. By Zair! But my Delia is loved by her people!

Then a great outburst of shouting and laughter dragged us back from the lip of mawkish sentiment. The two hotheads had laid each other out, their wooden swords clattering onto the cobbles. I barely saw. My Val! My Delia—she demanded everything of me I had to give. Everything...

Seven

Sacrifice

When Turko and his army were safely on their way north, that, I made up my mind, would be my cutoff point. Then I would take off for Hyrklana to bring back our friends. During my recent absences from Vallia the country had been run by my son Drak, the Presidio, the Lord Farris, with the expert and unstinting help of Larghos the Left-Handed and Naghan Strandar, chief among the other pallans. Yes, that was what I decided.

Jilian had not returned. The Wizards of Loh, although in communication by messenger, had still not penetrated through whatever dark veil of sorcery that arch devil Phu-Si-Yantong had thrown over us. The army needed an overhaul. The harvests remained good. So with a small suite I took myself off to the rocky island of Chandror, off the south coast of Gremivoh. We took one of the sailing fliers and made good progress. On Chandror the new gold mines were yielding ore of a rich red lusciousness. Gold is just a metal; but it has its uses.

Chandror was an imperial island. There was little there, beyond the goats that leaped from crag to crag in the interior, untold millions of sea birds and a few fishing villages with stout stone walls. I suppose none of the nobility in the past had coveted Chandror, and the emperor had simply accepted it as part of his domains.

Now that gold had been discovered—and kept secret—the island figured afresh in our calculations. We had to pay vast sums abroad for supplies, and we had to make sure we did not overly inflate our own economy with what amounted to cheap money.

The old saying in Havilfar has it: "Money does not drop from fluttrell's wings." But it seemed to me, as our sails slanted with the breeze and we began to drift down, that had happened. These gold mines were delivered into our hands by sheer chance; a strayed ponsho, bleating and baaing and falling into a pit. And the shepherd crooking him out and with him, a ponsho fleece of gold. The old stories are the best...

A sudden hubbub of laughter and good-humored chaffing erupted at my back. I did not turn, watching the island grow ahead. I knew the voices. These were two lively youngsters, twins, the sons of the son of Genal Arclay, Vad of Valhotra. One day, Opaz willing, one of these two skylarking lads would be Vad in his turn, the other the vadnich.

Valhotra, a lush land, rich in agriculture and husbandry, lay immediately to the east of Vondium and the southern extension of the imperial province of Hyrvond along the Great River. As a matter of sound common sense Valhotra and other provinces close to the capital were held by nobles loyal to the emperor. These twins, Travok and Tom Arclay, could look forward to a glittering future. But, first, they had to serve as aides, pages, raw-edged young coys sucking in all the information they could. And while they were doing that, they thoroughly enjoyed life, always up to tricks and jests, into scrapes and roaring with laughter all the time. They were devoted to each other.

The sailing ship of the sky slanted down through thin air. The island below spread in grays and browns on the sea. The water rippled silver in lapping waves. From the crags the sea birds soared as we swung down, filling the sky with the beat and flutter of their wings.

Turko was laughing, and Korero was shouting something about its being more convenient to have four hands with imps like these. Still I gazed over the rail at the scene spread out below. There was all the need in Kregen for laughter...

We made a reasonable landing with the sailer of the skies, which meant we got down and threw the anchor out without smashing anything too serious.

The island was garrisoned by the Ninetieth Regiment, a kind of gendarmerie outfit mainly recruited by Naghan Vanki. We wanted to keep knowledge of this treasure trove as secret as we could. An assistant pallan,

Noivo Randalsh, welcomed us. A calm, competent man with a habit of moving his head back and forth when he spoke, Randalsh had Chandror well-organized and producing gold. We saw the workings and I made damned sure I talked to the workers, and not a slave within many a mile, and discovered their grievances, if any, and checked on their work conditions. The gold came up out of the pit the ponsho had found with gratifying ease.

Because of the importance of this gold to Vallia, Farris had spared a sizable airboat to ferry the bullion to Vondium. We watched as she took off, turning to vanish into the north.

"You are doing well, Pallan Randalsh."

"Thank you, majister. As a mark of your visit I am authorizing an extra issue of wine—"

"Sore heads in the morning?"

We laughed.

"It will be worth it. Your words mean a great deal to us. The workers understand better now."

I turned away, losing my smile.

Turko stepped in.

"The Ninetieth have prepared a feast. I am sure they do not want death's heads at the table."

So, brisking up, I enjoyed myself at the feast given by the Ninetieth Regiment of Foot. And we sang. Well, swods on Kregen always sing, as you know...

The following afternoon, having seen what we had come to see, we took off, spreading the canvas, hoisting the anchor, letting those magical silver boxes lift us up into thin air. The name of this sailing ship of the sky was Opazfaril. She was a fine craft. We waved and shouted down and the Ninetieth in their ordered ranks let rip with the wild war whoop that revealed that all the spit and polish, all the drill, could not entirely conceal their wild warrior origins. The workers shrilled the remberees. So Opazfaril sailed up into the glory of the suns.

A moment later the aft lookout called, and we all looked up.

Up there, erratic in the streaming radiance playing among the clouds, a nimble airboat gamboled. We looked closer. Three other airboats circled about the first, catching her up, diving to attack.

The pursuers were trying to cut off the boat which fled madly. And now we saw she was making determined efforts to fly down toward us.

A warning note in his voice, Turko said, "Is it any business of ours?"

"It is taking place in Vallian skies."

"All the same—"

I shouted at Captain Dorndorf. "Beat to quarters!"

The drums began to roll through Opazfaril. Men ran to the varters, the snouts of the ballistae frowning along the broadside. Other men carrying bows climbed the rigging. We prepared for battle.

Korero appeared at my side. His four hands grasped two massive shields. His golden beard jutted.

"Yes, yes, Korero," I said, before he could speak.

And then Turko appeared, with his shield uplifted.

Korero the Shield. Turko the Shield. Well, that problem had been solved. But right here and now as we went flying into action, these two comrades might have a little ding-dong among themselves, arguing who was to stand at his back with shields upraised.

"One each side," I said. "And don't get in my way!"

My surprise was perfectly genuine when they both cracked out a "Quidang, majister!"

By Vox! But I must have snarled it at them to evoke that response!

The apparent confusion as the crew of a fighting ship ran to action stations rapidly sorted itself out. The smell of the sea bore in on the breeze. Our canvas swelled. Up there the fliers spun, weaving patterns between the clouds. The mingled radiance of the suns fell in an opaline glory.

"Does anyone recognize the cut of their jibs?" I bellowed.

No one replied.

The vollers were of a style new to me, new to everyone else in the ship too, it seemed.

Then, with only a slight hesitation, Korero said, "I think—I would not swear to it—I think they bear some resemblance to airboats from Balintol." He stared up, concentrating. "Not Balintolian, though. But like it."

As the vollers approached it was possible to make out the profusion of carving and ornamentation smothering their hulls. The three pursuing were much larger than we'd at first thought. They were stuffed with men. We could see the round helmets and the thick forests of upraised spears over the bulwarks.

As I had not gone below, Deft-fingered Minch, my orderly, brought the armor on deck and helped me into it. I wanted nothing heavy or fancy for the kind of work I anticipated lay ahead. The supple mesh links of that marvelous coat of mail I had fetched out of the Dawn Lands and a close-fitting helmet would suffice. All the same, Minch saw to it that a tall and waving panache of scarlet feathers sprouted from the top of the helmet. Perforce, I allowed that, seeing it was expected.

Now the fleeing airboat, by the execution of a pretty piece of flying, won free of her pursuers. In a wide skating curve she threw them off to starboard. They swerved around, the pennants and flags fluttering from many flagstaffs. But the smaller airboat slid down and away from them for just enough time to stand a chance of reaching us.

"He'll make it," said Korero with perfect confidence.

"Just," said Turko,

Weg Wegashtorio, the Bowman of Loh I had selected for an important task, glanced across.

"A few heartbeats more, majister—"

"Aye, Weg. Loose when you are ready."

He nodded, turning back to his little rank of bowmen. He had ten of them, ten Bowmen of Loh that Seg had insisted I use. Each man was a veteran, a kampeon who had served faithfully and was now a citizen of Vallia, and no longer a mercenary. Other archers with the compound reflex bows settled themselves comfortably in the fighting tops. The space between the fleeing voller and Opazfaril narrowed.

This situation, of course, presented just those kinds of problems that beset me when I was dumped down, naked and unarmed, somewhere or other on Kregen to sort out a problem for the Star Lords. Why should we assume the fleeing boat needed to be rescued? Could not those three grim pursuers be chasing a criminal, a render, say, an aerial pirate of their skies?

By chance it happened that the officer and the duty squadron with me were Jiktar Rodan and his men. I did not need to give him a look. The squadron of the 2ESW waited calmly, not in ranks but taking up good fighting positions about the deck, ready to loose the bow or ply spear or sword as the occasion warranted. The Emperor's Sword Watch was a regiment that fought astride saddle animals, on foot or in the air. Their task was to protect the emperor.

The problem of which side to take in this coming fight, if side we had to take, was rapidly solved.

Jiktar Rodan flung up a hand, pointing to the flags streaming back from the staffs. Wind pressure had concealed their devices from us. Now as the fleeing voller turned in close the banners fluttered bravely into view. By color and symbol, device and design, you can get to know the Treshes of Kregen, and thereby know with whom you are to deal... And just as surely, it would take a lifetime of lifetimes to learn them all!

Staring at those flags as they flew fluttering back I realized I had not instinctively tightened my grip on my sword.

Every flag was green.

Dark green, those standards with purple and gold embroideries, and the tiny little jolt I would ordinarily have experienced was absent.

Rodan shouted, "From Persinia!"

Everybody strained to look, and many stared owlishly across the wind-streaming gap.

Vallia had strong trading links with Persinia, although much weakened now after the Time of Troubles. A deal of that red gold we dug from Chandror was on its way to more than one nation of Persinia to buy supplies and to purchase totrixes and nikvoves.

I looked up at Korero, at his superb face fixed in a trifle of a scowl, the golden beard and moustache bristling.

"Friend or foe, Korero?"

"Who can say? It is like a stewpot there, allied one day and at each other's throats the next. They are always on the go."

"You sound as though you are describing the Dawn Lands of Havilfar!"

"They are something like that in Persinia, although on a smaller scale. Those flags, I think, are Pershawian. The purple and gold nikvove on the green field."

Korero was from Balintol—which remains a mighty mysterious place, by Vox!—and that subcontinent stretches down from Segesthes. Persinia is the southern protrusion of the coastline to the west. It lies to the north of the Undurkor Islands. Because the river which flows in a loop north and west from the mountains of Balintol reaches the sea far to the west at Zenicce, it effectively cuts off these southern lands from the Great Plains to the north.

The flier looked to be in trouble. Her flight turned into a series of blind lurches through the air.

Rodan said, "She is from Pershaw. And it looks as though she will go no farther."

We had been buying nikvoves from Pershaw. This fleeing voller bore grated openings along her side, two decks of them, and safely penned inside would be a consignment of nikvoves. Those wonderful eight-legged saddle animals, although not as powerful or fierce as the superb voves themselves, were sorely needed by our cavalry. And in the nature of things, they would have already been paid for.

Perhaps that petty financial reckoning made up my mind.

"We must save the flier," I said. "Captain Dorndorf, it is up to you and your helmsman. Maneuver to mask her."

"Quidang—" There was no time for the tiresome majister. Opazfaril took the breeze and surged ahead, the silver boxes buried deep in the hull exerted their influence upon the lines of ethero-magnetical force, as the wise men say, and we swung up and past the staggering voller and hurled ourselves full on the three pursuers.

Now your real voller is propelled along as well as lifted by the two silver boxes. These three could pirouette about us like hounds about a stag. Our only motive power came from our canvas spread to the breeze. Well... not quite only.

There was one other power, an awful force of nature, that together with the ship designers of Vallia, I had calculated to use in battles of flying sailing ships against vollers. That power had been used to grim effect on the long flight of steps up to Esser Rarioch, the strom's palace and castle on Valka...

Captain Dorndorf proved a fine shipmaster.

Opazfaril got in among the three vollers. Then the canvas came in, with just enough spread to give us a trifle of forward momentum, and we settled down to act as a solid fortress and shoot it out. These airboats from Persinia were not too well equipped with varters. Our varter crews bent to their work lustily, twirling the windlasses, drawing back the heavy bows, sliding in the lethal darts or the ugly chunks of rock, letting fly. The Vallian gros-varter is a king among ballistae, and we had four of them among the smaller projectile weapons.

The archers shot. Down in the fighting galleries along the keel the bowmen loosed, up in the fighting tops and the walkways between the masts, the archers showered their steel-tipped death. Return shots came in. Our bulwarks were thick and high, our mantlets arranged just so, and for this kind of work Opazfaril was just as well suited as the vollers. If those lean hunting hounds sought to drag down this stag, they found she had needle-sharp horns everywhere and not just adorning her forehead.

The lookouts on special duty posted in a relay chain kept calling the positional information up, along the relay, to Travok, grandson of the Vad of Valhotra, positioned near Captain Dorndorf on the quarterdeck. Travok's twin, Tom, was up in a fighting top, screeching his lungs out.

"I leave the moment to you, captain."

"When the trumpet blows, majister—do you grasp hold!"

"Aye!"

Arrows sprouted from our masts. Our hulls overside must have looked like pincushions. But our varters were striking home in ruthless fashion. Chunks of the vollers splintered stern, bulwarks, hull, beams. One or two lumps of rock whistled across our deck and a young cadet, Bolan the Tumbs, brought one across to me. I weighed it on my palm.

Captain Dorndorf nodded. "Small."

Korero said, "Enough to knock your head off."

Turko said, "That's why—" and stopped.

An arrow stood in his shield.

He broke it off and we looked at it. Not a Lohvian shaft, but long and deadly and tipped with steel. The feathers were undyed, being browny-white from the Oraneflut, a useful bird of graceful body and broad wings.

"I've been shot at a few times with those," observed Korero.

The fight brawled across the sky as Opazfaril sailed slowly and steadily on and the vollers swirled like leaves in a hurricane about us. The flier they had been pursuing snuggled in along our flank, grapnels flew and men went across to shoot on that side. A number of crossbow bolts snicked in among the arrows. I began to think the time when the boarding attempts would be made must be near. I told Dorndorf. He nodded, and drew a short, stout, thick and extremely nasty-looking axe. He ran a thumb along the edge.

"Soon now, majister, yes."

"Find out about the voller."

Cadet Bolan the Tumbs ran off, like an alley cat, leaping the cumbered decks, disappearing over the bulwarks to shinny down onto the grappled voller. His freckles had blazed with his passionate enthusiasm.

Travok Arclay yelled.

"One is swinging in below!"

Certainly, there were only two vollers circling above us and trying to drop nasty objects on our decks. Stationed at the end of the chain of men reporting from the lower fighting galleries, Travok kept looking up at the top where his twin screeched with excitement and hauled up barrels of arrows.

I wondered if these harum-scarum lads were disappointed that the thought that crossed our minds on first sighting the strange vollers had proved false. The island below was rich in gold. Well, then, if the secret got out, wouldn't you expect hordes of renders to come sailing piratically down? Of course. But there was a lot more to this little fracas than mere piracy.

The nearest flier was close enough now to bring a catapult into play that hurled larger and altogether more unpleasant chunks of rock than their small varters. A section of our bulwarks broke in and men staggered away yelling. Portable mantlets were dragged across to give shield cover against arrows and crossbow bolts. Lookouts tried to spot the catapult on the crowded enemy decks and shooters tried to knock out the crew. The fight was becoming personal.

The crash splintered through the uproar and a barrel of arrows burst and showered shafts skittering across the deck. A rock had cleanly severed the rope by which Tom Arclay hauled up replenishment arrows. At once he started to shinny down the line, swinging like a monkey down to the deck, ignoring both the ratlines and the ladder affixed to the mast for landlubberish soldiers.

"He's almost under us!" Travok jumped in excitement Tom hit the deck near him. They were both wrapped up in their work.

The lookouts below reported the progress of the airboat almost under us. Probably the voller captains were quite unsure how to deal with us, a weird contraption the like of which they had not seen before. They must quickly have realized we had no power and were wind-driven. That made them incautious. No doubt they sought to fly in below and swing up, judging it nicely, and land boarding parties along our keel galleries. They would be in the ship far more easily and quickly that way than by any attempt to land across our mast and rigging-encumbered decks.

If this captain below us wanted to try that, he was welcome...

"Another few murs!" shrieked Travok.

Tom glanced across at his twin.

The bulwarks broke back just by the two lads. Yellow splinters of wood whirred murderously. A bowman screamed, transfixed by a shaft ten times thicker than those he shot. The two boys were down, rolling on the deck. A trumpet pealed.

The trumpet rang above all the noises of the combat.

Instantly, Opazfaril dropped like a stone.

The silver boxes had been thrust apart, the lifting power vanished, the ship fell. She fell crushingly down upon the voller under us. The noise racketed maddeningly. But I saw the Arclay twins, rolling on the deck, sliding toward the shattered side and the awful drop into nothingness.

Somehow I was there. There is no memory of leaping across the planking. I grabbed Tom, who was nearest, and threw him back. He pitched over and reached out, grasping for a handhold.

A smear of blood across the wood told of some poor devil who had been in the way of the flung rock. Travok was over the side, gripping with his fists into the folds of the netting, the tarred cordage biting. He was slipping down. The net was running out, ripped through on its eyelets.

His head vanished below the shattered bulwarks. In only moments he would fall free of the ship as the net and its supporting booms collapsed away.

Four long leaps should carry me to the side and the slipping net, and the grasping fingers of Travok Arclay.

Captain Dorndorf was a fine sailor of the skies. He understood the limitations and the possibilities of his ship. Opazfaril lifted a little. I felt that movement under my feet as I left Tom on the deck and began my leap for Travok. No one else was at hand; it had all been very quick. I felt the movement, I leaped, and Opazfaril dropped again, dropped sickeningly down. She hit the voller under us and the jar felt as though I had leaped down onto a marble tombstone. I staggered. My balance was gone.

Without a sound I pitched over the side.

Upside down I fell past the side of the ship.

A flailing hand welted out and caught bruisingly in the next net by the one to which Travok clung. His net's supports were broken through and he was slipping down. My net held firmly, and I got another hand hooked into it. I was quite safe. I looked sideways at Travok, to see how quickly I could traverse and grab him.

"Hold on, Travok! We'll soon get you out of this."

"I am not afraid, majister—"

Tom poked his face over the smashed bulwark above us. He looked down.

What followed followed fast.

Tom looked down and saw his twin brother, to whom he was devoted.

He saw his emperor. He saw us both and saw how we clung to our nets, and the way the nets swayed and ripped against their smashed eyelets.

He did not hesitate.

That was the thing that got to me, that screwed me up, that made—it is painful.

Without hesitation, Tom reached over and hauled on the net to which I clung, hauling it in until he could reach me.

I yelled.

"No! No! Get Travok!" I screamed it out. "Travok!"

But Tom Arclay doggedly hauled on.

I put my hand on a damned splinter in the ruined bulwark and I turned my head and looked down. Tom's face was wet with tears and I could not look at him.

Travok's net split. It parted down the middle and Travok Arclay fell and fell, fell away, dwindling to a little spinning black dot with tiny whirling arms and legs.

I could not watch him all the way.

All I could do was haul myself over the side. I couldn't look at Travok as he fell spinning down and I couldn't look at his twin, Tom, as he collapsed on the deck.

Truthfully, I could look at no man in that instant—least of all myself.

Eight

Zenobya

"Hyrklana!" I said. I shouted it savagely. We were back in Vondium and a lot had happened and I was raw, ravaged, contemptuously intolerant of myself. I didn't want fine young men dying for me, I didn't want fine young men having to make that kind of awful decision—for me. "I'm going to Hyrklana. But before I do I am going to do one thing—send Sans Fantor and Therfenen in. Bratch!"

Not often do I use that hard word, bratch! It means jump, move, get the lead out. Sometimes, perhaps, I should have used it more.

The messengers bratched.

When the two wise men came in they looked pale. No doubt they had heard that the emperor was in a foul mood. Everyone who could recall what emperors traditionally did when they were in foul moods would tremble. Shoulders and heads would have air gaps. In the old days.

"Sans," I said. My words were hard. "Come in. There is a task to your hands I will have done immediately."

Among the gorgeous rams of the imperial palace this audience chamber had been refurbished, the roof not having fallen in, and the throne—a mere marble affair with only about a sackful of jewels embedded in golden settings—replaced from where it had been toppled among rubble. It had avoided being looted by this, for although a mere sackful of gems is paltry when embellishing one of an emperor's collection of thrones, it is highly prized and valuable portable property to a reiving mercenary. This was the Chamber of Allakar, and it impressed the two wise men, who were more used to meeting me in my homely study or their workrooms.

"Majister?" They quavered like little old gnomes instead of acting as they usually did, as wise men and savants of the Empire of Vallia. I frowned.

"Take what is necessary of the minerals we prepare for inclusion in the next batch of silver boxes for vollers. Make up small boxes, in pairs. Attach them to strong leather belts in slides, so that they can be moved together or drawn apart. If anyone falls over the side of a flier again I want him to have some means of saving his life. Do I make myself clear?"

"Yes, majister..." And, "Aye majister..."

I sent them off with their promise of immediate production of the safety flying belts mocking me. If only Travok had had a belt!

The fight had not lasted long after we had come to hand strokes. We had captured two of the vollers—useful additions to the Lord Farris's fleet—and the third had flown. One of those we had captured—the one Captain Dorndorf had smashed his Opazfaril down on so ruthlessly—was not much good for anything. She could be stripped for her lumber. It was the silver boxes that were important. We would build a new and better voller around them.

There were prisoners. We in Vallia of the parts that had been liberated kept no slaves. The prisoners would have to be repatriated on flights back to Persinia. These fighting men were from Chobishaw and most wroth they were that they had failed to capture the voller we had rescued. These Chobishaws spoke in fine manly terms, but I didn't have time for their pleas.

"No," I said to their leader, whose impressive plate armor had been taken away, and whose face with its long down-drooping moustaches and thin nose expressed the utmost fury and scorn—baffled fury and useless scorn. "No. I will not yield up to you the Lady Zenobya. She is her own lady to decide her own fate. She asks help of Vallia. She—"

"The king has decreed her death! She has no claim to the throne of Pershaw—"

"I think the lady has a claim."

"If she has—and we do not agree on that—it will be canceled in death."

"Not," I said nastily, "while the Lady Zenobya appeals to Vallia."

"Vallia!" This Chobishaw laughed then, his thin nose arrogant. "Vallia! There is no Vallia any more. It is ruined!"

The damned devil! He was almost right... Almost...

But we had liberated much of the main island and the fringing islands of the coasts, and we would free the remainder.

"King Pafnut refuses to deal any longer with you Vallians. Chobishaw looks to other and stronger empires."

"By all means," I said, "if these can be found. Now go away and wait until we can send you home."

The dark blood rushed to his thin face.

He was wheeled around by my lads of 2ESW and then I called, "I am told you in Chobishaw are very clever with numbers and can make circles out of straight lines and tricks of that sort. But can you make vollers?"

He looked back at me, venom in his face. That thin nose, those down-drooping mustachios, that pallid face with the thin scornful lips— if they were all like that back where he came from no wonder the Lady Zenobya had found no joy of them.

"We do not need to make our own fliers. We can buy them from our good friends."

I resisted the impulse to retort. He was in all probability not speaking of Hamal, for Hamal desperately needed all the vollers she could make herself. Unless, that is, vast new factories had been opened. With mad Empress Thyllis, anything was possible.

All the same, I told Naghan Vanki to begin an investigation to discover just where these folk of Persinia did buy their airboats.

The story the Lady Zenobya told us was charming. She said she ought to have had a few more heads off, and then she wouldn't have needed to stow away in a flier bringing nikvoves to us. Her hereditary foemen from Chobishaw had only got wind of the stratagem at the last moment. Their pursuit had ended with the Lady Zenobya being received as an honored guest in Vondium.

Pershaw, of course, was now firmly under the thumb of King Pafnut of Chobishaw.

"I have many brave fighting men loyal to me, but they lack a leader, they lack instruction, they are bemused by what has happened."

Lady Zenobya spoke in a fierce way, like a zhantilla defending her cubs. A poised woman, beautiful—yes, of course—but she contained within herself a determination one felt gained its own ends against seemingly insuperable odds, and this lent her beauty an aura of power missing from those women who imagine beauty is skin deep. She was not from Loh, but she had red hair, a deep and lustrous auburn that shone splendidly in the lights of the Chamber of Allakar. We got to know the Lady Zenobya better later on—as you shall hear—and we discovered that her charm and politeness concealed a Machiavellian diplomacy and gift of misdirection that, combined with her forthright honesty, gave her a diabolical ingenuity.

Among the nikvoves brought in the voller in which she had stowed away she had contrived to arrange that her own favorite animal should be included. Mind you, his eight legs and powerful body were clad in an odd hide of black and white, with immoderate amounts of hairy mane, tail and hocks. His name was Sjames, and he was, so Zenobya claimed, supernaturally intelligent.

Whether the last was true or not seemed something we would have to wait to find out. For now, the Lady Zenobya looked splendid, riding her Sjames, cantering out into the countryside around Vondium, her auburn hair a flame in the lights of the suns.

The decision to go to Hyrklana was forced on me by that horrific occurrence in Opazfaril.

The process was not as clear-cut as that makes it sound. I was still confused. The sight of Tom Arclay hauling me in and letting his twin beloved brother fall to his death... No, I wanted nothing more of that for a space.

The shame crushed me. And, too, the deeply sensed and avoided feeling that an emperor to be an emperor must needs receive that kind of sacrifice, filled me with self-horror. To throw away your life in the heat of battle and sacrifice yourself to save another—yes. Mad though that may be, it is not as rare as the cynics would have us believe. It is a part of that battle rapture of which I hold such strong feelings. I dislike—to use a pale word—the red veil that clouds vision and sanity.

But Tom Arclay had acted coldly, determinedly, unswerving in his devotion to the Emperor of Vallia.

I had to get away.

The two Wizards of Loh had by means of pooled power forced a passage between themselves through the occult realms. The kharrna exercised by Phu-Si-Yantong was not, then, all-powerful.

Nothing fresh came to hand on the whereabouts of Voinderam and Fransha. Our schemes for Mavindeul were perforce frozen. Once Turko got up there with his army, liberated his new kovnate of Falinur, hooked left into Vennar and dealt with Layco Jhansi, we could link up with the Black Mountain Men and the Blue Mountain Boys. After that it would be the Racters of the north. Perhaps we did not really require Mavindeul to rise for us.

I felt we did. It would save lives.

The Lord Farris had promised air support for Turko.

We worked out the army he would take, and the Presidio, with that sense of grandeur I found slightly comic, christened Turko's force the Ninth Army.

The Eighth Army, which had won that battle centered around the thorn-ivy trap, the Battle of Ovalia, I had reserved to my own hand. Many of the same regiments would march with Turko. I held onto the army number.

Nine is the sacred and magical number on Kregen. Turko was pleased.

"It's all a foolishness, Turko," I told him. "You have a Phalanx and regiments of churgurs. Your soldiers are keen. Your spearmen are a little raw. But your archers are first class. Your kreutzin will serve you well. But do not get ideas of glory and grandeur just because this collection is called the Ninth Army..."

"If I didn't know you better, Dray, I'd want to know whose side you are on."

"You're taking a capital adviser in Kapt Erndor. He is an old Freedom Fighter from Valka and as cunning as a leem."

"I'm glad he is with us. I value his advice."

I nodded. Turko might have been made up to be a kov by me, and have fought in many battles, but he lacked the professional experience of a general in command. He'd learn, I made no mistake about that. And the truth was Turko had learned a very great deal regarding campaigning and logistics, strategy and tactics and the all-important field of operations in the wars in which we had fought together.

Units were being sent from both Drak's and Seg's armies to join Turko. I sent a messenger to tell Seg to take over command of both forces, the First and the Second Armies, and another messenger to tell Drak to come home to Vondium.

"I'd like to see Seg before I start," said Turko. "But I don't think it possible. By Morro the Muscle! I miss that man!"

"Me, too."

"And it's a pity Voinderam couldn't cork it until the legal bokkertu was settled. I was counting on him. He is rated as a swordsman—not that swordsmen mean—"

"Quite."

He smiled. "No, Dray. I mean Voinderam took up with the shield; he saw the possibilities early. He has gained a fine reputation as a churgur. I believe he would have put some useful regiments into the field."

"Sword and shield men are still thin on the ground, I agree. But the Vallians are learning."

And so was I. I tried to cram a hundred burs into every Kregan day, which Opaz has decided should hold but forty-eight. Drak and Farris and the Presidio ought to be able to handle affairs while I was away. By Vox! They had done it before, and for all my own long-faced doubts, what we had of Vallia was in better shape than anything seen for seasons. For all the work I did, I was not indispensable as an emperor. And that was the way I wanted it to be.

As always when Delia was in Vondium with me, the efforts proved not only more worthwhile but also much easier. Jilian trailed back to the city, swearing and swishing her wicked claw about, completely foxed. The elopers had run away and vanished.

The Lady Zenobya proved popular in the assemblies and balls. Filbarrka hung about the city, working on plans for the cavalry force of freedmen. Nath Karidge took delivery of his six hundred first-class zorcas and the EDLG grew as prime men came in.

Although I had promised myself I'd leave as soon as Turko flew off with his army, I now delayed my own departure until the EDLG had been properly raised, formed, and put into a reasonable state of readiness. This was one kind of excuse I did not need for myself.

Delia designed the uniform. I was delighted. It carried the brave old scarlet well, with yellow trim and a decent area of darker colors—varying with squadron—to set off the dashing effect. Guidons loaded with bullion were presented to the standard bearers of each squadron. The trumpets were of silver—we vetoed gold on the scores of weight and tone. Yes, the Empress's Devoted Life Guard, glittering, polished, prancing on nimble zorcas, looked a superb regiment. They were not mere ornaments. Each trooper was a kampeon. They would give of their loyalty to Delia; they'd fight for her. They'd fight to the death.

Turko and Korero had agreed to disagree. Turko, as a kov, had a task. But he kept on trying to tell Korero what to do, the better to protect me with his shields.

Korero pulled his golden beard with his tail hand and said, "It is just as well we are leaving."

And then Turko said the right thing, and they were friends again.

"I could do with a regiment like the EDLG with me, up in Falinur," said Turko wistfully, as the guidons were presented. Korero nudged him. At once, Turko went on, "But, by Morro the Muscle! The Empress demands the best there is in all Vallia!"

Because I am weak in some matters, I gravely acceded to Tom Arclay's request to accompany Kov Turko of Falinur.

I had done what had to be done over the death of Travok.

I will not detail the events, but I felt no slackening of my anger, my contempt. The world was not a just place, not Earth, not Kregen. And the fact that I had been in no real danger, hanging over the side of Opazfaril, must never be revealed. If Tom knew that he had sacrificed his twin brother's life in vain...!

So, in my weakness and selfishness, I was glad to know Tom would be flying off with Turko. That great Khamorro would look out for Tom Arclay, now, with a special fervor.

But he had something else on his mind.

We were sprawled on the mat in the gymnasium, having contorted ourselves in a few falls, and tied ourselves in knots. Turko sat up and blew his cheeks out.

"They don't go in for the martial arts in Hyrklana, Dray? No unarmed combat in the arena?"

I shook my head.

"It's edged and pointed weapons. When you are lucky enough to be given them. Sometimes in the Jikhorkdun you are sent against wild beasts with your bare hands."

"Well...? That would be—"

"Ghastly. I have seen it."

So he said, "So, my old dom, you keep well away from the Jikhorkdun in Huringa—"

I found a craggy smile. "Deb-Lu-Quienyin told me that our friends are involved with the Jikhorkdun again."

"No!"

"I shall gather more details before I go. It's not the arena in the Jikhorkdun that bothers me so much. I just hope fat Queen Fahia and her neemus do not get a scent of me."

Then we indulged in a few more falls, the skills and disciplines of the Khamsters pitted against those of the Krozairs, and both learning from each other. Queen Fahia's pet neemus, feral, treacherous, black as a night of Notor Zan, decorated the steps of her throne. I was not enamored of the idea of seeing Fahia again or renewing acquaintance with her pets.

The moment Drak arrived I knew I'd be surrounded by an orgy of back-slapping, arm-wrenching, uproarious hullabaloo as my comrades of the First Emperor's Sword Watch renewed their acquaintance with me. I knew they felt pushed away from me, almost slighted, but I'd impressed them forcibly with the notion that their duty lay with Drak, seeing that he was the one fighting the war up there. Now nothing would keep those ruffians of 1ESW from standing watch over me, as in the old days. Certainly, 2ESW would not. Nor would the Yellow Jackets, who would return with Drak. These kampeons felt they had a divine right to put their own bodies between me and the deadly shaft, the murderous sword. I was not happy about that, as you know; but I had to accept the needle, as they say on Kregen.

An interesting strand of the past was revealed to me at that time. Among the many people I saw every day on business of one sort or another there were always a score or so who came offering their swords, seeking a particular favor. I tried to accommodate them all, according to their merits.

One limber fellow was wheeled in during the bur I put aside for this purpose—the waiting room was always filled and Enevon would allow no golden corruption to seek preference—and I sized him up. The pakzhan

66

glittered at his throat. His pakai was coiled around his shoulder three times, that mercenary's record of trophies, the string of victory rings. His face was hard—as it would be, it would be!—and he held himself alert. He wore a tufted goat-like beard. He looked at me forthrightly.

"Koter Ian Vandrop, majister! Known to myself as Ian the Onker, for not having returned to Vondium sooner."

This could be flannel, of course. But he looked likely. More than likely. He was hyr-paktun, experienced, with his tally of kills.

I quizzed him on his service and learned he had served all over Paz, our grouping of continents and islands on this side of Kregen. He would find employment with me.

"But not as a mercenary. You are a Vallian."

"I almost forgot that, majister. But my father—"

"Vandrop?" There was the Bower of the Scented Lotus, a middling establishment at a crossroads of Southern Vondium, a fine place to take the Baths of the Nine. It had been smashed to smithereens in the Time of the Troubles. And Koter Vandrop had worn a goat-beard just like this strapping hyr-paktun.

"If I mentioned the names of Urban the Gloves and Travok Ott, Fat Ortyg—and the Bower of the Scented Lotus? Your father wore a goats-beard tuft as you do?"

He shook his head. "My father was clean-shaven, except when he awoke in the morning, a red-faced, serious, swearing man."

I was about to brush this misplaced episode from the past aside when the hyr-paktun Ian Vandrop went on.

"My grandfather, may Opaz light his days, had a beard like mine, so I am told, and he patronized the Scented Lotus."

Well, time flies, time flies. Grandfather...

"For the kindness shown by your grandfather, koter, I shall appoint you to the Emperor's Yellow Jackets, if you so desire. An ob-Hikdar to start with. You'll be a Jiktar in no time. There are recruits to train up—" I stopped as he looked puzzled.

"I thank you, majister, it is munificent. But—grandfather never said he met the Emperor of Vallia!"

"He is well, I trust?"

"He is with Opaz, majister, and well, I sincerely believe."

"He will be. He was a kind man. Opaz will have him in his keeping."

I mention this incident because it closed a past chapter—well, half-closed it. There were many men willing to serve. Vallia's prodigal sons were returning home. The word that Vallia no longer employed mercenaries had spread. Also, word that the Vallian army gained repute also spread. The lads who had gone overseas to seek their fortunes, adventures and gold, now flocked back to Vallia to stem the invasions of her foes.

67

Everyone was needed. Ian Vandrop was worth a regiment, because he would train and command a regiment in the bloody battles to come.

What I had visualized when those happy maniacs of mine returned to Vondium with Drak transpired. Oh, yes...

Talk about a riot. Carouse, bender, splurge, debauch—the uproar went on for a sennight, at least. Mind you, during the day I worked, as usual, and they went on parade, staying upright by the simple force of will. Their names you know—many of them. There were new faces in the ranks. The two corps, the Sword Watch and the Yellow Jackets, were not just pretty, dressed-up guardsmen or tough fighting men, they were very much cadres for teaching warrior skills and for infusing the spirit of the emperor's jurukkers into the whole army.

But that worthy objective must be seen in its true perspective, for the Vallian Army now possessed its own traditions and spirit. Created from nothing, building on courage and devotion, growing from guerrilla bands, the army flowered as experience matured it. Certainly the job would have been immeasurably harder had we not been able to call on the services and advice and training skills of my Freedom Fighters of Valka. And returning mercenaries, scarred with seasons of campaigning, added to our cadres. But the job would have been done. The Vallian Freedom Army was of Vallia. That was the lesson and the victory.

The daylight never lasted long enough; the lights of Kregen's moons shone upon our labors. And through it all, I began to see the approach of the day when I could leave for Hyrklana. Deb-Lu-Quienyin returned to Vondium with Drak and was long closeted with Khe-Hi-Bjanching. When they saw me they looked much more relaxed than I would have expected.

"We are now convinced that the interference of Phu-Si-Yantong—for it was he—had no connection with the elopement of the Lady Fransha and Ortyg Voinderam."

I stared. "Then, why did he exert all that force?"

They both started to speak, halted, and I said, "Deb-Lu?"

"We are aware of Yantong's insane desire to rule all of Paz, rule it physically, that is. Mad, mad. He has to try to break down the occult shield we have erected. The concepts are difficult for one who is not a sorcerer—"

"One who," put in Bjanching, "is not a Wizard of Loh."

"True. We are engaged in a battle on the ethereal planes, to put it crudely, and this attack was a reconnaissance in force."

"And there is no news of Fransha and Ortyg?"

"A Wizard of Loh needs knowledge of those he seeks in lupu—personal acquaintance, some artifact, a portion of themselves, the proverbial lock of hair, for instance—"

"But you discovered the whereabouts of my friends—"

"Yes, yes, majister. But they were sent to their destinations by sorcerous power." Here both Wizards of Loh looked uncomfortable. Well, I knew that the Savanti nal Aphrasöe scared the hell out of any sorcerer. "I could follow that. We thought Yantong had had a hand in this elopement and that we could follow his trail. But he did not."

"So Voinderam and Fransha are gone—and no one knows where?"

They nodded.

I said, "I shall reinforce Kov Turko's army. We'll have to hit Layco Jhansi so hard we start him running clear across Vennar and rush him up and into Racterland. And Kov Seg will attack from the east. It'll be a fine old argy-bargy while it's going on. But I'll be back from Hyrklana by then."

The sheer size of Vallia and our limited transport would give me ample time down south in Hyrklana to get our friends out and see about vollers before we hit Jhansi and the Racters.

It was at this time that the question of Barty Vessler's will came before the courts.

He had left everything to Dayra.

He had been the last of his line, the Strom of Calimbrev, and, as far as the courts could see, any other heirs there might have been were all dead. I sent three men to the island of Calimbrev to hold the place in trust for Dayra. Also, I arranged with Tom Tomor in Valka to send a few regiments as security. I sent Pallan Nogan Westmin, a loyal member of the Presidio. Although folk do not change much over their better than two hundred or so years of life on Kregen, there is an odd strain, probably non-hereditary, affecting hair. Some people, men and women both, go gray and then white. It has nothing to do with senility. Pallan Westmin had shining silvery hair. It is not particularly common.

I sent an imperial Justicar, Nazab Vantile, an energetic man bucking for a bigger province in the imperial service.

I sent Chuktar Logu Le-Ka, who as a Pachak had given nikobi, the Pachak code of loyalty. He was now a Vallian citizen, with an estate and a fair income, and as a commander in the army would take control of the forces in Calimbrev.

All this I did for my daughter Dayra, yes, to keep her inheritance intact from those who might seek to snatch it away from her. But I truly think I did it as much—even more—out of remembrance of Barty Vessler. He had wanted this. I would do my utmost to make sure his wishes were carried out.

There is a theory or philosophy—to dignify the notion—sincerely believed in by those who hold to it that all problems will solve themselves. They can point to planning and interference by government or whomever and call attention to the resultant shambles. They appear to have a strong case. Laissez-faire, as a system, has been discredited but the tightly planned economies that have attempted to replace that way of going on have fared no better. Dictatorship, where one person wields the chop, or democracy, where everyone gets to shoot his own arrow, as they say on Kregen, is not to everyone's taste. That old devil power rears his ugly and fascinating head.

A whole lot of folk just want to carry on drinking and singing and laughing and having a damn good time, and get paid fairly for what they work at, and leave the headaches of sorting it all out to somebody else.

Another slew want to get in the driving seat and crack the whip.

I suppose, as was forcibly pointed out to me by the good folk of Vallia—and before them of Valka and Djanduin—you have to have some Joe Muggins to blow the whistle.

If that was what I was, a work-burdened, worried, run-ragged referee, then that was what I was.

Oh, they called me an emperor and I had a lot of land and chests of gold and jewels and a few palaces—many of them burned down—and that collection of objects is no recompense. I did have good friends and blade comrades. And—there was Delia.

So the full circle was completed. I was the emperor and I was stuck with it, at least until Drak took over. I told him, this tall, serious, intense son of mine, "Drak, my lad, I'm off to Hyrklana to fetch our friends—Naghan the Gnat, and Tilly and Oby—and you'll run Vallia while I'm gone."

"You recall, Father, what I told you in the flier over Ba-Domek on the way to Aphrasöe, before you disappeared as you so frequently do? I said I would not be emperor while you or mother lived—"

I was brisk. I thought I knew this strapping son of mine and I didn't wish to make an issue of this now and harden attitudes.

"If your mother and I want to go off for a holiday, and I place the empire in your hands, will you refuse?"

"We-ell—no. But—"

"I was born a plain and ordinary fellow. I've been a sailor, a soldier and here and there an airman and a flutsman. I've done a heap of things. I've been slave. But you—you are born of a line of emperors, the son of an empress, and you are clearly not an ordinary sort of fellow at all. Your destiny is to be an emperor. I do not think that mine is."

"Father!"

"Your brother Zeg is now King of Zandikar. Well and good. He is a splendid man, a Krozair of Zy, like you and me. He will not challenge you for Vallia—will he?"

"I do not think so. But—"

"And your brother Jaidur. He is a tearaway, reckless and feckless. He hates my guts—"

"No!"

"And he has other fish to fry. I don't think he would seek to dislodge you from Vallia—would he?"

"No. But—"

"So that leaves you."

Drak's nostrils pinched in. He is sometimes an old sobersides, but he can be just as wild and barbaric as anyone whose name is Prescot.

"If you will let me get any words in at all," he said. "I will say that I will go to Hyrklana. I went to Faol and fetched back Melow and Kardo, and—"

I was very nasty to him. I screwed up my eyes and I said, "And Queen Lush?"

He did not flush. He stared at me. "Queen Lushfymi—"

"Oho! So it's Lushfymi, is it? Have you spoken to your mother?" I was well aware of the treacherous ground I trod. Delia and I wanted Drak to marry Seg's daughter Silda, for we had seen how Silda had behaved, and I had seen how Silda would have given her life, willingly, to save Drak.

But at the slightest hint of parental maneuvering, Drak would act—well, he'd be just as stubborn and pig-headed as I am, Zair forgive us both.

He said, very quietly, "I have the greatest respect for Queen Lushfymi."

"Good." I wasn't fool enough to ask, "And is that all?"

We were interrupted then by Delia coming into my study. She saw Drak's face, and my ugly old beakhead, and she sighed, and—how it was done remains a marvel and a mystery—we were all talking about the fancy dress ball that night and planning costumes. I ask you. Costumes for a fancy dress ball! And we'd been discussing the dynasty of an empire!

There is no need to go into a description of the ball. It was sumptuous, superb and splendid. Everyone seemed to be there. The thing of note, the event that rocked me back on my heels, took place as I was taking my leave with Delia radiant on my arm. I looked at the crowd, and every face was smiling and glowing, and every face belonged to a friend.

Ah! There is the wealth that no empire can give!

"I'm off to Hyrklana day after tomorrow," I said. "So I shall take the remberees of you now. Everything is arranged."

They let Korero be their spokesman. He stepped forward.

'That is good news, majister! A little adventuring will not come amiss. We are all ready—"

"What?" I said. An awful suspicion dizzied me.

"Oh, yes, majister. We're all coming. Why, you don't think we'd let our emperor go flying off into danger all on his own, do you?"

Nine

"You'll be just that, Dray Prescot! Arena fodder!"

The argument went on all next day.

"But," I said, "I'm the emperor. You're supposed to do what I say."

That was a laugh, of course, in a matter of this seriousness.

"You just cannot fly off to Hyrklana all on your own!"

That claustrophobic feeling of being trapped in a cage of invisible iron bars engulfed me. Hitherto when I'd been flung about Kregen by the Star Lords I had hungered to return home. Now that I had a serious task to perform, rescuing our friends, I was being mewed up and allowed out only with a great gaggle of nursemaids to hold my hand and wipe my nose. Talk about a cage!

They all wanted to come. 1 and 2 ESW. 1 and 2 EYJ. Nath Karidge insisted on bringing EDLG. Most of the slate of Vallian nobility were lining up. Applications poured in from all the regiments.

"Think of fat Queen Fahia!" I said. "She'll think we're invading her island!"

With a judicious air, Lord Farris said, "I can spare you enough fliers to take a thousand men. They'll have to draw lots to see who goes."

"Well, I'm going," said Korero, "and I'll fight anyone who tries to steal my place."

"And me!"

"And me!"

"By Vox!" I said. "This isn't like the old days."

"No," said Delia. And she smiled, the cruel and heartless woman. "No, Dray Prescot. You are the emperor now."

I groaned. Were the brave old days gone when I'd wrap the old scarlet breechclout about myself and take up my weapons and board a voller, richly stacked with wicker hampers provided by Delia's loving forethought, and fly off to find adventure, hurtling across the face of Kregen under the Suns of Scorpio?

"By the disgusting diseased liver and lights of Makki Grodno! I'm not having this! If I am the damned Emperor of Vallia then what I say goes! How can I work my way into the Jikhorkdun in Huringa and rescue our friends if there's an enormous lollygagging army of ruffians hanging around my neck?"

"Oh," they said, "you'll think of a way."

Sink me!

Turko, who hadn't left yet, talked darkly of sending north for Seg and Inch to come down and knock some sense into my obstinate vosk skull of a head.

"And then," I snarled, "I suppose they'll want to come, too."

"Probably," said Turko, and he flexed his muscles.

Despite all the lightheartedness of this there was a darker side. Oh, it wasn't anything to do with questioning the authority vested in me as emperor. If folk didn't want me to try to be an emperor, I'd quit, instanter, and they knew that. I'd told them enough.

But just suppose—just suppose the Star Lords took it into their super-human heads to whisk me up out of Vondium and hurl me down into some other part of Kregen, all naked and unarmed, to sort out a problem for them? The Everoinye had been silent of late. I'd not even seen their spy and messenger, the Gdoinye, flying high and looking down mockingly on my doings. If that happened now, what would be the reaction of the people of Vondium, of Vallia?

This time, my disappearance would be viewed in an entirely different light. In, I could see, an unfavorable light.

I said to Delia when we were alone, "Look, I can't manage the Jikhork-dun with that crowd along! Surely they can see that?"

"I am not sure you should risk the arena at all."

"But—we want Tilly and Oby and Naghan back, don't we?"

"Of course! But, dear heart, there has to be another way. An embassy to Queen Fahia—"

"She'd laugh at them. She thinks she is the leem's claws. Hamal won't bother her now because Hamal is so tied up with Thyllis's mad schemes of conquest. Hyrklana must be doing very well, very well indeed. And their agents will be scouring the world for human fodder for the arena."

"And you'll be just that, Dray Prescot! Arena fodder!"

"Better me on my own than a great gang of—"

"No!" Delia put a hand to her heart.

After that, for a space, we were occupied. But, all the same, nothing was solved regarding my expedition.

The same difficulties that stopped Hamal from invading and conquer-ing Hyrklana—as mad Empress Thyllis probably longed to do—prevented us from flying there in sufficient force to do what was necessary. We were overstretched and our resources were committed. Hamal had invaded north and south, although her invasion to the west had withdrawn. We were fighting to regain Vallia. Both empires grappled with problems that overtaxed their strength.

"All right," I said, "then I shall not go to Hyrklana."

I said that. I did not mean it. I had a plan.

In all this furor the Lady Zenobya continued on in her serene and yet enthusiastic way. She was a many-faceted individual. She clearly expected Vallia to give her assistance to regain her lost lands in Pershaw and kick out the Chobishaws. The Presidio was in sympathy with her. All the evidence we had, supported by reports from Vanki's spies, indicated that the right of the case lay with the Lady Zenobya. But how, in our impoverished state, were we to help?

Certainly, our gold would buy mercenaries.

"Yes, and I thank you," said the Lady Zenobya. "I shall avail myself of your kindness and use the gold, and you will be repaid, in full and with interest, in specie or in kind, when I am firmly established in Pershaw."

So that was decided. The Lady Zenobya had very definite views on the type of warrior she required.

"The men must be well-armored," she said, with that toss of her red-haired head that indicated she knew exactly what she was talking about. "They should have lance and mace. Under the armor they need a good thick cloth and where it shows, divided and out of the way above the legs, it should be heavily embroidered for the battlefield."

We stood with a group of my rascally henchmen from 1ESW bellowing unkind orders at a bunch of coys, out on Voxyri Drinnik. The recruits were riding marlques and they kept tangling out of formation. It was lucky for them the spears were blunt. The Lady Zenobya had given the recruits a comprehensive look and, no doubt, dismissed them from any consideration for a season or so. A zorcaman rode slowly toward us from Voxyri Gate. The suns shone, the breeze blew, the dust and animals and oiled leather filled the air with familiar odors.

"The trouble with a cataphract with a kontos is that he's a bit slow." The Lady Zenobya was staring at the approaching zorcaman. "Cataphracts are a delight, of course. But you really need lights for scouting, and air, if possible. I'll have to find flutsmen I can at least trust while they are paid. Their crossbows ought to keep them out of trouble with the Chobishaws—although their crossbows are wicked."

The zorcaman turned out to be Filbarrka na Filbarrka.

His beaming face was a welcome sight. He was incredibly smartly turned out. His zorca was tremendous.

"Lahal, majister!" he called. And then his cheerful voice changed in tone to a remarkable degree. "Lahal, my lady."

"Lahal, Filbarrka," said the Lady Zenobya, and her voice, too, held a different, huskier note than the voice in which she spoke to me or anybody else.

Some poor wight out on the parade ground dropped a spear and the wrath of his Deldar was awful to behold.

"They won't drop their kontoi in Pershaw when I'm through with them," said Filbarrka.

I raised one eyebrow at him.

"I have asked Filbarrka na Filbarrka," said the Lady Zenobya, her laugh exquisite, "if he will command my forces."

Filbarrka's fingers grasped the reins, otherwise they'd have been entwining like a nest of rattlers. "I have set up the whole organization for the second-line cavalry. My lads from the Blue Grass country are training 'em hard. You'll have a good, dependable—if a trifle brittle—force there in no time at all."

"Thank you, Filbarrka," I said. "And so you are off to Pershaw with the Lady Zenobya?"

"Aye!"

And, of course, there was more to it than that, as was very obvious. Later on, Delia told me, "They make a superb pair, do you not think, my love?"

"Oh, aye! Filbarrka is getting all the fun, going off to adventures overseas, and I'm stuck here—"

"Hush!"

For just about the first time on Kregen I had the hankering for the damned Star Lords to seize me up and dump me down somewhere. I'd sort out their nonsense for them and then I'd be a free man, able to go to Hyrklana on my own, able to do what I wanted. Of course, there was Delia...

She would welcome the return of our friends from Hyrklana. And I did not want, most certainly did not want, my Delia risking her life anywhere near Queen Fahia's Jikhorkdun!

This plan was typical of Dray Prescot. It was simple. When necessary I can invent complicated plans of fiendish subtlety; I prefer them simple. Although I am told my face is of that fierce damn-you-to-hell kind, I am able to assume an expression of near imbecility. This has served me well in diverse escapades. Now Deb-Lu-Quienyin was able materially to improve on nature.

"It is all a matter of muscle control," he told me as we sat privately in my study. "You have attained a fair degree of control. I think I can improve on that."

He made me do exercises with my ugly old beakhead. Also, without doubt, he exerted some of his supernatural powers. I do know that after a sennight he had me so composing my features that I did not recognize myself in the silver mirror.

"It is a miracle, San—"

"Not a miracle. A matter of tone, of muscle, of enhancing features and of reducing them. With practice an adept is able to suggest what his face is like. People do not see what they look at; they see what they expect to see."

"True. So—?"

"So they see your clothes and they fit the face to them. Where are you going?"

I half-turned. "I'm going to test this out."

He let his laugh ripple out like a tree branch splitting from the main trunk. "Beware lest Folly and Pride lead to Perdition!"

"Aye—and Hunch and Nodgen have been saying that they're going to Hyrklana with me. I ask you! Can you imagine our Hunch in the arena?"

"The mere thought leaves me cold—and also—amused."

Wearing a simple gray tunic, with a leather belt from which one of the long thin daggers of Vallia swung from plain bronze lockets, with sandals on my feet, I put on a new face and stalked from the study. I passed along corridors and soon people were there, passing me without a second glance. People I knew! People who knew me!

Diffident about how long this would work, how long I could keep my facial muscles holding the new face, I returned to my study. One or two people looked at me more closely as I walked back, and I had to duck into a cross-corridor and let my face relax. By Zair! It was hard work. I ached as though I'd been stung by a hive of bees. But, with practice, I'd be able to hold these new faces for longer periods.

Deb-Lu studied me as I walked in.

"Hurt?"

"Yes."

"That will pass."

"I hope so. If I'm to get out of the palace without one of my rascals spotting me, the face I put on has to last me. The security system here is now first class. No assassin would last a couple of heartbeats."

"And you mean to leave? Just like that?"

I nodded. "By Zair! Do I not!"

"The empress...?"

I glowered. "She will be left a message and she will understand... I know that to be so."

Then Deb-Lu-Quienyin shook me. "I am a Wizard of Loh, and all men fear us. And rightly so. But I think I might be tempted to relinquish all my arts and all my knowledge for the love of a lady like the Empress Delia."

"You old devil!" I said. But I spoke in affection.

I was sure, absolutely hell-fire sure, there was nothing in two worlds that could tempt me to abandon Delia.

By this time along I was shedding the work load as fast as was seemly. Ever since the first days when I'd realized there was work to do for Vallia I had, as you know, arranged for people to take over when I vanished. On Valka the Assembly was able to run the island stromnate perfectly. And, as my tasks sensibly lessened, with the people appointed by the Presidio shouldering more of the burdens, another little part of the puzzle about power fell into place.

If you have an emperor who is not allowed to do anything, has no job to do, then he will, like anyone else, become bored. And he'll start looking around for something to get up to, to while away the time. Well, by Djan! And hadn't I looked around, when bored, for something to do in Djanduin, and wound up king as a result? Keep an emperor busy and he will discipline himself, that was the theory.

In order to reward the many folk who had worked so hard for Vallia, the Presidio had instituted a whole fresh ranking of minor nobility, whose standing was a little below the already existing minor nobility. The main difference between this new hierarchy and the older minor nobility lay in the absence of lands or estates attached to the titles. The titles themselves had resounding names, which you will hear when a recipient enters my story, and usually a generous pension. By this means a non-endowed but wealthy peerage was established loyal to the country and to the emperor.

Again, I took the selfish pleasure of rewarding men and women, and seeing their pleasure. Maybe this is petty, maybe it is just another manifestation of the power syndrome, all I know is that when a fellow who had done well for the country received his new title of spandar or chornuv and his five or ten thousand golden talens, and started thinking about his new coat of arms, I felt his happiness as my happiness. And this despite my profoundly held ridicule of all titles and pomp.

The simple plan I had concocted—simpleminded, probably—demanded that I get to Huringa, the capital of Hyrklana, and then simply join the throngs flocking to the arena. Once there I would find out which of the four colors in eternal competition now commanded the allegiance of my friends. We had fought for the ruby drang. Then, once they had been located, I'd just boldly go in, carrying disguises, and have them out of it and into a borrowed voller and whisk them away home. Simple.

The major problem, as I saw it, was stealing a voller from the Lord Farris. He was not as young as he had been—by Vox! who is?—but he was just as punctilious in his duty, the perfect emperor's right hand, a treasure, and a confoundedly difficult fellow to steal a flier from.

Barty Vessler had taken a voller. True, it had been his own. I let my eye fall on the Lady Zenobya's cage voller. But that was too large. Anyway, she and Filbarrka would require the use of the craft. She'd said that Pershaw had bought fliers from Hamal before the supply dried up, and the pesky things broke down, a familiar story. Where Chobishaw was buying vollers from now she did not know.

So I put on decent Vallian buff, the wide-winged tunic and the breeches, and drew on a pair of the tall black boots. The broad-brimmed Vallian hat, with those two slots cut in the forward brim and the jaunty feathers flaunting, shadowed the new face I assumed. I sallied out and tried to bribe an attendant at the vollerdrome.

Well!

After they unchained me and stood me on my feet and dusted me off, I had to invent some rigmarole about checking security of the flierdrome.

My face had slipped during the dust up. It was a miracle nobody was hurt.

It happened to be the 1EYJ on duty at the flierdrome that night. Now Clardo the Clis and Torn Tomor stared suspiciously at me. As you know, the two corps forming the emperor's guard ran themselves, their officers alternating as to duties and leaves. Now these two looked at me as though I'd tried to make off with the crown jewels.

"Yes, majister," they said, and, "Certainly, majister."

But they knew!

The devils, they guessed right away what I was up to.

So, after that contretemps, I was faced with the problem of finding alternative means of transport.

It really was a bit thick. When an emperor can't quietly sneak off for a spot of adventuring, hurtling along under the Moons of Kregen, life tends to be dull, dull...

Not that life was dull, as you have heard and will hear. Naturally, much happened I have not so far apprised you of. The son of Trylon Lofoinen, for example, being enamored of a certain lady, hired a band to serenade her outside her father's villa. And his rival, the son of Strom Nevius, got to hear of it and arranged for a dung cart to run down the hill, all over the band, Lofoinen's son, and whoever else was in the way. That whoever else happened to be a solemn procession of adherents of Mev-ira-Halviren, going chanting to see their idol open its mouth and give forth prophecies.

The resulting uproar, not to say scent, enraptured the neighborhood.

The two lads were sent packing up north to join Seg's Second Army. He wrote that they were being kept buckled down to their duties—and had each found a little shishi already. This was an unsavory story—pungent ibroi was in short supply in that neighborhood for a sennight—and not necessarily typical of the amusements afforded by Vondium. Crude— of course. Funny—possibly, depending on your station vis-à-vis the wind. Perhaps it is best to leave the story to molder where it lies.

The crusty, bearded kampeon who had bossed my field quarters in the Eighth Army, Deft-Fingered Minch, possessed what was to me an amusing and endearing habit. He had fought with tremendous gusto in the ranks and had made shebov-maztik, before coming to my notice. He ran a field quarters with a competence I recognized as being akin to what was expected of a first lieutenant of a ship of the line in Nelson's Navy. I ought in parentheses to say that junior noncommissioned officers in Vallia were maztiks. Matoc is a Havilfarian name. And, anyway, they aren't like NCOs or noncoms; they are more like those special privileged fellows in the legions of Rome. More or less. Minch's endearing habit was simply this: Every time he encountered Emder in the course of his duties he would draw himself up and deliver himself of a chest-crushing salute. Emder, quiet, gentle, courteous, was treated as though he were a Jiktar at the least, and more probably a Kapt. Minch was serious, I fancied, but Emder wasn't quite sure how he should receive these military honors.

This was a case of the rough diamond respecting the cut and faceted gem.

One day Minch fairly cracked his fist against his chest, as Emder appeared in the corridor. Neither man saw me. I started to smile and then Minch broke with tradition.

"Jen Emder! A word!"

I will not attempt to reproduce the conversation word for word. What it boiled down to was Minch's desire for more information on my civilized habits. Emder did everything in the palace; Minch was the out-of-doors camp-king.

"For, Jen Emder, when we get to Hyrklana the emperor will be living in surroundings much like this. Is it possible you will accompany him as well as me?"

Emder made some reply. I just stood there. This was getting right out of hand. Plans, plans—how could I just go off and leave them all now? There was left to me one person, and one person alone, who could cut this knot.

So I went to see her.

"Delia," I said, "this nonsense has to stop!"

"Yes, dear. How?"

"That's for you to tell them all! By Vox! You are the empress, daughter of the old emperor! You know about these things. Tell 'em. Or, I swear it, I'll just take off one dark night and—"

She smiled. "The Sword Watch and the Yellow Jackets have very good eyes."

"Maybe. But when my mind is made up, my mind is—"

"Like a weathervane. We must hold a conference."

I groaned. "When did chitter-chatter solve anything?"

"You'll see. I promise."

So Delia called her famous conference. As I say, she is not only the most beautiful and most wonderful person in two worlds, she is also the most clever, the most tactful—the most downright cunning.

The decision was this: Farris would supply vollers to take a reasonably sized party, lots would be drawn, I would not be allowed to travel alone. When they started politely putting forward reasons why the speakers in turn had a special and undeniable duty to be among the participants, I left. All that reasonableness and fair-speaking frightened me. These were hairy warriors, as ready to slit your throat if you offended them as to wait for an apology—and they were all sitting neatly in rows discussing the point like a girl's grammar school debating society. But, you see, they were sitting there so docilely under the eye of Delia, Empress of Vallia.

These incidents did make me form a resolution. In future when I wanted to go off somewhere to get something done, I'd keep the fact to myself, and just go.

Delia would be told, of course. She had lived for far too long in the shadow of these mysterious absences forced on me by the Star Lords.

The thing was settled and I had to put the best face on it I could. So I took myself off and stood before the silver mirror in private and put on more than one best face. The bee-sting pains attacked me less and less, and I could hold a face for gratifyingly longer periods. Two things happened, and then we could leave.

Young Bargom, an old comrade, a Valkan, requested the pleasure of my company at the reopening of the Rose of Valka. By Zair! How that took me back! So, dressed to kill, I went down to the Great Northern Cut and took part in the ceremony consecrating the new inn and posting house. We had a right old night of it, and we sang that song "The Fetching of Drak na Valka" until the stars paled in the sky.

Among the singers a couple of Pachaks were, despite the presence of the emperor and the joyful ructions, far more interested in themselves. This was right and proper. They were Donal Em-Da, a Hikdar on leave from one of the Valkan regiments, and his affianced love, Natema Na-Pla. They sat in a corner—there were no quiet corners—with their right arms and two left arms each entwined. Their tail hands took care of the wine. I like Pachaks. I was told they planned to marry before Donal Em-Da marched out to rejoin his regiment, somewhere up north at the front. Then I learned something that brought me across to stand before them, finding a smile, hushing them back into the seat as they began to stand up.

"Now, Kotera," I said to the Pachak girl, giving her the full title of lady of Vallia. She was charming, blooming with health and youth, dressed in a simple laypom-colored gown and with only the brooch that was the badge of her fiancé's regiment as ornament. "Natema Na-Pla. The Pla from your father's name is that of Planath, is it not?" I was teasing her, for I had been told just this moment.

"Yes, majister—" She did not flush but her eyes were wide.

"Did he not tell you of the standard he bore?"

"Oh, yes, majister. Many times. He was proud."

"And I promised Planath Pe-Na that I would dower his daughter." That wasn't quite the word, but the idea was much the same. I remembered Planath Pe-Na. He had been my standard bearer at the affair of the Burned Man at Twin Forks, and at the Battle of Tomor Peak. So I bumbled on and the meeting somehow heartened me. Many fine men, apim and diff, had sought and succeeded, sought ways of serving Vallia and succeeded in giving their service to the best of their ability.

That was made my first duty next day. I gave Enevon instructions to present a seemly sum—not trifling, and yet not stupidly embarrassing, for Pachaks have that berserk streak, true or false does not matter, and their honor means much. Then the day's work could begin and Naghan Raerdu, Naghan the Barrel, was first on the agenda. Turko was present.

"Majister—word from Chuktar Mevek. The gold we sent has been well used. But it is detestation of Layco Jhansi that matters more." Naghan's laugh broke out, and he shut his eyes and the tears squeezed forth. "By Vox, majister! Jhansi seems to have taken leave of his senses. His mercenaries show no mercy and grasp the whole of Falinur in a grip of iron, trying to squeeze blood."

Turko looked grim, and it was easy to guess what he was thinking.

"So I march?" was all he said.

"Aye, kov. The time is now."

I said, "Have a tenderness for the stromnate of Balkash, Kov Turko. It acknowledges you as its legal lord, or will when Jhansi is thrown out. But, well, you know."

"Aye," said Turko, easily. "Balkash remains the stromnate of Dray Segutorio. I count it a joy to me to have Seg's son as a friend. And he will be home soon, so I believe."

"The quicker the better. Silda wants to see him."

Now there was nothing to hold me back. Turko was all ready. We stood to see him off. I own I half wished I were going with him, but by the time he had his army positioned and Seg had swung across, I'd be back from Hyrklana.

Farris provided a medium-sized voller to take the hundred who would go. Delia was there. So, thank Zair, was I. With the remberees thundering in our ears, we lifted off. Flags fluttered. The suns shone. And the flier turned over Vondium and headed south, south for Hyrklana, and Huringa, and the Jikhorkdun.

I was the emperor of Vallia, and constrained by these hundred stalwarts who had drawn the luck in the lottery. But I just could not see how I was to organize them when it came to the arena. But, also, I was Dray Prescot. I fancied—I hoped, I prayed—that the old Dray Prescot, Lord of Strombor and Krozair of Zy, might turn a trick or two to get himself unlumbered.

Then, why then it would be a skip and a jump and some headlong action before the game was played out.

"By Kaidun!" I said to myself. I looked calculatingly at these hundred companions of mine. I looked at Delia. "By the glass eye and brass sword of Beng Thrax! Now I'm not a cunning old leem hunter if I can't fashion something out of this!"

Ten

Unmok the Nets

Standing right in the eyes of the flier with the wind rushing in our faces, Delia and I grasped the rail and stared at the sea far below. Splinters of silver light rayed back and the streaming mingled radiance of ruby and emerald added touches of fire and viridian to the scene. We could see no ships down there.

"Listen carefully," I said. "If I am—taken—as I may well be—"

"Those dreadful Everoinye?"

"Aye. If I am, promise me you will not fret—well, that may be foolish. Promise me at least, that..." And I stopped, too muddled to go on.

Delia gripped my arm. "I know what you mean. It is hard, it always has been hard and it always will be hard. But I know. If you have to go away to your silly little planet with only one tiny yellow sun and one tiny silver moon and no diffs at all, only apims, why, then—"

"By Zair!" I shivered in the windrush. "I don't want to be sent back to Earth!"

"No. But if you go away, I will understand. But that is all."

I swallowed. "Promise me you will not go to see Queen Fahia. She is fat and unhealthy; she is also dangerous. Our hundred wild men will not stand against her army forever."

"You mean you may be sent somewhere else?"

I spoke the truth, for if I was called by the Star Lords they would send me somewhere else about their business.

"Yes. You must promise me not to go to Huringa."

"Very—well. But—"

I looked at her.

She sighed.

"Very well, my heart. I promise. I see the sense of it. It is so unfair, though, so damned hard!"

"Life is unfair. It is always hard."

So, you can see into what kind of low-class skullduggery I had fallen, what a proficient liar I was forced to become. But I wasn't having Delia going anywhere near that horrific arena. No, by Zim-Zair! For I and our friends had been lifted to safety from the blood-soaked silver sand, and Delia was all naked and chained to a stake at the center. I shuddered. That had been an experience I would not willingly repeat. Enough of that horror was enough.

Then she said, "You have seen the golden and scarlet bird?"

There was no need to lie. The big one had been put across, all else merely followed. "No. But I sense that I may be called. Try not to let this—" Stupid, stupid! Of course my going away would upset her! "You'll have to convince this gang of cutthroats who invited themselves along."

"They will listen—"

"They'll listen to you. I expect Turko will find them of use." I glanced back at those fighting men crowding the decks. "It seems to me whoever rigged the lottery was a master hand."

Delia laughed. She was determined to throw off all cares until the causes of those cares arrived. "I do not care to inquire too closely into the legality of the lottery. But I agree, there are a suspiciously large number of..." She hesitated.

"To find the right word for them is difficult."

They were all our staunchest comrades in this voller. If the lottery had not been fixed, then Five-Handed Eos-Bakchi, the spirit of luck and good fortune called on in Vallia, had answered a goodly number of calls from the ripest fruits of the ESW and EYJ and EDLG. By Krun! And from the sprigs of the nobility whose business had brought them to Vondium at this time.

Looking at them, I considered my plans had just about matured. All that was necessary now was the timing.

Looking back as I relate my narrative I suppose I can afford a wry smile. It must be clear to you listening to my words, as it is clear to me—now— that I was living in a dream world.

Even my Delia was a part of that dream, for she had promised me without overmuch demur. But I was wrapped up in my own schemes. Onker, as they say on Kregen of that particular kind of idiot, onker of onkers, get onker. The Gdoinye liked to call me an onker, and I'd call him one back, too, in those slanging matches which, I suspect, if the stakes had not been so high I'd have enjoyed as much as he did, the onker!

Southeast we flew, out over the Sea of Opaz which separates Vallia from the island of Pandahem. We would not fly over this latter island, for the Pandaheem, besides their longstanding antagonism to Vallia, were now in the merciless grip of Phu-Si-Yantong. Ever southwards we flew across the Southern Ocean, passing just clear of that lonely island group, Astar, where once the Leem-Lovers, the ghastly Shanks from over the curve of the world, had set up a base to raid and harry and kill the peoples of the shorelines of Paz. A garrison held the islands now.

"Do we fly direct to Hyrklana, across Hamal?"

I shook my head. "No, Delia. We avoid Hamal like the plague. We will fly around the coast, out of sight of land. I think we can risk crossing the Risshamal Keys." These stretch out like skeletal fingers from the northeastern corner of Hamal. Hyrklana lies due south of them, past Arnor and Niklana. To cut across them would save time.

So that is what we did. Perhaps, had I been less cocksure, less confident and taken us all the way around, well—then it would have been a different story, by Zair...

Any Kregan needs his six or eight square meals a day and we were capitally provided for. I refused to blink when Deft-Fingered Minch produced a delicacy that was a particular specialty of the palace kitchens. He had spoken to Emder, that was clear.

Down below us the Keys passed, gray and brown, narrow and humped, some barren and some choked with jungles, for we flew with the equator just to the north of us. On those strings of islands lived among a multitude of races the Yuccamots, a web-footed, thick-tailed race of diffs who lived by fishing and were kind and friendly by nature. And that made me think how Vad Nalgre Sultant, of Kavinstok, who had proved so unpleasant a character down there, had rallied around the Racters when Vallia herself passed through her Time of Troubles.

"Look at the weather up ahead," said Korero, flicking his tail hand.

"Aye. It looks murky."

The horizon ahead held that brazen copper look, as of a furnace glowing with the fires of hell. Black clouds boiled. If we were in for a twisting blow we'd best batten down, or get down. I measured the extent of the gale—typhoon, hurricane, call it what you will. It pounced with monstrous speed. One moment we were apprised of its presence, the next we were starting to descend and in the third we were caught and shaken like a ponsho in the jaws of a leem.

The blackness enveloped us like the cloak of Notor Zan.

The wind shrieked about us. We were hurled across the sky, blown like a pip from the mouth of a giant. End over end, whirling, we were buffeted and deafened, crushed, by the violence of the elements.

The voller was well built, one of those we had secured from Hyrklana, that being thought a clever notion as we were flying to that island realm. She was broken in two as a child breaks a reed boat. Chunks fell off. Men fell. We were all wearing the safety belts produced just in time by the wise men of Vondium, and as the voller broke up and we were cast adrift, so we went sailing independently across the sky, mere helpless chips in a millrace of wind.

The suns might not have been shining in the sky. The darkness blustered about us. For a few moments I caught sight of other hapless wights being hurled and tossed about and then I was swept away into the blackness. Night was not far off. The wind tore at me, filling my mouth and ears, screaming. The twister curled a tail around and the hurricane of wind coiled devilishly, spinning me away—somewhere.

The time passed in this nauseous inferno of black noise. The howling went on and on and on. End over end I pitched away, one of a hundred separated and scattered leaves in a whirlwind.

The chances of making a safe landing in this were practically nil. Anyway, I'd probably come down into the sea, for my bump of direction told me I was being hurled toward the south. How long it all lasted was easy to calculate after the event. While I was being driven hither and thither, swung up and belted down, the time stretched so that it seemed I'd spent all my life being tossed about in the black gullet of that blow.

That blow!

Afterward I learned that a whole fleet of argenters, stout, beamy craft, had been lost. A squadron of swordships had been tossed onto the rocks of one of the Risshamal Keys and thoroughly reduced to flinders. And a wing of the massive skyships of Hamal had been contemptuously smashed into the ground. The gale broomed sea and sky and swept them both clean.

The end of it for me was a sensible lessening of the wind and the sight of a flake of the Maiden with the Many Smiles, gleaming fuzzy pink light through cloud wrack. For the rest of that night and the following day I was tumbled along southward. Sea, and only sea, stretched below me. I was hungry and thirsty—I was thirsty, by Krun! But there could be no hope of letting down to the sea. All I could do was hope to last out and put the thirst torturing me out of my mind and so let the wind hurl me on.

The second night was unpleasant.

If these wonderful belts we'd invented had possessed the power of independent movement through the air... But, then, that was the secret we still had not fathomed, the prize Hamal and all the countries who manufactured vollers kept close.

I tried not to worry overmuch on the fate of Delia. My friends were a hundred tough and resourceful desperadoes, and if I'd been chucked off by the wind, I trusted that some of them had been able to link up with Delia. Korero had been with me when the voller broke up. But I was alone, singled out, a tiny speck in the vast sky above the vast ocean.

When the island came into sight, far to the south, a mere black smudge upon the glittering sea, I heaved a sigh of relief and then started paddling desperately to strike a course for that haven. If I missed it...

The fates, or whoever has charge of handing out favors or black marks—certainly not, I fancied, either the Savanti or the Star Lords—guided me near enough to the island for me to slide the silver boxes apart along the belt and drop gently into the sea. Then it took me a couple of burs to swim in.

The beach was white sand, smooth and inviting, and only twice I was forced to lift up on the safety belt to avoid gaping jaws and serrated teeth from some hungry predator of the sea. I lay on the beach, spouting water, breathing easier, and then rolled over and surveyed what I'd dropped and swum into.

Practically every coastline on Kregen—not all—is festooned with islands, large and small. It was perfectly possible that this little beauty appeared on no maps anywhere at all. But the ground was solid underfoot as I rose. Then I realized the wind was still strong, still blowing half a gale, and I went running up the beach, half propelled by the wind and half drawn by the fruit hanging on the trees.

That fruit tasted good, by Krun! My thirst tended to be fierce, and my face was smothered with fruit juice. Water was a prime requisite, and I struck along the coast looking for a stream. Tropical islands are veritable paradises—if certain things are available and certain things are absent.

Well, I found water, and drank—cautiously. I bathed the salt off my skin. I perked up. A craggy mass of rock chopped off the next bay and, after a time, I rolled along to have a look-see.

An argenter floated in the bay, bold as brass, real, no mirage, four anchors out, and the rocky headland giving her beautiful shelter. I studied her most carefully before I walked down to the waterline and hullooed across.

She bore the colors of Hyrklana. Mainly green, of course, seeing that Queen Fahia was a fanatical follower of the Jikhorkdun and her chosen corner was the green, the emerald neemu.

"Ahoy!"

A head poked over the bulwarks. A spear point glittered.

No doubt they wouldn't be surprised to find a cannibal. After all, desert islands are desert islands and have a reputation to keep up.

In any event, they took me aboard Pearl of Klanadun and instead of killing me out of hand fed me two square meals and a gallon of Kregan tea. If I treat this whole episode matter-of-factly, that is the way I tried to treat it while it was happening. But it was a fraught old time, I can tell you.

Drifting over the sea, nothing in sight save sea and sky, slowly starving and thirsting to death—no. No, I do not believe I enjoyed that.

Because I did not usually wear a Krozair longsword when not engaged in something strenuous, I was not carrying one with me now. I'd been talking to Korero, digesting a good meal, and dressed in a light tunic for the tropics. Naturally, I had a rapier and main gauche. Well, they—the Jiktar and the Hikdar—tend to grow on a fellow after a time, so it seems. I was extremely careful to let these folk in the argenter see that I had no intention of drawing weapons against them.

Pearl of Klanadun held a smell, a wild-animal smell that wafted up through the gratings in her wide decks. Down below in her capacious holds the owners of that wild-beast smell were caged in iron bars.

"Yes, Horter Jak," said the captain, bluff and genial, rotund of belly and purple of nose. "This is what I am reduced to." A vein throbbed alongside his nose. "I cannot lay the blame at the feet of Havil the Green, for I am a religious man, and mindful of the obligations a sea master must never forget. But, all the same—" And he gestured in a manner at once helpless and comical at the gratings. "A mere freighter of wild animals for the Jikhork-dun! Is this my reward for a hundred years of sea apprenticeship?"

"But, Captain Nath," I said, "there are many men engaged in this work. The Jikhorkduns of Hyrklana are never satisfied."

"True, true. My brother, who commanded our late father's ship, was gored to death by an Ilurndil—the second horn went clean through here." And Captain Nath the Bows jabbed a thumb into the side of his stomach.

I didn't much care for Ilurndils, six-footed battering rams with leather hides you could make roof tiles out of—that roof tiles were made out of—and a pair of horns superimposed between piggy eyes. As for Nath the Bows, as he said, his father's name was Nath and what was good enough for him was good enough for his boys. They were twins, Nath the Bows and Nath the Stern. It wasn't new.

Pearl of Klanadun was a natty enough argenter. Her topmen were Hobolings, among the best in the business. She had a lot of Brokelsh in the deck hands. Her marine guard consisted of half a dozen Undurkers with their canine faces and snooty looks and smart bows and notched arrows. We sailed along as soon as the storm abated enough to make passageway comfortable for the wild beast cargo.

Down in the saloon I met the owner of the cargo. I was fully prepared to dislike him on sight. After all, running animals in for the arena, where they would first of all chomp up criminals and condemned slaves, and then be cut to bits by kaidurs who knew how to handle weapons, is not the kind of occupation guaranteed to endear any man to me.

But it was extraordinarily difficult to dislike Unmok the Nets. He was an Och. He did not, however, have six limbs like Ochs are supposed to have. As he said, "There was I, minding my own business—I was in selling beads and bangles at the time, not much but a living—and this chavonth came at me. Chewed out my middle left. Still feel it twinge come rainy days. Took sinews outta my lower left, too. Dratted chavonth. All teeth and claws and that mess of blue-gray and black hexes."

Unmok the Nets limped. As an Och he stood shorter than Hunch, who as a Tryfant had to stand on tiptoe to look over the big guy's bar. His Och head was the usual lemon shape, with puffy jaws and lolling chops, although he favored a kind of heavy woolen muffler.

"Since that danged chavonth got me I feel the cold."

We were only a few degrees south of the equator here.

He liked to talk. I cannot repeat most of it, all small talk larded with dollops of Och wisdom, which might suit a small race of diffs with six limbs; it's only marginally applicable to an apim with only four limbs. I tried to remember some to tell my Djang friends.

He started to tell me how he'd got into the wild-beast catching business when we went down to the dinner table to eat, and he went right on, interrupting himself and going off into unrelated subjects and getting back to the point. He never did finish. I gathered, more as a matter of guess-work, that after his mauling by a savage big cat he rather wanted to get his own back. For a little crippled Och, well, that took some doing, petty and vindictive though some folk might take it.

There was always a demand for wild animals in the arena. And for human fodder. We sailed on down south toward Hyrklana and, despite some of my chaotic feelings, Unmok the Nets and I got along famously.

And he told me about the animals.

He had a team of harum-scarum diffs and apims to assist. Some knew how to handle the beasts; others simply used the whip and the torch and lived scared half to death most of the time.

"Get rid of them as soon as I can, Jak," he told me. "Poor trash. You have to know how a beast feels to trap it, and then how to keep it alive. Some just curl over and die if you don't treat 'em right."

"You're making for Huringa, of course—"

"Gotta pick up a consignment of thomplods first. Had 'em shipped in to Hyrklana South. They'll fetch a fortune."

He said thomplod, which is the vernacular for the animal I always think of as a haystack on feet. Twelve feet, six a side. And the smell—well, I can't smell it, not many men can. But other animals—well, now. That dung cart of the son of Strom Nevius that ran away with the band and the son of Try-lon Lofoinen and the solemn procession of adherents of Mev-ira-Halviren, that didn't create half the stir among the neighborhood that a single thom-plod could churn up among the animals of a sizeable town. No, sir!

Not all the animals. Mostly saddle animals. Some riding animals seemed to be immune to the smell; most are not. Unmok was going to have to arrange transportation for his menagerie. The carts would be pulled by Quoffas, and those huge-faced shambling hearthrugs would patiently haul and not care a fig for the thomplods. But no one was going to ride a totrix or a marlque or a hirvel, not with a thomplod within sniffing range.

Well, Unmok and I got along and pretty soon he was suggesting I might like to throw in with him. This often happens to me, on Earth and on Kregen. Delia and I had taken a few handfuls of golden deldys, one of the more usual currencies of Havilfar, and I had a walletful. I thumped a purseful on the table and Unmok sniffed and allowed that Havil the Green or some divine spirit had answered his prayers. He was a little short, did I see, and we were partners. We shook on it, in the Kregan way. As I say, I was surprised myself.

I was to be a working partner.

Captain Nath the Bows kept well out to the east giving the coast of Hamal a wide berth. Sailing direct to Hyrklana South was not so much out of our way, after all.

"Those devils of Hamal can't pay for animals for their Jikhorkduns now," observed Unmok. "That stupid war they've got themselves involved in. Oh, they have plenty of prisoners. But they're short of prime cargoes of animals."

A few days later a voller passed high overhead, traveling fast toward the south. Unmok screwed his chops up and stared aloft, tense, hopping on his one good foot. Then he relaxed. A single glance had told us the flier was Hyrklanian and not Hamalese.

"Thought it might have been a cage voller." Unmok visibly relaxed, and the breeze blew the feather in his cap askew. "That'd mean tough competition." He admitted, seeing I was now his partner, that he had been a trifle strapped. He had planned on selling a few beasts at the wharf side, and damn poor prices, too, to pay for the passage. "One day," he said darkly, "I'll have me my own cage voller. Then you'll see!"

As soon as we reached a stylor, he said, the bokkertu could all be written up in due legal form.

"And if that was Maglo the Ears, why, I'll—I'll—"

"Who's he?"

"The biggest rogue unhanged since Queen Fahia grew her moustache." Then he looked about swiftly, to see if anyone had overheard this flagrant example of lèse majesté, as they say.

"Maglo the Ears preys on honest traders like me. He is welcome in the Jikhorkdun because he can sell at cut prices. Of course he can, the yetch! He steals what honest men have worked for."

No matter what trade or profession you go in for, it seems on two worlds, there are always the fly-boys, the get-rich-quick merchants, the unscrupulous to twist a profit out of villainy. Unmok heaved up a sigh and cut phlegm.

"And the Jikhorkduns can afford to pay. Hyrklana has never been richer. Hamal pours out her treasure for war and we profit. Mind you, they drive a hard bargain when it comes to selling a few hundred people for the arena. They have a good supply, as I said, and we still have to send out parties and scratch and scrape to find men suitable—"

I started to interrupt, harshly, unpleasantly, and forced myself to calm down. But for his trade and its singularity, Unmok the Nets was a simple ordinary trader, wasn't he? Hyrklana needed men like Unmok. Others like him, probably much more unpleasant in their habits, would be out now scouring foreign countries for arena fodder.

Korero and I had been talking up in the prow of the voller when she smashed and I could only hope the others had been able to stick together. Certainly, if some slaving rast from the arena tried to capture my hundred lads, he'd be eating his teeth, and digesting a length of steel through his guts.

If there exists a demand men will be found to supply it.

That is no excuse, never has been. But Unmok cared for the splendid wild animals in his charge, mindful of not only their physical comfort but seeking ways of easing their rages at confinement. He disliked the whip. He checked a shaven-pated Gon who slashed a strigicaw, and the Gon sulked. Unmok heaved up one of his feather-whiffling sighs, and promised me he'd discharge the useless lumber, as he called them, and hire fresh beast handlers in Fanahal, the chief port of Hyrklana South.

Unmok's chief assistant, a strong-bodied Fristle, whose cat's face was missing a sizeable portion of fur so that the membrane glistened pinkly, provided the strong arm necessary. This Fristle spoke little, spat often, and was called Froshak the Shine.

Froshak saw my sailor knife in its sheath snugged at the back of my right hip, and asked to examine it. I let him hold the knife, and he turned it over, and felt the heft. Then he handed it back and whipped out his own blade. The knives were very similar.

"Good," said Froshak. "Good for slicing guts." I agreed. Out of politeness.

He gave no trouble that I had been taken in as a partner. As I say, I was a working partner. Unmok's system was simple and neat. One empty cage at the end was cleaned and swabbed out and provided with fresh litter. The gate to the adjoining cage was opened and the occupant of the second cage enticed, cajoled—whipped—into entering the first. Then with the gates shut the second cage was cleaned out. The process was repeated until the end of the line, when on the following day the end cage was prepared and the process repeated in reverse.

I took my share. I cannot say I came to be overly familiar with the wild animals; but the education was formidable. Mostly I'd been on the receiving end, with a sword in my fists.

Unmok had three leems. He was proud of them. No one else relished the idea; but they were valuable, and we needed to eat.

Pens up on deck held tame livestock. Preparing them for the beasts' dinners was not a pleasant job. On a long sea voyage rations were tightly arranged, anyway. Unmok had lost only two of his stock, as he told me sorrowfully, a fine graint and a chag, which had been weak anyway. He took particular care of the four splendid specimens of neemus. These black, vicious, treacherous beasts with their round heads and flat ears and slanting slits of lambent golden flame for eyes were to be sold to Queen Fahia. Unmok was confident of that. I could just imagine them, scented, pampered, chained with silver links, sprawled on the steps of her throne.

And I must mention the werstings. These white and black four-legged hunting dogs were just about trained. They remained savage. Unmok owned five couples, collared with bronze, bearing his mark. I doubted if even a wersting would be able to check these wild animals if they broke free, but Unmok informed me that these werstings, toward whom he held an ambivalent attitude, were as much for his own protection against grasping rogues like Maglo the Ears as against escaped stock.

He had no Manhounds, and I was not sorry for that, I can tell you!

The Suns of Scorpio blazed down, the breeze blew, we made a good passage and came up beautifully to our landfall, making boards in to Fanahal, and we saw not a sign of another craft until we were in the coastal sea-lanes.

The port gleamed pink and green over white in the blaze. The water glittered. A busy confusion of ships and boats congested the roadway. We were hauled in by a ten-oared tug manned by Brokelsh, and the local dignitaries came aboard to the ritual wine, bribes, and signing of papers. The noise of the wharves and the smells had to be adjusted to after the long windblown reaches of the ocean.

I had arrived in Hyrklana.

Eleven

A Shot at a Swordship

One thing you could say for Unmok the Nets—he was a businessman. He discharged the useless lumber—the shaven-headed Gon would have been a nuisance, but Froshak the Shine clicked his sailor knife up and down in the sheath. The Gon departed. Unmok worked at a high pressure. The thomplods were loaded into a second vessel, little more than a sailing steerable raft for coastal navigation, fees were paid, bribes were distributed, stores taken aboard, and we set off northward around the west coast of Hyrklana.

Everyone was jumpy.

Hyrklana is a large island shaped rather like a pear, or a flint arrowhead. From north to south it measures around thirteen hundred miles and across the broadest part just over eight hundred. The coast of Havilfar to the west curves in a bow shaped to fit the bulge of Hyrklana. The Hyrklese Channel is approximately three hundred miles across.

These waters, wide though they were, were infested with pirates. Renders from the coastal countries of the Dawn Lands, ships searching for plunder, attacking and looting anything else that sailed the seas, the brethren were an odiferous bunch. A deal of policing had been done; but the current wars had made supervision too costly. It was every ship for herself.

So we had taken aboard Unmok's hired guards at Fanahal to reinforce Captain Nath's Undurker marines. We made as fast a passage as we could, giving the contrariness of Whetti Orbium who under Opaz's beneficent hand runs the weather on Kregen. Propitiations were made, of course, and the low-domed temple with the ships' figureheads set up outside in ranks and rows took in another tidy little heap of gold coins to the old-age pensions of the priests.

Money began to figure now. My store of gold, although mere handfuls, as I have said, was in these circumstances considerable wealth. All the same, it would not last for ever.

Unmok had been careful with his hired guards. They were mostly Fristles and Rapas. He had contracted to pay them five sinvers per sennight. Although, contrarily, I give the word sennight for a week of six days, it seems to me to fit. Across in the Dawn Lands I'd hired out for eight broad strebes a day, and even there a Fristle or Rapa could get the standard one silver coin per diem. Unmok, as I say, was shrewd.

There were no Pachaks or Chuliks in the bunch we hired. Ten of them, and one Khibil. His fox-like face drooped instead of bristling with the natural arrogance of a Khibil. He had been given a nasty—a very nasty—blow in the middle at some time and it had broken some spiritual spring deep within him. He was an archer; but his bow, although compound and reflex and an admirable weapon, pulled lightly. But, for all that, he remained a Khibil.

"I am a Khibil," he said, as he stood before the table where Unmok sat with the leather bags of silver sinvers, some spilled casually out across the wood, glittering. "I hire out for nothing less than eight."

Looking at this Khibil, Pondar the Iumfrey, I was forcibly reminded of the time I'd hired out over in the Dawn Lands, and of Pompino demanding more because he was a Khibil. The contrast between this Pondar before me now and my comrade Pompino could not have been more marked. And, by Zair, where was Pompino the Iarvin now?

"The Rapas and Fristles have settled for five," pointed out Unmok. "But, yes, you are a Khibil. I will pay you one silver sinver a day. No more."

"Done."

Pondar the Iumfrey affixed his mark.

Men were not easy to find. Good men were scarce. But they still existed, carrying on in the old ways and refusing to be drawn into foreign wars. Hyrklana liked to be an island and cut off from the rest of Havilfar.

So we sailed up the Hyrklese Channel and kept our eyes skinned for renders. Pirates are a pain in the neck. When we saw our swordship, her single bank of oars driving deeply, surging on toward us, sheeted in spray like a half-submerged rock, the old wailing cry went up, filled with horror.

"Swordship! Swordship!"

We were, therefore, in for a fight.

I said to Unmok, "Is there a spare bow and a few shafts?"

He lifted his shrewd Och head up above the companionway coaming. He waited for no man on his descent below decks.

"Bows? Shafts? Jak, what are you dreaming of?"

"We have to fight them off—"

"They do, the hired mercenaries. We don't!"

I didn't blame him for scuttling below. He was better off out of the coming fight. It wasn't even as though he had all his limbs, was it, now? But he shouted that there was a bow of sorts in his cabin and I was welcome to it.

The bow proved to be a compound job of wood and sinew, with a little horn, and the reflex curves made only a halfhearted stab at the double-reflex curves of the bows of Valka.

But I took it up and strung it and heaved on the string. The shafts were iron-tipped and fletched with the yellow feathers from hulfoo birds, a kind of Hyrklanian goose. They looked to be reasonably straight.

On deck, having seen Unmok stowed away safely below, I found the Khibil, Pondar, arguing with a heavyset Rapa, whose red wattles congested and whose dark eyes snapped anger.

They were arguing as to who was to be Jiktar of the mercenary guard. Of course, Jiktar was just a name, a kind of Kregan relative to saying the captain of the guard.

I said, "You know your posts. Take them. Pondar, take the stern. Randalar, take the bows."

The swordship looked as though her captain meant to hit our port bow. The Rapa and the Khibil wanted to continue their argument, but I told them to get on with it, and they did.

We possessed but one varter. It looked as though it might fall to pieces the moment the windlass was wound, even before the missile was discharged. Captain Nath stood looking at it and pursing his lips.

"Well, I don't know..."

Without a word I started to wind the windlass. The old wood creaked and groaned. But the plaited string inched back and the bow bent. I did it cautiously, I may add, out of respect for my own hide. A broken varter string can whip out your eye better than a diving blood-lance.

I won't go into the details of the fight, mainly because there were so few. Even this antiquated and dangerous varter could out-range a bow. Before the two ships closed the range for archery I swung the varter on its swivel and lined up the ugly beak of the swordship. We were going up and down and the renders' vessel was pitching like a maddened totrix.

Froshak the Shine dumped a chunk of rock into the chute. I waited until Pearl of Klanadun rolled, and pulled the trigger. The rock flew.

Just what it did I do not know. But the swordship stuck her bows under the next wave and the sea washed back in an unbroken green tide and she didn't right herself. She just went on and in, with all her oars driving lustily.

We sailed on, and it was as though the swordship had been just a bad dream.

We didn't even stop to see. That would have been very difficult with a plunging, wide-beamed and unhandy argenter.

The outcome of that was that the men started calling me Jak the Shot. I'd given the name Jak, for obvious reasons. I made no demurral on the Shot business, just let it ride.

Swordships are cranky craft at best, and seem to spend as much of their time under the water as above it. "Now if that had been a Vallian galleon..." I said to Unmok.

"Oh, them!" He sniffed. "I've been married a couple of times and one of my sons went off to Vallia. Never got to be a paktun, got himself killed somewhere in Pandahem, so a comrade told me. My lad said the Vallese are a strange lot. Haven't got a soldier among 'em. All pot-bellied money-grabbers. Then he laughed. "Like me—with pot-bellies!"

I forbore to bring Unmok up to date. But I warmed to his honesty. What he did he did because that was the way he made his living. Among his chatter he spoke often of buying a cage voller, of making his fortune and going into a new line of business. This varied with each recital of his dream.

Froshak the Shine came up. "Varter's busted. We were lucky."

We looked. That ballista would never loose again. One of the arms was cracked through, and the wood was black rotten for three-quarters of the crack, and pale yellow the rest.

"Lucky," said Captain Nath the Bows. "I'll have to replace her. Money, money, money...!"

"Praying again," I said, and—refreshingly—we all laughed.

Huringa, capital of Hyrklana, stands on the south bank of the River of Leaping Fishes, some thirty dwaburs up from the mouth. The river is not navigable past about the halfway mark, so we had to hire quoffa carts to take us the remainder of the journey. Hyrklana is a civilized country. As civilized, that is, as any civilized country on Kregen.

"We ought to be in the city in good time, Jak," said Unmok as Pearl of Klanadun and the coaster unloaded, the carts carrying the cages lumbering along, the men yelling and the whips cracking, we started. "But there is the Forest of the Departed to pass through."

In these gloomy woods uncounted numbers of past inhabitants of Huringa and the surrounding country had been interred for centuries. The place was a forest, yes; it was also a giant mausoleum. Froshak picked his teeth, spat, and said nothing. I eyed Unmok.

"Maglo the Ears?"

"Him, and a score of drikingers almost as bad."

Bandits are bad news anywhere.

Those drikingers I had employed in Vallia, clearing out aragorn and slavers and the iron legions of Hamal, had been driven to banditry against their foes. Your hardened, throat-cutting, purse-slitting bandit is a different matter.

Naturally, the mercenaries demanded extra pay. Unmok started to chitter-chatter, and I said, "Pay 'em," and so we did. We were eating bread sliced thin already. No sense in throwing the loaf away because of that.

Our ten thomplods lumbered along, thomp, thomp, thomp, their twelve legs apiece shaking the ground. The carts groaned, the wild beasts screeched and yowled and spat. We walked on, weapons in hand, staring every which way. In the Forest of the Departed are many grassy rides and wide open spaces lined with long-abandoned tombs. The shadows dropped confusingly down. The leaves rustled, a tiny hot wind blew, the smell of the forest fought the stinks of the caravan. We plodded on.

Looking at Unmok the Nets as he limped along, occasionally agreeing to ride aboard a cart, I reflected that this was one way to earn a living that was not for me. But we neared Huringa and the Jikhorkdun and the reason for all this.

The bandits hit us just as we were thinking about making camp.

We were crossing a wide grassy expanse where there was no hope of our seeking shelter among the trees, and the drikingers came howling and yelling along a ride at right angles. They carried spears and swords and axes, and they urged their totrixes along with spurs. They would have cut us into little pieces, gone slap-bang through us and then turned, pirouetting, to finish us off at their leisure.

Instead, they went careering madly across our front, swerving away. Men struggled to stay in their saddles. Spears fell to the grass. Men fell, too, to be trampled in the stampede of maddened totrixes, their six hooves battering helmet and breastplate and pulping out the red ooze.

"The thomplods!" screamed Unmok. He danced in ecstasy. "I hope that's Maglo the Ears, may his guts dissolve into green slime!"

The bandits could not control their mounts. The attack was a fiasco. Perking up, our guards loosed off a few shafts and this finished the business. Yelling and swearing, the drikingers vanished among the trees.

"If they come back," I said loudly, "we will serve them steel stew!"

"Aye!" shouted the mercenaries. They were almighty puffed with the victory. But not one had the temerity or stupidity to mention a Jikai. There are limits...

Although our hired guards had not yet been offered the opportunity to display their quality as fighting men for us, they were not slow in behaving as any good paktun will and doubling across to loot the corpses. This is a mere part of life and death on Kregen, a facet of the economy.

The idea of perfectly good swords and armor being allowed to rust uselessly away goes against the grain.

Wandering across, I found myself a useful-looking thraxter, the straight cut and thrust sword of Halivar. The grip was plain, the hilt unadorned, and the blade not too heavy. One needs something a little more robust than a rapier in a nasty little fracas of this kind. As for armor, two kaxes I looked at were both pierced through by arrows. I retrieved the arrows from the corselets; one was broken and the other I stuffed back into the quiver I had kept after being dubbed Jak the Shot. In the end I found a leather jerkin with bronze studding. It clothed a dead apim and by letting the thongs out to their fullest extent I was able to get it around my shoulders. Had it been the slightest tight on me I'd have not touched it with a bargepole. But the dead man was of a goodly breadth across the shoulders. He had died of a totrix hoof in the head.

The mercenaries were busily hacking off fingers and ears to get at rings. I wasn't particularly interested in that. In the normal course I wouldn't have bothered any further, but Unmok and my partnership was a trifle strapped. A Rapa lay pitched onto his vulturine nose, and the gleam of a fine scarron necklace attracted me. I went across and turned him over and nodded. The gems were valuable, loot, no doubt, from some unfortunate woman trapped in a destroyed caravan. I started to unhook them.

A Fristle wanted to dispute my claim. I pointed to the arrow through the Rapa's eye. The feathers were yellow from a Hulfoo bird, that Hyrklanian goose. "Mine, I think."

The Fristle spat a little, ruffled up his fur and then went off farther into the trees after easier pickings.

Unmok was delighted with the scarron necklace.

"You could make a play about that," I said, and I found my ugly old beak head itching, almost as though I smiled at a jest.

Shadows now cloaked the clearing and occasionally the last of the twin suns shafted a smoky twinkle between the trees. Myriad insects whirled and gyrated, chips of flickering light in the rays. We set about pitching camp and came alert again, quivering with fresh alarm, as the jingle of harness and the clip-clop of hooves heralded more jutmen. But they were zorcamen, a regiment out from Huringa and not caring overmuch for the duty of bandit-chasing. They'd be back inside the city long before midnight.

Unmok spoke to their Jiktar, graphically describing the bandits' attack. The soldiers poked around among the remains. They took a few of the bodies with them, so as to look good on their report, I judged. I kept away from them. They were smart and could march with lances all aligned; but I didn't trust them.

What had been going on in Hyrklana that bandits could exist, and with impunity so close to the capital city? Even in a dense and gloomy place like the Forest of the Departed?

The ominous growls from the big cats and that whiffling, snorting, bubbly hullabaloo from the thomplods cut short my theories of political upheavals. Dripping hunks of meat were served out, and the growls changed to grunts and snarls and digesting noises of pleasure. Thomplods eat a good deal, naturally, giving their size. Luckily they eat almost anything and we shepherded them under suitable trees where they quickly ripped and stuffed, ripped and stuffed, until the tree was as bare of leaves as high as the muzzles could reach. Then on to the next tree. As for grass, that went down by the mawful.

Unmok, like most folk standing in those parts of Kregen not so far converted, kept a slave or three. His camp chief, Nobi, was a little Och with a villainous face and no teeth. He kept a little mincer on a string around his neck. Now Nobi pushed and harassed the other two slaves into serving the evening meal. Fragrant scents wafted. The wine was poured. After a hard day we could relax.

Then a dratted strigicaw broke free.

Absolute bedlam. Pandemonium. We all ran this way and that, banging gongs and old brass trays, yelling and screeching, and scared right down to our toenails.

One thing about hunting-big-cats in captivity is that being fed by chunks of meat flung at them, they are half tame and half wild, and will eat meat they haven't killed themselves. We found the strigicaw with his head buried in the intestines of one of the Rapa casualties of the bandits' attack.

His brown and red hide glimmered splendidly by the light of our campfires and the scattering light of She of the Veils, pink and golden among the trees. Striped in the foreparts and double-spotted in the rear, with six pumping legs shading to black at the clawed paws, the strigicaw is a powerful and fast-running carnivore. We lassoed him from a respectful distance, and hauled, pushed and prodded him back to his cage. He kept his talons fast sunk into the remains of the Rapa.

"Still hungry," commented Froshak the Shine. "Meat no good."

"Then lucky we are it's all gone," said Unmok. "Tomorrow we'll be asked to pay good money for supplies. And if I know that camp manager, he'll cheat us rigid."

Froshak touched his knife. "Let me talk to him."

Unmok laughed, and then winced, and cradled the stump of his left middle. "What, Froshak, you leem hunter! And have the queen's guards lock us all up on that pretext, and drive us out into the arena to be gobbled up by our own stock?"

"She would too," said Froshak. "She-leem."

And he didn't even bother to cast a guilty glance over his shoulder.

Next day a bur or so after the hour of mid we rolled up to the gates of the transit camp. A slope of a hill ahead cut off any view of Huringa. I should have expected this. But I had been firm in the belief that we'd just drive the stock up to the Jikhorkdun and be let in. Easy.

The formalities were formidable. Paperwork threatened to bog us all down. Certificates had to be produced. The medical men checked the animals thoroughly. Some were put to one side as being second-class specimens, and these would find their way to other Jikhorkduns. Only the best were good enough for Huringa.

Perforce, I sweated it out as Unmok drove the hardest bargains he could. The managers and the inspectors insisted on everything being done correctly, which meant being done their way. An attempt at bribery was met with an impossible demand. There were other wild-beast purveyors to be thought about. There were a few of the inevitable fights. I stayed well and truly clear.

But, slowly, we and our stock were processed.

We received permission to take the thomplods in to Huringa. Enough nobles were interested. Money was paid over. Unmok was able to discharge the mercenaries, who would soon find fresh employment. Froshak was left in charge at the camp. Unmok looked me over.

"Best foot forward, Jak the Shot. Best clothes. We have to create an impression."

"My wardrobe consists of the tunic in which you found me, after I was washed overboard, as I told you. And a jerkin from a dead drikinger."

Unmok guffawed. "We'll outfit you, Jak."

"One thing puzzles me. What happens to the totrixes and the other juts when these thomplods enter the city?"

He winked, in that foolish yet extraordinarily knowing way Ochs have. "The managers of the Jikhorkdun know all about thomplods, and all the other animals you care to name. They will give us a phial or two at the city gate."

So, and with an excitement I did not bother to mask, I went with these meandering haystacks down toward Huringa, which is the capital city of Hyrklana, where they joy in the Jikhorkdun.

Twelve

Beasts for Huringa

Huringa had grown another enceinte since I had last seen the place. The outer lines of walls were not, to my perhaps too-critical eye, quite tall enough. We thomplodded along the dusty road and left everything smothered in the white dust as we passed. The new walls stretched out of sight on either hand. Built of a gray-white stone, they looked impressive, curtains relieved by towers in a long sweeping curve to north and south out of sight. Beyond these walls rose the older walls. Beyond them the remains of the old walls were visible here and there. The city jumbled. Dominating it all, of course, the high fortress of Hakal.

Rearing from the solid rock, tall, dominating, the high fortress of Hakal brought back a host, a flood, a tempest of memories. The lip of the Jikhorkdun was visible, and a hint of the many walls separating off the practice courts, the smaller arenas, the secluded gardens, the ball areas.

During the day the gas jets along the four main boulevards would be extinguished. Vollers crisscrossed through the air above the rooftops. The sense of bustle and urgency, of people about their daily business, of life being lived, gave a zest to the scene—a spurious zest in my view.

Slightly offset from the old Boloth Gate in the inner walls—what were now the inner walls—the gate giving ingress through the new walls lofted immensely. Massively serrated architecture allowed many arrow slits to frown down and murdering holes to dominate the gate's main tunnel. The thomplods passed through the opening with room for two more at each side and above and to spare.

"The Gate of The Trompipluns," said Unmok. He sniffed.

I gathered that though he valued his thomplods, he would dearly love to have brought a dozen trompipluns into Huringa.

Officials, backed by blank-faced guards, halted us. The arrangements were made and a boskskin bag containing golden deldys changed hands. The phials, buckets and water were brought.

Then we emptied the phials into the water and sloshed the resulting mixture all over our perambulating haystacks.

A few casual inquiries, a coarse joke or two, and the chingle of deldys brought me the information that the phials contained jutblood mixed with a variety of herbs. I let my memory jot down the names and descriptions. Unmok's tame slaves jabbered and scurried and the buckets were emptied. I could smell nothing fresh, but when we went on, a string of calsanys and a group of totrixes took no notice of us at all.

Unmok had brought just one couple of werstings with him, two dogs he particularly favored, and they stalked along, black and white terrors from which people automatically shrank to allow their sharp white teeth plenty of passageway.

The noble with an interest in the thomplods turned out to be Noran. A strom no longer because his father had died, he was now Vad Noran. He did not recognize me. Why should he? He had seen me for perhaps a couple of burs many seasons ago.

Noran had lost that first bright flush of youth. Lines indented his forehead. He was thicker in the gut. But still he retained the awareness of his position as the leader of his particular set.

"By Gaji's bowels! And these are the famous beasts I have waited to see! They are a mangy lot."

The thomplods stood with drooping heads in the walled courtyard of Vad Noran's villa. Missal trees lent a merciful shade. The sanded area was neatly raked. Watchful guards, mostly blegs and Rhaclaws, stood at the gates. Noran was bright and contemptuous and he did not deceive Unmok.

"The queen..." said Unmok, and paused, artfully.

"Yes, yes, I shall buy them. But the price—"

Casually, I eased away and walked a little space as though to examine the ornate well in one corner. A slave—she was a Fristle woman much bent over—hauled up the gleaming copper bucket and poured water into a copper bowl for me.

I placed an ob on the stone coping. The small coin vanished into her ragged slave breechclout like a fly on a lizard's tongue.

The haggling could be left to Unmok. That was his trade. As a beast purveyor he had no real need to wear one of the colors of arena allegiance. Just about everyone in Huringa wore a favor. A man sauntered across to me. He wore fancy clothes and his thraxter in an embroidered scabbard thumped his thigh. His face was over-red, filled out and petulant. But he was still Callimark. Again, I had absolutely no fears that he could possibly remember me, a man seen for a few burs one evening seasons ago.

"You wear no favor, horter." His own red cockade shone.

"Lahal," I addressed him, and by omitting the double L indicated his lack of politeness. His eyebrows drew down, but I went on smoothly, "I have had my red so long its stitching has quite worn through. It lies somewhere now, no doubt being trampled upon by a green, or a blue or—"

"By Clem! That is not to be borne!"

Instantly, by reason of this exchange, we were on friendly terms. He rummaged around in his scrip and produced a red favor, small, crumpled, but wearable.

"You would do me the honor—" he began.

I found that grizzly old smile and nodded, and took the red favor.

"I am in your debt, Horter…?"

"Callimark."

"Jak."

Unmok had completed the preliminaries, and Callimark, looking across, called out cheerily. Noran and Unmok joined us and there was mention of sazz or parclear, depending on one's preference for white or colored sherbet drinks, and palines, and perhaps banber sandwiches. Unmok winked at me. The atmosphere was genial, and that augured well for our partnership's financial well-being.

Here in Hyrklana we were somewhat closer to the equator than we would be in Vallia, but because of the enormous spread of Kregen's temperate zone the temperature remained comfortable. Noran's villa proved to be the sumptuous palace one would expect. We sat in cane chairs in one of his refectories and drank our sazz and talked. The conversation quickly turned on the execution—in the arena, of course—of the criminal lunatics who had attempted to burn one of Noran's voller factories.

I perked up.

"By Gaji's slimy intestines!" exclaimed Noran, flushed, vindictive. "They may not like the queen, but that does not mean they have to destroy my livelihood!"

"No, indeed, Noran," said Callimark, sipping parclear.

Now, seasons ago I had told these people I was Varko ti Hakkinostoling. The name was mouthful enough, the land far to the south had been ravaged; no one was going to bother overmuch about it. I had learned enough to pass muster, and indeed, had told Unmok that I was from Hakkinostoling.

So it was that I could venture an informed opinion.

I said, "Surely they do this, vad, as much in resentment of Hamal as of the queen—"

"Yes. You have it right, Horter Jak. But it is I who suffers!"

"The vad is constrained to sell to Hamal," put in Callimark, acting perfectly the part of the confidant to one in high position. "The Empress Thyllis is quite mad, of course, quite unlike our own dear queen. We must stay out of the insane war she wages."

"Yes." Noran exerted his own authority, overriding his friend. "We profit by her stupidities. But the thought of Hamalese skyships over Huringa— no. Better to sell to Hamal."

Now a vad is a very high rank of nobility, and Noran was being very gracious and condescending in his manner. This, I judged, was to impress Unmok and to bring down the price. So I risked another shaft…

"I agree with you absolutely, notor." I spoke in a soft, almost philosophical voice and trusted he would take no offense. "This, I am told, is the queen's wish. The only trouble is that this makes Hamal stronger."

101

Noran nodded. He didn't like it, but it was the truth.

"If only—" he said, and stopped.

I went on, "If we could sell to other countries we would benefit Hyrklana immensely."

"I know that! By Flem! It is enough to make a man take up sword himself!"

"Perhaps one day you will be afforded that opportunity."

Both Noran and Callimark looked sharply at me. I saw their reactions, transparently reflected in their faces. The next moment might see a little hop, skip and jumping...

Unmok was a mere beast purveyor, but he had standing.

Slowly, Noran worked his way around to what he fancied might be an answer to my manner.

"You speak as though—" he started, and then: "You do not talk like a beast handler, Horter Jak."

"The queen—"

"Ah!"

Unmok was looking at me as though I'd started spitting fire like the Spiny Risslacas.

I said, "A man has to turn his hand to many things in life, and must do what those in authority demand, in loyalty and affection. This is so, is it not, Vad Noran?"

"This is so, Horter Jak. But if you are not here as I had thought, have you anything specific to ask?"

This was brass-tacking with a vengeance.

"At the present moment, no. But your sentiments do you credit—and I mean no disrespect, as I hope you will understand."

"Go on."

Go on! I was fishing around desperately as it was, filling the air with noise. Go on... I'd had a hard time getting here! So I leaned back in the cane chair and sipped my drink and looked wise—emperors are good at looking wise when their heads are empty—and told him, "The time will come, and I hope soon, when the queen will make her decision."

That appeared to satisfy him, for he banged a little silver gong, and we all rose as the slaves advanced to clear the tables. We went out to the courtyard and the business of the thomplods was concluded. As Unmok said to me, "Whatever was going on in there, Jak, he didn't haggle afterward."

So I said, "That's what partners are for, Unmok."

Thirteen

Of an Encounter in a Skyship

During the considerable time I had spent in Ruathytu, capital of Hamal, I had rarely visited any of the arenas there. Huringa was not so large a city as Ruathytu, and life was to a far greater extent dominated by the arena. Everywhere were reminders. Folk wore their colors of allegiance as a matter of course. They might live cheek by jowl, the baker being a follower of the diamond zhantil, and the cobbler an adherent of the sapphire graint, but always they were aware of the corners in the arena for which they shouted.

And they shouted. By Krun, but they made a din!

When the games were being staged the noise was clearly audible all over the city.

"For my part," said Unmok the Nets, during the next games when we could not bring in any of the remainder of our animals, "I do not care to choose a color. I do my work, and although it does not please me, it gives me a living." We were heading for an open-air eating place where we looked forward to roast vosk, momolams and enormous helpings of squish pie. "Now, when I get me my cage-voller..."

The people moving slowly on the boulevards and sitting at the tables all wore a pinched look, a grayish cast to their gizzards. They spoke in high-pitched voices, and laughed a great deal, with exaggerated gestures. They fooled no one. They were not in the Jikhorkdun, and therefore were, for the time being, out of the main pulsating current of life.

We sat down to eat. This was a good time for service. Nothing much happened outside the Jikhorkdun when the games were on.

The Jikhorkdun itself comprised all the inner courts and practice yards, the barracks, the cells, the animal cages and, as the focal point of all the effort, the arena within the great amphitheater. My job was to get Tilly, Oby and Naghan the Gnat out safely. Before that, I must make sure of a voller. Despite the importance of airboats to Vallia, I would not jeopardize my task of freeing my friends for the sake of a single flier. First things first.

"I am not an overly religious man, Jak," said Unmok, leaning back, "but sometimes I question the judgment of Ochenshum in arranging my life for me. As for Havil the Green, I think his days are numbered."

"How so?"

"Why, did you not hear that Vad Noran and his crony. Callimark? It was Flem this and Glem that, and anything-lem, all the time."

I knew exactly what Unmok was talking about. I felt the hateful repugnance for the evil cult of Lem the Silver Leem. I looked hard at Unmok, hoping he was not involved with that blasphemy. Right or wrong, my friends and I had determined that Lem the Silver Leem should never sully Vallia.

"Some secret religion of theirs. I've heard of it vaguely." Unmok's middle left stump twitched. "I know nothing of it and wish to know nothing. But there's a lot of it about."

"From what I know," I said, speaking with caution, "I fancy even Havil the Green is preferable."

"Every week you hear of babies gone missing."

I buried my face in squish pie. My thoughts were far too black and my face would have expressed my murderous feelings for the monsters who butchered babies to the greater glory of the Silver Leem.

We had managed to rid the martial race of Canops of the cult of Lem the Silver Leem, and the whole nation had been peacefully resettled on the island of Canopjik, situated at the mouth of the Gulf of Wracks which leads from the Ocean of Clouds into the Shrouded Sea. The island was considerably larger than their original home of Canopdrin and they flourished and maintained friendly relations with Migladrin, among other peoples and nations of the Shrouded Sea and the Dawn Lands.

When our meal was finished, Unmok said he would go to see a client who, because of an indisposition, was confined to his bed and unable to take his reserved seat in the amphitheater. I excused myself with a vague comment that Unmok would make a better fist of it than I. I sauntered along the boulevard with the infernal din from the arena booming like the thunder of the Ice Floes of Sicce. The noise rose and faded away and each punctuation marked the end of some poor devil on the blood-soaked silver sand.

Vollers cost money.

After my adventures the money remaining would not buy me the kind of voller I required, even if I could find someone to sell the craft. Production was tightly controlled, and the information that Vad Noran was engaged in voller manufacture came as a revelation to me.

So that meant I would have to liberate an airboat. I have done this before and was to do it again. All the same, I fancied in this case I'd recompense the person from whom I borrowed the flier. That seemed only fair. Vallia was not at war with Hyrklana. Ludicrous though the notion may be, it does have weight, this idea that stealing from one's enemies is not stealing in the true meaning of the word. Well, it is not, true, but you have to ponder the question and, sometimes, come up with unpalatable answers.

While the blood-antics went on in the arena was as good a time as any and better than most for work of this nefarious nature. The flierdrome I selected lay beyond the Walls of the Sapphire, between them and the new walls. The suns burned down as I walked gently along. Unmok had been as good as his word, and I wore decent Hyrklanan clothes: a blue tunic, a gray wraparound and high-thonged sandals. I wore only the thraxter—and my old knife, of course—and had left the rapier and dagger at our camp.

Many roofs jumbled below me in a little valley. On the flat ground to the side rested many airboats, of different descriptions but all of a moderate size. It slowly dawned on me as I approached that this was now a factory as well as a flierdrome.

Large numbers of slaves were in evidence as well as men of the artisan class, those they call guls in Hamal. The place looked busy. Here they built airboats for Hamal. Guards patrolled, mostly Rhaclaws and Rapas; but I fancied I could elude them for the vital amount of time required.

The blue tunic and gray wraparound were detestable garments. But they had their part to play. Passing through the shadows of an outlying block with a gate and a guard before me, I stopped. Because there are two suns in the sky of Kregen everyone expects everything to have two shadows. So the word for shadow, umshal, is a plural, rather naturally. In a room where there is a single lamp, or at the times of solar eclipses, when a Kregan wishes to talk of a single shadow, he will say a nikumshal, half-shadows. In the shadows I put on a new face, as Deb-Lu had instructed me. The bees began to sting, but I would have to endure that. I marched briskly on.

"Lahal, dom," I said as I came up to the guard. He was a cat-faced Fristle, bored and yawning, wishing he was in the Jikhorkdun—as a spectator! My use of the familiar word dom, pal, half disarmed him. I rattled on. "Vad Noran sent me, urgent word within—you know how it is with these notors."

"Aye, dom, I do know. What is the latest?"

I had my wits enough about me to know what he was on about. I improvised as only an old kaidur could. I told him that one bout had seen off twenty Brokelsh coys and not a hair of the heads of their opponents scratched. This Fristle wore a blue favor. So I added to flavor the dish, "And the blues are doing well so, as a red, you will pardon me from laughing."

He laughed and opened the gate and I went through.

Strutting along with the importance of the petty official about business, I penetrated between the buildings, and penetrated is a good word, there, by Krun! The place was alive with men and women scurrying about. The slaves ran. The guls walked to show their free status. The sounds of hammering and sawing floated from various buildings. This was Sumbakir on a large scale.

If I knew nothing at all about voller production, I knew that the silver boxes would not be made and filled here. They'd be freighted in for fitting to the vollers. Rhaclaw guards prowled. I ignored them, and my nose went up a few inches. The right petty bureaucrat, me!

My face was beginning to sting uncomfortably, but I did not want to relax in case I did not put on exactly the same face again.

Rounding a corner I looked up at the edge of the flat area. Steps led up. Only one Rhaclaw guarded them, and he was more interested in the lines of slaves hauling half-built vollers up to the finishing sheds crowning the edge. The slaves made a din. I judged that the valley had been chosen as the site because it was thought easier to defend against aerial attack. Towers studded the place, and archers moved in the fighting tops. They'd shaft an aerial attack, and they'd shaft runaway slaves. And—they'd shaft clean through anyone who attempted to steal a voller.

My lips drew down in that new face. This was not looking good.

Well, as long as I was here I might as well see how far I could get.

Now the weird thing was, and I swear this is absolutely true, as Zair is my witness!, the fact of stealing a voller and the story I had told, or rather hinted at, to Vad Noran brought vivid impressions into my mind. As I started up the slope I was thinking of Prince Tyfar and of Jaezila.

Prince Tyfar and I had gone through a few adventures together and he was a good comrade. Also, he was a Prince of Hamal, which was unfortunate. The son of Prince Nedfar of Hamal, Tyfar was intelligent, studious, a lover of good books, honorable and upright. Also he was a superb axeman. He'd gone back to Hamal after our last adventures and, I confess, I missed his company.

As for Jaezila—well, now! That commanding and beautiful woman, mistress of the bow and the sword, had plagued Tyfar cruelly with her manner and her willfulness. She worked for Hamal, although I was not certain she was Hamalese, and had been attempting to obtain fliers for the Empress Thyllis. She was a marvel, that girl, ravishing, alluring and damned temperamental, as Tyfar had discovered. When we'd been forcibly parted she could easily have gone with Tyfar back to Hamal, and there made the shattering discovery that the ninny she so contumed was a noble prince and highly thought of. I'd have liked to have witnessed that revelation, by Vox!

Maintaining that brisk gait I ascended the stairs. The Rhaclaw half turned to look. His leather armor was liberally studded with bronze and he carried a stux, one of the throwing spears that can burst clear through you. He was a Rhaclaw, a race of diffs more commonly found in Havilfar, with the enormous domed head fully as wide as his shoulders. He looked at me suspiciously.

I started my rigmarole of bearing a message as I neared him. As I reached the top, I paused, theatrically holding my side and gasping for breath.

"My Havil! That climb takes it out of a fellow."

"You have no business here—"

Beyond him and beyond the edge of the finishing sheds I could see row after row of vollers. These were all the same, over at this end of the field. Six-place fliers, they were military craft, most useful for scouting purposes with enough punch if they got into a tight squeeze to scrape clear.

"Wait a minute, dom, till I get my breath."

"You have no business." He didn't bother to finish talking to me. He half turned and opened his letter box of a mouth. He was going to holler for the Deldar of the guard.

So, unwillingly, I leaped forward and laid him down gently enough, and then ran on leaving him slumbering.

Security at this voller factory was not so slack as I'd assumed.

A hell of a racket began. As I ran I realized this was a bedlam of bells and gongs and ratcheted clackers, all kicking up their own brand of inferno. A file of Rapas doubled around the end of the finishing shed. Evidently, each sentry post was overseen by the next. Some system of checking could alone account for the rumpus.

If I could reach a voller...

Guards were running from every which way. They sprang up all over the field like dragon's teeth.

I'd never reach a voller now... The finishing shed was the only cover. Instantly, I turned and hared off for the shadows.

Once aboard the voller and the girl is mine... The silly jingle kept running around in my head.

For a factory, the finishing shed proved to be a handsome building. Its eaves projected. I went into the shadows like a fish diving under a weir. Inside the shed the dimness could not be allowed to hinder me. Slaves started to yell, and the evil sound of whips and that hateful word "Grak!" burst out. I straddled three overseers who would awake wondering what had hit them. I hared on, running flat out, making for the far end.

Down both sides of the shed the bulks of vollers lay waiting for the final touches. No doubt here was where the silver boxes were fitted. If I got out of this in one piece it might pay to return here and investigate the mysterious silver boxes. A Rapa leaped at me, his thraxter a glimmering bar of steel. I slid his brand, chopped him in the wattles, jumped and ran on.

The pack hullabalooed after me.

If this was an example of how Dray Prescot liberated a voller, then Zair help him!

Out the far door, no time to blink at the blaze of suns shine. The next shed's open door gaped an invitation.

Inside this one they were building a very large vessel. Very large indeed. Although not as huge as a Hamalese skyship, she towered up to the beams of the roof, and her bulk swelled to allow an alleyway at each side. Here slaves and guls labored to put the finishing touches to the hull.

There was no time to stop.

Then the thought occurred to me. Up to now thought had played little part...

I went up the nearest ladder and dived into the ship.

She was a fine craft. No doubt of that. Even in this uncompleted state, with holes in the decks and planks and ladders everywhere, sawdust and shavings strewing the decks, paint pots and buckets and all the bric-a-brac of ship construction lumbering the clearways, she still held a good line, still conveyed the sense of the power she would wield in the skies.

Noises inside echoed like gongs in a cathedral. Light fell confusedly. I hurried along. My face was now a blazing pain. To hell with it! With a feeling of enormous relief I let my new face disappear, and my own old beakhead of a face glowered out. Disguise is all very well. But there are limits...!

The gray wraparound had served its purpose. I unwrapped it and chucked it into a waste bin among oily trash. Now I looked like any horter, with a decent dark-red breechclout and a blue tunic reaching to mid-thigh. I hitched up the thraxter. The weapon had not yet been drawn.

A deal of noise spurted up from aft and below. This was noise not of slaves arguing among themselves or guls telling the slaves what to do, but of guards searching around for their quarry which had—for the moment—eluded them.

One thing I was certain of: I'd done the right thing in running. I'd never have talked my way out of that mess.

Down a corridor that was just about finished, apart from a lick of paint, I marched on smartly. At the end there would be a companionway down and I could emerge from any of the holes being filled with varters, or reach the lower fighting galleries and descend to the shed floor from there.

Voices reached me from ahead. I did not stop. Now I could bluff from an entirely new hand. News would not have reached this far yet.

Light shafted down from a broad opening in the deck above. People stood in a group in the center of the radiance. Some held plans, which they slanted to catch the light. A big fellow with a mass of dark hair was gesticulating around and jabbing the plan. Another man was standing a little to one side looking at the carpenters' work on the near bulkhead, and he turned back to speak to the big fellow with the plans.

"...Not good enough," said this young fellow. He spoke in a pleasant enough voice. He wore decent clothes, of a neat cut and of blue and gray, with gray trousers. I saw those trousers. At his side swung a rapier, and a main gauche would match it on the other, of that I felt sure. He looked lithe and Umber, with a handsome, keen face, and I sighed.

As I said, I'd been thinking as I ventured in here of Prince Tyfar...

I walked forward boldly into the light.

One or two of the group looked up as I appeared.

The woman—the girl—was there, this time dressed in dark blue, and a rapier swung at her side, too.

"Lahal," I said cheerily. "I am sorry for my lateness. But there was some disorder, something about a man running down there. I trust you are well?"

I used no names.

Prince Tyfar gaped at me. Jaezila stared.

Then she smiled. "Lahal, Jak. We are pleased to see you."

Fourteen

I Amuse my Friends

As I was a member of the delegation with Prince Tyfar of Hamal there was no trouble about my leaving. He had with him two grave-faced men, high officials of the department in Hamal charged with voller procurement. Also he had Barkindrar the Bullet and Nath the Shaft. With Jaezila was her retainer, Kaldu. They merely nodded to me and smiled. They took their lead from their master and mistress. Anyway, we had been comrades together, blade comrades. There was much between us.

So we went down the steps and the furor continued as the guards hunted the fugitive. The wildest of rumors flew about.

As we walked together, Jaezila smiled. "You, I suppose, Jak the Sturr?"

"Aye, my lady, me. And my thanks—"

Prince Tyfar half turned, the epitome of a handsome young prince.

"You observed the skyship, Jak. Your opinion?"

"A fine craft, Prince." I'd heard the others address him thusly, so that was one hurdle out of the way. He was here with the delegation officially from Hamal buying fliers. "She will serve admirably once she is completed."

"My thought, exactly, except—"

I chanced a shaft. "The varter positions on the upper deck?"

"Precisely."

A little technical discussion ensued, in which I was able to insert my oar from time to time. Tyfar was a right tearaway in that he'd chanced dropping me in it. But, I fancy, he had taken the measure of my mettle as I'd taken the measure of his down in the Moder, among other fraught places.

The big fellow with the hair and the plans appeared anxious to please. He was the manager, Nalgre Orndalt, and he heaved up a sigh just before we said the remberees.

"The ship will be only two weeks behind schedule, Prince. You can't get the quality of workmanship like you used to. And I'd as lief be in the stands of the Jikhorkdun as working this afternoon."

Rather sharply, Tyfar said, "You perhaps object to working for Hamalese paymasters?"

Nalgre Orndalt's thick fingers clenched on the plans. The paper ridged and creased. Then, slowly, he said, "No, Prince. There are some, as you know, who... No, I do my work and take my wages, and leave politics to the queen."

With her brilliant smile, Jaezila said, "Well, Nalgre, perhaps you could hasten the work. Improve on the two weeks?"

"I will try." He did not say, "For you, my lady." But the impression of his having said that remained. I did not wonder. Many men would move mountains for Jaezila. I did not think she would treat them like dirt beneath her sandals, but if she did they'd be grateful for the attention.

When we were safely outside the gates and walking slowly toward the lines where the zorcas were stabled, Tyfar said to the officials in his delegation, "I believe you expressed the desire to witness the games? There will still be some games left. Of the more barbarous kind." His face expressed his distaste. He had told me he did not care for the Jikhorkdun in his native Hamal.

"Thank you, Prince." The officials and their aides mounted up and rode off. We looked after them, waiting for them to leave. Kaldu, big-boned and powerful, his brown beard trimmed to a point, kept away from me. He would not look at me.

I moved to stand at his side. "Do not blame yourself, Kaldu. You did right—"

"But we left you to certain death—"

"The death was not certain. For I am here. Now, for the sake of Havil, cheer up! Your duty was to the lady Jaezila. You did right, and you would do the same again."

He had forcibly taken Jaezila aboard the voller and lifted away to safety as I had been ringed with steel.

"Aye, Jak. Aye. I would do the same again."

"Queyd-arn-tung!" I said, which means no more need be said on the subject.

And Kaldu passed a broad hand across his beard and smiled.

Then it was Tyfar's turn to attempt to apologize for leaving me. In all the kafuffle of the attack he had not been in any position to contribute. I told him so, and added, "And now that you are here and I am here, in Hyrklana, we have a lot to do."

"And Deb-Lu? And Hunch and Nodgen?"

I moved my hands. "I assume they are safe. They lifted away in good time."

"I pray they are safe. I set much store by Deb-Lu-Quienyin. And as for Hunch and Nodgen—"

"Hunch, at least," put in Jaezila, with her laugh, "would have trembled in his shoes up there."

We all laughed. Even I laughed, for that seems the right thing to do when Hunch the Tryfant comes into the conversation. And he had been a good companion to us, with his comrade Nodgen...

I was not going to tell Tyfar or Jaezila that Quienyin and Hunch and Nodgen, and the Pachak twins, Fre-Da, had reached Vallia. Tyfar and Jaezila were Hamalese and thought I was working for mad Empress Thyllis as were they.

That was the explanation I gave them for my presence. As I expected, it worked like a charm. If you understand that I felt a twinge of guilt at telling that kind of untruth to two people for whom I entertained the highest respect, admiration and affection, you understand aright. But as with Rees and Chido, personal friendship beclouds the supposedly greater issues of patriotism. And I had already vowed that patriotism, for all the demeaning postures now understood by that word, would not be allowed to harm Tyfar or Jaezila.

Not while I lived, by Vox!

As we mounted up—I've no idea to whom the zorca I so airily made use of belonged—I thought if only these two were not Hamalese!

We had a deal of mileage to make up. Through downright cunning use of my supposed secret assignment from Empress Thyllis I was able to bypass most of the awkward questions. I let them understand I'd got out of that scrape back there in Absordur with the Vajikry-mad trylon by telling the truth. When I mentioned that infuriating game of Vajikry, Tyfar threw back his head and laughed uproariously.

"You, Jak! Vajikry! But you're a Jikaida man."

"Surely. I was hard put to it to survive." Then I told them of the gambit I'd used to win free, whereat they laughed the louder.

I could see the funny side of it well enough, but I said, "It was a good laugh afterward. But at the time, and what with that oaf singing his damned dismal song, the "March of the Skeletons," well, it wasn't so—"

Jaezila interrupted swiftly, turning to me from her saddle. "Jak! We are thoughtless and cruel to laugh so!" And then she couldn't stop bursting out with a snorting laugh she tried to stop and only made worse.

Comrades. Blade comrades! I warmed to them.

And their adventures had been a trifle fraught, also. They'd had a few fights and helter-skelterings of that kind winning free and reaching Hamal. Kregen offers unbounded opportunities for skull-bashing if you have a mind to that kind of frolic, which I have not. Then it was my turn to laugh as they described Jaezila's surprise—her consternation—when she discovered the ninny she so put upon was a prince, a real live prince of Hamal.

"Ah, but Jaezila," I said, "you should have seen him down the Moder. He was like a zhantil."

"Oh, now, come, Jak, really—" protested Tyfar. But he gave a glance at the girl—the woman—who rode so straight and proudly at his side. And I, nodding to myself, fancied the future held prospects there that would have astonished just absolutely everybody when we were crossing the Dawn Lands.

"And the quest for vollers proved negative there," they told me. "And we were ordered to speed up production in Hyrklana."

I made a face. "But can you order another country like that? You know they do not like the Hamalese."

Now it was Tyfar's face which changed. He looked at once savage and dismayed. "I know. I deplore what we are doing with our army and air service. We attack, it seems, at the whim of the Empress Thyllis—may Havil forgive me if I speak out of turn, Jak. But I cannot much longer remain still. My father keeps his own counsel. But—"

"You know my opinion of Prince Nedfar," I said. "He is a great man. He will always strive to walk the path of righteousness." I did not use those exact and somewhat mawkish words; the sentiment remained true.

"Aye." Tyfar's eyebrows drew down and his forehead wrinkled. "Aye. I pray he does not run into trouble."

"If the iron legions of Hamal are stopped," said Jaezila, and she spoke on a breath, "what will Thyllis do then, d'you think?"

We didn't know. But we all felt it would be something exceedingly dire.

I forbore to inquire who was going to do the stopping. Up in Vallia we had made a good beginning in that direction...

They asked me where I was staying, preparatory, I guessed, to inviting me to stay with them. I said I was living outside the walls, and doing very well. I did not particularize.

There were three or four small townships, not quite suburbs, outside the walls, and all at least two varter shots from the walls. This was a common-sense precaution. They assumed I was staying in one of these suburbs.

"We have been put up in regal fashion with Pallan Mahmud nal Yrmcelt," said Tyfar. "He is the queen's chief pallan."

"Ord Mahmud," I said, thinking.

Tyfar looked surprised. "Why, no. Orlan Mahmud. You have his name wrong. Beware, he is high in the queen's favor."

"I believe I have heard." said Jaezila offhandedly, "that Orlan's father's name was Ord."

I nodded and let it pass. Time flows, time flows...

It seemed to me he would not remember the descent of a slate slab and a scarlet breechclout. He might. If he did I fancied he would wish to forget. After all, at the time he had been involved with a group plotting the downfall of Queen Fahia. Perhaps, I surmised as we jogged along, perhaps Orlan Mahmud nal Yrmcelt was still opposed to the queen, and taking over his father's position as chief pallan, sought-to work from within the establishment. It was a possibility.

Also, it was quite likely to be mere wishful thinking. Men as they grow older, on Kregen as on Earth, often change from being red-hot revolutionaries to straitlaced pillars of the community. The thought, the fact, is not new.

The games still proceeded and the beast roar of the crowd swelled over Huringa. Tyfar declared his throat was as dry as that infernal desert we had marched through together and so we reined in at a convenient hostelry and, dismounting, saw that the zorcas were led off by slaves. Then we sat around a table, with the retainers at a respectful distance.

This was nonsense for us, for we were all comrades-in-arms. But we had no wish, for our various reasons, to attract undue and unfavorable notice.

As we sipped the wine, for it was just time, I reflected that this was all very fine and wonderful; it brought me no nearer to securing a voller for the escape I planned.

Overjoyed though I was to meet up with Tyfar and Jaezila, I could not, must not, allow them to deflect me from my purpose in Huringa.

We had a deal to talk over. Prince Nedfar, Tyfar's father, had reached Ruathytu safely. I was relieved to hear this. Tyfar, again, expressed his unease over the policies being followed by his country. Jaezila, her color up, her splendid eyes fierce, observed that, by Krun! Hamal trod a dangerous path. But she, like Tyfar, would not commit herself to any definite statement. They worked for Hamal, as I worked for Vallia. The thought saddened me.

My explanations, although lame in my ears, satisfied them when I said I would have to return to my quarters. We enjoyed a slap-up meal before the Jikhordun turned out and the taverns became choked with excited patrons discussing the details of the games. I gathered that the yellows had lost their place of preeminence, and the blues had, as I had told that guard, achieved the highest position.

Mentioning the lady Ariane nal Amklana, Tyfar said he had not seen or heard of her since entering Hyrklana. The lady Ariane had not, in our opinion, biased though we might be, turned out too well in the Moder. Much might be forgiven her, but Tyfar was too much the gentleman, the true noble, to dwell on that. She was, he said he had discovered, well-known in Huringa, visiting there from time to time. She was a vadni, the Vadni of Amklana, and her husband, like Queen Fahia's husband, King Rogan, was a nonentity.

"I heard once—oh, a mere whisper—that King Rogan might seek to take the reins of government into his own hands." I said this in the quiet expectancy of immediate and incredulous disbelief. My expectations were not disappointed.

"He is a nothing," declared Tyfar. "Poor fellow."

"It is true. I do not know where your whisper came from, Jak," said Jaezila. "But it is surely false."

"Aye. It was probably a pious hope. A wish that he might prove a better sovereign than fat Queen Fahia."

No one outside our circle heard me, which was just as well.

Pleasant though it was to sit in the radiance of the declining suns and eat and drink and talk with my comrades, I had work to do. I stood up. Tyfar instantly stopped my attempts to pay the reckoning, with princely grace quietly insisting he would settle. I made an arrangement to meet them on the morrow, expressed my regrets I was called away and walked off. My twin shadows preceded me as I walked along, heading for the Jikhorkdun.

In that warren of evil and horror and high courage three other friends awaited—all unknowing—the chance of escape I trusted fervently I was bringing them.

Fifteen

Of Questions and Reminders

"No. Never heard of him."

"A little fellow. Very cheery. The best armorer you could hope to find."

"Sorry, dom."

I turned away. This was the fifth dead end. Around me the familiar— hatefully familiar—sounds of the practice rings rose into the evening sky. The bulk of the amphitheater cast deep and imposing shadows. The smaller courts blocked off the last rays of Zim and Genodras, which in Havilfar are known as Far and Havil. The clink of steel on steel, the swift stamp and scrape of foot, the hoarse intake of breath, all these blood-quickening sounds served on this evening only to depress me. The Jikhorkdun was vast. It was a labyrinth.

This maze might not be quite as dangerous as that labyrinth within the Moder, down which we had ventured, braving monsters and sorceries; it held its own evil brand of danger. There had, it seemed to me, been nothing else for it but to ask for Naghan the Gnat by name. Yes, there was inherent peril in this. He might be using another name. Strangers who asked around for one particular person would be looked at most carefully. But—how else was I to find Naghan?

Deb-Lu-Quienyin had assured me my friends, although of the Jikhorkdun, were not involved in the arena. Tilly, that beautiful golden-haired Fristle fifi, might be anywhere in the immense barrack blocks. Oby, who was no longer a young tearaway and who might now prefer his name in full—Obfaril—had given up all desires to be a kaidur. In Valka he had become obsessed with fliers. He was an expert in vollers. Now, I trusted he had not been given the chance to fulfill his youthful ambitions.

As for Balass the Hawk, that doughty fighting man would have been sent back to his native land of Xuntal. I did not expect to find Balass here.

The promenades were crowded with folk come to see the kaidurs at close quarters. Even a day of surfeit in the arena could not satisfy many of the aficionados. Time would never dull for me the impression, the emotion, the passions of the arena. I'd been through the mill. I thought I knew.

Partisan devotees would come to admire and to shower gifts on the kaidurs who had been victorious. Wagers were arranged, and the bets were enormous. The trainers would display their new men; the backers would look and whisper behind their hands, pomanders well in evidence. It was a flesh market, of course, but at the same time the young sprigs of the gentry and nobility would take up a sword and set to with a renowned kaidur. The steel rang and scraped. I knew no kaidur was going to use all his skill to show up some popinjay. All the same, nasty knocks could be taken—aye, and given!—in these pretty little private matches.

The Jikhorkdun has its four color corners, plus the area reserved for the queen's kaidurs, and I went first and naturally to the reds. And, again naturally, I sought the armorers and made my inquiries. After the fifth dead end I changed my tune about Naghan being the best armorer you could find. It was true. I have mentioned other armorers who had worked for me and who were comrades, and there were many—particularly in Valka— who were superb. Naghan the Gnat took his place among the finest. But my questions would be met with scowls and black brows.

So that little man with the great heart became just Naghan the Gnat, an armorer.

And still I found no trace at all, not even a memory. Well, that is passing foolish on my part, for by the nature of its trade, being a kaidur means you do not make friends. They tend to die off quickly, and you take your turn in that dismal procession.

About to chuck the reds and try my luck with the blues, for unless you volunteer to walk into the arena you do not often have the chance of choosing what color you fight under, I saw Cleitar Adria talking to a pot-bellied man loaded with gold chains. I thought it was Cleitar Adria. I stopped, looking without appearing to stare.

By Kaidun! It was Cleitar.

We'd been captured as slaves together, and given the opportunity to fight in the arena, and taken it. Cleitar had prospered as a kaidur as though wedded to it. It had become his life—and I own I was glad to see he was still alive. He had the marks of the Jikhorkdun upon him.

The dead tissues of the scar bisecting the left half of his face glistened like white ceramic from Loh. That scar started at his hairline and finished at his chin. His left eye socket was simply dead scar tissue.

I fancied no one called him Ob-Eye Adria.

He had not been a particularly close comrade. I had rubbed along with him out of pure self-interest, to avoid a fracas, and cheered his victories because he fought for the ruby drang.

It seemed to me he would not recognize me. But, just in case, I moved to one side and began to compose my features as Deb-Lu had instructed me and started to put on a new face.

Something soft and padded, and containing something hard and edged, thumped me in the middle of the back. I did not fall. Balance is important to a fighting man, even when he is in the middle of half bending over to change his face. I straightened as a bull roar broke out, a bellowing, hectoring, vicious torrent of words.

Some pot-bellied, swag-jowled, bloodshot-eyed, gold-bedecked oaf had bumped into me. The objects I had felt had been his guts and his sword. I will not repeat what he said.

The tide of invective poured on. I did not know who he was. The uproar attracted attention. He clearly felt himself to be an important man.

Even as I plucked my fist out of the air and slapped it down, opening my hand out to clamp around my thigh, I turned away. Hitting him would not help my three friends. And, somewhere in the limbo of the unborn, that new face of mine howled for a body.

By Zair! But I know my own face must have looked a sight—that devil's look that stops a risslaca in its tracks.

I dodged down a side alley. Toward the end a cage held half a dozen werstings, and the black-and-white killer dogs prowled around and around, tongues lolling. Poor old Unmok the Nets had been in a quandary about his werstings. He put great store by them, and pampered them, and did not want to sell them and, because the rest of his merchandise was of top quality, had received offers. The quandary lay in this—his werstings were now soft. Pampered, overfed, overweight, perfumed and silk-ribboned, they would not last a heartbeat against real killers.

Mind you, I hold no brief for werstings. They have taken the seat out of more than one pair of breeches before I could jump clear. They and stavrers, both...

* * * *

The noise rose into the sky. The suns were gone and the gas lights jetted. Under the arcades all manner of unholy trades were going on, fruits of the excitement of the arena. The crowds jostled, taking the opportunity for a last look at famous kaidurs before the evening's entertainments took on their more familiar aspects—taverns, theaters, dopa dens, girls all beckoned the raffish sets of Huringa.

In the shadows under the wooden swell of tiered seating of a small private arena I halted. Footsteps padded after me. Three drunks passed in the opposite direction, and I used their stumbling bodies as a shield to turn to confront whoever it was who stalked me. A man stepped forward.

"Lahal, Drak the Sword!"

"Lahal," I answered firmly. "You would do yourself a good service, Cleitar, if you omit the Sword from my name."

His one eye disappeared as he winked—or blinked—who can say in a one-eyed man?

"I understand. I thought you dead. You left—I recall it as though it were yesterday."

"And, when that fat oaf bumped into me, you saw...?"

"Aye, Drak. One does not easily forget that look—"

"So I am told."

"By the brass sword and glass eye of Beng Thrax! I am glad to see you. These young coys are all flatfish these days."

I digested that. So much came out there. Cleitar must know we had not been blade comrades. But we had been comrades fighting for the ruby drang. I nodded. "Can you...?"

"Oh, I am a cheldur now and may come and go as I please."

As I try to explain it, a cheldur is not quite like a Roman lanista. He is a trainer, above all, responsible for his barracks and for the production of kaidurs. He does not really possess the lanista's privileges of arranging affairs.

Cleitar gestured to his face.

"This was a blessing in disguise." He went on to describe in gory detail the fight in which he had received his wound. We walked on to where he said we could find wine or dopa. "After that they said I could be a cheldur and no longer fight. Well, by Kaidun! I have done well—"

"The ruby drang sits at the bottom of the staff."

He looked savage. "Aye! The sapphire graint lords it now!"

So, weirdly, weirdly! I was back thinking and passionately thirsting for the ruby drang to be triumphant. I recalled how we reds fought and shouted, cat-calling the other colors, contemptuous of them all alike, how we crowed at our victories and screamed and rattled weapons along the iron bars at our defeats. Oh, yes, I had been a hyr-kaidur and one does not easily forget that, by Kaidun, no!

And, the other weird thing was, here we were, walking along and talking almost as though so many seasons separating our last meeting meant nothing, had never existed...

He wanted to know all about that dramatic escape in which a monstrous skyship had descended into the arena and plucked us from the silver sand. I told him a little—very little, as you will easily imagine. Then it was simple to go on talking about Oby and Tilly and Naghan the Gnat, for they, with Balass the Hawk, had been rescued along with me.

He had not heard of them, any of them, from that day to this.

So, I said to myself as we went into a vile-smelling place filled with wooden benches beneath a training ring, that means Naghan has to be armorer to another color.

"In here, Drak—" Cleitar said, ducking his head to pass under the lintel. I took his arm and held him back.

"It would be a good idea to call me by my name," I said. "I am Chaadur, sometimes called Chaadur the Iarvin."

He looked nonplussed for only a space, then he nodded, and we went in. He well understood that Queen Fahia would like to get her hands on me. Her pet neemus would have a feast then. And I was aware that he had to be watched.

As for the name Chaadur, this was a name I had used once in Hamal. And Iarvin—well, Pompino wouldn't mind if I borrowed that, would he now?

The impression I took that Cleitar Adria hankered after the old days when he had been a hyr-kaidur strengthened. He spoke offhandedly about the new men he had to train up. Not one, he said, banging his fist on the table, not a damned one was fit to latch the sandals of the coys in our day!

It occurred to me that, as the ploy had been successful already here in Huringa, I would try it again. By innuendo and hint I got across to Cleitar that, far from the queen being angry with me and seeking to have me killed, quite the contrary was true. I even went so far as to suggest the skyship had been a part of the plan.

"And I am here in Huringa, and Fahia—" I said Fahia and not the queen or Queen Fahia to impress him "—has been graciously pleased with my work for her. So, Cleitar, keep the old black-fanged winespout stoppered. Dernun?"

I said dernun in a nonviolent, inquisitive way, and his immediate response of "Quidang" carried also that note of conspiracy. And, at that, he got a thrill out of feeling in touch with skullduggery for the queen.

Dopa, that fiendish drink, was being drunk by other men in this malodorous cavern. Cleitar bellowed for purple Hamish wine and I was quite startled when it was forthwith produced.

He nodded, slyly. "This is more like it, Dra—Chaadur. We do ourselves well, out of sight, like. Better than Beng Thrax's Spit, yes?"

"But you are surely allowed into the city?"

"Of course." He poured. "But well—I have grown used to the Jikhorkdun. It is my home now. Far more than my real home ever was, when I was a quoffa handler."

We talked over the old days, remembering past kaidurs and hyr-kaidurs, and the great kaidurs they had performed in the arena. Just how much he really believed of my story about the queen I wasn't too sure. But I fancied he wanted to believe. He was a very lonely man in these latter days.

This dopa den was not patronized by kaidurs, of course. Here congregated the men involved in the ancillary details. Here sat and drank beast-handlers and slave-managers, cheldurs and armorers, the quasi-privileged of the arena. If they wanted to sing or fight, as is the habit in dopa dens, I did not care, being in the mood to oblige either desire. I gave Cleitar to understand that my reason for being here this evening was to pick up a few tips. I'd been away, I said.

He gave me the names and rankings and running odds of various of his kaidurs. The reds were down in the mouth these days.

"We have a new batch due in, coys as green and raw as uncropped corn. Maybe out of three hundred I will find three who will do. Eh, Chaadur! You remember how we began, me and you and Naghan the Gnat?"

"I do."

By Kaidun! I did! And I had to get about finding Naghan and not sitting like a putative sot drinking purple Hamish wine.

So, with excuses and promises to return, I took my leave.

And, and I say this with all sincerity, it had given me quite a jolt to meet Cleitar Adria again and talk over the old days. Quite a jolt. As I say, when you have been a hyr-kaidur in the arena, you never lose the cachet, odiferous though it may be.

The partnership with Unmok proceeded splendidly, but he wanted to save the incoming money. I agreed. So instead of buying ourselves zorcas to ride about we purchased urvivels. These are sturdy animals, although not in the same class as zorcas. I walked across the patio toward my urvivel, patiently awaiting me, and two shadows closed in under the lights. We went outside the Jikhorkdun. The people had mainly streamed away along the boulevards. Suddenly, this patio was deserted of all save me and these two.

"By Rhapaporgolam the Reiver of Souls!" quoth one, very merry. "I do believe we have a chicken to be plucked!"

"By the Resplendent Bridzilkelsh!" chortled the other, very darkly. "I do believe you have the right of it!"

They bore in, bludgeons upraised. One was, as you will perceive, a Rapa, and the other a Brokelsh.

I turned to face them. "A chicken, my friends? Oh, you famblys, I have no feathers left!"

So, joyfully, we met in combat—they to take my gold and slit my throat or bash my skull in if they had to, and I to prevent them. The first bludgeon blows hissed through air instead of rattling my brains in my skull. The first knife was drawn in exasperation. They were a right comical pair—I've no idea what their mothers called them—and they went to sleep, slumbering like the babes they once had been. I looked down on them and shook my head, in sorrow rather than anger.

"Thank you, my friends," I said to their unconscious bodies. "You serve to remind me that life is mutable and that the suns may rise over Kregen as ever—but not for everyone."

And with that, I mounted up on the urvivel and ambled off to our camp outside the city, and to a fine old argument with Unmok the Nets.

Sixteen

An Armorer Raises an Echo

The argument erupted into a rip-roaring row.

"But we're partners, Jak!"

"Yes. But—"

"The animals are sold. There is nothing to detain us here. I do not like the Jikhorkdun—"

"No more do I!"

"Well, then! What ails you, Jak? Let us clear out. I have good suppliers lined up and we can fetch in a fresh consignment—"

"What about your cage-voller?"

Unmok lifted his upper left and middle right. His upper right held a goblet of cheap wine.

"Not yet. I do not have the cash. But our money is safe with Avec Parlin, who has banking connections—"

"Yes, yes. But—"

"And this voyage will see it, Jak. It will! Then we can buy a cage-voller and set up properly in business."

"I thought you were giving up? What was the last scheme—totrix breeding in Haklanun? Or was it a return to the beads and bangles on a vast scale—?"

"You mock me! We are partners, Jak!"

It went on for some time. I couldn't leave Huringa now, of course not, and Unmok couldn't see why not, and I couldn't tell him. We went to sleep in an uncomfortable silence that all our attempts to come to an understanding only made worse.

In the morning we breakfasted with only the stiffest and politest of words between us. Froshak the Shine kept well out of it, and so opened his mouth as to yell more than twice at the slaves, which clearly indicated all was not well with Ms world.

"I have to see Vad Noran," said Unmok. "No doubt you will be about your business—whatever that may be. I will see you tonight?"

"Yes. I will not—yes, I will see you tonight."

I'd been about to say I wouldn't leave without saying the remberees. But that would only arouse a fresh storm.

Riding the urvivel into Huringa, I pondered the problems. Today I intended to try my luck with the blues. The sapphire graint was the top color these days. Maybe Naghan had a hand in that. The guards at the Gate of the Trompipluns let me through—trompipluns means yellow feet—and I cantered to the inn where I would leave the urvivel for the day, preferring that to a public stables. The inn was The Queen's Head. That has ominous overtones, if you like. It was situated right next door to the Arbora Theater where all this month of She of the Veils they were presenting The Vengeance of Kov Rheinglaf, from the Third Book of The Vicissitudes of Panadian the Ibreiver, by, as you are well aware, Nalgre ti Liancesmot. These ordinary events went on, the inn was patronized, the theater attended and all the time the Jikhorkdun lowered its shadow over all.

The noise of a busy city arose on the morning air. Slaves were hard at it. Guls were earning their hire. The gentry and nobles were thinking of getting up and facing the day. Carriages were already abroad. The hectic activity of the night in which the country carts trundled in with the produce to sustain the city's life had ceased and given way to the equally hectic business of the day.

And I had a Gnat of an armorer to find, and a beautiful Fristle fifi, and a right tearaway who passionately loved vollers.

This early in the morning the environs of the Jikhorkdun held an exhausted, gray, hung-over look. The guards shuffled. I had scrounged a piece of blue cloth from our camp and had replaced the red with the blue. I walked up as though I owned the place.

Well...

At that time of day it was not too hard to find a way to let a gold coin change hands; a wink, a smile, and I was into the outer courts. Nothing—or very little—would get anyone into the inner courts. You had to be of the arena to be allowed there. I began my inquiries.

"Naghan the Gnat?" said a Khibil guard, his burly body straining his leather armor, his alert foxy face shrewd. "Well, now..."

Another gold coin changed hands.

Always fancy themselves a cut above the ordinary run of diffs, Khibils. I get along with most of them. Their ruddy whiskers, their bright eyes, their keen fox-like faces, have been a comfort to me on many a battlefield. The gold vanished.

"Yes, dom. Naghan the Gnat—" He hesitated.

"Yes!"

"Aye, dom. Yes. I know him."

I quieted down. Maybe there were two men with the name of Naghan the Gnat. I nodded and the Khibil went on.

"See this thraxter?" He drew his sword and showed it to me. He pointed. The rivets of the hilt were indeed beautifully forged and fitted. I thought—I would not, dared not believe—they were Naghan's work. "He did that, the little feller, after I wrecked the blade on the armor of that bastard of a Rapa who—"

"Where is he?"

"I'm telling you, aren't I?"

"Yes." I made myself speak meekly. "You are, dom."

After all this time I was really going to find Naghan!

"He wanted to work for the reds. Course, the managers wouldn't have that." The shrewd fox face lowered on me. "I c'n tell you that we're doing well now because Naghan's armor is the best in the world. That's why. Course, he works hard. Has to, d'ye see? They whip him if he don't."

My fingernails bit into my skin, but I held still.

"Where is he?"

"Where? Why, where d'you expect him to be?"

I suppose, just about then, this smart Khibil more or less took a closer look at my face. He swallowed. His stiff red whiskers bristled. Then he said, rather quickly, "Why, he's in his forge, of course. Where else would an armorer be?"

Of course. The blue section might not be laid out in the same way as the red. I caught my breath, and then in what I considered a neutral voice, I said, "Tell me where the forge is, dom."

The Khibil jumped.

He pointed. "Down that alleyway between the barracks and the second training ring. You can't miss it—stinks of charcoal and smoke and oil—"

I walked on.

The sound of a two-pound hammer in that particular rhythm: chang, ching-ching, chang, ching-ching, met me as I walked along. The smells were there, charcoal and smoke and oil. The furnace glowed cherry red. Three miserable-looking slaves cowered out of my way, carrying baskets of charcoal. I walked on. A man stood at his anvil, half-bent, striking neat, tidy blows, working with the utter absorption of a master craftsman.

This was no dramatic confrontation. There was no hectic rescue amid showers of arrows, no smiting away of sword blades to snatch Naghan to the saddle and gallop madly into the sunset.

I just walked up and said, "Lahal, Naghan, my name is Chaadur and—"

He whirled. He was just the same, thank Zair.

The hammer fell from his nerveless hand.

His stained leather apron with the marks of the fire on it, his small body all gristle and bone, his lively face, with the soot marks of his trade, sweating already, and his whole astonished gape endeared him to me all over again.

He began to stutter, and swallowed, and: "Dray!" and he would have gone on.

I said, "I am Chaadur the Iarvin. Best you mind that."

"Aye," he said. "Aye." He shook his head, and bent to retrieve his hammer.

"Talk later, O Gnat. Are Tilly and Oby here?"

"No." He wiped his nose and left black smudges. "Oby is with the yellows. I am not sure about Tilly. But, but...!"

"Later. Does anything detain you here?"

"Not a damn thing."

"Then bring your hammer and a few tools. Walk casually. We are on an important task for a great lord. Dernun?"

"Aye, and thanks be to Opaz—"

"Come on."

So we walked along the alleyway. We did not pass the way I had come, for gold would not have quieted that Khibil guard. When Khibils hire out as guards they hew to their own codes of honor.

"I can't just walk out, Dr—Chaadur!"

"You can and you will."

We went along past the second training ring, briskly, Naghan two paces abaft me.

The gate I chose for the exit was guarded by a Rhaclaw. Rhaclaws possess immense domed heads; that does not mean they have any more brains than any other race of diffs.

"Hey, dom," I said brusquely. "Here is a pickle. The kov needs an armorer at once—at once, mind—and if I do not fetch him a miserable slave I, and you, will rue the days we were born."

"Kov?" said the Rhaclaw. He looked at me vacantly. "What kov?"

"Rast!" I bellowed. "Do you bandy words with the kov! You are a fool if you do. Out of the way before the kov has you strung upside down and your head in the fire."

He blanched.

He lifted his spear and I brushed it aside, as one would brush aside a hanging branch in a garden, and walked on. I bellowed at Naghan.

"Yetch! Grak! The kov will have your tripes for harness points if you don't jump!"

"Quidang!" yelled Naghan, playing up nobly, and we hurried past the Rhaclaw and left him trying to regain the balance of his spear.

Mind you, the moment we passed beyond the angle of the wall we both did a quick right turn and darted into the shade of a few dusty tuffa trees, all wispy and drooping and springy.

"What—?" began Naghan.

"See that fellow walking toward us?"

"The man with the striped apron and the tray upon his head?"

"Yes. Fall down and writhe. Yell—but only a little."

Naghan immediately dropped to the ground, curled up and kicked his legs. He shrieked—but only a little.

The butcher's arm came over balancing his tray. He looked down. "What ails him? Is it catching?"

"Yes," I said, and put him to sleep. I caught the tray as he fell. Naghan put the lad's clothes on—they were not too big to pass muster—and he balanced the tray on his head.

"Throw the meat away, for the sweet sake of Opaz!"

"Aye, aye." Naghan tipped the tray over. "You wouldn't take meat out of the Jikhorkdun, now, would you?" And he laughed.

"Walk a little ahead. I am not with you."

"Aye. How did you—?"

"Two things, O Gnat. One: gold. Two: a kaidur's knowledge. Talk later."

We walked on in the bright morning, just a butcher's man, probably a slave tricking himself out with a striped apron, and a hulking great fellow who'd as lief knock the butcher's lad over as not if he got in his way. We went along smoothly until we came to an area where the stalls and booths were shuttered and quiet. When the gas jets were lit this place would teem with people on their way to visit famous kaidurs, perhaps idling for a few moments and spending money on knickknacks. At least, we were clear of the inner precincts. Then I noticed that Naghan, balancing the tray on his head with one hand, kept a fast grip upon his leather toolbag with the other. The head of his hammer protruded at one end and the business end of a pair of tongs at the other.

Before I could hasten my steps four Rapa guards rounded an emporium which, although shuttered, proudly proclaimed on bills and hoardings that here the mysterious potions that gave love where it was sought might be purchased. The four Rapas were quarreling—well, that was their privilege. But perhaps because of their quarrel they chose to pick on the butcher's delivery lad.

"Hey! C'mere!"

And then, of course, they saw the leather tool kit, and immediately diagnosed the situation. This thieving rast of a butcher's slave had stolen a valuable bag of tools!

Because of the very ordinariness of the tool bag being picked up by Naghan, I had not noticed. Mea culpa! Again I considered that if this was the way Dray Prescot went about rescuing his friends, Zair help him... And then it was all a flurry of action, and skipping and jumping and of skull bashing.

The four Rapas, out to earn their hire, clearly expected Naghan to run. They began to race toward him and, as I started off, so Naghan whipped the hammer from his bag, the tray going clattering into the Rapa's running feet. The hammer circled once and slogged into the first Rapa's middle. The second slashed his sword down, and then I slid the blade on my own thraxter and, regretfully, turned my wrist over and let the sword strike through.

The third and fourth yelled and plunged in and Naghan dropped to his hands and knees and chingled his hammer against the next Rapa's kneecap. I felt that for the poor devil of a Rapa... Very nasty. My thraxter revolved in the air, the blade swept the last Rapa's weapon aside and the flat thunked down against the side of his head, spreading the feathers, and spreading the Rapa, too, sending him sprawling across the stones. Naghan stood up.

"Run," I said. "Yes, I think we should run now."

So we ran.

We got to the next courtyard and then slowed our pace and walked out across a roadway where they were exercising a gaggle of totrixes. The lumbering six-legged riding animals went clip-clup-clop past. Totrixes are used in the arena. No true lover of the marvelous saddle animals of Kregen cares for that.

We squeezed along out of the way and crossed the road and went toward the gate where only a Fristle stood guard. Most of the outer sections, open to the public, needn't have been guarded at all. But this passion for posting sentries everywhere is quite practical. For one thing, it impresses the common folk. And, for another, it gives the bodyguard something to do.

The Fristle was brushing up his whiskers with his little personal brush, all smothered in tawdry imitation jewelry, and twisting his head about the better to get just the right angle he wanted. He had taken off his helmet. His fierce cat's face was contorted with the effort of seeing his whiskers in his pocket mirror. When we hove up he cocked an eye at us, in annoyance. I suppose, logically, that Fristle was near to death, in a cold and calculating way. Had he spoken out of turn, had he tried to stop us, had our blows just missed being non-lethal, then he would have died. Instead of all that unpleasantness he waved the brush at us and went back to his cat's whiskers. We walked through the open gateway.

That Fristle possessed remarkably fine whiskers.

"They're a poor lot of mercenaries, aren't they, Naghan?"

Naghan kept the striped apron. He wanted to skip and jump and I put a hand on his shoulder and pushed him down.

"Yes," he said at last. "Outside. But, inside—!"

"I know."

Halfway to The Queen's Head Naghan discarded the striped apron. He wore shabby old clothes, a holey tunic and a pair of sandals that were falling to pieces.

"Shove the tools into the bag, so they don't show."

Naghan pushed the hammer down and then, as we approached the inn, looked up. "You'll never get me in there!"

"Not like that, no."

We went around the back and I told Naghan to wait quietly as I dug into my urvivel's saddlebag and produced the clothes I hoped would fit Naghan. He put them on, a decent dark brown tunic and a pair of almost brand-new sandals, and then he flexed his arms and hung his tool bag alongside the saddlebag, turned to me and said, "Now what?"

"I have hired a room in the inn. It is quiet. You can stay there without attracting attention. I'll leave enough silver." I spoke matter-of-factly, having worked all this obvious detail out already. "Now, tell me all you know of Oby. His whereabouts. You said he worked for the yellows?"

Naghan the Gnat put his hands on his hips. "No," he said.

I glared, shocked. "You—" I began.

"You may be the prince majister of Vallia. All very well. But Oby and Tilly are my comrades, as well. I shall not tell you what little I know of Oby's whereabouts unless—"

I managed to close my mouth. I said, "Unless?"

"Well, it's obvious, isn't it? I'm not letting you go running off to rescue them on your own."

Talk about an echo, bouncing between Naghan the Gnat and those fearsome fellows of my Guard in Vallia!

Seventeen

Of the Eye of a Vollerman

There is little communication—for obvious reasons—between the four color corners. Each corner is a world to itself. And the area reserved for the queen's kaidurs is, in those terms, a double world to itself. We found

Oby flat on his back under a half-dismantled voller. He worked—as a slave—for one of the managers of the yellows who fought for the diamond zhantil.

Naghan kicked his foot. He bent down.

"Oby! Come on out—and quietly."

"Go away, rast, whoever you are," said Oby's familiar voice. He had been a mere youngster, and now he was a man, nimble, strong, adept with a knife, obsessed with vollers.

I said, "I am Chaadur the Iarvin, and Naghan the Gnat kicked your foot, for he is no respecter of persons."

Oby came out so fast he hit his head a crack on the rim of the voller. He rolled out and looked up, swearing. "By Vox! It is—but—but—"

Oby's left eye was puffed and swollen and closed to a mere tear-oozing slit. It was a shiny purple color, with tasteful admissions of green and black.

"Damned overseer gave me that... Naghan? And..."

"Chaadur," I said. "Make no great fuss—"

"But the guards?" Then Oby saw the four Fristle guards slumbering at the foot of the trestles on which the voller was supported. The wooden shed allowed a mingled radiance of the suns to fall through cracks between the warped boards.

"Precisely. Now gather what you want. We will leave here now."

Oby's wits had always been like quicksilver. He was off the platform, scooping up a raggedy cloak of off-cuts of ancient gray blankets sewn together. He, too, picked up a leather tool bag.

"D'you know the way?" He was, at once, apprised of the situation.

"Yes. Talk later."

So, quietly, we went out from that area of the yellows. We did, this time, tend to leave a trail of unconscious guards. But I was in a hurry. A single quick question and a surly answer elicited that Oby had no chance, no chance in a Herrelldrin hell of stealing a voller.

"You'll have to ditch that cloak."

Oby looked annoyed. We walked not too close together along an alley-way between booths on one side and cages on the other. The wild-animal smell remained strong and evocative, but all the cages were empty. Tame slaves scurried with buckets and brooms and pungent ibroi. The disinfect-ant smell battled feebly with those primeval odors of the wilds.

"It took me a season and a half to collect all the scraps of blanket and sew them together. But if I must, I must."

The multi-gray cloak went in an arc into a trashbin where the slaves dumped what they cleared out of the cages. We walked on. When, at last feeling free, Oby and Naghan reached my urvivel and I could fish out clothes for Oby that only just fit, they began to jabber. They could have talked all day and all night.

"Yes, I know," I said, interrupting. "When you found yourselves sorcerously transported back here. But we aren't out of the woods yet. There is Tilly."

Oby looked up from the knife I had, as a matter of course, included in the kit I'd brought for him.

"I know where they took her. She is a serving wench in the household of a nulsh of a noble called Noran. Vad Noran."

"I know him." I felt the glow of successful accomplishment. "This is good news—if Tilly remains unharmed."

"She has sharp teeth—and her nails." Here Oby shook his head. "Fristle fifis can scratch a fellow's eyes out."

"If they've a mind to it," added Naghan, comfortably.

"That is all well and good. Now you two will stay—"

"I have given you my thoughts on that, prince," said Naghan, very stuffily.

Oby said, "I do not think I shall stay behind—prince."

When these two princed me—for they did not know I had become the emperor—they were pulling my leg, being sarcastic, in modern parlance, sending me up rotten. I sighed.

"I own I am glad to have you with me, but..."

"That's settled, then," said Oby briskly.

You may be sure there was much to talk about, fathoms and fathoms of it, as we took ourselves off to the sumptuous villa belonging to Vad Noran. I wondered what I would do to him if he had harmed Tilly. I had no doubts at all what Oby and Naghan would do, no doubts whatsoever.

Our new clothes made us look respectable horters of the city, gentlemen with a purse of gold and a cutting way with slaves. Any searches for runaway slaves from the arena would take time to be mounted outside the Jikhorkdun. As Naghan said, "They'll wonder, at first. They'll not believe we could have won free. There is a little time."

"We will make the time," said Oby. I glanced at him, seeing in his dark, scowling face with the strong lines that suffering had etched there but a pale ghost of the sprightly lad I had once known.

Then he laughed and said, stretching his arms wide, "By Vox! What it is to feel free!" As he spoke his whole face changed, the scowling lines vanished, his mobile lips curved and he looked like his old self. Then he winced and swore again, feelingly. "My damned eye!"

When I explained that as soon as Tilly was with us we would have to take a voller to fly to Vallia, they treated it as the most natural thing in the world. Oby said he could fly anything that flew, and repair anything that was broken—always excepting the silver boxes.

Naghan said, "I suppose some fat notor of Huringa will miss his voller. I'd like to roast 'em all!"

When you looked at it like that, at the fact that the man from whom we would steal the voller sat in his plush seat in the amphitheater and howled with glee as some poor wretch was disemboweled or pierced through... That did tend to reorientate my pious doubts. All the same, and I did not confide the decision to these two, I would reimburse the man for his flier. Even if he was...

I said, "It might be possible to seize a voller from this Vad Noran."

"Capital!" said Naghan.

"Diashum," said Oby. And, indeed, the thought was rather magnificent, rather capital. So we walked on in the strengthening rays of Far and Havil, and the hour of mid approached and I licked my lips and cocked an eye at them.

"There will be time," said Oby.

"I am dry," said Naghan. "And it is a long time, a very long time, since I have tasted anything respectable."

So we went into a moderate eating establishment and I watched these two stuff their faces. The place was decent and doing a brisk trade and we attracted no attention. The clepsydra on the shelf dripped away.

As a simple precaution I had provided us with red favors. This might not fool the searchers for long if Oby or Naghan were recognized, but it might give us a mur or two in which to jump.

When we went out I began to feel itchy. I know that feeling. It comes over me when I shilly-shally, and yet I was not delaying now, was I? So why should I feel this unease?

There was no denying that uncomfortable sensation. I was in the throes of one of those itchy sessions when I shilly-shally. The suns shone, there was a pleasant breeze, we were comfortably filled with good if plain food, we could jingle silver in our pouches, we were armed with thraxters taken from slumbering guards. And yet... Yes, we walked the streets of a hostile city that would show no mercy if we were caught. The stink of the Jikhorkdun pervaded the place. But that should not trouble me overmuch, surely? A whiff of peril? Never...

Something was itching away at the back of my old vosk skull and I was too dim-witted to grasp it and drag it forward into the light.

Unmok!

I stopped.

Naghan and Oby stared at me.

"How would you two," I said, "like to be slave again?"

I gave them just enough time to start reacting nicely, and then I said through their gapes, "We need to find three juts at once." I did not specify the type of riding animal we would take, saying jut covered anything we picked up, from a totrix to a preysany. I started off walking rapidly toward the nearest tavern. They hurried to keep pace, and they did not expostulate or call out questions. We needed to remain inconspicuous, and they were probably more aware of that than I was.

We found three freymuls—the poor man's zorca—their hides sleek and well cared for, tethered up at the side of the tavern. We slit the leather hitching thongs and mounted up. At a sedate walk we went out and along the avenue, mingling with the traffic. We looked so ordinary that no one was going to remember us, particularly as a Hyrklanan hat was hung over the saddle of my freymul. I put it on and pulled the brim down and slouched in the saddle, and we rode out to the camp where Unmok was busy working himself up into a frenzy.

"It seems to me," I said as we reined up and dismounted, "that you, Naghan, had best be Nath the Long (which is another example of the warped Kregan sense of humor) and you, Oby, had best be Nalgre the Eye." I started off for the tents and then swung back. "Oh, and I am Jak the Shot, here. Remember."

People on Kregen do remember names. They know if they forget too often the chances are they'll wind up with a length of steel in their guts investigating their backbones.

Unmok's middle left stump quivered. His little Och body quivered. His face quivered.

"And you've come back, Jak, to—"

"I come in friendship, as ever, Unmok." I made the pappattu, introducing Unmok and Nath the Long and Nalgre the Eye. The Llahals changed to Lahals. "There is no time for me to explain, Unmok. You know I have work to do."

"Aye." Unmok eyed my two companions, and Froshak eased nearer, his hand on his knife hilt.

"Your werstings. If you have not yet decided to sell them to Vad Noran, then I will buy them from you and sell them to him. I warn you—I will sell for more than I buy."

"Naturally."

He digested this. Then: "When?"

"Now."

"Well—"

"Now. Right this instant—as soon as I take them in."

"But, Jak, why?"

I breathed in, then out. "I have to see Noran and this is the surest and quickest way. You know how he hungers for the werstings."

Unmok clasped his upper right over his stump. "Then we are still partners? You will make the next voyage with me?"

Now, as you know, I am a rogue, a reprobate, a sinner among men. I have done things for which I am heartily repentant; but in the same circumstances I know I'd probably do the self-same things again. I try not to hurt people. Now I thought I understood what that itchy feeling had been about. Struggling to answer Unmok's unanswerable question, I saw. I said, "A moment, Unmok." Then, to Oby and Naghan: "You came here together? You know what I mean. Tilly was with you?"

They nodded. "Yes. We were taken up into slavery together." They had evidently decided not to risk names at all.

So that was it, that was the cause of my unease.

"There is no time to lose." When you say that and mean it, it sounds damned different, let me tell you!

Oby saw it, and then Naghan. "They'll know! They'll put two and two together...!"

"Yes." I turned back. "Unmok. We have been partners, we are still partners. I must see Noran—at once!—and the werstings will turn the trick. Please. We will talk about our future plans afterward."

He did not look convinced. "Have I your word?"

I shook my head. "No, Unmok. For any one of the many gods in their mutual wisdoms might strike me down. I must go. I will take the werstings."

My thraxter flicked out. Froshak halted at once.

"Froshak the Shine! I value your friendship. Do not seek to prevent this."

Froshak said nothing, as was his wont. But his knife, that knife so like my old sailor knife, slid up and down in its sheath.

Oby looked shattered. "By Vox," he said, and he spoke in a shaky whisper, staring up at me. "I've been saying we had plenty of time, speaking so grandly. We've plenty of time. Fool! Onker!" He began to curse himself then, and with a manic spring leaped for his freymul. He was up on the animal's back and driving in his heels as I got to him.

"Still, Oby! Wait! Think!"

"I've waited too long—if they've—Tilly—"

"Think! This rast Noran will not let us in—he thinks I spy on him for the queen—we will only enter by a subterfuge."

All the time I was holding onto him and dragging at the freymul. Naghan ran across and joined in. It took a little of the precious time we had been squandering; but we calmed Oby down.

"No time to fix you out as slaves." They had incontinently thrown their gray slave breechclouts away when they'd donned the clothes I'd brought. "Unmok!" I bellowed. "In this show me the value of your friendship! Let me have the werstings and the slaves to run them." I turned my face to Oby and Naghan. "You run the slaves running the werstings."

Unmok hovered, pitched to a frenzy between despair and hope. I felt for him. Also, I feared—oh, how I feared!—for what might happen to golden-furred Tilly while we delayed.

I picked up the thraxter, for that had been dropped any old how in my spring after Oby. Froshak had not moved.

Unmok unwrapped himself, letting his middle left stump jerk up, his right upper lifting. His right middle joined his left upper, and then spread wide. He bowed.

"Very well, Jak the Shot. For our friendship—new and yet of great value to me. Take the werstings. Froshak also. And, Jak—" Here his little Och face screwed up into a fearsome grimace. "I shall come with you to make sure we get a good price from Vad Noran."

There could be no further argument.

So, mounted up, urging our mounts on, we left that deserted camp. We followed the slaves who ran fleetly, dragged along by the werstings. The killer dogs howled and barked and ululated, racing ahead, straining in passion against their collars and the long leather leashes.

Eighteen

In the Recalcitrants House

"Obfaril!" said Naghan the Gnat. The sword smith spoke with a tone of sharp rebuke. We roared along after the slaves and the werstings, Huringa and a beautiful golden-furred Fristle fifi ahead. "Young Oby!" said Naghan. "The managers will not connect us that quickly. Yes, they will in time—"

"We have no time, Gnat!"

"Time. It will take them time to connect. Two mangy slaves run off—they'll expect to recapture them very quickly. Only when they do not will they think to look deeper. Then the records will be hard to find—there will be time." Naghan clenched his fists around the reins and lifted his head defiantly. "Dear Opaz! There has got to be time enough!"

The mention of Vad Noran's name and the business that brought us to the city did not perhaps carry as much weight with the guards as the bright fangs and lolling tongues of the werstings. Their howls echoed under the arch of the city gate.

"They'll have to be muzzled in the city." The Deldar of the guard swelled his chest against his armor. He wore a scale-metal kax, and was no doubt proud of that. "You know the laws are strict—"

I was about to knock him over, not having time to argue about the matter, when Unmok said quickly, "Of course, Deldar. The slaves are doing it now." I looked. They were. They did not have too much trouble fitting the bronze muzzles, and the dogs' tongues still lolled, evilly. Unmok knew his business. Had he not accompanied us with the tame slaves...

We pressed on, striking directly toward Noran's villa.

Noran loved ostentation. His villa, a palace in miniature, was equipped with all the paraphernalia for gracious living. He boasted his own swimming pool, his own ball courts and his own small private arena. The cadade happened to be in the courtyard into which we were ushered, talking to four or five of his men, and I heartily wished him and his men a million dwaburs away from here. Oby glanced at me, and Naghan licked his lips.

"The master will come at once, almost at once, I feel sure," said the majordomo, dancing on pointed toes as he led us through. His retinue of slaves and fan-wavers and scroll-bearers, with a hefty Brokelsh to keep them in order, tagged on. Our slaves stayed with the werstings in the yard. My plan, if you wish to dignify the scheme by that name, was for us three to slip away and get into the slave quarters. We would pick up three slave breechclouts from the first three to walk by. It is easy enough to become a slave on Kregen, the trick—and it is often a damned difficult one—is to become free.

Oby nodded his head toward the cadade. The man was big and rugged, with a florid face. He was apim, like us, although some of his men were diffs, as was normal. He wore a splendid bronze kax, trimmed with silver, and his helmet bore a panache and plumes. He happened to be a Jiktar—well, a noble in Noran's position would have to employ a reasonable rank as the captain of his household guards—and he looked useful. No doubt it was sure that Noran paid him far more than the cadade could earn by hiring out as a mercenary in the wars.

As we padded along I reflected that I could not understand the attitude of many of the nobility on that score. Mercenaries fighting a war are one thing, but they are not as important as the mercenaries you hire to protect your skin. No, sir! Not in many parts of Kregen!

I didn't want Vallia to go down that road.

We walked past a clump of gregarian bushes and Unmok said in a throaty whisper, "Leave the talking to me."

"With the greatest pleasure," I said. "But, Unmok, we will not be with you. When we vanish you need not mention us. If asked, you say we must have returned to the werstings."

He cocked his face up at me. "But, Jak—"

"Around that column with the statue of Mahgoh of the Two smiling at the top. There we will leave you."

"What will—"

"You must, if necessary, deny me. Say the truth, that we have only recently become partners. Froshak will bear witness. Talk your way out of it, if necessary, man of the nets."

"But—Jak—!"

The statue of Mahgoh of the Two cast a large shadow. We entered the shadow from the left side and as the others walked on into the mingled rays of the suns shine we three skipped away around the corner and vanished from their sight.

The vanishing trick was, if I may say so, neatly done.

The urgency began to bite into us. Not one of us liked the idea that the cadade had been in the outer court. Perhaps news of the runaway slaves had already been received? Perhaps the guards from the Jikhorkdun were even now closeted with Noran, telling him, hatching a plan?

No immediate signs of the household being aroused alarmed us. Slaves came and went with the usual hurried slave shuffle. The shadows rested on the walls and paths, tinged with green and red, and the muted surf roar of the villa continued. In ten murs or so we had three slave breechclouts, and three slaves slumbered under the hedge. Poor devils, that was probably their first decent rest in months.

We carried our weapons and gear bundled up, acting the part of slaves carrying a burden for the master. Then we plunged boldly into the slave warrens.

Our very first question had elicited the reply, gasped out with a fist around throat, that, yes, the golden-furred Fristle fifi was here, quartered in the Recalcitrants House.

Not a one of us liked the sound of that, by Vox!

Outside the Recalcitrants House a hefty Rapa, stripped to the waist, was flogging a Xaffer. I stopped.

The walls lofted here, with spiked tops, and the house itself was pierced only with small windows, high up, barred. The courtyard echoed with the Xaffers shrieks.

With his nervous laugh, Naghan said, "It is no business of ours."

"No." I forced myself to walk on. "But what kind of insensitive offal orders a Xaffer flogged?"

Xaffers are diffs of a strange remote race, vague, used when slaves as stylors and in other like capacities. They never—or practically never—give trouble. We passed the wooden triangle and I saw the dark bloodstains fouling the wood. The Rapa went on lashing, and a stylor in a blue tunic at the side chalked down the strokes on his slate.

The door of the Recalcitrants House was narrow. A Rapa guard held his post there. I took Naghan by the ear and ran him up to the guard.

"Here's another one—and I'll get an extra portion of palines for bringing him in." Naghan was squirming most realistically. Oby chipped in and gripped his flailing arm.

The Rapa hawked and spat. His feathers quivered.

"You scum—sell your own mothers for a bowl of porridge."

"Yes," I said, approaching fast. I let go Naghan, who spun away in Oby's grip, kicked the guard betwixt wind and water, and caught him as he fell. We all bundled inside. Oby had the guard's spear out and pointing along the corridor. It was deserted and all the doors were shut.

"So far, so good." I picked the Rapa up by his wattled neck. His eyes were unfocused, and spittle ran out of his vulturine beak. "Tell me where the golden-furred Fristle fifi is chained up, and you may live."

He gabbled.

I shook him.

His eyes popped. He slobbered. Then: "Cell eleven."

"Cell eleven," I said to Oby.

Naghan rubbed his ear with his left hand and lifted the key ring from the guard's belt with the other. Then he and Oby padded off along the corridor.

"I see you wear a red favor, so do I," I said to the guard, trying to make refined conversation. "I hope our fortunes improve soon."

He boggled away, and then he spat out, "You are mad."

"Oh, aye. And my friends. Believe it."

The clitter-clatter of keys followed by the wheeze of a heavy door drew my attention. Oby and Naghan went into cell eleven. Presently they came out. Between them walked Tilly. I own to a throb of thankfulness—she could walk. She looked dazed. She was trying to rub her wrists, and wincing. Much of that glorious golden fur had been rubbed away, the skin raw. Oby and Naghan supported her.

"But—" she was saying, half laughing and half crying. "But—dear Oby—dear Naghan—"

This was all going splendidly.

With Tilly safe, why, what was there that would stop us now?

The Rapa guard gave a twitch and I shook him, just to remind him. Tilly saw the guard, and she saw me.

"Hush, Tilly," I said. "I am Chaadur the Iarvin."

"Yes," she said. "They told me. But it is all so, so—" Then she broke open those inner springs that men are not supposed to have and that they do have, witness the feelings they try to hide. "I have been chained, master, and not in silver chains, and not by you."

By the disgusting diseased liver and lights of Makki Grodno! But that took us back, Tilly and me, and her flirty golden tail, and our talk of silver chains for impudent fifis!

I swallowed.

"You're going to be all right now. You're safe. All we have to do is find a voller—and we're free and flying."

"Yes, master."

She knows I detest her calling me that.

"Let us clear off, then," said Naghan. He looked about as though the shadows would leap on him.

Tilly held onto Oby and Naghan. "There is a Fristle—he has tried to be kind to me here. I am new here. He is called Fordan. He is locked in one of these cells."

"Open them all," I said. "But step lively. I do not think these slaves will break for their freedom, being cowed. But it will add a complication." The Rapa in my fist had swooned away so I dropped him. "Start at the far end and warn 'em all to silence. Not that they will."

The doors opened one by one. A motley collection staggered out when the chains were unfettered. Some refused to budge, aware they had no hope of extended liberty and fearful of the flogging at the end. We could not take them all. The corridor turned with a dog leg at the end, and there were more cells, some holding more than one inmate. We opened them all.

Fordan turned out to be a strong-bodied Fristle, his cat's face bewhiskered splendidly, his fur a lustrous ginger with gold and black patterns. I liked the cut of his jib, even though his face was swollen from beatings. My dealings with Fristle men had often been ambivalent at best, and downright hostile at worst. Probably, I considered as we went along opening doors, probably Tilly's quick and instinctive gesture of pleasure at seeing Fordan, and her little squeal of horror at the state of his face, predisposed me in his favor. "I thank you, notor—" he began.

"Thank Tilly," I said. And then, with meaning, I added, "My friends and I will gladly kill anyone who hurts Tilly."

And Fordan, quickly, on a breath said, "And I, too!"

"Then stand just inside the doorway and keep watch."

"At once, notor." He went off, limping, making nothing of the pains he must be suffering from his swollen face.

I said to Tilly, "A likely lad."

Her little chin went up. "Well—I like him!"

A small crowd gathered in the corridor, bemused, wondering what to do for the best. I threw open a door and said to the golden-furred numim who attempted to strike me down, "Steady, steady, dom! We're letting you out—no noise."

The lion man let his clenched fist drop. He reached the end of his chain. Quickly I unlocked him. He looked savage, fierce, with such anger in him as boded ill for those who had chained him and abused him.

"Letting us out—where to?"

"That is for you to decide. I have no love for Noran, nor have you, as I judge it. If we can break free, then you are free. If not, then you are slave again."

"I shall not be slave again!"

His lion face expressed absolute determination. He must have put up a fight before they chained him. He flexed his muscles, no sign of the pain reflected on his features, and pushed past to the door.

"Perhaps you would like to stand at the outer door, and—"

"Aye."

He went along to stand with Fordan. Fristle and numim stood side by side, concealed, looking out. I fancied if a guard walked unwarily by he would face two formidable opponents in these two. They did not speak to each other, and I guessed they were strangers.

Only a few doors were left.

The crowd grew restless. And who can blame them? If they were going to break free, they wanted to start now.

For every one who stayed miserably in his cell, too frightened to venture forth to certain punishment, there were two who came out filled with vigorous determination to run for it and never be caught again.

There were only two doors left.

"Let them go," I called to Fordan. He nodded and stepped aside and the crowd ran out. Pretty soon their uproar would attract the guards. We would be well away by then, taking our own chances. Most of the slaves made up their own minds what they would do; it was every man for himself, sauve qui peut, and to the devil with the hindmost.

A girl tottered out of the last door. She looked in a distressed state. She wore the remnants of fine clothes, and there were weal marks on her naked back. Her hair tangled in an untidy mess about her face, and tear streaks cut through the grime. She saw me. Her eyes, wide brown eyes, closed. She tottered and Naghan went to catch her, thinking she was about to fall. But she was not falling; she was going into the full incline.

I said, "My name is Chaadur the Iarvin. Remember that, Fransha. Now we are taking you home."

She started to cry.

Tilly put a hand out, and the gesture of friendship from the Fristle girl spoke volumes. One distress called to another.

"You know her?" Tilly did not sound surprised.

"Aye. The Lady Fransha, who ran off with her lover and put all Vallia into a turmoil—"

"No!" Fransha looked up, shaking. "No, majis—no, Chaadur! Voinderam and I were kidnapped! By the Racters!"

I felt the ice clench around my heart. The damned Racters!

"Tell us as we run, Fransha. You are with friends, now."

We stepped over the Rapa guard. The suns shine smote down. The dwindling uproar from the slaves indicated they had split up, as we had anticipated, and were running every which way. Some of them would be running in circles, I had no doubt. But some, too, would win free.

The Rapa who had been flogging the Xaffer lay with his whip wrapped around his throat. There was no sign of the stylor and his chalk and slate. The Xaffer was gone, too.

We crossed the open space swiftly, and now we ran with naked steel in our fists. Fordan stayed close to Tilly.

"The Racters sent a note to each of us, saying the other must desperately meet. So I went to the meeting place, and Ortyg went too, and—"

"The Racters surprised you and kidnapped you, and sold you as slaves!"

"Yes and no." We slowed our run to a walk and Fordan assisted Tilly and Oby and I helped Fransha. "No, Strom Luthien wanted to kill us out of hand—"

"He would."

"But the Kov of Falkerdrin would not permit it. He said we would go to his estates and be held prisoner until the Time of Troubles was over."

"Nath Famphreon, you mean? The son of Natyzha?"

"Yes."

"I know him. In this, he acted as I would expect, I think. He has notions of honor and loyalty. The pity of it is, in one cynical sense, that his loyalty is to his mother."

"He was kind to us. He apologized for what had been done. And I believed him."

We went down an alleyway between hedges, heading toward a squat, flat-roofed building supported on many thick pillars. That had the look of a landing platform.

"Nath Famphreon betrayed you?"

"No." Fransha was now gaining better control of herself. Her memories of what she had gone through were being pushed aside as she spoke of the very beginning of her ordeal. "No. Our airboat had to come down—well, you know how unreliable they are. We were captured by flutsmen. The kov was not with us, and his men fought, but they were overborne. He employs mighty paktuns to work for him. But some were slain and others were captured. We were sold..." She stopped. She did not like to recall this part of her adventures; it brought back the hideous nightmare, and she shook.

Tilly said, "Leave her alone for now."

"That is the platform," said Fordan. He carried the Rapa guard's thraxter. I was pleased to see he gripped it in the fashion of one who knew how to use the sword.

"No, Tilly." I spoke as gently as I could. They all jumped anyway. "No, there is yet one more thing I must know."

Fransha laughed, too shrilly. "Ortyg? My love, Ortyg Voinderam?" She was shaking so much now her hair swung and matted before her face. "I do not know. I have not seen him since they brought me to this hideous place!"

The racter party had been very clever. They had spiked our guns in the matter of our plans to invade them. But, all the same, I was glad to have confirmation that Phu-Si-Yantong was not instigating this latest plot against us in Vallia.

We paused in the shadows of the landing platform. An ornate staircase built of stone, with iron balustrades and chemzite facings, led up to the roof. Hyrklana is rich in iron. On the roof the overhanging eaves of hangars for the fliers told us the private flierdrome was of some capacity.

"Listen," I said. "Other escaped slaves will probably come this way, seeking vollers. You, Naghan, and you, Oby, will see to it that our party gets onto the roof and into a voller. Fordan will care for Tilly, I feel sure—"

The Fristle nodded. "With my life."

"So that leaves the Lady Fransha to you two."

"And you?"

"Listen! Take a suitable voller and lift off at once—"

"Now just a minute!" started Oby, furiously.

Naghan began expostulating.

I quieted them down.

"Listen, you two! I want you up and away and out of it, with the two ladies. There are still chores I must do here. For one thing, I can't just walk off and leave old Unmok the Nets, can I? He risked it all coming here with us. And there is Ortyg Voinderam. If he is here I want to find him. That is for the good of Vallia." I did not add that, also, I had an appointment with Prince Tyfar and Jaezila and their retainers, Barkindrar the Bullet, Nath the Shaft and Kaldu.

"But we can't just fly off and leave you!"

"You can. And you will. I came to Hyrklana to get you three out of the Jikhorkdun. Thank Opaz, that has been done—or nearly done as soon as we bag ourselves a voller. And we've found the Lady Fransha, which is a blessing, and unexpected, although all of a piece, given the habits of flutsmen and slavers. But I have other things to do."

Well, there in the shadows, with the shouts of guards beginning to rise from the grounds of the villa, these two wanted to start a fierce whispered argument. I wouldn't have that. I was somewhat fierce.

In the end we padded up the stairs and knocked over a few guards who wanted to stop us, and we found a palatial voller with a cabin amidships and a steeply lofting poop aft. She had fast lines. She was worth much gold in Hyrklana and a small fortune in Vallia. Oby said she would do.

"No more arguments! Up and away. All the way home to Vallia." I gave them a very rapid rundown on the altered state of the empire, and cautioned them to beware of everyone until they reached the imperial palace in Vondium. I did not think that would have fallen again. They wanted to know all about the Time of Troubles, but Fransha said she would explain. She called me majister as a matter of course. When, in his biting tones of argumentative sarcasm, Naghan addressed me as prince this and prince that, Fransha looked alarmed.

"But, Naghan—this is the emperor!"

Naghan looked at me. Oby shut his one good eye.

"Emperor?"

"It doesn't matter," I said impatiently. "For the sweet sake of Opaz! Take off. Guard yourselves. I'll be back home in Vondium in no time." I told them that Delia and a gang of cutthroats might be following me and added that they were to be told what I'd told Naghan and Oby. Privately, I hoped the two parties would not meet up. If they did I knew what would happen. The whole raving bunch would come roaring down to Huringa ready to take the place apart stone by stone.

Of course, that might be a Very Good Thing, as Deb-Lu might say; it did not happen to fit in with the plans we had for Vallia. First things first.

"Now," I said, and a brusqueness harshened my voice. "Get in the voller and take off!"

And then a party of slaves ran shrieking into the area below the landing platform. That did it. Fordan helped Tilly up into the voller, and I noticed how they both observed the fantamyrrh as they entered. Oby turned to Fransha. But she was looking over the parapet, her fists gripped on the stone.

"Ortyg!" she said, choking, shaking, trembling uncontrollably. "My love! Ortyg!"

Down there vicious guards were herding slaves into a huddle. Whips rose and fell. Shrieks rent the air. And, clearly in the mess of slaves, beaten to his knees, Ortyg Voinderam staggered and fell.

Nineteen

Mazdo the Splandu

What a confounded mess!

I swung to glare at my friends.

"Stay here!" I spat it out. I know my face must have blazed that old devilish look, I know I sounded like the craziest of all mad emperors. "Stay here. Keep a watch from the voller. Slay any guard who tries to molest you. If I fail—lift off."

"But...!"

"We will..."

"We won't let you..."

"By the Black Chunkrah! Will you do as I ask?" Then, cunning with the frantic pressures of the moment, I bellowed, "For the sakes of Tilly and Fransha!"

They had not seen what I had glimpsed among the trees and shrubbery beyond the corner of the landing platform. A small stairway led down over there. Without giving them any further chance of argument, I leaped away, raced across the roof.

Their faces must have shown shock and horror in that fraught moment—for I ran away from the ornate stairs with their iron balustrades and chemzite facings. I ran away from the brutal guards and their whips below. I ran away from Ortyg Voinderam, so cruelly beaten into the ground.

I, Dray Prescot, Lord of Strombor, Krozair of Zy, must have seemed to them to be fleeing.

Just as my head whipped below the level of the platform I half turned and bellowed, "Do as I say as you value your lives—and my friendship!"

Then I was down, haring like a maniac for the secluded path leading to the space before the landing platform.

Along that path, hurrying, came the cadade.

With him half ran, half scurried, a gesticulating guard, a Fristle, who had evidently brought the bad news to the cadade. The florid face was more flushed still, the eyes mean, the jaw fiercely set. Sweat dripped from the brim of that splendid helmet with its panache and plumes. He hurried. But he would not sully his own dignity by running.

That pompous self-esteem of his gave me the chance to get down the little back stairs from the landing platform and into the corridor between the hedges.

There was little time for finesse. The Fristle saw me coming and started to yank out his sword. He was slow.

The cadade let rip with a blinding bellow of rage and ripped out his own over-elaborate sword.

Now, I had no wish to slay them, either of them. But this had to be done nip and tuck. I belted into the Fristle, slid the blow of the thraxter, slammed his head back with a simple and unsubtle right cross. Before he slumped to the ground I'd ducked, spun, kicked the cadade and then dug my thumb into his windpipe. After that it was a mercy to tap him alongside the head—having first picked up his sword and tipped off his helmet. He went to sleep.

A voice said, "By Opaz! As neat a piece of work as—"

The voice stopped. It stopped abruptly and on a choked grunt. The reason for that was my fist wrapped around the throat of the speaker. I recognized the golden-furred numim we had released from the Recalcitrants House. I let him go and stepped back and instantly bent to the unconscious cadade.

"You were nearly a dead man there, dom," I said, matter-of-factly, stripping off the ornate bronze and silver kax, ripping the silver-tissue vest away, getting at the blue tunic beneath. The kilt was mostly bronze and silver. That went on me first, wrapped and thonged with swift and sure knots. I was driving my arms into the tunic before the numim got his breath back.

"You—you are mighty quick, dom."

"When necessary." I still did not pause, dispensing with the silver tissue—it had ripped clean across, anyway—getting the kax on. Without being asked, the lion man stepped up and helped me buckle up the straps.

"My thanks, dom—"

"I am Mazdo the Splandu." He spoke the name simply. But I grasped much by the cognomen—not that there was time for the pappattu. I had to get out into the open space among the slaves before my bunch of revolutionaries came boiling down those ornate stairs to rescue Voinderam themselves.

"There are vollers up there. You had best take one swiftly—I have other work to do."

"I shall take an airboat from these rasts. But, cannot I help—?"

"Again, my thanks, Mazdo the Splandu. But—no. Best for you to take your freedom while it is still on offer."

The cadade's sandals would have to be high-thonged, of course. I slapped the leather thongs about as fast as I could. My heart was beginning to let me know it could beat a right old tattoo. The sword belts, the last check to make sure everything was shipshape, and finally, grabbing the helmet and lifting it up and feeling the weight, and settling it on my head. The kax strained as I raised my arms. But the cadade was a big fellow, as I've said, and I could wear his armor albeit with some constricting discomfort.

"You—"

"If you must, call me Chaadur. Now I am off. Remberee, Mazdo the Splandu. We may meet again."

I bustled along, half-turning, and then banishing that superb specimen of the race of diffs we call numims—lion-men—from my mind. He called after me, soft-voiced, "If we do meet again, Chaadur the Sudden, I stand in your debt."

I lifted my arm, not looking back, and so rounded the last hedge.

Here I concentrated. I knew the lineaments of the cadade. I forced my face into an approximation, thinking of what Deb-Lu-Quienyin had said, pumping up the blood, getting a flush to spread. Mind you, that wasn't difficult, not after the rushing about I'd just been doing. I was not exactly panting, but I was breathing faster than usual when I rounded the end of the landing platform and paced rapidly out toward the knot of cowed slaves and the belligerent guards.

They sprang to instant attention as the glory of the bronze and silver kax, the waving plumes, the glittering helmet, bore down on them.

Now for it...

I started bellowing in the hoarse commanding voice I had heard in the outer courtyard. Deb-Lu was right. Habit, acceptance, seeing the clothes and hearing the vicious words of command, all these things added up to the cadade to these guards. I was the cadade. Who else?

This was quite clearly a random collection of slaves. They'd been going about their unending labor when the guards had rounded them up. Quite probably there was not a single one of those who had escaped from the Recalcitrants House.

I stalked across, giving the guards the rough edge of the cadade's tongue—for a few moments of listening to him in the outer courtyard and experience of his kidney before had given me his measure.

"Take them away," I foamed. "They are not the ones—fools, dolts, onkers! Nulshes! Pick up this one." I pointed at Voinderam who lay, a dark trickle of blood staining his pale face. He looked in a bad way. "Bring him. I will question him. He will know the answers."

Peremptorily, I indicated that two Rapas should drag the slave I had picked out. "The rest of you—about your business, or I'll have the skin off your backs jikaider! Grak, you yetches, grak!"

The guards started to lead the rest of the slaves off. The two Rapas, blank-faced, petrified with fear, followed me. I headed for the ornate stairway. Halfway up I turned and bellowed down, "What are you skulking for! Hurry, you cramphs! Bring him up here!"

They hurried. The sounds of the others receding gave me little comfort. But, by Zair, a man can do only so much in this wicked world.

At the top I walked half a dozen paces across the roof. The two Rapa guards, shaking in their sandals, started after me, dragging Voinderam between them. His shoulders stuck up like windmill sails, his head hung down, draggling. I quelled any feelings of pity—for anyone.

"Thank you," I said, and turned back and with a simple one, two, put the Rapas to sleep. I managed to catch Voinderam before his face hit the paving of the roof. A scuffle at my back brought me around—it was Oby with Naghan. Half hysterically, Fransha threw herself forward. Between us, we levered her free, carried Voinderam across to the voller, pushed and pulled Fransha into the airboat.

"Now, take off, keep low, and then go fast. Go as fast as you can. And may Opaz go with you."

My face did not hurt, and I realized that somewhere up those fancy stairs I'd been forced to let the cadade's features slip away. I looked at my friends, and I felt the glow of comradeship. Then they started up their protests again.

"I will not tarry long. But you would not—in honor—have me abandon Unmok? Surely?"

"But we should go with you—"

"I am not starting again. By Vox! I left Vallia to get away from that!"

Well, there was little time. A group of slaves ran up the back stairs down which I had gone, and I saw that one carried a bloodstained sword. I fancied he'd got that from the Fristle I'd knocked unconscious. So one did not need to be told whose blood sullied the blade.

The slaves simply raced for the nearest voller, clambered in, and in heartbeats she lifted.

Among that group of ex-slaves maddened by near despair and now gripped with the determination to be free, there was no sign of the splendid golden numim, Mazdo the Splandu. I fancied he'd make his own way out of Noran's villa, aye, and crack a few heads in the doing of it.

"That does it." I had to make my friends grasp the essentials. "That lot will arouse the dead. You must go now!"

Finally, reluctantly, but anxious for the welfare of Tilly and the Lady Fransha, they shouted down the remberees and the voller lifted off. I did not intend to lollygag around. The flags of the roof were hot underfoot, bathed in the mingled streaming radiance of the Suns of Scorpio. Shadows lay hard and tinged with the old emerald and ruby fires. I darted across into the shade of the hangars, caught the first lifting yells of approaching guards and raced flat out over the roof for the other small stairway, twin to the one down which I had descended on the cadade. As I reached the top and bolted down the first guards boiled up onto the roof.

Below me stretched a maze of little outbuildings. Vegetation smothered the alleyways. This was a relatively neglected quarter in Noran's villa that offered capital concealment. I stripped off the fancy armor and chucked it down under a bush. With my own clothes once more revealed I sprinted on, twisting and turning, heading back for the outer courtyard, and Froshak and the werstings.

Slowing to a walk and going along briskly but with caution, I angled around the main buildings and so came up to the courtyard from the flank. The uproar in the grounds of the villa really was rather satisfying. Slaves looked uniformly scared; which did not please me. I saw no guards until I reached the courtyard, and they were all staring the other way. I looked, right along with them.

"No," Froshak was saying. "Not me. Know nothing."

He stood in the grip of two Rhaclaw guards. By reason of their immense domed heads, Rhaclaws are often badly served in the way of helmets. These two wore helmets fashioned from strips of iron, filled in with boiled leather. They held Froshak firmly.

Callimark, nervously pacing, fiddling with his sword, looking agitated, swung back to glare at Froshak.

"I do not believe you! By Flem! If you're lying..."

"Know nothing—notor."

The werstings, still handled by our tame slaves, were being herded into wheeled cages. The pampered dogs, killers or not, went in eagerly enough at the sight of the red meat within.

I walked slowly forward.

This might be a little tricky.

I was still unobserved.

The well where the old bent-over Fristle woman had drawn me a copper bowl of water partly concealed me. The stone coping was dry. No drier, perhaps, than my mouth.

"Take his weapons, nulshes!" Callimark had made up his mind. The Rhaclaw guards snicked out Froshak's knife. He made a single gesture; then he remained still.

Callimark pulled his thraxter around. "Guard him. I shall consult the vad in this." So saying, Callimark marched off. He took with him, I noticed with amusement tinged with concern, an audo of his guards, the section—not a rank—of eight men marching along closed up around him. With his going a visible relaxation took the guards left. As for the slaves, they chittered and chattered about their business, and the dust plumed and the suns shone and, for all I could see, no one here cared aught of a mass escape of slaves from the Recalcitrants House.

A bronze bell rang above the outer door.

The noise among the trees and pathways fluctuated as the guards searched and this outer courtyard must have been checked over at the very beginning. Certainly, as I observed, no one, slave or guard, gave sign of excitement or concern over that escape. The escape that concerned them had taken place here earlier. The bronze bell rang again and with its second summons the majordomo and his retinue who had admitted us appeared, hurrying toward the gate. He had to pass by the cage which lay on its side, its iron-barred door flapped open. At first this had seemed to me to be a wersting cage, but it was not, as I looked closer. Something had been brought into the courtyard in that cage and the cage door had been opened and the something—or somethings—had escaped.

So that was why Callimark questioned Froshak the Shine.

The outer gate was thrown open and a file of slaves entered. They carried sacks and pots and their backs were whipped every now and again to urge them on. They scurried beneath the trees away toward the vad's storerooms. Despite the noise the business of the villa had to go on.

One of the Rhaclaw guards gave Froshak a prod. Just why he did this I do not know; all men in these positions of petty power are not insensate beasts—of course not. But some are.

Froshak reacted. He twisted away, violently, avoiding that prodding sword.

The other Rhaclaw guard joined in, bellowing his anger.

The swords beat down. Froshak defended himself, pushing up his arms, taking the blows as best he could. He saw the open gate. If he broke free now—he and I were both aware that any resistance the Fristle might make would be punished, he could be killed, and no one would bother overmuch. The vad's writ ran here. The Rhaclaws used the flats of their swords. Froshak would have to take his punishment, take his beating, or make a break for it.

The slaves took no notice. The other guards guffawed.

Froshak tried to grab a sword arm, and missed, and the thraxter came back and belted him alongside the ear. He tumbled over. I saw his right hand. It snaked down to his belt and an expression of anger was followed swiftly by a look of bafflement so furious I felt for the Fristle. His knife was not sheathed at his belt. He crouched, glowering. The Rhaclaws taunted him, obscenely, savage in their enjoyment of his frustrated savagery.

I drew my own sailor knife.

"Froshak!" I called in a voice directed to the Fristle. He looked up. I threw.

The knife glittered once as it flicked across the intervening space. Handle first it flew. Froshak put his hand up and—thwunk!—the knife slammed into his fist as though grown there.

One Rhaclaw yelled in abrupt alarm, and then Froshak slid the knife in, and out, slashed at the other Rhaclaw, and was on his feet and running. He was quick, by Krun! The Rhaclaws staggered away, dropping their swords, the blood bright upon their legs. There was little point in hanging around any more. Froshak ran out through the opened gateway, and I dodged back the other way around the well, keeping below the coping, faded back into the bushes.

Very little time had passed since I'd hurtled off the roof of the landing platform.

Finding the statue of Mahgoh of the Two was not difficult. The lady was a somewhat prominent landmark. Beyond there a curving arcade led on and I padded along. Froshak the Shine was a tough and resourceful customer and I had no doubt that he would win free. What he would do thereafter I could not guess. He'd recognize the knife, for sure. He'd know who had thrown it to him.

The shrubbery at the side of the path flanking the arcade rustled. Bright green leaves moved aside and a couple of men staggered out, locked together. One was a slave, a Gon with a bristle of white hair over his scalp, the other a Rapa guard. The Rapa could not cry out because the slave's fists gripped a length of the chain about the feathered neck. The Gon struggled silently with his work. They pitched onto the pathway, flailing about, and the Rapa's struggles weakened.

I stopped in the shadow of a column.

The Gon stood up. He touched blood on his left arm, and along his ribs. He was panting raggedly.

I said, "I'll give you a hand to stow him in the bushes, dom."

The Gon spun about, his hands flicking the lethal chain up.

"You'd best hurry—there will be other guards." And I jumped across, grabbed the Rapa and started to heave him into the bushes. The Gon drew a breath.

"By Havil! You are a—"

I was ripping the Rapa's sword belt free. His thraxter was a plain and simple weapon, much like the one I had been forced to abandon when dressing up as the cadade.

"No time for jabbering! Listen!"

The sound of heavy footfalls reached us around the curve of the arcade. The Gon looked wild. He would not touch his bristle of hair, as another man might have done, rubbing his hand across his hair in perplexity.

"I'm off—"

"May Havil the Green go with you, Gon."

"You will need the protection of Havil more than me if you stay here." The Gon shoved into the bushes, panting, holding> his left arm where the blood ran. "Run, apim, run!"

He vanished between the leaves. I straightened my clothes and walked on a few yards past the place where blood drops might prove tricky to explain. Mingled with the oncoming tramp of studded sandals, the ominous clash of weapons indicated guardsmen. I finished buckling the Rapa's sword belt about me, flicked my fingers and walked on.

Vad Noran in the lead, Unmok bobbing along at his side, the party rounded the bend and bore down. He had a score of guards. Noran looked murderous. At his other side, Callimark, looking agitated, was fluttering his hands and trying to explain.

I stood to one side, looking at them, and—I own!—I drew my stomach in and pulled myself up and got ready to lie like a trooper for our lives.

Twenty

Combat, Blood and Death

The lies tripped off my tongue smoothly enough once I'd figured out what the hell was going on.

In addition, I was now pretty sharp set. The thought of a slap-up meal inside me to fortify the inner man against the hazards ahead tantalized with its unrealizability at the moment.

"...malignancy, and he'll be flogged jikaider if I have any say in the matter,"

Callimark was saying. He looked like a man bluffing away, blustering to conceal his own lapse in duty.

"When the truth is established, Callimark, we'll flog to your heart's content." Noran's face bore a most unpleasant expression.

"The schrepims have not been found—"

"Your pardon, notor," said Unmok, his middle left twitching. "But there could be no reason for Froshak to let loose the schrepims! Believe me, notor, we are too conscious of your kind patronage—"

"As to that, Unmok, we shall see. I paid good red gold for those four schrepims and I intend to have my money's worth!"

Now it was plain. The overturned cage with its iron-barred door flapped open had contained four schrepims, and these diffs, rather like overgrown lizards with cunning and intelligence, had escaped. I, too, doubted that Froshak would have done that; there was no reason for it. Well—no reason beyond the ordinary person's aversion to schrepims. It was reputed that these scaled men had the powers of the Dark, that they could scry almost as well as a Wizard of Loh—that, I did not believe—and that their cold reptilian natures set them always in opposition to the ways of the gods of Kregen.

I stepped forward.

Unmok twitched. Callimark cast a worried look at me and then started to argue his case again with the vad. Noran did not stop. He went to bustle past without even looking at me.

I said, "Your pardon, notor." I went on very quickly. "I believe there has been an escape of slaves, and they overturned the cage and the schrepims escaped in the confusion."

Now Noran half stopped and regarded me as he continued on along the curving arcade.

"And you?"

"I do not know for sure, notor."

"If you are right this Froshak may keep his head—and Unmok here and you may escape a flogging."

That was as cold as the Ice Floes of Sicce.

Noran stopped. He eyed me up and down.

"The schrepims cost me money. They are renowned kaidurs—hyr kaidurs. They must be coddled. If they are damaged before I see them fight... By Glem! Am I or am I not the vad!"

Everyone around him hastily assured Noran that, indeed, he was the vad.

Up to now on Kregen I had not much faith in receiving any help from the Star Lords or the Savanti. Oh, yes, there had been times during which I thought that, well, perhaps either the Everoinye or the Savanti might have arranged things to favor me. But these occasions were few and far between. As far as I knew, and as far as I was concerned, I was battling along alone.

Now, a large missal tree overhung the arcade a few paces along and its leaves brushed the tiled roof. The arcade curved around Vad Noran's private arena. A movement among the branches of the tree drew my attention, and then the quick looks of the others.

Up there, quickly glimpsed and vanishing, the green-scaled visage of a schrepim glared down on us.

As I say, it was probably mere chance. But, perhaps, just perhaps, the Star Lords did have a hand in it...

"They have run into the arena!" shouted Callimark.

Noran swung to bellow at his guards.

"Go and round them up—and treat them gently until I get there." He guffawed then, suddenly back in good humor.

"After that you may fight in my arena as though in the Jikhorkdun!"

There were a score of guards. They ran off obediently enough, but it was very clear they did not much fancy the task ahead of them. I felt a stab of pity. Schrepims are the very devil as antagonists. They are quick and sudden, skilled with weapons, able to take a great deal of punishment before they are killed. Their vigorous energy is cold and reptilian, and exceedingly vicious.

The memory of that time over in Higher Ripolavi where we'd been forced to fight a roaming band of schrepims came back to me. There are schrepims and schrepims, and that lot had been of the Soparan race. These four who would give the twenty guards a nasty time, as I judged, I gathered were of the Saradush race. Over in Ripolavi we'd lost Nath the Langon and Nalgre the Forge before we'd even got properly to handstrokes. We'd lost half a dozen more good men before we'd seen the scaled fighters off, and there had been only thirty of them in the band.

Noran was rubbing his hands together. Callimark was looking relieved.

"We will go up into my arena and witness the fight." said Noran. "It is what I paid for, and I will not be balked of my pleasure." He set off at a brisk trot around the arcade toward the flights of steps leading up to the stand seating. We followed.

Managing to fall in beside Unmok as we trailed along after the vad, I said, "Froshak got away."

"Thank his Fristle gods for that! We're like to have our heads off if—"

"No, Unmok! It will turn out all right. Remember the werstings."

"I do. Money will not stitch my head back on my shoulders."

Noran's private arena had been built as a miniature copy of the arena in the Jikhorkdun. Strewn with silver sand, ringed by comfortable seatings, shaded by a velarium which could be pulled across on its yards if the suns burned too hotly, it waited in the true style of an arena—an area dedicated to combat, blood and death.

He even had the four quarters arranged with their various colors, each with a prianum to receive the trophies of victory and the four staffs with the colored symbols. At the moment the ruby drang lifted highest. Noran was of the reds. The sapphire graint, the diamond zhantil and the emerald neemu were all at the bottoms of their poles. I wondered if he altered this when he invited guests of different color persuasions.

His own box, although lavishly appointed, flanked by columns garlanded and wreathed and with sumptuous hangings of cloth of gold and ruby velvet, did not dare match the opulence of the royal box in the great arena of Huringa. Queen Fahia was conscious of her regal dignity and touchy on matters of etiquette. But the display of wealth was dazzling.

Noran took his seat. It was a throne in everything but name. We settled alongside on the lesser seats. Each one was softly upholstered, with padded arms and back, and with a small table alongside with wine racks beneath. As I sat down and looked out across the suns shimmer along those silver sands I caught my breath.

Here I was, looking out over the arena in Hyrklana instead of being down there, with a sword in my fist, facing death for the entertainment of gilded trash in the stands and the howling crowds!

Sitting in those plush surroundings with the waiting oval of silver sand spread out below me, I wondered what was going to happen next. My thoughts veered off to a vision of this kind of obscenity finding a place in Vallia. The bloody tradition of the arena flourished in many countries of Havilfar. Even the games of Jikaida City were in truth an offshoot of the Jikhorkdun. No, in Vallia we drew spiritual sustenance and refreshment from other sports. There were precious few Vallians I knew who would wish it otherwise.

Three of the escaped schrepims moved into view below. They stepped cautiously backwards, feeling back with each foot in turn, moving with the reptilian grace of their kind. Following them in a curved line, the guards advanced cautiously. There was a sense of hunting animals closing in for the kill in the way that semicircle of guards shuffled steadily forward. But it was clear to us all that they were in no hurry to get to grips with the scaled men.

Noran picked a candied fruit from a box on his table. He bubbled now with good humor.

"This is more like the way life was meant to be led." He popped the fruit into his mouth. His cheek distended, glistening. "I paid my money, now I want my entertainment."

"The guards are not happy," commented Callimark. He, too, sat forward in his chair to watch, and a lick of spittle drooled from the corner of his mouth.

"Get on with it!" Noran abruptly shrieked down. He waved a fist at the guards. "A dozen gold pieces for the first to attack!"

My small knowledge of the fighting habits of the scaled men told me the guard who accepted the offer would not live to collect his dozen gold pieces.

I studied the schrepims.

Their greenish-grayish scales were dull. Different races have different shapes and colors of scale, of course, and the edges glister with different contrasting colors. These three had orange edges to their scales under their fighting harness. The straps were all of scales. Their armor was scale. But their swords were solid thraxters, efficient weapons in the hands of experts, although in nowise the finest swords of Kregen, as you know. The tails of the schrepims were thick at the root, and heavy, flat, flailing instruments. They were nothing like the supple whip-tails of Katakis, for instance, or the superb handed tails of Pachaks or Kildois.

"What are you waiting for?" bellowed Noran again.

The guards shuffled forward, swords pointed, shields up, the visors of their helmets pulled down.

"They're all jikarnas,"* said Callimark. He beat a fist on the marble coping before him. He looked contemptuous.

No one sought to contradict him. Also, no one suggested he might like to hop down there and set to himself.

The aura of the scaled men exuded a menace that comes as much from their reputation as from their mere presence. Ordinary mortals steer clear of them, and they have their own ways on Kregen.

"Jikarna!" Noran shouted the word down. It made no difference. Slowly and steadily the guards advanced and as steadily the three schrepims retreated. It was quite clear the guards had decided that no single one would rush forward—the notor's dozen golden deldys or not—but they would attack together, in a bunch, and overpower all three in a final massive onslaught.

That made the sweetest of sweet sense to me, by Krun.

The three scaled heads, so much like those of lizards, turned this way and that, in purposeful summing up of the situation. When the action began the speed of the schrepims would be blinding. And, I own it with some diffidence, I began to calculate just how many guards might be left at the end, or even if any would be left alive, and whether or not the scaled men might win free.

"Fifty deldys," roared Noran.

One of the guards, a Khibil, reacted. Khibils with their overbearing ways and haughty fox-like faces always consider themselves to be a superior race of beings. Well, I own to a fondness for Khibils that, although of a different nature from my affection for Pachaks, shares much of that fellow feeling. This Khibil hoisted his shield, whirled his sword—and charged.

He shrieked as he went in, boring dead for the center scaled man. "Fifty golden deldys!" he screamed, and with all the cunning of the fighting man

---

* jikarna. Arna is a Kregish word having the meaning of "absence of." Hence Gilarna the Barren—the Absence of Pleasure. So that jikarna can be translated as the absence of warrior qualities, i.e., coward. *A.B.A.*

sought to overpower the center antagonist before the two flankers could strike at him. Taking his onslaught as the signal, with equal cunning the other guards rushed forward.

The Khibil had time for one stroke. It was a bold, slashing blow that would have taken the head off the schrepim had it landed. But the schrepim was not there as the blow whistled past. A superb sliding glance of the scaled man's body, a glint of greenish gray, and the wicked sword smote once, and was still.

The Khibil staggered away, his shield falling uselessly, his sword dropping. His foxy face was a mere mask of blood.

The remaining guards howled and flung themselves on. It was all a flurry of blows, and the quick scrape and ring of steel on steel, the screech of steel on bronze. How they fought, those schrepims! Superb in their reptilian strength and speed they danced on their massively muscled legs, balancing on those thick tails, striking and avoiding, chunking into the guards and slashing and hacking, and withdrawing with bewildering rapidity.

Yes, oh, yes, I remembered their style of fighting!

Four guards were down, then three more, their throats slashed, their unshielded sides cut through. Blood smoked on the silver sand. The uproar deafened. Three more guards staggered away, their legs unable to support them, sinking to the sand. Three more—and yet three more. The four remaining waited no longer. They cast down their shields and ran.

With long reptilian strides the schrepims chased them.

Swords lifted and blurred down in savage blows.

The last man, the single survivor, screamed and ran blindly.

One of the schrepims tossed his sword into the air. He caught it by the forte. His arm went back and he hurled, a vicious, cunning, superlatively destructive cast. The running man staggered on for four paces, lurching, before he fell with the sword burst through heart and lungs.

"By Havil!" Noran was on his feet, one hand to his chest. His face was flushed. "By Glem! They were superb, superb!"

"Money well spent!" declared Callimark.

I looked at these two with interest. None so blind...

Unmok nudged me.

"Jak! They'll—!"

"Yes," I said.

Rich blood puddled the silver sand.

Vad Noran was suffused with pride. This villa was a palace and a fortress. Within its walls his will was law. My early impression had convinced me that it would take far too much time to break an entrance in my own old swashbuckling way. The trick with the werstings to gain us entry had been essential, and had worked. But, also, that very impregnability of his villa meant Noran, standing now flushed with the excitement of the combat, had no fear of the three schrepims. He looked down at them as they walked alertly back toward his box.

"Well done, Slacamen," he shouted, giving them a nickname common among diffs and apims, a name, incidentally, I had heard the Schrepims often chafed under. "There will be much gold for you, aye, and rich foods and fine clothes."

Still the three advanced, silently, across the sand. The blood glimmered most evilly upon their blades.

Unmok the Nets choked out some unintelligible comment. He started to scrabble over the back of his chair.

Noran did not turn.

"Sit quietly, Och! These Slacamen cannot climb up here."

Unmok collapsed onto his seat. He was quivering.

"You are sure? Notor—you are sure they cannot get at us?"

"Of course. Why should they?" Noran's contempt seemed to me to reveal a sudden and unwelcome thought—the kind of thought he would not allow himself to think.

The scaled men couldn't climb up here, could they?

From my own experience I fancied they could—and would.

I said, "Van Noran! There are three down there. Were not there four in the cage?"

Callimark let out a squeal of pure terror.

"By Flem! He is right!"

"They will not harm me!" Noran bellowed it out. He put a beringed hand to the hilt of his sword. "I am Vad Noran! I bought them to fight for me! I pay them and feed them—they owe their lives to me."

"I do not think they see things that way." I looked along the seating, left and right. There was a fourth, and I did not think he would have run off and left his fellows.

The throaty sound of breathing, hoarse and rasping, came from Callimark trying to nerve himself. Unmok crouched in his seat. Noran yelled down, "I am Vad Noran! I pay you gold to fight for me, Slacamen!"

Left and right, along the seating, and up to the lip of the arena wall, along the trees, and down again, to the ornate entrance. My gaze flicked about. No sign... No sign, yet...!

Very quick and sudden, schrepims, very fast and deadly.

But although Vad Noran's guards were not, in the judgment of a hard old fighting man, worthy of their hire, some, at least, of that score who had died in the arena had struck shrewd blows before they perished. Two of the schrepims bore wounds, from which a green ichor leached. Hard to kill, these reptilian humans, but die they could, given courage and strength and skill and the effort of willpower to pit against them.

Around the arena I looked, carefully, seeking a glimmer of greenish scales along the seatings or up among the overarching trees. Callimark continued to breathe noisily. Unmok sat up straight and hauled out his sword.

"I am not in the habit of doubting the word of a noble," he said, and there was an edge to his voice. "But it seems to me the schrepims will climb up here and we will die. I will strike a blow first, by the golden jeweled cup of the Och Kings!"

"Nulsh!" said Noran. But his voice faltered.

Around and around, searching, searching...

The three walking toward us across the blood-puddled silver sand gave off that aura of menace that breathes from reptilian things. They walked easily and their thick tails were lifted high. You did not cut off the tail of a Slacaman as easily as that of a Kataki. Although the contest between Kataki and scaled man is instructive—in a gruesome way—and conducive to many serious lessons, it remains for all that a spectacle I would not cross the road to witness. All the time as these three advanced and Noran began to gnaw his lip and Callimark tried to get himself under control and Unmok quietly whistled his sword about to get his eye in, I twisted my neck and stared about, up and down, along and around, searching, searching...

"Perhaps, vad, we had best depart," said Callimark, and his voice pitched up and down the scale alarmingly.

Give Vad Noran his due—he just could not understand why men he had bought to fight for him, men recommended to him as hyr-kaidurs, should want to slay him. That was too personal. He delighted in the atmosphere of the Jikhorkdun, living its thrills and glorying in its valor and blood. But he hadn't considered that his own blood would be risked in any valorous combat. He would enter the ring to a challenge from an equal, he would fence with a professional kaidur, but that would not be for real, not for blood and guts real.

Just when he realized the schrepims would—damned well would!—climb that barrier and leap on him with lifted swords, with fang and claw, I do not know.

But, in the instant I spotted a staggering group of slaves boil out of the entranceway and totter, sprawling, shrieking, groveling, scrambling any-old-how along the seating, Noran's nerve broke.

Blindly, drawing his sword and thrashing about with it as though he slashed weeds, he bolted.

I said to Unmok, "Time we were leaving." The little Och came up out of his chair like a gazelle. "As Ochenshum is my witness you speak sense." He joined me as we moved back from the ornate seating. The uproar farther along grew. "But, Jak," said Unmok, and the avaricious old devil looked green. "This great noble, Vad Noran, has not yet paid me for the werstings!"

The slaves had scattered, shrieking, and Noran was rampaging along toward the exit with its curious carved nymphs upholding torches that were, at this time of day, as yet unlit.

"I think, Unmok, my friend, we will not get paid at all from that one." And I started to run.

Unmok let out a screech. Callimark took to his heels and ran the other way. Noran staggered back from the exit. He waved his sword about drunkenly. The schrepim who moved out of the opening between the torch-bearing nymphs looked no different from his three brethren in the arena. The same reptilian-snouted face, the heavily hooded eyes, the snaggle of sharp teeth, the same grayish-greenish scales with their bordering of orange. His clawed hand grasped a thraxter. His left arm was concealed by a shield. That, as I judged it, was the only difference.

Unmok screeched again. "Jak! They climb the barrier!"

Time for a single swift glance back. It was all there, the picture I remember and hate to recall. Callimark was flung across an ornate chair, his body slashed almost in two. The three schrepims leaped like lizards over the seating. Unmok was running toward me. Ahead Vad Noran, screaming in a paroxysm of fear, blundered back. The fourth scaled man followed him purposefully.

No doubt now remained that the schrepims would kill and go on killing until they were stopped.

I stopped running toward Noran. Unmok was my first concern. Noran would have to take his chances.

And then—and then, by Zair!

As I stared at the three scaled men in one direction, and was aware of the fourth in the other, I experienced for a fleeting moment of horror an image, scorched on my brain, of a splendid golden Kildoi, four-armed, tail-handed, brushing aside with superior swordsmanship all my efforts at swordplay.

Damn Prince Mefto the Kazzur!

But, with a little crippled Och to save, there was no time to blither-blather about the past and what was dead.

Not that Mefto the Kazzur was dead...

Noran was screaming in a crackling voice for the cadade. I did not know if the cadade was dead or not, but he wouldn't be turning up here.

"Out of the way, Noran!" I said. My voice must have penetrated the scarlet fear cloaking his senses, for he jumped, shivering, and then fell over the backs of the row of seating, tumbling among the bright cushions.

The schrepim didn't mind whom he killed first. Just so long as he could get his sword into someone, just so long as he could vent the frustrations of being taken up and forced to fight as a kaidur in the arena, chained, caged, whipped, sent out to fight like a wild beast—and he a man!—and then caged again if he lived, and dragged off with a hook through his heel if he died.

He came at me with the flashing speed of a reptile.

Whatever happened with him must happen fast. His comrades were breathing down the back of my neck.

He used his shield with skill, for he was a hyr-kaidur, and I had to skip and leap and parry for longer than I liked before my thraxter managed to loop inside his. I shoved the shield up and the rim took him under that ferociously toothed snout. He grunted. His squamous body was like a wriggling eel. But the thraxter went in, punching through scale, sliding on, cutting. I withdrew at once, green ichor sliming the blade, kicked him as he went down and then jinked sideways without looking back. I leaped over the chair upward from the rank, landing and spinning about.

That dramatic exercise had been necessary.

The leading schrepim's blow chunked stuffing from the chair seat.

I leaned forward to strike down on that sleek scaly head, but with lizard-like swiftness he recoiled.

For an instant we glared, eye to eye.

The fourth tooth along each side of his lower jaw protruded up at an angle. Larger than the other teeth, it slotted into a groove outside the upper jaw. The jagged line his jaws made as they clicked together gave him a ferocious aspect, almost as though he grinned at sight of his prey. The scales hooding his eyes looked like monk's hoods. Just below and closer together than the eyes the two deep pits of his heat-sensing organs were no doubt picking up my sweaty radiations and helping him to locate me even more exactly. Although his eyes were dark, the pigment, rhodopsin, in them which gave him good night vision would appear to glow an eerie red-orange at night from any reflected light. To see the eyes of schrepims glowing at night, the Kregish saying runs, is to look on the watchfires of hell.

His thick tail thumped the ground between the seats. I did not wait but leaped to the side. Using his tail as a lever, he soared up, his sword flashing out at me. I landed first. With solid ground under my feet I was able to roar forward and slash him while he was still in the air. Green ichor gushed from his side. He fell awkwardly.

Now he uttered sounds, a spine-chilling hissing, a spluttering rush of words and a ferocious shrilling.

Schrepims mostly speak their own language, their forked tongues giving a sibilant quality to their words; but they are well able to speak the universal Kregish language. By reason of that genetic language pill given to me by the Savanti I am able to understand tongues. Even as he fell, he was shrieking, "You will be caught up in the coils of Ratishling the Sinuous and crushed until your bowels smoke, apim, for the indignities you heap on me."

Oh, yes, I could feel sorry for him. But his two fellows were leaping like lizards along the seating toward me, and I knew their rage was such they'd prefer to use their fangs and claws on me rather than the swords they wielded. The wound in this one's side leaked green; but that wouldn't kill him. I aimed a delicate cut along his neck, where the scales smoothed and were more tightly fitted and of a lighter hue, just above the black scales of his harness. The thraxter bit and drew, cutting cleanly.

I leaped away.

Noran was shrieking and blubbering, and that old devil Unmok the Nets, his sword gripped in his two right, upper and middle, hands was struggling up from the tier of chairs below to get in the way of the charging scaled fighters.

"Get out of it, Unmok, you fambly!"

"Jak—if we are to die—"

"We're not!"

And I fairly hurled myself forward. Just in time I got the sword before Unmok and swept away the first blow from the leading schrepim. They were so damned quick! He came back, screeching, and there was no time to play him, for the first and fourth were rampaging up, and now they, too, were shrilling. They filled the air with fearsome promises of what Ratishling the Sinuous would do to me and all non-schrepims.

Well—you couldn't really blame them, could you? But I do not like to stand still while someone tries to kill me, never have and, by Krun, never will, I daresay. So I fought.

That was a fight of which the details remain hazy to this day.

Instinct, pure primeval instinct, and skill and utter dedication to the Disciplines alone could aid me now.

The swords clanged and chirred, and one schrepim was down and his dark green blood flowed from a mangled neck.

The other two bore wounds, as did I, and I'd falter and grow weak long before they'd even realize their scaly hides had been punctured.

One of them swept in and tried to fasten that rat trap of a mouth on my left arm. I got away just in time, with a long shredding of skin hanging from between his ugly fangs.

I leaped sideways and his thick tail swept around like a barn door closing and slogged into me and I went end over end down among the seats. How I didn't crack my head open I don't know. He scuttled after me and with a long, low lunge I kept down and so, left hand pressed against the floor by the seats, stuck the thraxter up into him. He sailed on and over me, as though pole-vaulting in just about the most uncomfortable position for the pole you could imagine, and he did not drag the sword from my grip. It came out with a wet slurshing sound. No time to watch him writhing in agony, no time, no time!

The last one jumped the seating to get at me.

To dream he was the last would have been a mistake on my part, and one I did not make. He was the last one to come into action, but the others were not out of it. Oh, no! Slit throats, deeply punctured wounds, impalements, that kind of punishment does not stop your schrepim. Their dark, insensate energy, the vigorousness of their attack, the febrile swiftness of them—they have to be killed and then killed again before they are dead.

Our swords crossed, I used, as I recall, a middling clever passage and hit him clean across the snout.

My thraxter broke across.

Instantly, I raced away, drawing him with me away from Unmok.

The thraxter had been my only weapon. Never laugh at or decry the great old Kregan custom of carrying an arsenal into battle! If ever I'd needed a selection of weaponry, it was now...

I ran.

The Sorzarts of the inner sea, the Eye of the World, do not compare with schrepims. The Phokaym do, of course; but they are of a world apart, there by that noxious cleft in the earth called the Klackadrin. Cousins in the realm of reptiles, Phokaym and schrepims. I ran and Unmok let out a screech and I half turned as I ran. The pursing scaled fighter was almost on me. Unmok's sword arched in the air, spinning, sailing up and over the schrepim's scaly head. It spun down toward me.

That was a tricky catch.

The sword hilt thumped into my fist and I failed to grasp it cleanly the first time and the schrepim slashed. I ducked, felt my sword that had been Unmok's slipping away, and grasped again. I put my foot into a scaled belly, thrusting, and then jerking instantly to left and then surging right.

His wicked tail lashed where I would have been.

The sword snugged into my fist. I thrust.

The blade squished in deeply. I drove it on, grinding it around, sawing on it, and I smashed my fist across his snout, driving back those wicked fangs.

He screamed and struggled to get at me past that steel tooth. I got a grip around his throat with my left hand and squeezed. I spat in his eye. If I'd had fangs I'd have ripped his throat out.

I kicked him, and we hopped about, locked together.

Somewhere out of the scarlet haze Unmok's yell: "Behind you!"

With a supreme effort I managed to spin us about. The blow hit the schrepim on the back of the head. If he noticed it, I do not know. It was a blow that would have split an apim's skull.

The fellow who had struck the blow drew back, setting himself for another try. His scaly body was slimed green with his own blood. He moved at a speed a normal eye could follow. He was dying. He didn't know that, or, knowing, pushed it aside in his insensate desire to kill me.

I shoved my man back, drawing out the sword with a loud sucking noise.

The two schrepims staggered together. I was just about done for now. As the two collided I jumped. The sword went around in an arc of greened silver.

Two blows, two blows delivered with the failing dregs of my strength. Two reptilian heads popped off to roll thumping down the stairs. I turned wearily and saw the other two, who should be dead, advancing on me. I noticed the red blood on their swords, and gazed stupidly at the green ichor fouling my blade.

Unmok appeared at my side, carrying a sword. The thraxter was most ornate. I realized it was Noran's weapon.

"I would not believe, Jak the Shot—but..."

"Do you stand aside, Unmok the Nets. They may pass me, but they will be dead doing it."

"And, my friend, so will you."

"If it is my time for Zair to whisk me up, my friend, then up I will go, and nothing on Kregen will prevent that."

A flash of gold just beyond the scaled men, a glitter of steel. The first schrepim bore on for me, but the second swung back, not as quickly as he had once moved, to face the golden numim who leaped on him, sword held just so.

The two combats finished with a speed that astonished me.

My schrepim died, at last, poor devil, and I swiveled to see Mazdo the Splandu finish off his with a slicing cut that left the schrepim's head all a-dangling before he fell.

"Jikai!" called Mazdo. "Jai, Jikai!"

"Maybe," I said in a grunt of exhaustion. "I give you the Jikai for your help—and, my thanks—"

"You did it all. I merely brushed up the crumbs."

And Mazdo the Splandu ran fleetly off along the seating to vanish past the curious carved nymphs. After that the guards turned up. I do not know if they had waited to see the outcome of the fight. But Vad Noran, shaking still, his face as green as the green ichor staining the seating of his private amphitheater, slowly came back to his senses. He started bellowing orders.

His guards, who may have waited and who may not have, were in for a very rough time of it. A very rough time indeed.

Presently, when the poor shredded schrepims had been carried away, and Noran had been petted and fussed over by his tame slaves, all aahing and oohing, and blandishing him with exclamations of admiration and praise for his valor—at which Unmok and I wisely held our tongues—we all went into the villa. Little to add to that. Unmok, brisking up, mentioned payment for his werstings, and Noran paid. He looked at me.

"I shall reward you, Jikai—handsomely. You are, I think, a hyr-paktun. Will you fight for me in the arena? There will be much gold. You will be a hyr-kaidur very quickly, I know—"

"Much as you honor me, notor, I am not able. I am sworn."

He looked disappointed, but he had the sense not to press.

It was quite clear to everyone that Noran must have fought like a leem to have slain all the schrepims with my and Unmok's assistance. Unmok started to protest, but I hushed him.

"Give us our gold, notor," I said. "We have a cage-voller to buy and fresh animals to find."

"Yes, yes. You shall have gold—" He swallowed. "My life is precious—" And then he said, "I cannot understand the ingratitude of those vile Slacamen! I paid for them, I would have treated them well! Why did they choose the path of murder?"

His personal needleman had patched me up and stuck a few needles in to deaden the pain. I felt half alive. I said, "They are men despite all, despite what diff and apim may think of them. No man cares to be chained and caged and forced to fight in a battle that does not concern him."

"You speak foolishly, Jak. Men like that have only their swordarms to sell in the market. And I pay them well!"

You couldn't argue with him. At least, I couldn't at that moment. I nodded.

"Thank you, notor. Now we will take our leave."

The vad's palatial quarters reflected his tastes well enough. The fellow who so far had sat quietly in a deep armchair by the window, idly pulling leaves off a plant in a bowl at his side, looked across. He was a spare man—by Krun! he looked like a starving ferret!—and his tastes were most certainly not reflected in the sumptuousness around him.

"You sound as though you sympathize with these Slacamen."

I shook my head and waited for the Bells of Beng Kishi to subside. I had taken a few fair old knocks. "No, notor. Just that they made the mistake of not knowing when to stop killing."

"One that you will not make?" His voice was like oiled steel.

I agreed, in the same deferential way I was talking, for I wanted out of here. He wore supple mesh mail from the Dawn Lands, and his dark hair was cut savagely short. His left eye was covered by a patch, a thing of crusted diamonds and emeralds. The stillness of him as he sat there, the deliberate movements as he stripped the plant, all conveyed the sense of suppressed energy. He was a man I would not seek to cross, and if, inadvertently I did so, would guard my back and put him down as quickly as possible.

He said, "You will not leave without the vad's permission."

"Assuredly, notor."

He turned his one good eye, sunken under a black brow, up to Noran. "I would have given much to have seen the contest in the arena, Noran. And more to have put my sword-arm alongside yours in your battle with these yetches."

Noran laughed. His voice pitched a trifle high, his face was flushed, his eyes bright. I did not look at Unmok. I just wanted out. We had gold enough now to buy the cage-voller.

About to open my mouth again, I was brought to my senses by Unmok's grip on my arm. The two lords missed the byplay.

"Shut your black-fanged winespout, Jak!" Unmok's whisper was fierce and frightened.

Noran was speaking, trying to sound offhand, casual about his fight and yet driven by what the pretense demanded.

"I would have joyed to have had you at my side, Gochert. It was a High Jikai!"

I kept my craggy old face impassive. By Zim-Zair! The presumption! Not in claiming what Noran claimed—that could easily be understood, and excused, on the grounds of his natural vanity and the position he found himself in. No, not that. But to use those great words, the High Jikai, in this context... No, I wanted out, by Zodjuin of the Silver Stux!

Then another portion of the puzzle that I sensed—and with a chilling unease, too!—was going to influence my life in the immediate future, dropped into place. This jewel-eyed Gochert had finished with the plant. It was now a mere stiff skeleton of twigs. His deliberate fingers began to slide over the pommel of one of his swords as though it were a netsuke. This was his thraxter. He wore also a rapier and his left-hand dagger was larger than the usual main gauche. All the weapons looked to be plain and workmanlike.

Gochert's one good eye appraised Noran. He waited before he spoke, and that small pause was just not quite long enough to be insulting.

"A Jikai," he said. "A High Jikai. By Spikatur Hunting Sword, Noran, I think you are right!"

Even if Vad Noran's jaw drew in until his neck creased and his shoulders went back, he took the remark as a compliment. He had no desire, apparently, to cross this jewel-eyed, ferret-faced Gochert. He waved his hand to dismiss us.

I said, "With the vad's permission." Then I added, "It is now clear that Froshak the Shine did not release the schrepims."

"By Glem! Is not that what I have already said!"

He hadn't, but I did not wish to argue the point. We went out and I took a last good look at this Gochert fellow, who scared Vad Noran and who talked of Spikatur Hunting Sword. The gold weighed on us, and I, at least, was ready to fight for it. But Unmok knew what he was doing. He might be scared of the protocol surrounding nobles, but he assured me that Noran would honor his promise and payment. So we collected the tame slaves from the outer courtyard and left Vad Noran's villa and its secrets, and walked down into the busy bustle of Huringa.

In a weird way, somehow or other, I seemed to hear the echo of clanging iron bars back there in that villa.

As we walked along Unmok regained his usual perky self. "A cage-voller!" he said. There was awe in his voice.

"You told me you did not much care for this beast-caging life, Unmok."

"So I did, Jak, so I did."

"So why continue? We have enough gold. You could set up in business." I refrained from mocking him on what might be the current nature of that business.

He stopped and twisted to stare up at me. His middle left jerked in excitement. "It is your gold, Jak! You fought the Slacamen, not I!"

"Are we or are we not partners?"

"But—in this!"

"You'll find Froshak again all right?"

"Yes, yes. But tell me fair what is in your mind."

"I will, Unmok. I will—but..."

The plans I had for Unmok and Froshak were dreams they would consider impossible. I did not want to force their destinies upon them, become an arbiter of their fates. If they wanted to go with me to Vallia, they would have to make the decision themselves. I was fully prepared for a refusal. Their lives were their own.

Amusement touched me at the thought of Noran and the pitiful figure he cut and his desperate desire to hold onto the reputation of a Jikai he had acquired over the affair with the schrepims. The honor in his life was now caged up, locked with a lie.

As for my life, well, I had broken free of my iron-barred cage, if only for a time. Delia and my gang of ruffians were safe, for no warning of danger had reached me from Deb-Lu-Quienyin, but there was cause for concern over the safety of anyone foolish enough to stand in their way.

Tilly, Oby and Naghan the Gnat had been rescued. Voinderam and Fransha were on the way home to confound the plans of the Racters. Vondium and Vallia would stand. We would struggle through, that I passionately believed in, even against Phu-Si-Yantong. Life would open out for me again, the iron bars forgotten. Whatever Unmok and Froshak decided, I would find myself a handsome voller and fly home to Vallia through the streaming mingled radiance of the Suns of Scorpio.

There were Prince Tyfar and Jaezila to bid good-bye to first.

Saying the remberees to them would be painful, but, after that wrench—Vallia!

Vallia and Delia!

Rebel of Antares

The Suns of Scorpio

Dray Prescot is a man scarred by a destiny that has hurled him four hundred light-years from Earth to the exotic world of Kregen orbiting the double star Antares. Assured of long life and vigorous health by the well-meaning Savanti nal Aphrasöe, now he is entrusted with the task of reuniting the island empire of Vallia and resisting the ambitions of the Empire of Hamal. From time to time he is called upon by the superhuman Star Lords to serve their mysterious purposes, and his relationship with them is entering upon a new phase.

To survive on Kregen Dray Prescot needed to be strong, resourceful, cunning and courageous. Yet there are more profound depths to his character than are called for by mere savage survival, and the tasks set to his hands and his experiences have changed him markedly. Educated in the harsh environment of Nelson's Navy, he is a man above middle height, with brown hair and eyes, the quiet movements of a hunting cat and a physique of exceptional power. Although he describes his face as "an ugly old beakhead," other sources state that his face is "noble and fierce." Expert with weapons and a master swordsman, he knows his own limitations. That he so often transcends them is a testament to his attitude toward life.

Prescot's loyalty to his friends is unbreakable. In the island realm of Hyrklana, off the east coast of the southern continent of Havilfar, he may now return home to Vallia. Many of the incidents of his varied career on Kregen are now falling into place in the grand design, and the reasons for his involvement are becoming clearer. At once, as is the happy way on Kregen, he is hurled headlong into new adventures under the Suns of Scorpio.

One

Sorcerers in the Souk

I have often been in two places at once; the superhuman powers of the Star Lords can arrange that little trick without trouble. Less frequently have there been two different versions of myself in the same place at the same time.

Walking along in the bustle of the city of Huringa, I was under the impression that to solve half of the problems confronting me I had only to bid farewell to my comrades Tyfar and Jaezila, secure an airboat and fly home to Vallia. The other half of the problems limped along spryly at my side, chattering away, and without a doubt presented the much more intractable half.

Unmok the Nets and I had become partners in the wild-animal business, dealing fairly with each other, and he expected us to set off on a new voyage to collect a fresh selection of savage beasts for the Arena. If ever there had been an occasion for two of me to be in the same place at the same time—then it was now.

As we passed under a balcony from which a cascade of multicolored flowers scented the air, I said, "Don't look back, Unmok. There is an unpleasant-looking fellow dogging our footsteps and I think he means us a mischief."

That, then, was an extra little problem for the evening.

Presently Unmok contrived a glance back as we neared the arched entrance to the Souk of Trifles. The twin Suns of Scorpio were almost gone and the sky blazed in cloud-banded jade and ruby.

"A nasty, devilish-looking customer, Jak."

"Just walk along quietly. We'll dodge into the Souk of Trifles. It might be interesting to play this fellow. Find out why he follows us like a burr in a blanket."

"Aye, it will be fun to bedevil him—"

"I said nothing about fun."

Unmok had no need to laugh. He might be a little six-limbed Och not above four feet six inches tall, and with a stump in place of his middle left limb; he was accustomed to handling the ferocious beasts employed in the Arena here.

"I know you, Jak the Shot," he said, sidestepping a man rolling an amphora along, single-mindedly concentrating on his rhythm. "You will play him and suck him dry, aye, and have fun in the doing of it."

"And if he is an assassin?"

"You have your sword, as I have mine."

Torches threw ragged light into the shadows cast by the declining suns. People bustled everywhere, intent at this time on finishing up their labors and enjoying themselves, and on offering a multitude of services to entertain and to relieve their customers of their cash. The Arena had, this day, remained empty and silent. People were dry-throat thirsty for sensation. At the entrance of the Souk, situated between three-story buildings of gray brick, the nearest stall furnished, as it were, a foretaste of what lay beyond. This stall, partially covered by a striped awning, piled with ankle-bells whose qualities were touted in un-bell-like bellowings by a woman whose bodice strained with lung power, offered us concealment as we struck off down the Souk. At once we were engulfed in a jostling tide of humanity.

"Perhaps," said Unmok as we edged our way through the throngs, "there are others with him."

"The thought is in my mind."

The noise of hundreds of people shouting and laughing, chaffering and bartering, bounced from the crystal roof. With the last of the daylight, the mineral-oil lamps were lit. They depended on brass chains, high above, and as the agile monkeylike girls and boys clambered among the girders and chains with nerveless skill, the light within the Souk brightened. The vista of those long lines of light, the hanging chains, brought a vivid image of the Swinging City of Aphrasöe to my mind.

"Well, I can't see anyone else with the rast."

"They'll hang back and await his signal—if there are any more assassins with him." I could feel the soreness of the wounds I had taken still on me. I would not welcome another fight. All day Unmok and I had spent resting at our camp well outside the city walls, and we needed that rest. Froshak the Shine and the slaves waited for us, and Unmok had insisted he would go with me into Huringa. As for our gold, that was buried just outside the camp. If these assassins dogging our footsteps wanted that, they would be unlucky.

"So," I said, continuing the thought, "what does this fellow want of us?"

Unmok dodged a blundering Gon carrying a tray filled with sweetmeats. His little Och face screwed up. "Rather, who would want us killed?"

"Noran, for one. Vad Noran, for falsely taking the credit for fighting the schrepims in his private arena yesterday. His honor was very touchy on the matter."

"Perhaps. I was convinced when he paid us, for the animals and for the fight, that was the end of it. But you never can tell with these nobles."

"Aye."

This Vad Noran, a puffed-up bladder, but a bladder with much power, had bought many of the animals Unmok and I had brought into Huringa. When the schrepims, fearsome scaled warriors, had broken free and sought to slay anyone in their path and we had been forced to put them down, Vad Noran had, willy-nilly, been credited with the victory. It had been called a Jikai, a warrior triumph. Perhaps he wanted to shut our mouths, in case we talked and revealed the hollowness of his claims.

An excited bunch of people wearing blue favors crowded in a rowdy uproar, laughing, already very merry, a whole mixture of races united in their partisanship for the Sapphire Graint. The blues rode at the highest point of the victory totems just now, their prianum filled with trophies of triumph. This mob was celebrating and didn't mind who knew.

"The Sapphire Graint! Kaidur!" they yodeled, reeling along, shouting, waving bottles, pushing people out of the way. It was all good-natured fun, and nothing untoward. I looked back.

The man who followed us so tenaciously persisted, waiting by a booth, crossing to the other side of the Souk, forcing his way through folk who, after one look, gave him plenty of room. He was an apim, a member of Homo sapiens, wearing nondescript brown clothes, a brass-studded jerkin and pleated kilt and with a Hyrklanian hat pulled low. I caught only the jut of a dark beard. He wore sword belts strapped diagonally over his shoulders.

"He sticks with us." Unmok's middle left stump gave that small characteristic twitch, a reflex he could not control, a pointer to his state of mind. That limb, the middle, set between the upper and the lower, is used as either a leg or an arm by Ochs, who are sprightly, agile folk. Unmok's middle left had been chewed off by a wild animal—before he earned the sobriquet of Unmok the Nets.

"He knows his trade."

"And I know mine. He is ripe for netting, that one."

Along each side of the Souk extended arcades, each a heaped treasure-house of Trifles. Extending the illumination of the high suspended lamps, myriad torches and cheap mineral lamps cast ruddy light upon the scene. Multicolored clothes, the glint of jewelry, the massy banks of hanging carpets, the furtive glitter of teeth and eyes, the smile that concealed, the merry jingle of coins, the uproar of bartering, all the normal everyday chaos of a busy bazaar flowed about us. The smells were quite comfortable, spicy, tangy, quite unlike some of the more odiferous of the Souks of Huringa.

"Out at the other end, Unmok, then double back and—"

"And find out what his tripes look like."

A sharp-toothed angerim, all hair and ears, spat at us for jostling his stall, where an untidy mixture of pots and pans and cutlery rang and chimed together. Angerims as a race of people are singularly messy in their life-style.

"Easy, dom," said Unmok quickly. "No harm done."

"Fuddled Ochs, clumsy apims," said the angerim. And then: "Buy a pot—here is a fine brass pot chased in Cervantern style, cheap for you, doms, a quality piece for your fire."

We walked on past hanging drapes of cheap cloth of brash color and pattern festooning the next stall. The angerim spat after us, wiping swatches of hair across his ears. The man who patiently dogged our footsteps padded on, keeping to the shadows.

The uproar within the Souk of Trifles continued and increased. A multitude of people from many of the fabulous races of Kregen presented an unforgettable spectacle, vivid with life and energy, laughing, bartering, quarreling, shouting, but alive, alive! At the far end the Souk opened out onto the Street of Running Werstings. Other bazaars riddled this area with noise and color and confusion. We passed under an overhanging balcony protruding from the level over the arcades, which are often called Monhan terraces. A woman leaned over and emptied a pot. To her evident disappointment, the pot's contents missed us. The splash cleared a circle.

A mob of people running wildly and screaming in fear scattered back from the exit to the Souk. They were all a mixture of races and colored favors and they pushed on blindly, their faces contorted, their eyes staring, their mouths open, screaming. The throngs picked up the panic. They began to recoil, and turn, and join in the flight. An enormous Rapa whose beaked face stuck up, surrounded by bristling feathers, blundered past and knocked Unmok flying. The little Och skidded back into a confusion of basket-protected amphorae. He flailed about, trying to get his balance, as the crowds streamed past. I had to skip smartly to get out of the line of stampede, and hitched myself up under a beam from the arcade.

"Hold on, Unmok! Stop thrashing about like a stranded fish."

"That Rapa—I'll—"

Unmok got his feet under him and staggered up and was immediately knocked over again by a fleeing Rhaclaw, whose immense domed head tried pathetically to twist on the pitiful plate of gristle that passed for its neck to stare back. The Rhaclaw wore armor and swords, and he ran with the rest, ran in blind panic.

The words the crowd was shouting spurted up mingled with the shrieking.

"Sorcerers! Wizards! Run! Flee! Sorcerers!"

Well, I generally steered clear of sorcerers myself, unless they were friendly.

The scattering of basket-protected amphorae dislodged by Unmok at last made a kind of breastwork. He staggered out, wild, flailing his arms about. When folk with three or four arms do that it makes you blink. He looked down the Souk and then up at me as I dropped down to join him.

"The rast is still there, Jak. Crouched in a doorway on this side—"

"I saw him. And his fellows are with him now."

"Aye."

"Do you fancy assassins or sorcerers?"

"You give a man a hard choice. If there is nothing else for it—"

"Unless you can batter a way through the walls."

He took the suggestion seriously, in that dour way some Ochs have, but he knew the thickness of the walls needed to uphold the overarching crystal. "Unless we find a door, we'll never knock a hole through in time."

"I judge the same."

The rout streaming past thinned and a last few crazed individuals fled past, sobbing, casting agonized glances back. We looked along the Souk under the lights and the crystal roof toward the end that gave egress onto the Street of Running Werstings.

Two beings stood there in the puddled light, facing each other. It was a Confrontation.

One of the figures stood tall and robust and encased in a solidly glittering robe. A splendid figure, a dominating figure, one who commanded and knew nothing of disobedience, one who wore splendid vestments of silk and gems and gold thread, this one was a Sorcerer of the Cult of Almuensis. For the briefest of moments I fancied he was San Yagno, who had disappeared down the Moder, but he was not. His face, lined with the seasons of knowledge and power, bore a fierce, predatory look as he intoned the spells from the great book in his beringed fingers. The book was covered in lizard skin, gold-bound, gold-locked and fastened to his belt by golden chains. From this book, this hyr-lif, came the sorcerer's very real powers.

The Sorcerer of the Cult of Almuensis sparkled with the radiance of power within the lights of the bazaar.

The other figure presented the most marked contrast.

This was an Adept of the Doxology of San Destinakon. His gown swathed his figure in a drab but bewildering array of brown and black lozenges. The hood peaked to his right, for a woflovol perched on his left shoulder, the little batlike animal's membranous wings now extended and fluttering in echo of the rage suffusing his master. The woflovol was chained to the Adept's waist by a slender bronze linkage. In the sorcerer's right hand, a hand devoid of ornamentation, a wooden-hafted bronze flail, a scourge, was uplifted, for the followers of San Destinakon are not above the outrage of physical chastisement. Now the bronze flail hung limp, but it quivered with the passions of the Adept.

169

Two figures in marked contrast, yes. But they held and controlled power, undeniably. Between them, shimmering and sparkling, grew a dish-shaped circle of light. Constantly changing in color and texture, shooting forth rays of brilliance, the center of the conflict between the two sorcerers shifted back and forth and spat fire, crackling with the dissipation of energy.

Unmok gulped.

"An Almuensin and a Destinakon! This is no place for an honest man, Jak. Let us—"

"Loosen your sword and let us hit the damned assassins first—"

"Yes! As Ochenshum is my witness, let us die by an assassin's hand as by the malignancy of a wizard!"

Just like Unmok the Nets. I knew him to be brave and loyal, but brave only when he had to be and loyal only to those he valued. If he could have paid some of his good red gold to a fine gang of cutthroats to insure his safety out of here, he would have done so, faster without another thought. Well, and wasn't that the sensible course?

"Sink me!" I said. "We won't get ourselves killed. Come on. Let us hit them fast and break through and then—"

"Run!"

"Aye!"

Then a noise broke about our heads like the last trump. The colossal smash of sound bore in on us and made our heads jump on our shoulders. I thought the sound more like a battery of thirty-pounder Parrotts all firing together right beside us than a battery of twelve-pounder Napoleons. The air in the Souk was thick and the noise bellowed along, amplified and channeled and directed personally, so it seemed, at every individual's eardrums. But, on Kregen, they had not yet developed gunpowder or guns. This was no battery of cannon firing, this was sorcery venting in deafening discharges the overflowing plasma of thaumaturgy. I glanced up.

The crystal roof split.

In spinning sheets of crystal, in razor-edged plates of shimmering fireglass, the roof collapsed. It rippled as though shaken. The metal supports buckled. Over an area a full hundred paces long and the full width of the Souk, the roof fell in.

Unmok let out a screech and dived for the upended barrow that had contained the amphorae. I wasted no time in joining him. Together, heads down, we crouched in the hellish din.

Sharp slivers of crystal slashed into the paving. Chips flew like shrapnel. The uproar smashed at us so that we gasped for air. The barrow and the amphorae clattered with the scattering crystal chips. Amphorae exploded. Wine gushed forth, staining the basketwork and the straw and running gleaming red across the paving. The whole place quivered as though in the grip of an earthquake.

The avalanche of crystal thundered down for what seemed an eternity of Kregan nights and days. At last in a final clashing of shining slivers the noise ceased. Unmok lifted his head.

"If that is what the end of the world is going to be like, I do not believe I will wait around to see it."

"Sensible," I said, brushing dust from my clothes.

We crawled out from under the barrow and shook our heads, bloated with sound.

The order in which we took stock of the situation might have reflected a mutual dependence in a coming battle; it could just as easily have revealed our nervous preoccupations. Unmok peered through the swirls of dust toward the two wizards. I looked back into the Souk for the assassins.

Assassins are hardy souls, the stikitches' trade being of a demanding nature, and two leather- and bronze-clad men still sheltered in an arcade opening, peering out at us. Their beards showed black against the pallor of their skin. The rest of the gang had fled; at least, they were nowhere in sight. Leaving my observation of the assassins and that problem, I turned to look where Unmok stared, rigid with a terror he made valiant attempts to conceal.

The two sorcerers had by no means finished their altercation. The disc of light spun between them, coruscating and throwing off streams of radiant matter as though a Catherine Wheel spun to a crazy destruction. The shards of light struck the walls of the Souk with thunderclap noises. Chunks of masonry were blasted away. Dust sifted among the wreaths of smoke.

"Let us—" said Unmok, and he swallowed and wet his lips before he could continue. "Let us get away!"

I nodded. The wizards' quarrel was no concern of ours and we were like to be harmed by its side effects. The assassins presented a simpler and more approachable problem, for all that I had looked their way first. I have no truck with sorcerers unless I count them as friends or must use them despite all.

We began to move back down the Souk.

The crackle of splintered crystal under our feet sounded like mahogany leaves. The assassins eased out from their arcade.

"Two," said Unmok. "I think we will be able."

The assassins bared their swords, the weapons glinting in the light of the sorcerer's quarrel.

The Souk presented a melancholy spectacle, empty of people apart from us four, with the paving strewn with smashed Trifles, stalls over-turned, bales of cloth unrolled and abandoned in serpentine meanderings, smashed glass and pottery, feathers and ivory and knickknacks scattered everywhere. The noise and light at our backs persisted. We moved on.

"Are they assassins?" asked Unmok, as the two men ahead of us hesitated. They began to withdraw, steadily, their weapons lifted, going slowly, but they drew back before us as we advanced.

Without looking back, and just to cheer up Unmok's little Och heart, I said, "They need not be retreating because of us."

Unmok burst out with a comment that almost made me smile. He whirled to look back.

"The sorcerers still fight, Jak—you devil! You had me going then..."

"True."

"Tell me why I shouldn't throw you into one of my wild-beast cages."

"Riddles were never one of my easiest marks."

The assassins—if they were stikitches—halted again and then once more drew off. They moved with purpose.

"It could be they seek to lure us on—"

"On to our doom!" Unmok cast another look back. "Well, there is no getting out that way."

Keeping a very sharp lookout in all the nooks and crannies of the Souk, bathed in that supernatural fire, we pressed on.

The occult radiance drove our shadows ahead of us, long and dark and leaping, seeming to draw us on as the fires forced flames and smoke into the Souk. The mineral-oil lamps cast gobbets of flame as they fell in the continuing crashing destruction of the roof. We were running now, leaping obstacles and diving past overturned stalls as the crystal burst and the lamps showered down and the fires raged.

We must have looked like two phantom figures bursting through veils of smoke from some time of forbidden lore, some realm of ancient magic. The assassins hovered, their steel glinting. Then they swung away, looking back for only heartbeats; Unmok ripped out his sword and waved it—and the assassins fled.

"That," said Unmok with immense satisfaction, "has seen them off."

"By Harg!" I said, leaping forward. "I want to know more about this—who sent them—what the hell they're up to!"

"Jak—"

The backs of the assassins leaped and dived among the Trifles scattered over the Souk. The roof fell in successive crashings. The fire crackled. Smoke streamered in long layers, stinging the eyes and making us cough. I roared after the fleeing assassins.

The whole area had been cleared of people, and any thoughts that the first roof-falls had finished the business were now seen to be ill-founded. What the sorcerers had begun the fire and the domino effect along the roof would finish.

One of the men running ahead of us skidded on a mess of squishes upended from a basket. His arms flailed. He staggered into a rack of cheap zorca trappings, and before he could recover I put my fist around his neck. He squeaked like a rabbit.

"Let me go!" he shrieked. "The sorcerers—"

I let my dagger make an acquaintance with the space between his third and fourth ribs. "Do not fret over the wizards, dom. They quarrel between themselves. You should rather fear for your fate—" the dagger twitched "—here and now."

He gasped, twisting, trying to kick, trying to bite. I moved the dagger.

"Tell me who sent you, and I will let you live."

"I cannot—"

"Very well. You have your stikitche honor. You may adhere to your code and die, here and now. I do not care. I will find your comrades. One will tell me."

"You devil!"

"So I am told."

"I cannot tell you!"

"You mean that for a short moment you will not."

"Listen, dom—take that dagger away. It is sharp!"

"A blunt dagger is like a grave without a corpse."

He knew that old Kregish saying, which may be taken in two ways, both of them apposite. He went limp in my fist.

"If—"

"Just speak up."

"I am no stikitche."

Unmok arrived then and made a disgusted sound.

"We guessed as much. As assassins you would make passable dung-sweepers."

"So," I said, "Vad Noran sent you. And you've failed him."

I felt the quiver of him in my grip. "I did not tell you that! I did not! As Havil is my witness, I did not speak!"

I gave him a resounding kick up the backside and let him go. He had merely confirmed what we suspected. I bellowed after him as he scampered off.

"If you dare to face Noran, tell him we will keep our silence. We will keep that and the gold. Tell him."

He did not answer, did not look back. He just ran.

Unmok rubbed his middle right across his face; his upper right still gripped his sword. "Now that I've seen him close to, I do recognize him. He's one of Noran's men, all right. They call him Hue the Grasshopper. But the others with him..."

"Of a tougher frame of mind, I would think. But if they are not assassins, I, for one, am profoundly grateful."

There was no need for me to elaborate. Once stikitches take out a contract, they will, within the framework of their so-called honor codes, fulfill it, or arrange the recompense on annulment. If I was to do what I had to do in Huringa, I did not want a horde of hairy, unwashed assassins breathing down my neck all the time.

What I had to do now was to find some way of taking my leave of Unmok the Nets so that I could bid farewell to Tyfar and Jaezila. If one problem had been resolved the rest remained.

All the same...

"I wonder—" I said as we dusted ourselves off and started off toward the far end of the Souk. "I wonder what the quarrel was between the two sorcerers."

Unmok gave a little cluck of sound, a dutifully respectful and at the same time dismissive appraisal of all wizardly doings.

"Who can say? They are unto themselves—thank all the gods."

People began to move about at the far end, creeping out of hiding places, standing up to look with bewildered horror upon the catastrophe. The fires burned fiercely at our backs. We went on and found an arcade with an opening onto a narrow side alley. One or two people evidenced a desire to talk to us; we had no wish to engage them in conversation. By Krun, no!

The fires burst through between the empty walls and threw orange and crimson weals against the evening sky. We dodged along the alley and turned right and then left between shuttered buildings and came out onto the Street of Condiments where people stood about, staring up, talking among themselves, watching the fires. The conflagration would be brought under control by fat Queen Fahia's officials, for like most monarchs of important cities, Fahia kept up services to deal with emergencies of this kind.

Ashes blew on the evening breeze. We went through the throngs, their eternal chatter about the Arena for the moment forgotten, and thought about a wet.

"My throat is as dry as a Herrelldrin Hell," said Unmok.

"There's a swinging flagon."

We went into the low-arched opening and sat at a wooden table, and the Fristle fifi brought us a jug and two flagons. Unmok poured and we drank. By Vox! I was thirsty. My Och companion scattered a few copper coins on the table, a handful of obs, and we refilled the flagons.

"Talking of money," said Unmok, which was a perfectly logical process of thought for him, "I am in poor case to see Avec. He will think my talk of gold a cod to catch him." He started again to bang at his clothes and to pull and tweak them about to make them fit better.

"We have the gold now, Unmok, and no man will quibble when his hand jingles the bag of yellows. Just tell him straight out."

"I will. You are right."

Unmok the Nets was a wily enough fellow when it came to money matters, and his banking connections with Avec Parlin, I fancied, would not altogether favor the banker. Unmok's burning desire now was to buy a cage voller, an airboat fitted for the carriage of wild beasts. With such an airboat in his possession, with his connections, he ought to make money like wildfire.

The Fristle fifi in her yellow apron—for she was not a slave—came over with a wooden tray filled with odds and ends of munchables, and we popped a few into our mouths and chewed as we talked. The wine, a middling Stuvan, lowered in the jug.

"Avec will know the best bargains," said Unmok, with confidence. "We need a large vessel, but she must be economical to run. A few deldys more on the initial costs to insure that will pay dividends."

I fretted within myself, for I had more or less promised Unmok I would ship out with him on his next voyage, and yet I could not in all conscience do so. I knew that, although my own country of Vallia was in good and capable hands, I wanted to return there and finish up the business of uniting the land and turning out the villains who had so destroyed and brought low the Empire of Vallia. I sipped wine to conceal the turmoil of my thoughts, and Unmok burbled cheerfully on, already in command of his famous cage voller and soaring through the skies with a full cargo of fearsome, snarling, savage beasts.

Then he stopped talking, and his jowly Och face changed, a frown of concentration drawing down his brows.

"Hue the Grasshopper—Vad Noran's man you lifted up to inspect—may not have been a stikitche, being at best a stable hand. But the man who followed us, dogging our footsteps—he was an altogether more ugly customer."

So I guessed Unmok had seen this altogether more ugly customer pass outside the tavern, still seeking us, no doubt.

I felt relief.

The persistence of this tracker afforded me a chance to postpone telling Unmok that I would not be shipping out with him, that our partnership was ended unless he chose to go with me. I stood up.

"Jak?"

"You go and see Avec Parlin. Make sure he lays his hands on the very best cage voller we can afford. All the gold is yours. I may not be able to ship out with you—"

"Jak!"

"—But I will see you again. You know you have my word on that. Now, which way did this ugly customer go? I will sort him out—"

"Jak!"

"—So there is no good arguing, there's a good fellow."

Unmok swelled out those jowly Och chops and tilted his head back to look at me. He did not stand up, and in that I felt the smaller of the two of us.

"He went along toward the Avenue of Sleeths. No, there is no profit in arguing with you. You have secrets, that I do know. I will see Avec and arrange the cage voller. After that—you must decide. As for me, we are partners, and remain so."

Little, are Ochs, puffy and with six limbs, and not apims like me at all. But in that moment Unmok the Nets displayed a dignity surpassing many and many a blowhard apim lout I have known. And that thought should surprise no one in two worlds.

"Although—" and here Unmok shivered his whole body, as though gripped by a vampire spider of Chem. "Although if you go away I will take it hard. We have been partners for only a small length of time, as these things are measured, and yet in that time we have been through much together. It is of value to me to think of that, and those times..."

"It is of value to me, also. I think you know that." The lamplight glittered on the bronze studs of Unmok's jerkin beneath the opened fold of his tunic. "Secrets—yes, we all have secrets. It is difficult for me to explain. I believe you would find it well-nigh impossible to credit. But explain I will. I will."

His regard of me did not waver.

"May the hands of all the gods rest lightly on you, Jak the Shot, and may Ochenshum have you in his keeping."

I nodded and without the usual remberees on parting, I went out and along the street toward the Avenue of Sleeths.

After all, as I tried to tell myself with some hollow vehemence, how could a partnership with a little Och wild-beast catcher and a half-promise to him possibly weigh in the balance against the preoccupations of an emperor and the fate of an empire?

Two

A Rapier Twinkles at Dinner

The quarrel between the two sorcerers and the resultant disastrous fire forced animation on the people of the city. Parties of the queen's guards galloped along the streets. The flames continued to light the night sky. People talked of the catastrophe, agog, joying that their premises had not been consumed. I walked along at a good pace, heading west out and along the street toward the Avenue of Sleeths.

Huringa, the capital city of Hyrklana, is not one of the largest capitals of Kregen, but it is impressive in its own way, dominated by the imposing pile of the queen's palace, the Hakal, with the ominous bulk of the Arena, called the Jikhorkdun, alongside. From the Arena the four main boulevards, lighted by gas, stretch toward the cardinal points of the compass. I saw no sign of the man who had been following us and whom I now followed in order, as I had told Unmok, to settle this business. I did not know, myself, if this were true...

Anyway, if I did not find him I was going in the right direction for the promised meeting with Tyfar and Jaezila.

The idea that I ought to take a part in the fire-fighting occurred to me. I dismissed it immediately. The authorities, charged by fat Queen Fahia with fire-fighting duties would be adequately capable. She'd have them thrown to her pet neemus if they were not.

Moving along among the folk out strolling in this early evening preparation period for the night's entertainments, I kept a wary lookout. The fourth moon of Kregen, She of the Veils, sent down smoky pinkish rays, wavering and erratic in the smoke pall, paling beside the lurid glow of the fire. Keeping out of the way of sorcerers had always seemed a sound practice, and this latest imbroglio merely confirmed that. The disc of radiance balanced between the two opposed powers of the wizards and casting off the chunks of incendiary material was in itself a potent force. That occult disc of light is called The Quern of Gramarye. When it grinds opposed magics the very fabric of time and space is distorted and fractured.

The Avenue of Sleeths ran straight between private houses fronted by gardens for over five hundred paces. Here lived some of those inhabitants of Huringa who were bracketed in the middling wealthy class, with slaves and carriages and fine clothes, whose tables were well-laden. Down at the far end, a crossing place where the Street of Sleeths joined the east boulevard was always crowded with idlers and ruffians patronizing the taverns and inns there. So it was from gentility into abandonment I walked. And still no sign of the fellow who had dogged our footsteps.

Many torches and lanterns lit up the crossing place which formed a kind of square or kyro, and the taverns stood cheek by jowl. Most strollers approached this place, the Kyro of the Happy Calsany, along the boulevard. When the amphitheater turned out after the games, the place became choked. Amid all the uproar I fancied there would be little chance of spotting my man, so I set off directly for the tavern, the Faerling's Feathers, where I was to meet Jaezila and Tyfar.

The great cross of the boulevards, with the Jikhorkdun and the high fortress of the Hakal at the center, imposed a certain order on Huringa's street planning, but the mixtilinear walls made of the alleys and streets in the outer portions of the quarters a mass of interconnected labyrinths. A general assault on this city would be held up there unless airborne troops could land in rear of the defenses.

Wondering why that particular thought had crossed my mind just then, I walked up to The Faerling's Feathers. We of Vallia had no wish to go to war with Hyrklana; quite the reverse. Tyfar and Jaezila were talking together, engrossed in each other's company. I looked at them with great pleasure. And I was come to say good-bye!

They sat at a small table under a climbing vine smothered in blue flowers; above their heads a balcony depended silken shawls and tasseled scarves. The light from She of the Veils glowed warmly from the stucco wall. The table was set for three; the empty chair waited for me.

I shook my head as though to clear away cobwebs. I knew that saying good-bye to these two would be a wrench, and now that I watched them as they talked so closely, I realized afresh just how much I did not want to part from them. Blade comrades are rare, and I have been blessed and more than blessed with true blade comrades on the wonderful and terrible world of Kregen. For a true blade comrade one would lay down one's own life without a second thought, and for these two, for Jaezila and Tyfar, I would—with only the first thought for my Delia to halt me—go through the fire. Delia, Delia of the Blue Mountains, Delia of Delphond, always stood foremost in my thoughts, and against our love I measured all my actions.

The task of saying good-bye would not be easy for another reason. Prince Tyfar, with his shining honor and ideas of upright dealing with all men and women, and Jaezila, with her willful ways and quick bright grasp on living, would certainly attempt to detain me. They had work to do here in Huringa for their own country of Hamal. Hamal was at war with my own country of Vallia, and that was all a stupid nonsense; these two were comrades and we had lived and walked close to the edge of death together.

Jaezila tossed her head back so that her brown hair rippled all gleaming in the moonlight. She laughed full-throated. And, so laughing, saw me.

"Jak!"

"Well, Jak," said Tyfar, scraping his chair back and standing up to greet me, "and have you freed yourself of your entanglement outside the city? Do you come to stay with us?"

"Lahal, you two," I said, walking up and grasping Tyfar's hand, leaning down to kiss Jaezila. "No. I'm not clear yet." I sat down and the wine was poured as I pulled the chair forward. "But I joy to see you—"

I had told them only the most superficial account of my true life and circumstances out of necessity. They knew I was happily married, although

I had—prudently—given Delia a different name. I had said—and I would not want Delia to learn this too swiftly—that her name was Thylda. That was a good name in Hamal. You see what petty shifts one is driven to when friendship is sullied by these monumentally idiotic politics of war! So they knew that my entanglement outside the city was not with a woman.

I asked after the fliers they had come here to buy, and heard that the work proceeded slowly, for the people of Hyrklana deeply resented having to build airboats for Hamal. Only fear of that great empire on the mainland opposite, and its mad Empress Thyllis, kept the Hyrklanians polite to Hamalese in their midst.

"Although," said Tyfar, looking flushed and annoyed, "a factory was burned to the ground today—ten fliers were lost. They go in for fires in Huringa, I see."

I told them that the fire in the Souk of Trifles had been started by two sorcerers quarreling.

"Their damned Quern of Gramarye, I suppose?"

"Yes."

Now that I had joined them, the slaves could bring the food. One thing was sure, despite the enormous difficulties, when Vallia had triumphed over Hamal—as we would!—we'd stop all this slavery. The transformation of a slave-owning society into a free society was causing difficulties in Vallia, and the problems would be worse in Hamal. But in Opaz's good time, the task would be done.

Jaezila wore a deep crimson evening robe, just such a gown as Delia had once worn here in Huringa, and with a narrow golden belt from which swung not a silly ornate curved dagger but a solid workmanlike rapier and main gauche. She looked stunning. And yet still she teased Tyfar, and tweaked him and, as I looked at them and saw, she was more attached to him that she probably realized. As for Tyfar, his dark blue evening robe concealed a harness of mesh link, I did not doubt; his rapier and main gauche swung from his belts outside the robe. Under the folds of cloth I also did not doubt he had his axe about him. He was not willingly parted from that axe, was Prince Tyfar of Hamal.

Toward the end of the meal he kept darting puzzled looks over my left shoulder. A wary expression crossed his face and then he returned to the squish pie. But again he looked up. Open and frank, bold and fearless— these words describe Tyfar as he carried himself with us, for we were comrades. With his father, Prince Nedfar, and the high notables, Tyfar tended to the withdrawn, the aloof. A bookish man, he had taken up the axe as a kind of defiance of those forces seeking to mold him into the run-of-the-mill Hamalese prince. A good man in a library and a good man to have at your back in a fight, Prince Tyfar.

He said, "I think—"

Then he stood up, very quickly, overturning his glass of wine. His rapier snicked out and thrust past my ear as he flung himself forward. I was off my chair and rolling on the ground, without thought. I heard the scream of surprised pain and then I was up, rapier in hand, to see that damned assassin fellow who had been following Unmok and me writhing with Tyfar's rapier through his guts.

Jaezila's own sword flicked about, checking the sudden surge of interest from other diners at adjoining tables.

The wretch skewered so neatly fell down. Tyfar withdrew.

"Friend of yours, Jak?"

"My thanks, Tyfar—not exactly. He's been following us—me—around Huringa tonight. I'm glad I know where he is now."

"He's on his way to the Ice Floes of Sicce, that's where."

"May his ib rest in peace—although I do not think that likely."

"Pay the reckoning, Ty, and let's go." Jaezila spoke evenly.

"Agreed."

I started to shuffle coins out and the prince checked me, as he always did in these matters. He was a real prince.

The landlord waddled up, protesting, but a dead man who might or might not be an assassin was no new thing in this Kyro of the Happy Calsany. A few gold coins jingling, a smile and a word or two, and the matter was settled. We were known to be strangers, and rotten damned Hamalese at that, but gold was gold.

We walked away, and Jaezila picked up a ripe shonage to eat as we went along.

So I told them about my dealings with Vad Noran.

"Unmok the Nets and I sold Noran a parcel of wild beasts. We were up at his villa when the slaves broke out." I didn't tell him why the slaves had escaped. "Some schrepims were released from their cage and the reptilian warriors went berserk."

"Schrepims," said Tyfar. He pursed his lips. "Nasty."

"Quite. Unmok and I managed to beat them off with the aid of a lion-man, and this great Vad Noran appeared and was given the credit for the fight. We did not care. Unmok just wanted his money and to get out, and the numim escaped, for he had been a slave there. So now, I think, Noran wants to shut our mouths in case we spread the true story. He has been dubbed a great Jikai because of his supposed fight—"

Jaezila laughed, striding along, munching shonage, the juices running down her chin. "It is strange, for we have heard of the Jikai Vad Noran performed. And it was like that!"

"We heard more about this Noran, also," said Tyfar, and he spoke seriously.

"He builds vollers and no doubt sells the airboats to you?"

"Yes. It was not his factory that was burned to the ground. But—"

"But he seemed most pleased that the vollers had been destroyed." Jaezila wiped juice. "No. Not seemed. He was damned pleased—and it is easy to see why."

These two blade comrades of mine believed that I worked in secret for the Empress Thyllis—a lie I had been forced to for the sake of friendship and a whole skin—and that I was Hamalese as they were. At least, as Tyfar was. Jaezila might not be Hamalese but she labored for that evil empire just the same. So I could say, with a grimace, "Because they hate us."

"They do hate us. And again, it is easy to see why."

Once more we were on thin ice. I guessed that Tyfar's father, Prince Nedfar, did not share the grandiose ideas of conquest harbored by Thyllis. Hamal had extended out to north and south, laying waste lands and islands, sending her iron legions to destroy all the might sent against them. Well, we in Vallia were checking that onward march. But south of Hamal, in the Dawn Lands, the Iron Legions of Hamal surged on in blood and death. The invasion to the west of Hamal into the Wild Lands had been halted some time ago. To the east, across the sea to the island of Hyrklana... Well, would not Hamal seek to conquer Hyrklana in the fullness of time? Unless mad Empress Thyllis was stopped? There must be many men in Hamal who wished to check the empress and could not. And I had said—or implied—that I worked secretly for Thyllis. Tyfar's father opposed Thyllis—again in secret. Yes, thin ice, damned thin ice...

"The empress is like a dark center of contagion," said Jaezila. I looked at her sharply. Tyfar's face remained wooden. I guessed they had talked long and deeply on this. Now, how was I supposed to react?

"I once said that revolution might not be the way. I once said—"

"Yes, Jak the Sturr?"

"I do not like wars and killing and all the horrors they bring in train. If they could be halted... " I paused. "If they could, the world would smile again."

"But Thyllis is strong. My father extends feelers, but he must move cautiously." Tyfar looked at me and his brows drew down. "We are blade comrades, Jak. Yet you work for the empress, personally—"

"We are blade comrades. You are aware that my opinion of your father is that he is a great man. I would like—" Again I paused. "Prince Nedfar is a man among men." Was the idea so ridiculous, so impossible? Would it be beyond the bounds of reason to imagine the Empress Thyllis deposed and Prince Nedfar installed as king and emperor? The war would end then, instantly. Vallia and Hamal could shake the right hand of friendship and turn to the more pressing problems of the reivers from over the curve of the world, the dark cloud of horror that threatened all these bright lands of Paz on this side of Kregen.

I harbored the suspicion that Tyfar's sense of honor would prevent him from raising his hand against his empress.

Feeling cautious, I said, "It is said in many of the old writings that a man's allegiance to his country must outweigh any friendship for an individual." Tyfar remained unresponsive. "Other wise men say that friendship overrides all other considerations. Does loyalty without friendship constitute reason enough?"

"Loyalty—" Tyfar would have gone on, but Jaezila burst out passionately: "I hate this stupid war. Thyllis should have had her backside slapped when she was younger, been made to realize a few things."

"Now, Zila..." Tyfar was not so much outraged as amused. I perked up. For a high and mighty prince of Hamal that was a good sign. And Tyfar was no high and mighty prince in that petty and world-weary way; he was alive and eager and filled with the conviction that, as the gods had seen fit to make him a prince, he was obliged to honor that position of trust.

We had talked up the east boulevard heading west, toward the somber bulk of the Arena. The outer courts of the Jikhorkdun would at this hour still be crammed with throngs seeking a continuation of the thrills of blood and death, catching a glimpse of their favorite kaidur, seeing an animal trainer, doing business with a slaver, organizing the eternal wagers, perhaps taking up swords and venturing into small practice rings to pit strength and skill against professionals.

Now shouts lifted at our backs and we turned about, wary and alert to possible danger. It was just a miserable coffle of arena fodder, being prodded along toward their destinies.

"Klactoils," said Tyfar. His face expressed a distaste I knew to be for the institution of the Arena and which people who did not know him and reacted as the common run of folk react would have taken for disgust at these chalk-white Klactoils. A strange kind of diff, the Klactoil, parchment white, only around three feet tall, with a thick ridged array of spines down the backbone and a walloping great tail that could take your ankles off. There is a fishy look to a Klactoil's face quite different from most of the faces of Paz. They keep themselves to themselves in out-of-the-way places, ruins like the Lily City Klana were infested with them. It was said—and at the time I was not aware any more than anyone else of the truth of the saying—that they were either a decadent remnant of a marooned band of marauding Shanks from over the curve of the world or else and more darkly a product of miscegenation of Shanks and some doomed race now long extinct.

Whatever the truth of that, these Klactoils were whipped and prodded along the boulevard headed for the Arena. The guards did not spare their whips. Most of the time I noticed that the lashes fell relatively harmlessly across that barrier ridge of spines along the diffs' backbones.

"Let the bosks at them!" a fat man declaimed, licking his lips. "That'll be rare sport!" He watched, safely away from them.

"No," disagreed his companion, nudging him. "Let the chavonths chew them up."

"If you ask me—" said a thin woman with a down-drawn mouth, one or other of the men being unfortunate enough to claim her for wife. "If you ask me, they should be tied two and two, and then tied two and two, until there is only one left."

"Yes?"

"Then let your bosks or your chavonths at him."

Jaezila made a disgusted sound, and we walked on. No, the institution of the Jikhorkdun in Huringa, the capital of Hyrklana, was not a pretty affair at all.

Of course, it was not beyond the bounds of possibility that one of those Klactoils might succeed in the Arena, might win his victories, advancing from coy to apprentice, to kaidur, and then, if the gods smiled on him and he trusted in Beng Thrax, he might become a hyr-kaidur. Then his fortune would be made. Of the fifty or so I did not think more than one percent would do that; which meant not one would succeed in the Jikhorkdun. The opposition would be just too fierce, from savage animals and giant beasts to extraordinary proficient and cunning kaidurs who'd have their tripes out as they stood on the silver sand gawping at the crowds and the color and the noise and the whole impressive and diabolical display.

The life of a hyr-kaidur could be alluring. I knew that. Once you had made your mark, achieved your victories, stayed alive, you were a man set apart. The life could suck you in and overwhelm you with sensory impressions, with the fierce surge of combat, with the ferocious partisanship and courage that sought victory for your color. The Mystique of the Arena might possibly transcend areas amenable to reasonable analysis; it existed. I had been a hyr-kaidur in Huringa at a time that, with the stink of the place in my nostrils, did not seem at all long ago... Yes, the Jikhorkdun possessed its aura, and between harshly defined limits the Arena did have a genuine feeling, a sense of passion in victory, an involvement with means which, in themselves, created a mystery above reason, even if the ends were despicable to me. I wanted nothing more of the Jikhorkdun, where I had been known as Drak the Sword.

Jaezila threw down the remnants of the shonage. "All the same," she said in her bright, no-nonsense voice, "the Jikhorkdun in Ruathytu is far more bloody than the one here in Huringa."

Tyfar hunched a shoulder. "True."

Ruathytu, the capital city of the Empire of Hamal, was well-known to me. I had visited the arena there, unwillingly.

"We were interrupted at table," I said. "Let us find a fresh bottle."

"And we can talk more about this Vad Noran. You know him well?"

"No, Jaezila. Only to sell wild beasts to." I laughed, shaking off the dark mood. "Oh, and to provide him with a vicarious Jikai." We jested, between ourselves, in an easy companionable way, and made light of ponderous matters. But the ponderous matters pressed in hard.

We found a small tavern that was not too congested and a bottle of red Corandian, very low in alcoholic content, and split it between us. "And did you see this mysterious swordsman, this Gochert with one eye and the other all covered with crusted diamonds and emeralds?" Jaezila lifted her glass and before she drank, added, "I am intrigued how a one-eyed man can be so sure with a blade."

"As to his prowess as a bladesman, that I cannot say," I said. "But, yes, I did see him. He moved with a deliberateness, rather like a stalking leem, very quiet and smooth. He wore good blades. He dressed austerely. And he was thin, by Krun! At the time I remember I thought he looked like a starving ferret."

Jaezila laughed. Tyfar nodded. "Such men are quick with a blade."

"I'll tell you one thing. He gave Vad Noran the Jikai* for the fight with the schrepims. But I don't think he could believe Noran had really done what was claimed. He looked at me with his one eye, very fishy."

"A Klactoil eye!"

"Precisely."

"But he was apim, like us?"

"Assuredly. What do you know of him? For I confess, he intrigues me."

"I know little and that little bodes ill for Hamal." Tyfar lifted the bottle, which was empty, and signaled the serving girl, who was a Gonell slave with silver hair wound around her body three times. The fresh bottle opened, Tyfar said, "My people here keep their eyes and ears open. They tell me this Gochert is a part of a conspiracy against Hamal."

This sounded promising. Maybe Gochert had been too harshly judged. Anyone willing to strike a blow against Hamal would, in Vallia's present circumstances, be regarded as an ally. And then Jaezila put the question that was crucial for any decision.

"Against Hamal, Ty? Or against the empress?"

"That, by Krun, I do not know. My people have done well to discover what they have. There was a spymaster here in Huringa I could have called on for assistance. Unfortunately, he disappeared before we arrived. Our ambassador here is jolly and fat and sweaty, as you know, Zila, and more than a bit of a ninny."

"Well," I said, putting the boot in, "the empress chose him."

---

* Jikai: A word of complex meaning. Used in different forms means: "Kill!" "Attack to the death!" "A warrior." "A noble feat of arms." "Bravo!" and many related concepts to do with honor and pride and warrior status. A.B.A.

"For a purpose, Jak. The Hyrklese hate us. Fat jolly Homan ham Ambath is a man difficult to detest. I think in this Thyllis chose wisely."

So that chopped me down to size. But Tyfar was right. Thyllis might be mad and bad; she was also shrewd and cunning and utterly ruthless, and therefore uncaring of ways and means just so long as the ends were her ends. And then Prince Tyfar said something that made me hold my glass motionless at my mouth just a little too long.

"It would solve many of our problems if only Hyrklana were a part of the Empire of Hamal."

Oh, no, my bonny prince, I said to myself, in that, my blade comrade, you are totally misguided.

Three

Unmok and I Agree to Quarrel

"Wriggled like a beetle stuck through with a pin, did he?" Unmok spoke with great satisfaction. He was not a bloodthirsty man, as I well knew, and he'd always avoid a fight and pay someone else to take the knocks if he could. If he had to fight, then he would take his part bravely. "Serve him good. Although, to be sure, Jak, I didn't know you had friends in Huringa."

"The capital is big enough to take in all kinds."

"I didn't mean that! And you know it, you hairy apim!"

"Well, that fellow may be gone. I wish we knew if Noran intends to send anyone else after us."

We sat at the table in our camp with Froshak the Shine, Unmok's big Fristle assistant, and now Froshak, who spoke so seldom as to be regarded as Froshak the Silent, leaned forward and spoke.

"We ought to slit Noran's throat."

"Ah—yes..." said Unmok. "But—"

The tame slaves set up a caterwauling by their fire, and Froshak turned his fierce bewhiskered cat face toward them, whereat they became silent on a sudden. A useful man with a knife, this Froshak, silent and swift and devoted to Unmok and bearing me no malice that I was the partner merely because of gold. Well, not merely. I was, after all, a working partner in the wild-beast business.

"I had some news that ought to get us out of this pickle," said Unmok, scooping up the last of his vosk rashers. The fat shone on his lips. The suns were up, shedding their mingled ruby and jade lights, and the morning air smelled sweet with the fragrances of the countryside—ah! A dawn on Kregen, that marvelous and mysterious world four hundred light-years from Earth, is like no dawn on any other planet of the universe.

"News?"

"I saw Avec, and the cage voller will take time. It seems all the shipyards are building as fast as they can for Hamal."

"That is to be expected. A second-hand voller?"

Unmok wiped bread around his plate. "Difficult. But Avec is putting out inquiries. However, I heard—and this is in the strictest confidence—that Noran is mixed up in some plot against Queen Fahia. If he is, then his head will come off and we'll hear no more of him. So—don't worry!"

"If Avec Parlin knows and told you, then with all due respect, Unmok, the news is general. I mean—"

"I agree, Jak. If they are conspirators, then they conspire damned foolishly."

"So Vad Noran's head—"

"Will come off in the jaws of a leem in the Jikhorkdun!"

"Or she'll toss him to her pet neemus."

"But in the matter of my agreeing with your conclusions that the news is general—no. No, I do not think so."

"Oh?"

"Avec is a good friend as well as a banker. He was approached to contribute financial assistance and refused, having a regard for his own head and no liking for the idea of walking out over the silver sand. He is safe, he assures me, for he holds papers against Noran and Dorval and others of that ilk. He knew I had done business with Noran and so he warned me in friendship. I agree the conspirators are foolish. I do not think that news is general knowledge."

"For your sake, I hope not—"

"My sake, Jak! Have I not just explained—?"

"Noran strikes me as a weak man who vents his pettiness in vicious attacks against those weaker than himself. If Avec dies, the papers may burn."

"Not Avec Parlin. He is too shrewd for that." But I could see the notion did not please Unmok. He twitched his middle left stump and threw his plate at the slaves with his middle right, at the same time picking his teeth with his upper right. His upper left brushed worriedly over his forehead where the lines stood deeply incised.

"Slit his throat," said Froshak the Shine.

This Froshak had been about to be put to the question, up at Vad Noran's villa, when the schrepims escaped. I'd thrown him my knife and helped him escape, and in the subsequent action he had been exculpated

186

of the crime of freeing the schrepims. I viewed him with favor, for we had fought shoulder-to-shoulder, and I think—I hope—that he bore me a certain fellow-feeling.

Where your normal camp boss might have stood up and said something like, "Well, time to be up and doing," Froshak the Shine just stood up and got on with it. The cages stood about, empty. Our mercenary guards had been discharged and the few tame slaves, who had been with Unmok some time, had little to do. The institution of slavery is abhorrent to me, but in this instance of Unmok and his tame slaves, a relationship had developed that, while still unpleasant, is perhaps less of a blot on humanity than slavery as a whole. Certainly, this kind of valued family-retainer kind of slavery is often trumpeted in extenuation of the whole vile business. As far as my friends and I in Vallia were concerned, it wouldn't wash. Slavery was going to be eradicated."

And there spoke the great idealist with stars in his eyes and blood on his hands and mud on his boots, by Vox!

A pottery dish of palines afforded Unmok the chance to remain seated, looking at me. He popped a paline into his mouth and chewed. I followed his example, savoring the taste. Chewing, he said, "I spent some time thinking over what passed when we first went to see Noran and sold him the thomplods. I think he believes you are employed in some secret capacity by Queen Fahia."

"I gave him that impression. It helped the bargaining."

"It did that all right. But Jak, if he is plotting against the queen then he will regard you even more as an enemy to be put down."

"You could have the right of it, Unmok! It could be that is why he sent those assassins, and not to silence our mouths about his vain claim to the Jikai!"

Solemnly, Unmok chewed and nodded.

"Then until this matter is settled, you and I must part company. He has no quarrel with you."

"If you think, you hairy apim, that I will—"

"I know. I had promised to introduce you to my friends this afternoon. But now, I think..."

Saying good-bye to Tyfar and Jaezila had been pushed from my head by what they had said. Huringa seethed with plots and moils, and now Unmok was telling me of another. If fat Queen Fahia could be brought down and I could play a part in that, then this was where I belonged. Vallia was in good hands, as I kept on telling myself, fretting that I was not there. Tyfar was expecting news this day, and from what he said the news might give us the chance to join in a plot that was, so Tyfar said, the most promising. The future filled with visions. There was much to be done here. But—

"If word is spread about that you and I have quarreled, and I have left the partnership, Noran should not trouble you further."

Unmok stared at me in comical dismay.

"You—you—if only we had that damned cage voller!"

"You have all your equipment, the cages and the draught animals and the beast handlers. Froshak is a good man. You can start a fresh trip right away. Or," I said, jocularly scathing at his funny ways, "you could take up the latest scheme you have to change your profession."

"Jak! You wound me!"

"I intended to."

"Well, you won't break the partnership like that."

"You are always talking about giving up the wild-beast business and going in for a new line. Or an old one. They are never the same two sennights running. Now is your chance."

He clamped down on a handful of palines, the rich juice spurting, and he glared at me in his funny Och way.

I sighed.

"Look, Unmok... It makes sense."

Suddenly he brightened. He swallowed. He jiggled with excited realization. "I have it! We spread the story of this quarrel and our parting. I take the cages back to the coast and there you join me and we sail off together! Capital! Capital!"

The immediate thought that shot into my head was vile. I couldn't do that to Unmok, could I? But, a little Och and a partnership, against the fate of empire? Could I?

I stood up. Emperors have to make decisions all the time, right or wrong, it is part of the job. Given the importance in material terms of the two conflicting courses open to me, I knew I was choosing the right one. In almost any other terms I chose wrong.

"A good idea, Unmok. I'll draw Noran off. He ought not to molest you and you can get the caravan down to the river and hire craft to take us to the coast. I'll meet you on the waterfront. And you mind you take care. Froshak—"

"It is in my mind to hire guards now. The caravan will be empty, worth nothing, but a few hired swords will afford a comfort to a five-limbed Och."

"Yes. I won't pick you up at Ingadot where you contract for the ship but at the mouth of the river. They always take on water last thing. It will be safer. And Unmok, watch out for the Forest of the Departed."

"I will. But it is caravans coming the other way that interest the bandits."

"And because of that, if you hire swords, keep them out of sight. They will make the bandits think you conceal wealth in what appears to be an empty caravan. Yes?"

"You are a good partner, Jak."

"Unless," I said, continuing the thought, "being a little five-limbed Och, you hire so many guards they would frighten a queen's regiment of crossbowmen away."

He threw the paline dish at me, whereat I felt the enormity of my underhanded treatment of him, for, of course, I had no intention whatsoever of meeting him where the ships took on water.

Unmok remained very cheerful as we said the remberees. We thought it prudent to begin the deception at once; thus, when we went down into the city we went separately. Froshak the Shine was apprised of the plan, and he said, in his usual way, nothing. I left the camp which had been moved away by the officials from the transit area. Once a caravan discharged its cargo it must make way for a new. We were a thousand paces or so up the road, sheltered in a nice little nook between fragrant clarsian bushes and the next nearest camp a good five hundred paces off. A stream ran paralleling the road here. I looked back as I crossed the rustic wooden bridge, looking at the row of cages, the tethered draught animals, seeing the huge, patient old quoffas with their wise enormous faces, seeing the thin stream of smoke from the campfire, and Froshak busily polishing up a krahnik harness brass. Well, I was saying good-bye to all that, and damned unhappy about the way of saying it.

I nudged the urvivel between my knees and he clip-clopped on across the bridge. Unmok and I had decided not to buy expensive zorcas as mounts, and I'd left him the freymuls. So astride an urvivel I rode along the road toward Huringa. We'd felt that the preysany was, just a little, not up to the impression we'd wished to create as businessmen. Kregen teems with splendid animals of all kinds, and all kinds are used, by Vox, for riding, flying, hunting and sport. For work the choice is just as vast.

My head was filled with jangling thoughts as I rode along, grandiose schemes to topple Queen Fahia and encourage the island realm of Hyrklana to resist the Empire of Hamal. Hamal's iron laws held sway over many lands, but by that token, resistance must exist. We in Vallia resisted, stubbornly and savagely. If Hyrklana could be coaxed into defying Hamal, one course of supply of the vital airboats would be cut off. If, then, Hyrklana would sell her vollers to Vallia...! That was an old dream. I knew my people in Vallia had tried to do business with Hyrklana, but the threat of Hamal had brutally snuffed out all hopes of that.

The rounded hill which obscured sight of Huringa from the transit camp unrolled its dusty road and gradually the city came into view. The fires were out. Queen Fahia had been extremely wroth at the two sorcerers, Unmok had learned, and had they been persons of ordinary quality who had become such wanton incendiaries, they would have been roasted alive. As it was, they had been asked to leave the city. The glittering, imposing figure of the Sorcerer of the Cult of Almuensis, high-powered and haughty in his book-magics, had been indisputably humbled, so the story going the rounds said. The Adept of the Doxology of San Destinakon, by contrast, had been scornful, uncaring of the destruction, threatening retribution against the Almuensian, and of being told that the queen's court wizards would have to intervene if he did not obey. Fahia had gone in for sorcerers of late.

The urvivel was a good strong beast, brownish with yellow splotches and pricked ears, and he was called Snowdrop—why, I do not know. His saddle was cheap and a trifle uncomfortable and my gear in saddlebags and knap-sacks dangled alarmingly between his legs. As for weapons for what might befall me, I had the rapier and main gauche, still unfamiliar weapons in Hyrklana, and a Havilfarese thraxter, a good stout cut and thruster that had seen useful service. Froshak had returned my sailor knife. The small wardrobe Unmok had provided had, in the nature of things, expanded, but I took only a few clothes. I had the feeling that I would be involved in more than a little hop, skip and jumping and wanted to be encumbered as little as possible. On Earth there used to be a saying: "Clothes maketh the man." On Kregen you would be fully entitled to imagine that the equiva-lent saying might be: "Weapons maketh the man." But Kregans are more subtle than that. They are aware that clothes can make a man look what he is not but weapons speak a truer tale when it comes to the test.

These jangling thoughts of mine veered away from clothes and weap-ons and sorcerers. The concerns over my country of Vallia never lay very far below the surface. If only...! If only all this grouping of islands and con-tinents called Paz could join together in friendship, then the menace of the Shanks from over the rim of the world could be met and fronted as a union. But the Empire of Hamal sought personal aggrandizement, and many other lands were at each other's throats. Hamal had to be dealt with first. And very first of all, Vallia had to be made safe.

My son Drak, my eldest, stern and serious, could run the empire; I knew that, his mother knew that, he knew that. But he stubbornly insisted he would not take over while Delia and I lived. Well, I'd as pig-headedly made up my mind that I would renounce the throne and crown and hand it all over to Drak when Vallia was once again in a fit state. That was settled, at least in my mind. My middle son, Zeg, was now king in Zandikar, miles and miles away in the Eye of the World. And my youngest son, that right tearaway Jaidur, was Opaz knew where, gallivanting around at the behest of his mother and the Sisters of the Rose. That secret organization of women ran far more damned things than many a mere male would credit.

The Sisters of the Rose had educated the three twin sisters of those three strapping sons of mine. Zeg's twin, Velia, had died away there in the Eye of the World, and her husband too, Gafard, the King's Striker, Sea Zhantil. The black agony tortured me still, whenever my thoughts turned toward them.

As for Dayra, Jaidur's twin, I fancied the problems she presented would solve themselves in time. She was called Ros the Claw, as she wore a razored steel claw on her left hand. At Lancival they had taught her how to employ those talons to shocking purpose.

So that left my eldest daughter, Lela, to worry me, for I had not seen her for long and long. Zair knew where she was now. All I knew was that she was away adventuring for the Sisters of the Rose. Her twin, Drak, had failed to recognize me when we'd met again, and I did not think Lela would know me, as I was confident, to my remorse, I would not recognize her now that she was grown up.

What it is to be a father separated from his children and hurled four hundred light-years across the gulfs between the stars!

People moved along the road toward the city, and I gave them all a wide berth. I was in no mood for idle chatter. Among the farm carts and peddlers and business folk and those pressing forward eagerly for the Games, marched formed bodies of troops returning to barracks after the night's patrolling. No caravans of wild beasts were in sight. The suns of Antares shone, the air smelled sweet, music and laughter sounded all about me and I wore a blackly hating look and down-drawn brows, and, by the disgusting diseased liver and lights of Makki Grodno, I was in a right turmoil.

Unmok the Nets, stump left middle and all, could fend for himself, couldn't he? Of course he could. He had Froshak. He'd done it before we'd met and formed our partnership. And Vallia could fend for herself, couldn't she? Even with the outrages daily committed by reiving mercenaries and slavers? With great-hearted men like Seg and Inch, and Turko and Korero, and all the others, surely my Vallia could be trusted to them?

I hauled on Snowdrop's reins.

By Zair! Was I or was I not the Emperor of Vallia? Well, then, if I was, couldn't I trust my blade comrades there? I knew I could. Each one knew what was at stake. Each one would give his life for me and for each other. I sat humped on Snowdrop's back and twitched the rapier in and out of the scabbard, and scowled. A passing Relt squeaked and stumbled on, his beaked face averted, the features quivering. I must have looked a sight!

"Sink me!" I burst out. And: "By the Black Chunkrah!' And: "By Zim Zair!" How could a little crippled Och beast-handler stand between me and my manifest destiny as an emperor? How?

As I hauled on the reins and swung Snowdrop back the way we had come, I knew how—too damned easily how.

I'd given Unmok my pledge. Even an empire couldn't stand before that, could it? Well, of course it could. My pledge given to a foeman, or under duress, is broken as swiftly as a faulty blade in battle... Even my pledge to a friend, if greater forces supervene, would be broken. Regretfully. But then, I do not pretend to be your gallant gentleman. The only real regret I suffered as I started off back to the camp and Unmok was that I was delaying seeing Delia. But even then, you see, she'd probably be off about some derring-do for the Sisters of the Rose...

As I rode back to the camp quite expecting to see Unmok riding toward me on his way to Huringa to settle accounts and to hire mercenaries, I decided what I would do. It was a simple statement of alternatives, something I had been unable to do before. Unmok could make up his own mind. He could choose to carry on in the beast-handling business. Or he could choose to go to Vallia. I would not have to explain everything, merely indicate that my secret was of sufficient size to encompass his well-being for the future. Unmok and Froshak, both. Yes.

Feeling the weight of indecision sloughing away made me brisk up wonderfully. Shilly-shallying about was a sin to which I owned, and detested, recognizing the symptoms. Now that I'd made up my mind, the world took on brighter colors and the air smelled even sweeter and the laughter and music from the bands of people going toward the city fell on my ears most melodiously.

Even my urvivel, Snowdrop, welcomed this early return and he trotted along cheerfully.

The wooden bridge over the stream clattered a welcome as Snowdrop trotted across. But it was not quite the welcome I expected. One of Unmok's tame slaves lay on his face on the farther bank, with a tall brown-fletched arrow protruding from the middle of his back.

Even as I looked up from the slave's dead body toward the camp past the edge of the bushes, a cacophony of sadistic yells shivered into the air.

Four

Of the Simple Pleasures of Bandits

They'd locked Unmok into one half of an iron-barred cage with a savage beast in the other half and they were having great fun lifting the iron grille separating man and beast and letting it go, and lifting again, and letting go. Great fun.

As the chain rattled up, the wild animal—he was a hexagon-patterned chavonth—leaped slavering for Unmok, and down would come the grille with a crash. The great cat hit the iron bars in a bundle of spitting snarling fur, and a taloned paw raked through trying to reach Unmok. When the chavonth drew off, baffled, the chain would rattle again. His fur in the pattern of gray, blue and black hexagons gleamed in the lights of the suns. His six legs spurted sand as he sprang.

The grille dividing the cage lifted to chest height and as the chavonth leaped the iron clanged down, infuriating the beast even more and arousing it to frustrated frenzy. He was just a killer denied his kill. The men clustered around the cage and roaring their amusement as Unmok jumped in time to the grille were worse than mere killers in the scales of inhumanity. Froshak was tied insensible to another cage. Insensible or dead, I couldn't tell from where I watched from the cover of the bushes. The large area where fur was missing from his face revealing the membrane beneath did not glisten pink. It shone a vivid red. That was why Froshak was called Froshak the Shine.

There were eight or nine men taunting Unmok. I felt myself chill, there in the bushes. Not good enough. In a situation like this, an estimate of numbers was just not good enough. I counted more carefully. Nine. Right. I had no bow so could not fletch a few of them before I charged. Just how long I had before they hauled up the chain for good I didn't know. Judging from previous experience with unpleasant gentry of similar inclinations, they'd carry on the joke—their idea of a jest—for as long as they could. Probably until Unmok passed out.

Froshak presented a problem, but if he remained insensible he ought to be all right.

These men were the usual mix of diff and apim. They were dressed in gaudy finery, with much cheap jewelry and an awesome assortment of weaponry in the Kregan fashion. Their leader wore a bright blue and yellow tunic over a brigandine, and he was exceedingly hairy. He was an angerim and his enormous ears had been cropped. They were mere flat ridges alongside his skull. So I knew who he was from what Unmok had told me.

This Maglo the Ears preyed on honest traders. He took the wild beasts from their caravans and sold them in Huringa as his own. No one had caught him. He had a finite way with him. Also, I did not doubt that as he could sell at a hundred percent profit, he could afford to distribute bribes on a scale lavish beyond the means of traders like Unmok. I frowned. Our cages were empty. So that could only mean that Maglo, coming along toward Huringa with a stolen caravan, had stumbled across Unmok and was dealing in this unholy fashion with a man with whom he'd tangled before. That explained the presence of the chavonth. The grille lifted, higher this time, and Unmok stumbled back to the far side of his cage, and the grille came down only just in time to halt the chavonth in mid leap. The screech of baffled fury spat like the scintillant bolts from the sorcerers' Quern of Gramarye.

"Finish him off!" yelled some of the men.

"Play him longer!" shrilled others.

Maglo the Ears strutted. He wore three swords on his left side, and they jutted up all at different angles. He was a big man, a spitting barbaric angerim, and he gloated in his power.

Working my way around between the clustering clarsian bushes, I momentarily lost sight of the cage. I could still hear the shouts of the men and the spitting fury of the chavonth. When I was positioned directly abaft the cage and cautiously peered out, Maglo was just walking across to the men on the chain. I guessed he meant to pull the chain for the last lethal time himself.

My first leap took me to the cage. The second landed me on the iron bars along the top and I plunged down and sprawled out flat. The door at the front was fastened by an iron staple. The staple came out in a long screech of metal on metal. I hurled the staple full at Maglo. Without pausing to see if it hit him or not, I drew my thraxter and reached down through the bars and hit the chavonth an almighty thwack up the rump.

The beast shrieked and spat and then, in a single sinuous bound, leaped clean through the open door.

The men screamed, and ran, and fell over, and goggled terror. A Rapa's head went one way as a taloned paw swiped, and his body toppled the other. A big Brokelsh stumbled and fanged jaws crunched. Dust smoked into the bright air. The noise racketed among the bushes. Unmok yelled. Froshak dangled in his bonds, and began to stir, lifting his cat's head.

"Stay still, Froshak, as you value your life!"

The Fristle had handled big cats for a long time. He did not move a muscle. Of us all, now, Unmok was in the safest spot.

Being a prudent man despite all seeming to the contrary, I stayed where I was. The chavonth went about his task of destruction with the unleashed fury of a cyclone. Men ran or died. The chavonth was in no mood to settle down with a nice juicy chunk of meat between his paws. Treacherous are chavonths, and this one vented his spleen in awesome fashion.

He vanished up the road after the last of the fleeing men. I hopped off the cage and slashed Froshak's bonds free. Then the chain was lifted and Unmok walked out. He was dazed.

"That Maglo!" We walked across and looked down on the bandit chief—or what was left of him. The chavonth had taken a bite in passing.

"You've one less damned animal bandit to worry about now."

"Aye, Jak. And, but for you..."

"Say nothing—"

Froshak joined in. I said, curtly, "Is there a caravan?"

"Maglo taunted me." Unmok cradled his middle left stump. He'd had a shock. "Down the road a space, out of earshot. He sent my tame slaves there, all except poor Nog who tried to run."

"I saw him. Let us take weapons and pay a call on Maglo's caravan. It will have been thieved by him."

"And we," quoth Froshak, abruptly pleased, "will take it for ourselves."

"Well, now," said Unmok as we stared about. "It won't be as easy as that. But—" He brightened. "May Ochenshum be my witness! We deserve it."

So, making sure none of the bandits still infested the place, and keeping a sharp lookout for the chavonth, we set off.

After the initial shock, these two got over the incident quickly. In one way, that merely reflected the hard knocks of their lives. When Unmok asked me why I'd come back, when we'd concocted a plan, I merely promised to tell him when we'd sorted out the matter in hand. At that point we had to skirt the remains of a Fristle, and so we pressed on with our swords clear of the scabbards.

The late Maglo the Ears had parked his stolen caravan beside the road and the uproar from the animals brought a quick frown to Unmok's face. "They are starving! That bastard Maglo—he kills the caravan owners and steals their wares, and then he does not feed them! Froshak—we'll have to see about this."

"Aye," quoth Froshak. "If there is food here."

If there was not, that would present a poser. The slaves huddled at the side of the road. They'd found shoots in the hedge and were chewing them and spitting green. Froshak roused them and they went off to attend to the animals. There was no sign of any of the bandits or the escaped chavonth.

"He is no longer hungry. He will probably not return."

"If he does, his hunger will be appeased and we can catch him as we would any stray."

Unmok yelled at a slave, a stranger, hurrying past with a bucket and a broom. The slave trotted up, half-bent, cowed, a once burly Brokelsh but now a man much fallen away. He mumbled his jaws and clenched and unclenched his fist on the bucket handle.

"Yes, masters. Ungarvitch the Whip. He was our master. The drikingers killed him. There was much blood."

"So you are a masterless man now, until your late master's creditors sell you."

The slave merely blinked his granulated eyelids and nodded.

I said, "Get Avec to find a good lawyer. You will have a claim on the animals, at the least."

"I will, Jak, I will. And we do, we do. I think I will leave Froshak in charge to get things sorted out. I am for Huringa and Avec and the law. There is gold in this."

I did not smile, but I felt like smiling. Good old Unmok!

"And you, Jak. What is it all about, hey?"

Very carefully, I said, "If there were a certainty that you would be received with great honor in a certain country, where you could take up whatever profession you desired according to your abilities, and Froshak with you, and where your position would bring copious quantities of gold, would you give up the animal-catching business—as you have promised time and again?"

He stared up at me with his quizzical Och face only half-puzzled. If I chose to speak in riddles, he seemed to be saying, that was my business. As for him, he had important affairs to conduct. "Well, Jak, if you will not tell me, I must see Avec and—"

"I am trying to tell you, you five-limbed infuriating Och!"

"For a great hairy apim, you bluster tolerably well."

I had not really regarded Unmok as a blade comrade. But I warmed to him, I warmed to him. A thought occurred to me.

"I suppose you can fly a voller?"

"Naturally."

Well, it wasn't really naturally, but in Vallia it was uncommon among the generality of folk to find airboat pilots. Here in Havilfar piloting was much more common. And I fancied in this I could, as Seg Segutorio would say, take two korfs with a single shaft.

"I am hardly likely to buy a voller I could not test fly myself. Now, if you have enjoyed your jest—"

"I do not jest, Unmok. I give you my word on this. Before I decide what is best to do, we must thrash out the whole business of the partnership—"

"You wish to terminate our agreement?"

"No, by Harg, no!"

"Well?"

"Leave it until the arrangements with Avec are made. But think on my words. It is you who must make up your mind, you and Froshak. Think of what is offered—assuming—assuming—"

"Assuming what?"

"Assuming I live to tell you."

There was no answer Unmok could make to that beyond the conventional one that I should confide my fate into the hands of Ochenshum and Havil the Green—and any other gods who would look kindly upon me.

A hullabaloo broke out with much shouting and cracking of whips, and presently Froshak came up to say the chavonth had been taken and placed back in his cage. We all breathed easier.

Froshak looked tensed up with excitement, and he spoke at a rate that, for him, was loquacious. "Come and have a look at this. It is remarkable. Come and see."

Unmok regarded the big Fristle with his eyebrows drawn down. "Come and look at what? You're being very mysterious."

"Come and look!"

"Do I, Froshak, or do I not, employ you and treat you well and pay you out of all proportion? I do, indeed I do. So no more of this mysterious nonsense. Tell me!"

But Froshak's fierce cat's face wrinkled up, his whiskers quivered, his bald membrane glistened, and he just nodded his head and started off, beckoning to us to follow along the line of cages. Unmok looked helplessly at me, and I set off after Froshak, so Unmok trailed on, loudly lamenting the evil days and the way loyal retainers had fallen away in the duty they owed their kind employers.

Halting before a large cage, Froshak pointed. He had all the air of a proud proprietor showing off his choicest wares.

We looked into the cage.

Well.

Unmok swallowed. He swelled. Tears stood in his eyes.

"Poor Ungarvitch the Whip!" That was his thought. "To have secured such a prize, and then to be killed! How he must have regretted not being able to go into Huringa as he died!"

Froshak beamed, as though the proud proprietor had pleased his clientele. "She is a magnificent churmod, such a churmod as I have never seen before, and I have handled three in my time in the trade."

I looked at Froshak in genuine amusement. This savage and malevolent wild beast had roused him and loosened his tongue. Unmok continued to stare into the cage. He shook his head slowly, and I could see he could hardly credit his good fortune.

"Look at the way she puts her eight legs down, and the size of her, and the talons! She could rip a boloth to shreds! And those jaws—she will fetch a fortune." He glanced up at me. "A word of caution, Jak. Churmods are unpleasant beasts, surly and sadistic and vicious. Never trust one. Never take your eyes off one unless strong bars protect you."

"Aye," amplified Froshak. "Churmods are beasts from the depths of Cottmer's Caverns. Nasty."

"And valuable," I said.

"Queen Fahia. She, alone, must be offered this churmod. To do aught else would be foolish." Unmok waved his stump about, letting the excitement out. This ferocious and malignant wild beast would make a man's fortune. The lawyers Avec Parlin found on our behalf would fight hard for this prize.

The churmod turned her head and stared at us. She did not rise, but her eight sets of claws extended, curved and shining, and she stretched with arrogant laziness. Her hide was all a silky slatey-blue, uniform, without patterning, and she looked like a silent silvery-blue ghost there in the center of the cage.

Her eyes were mere slits of lambent crimson in the blunt head. She looked magnificent and, at the same time, profoundly repellent. She was larger than a well-grown leem; but much as I detest leems I found another altogether more pungent feeling of distaste for this churmod rising in me and, displeased on that account, as though it demeaned my own sense of fair play, I turned away abruptly.

"Yes, Jak," said Froshak in this new loquacious way, "they do work on a fellow. Just watch yourself with her, all the time."

Fascinating though this splendid and vicious wild animal might be, we all felt that repugnance, and soon we moved away and Unmok and Froshak fell into a one-sided conversation about the running of the caravan and camp while Unmok was away in Huringa. He suggested we ride in together, and fake our quarrel there before witnesses. This was agreeable to me. If we could draw off Vad Noran's antipathy from Unmok onto me, that suited me. Unmok, to give him credit, did not see it like that. He saw the practical side of being able to manage our affairs in peace.

We walked down the road toward our camp and this time the swords were safely snugged in their sheaths. As we went I turned for a last look at the menacing slate-blue form with those smoldering crimson eyes.

Five

Valona

"A churmod," said Jaezila. "Your partner will make a packet with him."

"She's a her. And I hope Unmok does. He deserves to."

"Just steer well clear of them, that's all I will say," said Tyfar, and his mouth closed up tightly.

"Agreed. Have you had the news you expected yet?"

"I await the spy—" Here Tyfar looked around quickly. We were not overheard. The twin Suns of Scorpio, Zim and Genodras, flooded down their streaming mingled lights and filled the air with glory. We stood at one of the little open-air bars, a mere hole in a wall with a counter, where refreshing drinks could be had for the price of a copper ob or two. No one else was within earshot, and the crone serving the drinks had gone into the back at the wailing cry of a baby. Tyfar went on: "Just what it is about I am not sure. But fat old Homan ham Ambath won't let me meet the fellow anywhere near the embassy."

"That makes sense," said Jaezila, and she sipped her sazz.

"It is just as well he did not arrange to meet near the Kyro of the Happy Calsany. I do not think we would be welcomed there."

"We are not welcome anywhere in Huringa in Hyrklana," said Jaezila. She drank off her sazz with a defiant gesture.

"And this stupid protocol demands that our comrades Kaldu and Bar-kindrar the Bullet and Nath the Shaft must wait apart from us merely because they are your retainers." I half turned to lean back against the bar and so looked across the suns-drenched square toward another bar in the adjacent building where our three comrades stood, drinking easily, and keeping a watchful eye out. These finicky matters of rank seem to mean—by Krun, do mean—a great deal to most Havilfarese.

As I watched, a slinky sylvie, exhibiting all the flaunted sexuality of the sylvies, undulated up to the bar and engaged the three men in conversation. They did not stop looking out and keeping an eye on us, but they were engrossed with the sylvie, which was natural, given that they were men and she was a sylvie. She wore a dazzling garment of a rich dark blue, slit to the upper thigh, and her gems—imitation, of course—glistened in the light of the suns. She was probably a respectable girl who worked locally, out for a breath of air and a break from routine.

Jaezila drew her brows down. "Many girls say that the sylvies make them feel less than feminine."

"I do not think your Kaldu will—" began Tyfar.

"No. Nor your Nath or Barkindrar. But who could blame them?"

They were laughing together over at the other bar. A file of slaves carrying amphorae wended past, and a totrix clip-clopped six-legged along, his rider slumped in the saddle with his broad-brimmed straw hat pulled over his nose. The day seemed perfectly ordinary.

Tyfar squinted sideways up at the suns. By the position of the red and green suns Kregans can tell the time with wonderful accuracy. "In a few murs he will be here, if he keeps his appointment punctually."

Even as Tyfar spoke, a bent figure in a brown tunic and straw hat walked slowly toward the bar at which we stood. He carried a staff with which he assisted his movements. He looked completely inoffensive. So, naturally, we all became alert.

The sylvie laughed and danced a few steps away, and then walked in that undulating way they have around the corner. The bent figure halted at the bar. "Is the sazz here good?"

"As good as the parclear," said Tyfar.

That, then, was the secret exchange.

"Follow me, horters, hortera. It is not far."

We finished the drinks and walked slowly after the man in the brown tunic. I own I let my hand brush across the hilt of my sword.

There was no doubt that Hamal kept up a secret network of spies in Hyrklana. That was mere common sense. If there were plots against Queen Fahia the Hamalese would demand to know what the plots were and how best they might profit from them. Tyfar, now, might decide to help bring down Fahia, or he might decide it was better for his country for the fat queen to remain in power. Despite my feelings of intense affection for Tyfar and Jaezila, despite that they were blade comrades with whom I had gone through the fire, in these intrigues I would put Vallia first, always providing no harm befell Jaezila or Tyfar.

The opposite side of the small square was occupied by an arcade of shops nearly all selling religious trinkets and votive offerings. The fourth side was dominated by the bulk of a temple to Malab the Kazzin. Part of the side wall had fallen in and workmen had been killed in a second fall during repairs. Blocks of stone and bricks in ungainly heaps filled the side street. No work went forward until the queen's inspectors had surveyed the fabric. Malab is a relatively respectable religious figure. He is often called Malab the Wounded, or Malab the Fount, his believers seeking mercy and wisdom, luck and health in the blood that pours from his wounded head. He is not, of course, Malab the Kazzur, for that means bloody, and Kazzin means bloody, although the two meanings are very different. Our guide led us past the tangles of broken scaffolding and piles of brick. Dust tanged on the tongue. We went in through a low-arched doorway. The interior struck gloomily after the brilliance of the suns.

"Loosen your swords," said Tyfar in a low voice.

He went first, as was his right as a prince, Jaezila followed, and I tagged along at the rear. At that, I kept screwing my head around to inspect the way we had come for hidden assassins.

We climbed wooden stairs that creaked. The dust lay thickly. I could see only one set of footprints in the dust ahead of us, going up. Broken windows allowed light to sift in.

We came out onto a landing and a corridor with doors leading no doubt to the cells of devotees, or the quarters of the acolytes. The whole place lay silent and deserted apart from us intruders and whoever waited for us.

At the far end of the corridor the guide pushed open a door covered in red baize and studded with brass buttons. The door creaked in protest. Light washed out in a fan.

The guide passed through the opening, followed by Tyfar and Jaezila. Both gripped their sword hilts although they had not yet drawn. I paused. A sound wafted ghostlike up from the corridor. I looked back. A glimpse of a fierce Brokelsh face, of intent staring eyes, told me Barkindrar the Bullet led on our comrades to afford us protection. And, I own it, I felt the comfort of that. I went past the red-baize door. I left it open.

A vaulted space lay before us, long and high. The slates had fallen from the roof some twenty paces ahead so that the blaze of suns light fell like a curtain across the chamber. The myriad dancing dust motes within the wall of light, the brightness of that radiance itself, contained in a narrow slot, prevented any clear impression of what lay beyond. The proportions of the room suggested the slates had fallen near the middle and there was at least as much space again beyond. The door slammed at my back.

Whirling around was, as usual in these circumstances, entirely useless. This side of the door was solid iron.

The guide half-turned and beckoned us on.

At once I knew. Jaezila and Tyfar, also, at once saw what that indifference to the closing of the door must mean. The guide, in his turn, realized he had betrayed himself. With a cry he leaped headlong, vanished like a plunging swimmer into the curtain of light. Tyfar ripped out his blade and ran after him with Jaezila at his heels. I followed and my brand was in my fist.

The light dazzled only momentarily, for I had half-closed my eyes against the glare. The space beyond duplicated the first and boxes and bales lay scattered about, with a two-wheeled handcart upended at one side. Tyfar stood peering about, looking this way and that, his sword snouting. Jaezila was nowhere to be seen. A hole in the floor between Tyfar and me puffed a little dust turning and floating and sinking.

"Jaezila!" I yelled.

Tyfar looked at the hole. I saw his face. The shock, the despair and then the anger flooded into that face of his. His rapier shook.

"I heard nothing, Jak! Nothing! She must have—"

"Yes."

I ran to the hole, carefully, for the floorboards might be rotten, and looked down. Only darkness down there. Not a speck of light. Our blade comrade Jaezila had fallen down through a devilish trapdoor in the floor.

Tyfar edged closer. He gathered himself. He was going to throw himself down, without hesitation, gathering himself as a professional diver gathers himself before launching off a high cliff into a narrow slot of rock-infested water.

Before Tyfar took that plunge a figure rose from the cover of an upturned bale at his back. A blade glimmered. The figure screeched wildly and hurtled forward, the sword aimed directly for Tyfar's back.

The trap had been sprung.

I cannot say if I shouted first or jumped first. Everything happened at once.

"Your back, Tyfar!" I leaped.

I leaped. "Your back, Tyfar!"

Whatever the order, Tyfar heard me and rolled away and I landed awkwardly on the edge of the trap and got my rapier up in time to parry that cowardly thrust.

The man was a superb swordsman, that was apparent in the first passage, and he pressed in again hard, silently, swirling his brown cloak with his left hand to dazzle me. I fended him off, feeling for a secure foothold at the trap edge.

"Jak!" Tyfar raged forward.

"Jaezila," I shouted, "go on, go on!"

Tyfar hesitated no longer. Instead of leaping in to fight with me, as he had automatically begun to do, being a blade comrade, he jumped bodily down through the trap. I did not envy him the decision he had had to make, but he had made the right one. When there are three blade comrades and you have to choose which one to stand alongside in a fight to the death, all the gods must needs smile for you to choose right.

A second figure joined in against me, and this was the guide, bent over no longer, but young and lithe and, his staff cast away, boring in with a skillful flourish of a rapier fighter.

Circling, I cleared that dangerous trapdoor. I foined and then a thrust intended to skewer the guts of the first fighter scored all along his arm as he riffled the cloak. He let out a yell and staggered back; in that moment I stepped in and, most unbladesmanlike, hit the guide alongside the jaw with my left fist. He fell down.

"So that is how you damned Hamalese fight!" said a light voice at my side.

I didn't hang around. I leaped away, ducking, and a blow from some solid gleaming object whistled past, missing me by the thickness of a copper ob.

"Gouge the rast's eyes out, Valona!" yelped the man with the gashed arm. He started to come in again, the cloak now wrapped clumsily around wrist and arm to stanch the blood.

The girl who, after her first blow had missed, had sprung back to clear a space between us, lifted her rapier in her right fist. Her left arm was held down behind her back. For a moment we stood, fronting one another.

"I can take care of this Hamalese cramph, Erndor. Get after that corrupt prince! Stick him! He is the man we want."

"Quidang!" said this Erndor. He ran and jumped down through the hole.

I said, "I admire your self-confidence, Valona. You Hyrklese hate Hamalese very deeply—or some of you." I wanted to annoy her. I studied her as she stared in open anger and contempt upon me. She wore a loose blue tunic and her legs were bare. Her legs were very long and lovely. Her brown hair was fastened by a fillet. Her face was regular and beautiful, with widely spaced brown eyes, and the redness of her lips in the radiance from the roof glistened with full passion. Some peculiarity in her face, some characteristic, struck me with a chord of memory. I did not know her, but I felt I ought to know her, although we had never met before now.

"The Hyrklese hate the Hamalese, some of them, as you say, rast. But I am not of Hyrklana."

And she sprang.

As she leaped so she foined with the rapier and then—and then! Her left arm whipped up. Her left hand reached for my face.

Razored steel flashed before my eyes. Her left hand was sheathed in talons, steel tiger-claws that could shred and rip and blind. And I knew she was exceedingly cunning in the use of this metal claw.

Without hesitation I leaped away, jangling the rapiers, and moving off and away from her. I did not wish to kill her. I could not, seeing she was of Vallia, and a sister of the Sisters of the Rose.

"I am not of Hamal," I said. I know I spoke breathily, caught up in the wonder of a girl of the SoR being here, here in the capital of Hyrklana.

"A cowardly lie to save yourself. You are Hamalese and therefore you will die."

"You are wrong on both counts."

I moved away, circling, the rapier up. I was ready for her next spring, rapier and claw working together sweetly, to lunge and to rip.

"Your armies have laid waste to my land and you, at least, will pay the price, here and now. Die, Hamalese!"

The rapier moved with precision, the feint lunge coming in exactly so, and the claw striking across with a glitter of steel. I made no attempt to parry but leaped away.

Again, we fronted each other.

"You are a man. Why do you not stand and fight? Do you fear my claw so much?"

"I am a Vallian—"

"You lie, rast! You lie!"

"I know you are of the Sisters of the Rose—"

"That is easy enough to discern. It is common knowledge, who I must be. Even you cramphs in Hamal have heard of the SoR—to your sorrow!"

This was becoming farcical. Here was this splendid girl trying to send me down to the Ice Floes of Sicce, and her deadly companions were off chasing Tyfar and Jaezila, and who knew how many more of them there were waiting below? I had to settle this, and settle it fast.

"Look, Valona the Claw—"

"That is not my name." But she hesitated.

"Valona, then. Listen, girl. Forget your preconceptions. Yes, the two who came here with me are Hamalese. But I play them, as I must. There is much at stake—you are here, far from Vallia. You must understand that... Perhaps you know of Naghan Vanki?"

"I know the name." Now her rapier lowered.

Naghan Vanki was the chief spymaster of Vallia. I wasn't going to say that, just in case she did not know. If she did not know I did not want her to have that information, and should she know, then Vanki was probably her employer. I knew he had spies in every country of importance to us.

And if she was one of Vanki's people, she would understand what I was talking about.

She swung the razored claw about. "My father has a friend called Naghan Vanki. Not that my father knows much about what I do. But I do not think I believe you. I think you are a damned Hamalese spy who knows more than he should. It is the Ice Floes of Sicce for you, Jak the Hamalese rast!"

She was going to spring in the next instant.

I said, "There is no time to waste any longer on you, young lady. I know that you have been through Lancival..." Lancival was the place where the Sisters of the Rose were trained up to use the claw, those that did so, for not all the girls of the SoR wore the claw. No one would tell me where the place was, would not even tell the Emperor of Vallia. But the name itself, alone, might cause this Valona, who was not Valona the Claw, to stop and think.

The hammering on the door that was subdued red baize with brass studding on one side and solid iron on the other increased. The door shook. It had been designed to keep out thieves from this store chamber, but Barkindrar and Nath and Kaldu would break it down in only heartbeats.

"I have met young ladies who have been trained up at Lancival before. I am honored they count me as a friend. Now do you—"

She had stopped dead when I used the name of Lancival. Now she broke in, roughly, flourishing her claw. "What do you know of Lancival? How could you know...?"

"Because I am what I told you I am! It is in my mind I know your father, for you bring someone to my mind. But there is no time for that now. I give you my most solemn oath, as the Invisible Twins made manifest in the light of Opaz are my judge! I am Vallian and dedicated to the Empress Delia."

"The Empress Delia! You dare use her name—"

"Stand aside from the men who are breaking the door in. For all your claw—and you have no whip? I see not. For all your razor-talons they will eat you up and spit out the pips. Now I am going down to try to stop honest Vallians from murdering those two poor damned Hamalese down there." I couldn't say that I was in agony for the fate of my blade comrades, my friends, Tyfar and Jaezila.

"I cannot believe you! You must give me more proof!"

"No time, no time."

I had worked us around during this conversation so that the open trapdoor lay at my back. I lifted the rapier in salute. She anticipated an attack and came on guard instantly." Then she saw what I purported—too late. She tried to get at me before I retired from the scene. Her exertions during the pseudo-fight had broken the latches of her tunic and as it gaped

I caught the sheen of black leather beneath. A real she-cat, tiger-girl, this Valona!

I could not refrain from calling, "You fight well, by Vox. Take your friend the guide and go, for those men breaking the door down will deal harshly with you. Remberee!"

Then I leaped into the open trapdoor and fell headlong into blackness.

Six

Froshak the Shine

The thump of landing was not overly painful. The place was little more than a closet, dark and dank. I kicked out and a wooden panel nearly broke my toe. The square of light over my head remained clear: I half expected Valona to jump down after me. I kicked again at the next wall, more cautiously. A distant crash from above was followed by voices raised intemperately.

"Where are they?"

"There goes someone—after them!"

"Get on, get on! The prince is in danger!"

I leaned more gently against the third wall and fell all sprawling out into a lighted corridor. I did not want Kaldu and Nath the Shaft and Barkindrar the Bullet with me now. I did not want those three blade comrades, Hamalese, assisting me to slay Vallians.

The panel revolved and shut. I looked up and down and saw a dead man slumped against the wall. He sat with his head on his chest and his arms lax at his sides. He wore inconspicuous clothes. I did not know him. I hoped he was not a Vallian and guessed he was probably the Hamalese spy Tyfar had come here to see. Valona and her merry men had gotten wind of the meeting, had slain the spy and sent their man as a guide to bring us to the trap. Well, the trap had not yet failed. I ran full speed in the direction pointed by the dead man.

I wondered how Erndor, whom Valona had sent off after Tyfar, would fare against that puissant prince of Hamal. The guide must have been shaken into sense by Valona and the pair of them run off to a prepared bolt hole as our three comrades burst in. Now, Erndor is a Valkan name, and I am the Lord of Valka. But, equally, as the Strom of Valka I cannot know the face of every Valkan, as everyone of that superlative island cannot know the face of his strom. The likenesses on coins are not reliable guides to recognition. If Erndor and Tyfar clashed, rapier against axe, it would make a pretty fight, a fight that would chill me to the core. I had to prevent that confrontation if I could.

The corridor ended at a door and I simply bashed it open and roared through. Torches in bracketed sconces lit up an area that curved in a subtle way like a crown rink, so that I guessed I was over the side porch of the great hall of Malab's Temple. Dust choked everywhere. I saw no more bodies, for which I was profoundly grateful.

A distant noise, like a clink of metal against stone, floating from the opposite side made me hare over the shallow dome, kicking dust. By the time I reached the opposite door, passing the ranked cubbyholes stuffed with skulls and skeletons, there was sign of no one. The torches were all burned low, some guttering. No doubt they afforded light to the watch-keepers of the dead. The believers in the power of Malab's Blood wished to remain in his temple when they were dead and not to be buried in the ranked mausoleums of the Forest of the Departed. As for Malab, your ordinary uncouth fellow like myself will quaff a good measure of Malab's Blood, and comment on the quality of the wine. Such is one belief to an unbeliever. As for Malab's Blood itself, as a wine I drink it when there is nothing finer to be had.

Stairs led down beyond the door. They would open up to the little porch that gave ingress to the major porch on this undamaged side of the temple. I rattled down the stairs quickly, but I went silently and my rapier snickered out before me as I went.

No one waited for me at the foot of the stairs.

Another damned door and this time I was out in the street.

The side alley was shadowed in the lights of the suns. I ducked back and went the other way, skirting around behind the pierced traceries, searching the ground floor of the temple. I could see no one, yet there had been that clink of steel on stone.

Back and forth I went, and nothing. Again I climbed, this time creeping out along the crazy half-exposed stairway where the other side wall had fallen away. Nothing. Back again in the vast and shadowed Great Hall of the temple, with all the fine furnishings removed, the idol missing from the alcove above the altar, the floor dusty and slick, I stared about.

Three men advanced toward me in the shadowed light.

I said—very damned quickly!—"It's me. Jak."

Barkindrar's sling stopped its whirling, and Nath's bow lowered.

"You were nearly feathered there, Jak," said Nath.

"After my shot had squashed his brains in," said Barkindrar.

"This is no time for a professional argument." I spoke more sharply than I intended. But I felt the pressures. "Where are Tyfar and Jaezila?"

They did not know.

So, once again, we went through Malab's Temple. Nothing.

At last I said, "Very well. They are not here. They will have escaped. They must have!"

"Of course," said Kaldu in his heavy assertive way. He was Jaezila's personal retainer, a big-boned, powerful man, who wore his brown beard trimmed to a point. He was capable of such anger when aroused in defense of his mistress that he could tear a savage beast in half with his bare hands, or so it was said. "All the same," said Kaldu, looking about. "It is passing strange."

"Deuced strange."

"They could have gone back to the tavern," said Nath. "But it is hardly likely—"

"They would not run off and leave us," said Barkindrar.

That, we all agreed, was most unlikely.

So, once again, we searched.

This time, in that same damned crown rink of a place above the porch, where the moldering bones glinted in the light of guttering torches, we heard a choked cry. Instantly Kaldu was tearing at the nearest heaps of bones, flinging them about in careless savagery. He hauled a pile of skulls away and Tyfar's face showed, the eyes fairly sticking out, the cheeks scarlet, and the gag partly wrenched away from his mouth. He was making the most ferocious sounds beneath the gag.

I stared at him. As they hauled him out I saw he was unharmed, if covered in skeleton dust. I felt such a heart-melting sense of relief I took a deep breath. So that made me say, "Just a moment, before you remove the gag. The prince may do himself an injury if he is allowed to vent his feelings too soon."

Barkindrar and Nath, being Tyfar's men, could hardly let their amusement appear too obvious. Kaldu, feeling with us all the same sense of relief, allowed a smile to cross his savage face.

Then I said, "Now, now Tyfar, my prince, rest easy. We will take the gag off as soon as we may, although the knot is difficult."

I thought Tyfar would explode. His eyes fairly bulged. When we got the gag off he took in a whooping breath, and stood up and flexed his arms, and then—and then he laughed.

"By Krun, Jak! You try a fellow sorely!" He looked about. "Where is Jaezila?"

Kaldu let out a screech and began to hurl the skeletons about in a paroxysm of rage. We joined in, searching among all the old bones, not uncaring that we violated sacred remains, since we were forced by the urgent necessities of the occasion. Jaezila was found, at the far end, piled under bones, bound and gagged. We pulled her out. She looked dazed. After a time we got it all sorted out, or as sorted out as it seemed possible to sort out so improbable a tale.

"All I know," said Jaezila, "is that I fell down a damned great hole and woke up under these skeletons."

"And I was leaped on by a man with a rapier and we were having a great set to, when three others appeared to assist him." Tyfar held his axe. The blade was steel bright. "One of them threw a brick at me." He sounded offended. "I was just about to enjoy showing them how an axeman tackles swordsmen when they ruined it all by throwing the brick. I woke up here, managed to chew or twist some of my gag away and yelled. I heard some fools blundering past three times. Three times. Before they heard me. I think I must still be suffering from concussion. Otherwise I would be extremely wroth with them."

Nath and Barkindrar found it necessary to study the angle of the roof above their heads with great attention.

Not for the first time I reflected that Prince Tyfar had grown in stature over the time of our adventures together. He had always been a man of honor, filled with noble ideas of virtue and right dealing, but now he was more contained, more sure, and where your run-of-the-mill prince would have lambasted into his men for failing to find him sooner, Tyfar could see the jest and relish it for itself. I looked on him with great kindness, and he looked at Jaezila with emotions far beyond kindness. She looked puzzled.

"I fell down the trap—and if it was a trap, why did they not kill us?"

We couldn't fathom out the answer to that.

Refusing to become maudlin over my sentiments for these two, I brisked them up. "We are not dead, thank Krun. Why we were not slain must remain for the moment a mystery. Now we had best go."

"Let us go to The Silver Fluttrell and get cleaned up," said Jaezila. "I feel positively grimy."

We were all smothered in dust and festooned in cobwebs. So off we went to The Silver Fluttrell, the quiet inn where they were waiting rather than avail themselves of the mansion they might have used as emissaries of Hamal. Their ambassador hadn't liked that.

When we were washed and they had changed into clean clothes, although I'd had to make do with giving mine a good brush, we sat in their airy upstairs sitting room, drinking superb Kregan tea, and eating a substantial meal—call it lunch, if you will—and talked the thing through.

"The devil of it is," said Tyfar, "we do not know what the spy was bringing." The man I had seen dead against the wall beyond the trap had been the Hamalese spy.

"And we do not know who killed him. Who it was who tried to trap us." I spoke normally, but the answers to those questions, known to me, must not be revealed to my comrades. Be sure I felt the degradation of this shabby double-dealing. But unless Tyfar and Jaezila ran into danger so great there was nothing else for me to do, I must put the well-being of Vallia first. I felt the coldness. By Zair! But they'd so nearly been killed. Why they hadn't been I had no idea. Certainly Valona had given Erndor sharp enough instructions, exact and explicit. Then why had those men simply chucked a brick at him and tied him up?

Presently I excused myself and said I must be going. If I was to play the spy in Huringa I wanted to settle the business with Unmok and Froshak. As for Vad Noran, I did not think he could have had a hand in the trap sprung in Malab's Temple. And if he had, he'd have killed the lot of us, and giggled in the doing of it.

"When you have finished this business with Unmok," said Jaezila, "then you will join us? Here, I mean."

"Thank you. Yes. And a thought occurs to me. This Vad Noran. I heard that he is involved in a plot against the queen."

They reacted to this very coolly.

"Of course," I went on, "it could be that plots like this are two a penny. There are many who do not like the queen."

"And many who will fight for her, in expectation of reward." Tyfar saw I had been a trifle put out. "But we ought to investigate every story. Suppose my poor dead spy was going to tell us of Noran's plot?"

"Entirely possible. But I hardly think it would be Noran's plot. There are stronger men using him."

"Gochert?" said Jaezila.

"Possibly. He struck me as a man capable of a great deal."

"Well, then," said Tyfar. He looked pleased, and lifted a handful of palines, holding them cupped on his palm so that the yellow berries rolled. "I have a plan of my own, that might serve. Also, it is time we had a plan of our own instead of others."

"Go on, Ty."

"I am here in Huringa to buy vollers. Everyone knows that. Vad Noran expects a visit from me at some time. I think I will pay him that visit and sound him out—"

"Oh—Ty!"

"Steady, steady," I said. I looked at Jaezila and saw she shared my concern. "If you are incautious you might find yourself minus a head, or loosed into the Arena—or thrown to Fahia's pet neemus."

It was very necessary for me to be circumspect. I did not wish to reveal the extent of my knowledge of Huringa, acquired during my previous residence here when I was Drak the Sword, a hyr-kaidur. But if my impetuous comrade was going to thrust his head into a noose, I was bound to loosen the rope, by Krun, yes.

"He would not move against me, surely?"

"Not openly. But he employs assassins, we know that."

"Then that settles it." Tyfar's air of pleasure increased. "If I convince him of our integrity, he will call off the stikitches he has set on you. So that is that."

"I see why he would do that." Jaezila put her head on one side. "But if what we suspect of him is true, he will prove a broken reed in times of trouble."

"I'll—" began Tyfar.

I stood up. "Promise me you will not sound out Noran until we have spoken again."

Jaezila nodded vigorously. "I agree."

Tyfar stared from Jaezila to me and back again. He flipped a paline into the air—and caught it in his other hand. Not for a prince of Hamal the indelicate business of paline popping in these serious circumstances. When he spoke he sounded somber.

"I take your meaning exactly. We are comrades, and we have been through much together. I think we value one another, and I do not intend to belabor the point. But I am a prince and if I see my duty plain I must do that. My duty tells me now that if I am able to get Noran to call his blood-hounds off you, Jak, then that is what I must do. And, betwixt you and me and Beng Dalty, I think he will listen to me."

"Oh, Ty!" exclaimed Jaezila.

"You—" I said. I took a breath.

"There is no more to be said." Tyfar placed a paline into his mouth and chewed. He chewed with great determination.

"All right. Then when you go to see him, I will accompany you—"

"And me!"

"And there is no more to be said on that subject."

Prince Tyfar of Hamal laughed.

When I took my leave of them I sought out their three retainers, who, scrubbed and polished, were stuffing themselves in their quarters at the side of the principal room. I was short and to the point.

"Very well, Jak. It does make sense." And: "Aye. Jak, we will." And; "Good, Jak. We will keep an exceedingly sharp observation."

So, satisfied that Kaldu and Nath and Barkindrar would not allow Tyfar to go wandering off by himself, I went out. If they knew where he was likely to go and he tried to give them the slip, they'd know where to find him. Or so I hoped.

The urvivel took me along to Tazll Kyro where the mercenaries temporarily without employment waited to see what turned up. Not for them the rigorous formality of employment bureaus; they would sit at the tables circling the square or stand at the bars, and they'd drink and ogle the girls and talk and quarrel and there'd be one or two fights per diem. People wishing to hire paktuns would look over these hard-swearing, ruffling, swashbuckling fellows, and take their pick, and haggle over the price. I looked but could see no sign of Unmok, and presently a one-eyed shaven-pated Gon with a kax fashioned from bronze, and two enormous swords, told me that, yes, a little five-limbed Och had been there and hired stupid Bargle the Drop and anxious Nath the Quick and cunning Kardol the Red who was a Khibil and would slit his grandmother's throat for a silver sinver.

I forbore to inquire why Unmok, if he had picked up so unlikely a bunch, had failed to hire this one-eyed Gon. I thanked him civilly and mounted up and clip-clopped back out of Huringa toward our camp. I would have preferred to have caught Unmok before he'd hired his mercenaries, but they could be paid off and no harm done—if Unmok agreed with my scheme.

Now you will have gathered by this time that I regarded Unmok as a very shrewd businessman. When I got back to the camp and saw what these mercenaries Unmok had hired were up to, I began to come to the conclusion that perhaps the one-eyed Gon had been right. They were certainly a pack of idiots.

An enormous spitting splintered the air.

Beside the cage containing the churmod the mercenaries were laughing and catcalling and poking their swords and spears through the bars. They were stirring the slatey-blue animal into a vicious temper. Her crimson eyes were mere slits of smoldering hate.

Jeering and taunting, the mercenaries tickled up the churmod and she slashed spitefully with her front two paws. The talons glinted. She knocked a spear away, the Brokelsh laughed and jabbed it back. When he withdrew, the tip showed a spot of red. The churmod hissed and slashed and the spear shivered in two.

A fire burned nearby with a cauldron bubbling away. One or two slaves stood, agape, transfixed by the behavior of these swaggering bully-boys. I cocked my leg over Snowdrop's back and jumped off.

Froshak the Shine appeared around the cage. He saw what the mercenaries were up to and he ran forward, shouting and waving his arms.

"Idiots!" he yelled. "Haven't you any more sense?"

He pushed the big reddish Khibil, who pushed him back.

"Keep away from her!" shouted Froshak, incensed.

He shoved up before the man, his arms outstretched—both to show he had no weapons and to shepherd them away. They sneered at him, calling that he was a spoilsport.

"Stand back!" shouted Froshak.

I saw it.

"Froshak, jump clear!" I bellowed with all the force of my lungs. "Froshak!"

The churmod's claws raked between the bars and fastened on Froshak's neck. Her other paw slashed around. She held the Fristle's body against

the bars, and her two second front paws menaced us. It was clear that Froshak was dead. He hung with her claws through his neck, and the blood
dripped from what had been his face. Then, holding him against the bars,
the churmod thrust her muzzle as far as she could and began to chew on
him.

The mercenaries stumbled back. They were screaming now.

Attracted by all the din, Unmok appeared. He saw. He did not fall down,
but he shook.

"Froshak!" But he could only whisper.

The horrendous grunts and savage snarlings of the churmod sickened
us. Froshak was being chewed up.

"We can't leave him—"

"Rather him than me!" said the reddish Khibil. He was not so red now.

I walked forward. I said in a voice that made them jump, "You are all
discharged, now, instantly, without pay. Get out of my sight. Get out now.
Or I will surely slay you all."

Then I took no more notice of them.

The fire crackled. I picked up the unburned end of a hefty branch and
swung it about so that the other end flared brightly. Holding the brand
before me, I advanced on the cage. The second pair of forepaws slashed the
air between the bars. It was death to reach out for the dead Fristle.

Savagely, as filled with bestial anger as the churmod herself, I thrust the
brand at her. I dug it in and jerked it back, and it flared and spat sparks
into those lambent crimson slits she had for eyes. She snarled and hissed
and slashed the air before me. I thrust the blazing brand and swung it and
scattered sparks. I reached out with my left hand and a set of talons raked
and I snatched my hand back. Again I thrust the burning branch. This
time I drove it with intent to hit the churmod in the face and force her
back, force her to relinquish her prey.

She flinched.

She snarled a bubble of hatred at me, and she released Froshak. The
dead Fristle fell in a heap. The churmod backed off. She looked at me.
Those twin slits of crimson spurted hellish reflections as though the flames
of the torch were caught and hurled back at me.

I stared malevolently back.

I thrust the fire through the bars, trying to burn her, making her back
off. Then, trembling, I controlled myself. It is often this way with churmods, and was why the mercenaries had taunted her when they would
leave a chavonth or a strigicaw alone. She slunk back, belly low, a smoldering silver-blue ghost of malignant power.

Froshak was carried away, tenderly, and laid on the ground. He looked
dreadful. Unmok stood beside the body of the cat-man he had employed,
and who had remained so silent under Unmok's proprietorial mewlings. I

stood by Unmok. There was nothing of any use or sense we could say to each other.

I looked at the little five-limbed Och.

Tears coursed down Unmok's face, and he dropped to his knees, sobbing.

Seven

Of Letters and Remberees

Froshak the Shine was buried with all respect and reverence in the Forest of the Departed. Unmok lavished his hoarded gold to buy and furnish a tomb that, as he said, was not good enough for his friend. The gold should have been spent on Froshak when he was alive; now that it was too late for that, Unmok would embellish the Fristle's tomb in sumptuous fashion and give his ib surcease in the long journey to his Fristle paradise.

Leaving Unmok for the next few days was quite out of the question. He had shrunk. He looked a small pale ghost of the shrewd, businesslike Unmok I had known.

We went to see Avec Parlin together and Unmok took no joy from the money he received for the safe return of Ungarvitch the Whip's caravan. The animals were sold off in the usual way and, not surprisingly, the chur-mod was reserved for Queen Fahia. Unmok's tame slaves were housed in a cheap lodging, for he would not avail himself of the services of the bagnio. During all this time the suns shone, Zim and Genodras, casting down their mingled ruby and jade, and the seven moons of Kregen rose and set, the stars glittered and the breezes blew and men and women went about their daily lives, and it might all have gone hang for Unmok the Nets.

Nothing would rouse him. Even when Avec Parlin announced that he had heard of a good-quality secondhand cage voller that was not required by Hamal for her Air Service, Unmok merely nodded absently. "That is nice," he said, in his choked whisper.

"And when will you heed her?" Parlin, the lawyer, an apim, treated Unmok with great civility. Had he not done so, I verily think, he would have had the rough side of my tongue, if not worse.

"When? Oh, I do not—I do not know—"

I said, "As soon as the sale is made, Avec, we will need the cage voller. Can you see that she is properly surveyed and then provisioned? You know the gold is available."

He nodded. Then he screwed up his eyes. "Unmok has told me of Vad Noran. You walk perilously, Horter Jak."

"I thank you for your concern. Tell me, does the plot against the queen prosper? Or is it all a phantom, a Drig's Lantern?"

We walked along the north boulevard and the streets were hot under the suns and few people were abroad. The beast roar from the Arena told where the citizens of Huringa were spending the day.

"The plot is real. I will have nothing of it. But as for Vad Noran—he is a man led by the nose."

"And who does the leading? Gochert?"

"Gochert? No." Parlin looked surprised. "My informant says that Gochert warned Noran most seriously. The one-eyed man refused to have anything to do with such a harebrained scheme."

That did not square with the impression I had received, but I let it pass. Gochert struck me as an antagonist worth ten Norans.

"Who, then?"

Parlin hitched up his shoulders and lifted his hands, palms up. "You are abrupt, Horter Jak. Such knowledge could bring a man to the Arena."

With the civility that was not altogether feigned, I said, "I crave your pardon, Horter Parlin, but the matter is of moment, as you understand."

"Assuredly. The fact is, I do not know. I have heard rumors that a great noble presses to take over the throne from Queen Fahia—"

"Someone with a legitimate claim? That would narrow the field."

"When the queen came to the throne she was severe with her family. Many died. Her husband is a nonentity."

I drew in my breath. "There is her twin sister, Princess Lilah."

In the long ago I had saved Princess Lilah of Hyrklana from the Manhounds. She had disappeared and no one I had spoken to had heard of her fate. Could she still be alive, and plotting against her sister? I devoutly hoped so, by Vox!

Again Parlin spread his hands. "It could not be. Princess Lilah disappeared seasons ago. Whoever plots against the queen and employs Noran as his tool is a man in the limelight who wishes to cloak his designs. That seems sure."

At another time and place in the long ago I had, because I was at first bored and then because I saw it was my duty, made myself King of Djanduin. Djanduin lay in the far southwest of the continent of Havilfar. The fearsome four-armed Djangs were among the most superb fighting men of all Kregen. They were fanatically loyal to me, as loyal as the ferocious Clansmen of the Great Plains of Segesthes. I did not toy with the notion that I, Dray Prescot, Krozair of Zy, Lord of Strombor, might make myself King of Hyrklana. I had done with titles. Now I would seek to exert my influence in uniting all of Paz against the Leem-Loving Shanks who raided our coasts, from the shadows and through emperors and kings and queens who saw the true path that the peoples of Paz must follow. Megalomania? If you wish. I did not care about that. All I knew was that if the Star Lords, who could fling me about Kregen on a whim or dispatch me back to Earth out of spite, left me alone to get on with the work which fate or destiny had set to my hands, I would carry on that good work with all the skill and dedication in me.

By Zair! The task was colossal and I a mere mortal man. But I could see no other reason for all the things that had happened to me. Well, as you will hear, I could see only a tithe, and a dark tithe at that, of what destiny had in store for me.

If uniting this great grouping of islands and continents in friendship was a fool's dream, then I was the fool, the onker, I have so many times been dubbed. I did not want a uniform grayness, a drabness. Havilfar was Havilfar, as Segesthes was Segesthes. Loh would remain a mysterious continent. The islands of Pandahem and Vallia would retain their identities. But we would cease from fighting among ourselves. We would turn all our energies toward ridding ourselves of the slavers and the aragorn, slavemasters and scum, and toward freeing ourselves of the grip of the Shanks. If that is idealistic nonsense, so be it.

At the time of which I speak, it was the guiding principle of everything I did and attempted on Kregen. Everything save one thing. And that was the happiness and well-being of Delia, Empress of Vallia. The welfare of Delia, Delia of Delphond, Delia of the Blue Mountains, and of our family and friends, for this I would see the rest go hang.

Such is the crumbling of high-minded principle when personal desires supervene!

As for all this not-really-but-almost nonsense of holding responsibilities in faraway lands by being the king or lord of them, as you will readily perceive, I was usually in constant communication by flier-borne letters and messengers with my folk in Djanduin, in Zenicce, among the Clans of the Great Plains. I knew what went on there, and the men and women charged with running those places to the standards we agreed knew my thoughts and carried out my wishes, as I confirmed my pleasure in their own ambitions and labors. On Kregen, with fliers to whisk you from one end of Paz to another, handling a widely flung empire was not anywhere near the enormously difficult undertaking the Romans had faced, or the Mongols, or Charlemagne. Napoleon would have relished instant news from Spain when he was in Poland—or, given that situation, perhaps not. The point is that although the image does not please me, I was like a spider at the center of a web, and I could feel the vibrations from all sides. Of course, when I went off adventuring, as I loved to do, the situation was more difficult. But now, with Unmok shattered by the death of Froshak, with my decision to send him to Vallia, and with a fine cage-voller to provide transport, I took full advantage of those assets.

A whole day was consumed in writing letters. I sent one of Unmok's slaves with a letter around to The Silver Fluttrell pleading that unexpectedly I had been detained. I would join Tyfar and Jaezila as soon as my duties were honorably discharged. I made no bones about it with Unmok. He continued in his dazed state, and I seriously considered flying with him back to Vallia myself. But that would be ducking what I had to do here in Hyrklana. Lackadaisically he agreed to go. He could hardly take in what I was saying, but I told him to go and see Enevon Ob-Eye. Enevon, as my Chief Stylor, would take care of everything. I fancied Unmok would get on better with him.

"And Unmok, fly directly there and do not land at all. Here is a satchel. Give it to Enevon. And guard it well."

"All right, Jak. But—"

The satchel bulged with a day's letters. Missives to my folk scattered across the breadth of Paz—but no letter addressed to Paline Valley, for that place lay in Hamal.

"Enevon is a good friend. The Lord Farris, too." I handed Unmok a separate, smaller letter folded and securely sealed. "If you cannot find anyone there—then take this letter to the empress or one of her handmaids. Otherwise—burn it!"

"Yes, Jak."

He shook his head. This was beyond him. But he would fly to Vallia in the new voller and there, as I devoutly hoped, he would begin a new life. As for me, I had plots and ploys to work here in Huringa.

As I looked ahead, the future appalled me. There was so much to do. The tasks to which I had set myself were enormous. And yet: "Sink me!" I burst out to myself. "It's got to be done! We have to scupper mad Empress Thyllis and smash Hamal so that we can turn to the more important tasks ahead." I could feel my fingernails gripping into my palms. I forced myself to relax those constricting fists. Hamal under the imperious sway of Thyllis was again growing stronger, and with sorcerous help could smash up Vallia. If Queen Fahia of Huringa was one of the keys to help unlock the torrent of opposition to Hamal, then Queen Fahia would have to turn, like it or not.

Much though I detest fighting and warfare, I admit that the thought of a powerful army from Hyrklana landing on the coast of Hamal and marching inland to Ruathytu filled me with what I see to be an unholy glee.

"You are—feeling all right, Jak?"

"Yes, Unmok. It is you who—" Trust the little Och to see I was burdened with other problems. I still had not told him what he so grandiloquently called "my secret" and he'd find out quite enough when he arrived in Vondium, capital of Vallia.

The cage-voller had been a splendid flyer; she was still sound but worn. The cages gaped emptily. Unmok's slaves would spell him on the flight. "You'll have to manumit your slaves in Vallia. But that will be no hardship."

"Agreed. And you are not coming?" Unmok cradled his middle left stump with his middle right, and wiped his upper left over his forehead. His upper right was extended toward me. "I don't know why I'm going off and leaving you, anyway. What am I doing?" He would have gone on.

There was no time for him to indulge in deep personal philosophy and inquiry. I bundled him aboard, saw that the slaves were all there, stood back, waving.

"Remberee, Unmok the Nets!"

"Remberee, Jak the Shot!"

The cage-voller lifted off, fleeted into the streaming mingled lights of the Suns of Scorpio.

Eight

We Plot Against the Queen

We threw ourselves into the business of plotting against Queen Fahia with tremendous zest.

We did go to see Vad Noran, and Tyfar convinced the nobleman that I was not a queen's man, that I worked for Prince Tyfar of Hamal, and that we ardently wished to assist Vad Noran in any way we could. He preened and primped and, because it was the easiest course, accepted our proposals. Money lay near the heart, of course, but the promise of swords tipped the balance.

No wonder Noran had been flustered when I'd suggested I worked for Queen Fahia! No wonder he'd tried to have me assassinated! Now he was revealed in his true colors, his attitude changed. We were all conspirators together.

I had given Tyfar and Jaezila the impression I worked for their mad Empress Thyllis; at the time the ploy had seemed clever enough and had served, as I judged, to ease my position. Later, when I gauged more accurately Tyfar's own tortured doubts of his empress and the course his country was set on, my own supposed cleverness was revealed as being too damned clever by half. I did not think that Tyfar or Jaezila would swallow any story I might try to sell them, that I had renounced allegiance to

Thyllis, in the same way that Vad Noran had swallowed the story I spun him.

Another side of Noran's character was revealed on the day when Jaezila and I went up to see him at his villa, Tyfar being obliged to inspect the latest progress on the airboats being built at another yard. Dorval, one of Noran's cronies and a man who did not recognize me, called me into the armory where he made a fuss over showing me some brand-new rapiers just arrived from Zenicce. I admired them. I whisked them about, feeling the balance. When, at last, we left the armory, I saw Jaezila marching along the covered gallery toward us. She was pulling her tunic up; its latches were broken. Her color was high, very high.

Going forward, careful not to appear overexcited, I said, "Yes, Jaezila?"

"That man!" Then, seeing Dorval going past toward the door from which Vad Noran was just emerging, Jaezila said, quickly and in a low voice, "Nothing. It is nothing, Jak. For the sake of Tyfar, leave it."

Vad Noran sported the beginnings of a fruity black eye.

Jaezila saw my hand twitch uncontrollably toward my rapier.

"Jak! Nothing happened! For all our sakes—please!"

Noran passed the matter off—something about a door being ajar—and since Tyfar's reactions would be well understood by Jaezila and me if he got into this, I, perforce, acquiesced, and let it lie.

To have made an issue of the incident would have impugned Jaezila's honor. She had requested me to do nothing. There was Tyfar to consider. So, even though it may seem strange conduct for Dray Prescot, nothing was what I did. All the same, Jaezila was relieved to be out of Noran's villa for that day.

"Do take the scowl off your face, Jak! Noran will—"

"Very well."

My old beak-head of a face can assume so ferocious an expression, so I am told, that it will stop a dinosaur in its tracks. So I am told. My comrade, Deb-Lu-Quienyin, who was now one of the two resident Wizards of Loh in Vallia, had given me the secret of altering my facial appearance. I say given and secret. By Vox! It was a most painful experience at first, like having a swarm of bees stinging me. But I had practiced and could now hold a new face for a goodly length of time, so that I could pass unrecognized. So now I assumed a face of docility that was still me, still Dray Prescot, in a mood of sweetness and light. Ha!

"Anyway," said Jaezila, "there is good news. Noran has arranged a meeting for the day after tomorrow. It does really seem as though we are getting somewhere."

Tyfar fired up at the news.

"At last!" Then his expression grew grim. "A new spymaster has been appointed. He flew in from Hamal. It seems that our operations here have been penetrated by those Vallian devils. They were probably responsible for the attack on us in Malab's Temple."

"Then," I said, desperately wanting to keep my Vallians and my Hamalese comrades away from one another's neck, "we had best keep our plotting to ourselves."

"By Krun! Yes!"

The situation in which I found myself was not an impossible one, although near enough to being impossible; it was most certainly a false position. This whole thing could explode around my ears, as the Quern of Gramarye had exploded the Souk of Trifles. I could be left surrounded by blood and dead bodies—and those corpses would be my comrades and my countrymen.

"This new spymaster has other disturbing news."

"Yes?" said Jaezila. She spoke casually. "What does he call himself?"

"Oh, Nath the Eye."

The name Nath on Kregen is like John on Earth. A pseudonym, without doubt. Jaezila nodded and Tyfar went on.

"There is something called Spikatur Hunting Sword."

I held myself still. I listened.

"Nath the Eye knows little. Some Hamalese nobles have been murdered, foully done to death. A man was caught. Under the Question he confessed to this Spikatur Hunting Sword. But he knew little, being a mere villainous hired stikitche, murdering innocent people for pay."

"I dislike assassins," said Jaezila.

"So do I." Tyfar looked angry and ashamed. "Yet, also, I dislike torturing people. Who can say that the answers are true, or shrieked in fear and agony, the poor wight saying anything he is led to say by his interrogators?"

I knew Tyfar well enough by now to know that his dislike of torture was not occasioned merely because the truth might not be extracted. He hated torture for the foul thing it was.

The reason for Prince Tyfar's mission to Hyrklana was to buy vollers and this was no fake assignment, for Hamal desperately needed fliers. Well, so did we all, by Krun. His involvement with the plot to topple the queen was a bonus on that. So, the next day, we went along to the voller yards where a ship had, at last, been completed. She was a fine large craft, with two decks and a high forecastle and poop, equipped with fighting tops and galleries. She could carry two hundred or so aerial soldiers, voswods, as well as her crew. Tyfar beamed on her proudly as the handing-over ceremonies were concluded. She fluttered a myriad flags from her staffs; those flags mocked me with the purple and gold of the Empress Thyllis. Had they been the new Union flag of Vallia, the yellow cross and saltire on the red field, I would have jumped for joy.

"A splendid craft," said Jaezila. She looked up expectantly.

The crew from Hamal who were to fly her back stood in a neat blue line. The shipyard workers, including many slaves, looked more sullen than Tyfar liked. But they could do nothing. Bands played. The breeze blew. All around the yard stood guards. Alongside the landing ramp the solid mass of a formed regiment of men from Hamal obtruded—brutally—the power of that empire here. They were here on the express invitation of Queen Fahia, so it was given out. As always, the swods of the iron legions of Hamal looked splendid, compact, formed and dressed, professionals to a man. They'd have short shrift with any disturbance. And, too, Fahia probably did not realize, these were some of the swords promised by Tyfar to Noran and his principals...

The crew stood in their neat line, but the voller began to lift.

People cried out. They pointed up, yelling. A man fell from the ship, his arms and legs spread-eagled. She rose slowly into the air. I saw Tyfar look aghast, and then furious, and then determined. At his side Jaezila gazed up with a ferocious expression I found difficult to decipher.

"She is being stolen!" Tyfar shouted. "Under our very noses!"

The band stopped playing. More bodies fell from the ship. We could hear the strife of combat aboard her, ringing out along her decks. I stared aloft, controlling myself, quivering with joy. I knew! Those gallant secret spies from Vallia had a hand in this! Perhaps Valona herself was up there, taking this splendid airboat for Vallia!

The ship hovered some fifty feet overhead. "If they don't get away soon," I said, aloud, wrought up, "they never will!"

Patrol vollers were shooting across. Soon the decks of the new ship would fill with fighting men and the handful of secret agents from Vallia would be slain.

"You sound—" said Jaezila.

"They're done for," said the owner of the yard, fat and ubiquitous Kov Naghan na Hanak. He was puffed up and proud with himself. "If a job has to be done, willy-nilly, then do it right, is what I say, by Harg, yes!"

"What, notor, did you do?" I spoke normally.

"Why, stuffed her with guards, hidden. I had an idea something would happen. Look—there they come atumbling down!"

I turned away, feeling sick. Those bodies falling to earth were Vallians—people who had thought to take away a precious airboat from hated Hamal. Now they were flung callously to the ground. The ship began to descend. I hoped, I prayed, that there had been few Vallians aboard. And, a treacherous and demeaning thought, I hoped Valona had not been among them.

Then Prince Tyfar once again proved himself. He looked somber. "It was a foolhardy attempt. A handful of people however brave and cunning, how could they hope to succeed? But I own I am sorry they died. They were a very gallant company."

Jaezila turned away.

Stealing airboats from Hyrklana had become a much more difficult and dangerous pastime than ever it had been, as I had discovered. Now, when—not if, when—I took a flier I would, besides paying the owner for her, concoct a plan that with much forethought and cunning could not fail. Whoever had made this doomed attempt had failed not from want of courage but from lack of planning. My Vallians! Reckless, gallant, and yet shrewd and practical men and women, accustomed to the ways of trade and commerce, they still had not fully realized that when you fight yourself for your country instead of hiring mercenaries, there are many painful and difficult lessons to be learned.

The men of the Hamalian Air Service boarded the ship; the guards positioned by Kov Naghan na Hanak marched out. You couldn't really fault him in that, although a few quiet words in his ear explaining the situation more fully might have helped in skyjacking his newly built flier. That could be a part of this wonderful plan it was necessary to concoct. And, too, the guards of all the voller yards of Huringa would redouble their vigilance now.

The rest of the ceremony went off without a hitch and the ship, flying her new colors, flew off to join the Hamalian Air Service. No doubt she would soon be in action casting down sundry nasties on Hamal's foes—on our allies! I swallowed. The day was coming. It had to be coming. The dignitaries accompanying Prince Tyfar had by now grown more accustomed to his ways, and so were no longer surprised that he withdrew from them, that he put up at The Silver Fluttrell instead of the embassy. We rode back in a silence that lacked some of the old companionableness, and this, without doubt, was caused by the tragic incident we had just witnessed. Tyfar took no real pleasure from dead men, whether or not they were Vallian or any other of his supposed enemies.

The moment we reached the tavern Jaezila excused herself and retired to her room. Tyfar glanced at the wall clepsydra.

"I have just a bur and a half to snatch a meal. Then I must see Orlan Mahmud. He understood that we could not impose on his hospitality for too long. He has a magnificent palace; but we find this tavern comfortable."

"As the queen's chief minister he must keep up appearances."

"You should meet him, Jak. You would like him."

I nodded. This Orlan Mahmud nal Yrmcelt was hardly likely to recognize me. He had seen me seasons ago for a brief space when the Star Lords had sent me to Hyrklana. I had held up a massive slate slab so that the conspirators against the queen, of whom Orlan had been one, could escape. My scarlet breechclout had dropped around my ankles, and I'd been taken up in nets and sent to the Arena. I did not think Orlan would recognize me. Even if he did, he would not want to acknowledge an escapade of his youth before he'd succeeded his father Ord as the queen's Chief Pallan.

A stir at the door of our room heralded the appearance of the landlord and a messenger from Vad Noran. The meeting had been unexpectedly brought forward. We were asked to go up to Noran's villa right away. Tyfar made a face.

"I must see Orlan Mahmud. You go on, Jak, and I will join you as soon as I am able. Jaezila must rest."

"Very well. I just hope it is good news."

"Things are moving, Jak. Things are going to go our way!"

"I'm sure you're right."

On the way up to Noran's villa I passed a gawping mob at a street corner. Riding Snowdrop gave me, even with an urvivel's lack of height compared to a zorca's, a vantage point. The crowd surrounded a sorcerer. He was going through his repertoire of tricks and surprises. He was a sorcerer and not a magician, as a single glance confirmed. His gown was liberally splattered with mystic symbols, and what he was doing was beyond mere magic tricks. I rode on. I had no idea of the man's discipline or what society of the many societies of sorcerers there are on Kregen he belonged to. Although it may sound unlikely to say a sorcerer was down on his luck, occasionally they, like any mortal, go through bad patches. Deb-Lu-Quienyin had been very down when we'd gone adventuring together. As a Wizard of Loh, among the most respected of all Kregan thaumaturges, he had bounced back and was now resident in Vallia. But the item that caused me most concern in this trifling encounter with a sorcerer on a street corner was its reminder that Queen Fahia now openly trafficked with wizards of all kinds. When we went up against her, we must be wary of occult powers arrayed against us.

In Noran's courtyard, the duty slaves closing the gates after me under the intolerant scrutiny of the gatekeepers, I walked across to the fountain. The Och crone gave me a cup of water and my ob vanished in its usual miraculous fashion. Noran had hired himself a new cadade to replace the old chief of his guards, but the new man, a Chulik, was not to be seen. I left Snowdrop in the charge of hostlers and went through with an underchamberlain to escort me. Cool shadows dropped down from the columns and arches. The streaming light of the suns lay across the stone flags. I followed the underchamberlain across one anteroom and we passed through double folding doors into a reception room.

The men, gathered into a group talking easily among themselves, swung around as I entered. I was aware of much finery, much gold and silver lace, a multitude of feathers, glittering jewelry.

A voice lifted, a strong lion-voice.

"Jak the Sturr! A spy! This man is a spy! Seize him!"

The group of men obeyed instantly. As one they unsheathed their swords and rushed upon me. There was no time to think, no time to cry out that

I was not a spy, for they would not have believed me. There was time only to rip out my thraxter and parry the first fierce blows.

The fashion in which the order had been obeyed made me realize that these men were disciplined, and now they tried to seize me as ordered and not kill me. So I did not make any attempt to slay them but beat away their weapons and sought a means of escape. The swords rang. The lion-man stepped to one side, reaching for a polearm leaning against the wall. I recognized the halberd as I recognized the lion-man, for this numim was Naghan the Doorn, whom I had last seen deep underground when we struggled through that subterranean vault of horror called the Moder. I shouted.

"Naghan the Doorn! I am no spy! I am here by invitation of Vad Noran. Call your men off before blood is spilled."

The swords flickered and flashed before my eyes. I leaped and swatted the blades away and circled back toward the door.

Footsteps sounded at my back.

There was no need to think. Instantly I leaped to the side and whirled, blade up. Two or three of the fine fancy young men rushed after me, and I was forced to thump a couple with the hilt. As they collapsed I saw that Vad Noran had entered the room, and with him, Ariane nal Amklana. I found no surprise she should be here, for the numim with the halberd, Naghan the Doorn, was her chief retainer. Ariane had not, when all was said and done, come out too well from the adventure down the Moder. Her yellow hair, secured by a jeweled band, fell to her shoulders, and her high-colored face turned toward me. She moved with all the old imperiousness. Her white gown did not fall sheer to her ankles but was cinctured by a broad golden belt. From the belt swung a thraxter in a jeweled scabbard. Even as I ducked a wild blow and so thunked the last one of that three and spun about to face any fresh attack, I reflected that the lady Ariane felt that to bear her part as a conspirator she must wear a sword. That was like her. Her gray-green eyes stared into mine for a heartbeat as I leaped away from the expected attack.

"My lady!" I shouted, in almost a yodel. "Call off your hound dogs before they are hurt."

Noran was fussing and throwing up his hands and exclaiming.

"Stop, stop!" he shouted. "What is all this trouble in my house?"

"Ask Naghan and his lady, notor," I yelled, skipping away and flailing a convoy of swords from my shins. Now that it was going to be all right, I could allow the stupid feelings of the ludicrousness of the situation full flower.

"Jak the Sturr!"

"Aye, my lady—Lahal. Now call your men off or I will strive in real earnest."

She had seen something of our fighting down in the Moder where we sought treasures and magics among monsters. She gave the order in her high hectoring tones, and the men fell back. I shook my arms and thrust the thraxter back into the scabbard.

"Lahal, Jak the Sturr. And you are one of us now?"

"Aye, my lady. As Vad Noran is my witness."

"It is true, my lady," babbled Noran. A single glance told me his sorry story and the state he was in. He was besotted with the lady Ariane, who as a kovneva, so I had been told, outranked him. If he could marry her and lay his hands on the estates and the money, he might aspire to rise a step and become a kov himself. "Jak is a valued associate of the prince."

"I never thought to see you alive again. You or the prince." She wrinkled up her pretty nose. "You must tell me how you escaped. We had a most dreadful time."

I forbore to mention the manner of her leaving us. I said, "The prince has been unavoidably detained. He will be here as soon as he possibly can."

At this Ariane pouted. It was clear she detested having her wishes flouted in the slightest particular.

Avec Parlin had been right. There was a powerful noble in the shadows masterminding the conspiracy and using Vad Noran, but it was not a man, it was a woman.

Much of the mystery surrounding this Ariane nal Amklana had been cleared up by this meeting. She had ventured down into the terrors of the Moder in order to secure some thaumaturgical advantage, and it was easy to guess why. If she was determined to overthrow Queen Fahia and take her place, she would need occult assistance to combat the queen's new sorcerers. And Noran would be her willing tool. As the men I had knocked down stood up, shaking their heads and looking miserable, Noran and Ariane moved on, just like a regal couple at a levee. Their words to each other confirmed my diagnosis of the situation. Ariane had Noran firmly wrapped around her little finger, wrapped and knotted tight.

Naghan the Doorn, stroking his whiskers, came over. The numim looked me up and down.

"You were nearly—" he began.

I said, "You are zealous for the welfare of your mistress. Just remember, I'm on your side."

Then he said something that, although it should not have surprised me, did so.

"When we left you and those others, down there in that underground hellhole, I was not—was not pleased. I am glad to see you escaped." He fidgeted with the halberd. "And the others? How did they fare? Did you all escape?"

"Yes, thank Huvon the Lightning. But it was a bonny time."

"I can imagine."

We talked for a space, and the men from Amklana went back to talking among themselves, and presently Prince Tyfar was announced. I wondered if all this open naming of names was the right way for conspirators to carry on. Certainly, other folk I'd tangled with had used cover names, and carried on deception as a mere simple precaution for survival. The answer—and at the same time as I delighted in it I felt the chill—must be that Ariane was supremely confident that whatever spell it was she had obtained would smooth her path over all difficulties.

During that meeting we began to flesh out the plans. We began to put forces in order, and decide where the bribery should be used or where the knife in the night was the answer. Men would march from Amklana and other of the provinces of Hyrklana inimical to the queen. Tyfar would assign his Hamalese soldiers. Soon specific functions were being allocated. It began to look as though these people not only meant business, but knew how to run it.

I caught the task of guard to the principals. That, on the face of it, seemed appropriate. Everyone assumed I would sell my life to protect Ariane and Noran, and joy in the doing of it to the greater glory of Hyrklana and the soon-to-be Queen Ariane. I did not disabuse them of that idea. If there was to be any laying down of lives on that account, it would be theirs and not mine. If Tyfar or Jaezila ran into trouble, that was entirely different.

The meetings continued on an irregular basis for the next few sennights, and I did not attend all of them. On the occasions I did attend I was aware of the forward movement of events. It seemed a sound idea to keep myself under cover as much as possible, and I did not venture too much abroad from The Silver Fluttrell and Noran's villa, and when I did I kept a sharp lookout on the backtrail. I was not followed, was not being spied on. I trusted this happy state applied to all the conspirators.

Ariane's men were close to the city; much gold had been spent. Noran, although a vad and not the highest of the nobility, a kov, was one of the richest men in Huringa. This, presumably, was the prime reason Ariane had selected him to be her dupe. She oohed and aahed well enough when they were together, but it did not take a sharp eye to see the true situation. He dreamed of becoming the King of Hyrklana. Fat chance!

Almost at the end of planning, for Ariane had matured her schemes for a goodly time, we met to discuss what was to be done with some of the important personages of Huringa who had refused to declare for the usurper to the queen. All they had done was to indicate their loyalty to Fahia, for Ariane had not revealed herself. The list was carefully considered. They came to the name of Orlan Mahmud nal Yrmcelt.

"He must be killed," said Ariane. She spoke spitefully, her words biting. "He is not devoted to Fahia, I know, but he refuses to aid me. And I have spoken to him. He detests the Hamalese, and would not aid me in my schemes when I am queen."

Tyfar looked upset. "Is it necessary to kill him? He could be banished—"

"No! Our alliance must be founded on rock, prince. When I am queen and you carry back word to Thyllis in Ruathytu that I will join with her in the glorious conquests, I do not want men at my back who will not support me, men who will work against me and the greater glory of Hyrklana and Hamal."

"I see that," said Tyfar. "But I do not like it. I think—"

I put a hand to my mouth. This woman Ariane would ally herself with Thyllis! She would place Hyrklana into bondage to Hamal! Yes, Tyfar would seize on this, as a good Hamalese. He was a prince of Hamal and eggs get smashed making omelettes, and no doubt he fancied Hyrklana's willing help would tilt the balance in favor of Hamal and thus end the war swiftly. As well it might. Hyrklana might be smaller than Hamal, but the island realm had been untouched by the war raging on the mainland and up north. The people were tough and hardy, certain with weapons, grown ferocious through the constant raiding by the Shanks, the fish heads, from over the curve of the world. My evil dream of bringing Hyrklana into the War was being realized—realized from the other side!

When we rose to leave, my thoughts were still in a turmoil. Noran spoke to Ariane, who nodded. She turned with her wide smile to Tyfar, to whom she was now exquisitely polite, seeing she had lost the influence she might once have had over him through her conduct in the Moder.

"Prince! The time grows nearer. Noran suggests you should live here until we strike. It seems a good plan to me."

Tyfar nodded agreement, so, perforce, I was to stay, too. Jaezila said she would see about collecting our things from The Silver Fluttrell, and Noran's majordomo saw about allocating quarters to us. The villa was palatial enough to have housed a regiment or two.

We settled in for the few days remaining. Tyfar was now possessed of an eagerness to strike very becoming in a proud young prince. I racked my brains to think of a way to scupper the plot. The obvious way seemed the best. When Fahia's guards burst in on my betrayal, I would see to it that Tyfar and Jaezila were safely away. I attempted to leave the villa, acting naturally, but was stopped. The new cadade, a Chulik, explained.

"No one leaves now. It is the vad's order. Security."

To have fought my way out might have served, once. I would only betray me, instead of the plotters. This night saw the last meeting. Kov Naghan na Hanak had at last decided to throw in his lot with the conspirators. We need wait no longer, for he brought a strong acquisition of strength. And I decided that I could probably deal more easily with Queen Ariane than with Queen Fahia. I'd let the plot succeed, and then see about stopping this ominous alliance of Hamal and Hyrklana."

By this time I knew my way around the less-private parts of Noran's villa. The meeting was to be held in a sumptuous reception room in the heart of the Strigicaw Complex. The room was a mass of crystal. Jaezila had brought all our gear from the tavern, so I could put on a scarlet breechclout, which still made Tyfar frown, and strap up a useful assortment of weaponry. Going down the stone stairs and out under the light of the Maiden with the Many Smiles, fat and pink through scattered clouds, I walked across to the Strigicaw Complex. I did hot feel at all like a conspirator ready to topple a kingdom and install a new queen. Jaezila and Tyfar came toward me as I walked in the light of the moon.

"Jak!" Jaezila's voice held an edge. "The lady Ariane bids you guard them well tonight. You are to take post at the far end of the colonnade."

I was surprised.

"Very well. That is some distance from the meeting place."

"If we do not hurry, we will be late," said Tyfar.

"There is time," said Jaezila. "I want to show you something you ought to see, a trinket they have here in a glass case. Come on, Ty! You will delight in it, for it is from Balintol, and then we can go into the meeting. Tomorrow—we strike!"

When one mentions a trinket from Balintol, which is a mysterious place, by Vox, one is always interested. Tyfar looked at the moon, telling the time, and then we went along the colonnade.

"This had better be good, young lady," said Tyfar. "To keep a revolution waiting!"

Noran's villa, like any well-furnished palace on Kregen, was stuffed with curios, objets d'art, fascinating treasures from all over the world gathered together through the centuries. We had time to inspect this item Jaezila had marked before the meeting began. The Maiden with the Many Smiles cast down a fuzzy pink light. Shadows burned pink, and the night air smelled sweet. The moonblooms were out. We walked along toward the building that formed an extension to the Strigicaw Complex, and a frightful hubbub broke out at our backs.

Tyfar whirled. We looked back along the colonnade.

"That's not Kov Naghan," said Tyfar.

Dark figures ran under the arches, and the sounds of wood smashing told us the door was being broken in. The jangle of steel broke brilliantly into the night.

He whipped out his sword and started to run back, and I caught him by his belt and hauled him in.

"Wait, Tyfar, wait."

"But—"

Those dark figures ran fleetly toward us. They looked demonic, agile, and the glitter of their weapons struck an edged note of horror.

"We have been discovered by the queen!"

"Then we must fight them!" said Jaezila. Her rapier gleamed liquid silver. She took two paces.

Tyfar put a hand on her arm and looked at me. I let his belt go. "You stop Jaezila, Tyfar, as I stop you. If we have been betrayed, there is nothing more to be saved by getting killed."

"But my honor—"

"I respect your honor, prince. But my honor says that you will take Jaezila and move back through the colonnade. I will hold them until you reach a good spot."

I stopped talking then for an arrow spat from nowhere and pierced Jaezila through her left arm. She did not cry out, but she gasped. She staggered. Tyfar caught her and glared wildly at me.

"There, you see!" I cried, annoyed. "Now take Jaezila and go! Do not argue."

I reached out with the thraxter and flicked a second arrow away. Dodging behind a column, I shouted most fiercely toward Tyfar and Jaezila. "She's in pain and you dillydally, prince? Where is your famous honor? Save Jaezila—that is your duty!"

"But—you—Jak—"

"By Krun! I've never met a man who'd argue when a girl needs to be saved."

I almost thought I'd overdone it. But he scooped Jaezila and ran like a scuttling locrofer, bent above her in his arms, and as he ran he flung back: "I will run and I will save Jaezila, Jak, you may depend on that. But for the sake of our comradeship I will not forget why I ran or who made me run away from a fight."

So I, Dray Prescot, laughed. In the next seconds my sword crossed with the first of the guards who sought to pass me and rush after my comrades and take them. The steel slithered and scraped. I took the first one cleanly and skipped away and so nicked the second. The third and fourth came on together and tried to sandwich me, whereat I let them come in and then, with the old one-two-hop, avoided them and clouted their heads together. They were Rhaclaws with domed heads as wide as their shoulders. They slumped to the stone floor of the colonnade. One remained, and he came on bravely, so that I dazzled him, and hit him with the hilt.

At the far end under the roof of the colonnade the shadows clustered. I trusted Tyfar would have the wit to keep on running. This was no time to hang around or make a stand. More guards were running up, and the noise from the meeting room smashed into the night air. Ariane's plot had been discovered and was in the process of being shattered.

There was absolutely no doubt in my mind what the lady Ariane would be doing now. She would follow the same course of conduct as that she had adopted down in the Moder where among the crazed mob she sought only to save herself and refused to aid others. Tyfar had seen that. Only his own code of honor maintained his civility toward Ariane. So now she'd be running and if Naghan the Doorn got himself killed protecting her, well, that was what he was paid for, and Ariane would soon hire a new retainer with a halberd. So I held no brief for her.

As for the other plotters, they must take their chances.

So, with slumbering guards strewing the stone flags of the colonnade, I took myself off. Tyfar and Jaezila were well away by now. Heading for a narrow alley between sumptuous buildings leading to the outside wall, I heard that typical ringing sliding susurration of bronze links above my head. I leaped. The net dropped on me. They are very cunning with metal nets in Hyrklana. The mesh enfolded me as an octopus engulfs its prey. I thrashed about, entangled, and they trotted up and bashed me on the head, just to be on the safe side.

Nine

Red for the Ruby Drang

The brilliance of the twin Suns of Scorpio, Zim and Genodras, beat down into the stone-walled yard. The sand strewing the floor was not the silver sand of the Arena, but coarse stuff suitable for a training area where coys were given a few rudiments of the craft before being sent out to face death. About two hundred miserable wights sat or stood about in the heat. I suppose I ought to consider myself lucky I was there at all, arena fodder, rather than lying in some pit with my head tucked neatly under my arm.

A certain amount of guile had been necessary to achieve this end. Using the painful art taught me by Deb-Lu-Quienyin, I had put on a doleful, moronic face and passed myself off as merely a hired guard who knew nothing—as Havil the Green was my witness!—of what went on among the great lords. Victims for the arenas of the many Jikhorkduns of Hyrklana were always needed. As a mere hired guard, who knew nothing, it was not even worth putting me to the question, and with the other guards captured I'd been packed off to the Jikhorkdun.

"Stand up! Stand up! Get in line, you no-good rasts!"

The bulky man with the whip walked along slashing about, and we cowed souls formed up into a long line. At the far end of the enclosure stood four men. They wore armor and carried weapons. Other arena guards were positioned at strategic points. We were all naked and weaponless, browbeaten in line.

As I took stock of what was taking place and the line shuffled toward the four men, I saw that as a coy reached the end of the line he walked to one of the four armored men in rotation, and then went through a doorway at the rear. The four men and the four doorways were marked. Over each door a splash of color stood out vividly in the suns. The four men each wore a colored favor. The line inched along toward the four men and the four doors.

A simple calculation told me that when I reached the head of the line I would, in my turn, have to walk toward the man with the flaunting green feathers in his helmet.

Now, had those feathers been yellow, or blue, even, I do not think I would have cared a jot. I'd simply have walked along and gone through the yellow or blue door. But green! Well, I had long since overcome my irrational, as it turned out, detestation of green. But, for some reason that I did not care to fathom out, I pushed in front of the fellow before me and checked him and so marched smartly toward the man wearing the red feathers. Again, I might in avoiding the green have walked to join the yellows or blues, and I do not think I would have cared. Fate, if it was fate, sent me once again to fight with the Ruby Drang.

"What are they going to do, dom?" said a young Rapa, his beaked face unhappy, his feathers limp.

"You have never sat in the stands?"

"No—I work on my father's farm, and—"

I said, "Do not lose heart, fight as hard as you can, and die well." I turned away. I would not make acquaintances, let alone friends, among men marked for death.

The manhandlers with whips and spears—and all wearing red favors—sorted out us fifty recruits who had been apportioned to the Ruby Drang. They went about their work with methodical thoroughness; this they had done many times before.

"You—over here! You—over there!" The whips snapped.

No one ran berserk, trying to escape. We were all too cowed. As for me, I had to bide my chances and stay alive.

"Spearmen, stand there. Swordsmen, stand there. Archers, here." They sorted us out and, after a moment's wondering if it might be useful to stand with the archers, I went over to the small group of men who claimed to be able to handle a sword. The managers of the Jikhorkdun had the nasty habit of sending archers up against unpleasant flying animals. Everything was carried out with punctiliousness and yet with an air of boredom, as though mere repetition dulled the alertness of the manhandlers. I knew that was false. One attempt to escape, a single try, and the retribution would be swift, I knew.

We were given red breechclouts and a cloth band to tie around our foreheads to keep our hair tidy and to hold a single red feather. The men stuck the feathers in awkwardly, talking in frightened whispers. Like a fool, I own, when I put the red feather into the cloth headband I felt—not a thrill, dear Zair, no!—but a kind of spine-stiffener, a flood of memories, a final reminder of where I was.

The blow on my head which had caused those famous old Bells of Beng Kishi to chime in my skull could be used as an excuse for stupid behavior. Not one of us was damaged goods, for the arena managers were strict; but some of us were in a sorry state, right enough. The face I now had was my own, if rather hangdog. The cheldur strutted out and stood on his pedestal and rested his fists on the wooden rail. His face was a mere mass of scars, although he still had both eyes. His red jerkin and his saffron kilt and his silver greaves made of him a figure of splendor. But it was his sword that marked him off from us, for we stood sullenly before him unarmed.

He shouted in his bullfrog bellow.

"Coys! You now fight for the Ruby Drang. If you live you may become kaidurs. If you die—die well! There is gold and wine and women and ease for those who live."

He swelled there above us on his pedestal. "I am Hundal the Oivon! You do as I say and you do nothing else. Or by the glass eye and brass sword of Beng Thrax you will do nothing else—ever!"

We believed him.

A sense of much greater speed in all the aspects of the Arena was clearly apparent from the days before the great war on the continent. We coys were assigned quarters and given some sketchy training with tricks and stratagems. But it seemed to me the blood fever gripped these people, clasping them helplessly in its grip. Spectacle was demanded, and more spectacle. The hunger for sensation, for blood and death, was insatiable.

Hundal the Oivon sweated over us. Like anyone closely involved with his color faction, he wanted the reds to win. At the moment the blues, devotees of the sapphire graint, were in the ascendant. We, we were informed, if we lived, would help to redress that balance and once again place the red of the ruby drang at the summit of the victory poles. These cheldurs who train up the apprentices for the Arena are singular to Kregen, it seems, for although they have wide privileges, they do not have the same opportunities as the old Roman lanistae. Hundal sweated over us—and he made us sweat, by Kaidun!

Well aware that the first fight I got into was likely to be the last, and that this first encounter out on the silver sand carried more danger by reason of the surroundings, I felt relief mixed with annoyance that a group of us was chosen to test out some apprentice yellows. It was to be a sword and shield encounter, a minor bout during a slack time, mainly to determine what quality the new material might be. Well, the spectacle of the amphitheater with the tiered seating lofting up into the sky, the rows of eager, blood-obsessed faces, the yelling and the infernal din, the stink of blood and animals, the smell of sweat and oiled leather... Yes, the Jikhorkdun can get under a man's skin, well enough, once he is a kaidur and understands what he fights for. I would have none of it. I intended to keep a whole skin and get out of here as fast as possible.

The coys went in awe of the kaidurs and hyr-kaidurs, who strode about like gods. To face one of those superlative fighting men would be the end, and yet, in many and many a breast beat a heart that would thrill to the kaiderin of it all, before it was stilled forever...

To perform a High Kaidur, that was the dream...

Preparations were still very thorough. Hundal chose an interesting mix of men; half were those who in training appeared more likely to cut off their own ears than their opponents', and the other half consisted of men who showed promise. We waited behind the iron-barred gate and the racket from the Arena, this close, dinned in our ears maddeningly. Fristle women poured the coarse red wine, called Beng Thrax's spit, into leather cups for us to refresh ourselves in the dust and heat. And I still did not know that drink was spiced with drugs that inflamed a man and turned him into an insensate fighting fury. So we waited until it was our turn to step out into that oval of death, a melting pot of passion, a crucible of conflict, and stake our lives for the enjoyment of the populace of Huringa.

The storm of emotions that hit me as I stepped out onto the silver sand! Instinctively I turned to look up at the royal box, glittering and high; the place gaped empty. Fahia would not waste her time on a program filler like this. As a devotee of everything pertaining to the Jikhorkdun, a woman who could recite the names of hyr-kaidurs for seasons past together with the kaidurs they had performed, she reserved her patronage for the best displays.

"By Havil, Chaadur! Don't stand gawping! Here come the yellows!" Norhan yelled at me.

Chaadur was the name I had given. I looked across the Arena and the yellow coys, shrieking and yelling and waving their swords, charged toward us. Hundal had warned us. "They'll come out like evil spirits from Cottmer's Caverns. Don't let that worry you. Just get stuck in."

So we did.

The fight proved Hundal's eye. The yellows' training had been just as thorough as our own in the time, I daresay. I recognized a few men who had waited in line with me to be chosen in the yard. Of the reds, we lost all those who had failed to measure up, and the yellows lost all except one, who ran shrieking about the Arena, under the wall, with the crowd yelling at him to stand and fight. A couple of our blood-crazed reds ran after him. It was left to a couple of the Arena guards to step out from a pillared area offset from the queen's box and feather him as he ran. He sank down, and that was the last of the yellows. The red totem would move up by a fraction of a notch. It would take a much more important kaidur than this to make any significant changes. Yet, as we walked back, feeling the aches and the aftereffects, Hundal greeted us warmly, and pointed out that we had lifted the ruby drang, not depressed the red, and that was as it should be.

Norhan, a shock-headed fellow with a twist to his lips and a remarkably evil eye, said, "You were moonstruck in there, at first, Chaadur. It is just as well I am quick-witted."

"Indubitably, Norhan. And my thanks."

He cocked that fishy eye of his at me and licked his lips, and we trailed off to the barracks.

During the next few days we trained hard and fought twice more, and Hundal and Oivon called me aside as we washed ourselves of the blood and filth after a grueling set-to with a pack of blegs of the blues. We'd drawn. And, with the old fever for the ruby drang hot upon me, I raged that we had not won.

"We are gaining strength, Chaadur," said Hundal. He glowered at me, a bluff, ruddy-faced professional cheldur. "I see you are of the reds."

"Aye."

"And also, Chaadur, I think you have fought before. You were a paktun, a mercenary, perhaps?"

That seemed the easiest thing to agree to. I nodded as I sluiced water. The basins ran red.

"You will make kaidur very soon. It is in my mind to try you single tomorrow."

Again I sluiced water, and nodded. The quicker I could rid myself of being a coy and apprentice, start to climb the ladder of victories, win my way to a position as kaidur, the quicker I would get a freer run of this place. We were prisoners. There was no easy way past the guards, as I well knew. I did not intend to rot here until I was killed. This was my route out.

"Tomorrow, then. You fight a churgur of the greens. As ever, by Kaidun, he will be good. I rely on you, Chaadur."

So it was fixed. I did not doubt there were wagers even on so small a match. The pairs paraded in their armor and feathers across the silver sand, the trumpets pealed, the suns cast down their mingled streaming lights, and we fought. Afterwards, as I washed myself again, Hundal said, "You may count that as your first victory, Chaadur."

We stood by the door and the noise of splashing water and yelling almost obscured the footfalls. I turned, warily.

Hundal said, "Lahal, Cleitar. Did you see Chaadur just now? Have you come to sniff him out for yourself?"

Cleitar Adria still appeared a little strange to me, with the dead scar tissue glistening down the left half of his face and the lifeless socket that had once been an eye. He looked just as tough and ruthless as he had when we'd been taken up together as slaves and fought in the arena. I had won free, with help, and Cleitar had gone on to become a hyr-kaidur and then a senior cheldur. I noticed Hundal's respectful attitude, despite his pointed remarks about another trainer looking over his men. I had to speak up sharply, and yet not arouse suspicions.

"Lahal, cheldur," I said. "I am new here, very new. It is all strange. But if you—"

And then Hundal's outraged bellow silenced me.

"Coy! You do not speak until spoken to! And especially to a kai-cheldur! Impudent fambly! Onker!"

But Cleitar had taken the message. He understood, for I had told him in a drinking den here in the Jikhorkdun that I worked in secret for Queen Fahia. As a story, I had taken some good mileage out of that, by Kaidun! Now he nodded, very much the superior officer, and said that he had seen me fight and was faintly interested. "All the new young coys are flatfish these days. It is pleasant to find a man who can use a sword."

"He can, Cleitar, he can," burbled Hundal.

They talked on and I stood back respectfully. Cleitar might give me considerable assistance to escape, and I was not going to miss that opportunity. They knew how to manage men in the Jikhorkdun, especially recalcitrant men.

The proof of that came very quickly when I got Cleitar alone for a few words. His scarred face sobered me, dashed my hopes. "Escape, Chaadur? No, dom, that is not possible. Not for you, until you become a hyr-kaidur again, as you will."

"In that case will you see that Hundal arranges fights? You know what I mean. I have to get out of here—"

At that, Cleitar's slashed lips curved into a mocking smile.

"Don't they all, by the brass sword and glass eye of Beng Thrax!"

My reactions might have puzzled me had I dwelled on them. I did not feel the biting sense of frustration I ought to have experienced. I was desperate to get away; and yet I felt that in a remote, disinterested fashion. It was not just that I was caught up again in fighting for the ruby drang. That was far below the worth of my feelings. But undoubtedly, although conscious of my duty to get away, I felt nothing was being lost.

"You were a hyr-kaidur once, Chaadur, when you fought under the name of Drak the Sword." I had known, then, that Cleitar Adria resented the bestowal of that name on me. "And you say you escaped by the queen's connivance? Then, why—?"

This, I had foreseen.

"Doing the queen's bidding is a hard road, Cleitar. I must get out of here and see her, for I do not think she can know I fight for the ruby drang again." That was true, by Vox! If fat Queen Fahia knew that Dray Prescot fought in her arena, she'd nigh choke herself laughing. Then—then she'd probably be highly unpleasant. She must by this time know who I was. It was not all gloom. Cleitar took in news of the outer world, and I learned that, yes, there had been a conspiracy against the queen, the latest in a long series, and the plotters had been taken up, except the ringleaders. They had escaped. It was known that Vad Noran was the chief criminal, and he was being sought over all Hyrklana.

"And the others?"

"There is a rumor, denied from the palace, which says that the visiting prince of Hamal was involved. It is a story not believed." Cleitar moved his shoulders. "I do not believe it."

"It is not very likely."

"No. Anyway, this prince has returned home."

My first and only genuine feeling was one of relief. Tyfar had gotten clean away, and that helped to make my own capture and incarceration and combats worthwhile...

He promised to do what he could to secure me promising contests. When I pointed out that, if Beng Thrax turned his glass eye favorably upon me and used his brass sword for instead of against me, Cleitar could pick up easy winnings, he merely smiled and tapped his nose and laughed, the scar glistening.

"That is what friends are for."

While not necessarily agreeing with that, I had to admit that friends are vital to both an emperor and a man trying to stay alive in and get out of the Jikhorkdun. Now I will pass rapidly over the ensuing period, for it was a simple round of combats in which I was concerned to keep a whole skin, and to pick up every scrap of information I could. By this time I was nowhere near the flamboyant fighter with the sword I once had been, although always preferring neatness and economy. Since my encounter beside the caravan with Mefto the Kazzur I had taken great thought to sword fighting. I was better than ever, but, as always, the thought remained with me that I could easily meet a man far superior to me out on the silver sand. If I did, if I met another such as Prince Mefto, then all my plots and stratagems would go for naught.

So I did not take this period lightly.

Norhan said, on one day of madness filled with the shriek of sword and the ragged swellings of death, "Chaadur! You are the simplest swordsman I have ever seen. You seem to do nothing, and yet you do everything."

I turned away. I remembered another man who had said that to me, laughing, bright, eager—Barty Vessler, who was dead. I turned back. "Better to be quick and safe, than showy and dead."

"True. I prefer a pot of combustibles, myself."

The guards were herding in a bunch of miserable felons, men and women shackled together and doomed. They were to be turned out with a short sword between two of them to face wild beasts. It would be horrible and unpleasant. And yet many had chosen this death to life in the Arena...

"That must be why they call you Norhan the Flame."

"Smart with a pot of the right stuff, and a light, that's me." His high opinion of himself, I saw, extended to his skill with combustibles. All the same, it was difficult not to respond to his brashness, for there was nothing repellent in it, nothing to make a dour old fighting man like myself dub him an empty braggart.

A woman fell among the chained ranks and was hoisted up and prodded on. This hideous aspect of the arena gave me always the chill of revulsion and of death. It was not necessary for me, one of the new and upcoming kaidurs, to interfere. As I stepped forward I was surprised that Norhan the Flame stepped up, too. We remonstrated with the guard, a burly Brokelsh, and although anything we could achieve in these circumstances was of ludicrous insignificance, as we turned away, Norhan said, "I don't think he'll prod a poor chained woman so quickly, next time." The Brokelsh sat up on the dusty ground, his mouth bleeding. Norhan sucked his knuckles.

And then I stopped dead in my tracks.

A man beside the woman, chained to her, attempting to help her, said, "It will not be long now, Mina, and, by Spikatur Hunting Sword, it cannot come too fast for me."

I looked back at the coffle. The chains clanked. The man looked exhausted, and his arms were broken and strapped up across his chest, so that he could do little for the woman Mina. A single step I took, and another, and then the furious form of the guard Jiktar roared down, purple of face, protuberant of eye, and the coffle whisked away between iron-bound doors that thudded dolorously together.

"What is it, Chaadur?"

I swallowed. "A nothing, Norhan. Let us—"

"Aye, by Sarkalak! Let us go for a wet."

That had not been in my mind; now that Norhan mentioned the subject it seemed the appropriate thing to do.

Ten

Of Spikatur and Princess Lilah

The first really hard information I obtained about the secret society calling itself Spikatur Hunting Sword came from a strong-faced swordsman who had parried a trifle too late, and taken a nasty thrust through his side. He had recovered and gone on to beat his man, a Rapa of the blues, but in the barracks he lay in pain on his pallet waiting for the needleman. I stayed at his side. He called for water and I fetched it. Helping to prop up his head so that he might drink more easily, I heard his sunken whisper of thanks. "By Sasco! I think I am done for."

"Nonsense, Pergon. The needleman will have you right in a trice." I bent closer. The stubble on his chin glistened. "Tell me about Spikatur. I do not think you are going to die, but—"

"I feel my death on me." His eyes rolled. We were alone in the barracks. He sweated with a chill that would be deathly if the doctor did not come soon. Norhan had gone for him and I had faith enough in the Flame to leave that in his hands. I knew that men who were involved with Spikatur used the oath "By Sasco!" In Pergon's weakened condition, near, as he thought, to death, he talked freely, telling me what he knew. What it boiled down to was not a lot. People had banded together into a hunting society, devoted to Spikatur, the mighty hunter, and they met in secret places in many parts of Hyrklana.

"And in the Dawn Lands, and in Pandahem. I cannot speak for the wild lands to the west of the central mountains of Havilfar, for that is remote and unknown. But Spikatur grows in strength—" He paused, and I gave him more water and wiped his forehead. I thought that he was going to die.

"All these lands," I said, "Pandahem, the Dawn Lands, Hyrklana where we are now—"

"Aye." He choked and blood dribbled down his chin, so that I thought the end had come and he would die before the needleman arrived to ease his pain. "Aye, Chaadur! We surround! We build. Soon we will strike!"

"Who leads you?"

"No leader." After that he became incoherent so that what he said was impossible to understand. He mentioned Faol and Ifilion, other countries of Havilfar. The doctor arrived toward the end. He was a crotchety old fellow, with a stoop, and he thumped his bag down and glared at Pergon as though the dying man had done him an injury. "This kaidur is dying. Nothing can save him. Why was my time wasted?"

I stood up. I looked at the doctor. I said, "Open your bag and take out your needles. Use them. Ease his pain."

He chomped his jaws in offended fury. He did not understand the situation. "I am a doctor! You are just a kaidur! Stand aside and let me pass, there is nothing I can do for this man."

"There is. I am a kaidur, and have nothing to lose. You are a needleman and have a deal to lose. I do not think you would relish inspecting your own backbone. Ease Pergon's pain, now."

"You are mad—"

"Do it!"

He did it. He inserted his acupuncture needles so that Pergon could die in peace. He kept muttering to himself. Norhan ran in with the basket of fruit he had stopped to fetch, and I shook my head. What had just occurred gave me no pleasure. It was symptomatic of the bestiality with which we were surrounded.

So Pergon died and was taken outside and buried along with the rest.

He was dead; but what he had said about Spikatur Hunting Sword lived on.

Norhan rubbed his jaw, which was lean and blue. "As San Blarnoi says," he observed, quoting a saint whose aphorisms are trotted out to confuse and offend, "'It is a flinty heart that is not softened by a fist in the jaws.' That needleman will ply his skill more freely in future, I think."

"Like the Brokelsh you took to task for hitting the woman? I wonder. Mayhap it will make them more savage."

"If they are they must be made to rue it!"

"You cannot run people's lives by fear, Norhan—"

He stared at me. "Fambly! How do you think the world turns?"

In no mood for argument, I let the subject drop as we went into the kaidur's drinking den and, avoiding dopa, which is the drink of fools, sat down with tankards of ale. Norhan knew nothing of Spikatur Hunting Sword. But two days later another man mentioned Spikatur—before he was chopped, so I guessed that a group of Spikatur's adherents had been taken up for the Arena. This made me realize that Fahia might know. Perhaps all the great ones of the world knew, and took steps to crush the Spikatur conspiracy. I might be the Emperor of Vallia, but I would not regard myself as one of the great ones of the world, for that way lay megalomania. All the same... If all I had to do to find out was ask one of my people in the Imperial Palace in Vondium...!

Somehow, I did not think it was like that at all.

By judicious arrangements, Cleitar assured that I met top-class opposition, and so rapidly made my way up the ladder. This was dangerous. Not just because I might get myself killed—that is an occupational hazard of those who step out onto the silver sand. But aficionados might cast their minds back and remember Drak the Sword. I had been a hyr-kaidur, yes, but my time here had not been too long, and perhaps the most spectacular fight at the end would be the fight that would be remembered. All the same, I fought along all the time expecting some well-meaning idiot in the stands to bellow: "Drak the Sword! Kaidur!" Then Queen Fahia would sit up on her silks and furs and peer down, and her fat jowls would quiver like those of her damned spotted strowgers as they chomped on portions of people's anatomies.

Talk about tightropes and razors' edges!

During these days the ruby drang lifted up the red totem on the victory pole so that we no longer rested in the lowest position. The blues still lorded it over the others, but the greens were giving them a hard tussle. Hundal the Oivon, our cheldur responsible for our barracks, had money laid out on us reds overtaking the yellows—which we had done and he had collected—and he reinvested his winnings on our taking the greens. He found many folk willing to take his wagers. The odds against the reds were quoted at variously high figures, for the strength in the ongoing tussle for the moment lay with the blues and greens. This continuing fascination was a part of the Jikhorkdun's aura, the partisanship that led to incredible feats of bravery in the Arena when the stands went wild. I had pledged myself I would have none of it, none of the blood and death and degradation; that meant I would have none of the high striving and the passion to excel and the sacrifice. I would have none of it. I was the Emperor of Vallia and I had a job to do, a daunting task to bring Hyrklana in against Hamal and then to subdue Hamal so that we might all stand shoulder to shoulder against the reiving fishheads from the other side of the world.

So be it.

But the passions of the Jikhorkdun got into my blood, and I rattled my blade along the iron bars, and shrieked out with the others when the reds triumphed, and roared and screamed when the reds went down to bloody defeat. So the days passed and I got to know Norhan a little more, against my inclinations, and Frandu the Franch. Frandu was a Fristle with a very high opinion of himself—hence his nickname—equipped with a sharp tongue. But he was a doughty fighter on the silver sand.

Because we were kaidurs of the middle rankings, we no longer had to face some of the more primitive horrors in the arena. We had fought our way through those perils. Now we were reserved for the professional combats, skills against skills, in which the most educated and knowledgeable of the Jikhorkdun aficionados delighted. We returned one day from an interesting confrontation with a group of Khibils of the yellows. We had bested them, even though the foxy-faced, reddish-whiskered Khibils are fine fighters. Queen Fahia had not been present, and at the end of the fights the crowd had been uncharacteristically generous, and the victorious reds had been allowed to give the beaten yellows their lives. That rarely happened when the queen graced the games with her presence.

"It was a bonny little ding-dong, by the Golden Splendor of Numi-Hyr-jiv himself!" quoth Frandu, spitting and taking an immense gulp of water. We sprawled on the benches waiting to return to our barracks. "And I recognized one of the Khibils and would have been loath to slay him, onker though he is."

"Not as smart as us, Frandu?" said Norhan.

"Not as smart as me, Norhan. I took him with the same cut I gave the Chulik who tried to spit him on the stairs when they tried to slay Princess Lilah."

I looked across. Names—well, there are many men and women on Kregen, and many of them bear the same names, as they do on Earth. I listened, saying nothing.

Norhan guffawed. "What do you know of princesses, Frandu?"

Now, the miserable folk herded into the arena seldom spoke of the reasons that brought them there. Sometimes, if they allowed themselves the foolishness of making friends, they would exchange confidences. Not often. But Frandu felt his honor impugned. He wiped water drops from his whiskers. His cat's face screwed up, all abristle, and his eyes looked dangerous, slitted, catlike.

"I guarded the Princess Lilah for many seasons, onker."

Norhan, offhandedly, taunting, said, "If you mean the Princess Lilah who was twin sister to Queen Fahia, then you surely jest. She has been dead and gone for many seasons."

"You are the onker!" Frandu was wrought up. "She was kept in a tower with her husband for season after season. I can talk of these things now, for we are all dead men. At the time I was sworn to a vow of secrecy, which I kept."

Norhan didn't believe the Fristle, and said so. Frandu's whiskers bristled. "She came back to Hyrklana seasons ago, and the queen immediately imprisoned her. Well, she would, wouldn't she?"

"Lilah is dead, onker."

"Yes, now. The Chuliks saw to that. And I am in the Arena."

I leaned forward. "Who married the Princess Lilah?"

"Who? Why, that silly fellow Arrian nal Amklana."

I sat back. It seemed to me that the clouds parted above the Jikhorkdun and the mingled rays of the red and green suns struck through, illuminating everything they touched. Here was the key. Here was the key to turn the lock—if nature's natural course had followed. I had rescued Princess Lilah from the Manhounds and she had flown home and no one had heard of her from that day to this. And now...!

I said, "And the child?"

"Her?" Frandu shook his head. "I am a Fristle and she is an apim, but I own I have seldom seen a fairer girl in all the world."

"She lives?"

"Aye. The Chuliks slew Lilah and Arrian, and I nearly came by my death. But little Princess Lildra lives safely."

A somber feeling of sadness for the senseless death and, from what Frandu said, the even more senseless life, of Princess Lilah kept me silent as the crowd roar burst out as the pairs on the silver sand battled down to a finish and the blues' victory notched up their totem yet again. Lilah had been marked, it seemed to me, for a woeful destiny, and yet—and yet— could I have done anything else than I had done? No—and the Star Lords had kept me working hard for them at the time. I would have liked to have spoken to her again. But—she had a daughter, Princess Lildra.

So, as we walked back to the barracks carrying our armor and weapons, the red towels draped over our shoulders—for we were not yet far advanced enough to warrant slaves to carry our armor—I said, "And Ariane nal Amklana hired Chuliks to murder Lilah, and Ariane's own twin brother as well?"

"She did, the bitch." Frandu nodded vehemently. "And they nearly did for me, too."

I pondered the inhumanity of woman toward man. By these dreadful means Ariane hoped to prove a spurious legitimacy to the throne. She would use the old means of force and coercion to gain lawful ends, what Kregans call the steel bokkertu. Her twin brother was married to the sister of the queen—was not that reason and proof enough, Ariane would claim, to take the throne, seeing that Queen Fahia was dead? Well, it hadn't worked out like that. I made up my mind to find Princess Lildra.

One other point needed to be resolved, although I doubted if Frandu would have that knowledge.

"Do you know what the queen did about the bitch of Amklana?"

"We rescued Princess Lildra and took her to a safe place. I worked for the queen for many seasons and obeyed her in all things. But then I—" He glanced at Norhan, who was not overly interested, and hitched up his armor. "If you laugh, Norhan the Flame, I will singe your rear with one of your own pots! A charming Fristle fifi and I were very happy and she got me drunk and I was late reporting. There was a great hullabaloo. There had been an attempt to rescue the young princess. I was instantly suspected of plotting—well, I hadn't been, but I was—"

"A credulous fambly!" chortled Norhan. "Falling for the oldest trick in the world! A little Fristle fifi—she could have taken your uniform and weapons and armor while you snored, aye, and your keys! She gave them to her lover and they broke into the tower—you are a fambly!"

"It was not like that—and I warned you—"

"Save it," I said.

They looked at me. Frandu took a breath and Norhan shook his head. Before they had time to lacerate me with their barbed wit, I went on: "This story is interesting. But unless you can tell me who it was who tried to rescue Princess Lildra from the queen's imprisonment in the tower, I am going for a wet—now!"

"We will go for a wet, too," rumbled Norhan.

"All I know," said Frandu, "for they beat me severely, is that I overheard one of the queen's guards say that it must have been a great lord, for the money and the skill and the knowledge. But who it was, no one could say." He looked across the dusty alley toward our drinking den. "And all this talk has made me thirsty, by Harg!"

We went into the drinking den to slake our thirsts before we went to wash up. Frandu might not know who the great noble was. It was not Vad Noran, for a certainty. But I had an idea I knew who had tried to bring Princess Lildra out of imprisonment so that she might be made Queen of Huringa. By Kaidun, yes!

Eleven

Concerning a Silver Sinver and a Water Jar

"Watch out!" called Hundal the Oivon, running into our barrack room. "Here comes Tipp the Thrax. Get lost!"

At once a scramble began to get out of the confines of the barrack room and into the labyrinth of alleys and arcades fringing the arena. Fifty men, all stout fighting kaidurs, struggling to run away from a little, limping, lopsided Gon! But, this shriveled-up, shaven-headed Gon was Kyr Tipp the Thrax. He was a Queen's Cheldur. We all knew what he wanted and we all prayed he did not have our names written down on his note pad. He had a gimlet eye, and a nose and chin in too close proximity, and Queen Fahia looked on him with great favor.

We scattered into the alleys between practice rings and yards, running under the high walls of barrack blocks and armories, even getting away toward the menagerie areas. If our names were not written down then we had a chance. If Tipp the Thrax could not see us, he could not lift that crooked staff of his and beckon us over. We'd have to go. Tipp fixed up the bouts for the Queen's Kaidurs, and as the youngest child in Huringa knew, the Queen's Kaidurs always won. Or nearly always. While it was true that the queen would more often allow a champion beaten by her kaidurs the opportunity of his life, out there in the Arena, than she would in fights between the four color corners, no one could be absolutely sure she would not condemn the vanquished. Of course, if a kaidur got himself chopped in the heat of combat, well—wasn't that always the possibility of this life? So, we rough tough kaidurs fled.

Frandu the Franch hauled up under a striped awning over an opening in the wall where soft drinks might be bought by those with money. Sometimes the cheldurs would give us small sums out of their winnings. Slaves moved about, busy as slaves always pretend to be busy, the suns shone, the shadows lay dark and slanting, and Frandu said, "By Harg! I'm not running anymore. If Tipp picks me I'll—"

"You'll come up against a Queen's Kaidur," said Norhan, "and he'll thrash you. They always do."

The queen recruited her own champions from the ranks of the greatest hyr-kaidurs. They were good, there was no doubt of that.

"One of these days, if I live, I will be a Queen's Kaidur."

"I wish you well of it, and may the glass eye of Beng Thrax smile upon you."

So they started another wrangle. The four color quarters within the enormous space of the Jikhorkdun were like small towns in themselves. If Tipp didn't have our names written down, selected by observance of performance, we were safe. This, of course, was another danger faced by any man aspiring to become a hyr-kaidur. But the managers selected promising material and would exclude them from those kaidurs sent up against the queen's champions. To do otherwise would have been folly. When I'd been a hyr-kaidur, as Drak the Sword, I had gone through the danger zone fast, and in part that was due to the personal fracas and reconciliation I'd had with Fahia. I didn't want to go through that performance again, by Zair!

Watchful guards prowled every exit from the secure inner sections, and to escape, as I knew, you'd have to have outside help. If you were a topman you had the run of the place. But I was not a topman, yet.

All the same, this incident together with what Frandu had told me of Princess Lilah's daughter, Princess Lildra, made me look again at the chances of escape. I left Norhan the Flame and Frandu the Franch arguing away by the soft-drinks counter and walked off. I had resolutely refused to make friends, and this attitude was common enough. So I walked along with a new spring to my step, reasoning that now that I had a lead to a promising fresh series of plots and stratagems, the quicker I got out of here and shed the false glamour and allure of the Jikhorkdun the quicker I could be about my proper business. And, to be perfectly honest, with this resolve to escape burning in me, I experienced a touch of disappointment that I would not be here to see the red of the ruby drang finally ascend to the top of the victory pole...

We had overcome the yellow of the diamond zhantil, and had almost reached the green of the emerald neemu. Then it was the blue of the sapphire graint—and triumph!

The decision to make a break for it, right here and now, was sudden and unexpected. It swept over me like a rashoon of the inner sea, the Eye of the World. By Zim-Zair! What was I doing, allowing myself to be sucked in by the excitement of the Jikhorkdun? Instantly, with no further hesitation, I knew I would escape—now!

It would have to be daring and quick and without doubts. It would have to be simple. I like simple plans. Swift and direct, childish, even, and I'd walk out of here.

In the shadows of a low-domed archway leading onto the outer sections of the area where the public came to see and admire their favorites after the games, and to stroll in the reflected glow of the Arena's thrills, I watched the guard. He was apim. He carried a stabbing spear as well as his sword, and his uniform might just fit. He was not alone. His comrade, a Rapa whose vulturine face appeared relaxed, laughed and picked up two pots swinging from long handles. He walked off with a casual remark about Beng Dikkane the patron saint of ale drinkers.

I looked back. Two slaves carrying a bronze cauldron on poles took no notice of me. A man stepped from the shadows of a doorway twenty paces back. He turned away at once, without looking toward me. At sight of him I bristled up, for he looked a fierce, barbaric, savage kind of man, in the way he walked and held himself, in the limber length of him and the breadth of his shoulders. But he took no notice of me and walked off. He was a man I'd not care to cross or to meet in enmity up a dark alley on a moonless night, by Krun!

I said to the guard, "I have found a silver sinver which is probably great wealth to the poor soul who lost it." I advanced, my empty hand clenched as though on a silver coin.

"That's funny," said the guard. "I dropped a sinver only this morning and you must have found—"

He did not say any more by reason of the fact that the clenched fist he so dearly wished to inspect put him peacefully to sleep. His harness came off in the shadows like the skin off a rabbit. I donned the leather straps and gear, buckled up the sword, settled the helmet on my head and seized the fallen spear.

Then I set off boldly, marching as though on parade, out through the public sectors. There would be more gates to pass through, but a guard obviously on business could, with a word or two of gruff comradely greeting, pass where a kaidur would be instantly stopped. There was no sign of the man's Rapa comrade. There would be time to get lost among the people out there and find myself a civilian's outfit. If this sounds easy, do not believe it. Escapees made the same old mistakes and were caught in the same old way. That apim guard had been lax—he had been lax and a fool. But then, a silver sinver...!

Had I mentioned a golden deldy, he would have been suspicious on the instant, and a copper ob would not have moved him. No, I fancied I had pitched it just right.

By the time I was dressed in a neat blue tunic with a silver hem, the distant sounds of shouting wafted across the intervening walls. The owner of the tunic slumbered under a bench against a wall. I slapped his thraxter down into the scabbard, for the sword was a private one, of fine workmanship, far superior to the issue sword of the guard. Then I put a simple, innocent face on, which stung confoundedly, and walked casually off toward the flight of steps leading to the nearest exit. The noise faded. The Rapa must have found his comrade, and now there was hell to pay. I felt sorry for the guard, but he had been lax in his duty, through greed, no doubt of it. That was no justification, of course, but I recalled the way Prince Tyfar regarded these affairs.

Walking up to the villa, which was as sumptuous as Tyfar had indicated it was, I felt the freedom. There was more to this feeling of liberation than merely walking outside the walls of the Jikhorkdun. The freedom was a liberation of spirit.

The day was on the wane. But there was no point in delaying. Escape wasn't quite as easy as I have indicated, and the Queen's Guards would scour the city. The civilian would describe his clothes. Any others I filched would likewise be traced. I had to press on as quickly as I could, trusting in the truth of my deductions.

The villa looked impregnable, but there would be a way in.

My face was now bedeviling me with a myriad bee-stings. I let the facial control relax, and that old beakhead that is Dray Prescot's glared out again. I'd put on another new face when the time was right. Getting over the wall was not too difficult, and only a few smashed frames and ruined fruit on the other side witnessed my descent. This was merely the outer wall. The man I wanted to see, if he was here, would be at ease in his own apartments. To reach those I could adopt the guise of a slave, or a guard, or try to bluff my way in as a horter on business.

Well, slaves get everywhere and are unremarked, especially if they are carrying something and look busy. There is the notorious case of the soldier who walked about camp all day carrying a piece of paper and looking important, and thereby escaped all manner of duties. The first slave I ran across was carrying a water jar. Now—laugh all you like—I realized I was extraordinarily reluctant to hit him. He had done me no harm, not even the negative harm the guard had done by merely being there. I looked the slave up and down and he trembled. "Slave!"

"Yes, master?" He was apim, with a gray slave breech-clout and he quavered, gray with fear. This was not promising.

"Is your master at home?"

"Yes, master. At home. I know, for Lettie told me—"

"Very well." My first ridiculous notion had been to ask him to give me his breechclout and jar of water in exchange for my fine blue tunic. I sighed, I said, "Slave, I bear you no ill will. But it is necessary that I hit you—"

"Do not beat me, master! I know I did wrong, but I have been punished enough—I was forced—"

So, in something of a state of self-contempt, I put him to sleep. I stowed the blue tunic and the sword under a bush and put on his breechclout. I picked up the jar of water and hoisted it. Then, with a hangdog look on my face, I trailed off toward the house.

One way or the other, I was not going to be long about this.

Considerable activity was taking place at the front, with carriages and saddle animals arriving and guests entering. This was bad news. I pushed on and went in through the slave entrance at the back, the jar of water concealing my face, and walked along bare corridors toward the front of the house. The door that led out of the slave quarters into the master's portions of the villa was marked by a hanging lamp and a thin-faced Rapa guard. I just hoisted the pot higher and walked on with that sad slave's shuffle. I went through without a word.

The villa was sumptuous. Tyfar had been right. The layout followed that of many of the better-class houses, and I decided that if I found an imposing series of doors along the next floor where an outside balcony ran the length of the house, I'd be on the right tracks. Slaves pitter-pattered past. There were a few guards stationed at various doors. A parcel of women, all beautifully dressed and dripping furs and jewelry, passed me and I shrank back. They were laughing and talking, refined, the great ladies to the life, and they just did not see me. I was grateful for that.

Their menfolk would be off somewhere talking business while they enjoyed themselves with gossip and scandal—and also with arranging affairs to suit themselves when they talked to their husbands again, I did not doubt. Two Khibil guards stopped me at a door studded with gold, and with golden zhantilheads for handles.

"Water, masters, water," I whined.

They let me through. They would be punished if they stopped the water being brought, as the slave would be if he spilled any on the priceless carpets of Walfarg weave. I walked on.

Voices sounded from the next room, which was large and domed, and with many lamps shedding a mellow light. I passed the open door and saw the men in there, brilliantly attired, full fleshed of face, assured, dominant. They were organizing the affairs of their world, without a doubt. I passed on and went through the small door at the side which would lead into the ablution area. My plan was simpleminded; it had worked so far, but now I was likely to come to a dead end.

The room was large and furnished with a variety of exotic wares—statues and ceramic pots of curious design, fountains and sinks of running water, ferns and flowers growing in tubs, and one whole area at the side was given over to the hot-air recreation lounge. The place was empty as I entered and, by Vox! I felt more than a little stupid with my pitiful pot of water. All the same, here I was, and no doubt in entirely the wrong place for the water jar. The door from the main room opened, admitting the buzz of conversation. The door closed. I busied myself with a mop snatched up from a corner, sloshing my precious water down and sluicing the mop back and forth. I did not look up. The two men talked in loud tones, ignoring me—not even seeing me, I had little doubt. Their conversation was of the foolish, fleshy, man-of-the-world kind so obnoxious in the real world. They finished up and looked about for towels. From a wicker booth offset to the side emerged a Fristle woman. She wore a decent robe of yellow, and there were thick-soled wooden sandals on her feet. She carried on a silver tray a pile of fluffy yellow towels.

She'd been there all the time, watching, waiting to perform her duty, and she, in her turn, had taken no notice of me.

The men left. The Fristle woman collected her towels and went back into her wicker booth. I let out a breath. The warm scent of perfumes on the air, the steam from the adjoining sections, the continual rush and susurration of running water, all added up to a weird rhythm. I blinked. I took a breath and the door opened again and a man stepped in. Because, I suppose, I was not bent over, mopping, or doing something slaves are expected to do, he looked at me.

He looked. My face was my own. He stared, and came closer.

He rocked back on his heels and looked me up and down.

Very calmly, I waited, looking back at Orlan Mahmud nal Yrmcelt.

He put a finger to his lips. His eyes were brilliant upon me. He wet his lips. "I do not—I cannot believe—Dray Prescot! It is Dray Prescot, that was Drak the Sword!"

Twelve

The Star Lords Astonish Me

"I did not think you would remember me—"

"Not remember!" He threw his head back, brilliant, laughing, suffused. There was a tremble in him that came from some hidden knowledge that gave him quick and sudden joy. "Not remember the man who, when we first met, told me I was an onker? Told me to run? A man who with a word might have had the queen throw me to her pet neemus?" He took his hand away from his mouth and looked back at the door. The heavy wood cut off all sound. "Not remember the man who threw the leem's tail? The man who fought the boloth and was taken up in a voller? My friend, you undervalue the stir you caused in Huringa those seasons ago."

"And yet you see me now wearing the gray slave breechclout—"

"I do not believe that. I have followed your story. Of course!" He replied to my surprised unspoken query. "I know you. And I believe it is Opaz himself, manifest through the Invisible Twins, who has brought at this hour into Huringa the Emperor of Vallia!"

"So you know—"

"I know a great deal. Not all. Not why you are here. We do not know each other, we met for heartbeats, and have not seen each other for seasons. But I have spies, I learn, I know what happens in the world, and how you thrash those Opaz-forsaken cramphs of Hamal." His voice thickened on the last words, and he almost spat out his hatred and contempt for the Hamalese.

I sighed. I had formed a favorable impression of Orlan Mahmud. He had been reckless and uncaring—yet he had been involved in a conspiracy against the queen. Now that he had succeeded to his father as the queen's chief pallan he still reminded me of the young man who had kicked me free of that damned great slate slab. He wore a costly evening gown, much laced with gold, of a deep plum color. His brown hair still clustered in curls and the fleck of green in his eyes still gave him that quicksilver look. A clever man, Orlan Mahmud.

"Why are you here to see me, majister?"

The way he said that, the way he brought out the "majister" in so unaffected a way, gave me pause. His quick words had lulled me. I could be in deadly danger. The Fristle attendant could now be bringing up guards. I stared at Orlan Mahmud.

"How was it you failed in your attempt to rescue Princess Lildra?"

He gasped and took a step back. It was not theatrical. He was genuinely shocked.

"Quiet, I beg you!" He looked about, and the color fled. "How—how could you know? If it is known—the Jikhorkdun—"

"Aye. She would have sport with you."

"Yes. I have come to detest the Arena of late."

"By your mien I guess you hold a meeting tonight with those who share the queen's favors—as do you—and not with those who share your true desires."

He nodded and said, "A formal reception. Tiresome. I am married and with two sets of twins. I have responsibilities. What do you know of Princess Lildra, whom Opaz preserve?"

"I fight—at the moment—against Hamal. I know of plots to bring Hyrklana into the Hamalese camp. For the sake of Vallia I do not care for that. I think if Queen Lildra sat on the throne instead of Queen Fahia, the world would smile more cheerfully."

"Then you know Fahia inclines toward Hamal, after all this time? She believes there is much gain for her. The ordinary folk do not like the Hamalese, as you know. I have much support."

I looked him straight in the eye. He drew in his chin, facing me, looking back. He was, after all, a queen's chief minister.

"Do you desire to make yourself King of Hyrklana, Orlan?"

"No, majister." His answer came back like a bowshot. I believed him. He had always exercised power from the background.

Before I could question him further, he said, "It is not safe for you to stay here like this. I will find clothes and weapons." Trust a good Kregan to bracket those together! "Then we can talk. After this damned reception. In my chambers."

"Very well. First—where does Fahia hide Princess Lildra?"

"The Jasmine Tower in the Castle of Afferatu."

There clung to him that quivering air of excitement. I suppose one could suggest, without too much megalomania, that he was impressed by having an emperor dressed up in slave's gear in his ablutions; there was something else, and that something else puzzled me. It seemed he was expecting me to say what he waited for me to say. I stretched my back and looked toward the door.

"Yes, it is a good idea for me to leave. I came here to see you. Is there anything else you have to say?" I studied him and, by Vox, he started to smile like a grinning lurfing. This meeting had been prosaic enough, Opaz knew. I said, and I own my voice was a trifle tinged with impatience, "You do not seem very surprised to see me."

"I am, I am. And, yet, majister—no." He laughed openly. "I am astonished to find you dressed up in slaves' gear when you could have come with an embassy to the front door. As the Emperor of Vallia you would be welcome—"

"I, Drak the Sword, welcome in Queen Fahia's eyes?"

"No. Of course not. But—why, majister, did you come if it was not to add to your son's pleas?"

I gaped.

"My son?"

"Of course. Prince Jaidur. He has been working on the lords and ladies of Huringa to bring them into alliance with Vallia, acting on your instructions."

Had I been wearing a hat I would have snatched it off, hurled it to the floor and jumped on it.

By the disgusting diseased liver and lights of Makki-Grodno!

"Jaidur—here?"

"You are telling me you did not know?"

Sometimes emperors have the opportunity to exercise a right which in others would be rudeness. I did not answer directly. I said, "Let me get into a safe bolt hole, with some clothes and weapons, and then I'll have a word with that young imp Jaidur."

"At once, majister."

The doors moved and then started to open and at once the blast of noise from the meeting burst in. Orlan looked stricken. He glared about like a hunted beast seeking asylum from the pack.

"You must hide, majister! Quickly—"

I just picked up the mop and bent over.

"Take no notice of me, and neither will they. Is the Fristle woman trustworthy? Not now. Later."

Four young men in high spirits caroused into the ablutions and began skylarking about, throwing water. Orlan stepped forward and the strongest desire in me to laugh had to be suppressed. The change in demeanor in those four foolish young men was remarkable. Well, as I had to keep reminding myself: Orlan Mahmud was Queen Fahia's principal minister. With a quantity of hangdoggery and sheep-facery, and quickly sloshed water, the four lads departed.

"All the same, Orlan," I said, when the door closed, "I will avail myself of your kind offer right away. Where do I go?"

"I will fetch you myself."

We went out through the smaller door into the corridors and anterooms, and as a slave I shuffled along half a dozen paces in rear. Orlan was clever. No doubt he had dealt with spies in a similar manner. Eventually, up a dark blackwood stair, I found myself in a small room, smelling faintly of dust and ripe apples, with a bed and table and not much else. Orlan closed the door, which was locked by a monstrous great bronze and iron contraption.

"You will be safe here. Only I have the key. I must get back to that tiresome reception."

"Assuredly. Tell me, before you go, what was Arrian nal Amklana like, as a man?"

"He was a friend. He was frothy, yes, but his heart was sound. He was with me in the cavern when you held up the slate slab so that we might all escape."

The feeling of satisfaction within me, almost like that of digestive juices moving, came from two sources. I was pleased that Princess Lilah had loved a man. Of course, when the Star Lords sent their damned great blue

Scorpion to snatch me up and deposit me somewhere else to do their bidding I more often than not remained in ignorance of just who it was I had rescued. I'd not known in this case; now I thought I did.

Orlan hesitated at the door and turned diffidently. "Arrian won Princess Lilah. He was a true man, and there was nothing I could say to that, for I loved her myself. He chose to go into captivity with her—as I would have done." And he went out and locked the bronze and iron contraption after him.

In the nal Amklana family, it seemed clear, the twin sister was the hard and ruthless one, the twin brother the easygoing and softhearted one. Perhaps his daughter would prove a broken reed; perhaps she would be embittered and vicious in her hatred of everyone. All I knew was that I had to rescue her and see about helping the rebellion along...

A most gorgeously formed Sybli wearing a slit shush-chiff of laypom-yellow material, her baby face bouncy with smiles, brought me food and drink. Through the half-open door I caught a glimpse of a giant Khibil, a massive glimmer of steel, dangling Orlan's key ring. So he did trust someone other than himself in his villa... In only a few burs, Orlan returned. He looked weary, and his face was whiter and more strained than it ought to be. He moved a hand despondently.

"The queen is set on her course, majister. We must depose her and install the Princess Lildra as queen!"

"Agreed. I'll get along to the Castle of Afferatu."

He sat down on the bed. "Yes. I will send word. We have people down there, but they are despondent after the last failure."

I thought to say, "Can you tell me anything of Spikatur Hunting Sword, Orlan?"

"By Harg! I was approached recently and I think other lords also. Then I heard nothing. And then arrests were made and men and women were sent to the Jikhorkdun. It was done by Kov Hogan who is a spymaster it would be better not to cross. He says he is a queen's man, but I know he has been bought by Hamalese gold. He hates me."

We talked for a space and I told him that Spikatur Hunting Sword was a conspiracy directed against Hamal. "They claim to have no leaders, which probably means local chapters each doing what it can and reporting back— but to whom? They assassinate Hamalese. They burn voller factories. They attempt to be a thorn in the flesh of Hamal and her friends."

It occurred to me that if the local chapter of Spikatur had not been broken up then Tyfar would have been in serious danger.

"What can you tell me of the plot formulated by Vad Noran?"

"He was betrayed. By whom, I do not know." Orlan spread his hands. "There are always plots and always, always, always, those who will betray for money."

"Or ideals."

"Those as well. It comes down to the same thing in the end. Men and women broken or turned out into the Arena."

"Yet you persist?"

"I must. There is no other way."

From this nighttime meeting in a small room smelling of dust and apples we both learned much. He was eager to ally with Vallia and Djanduin and whoever else would stand against Hamal. I spoke to him of the Shanks, or Shants, Shtarkins, the fishheads from the other side of the world, and he shared my dreams of a great confederation to stand against these leem-loving reivers.

"I have sent word to Prince Jaidur, and he will come, I have no doubt, as soon as possible to see his father. He is a busy young man."

"Aye," I said. "Busy."

The Sybli in her slinky shush-chiff, that alluring evening gown worn by Kregan girls on holiday or festive occasions, brought us wine and we drank a little companionably. Orlan left late, and I debated if it was wise for me to wait for Jaidur. He was still resentful that I was his father, although he had proved himself a fine young man and a splendid son to his mother. I'd give him until the morning, I told myself, and then I'd be off, and the little dusty-apple-smelling room tinged with a lambent blueness.

My first reaction was one of complete stupidity. Not stupefaction, for whatever tricks the Star Lords and their Scorpion got up to would not, I thought, surprise me. I shook my head. I slumped down on the bed. "Not now," I said aloud. "Not bloody now!"

And the gigantic form of the Scorpion leered down on me, gloating. Far larger than the modest confines of the room, that enormous shape glowed with blue fire, and I felt the winds sweeping me up and the coldness chilling my flesh and I went whirling away end over end, yelling my foolish head off that I wouldn't go, by the putrid diseased left eyeball of Makki-Grodno.

But—I went.

In the next few heartbeats I expected to be hurled down all naked and unarmed somewhere on Kregen's savage surface to rescue some poor devils at the whim of the Star Lords. The Everoinye, the Star Lords, cared not a whit for what I might be doing. If I rebelled against them I could be hurled back to Earth and left to rot. Once, I had rotted on Earth for twenty-one years.

Never again—not ever again, could I allow that...

By the exercise of willpower I had accomplished that defiance. My own puny mortal will had been set against the superhuman demands of the Everoinye. And I had influenced events. Mind you, they'd gotten their revenge in flinging me to Earth and leaving me there to molder away until, in the fullness of time and with the help of other forces, I had returned to Kregen.

So now, tentatively, I tried to resist.

Suppose I were thrown down into Segesthes, miles away to the east, or Turismond, miles away to the west? Suppose they dumped me down in the Eye of the World? I fought them. I had to go to the Castle of Afferatu to rescue a princess. The will of the Star Lords, I thought, being superhuman, must overwhelm my own desires. They were usually aloof, and although there was dissension among them with the young Star Lord, Ahrinye, demanding a greater share of power, they just did not bother about humanity. So I thought in my ignorance. And so, thinking that, I struggled against them.

A voice whispered in, like a dagger.

"You swore, Dray Prescot, there was a compact between us."

By three things I knew this was not the voice of Ahrinye. First: The blueness tinged with a deep crimson, and there was no sign of the acid green associated with Ahrinye. Second: The voice was not his, although superhuman and remote, not drilling in my head like a white-hot auger. And, third: I had no compact with him, and had at best a ramshackle kind of agreement with the Everoinye themselves.

So I said, "I hear you, Star Lords. Have I not done your bidding well and faithfully? And I know you have no thought or care for humankind, so that anything I might say will not move you."

Into the rushing wind swirling about me seeped that macabre silence and stillness found in the eye of a storm. The blueness of the Scorpion faded as the pulsating crimson brightened. I looked in vain for the first glimmerings of friendly yellow. The voice husked now, as though speaking in my ear, and yet I knew I sat on a bed in a dusty apple-smelling room in Orlan Mahmud's villa. All around me the crimson stretched, and gradually it coalesced beneath me and broadened and lifted above into a hollow vault.

"You have obeyed, Dray Prescot, although we know your resentment of us."

I marveled. These beings, although once human, were no longer a part of the human race. How could they be? I did not know. I was confused.

"What do you want of me now? I have work to do—"

"We released you for your work in Vallia. Now you will work for us in Hyrklana, as you did once before, just the other day. And your work here is goodly in our eyes."

I just didn't believe this.

"Goodly—my work? You mock me, Star Lords!"

"Mockery is for fools. No doubt that is why you mock others so much."

I clenched my fists. I was no longer sitting on the bed, I was standing on a hard crimson floor and the vault above blazed with white stars through the crimson curve. I stared, sick.

"What—"

"Listen! You will be sent to where you wish to go. In this thing our wishes coincide. Also, a bundle will go with you, for it grows heavy in the transubstantiated state. It seems to us, Dray Prescot, that you are not as other men. You are reckless, foolish, headstrong and cunning. Also, you have striven to resist us. As a Kregoinye, one who serves us on Kregen, you have done well despite yourself. Continue to do well."

I held myself in check. If I angered the Everoinye I could be back on Earth instantly, stranded on the world of my birth.

Yet I could not hold back: "I do not admit to being a Kregoinye—"

"Yet you are."

The hardness of the crimson floor seemed to me to be no illusion. A soft wind blew. I thought I could see distant shapes, insubstantial, gossamer, floating at the extremity of vision. I appeared to be standing on the floor of an impossible vast hall, vaulted with star-pierced crimson. Somewhere there was music. I breathed deeply. Was that a face, a face of enormous size, peering down at me? Were those eyes, as large as suns, shooting forth crimson light within the crimson immensity? I shut my own eyes, dazzled.

I felt the coldness of a damp wind on my naked skin and the earthly sough of tree branches stirred by wind. I opened my eyes and I was standing at the edge of a wood, dark in the light of two of Kregen's lesser moons hurtling past low above. I looked about. The breeze blew damp and chill. The grass was wet. The trees sighed, black masses flogging in the coming gale, and I sucked in a breath of air vastly different from the last lungful I had breathed in that supernal chamber.

My foot kicked a solid bundle, and I looked down. Wrapped in an old gray blanket, the bundle looked—odd. I bent and undid the rope knots and threw the blanket back. I stared.

That gray blanket reeked with a repellent odor of fish.

Inside, a short scarlet cape showed the typical thin and elegant gold embroidery of Valka. I lifted it aside to reveal a rapier and main gauche of fine Vallian manufacture. There was a first-class thraxter that had been taken at the Battle of Jholaix. I touched the old scarlet breechclout and fingered the broad lesten-hide belt with the dulled silver buckle. The breast and back gleamed with the luster of oiled armor, their chasings and embossings superb examples of the armorer-decorator's art. The helmet was really a plain steel cap with a rim of trimmed ling fur and a flaunting tuft of scarlet feathers I remembered I'd not cared for but had worn to show my position to my men in battle.

No surprise at all that the very first item I picked up, holding in my fists, and staring deeply, was that special sword Naghan the Gnat and I had designed and forged and built in the armory of Esser Rarioch, in Valka. That sword was as good a copy as we could contrive of the superlative Krozair longsword.

Well!

Yes, I knew this bundle of clothing and weapons. I'd last seen these swords, this armor, when I'd defied the Star Lords and been thrown back to Earth for twenty-one years. They had tried to bribe me then by hurling me down into action for them with my gear still intact. Usually—always—I was naked and unarmed. Slowly, I picked up the gear, looking at it, feeling it, expecting it to evaporate into moonshine as the pseudo-weapons from the Moder had done. But the metal felt hard and ridged under my fingers, the scarlet breechclout snugged neatly and the plain lesten-hide belt cinched tightly with the silver buckle.

I tore out half the flaunting scarlet feather from the steel cap and I hoped, as I donned the armor, that it would be taken as a favor of the ruby drang. For I was still in Hyrklana, and those lights beyond the curve of the wood must be the Castle of Afferatu.

With the rain-laden wind blustering about my ears, head down, I started off to rescue a princess from a guarded tower.

Thirteen

At the Castle of Afferatu

I should really have said to rescue a princess from a dragon-guarded tower. For her jailers had four captive risslacas, dinosaurs of ferocious aspect, chained up at the inner and outer gates. The walls towered. The arrow slits were narrow and deep. The moat was brimming and the drawbridge was up.

"No hope," said Dogon the Lansetter as we stood under a tree that dripped water on our heads and shoulders and down our necks.

The local rebels were very disheartened, dispirited, seeing nothing but failure ahead after their last failure. They'd been easy enough to find and identify from the information Orlan Mahmud had given me. We skulked in the woods and spied on the castle and we might as well have been on the first of Kregen's seven moons, the Maiden with the Many Smiles. There were perhaps twenty-five of us—I say perhaps, for I wouldn't care to try half of them in action. Men and women, boys and girls, both diff and apim, they looked up apathetically as Dogon the Lansetter and I trailed into the camp. Everything was sodden. There were no tents. And the waterproofs were wet inside and out. As for a fire—ha!

"There has to be a way to get in, to rescue the princess, and get out with all of us alive." I spoke commandingly.

A gap-toothed rascal looked across and unwedged his jaws from a cold ponsho chop. His gappy teeth showed as he spoke.

"We don't know you. You quote names at us—I say you are a damned spy come to trap us all without trouble."

"Aye!" shouted an apim with carroty hair and a spotty face.

The four Fristle fifis huddled under a blanket looked out wide-eyed. Pretty, they surely were. But now, they were wet...

"Which one of you organized Frandu the Franch?" At this there were squeals and giggling; then there were certain searching questions for me to answer. One of the fifis admitted to detaining Frandu, but: "Was no good. He didn't part with his keys."

"And we lost Naghan the Finger, and Ortyg the Lame and Hernon the Kramdu, all of them killed dead," said Dogon. He was a bulky fellow whose belt circumscribed bulges, but he was useful with an axe. He wore an iron cap. Most of the others had some kind of body armor, mostly leather, and an assortment of weapons. I refused to let my hope sink or to allow myself to become disheartened. After all, it wouldn't be the first time I'd ventured into dark and dragon-infested towers to rescue princesses, now would it? But I would prefer company on this occasion.

"By Harg! If only this rain would stop!" growled gap-tooth. He was not Gap-tooth Jimstye, for which I was grateful, but his mistrust of me, while perfectly natural, could have been awkward.

"We wait until tomorrow night," said Dogon.

I was fed up with waiting. I said so.

"Tomorrow we expect more men."

Gap-tooth cackled. "You could have more than a hundred men and you'd never bust in there. The castle's impregnated."

A girl with long fair hair started laughing. One or two others joined in. Gap-tooth glared about, not comprehending.

Then a blasted squall drove stinging rain onto us all and drenched us all over again. As I say, not a happy camp and not an auspicious start for a venture that should topple thrones.

The root words for impregnable and impregnated are not the same in Kregish either, but the minuscule jest remained, as if it were hovering in the rain-sodden air. I was still mentally dizzy from the encounter with the Everoinye. Superhuman beings of awesome power living God-alone knew where—yes, I feel I was entitled to be a little punch-drunk. There was no time for self-pity.

Circumspection marked Orlan Mahmud's dealings with people of this stamp, and I'd introduced myself to them as coming from him in his cover name of Klanak the Tresh. Tresh means flag, and Klanak is the name of a mythical hero of Hyrklana, so that Orlan was in effect saying, rise up and follow the flag of your greater past.

No, I could not wait around for this kind of rebellion. The rain pitter-pattered among the leaves and splashed among the huddled forms in their blankets. I looked hard at Dogon.

"What is the name of the guard commander tonight?"

"Now, by the belly and brains of Beng Brandaj, how am I supposed to know that?"

"Rebels have to know things like that."

Eventually, one of the Fristle fifis, not the one who had enticed Frandu, said it would probably be that lecherous Khibil devil with the big sword, Podar, who was a dwa-Hikdar now. Or, she added, her fur wet and bedraggled, or it might not be, and instead that passionate Fristle, Follando the Eye—and what an eye!—would have the Gate.

"If there are three guards in rotation, who has the third?"

"There is a Brokelsh called Ortyg the Bristle, and a Rapa called Rordnon the Andamak. They are ord-Deldars."

I did not chew my lip, for that would convey my own complete indecision. But I would not delay. They had no saddle animals, so I had to walk off in the rain to rescue the princess.

"Remberee!" they called. "We will try to rescue you from the dungeons only if—" I didn't bother to hang about to hear their stipulations.

Now the scarlet cloak and the armor I carried were not those of Hyrklana. A rapier and main gauche might be excused a dandyish officer who wished to be in fashion. The longsword was scabbarded down my back. There is a knack to drawing a blade from that position. But my equipment was clearly military and I was not inclined to toss it away and don a gray slave breechclout. For one thing, guarding a princess with your head forfeit if she escapes is vastly different from standing guard in a busy villa or palace; slaves would not be so free to move around in the Castle of Afferatu. I slogged on in the rain.

No handy soldier of the garrison popped up to be popped into the bag and his uniform donned. No one showed at all as I stood on the bank of the moat and helloed across toward the gatehouse.

The drawbridge lifted up, its bronze spikes very nasty. Lights shone from arrow slits. Everything looked gray and black and wet around those slits of light. The rain trickled down my neck. Among the vaguely discerned clumps of towers there was no telling which was the Jasmine Tower. As far as I could tell, I might have yelled my head off into Cottmer's Caverns for all the notice anyone took of me. There was no point in waiting further. The water of the moat rippled and danced in the slices of yellow light falling from the arrow slits. The rain pranced. It was all very wet indeed.

Only a few strokes took me across the moat. The water was not overly cold, for we were in Hyrklana. As for my weapons, during the time they had been in the care of the Star Lords they had been liberally coated with grease. Removing that protective covering from the hilts had been a thoroughly painstaking task. I hauled myself out under the rearing gray walls, running water between the stones, and unwound the rope I'd demanded and obtained from those miserable rebels. It was as slick as a buttered pole at a fair, so the knots would be vital. I looked up.

The rope would never reach the top of the wall. I crabbed along until I was below a slit in a tower. The first cast missed, the bronze hook clanging back with what sounded like an infernal din. No one heard. Or, hearing, took any notice. I cast again.

The hook lodged in the slit. Hand over hand, up I went.

Gaining the slit, I edged in sideways and braced myself against the smoother stone facings. Now for the tricky bit. The next upward cast would be blind. The hook swung below making a wide arc and then flew upward. I heard the bronze strike the stone, and down the thing plummeted. Seven times I cast upward and seven times the hook missed the arrow slit unseen over my head. Eight throws, and eight misses. I took a ragged breath. Nine...

On the ninth cast the hook caught and held. Not for nothing is nine the sacred and magical number on Kregen.

Dangling in the wind-driven rain over emptiness, up I went again and so wedged myself in the next arrow slit. Just before I gained that doubtful sanctuary I took a good though rapid look up and judged the remaining distance. Just, I estimated, just. This time the hook caught on the very first cast, for the top of the tower afforded a better purchase. The knots were hard-edged under my fists. The parapet bulged, with slits frowning down. I hooked a leg, crabbed out as though going up the Futtock Shrouds instead of through the lubber's hole, and so tumbled over onto the top platform.

A fellow muffled in a cloak stumbled out of the little canvas shelter the sentries had rigged up and tried to stick a spear into my throat. I swayed to the side, and as he rushed past helped him on his way. He went over the edge with a long wailing scream that was lost in the rush of the wind. I collected the rope and started for the head of the stone steps leading down.

Annoyance and regret over the foolish death of that fellow made me cross. Now I would have to find someone else to ask where away lay the Jasmine Tower.

The stairs curved down to aid defense and I paused at the landing to listen. The place might have been stuffed with corpses. At the foot the door was a tough oaken affair with iron bolts; they opened with not more than a regulation screech. The ward beyond lay rain-lashed, sodden and completely uninviting.

A few lights fell from interior windows, but most were shuttered. The rain sluiced down and the storm grew and the stars were expunged. What a foul night! Mind you, the very wetness of the night aided me. I recognize that. But the water trickled down my neck and my feet were sodden and my hair was plastered down to my scalp like a devotee of Curdium-Ferang's mud-oil caked hairstyle when they scalp the sacrifices.

"By Krun!" I said to myself. "The first door it is, and no mistake."

The first door led onto a stone corridor with a few cressets leading to a maze of storerooms. No one was there. Useless. Fuming, I barged out into the rain and plodded through pools of water among the uneven flags to the next door along. This was shut and bolted. I hit it with my fist, and then drew the thraxter and hammered on the thick wood.

"Open up! Open up!"

After a space the bolts shot back and the door eased in a crack. I put my shoulder to it and barged in. A man staggered back almost dropping his lantern. His hair fell over his eyes. His mouth opened.

"What is it? What's all the racket about?"

Beyond him in the dimness lay an anteroom of sorts with tables and chairs stacked against the walls, and tubs and barrels piled in the corners. A bed to one side showed where the man had staggered from. I lifted him up by the nearest portion of his anatomy to hand and said, "Where is the Jasmine Tower? You have two heartbeats to tell me before I push your face in."

He told me.

I put him gently on the bed and closed the door after me.

The second tower along, he'd said, the one with the lantern in a niche over the door. The lantern was out, drowned, as I hove up. I eyed the tower lofting above me, lost in darkness. Up there, in some room and well-guarded, waited Princess Lildra...

So far I had not been detected, but this was a busy castle where other things went on, I did not doubt, than the detention of a princess. Despite the rain and the foul night, guards would be changed, sentries prowl. Time was running short. The door was locked and bolted. I fumed. I bashed the sword hilt against the wood. After a time it pulled back and a light glowed dimly.

Before the man could say anything I bellowed. I was just a dark shape to him, lacerated with raindrops, squelching, foul of temper and brutal of tongue. I advised him of his antecedents and probable destination and roared on: "The lantern is out! You know the regulations! See to it before your backside is roasted, rast!"

He started to mumble and I bellowed him to silence. "You bungling fool! Out of my way." Then, pulling the name from the four given me by the Fristle fifi back at the rain-drenched camp: "Is Hikdar Podar awake, or does he sleep in a drunken stupor?"

"Hikdar Follando has the guard, notor, but, but—"

I was in. The light, weak though it was, dazzled. I squinted and took the fellow's throat between fingers and thumb. His face glared up. He was apim. The room was a mere box, pierced with arrow slits in three inner faces and with murdering holes above. I had little time to get out of this trap. The farther door stood open, with a wash of sorry-looking light across the stone walls.

Gently putting the man down, I stepped over him and went out of the door. The corridor led to the foot of the stairs in one direction. The other way the guardroom was open, without a door, and containing half a dozen men lounging on benches and half-asleep on tables. One shouted: "What was that infernal racket, Nath?"

I tried.

"The lantern is out—"

The man looked up from his folded arms. He was a Deldar, fleshy, an ale-lover, with an enormous mustache. His eyes went mean.

"Stand where you are, cramph." He lurched upright, dragging out his sword. "Seize him, you idiots!"

They were slow. If they subsequently blamed the tempestuous night and the pervading dampness, they might be right; more probably they subconsciously relaxed after the previous attempts to rescue Princess Lildra had failed. They were still standing up and drawing weapons as I went into them. My thraxter whistled about merrily. I thumped them smartly, on heads, behind ears, turning and dodging a few return blows and kicking out to finish the job. The six guards slumbered. I went back to the outer door and closed and bolted it. Then I started up the stairs.

Two guards came clattering down, all a jingle of weaponry, swords in fists, to discover the cause of the uproar below. They were tripped and fell headlong—always a nasty trick on stairs, that—and I went on and up.

The stone stairs smelled musty and fusty and damp as everywhere else, yet into that depressing scent scenery crept a strongly pungent tang of a smell I did not recognize. I sniffed as I padded up—something like old socks? No—that was from another time and another place. The smell reminded me of damp fleeces hung before a fire. The first landing was bare and with a torch sputtering in its bracket. Without needing a light on, I went up the next curving flight, alert for the next pack of guards to come rushing down. They were the queen's men, and they could be excused much on a night like this, but the fact remained, I'd not get out of this without a fight, by Krun!

Almost certainly Princess Lildra would be quartered at the topmost section of the Jasmine Tower. The next landing contained an enormous animal whose coat gave off that distinctive aroma, whose jaws opened and whose fangs gnashed—and whose yellow eyes regarded me malevolently from a face that was a mere mask of hatred. Instantly I hurled myself back, slipping on the damp stone, and the beast's charge carried him over the topmost step before the iron collar and iron chain hauled him up fast. He slavered after me, his tongue lolling and those glistening teeth clashing together.

His gums glistened black and his teeth stuck up like needles. His mouth spattered foam. Shaggy hair dangled like tangled seaweed. He growled and barked and snarled and leaped against the restraining chain. He was thoroughly at home on a vile night like this, being a hound dog from Thothangir in South Havilfar, and if he fastened those jaws in me he wouldn't let go without taking his hundredweight of flesh.

Then—and even I find this hard to credit—I heard myself saying, "Good dog, good dog."

He nearly took my outstretched hand off in one gulp.

Someone called down from above—a rough voice, most unfriendly.

"Quiet, Zarpedon, you hound of hell!"

The hound dog yowled and nearly tore his head off trying to get at me. I looked at him and drew in my breath.

"It's you or me, Zarpedon."

Even taking him with the flat presented an interesting problem, for he was quick. But then, I have been accounted quick also, and the sword blade thudded alongside his head. His eyes rolled. He fell over on his side and lay there, for all the world like a friendly collie taking a rest. I stepped over him, looking down, moving gingerly. Then I went on up. Zarpedon could not be blamed. He had raised an outcry, and the oaf above had taken no notice. Well, by Krun, that suited me.

At the head of the stairs I paused for a moment outside the door. The dog-abusing oaf had left it partially open, no doubt to hear if the dog made any more fuss, and to come out and shout again. I listened before I went in. That is a useful habit.

There were two voices, a woman's and a man's, and the dog-abuser was saying: "... hellhound. Worse than the risslacas at the main gate."

"Poor Zarpedon," said the woman's voice, a harsh, unpleasant croaking kind of voice. "You treat him shamefully."

"And you, you hag, treat him better than you do the prisoner."

"No worse than you, Charldo! No wors'n you!"

The sounds of a blow and a yelp were followed by dragging footsteps, and the woman's whining voice faded, mingled with the man's bad-tempered growlings. I pushed the door open and peered inside. Just an anteroom, with a few sleeping furs piled on a ramshackle bed and bits and pieces of furniture added to relieve the starkness. A light fell from a half-opened door in the far wall. Listening, moving soundlessly, I heard the man and woman grumbling again. But this time they had joined forces and were speaking in ugly tones to a third person.

The clank of iron and a heavy curse from the adjoining door made me realize that in there rested the guards. How many were there? However many, they would be considered by the queen to be up to the job of guarding her niece. I listened thoughtfully for a few moments, considering the thunderstorm outside, the dampness of the night and the hellhound dog below on the stairs.

"Now, then, missy*." The woman fairly snarled the words. "No more nonsense out of you. Drink it up or Charldo will take the strap to you again."

The sounds as of a leather strap being thwacked down into an opened palm made me almost instantly burst in. But I peered carefully through a knothole. Charldo was beating his palm with a leather strap. He was a most venomous-looking Kataki, a race of whip-tailed diffs with lowering faces and jagged teeth with whom I have had my fill of trouble over the seasons. Interestingly enough, he had unstrapped the bladed steel from his tail, and the flexible appendage coiled like a whip above the bed. The woman was a bent-over Rapa woman, missing a quantity of feathers, and her drab clothes bulged here and there, hiding the person who lay on the bed. The Rapa woman held a pottery cup in her hands. "Drink it, missy. Now!"

The Kataki's whip-tail flourished in time to the leather belt thwacking into his palm.

The girl on the bed spoke in a voice that trembled only a little, and the desperation in her and the low almost controlled words filled that dismal chamber with a courage anyone would respond to. Anyone except these two—and Queen Fahia and her guard.

"It is disgusting and I think it is taking away my reason. I will not drink it!"

Smack went the Kataki's tail down on the bed and that was quite enough of that.

"The princess will not drink your gunk today, kleeshes," I said, and jumped into the room—fast.

The Kataki fell down with a broken nose. I kicked him as he lay there as I grabbed for the Rapa to silence her. I got a hand wrapped around her mouth and her big beak clashed and she tried to nip me so I hauled her in, still gripping her tightly.

"I do not, princess," I said, "much care for striking women. But sometimes—"

"Let me," said Princess Lildra.

---

* The Kregish word Prescot uses here is tikshvu, which I have translated as missy with that word's ominous connotations of reprimand and temporary superiority threatening a girl who, powerless, yet insists on rebelling. A.B.A.

Fourteen

Princess Lildra

She stepped over the Rapa woman and started to run for the door and I took her arm and said, "We can't just run out like that, princess. There are guards."

"Of course there are guards. There are always guards." She looked puzzled, hurt, not afraid but withdrawn. "I have planned long and long what to do when my prince rescues me. So I know. We—"

I didn't listen to any more. I was too wet and in too foul a temper. She carried herself well and was young although fully formed, and her long white nightdress would be no garment for a night like this. In her face the lineaments of her mother, Lilah, could be plainly discerned. Also, there was more than a hint of the startlingly fair beauty of Ariane nal Amklana, her aunt who had ordered her killed.

"Are you a great Jikai or are you not? Who are you and why do you seek to rescue me if you are not my prince?"

"I see they allow you books to read in your imprisonment."

"You dillydally, fellow!"

"I am called Jak and have been called Jak the Sturr and Jak the Shot and Jak the Sudden. You may call me Jak the Onker, if you wish. Now, lady, put on some suitable clothes for a wild night."

She didn't care for my tone. I judged that before her parents had been murdered she'd led a life of some privilege, and these dolorous surroundings were relatively recent. As for her aunt, Queen Fahia, some credit—if credit is the right word—had to be given to that fat unhappy queen for refusing to slay her sister and sister's husband and child. And if we stood lollygagging around now we'd all wind up arguing on the way to the Ice Floes of Sicce.

"Get changed, lady. Move!"

She jumped and the flush stained her cheeks. But she went behind a holey curtain and rustles and clickings indicated she was putting on clothes better able to withstand the rain than her flimsy nightdress.

She still wore a dress, whereat I sighed. But perhaps she did not have anything else. I dragged a blanket from the bed and draped it across her head and shoulders. Her hair gleamed liquid gold in the lamplight.

"Keep your head down, keep behind me, and do not scream or run. Only run when I tell you to. And then, lady, run!"

She drew a breath and I took her shoulder, twisted her toward the door and started off.

The conventional view of a young girl in these circumstances did not require an intense imagination to visualize. Sympathy and a lively determination to escape safely with her might be all that was required of the average rescuer. But I fancied that her long absorption with the details of the rescue she was convinced would one day occur had acted as a kind of pre-sensitizing agent. Now that the long-awaited rescue was taking place the whole process acted on her as a drug. Her calmness, her decisiveness, the way she wanted this affair to run, all convinced me of her condition. As to my own expected feelings of sympathy and compassion—of course I felt them, as who, apart from those I have mentioned, would not? But Lildra's actions and ready acceptance of this rescue as a mere acted-out appendage to dream-planning afforded me the opportunity to move fast and not to fear she would collapse.

At the door she said, "The birds are stabled in the White Tower. They do not have them here. We must—"

"I do not think birds will relish flying tonight, lady. It is the rope for you."

Her eyes regarded me with a look I took to be incipient annoyance that her dream-plans were not going as expected.

There was little time before the guards below aroused themselves, but I said—and I own to a genuine curiosity: "How do you plan to reach the White Tower from the Jasmine Tower?"

Her head went back. "Why, that is simple. You will fight your way through and I will follow you."

The hound dog on the landing below sent up a throat-growling sound, very hackle-raising. Poor Zarpedon was feeling sorry for himself. The guards in the adjoining room gave no sign of alertness, and Lildra and I padded softly up the last little flight of stone steps to the roof of the tower.

She saw the rope and she understood. The rain pelted down. Her dress melted against her body in moments. I fastened the bronze hook on the stone and lowered the rope down, not dropping it. There seemed no point in explaining to her that if we could not find an arrow slit, and if we could not wedge ourselves into it, the last part of the descent would be ropeless through thin air.

She said, "When you burst in and knocked Charldo over I took you for a Jikai. But you refuse to follow the plan—I am not sure—"

"Just hold onto my harness. Grip tightly and do not let go."

I had to take her arms, wet and shining with rainwater, and place her hands on my leather gear. I cocked a leg over the parapet and let her weight come on me. The rope was like bristly butter under my fingers. Thank Zair the knots held! Carefully, with Lildra hanging from me, I started the descent.

My head was level with the crenelations when I felt a sudden and totally unexpected jolt and I slid down a hand's breadth. I looked up. The rope was slipping down the wall. In the rain the bronze hook looked a golden-brown smear against the stone. It opened. The bronze hook was bending open, the rope was slipping down the wall, and we dangled on the rope. In only a couple of heartbeats the bronze would straighten and we would plummet down.

One chance—just the one. My hands gripped the rope, found a knot, and hauled. The rope slid down and the bronze screamed on the stone. I got my left hand on the lip of the parapet and held. I dangled, twisting away, and the fire raked all through my arm as the muscles corkscrewed. We swung back. Lildra started to struggle.

"Keep still, girl!"

She quieted instantly, shocked into immobility.

Hanging from one hand, with a girl draped around my neck, I heaved up with my right hand. The rope fell. The rain hit me in my upturned face. Fingers scraping over stone, over rain-slick stone, I found a purchase, gripped, held. For a moment I just hung, dangling. Then I started to chin myself up.

At that moment the sky shattered itself into shards of jagged fire and vomited noise about our ears. Lildra jumped. The thunder and lightning sizzled and smashed again. Everything stood out in momentary flashes of light, the marching lines of rain glittering like the spears of a host. Then the night crashed us again in darkness.

Getting a knee over was difficult with the soft wet form of the girl in the way. But eventually, with cracking muscles and a final heave, we tumbled over the parapet.

Lildra sat up. She was a mere dark shadow, but the way she held herself told me she was furious.

"You should have done as I said, Jak the Onker! My mother told me about being rescued. I know. You seem to be very new or unskilled at being a Jikai."

Laugh! Of course—but later on, later on.

"You seem to have the right of it, lady. Just make sure you do not get yourself chopped."

"I will take Charldo's sword."

So, down the stone steps we went and back to her room. Charldo still slumbered, so rapid had been the fiasco on the walls. Lildra picked up his sword, and swished it about. I jumped out of the way. She had mentioned her mother. This time, this time I'd see the whole thing out, sorry farce though it might be. This time I was doing what the Star Lords wanted.

"Get those wet things off. The blanket was useless—put on some of your friend Charldo's gear that will fit."

Again the flush stained along her cheekbones.

"It will be wet again when we fight our way out."

"True. But all the same—do it."

"I—"

"You will find it more convenient not to have a dress encumbering your legs."

"In that case—very well."

Very much the great lady in her poise, upheld by the drug of her rescue, this princess, and yet heartbreakingly unversed in the ways of the world outside her stone walls. By the way she held the sword I saw she had had some lessons but was unskilled in the unpleasant arts of actually using the weapon to kill anybody.

She went behind the screen to strip off the dress and I unbuckled Charldo's gear. It would wrap twice about Lildra, but she would find it more convenient. And the door burst open.

The guards from the adjoining room broke in, cursing and swearing, swishing their swords about, raving to get at me. They had heard our quick conversation, no doubt of that, and I had been lax in not anticipating that they might be required to make regular rounds.

The blades crossed in the lamplit chamber and the first of them was down with a severed neck—a judicious slicing blow that kissed his skin—even as my sword leaped away to parry the oncoming blows. The metal rang and clinked. They were in no doubt that they would overpower me and we crashed across the room in a furious bundle of smiting blades and striking limbs. Two were Katakis, and one of the tails was chopped off from a neat little backhander. Its owner looked horrified and drew back, clasping the bloody stump in his hands. I wasted no more time on him but flashed my sword blade in the lamplight, dazzled the next long enough to sink the steel into his guts below the corselet.

The others still came on and I backed to make room and collided with the screen. Only by a reflex hop and skip was I able to clear the tangle. A sword swept down at Lildra's head. She was attempting to claw out of the screen and the racks of clothes, shouting not in terror but in fury. I parried the blow, twisted and sank a goodly length in Kataki flesh.

One of them, a bristle-pelted Brokelsh with the rank markings of an ord-Deldar, thrust past a stumbling Rapa to get at me. I parried his blow.

"Well, Ortyg the Bristle," I said, cheerfully, "either you back off and run or you spill your guts on the floor."

He showed his teeth and feinted cleverly and hacked back, but I wasn't where he expected me to be, and my sword was. So Ortyg the Bristle followed my prophecy in all things.

A sword flickered around my legs and I leaped away, swiveling, and Lildra slashed again, blindly. Her wet dress smothered her head. She had leaped up to get into the fray and the screen had gone over and now, here she was, raging and blindly slashing with the wetness gleaming silver and gold over her naked body. I said, "They are all gone."

She pulled the dress away from her head with a squelching sound. She flung it on the floor. She was mad clear through, panting, like a zhantilla aroused to magnificence.

"Why did you push into me, oaf! You knocked the screen all over me, old clothes and all!"

I pointed my blood-dripping sword. "Get yourself dressed. And be quick. They must have heard that racket by now."

She gave me a look that ought to have shriveled me and pulled on a tunic. She strapped up Charldo's leathers as I had said. Then, grasping the sword, she stormed toward the door.

She waited by the door, turning to glower across.

"You seem to forget I am a princess. I would not mention it ordinarily, particularly as you are supposed to be rescuing me and my mother was strict about that, but really—"

"Later," I said, going past and padding out onto the top landing. One thing gave me some hope; she had not fainted clean away at the sight of blood and dead bodies. Metal clanked below.

"They're on the way. Hurry, girl, we must reach the next landing before they do."

Her face expressed conflicting emotions, but there was no time. I seized her arm and hurried her along.

"Zarpedon," she said, on a breath. "He is fierce and will—"

"I sent him to sleep before, and will do worse if he tries to stop us now. Hurry!"

Down the stone steps we plunged and there was no need to steady Lildra. She ran fleetly. The shaggy hound dog glared with his demonic eyes and I jumped in, saying, "Good dog!" and clouted him again. He rolled over, stiff.

"You!" said Lildra.

"In here!" I pushed open the door to the adjoining room, which I expected to find deserted. There was no chance of making a stand. We had to get away. It is said, and with some truth, that a large number of lesser men may drag down one powerful man. True or not, I did not fancy our chances of fighting through the pack below with Princess Lildra to be guaranteed safe. The room was not empty—rather, as we entered it was empty, but the opposite door leading out to the ramparts opened and a crowd of guards from the next tower along broke through. They had come to find out what the disturbance was all about. It was possible they had witnessed my attempts at climbing down the rope.

In an instant we were at hand strokes.

The closeness of the room, the chill dampness of the stone, the stamp of bronze-bound sandals on the floor and the clangor of combat brought instant bedlam. It was not easy to keep Lildra out of it. She insisted on jabbing her sword at the guards from under my arm, or around my side, and there was a fair amount of skipping and jumping. These men were hired warriors, I judged, mercenaries and not soldiers of the Hyrklanian army. Fahia preferred this, for she could control absolutely any rumor or news of the imprisonment of members of her family. So these paktuns were fighting men all. We had a right to-do, slashing away, and with the occasional short jab sending men screaming and, retching, staggering out of the fight.

Working around and with my left arm curved back and holding Lildra, I managed to maneuver so that we had the door through which the guards had run at our backs. That way lay the ramparts.

"The way is clear, lady," I said, and took a Rapa's beak off. "Run out onto the ramparts—"

"And leave you? Never!"

"Run out and see if anyone else is coming. I don't want cold steel at my back, girl!"

She saw the logic of this and darted back through the doorway. I own to a sense of freedom when she went, not having to spend most of my efforts keeping her out of trouble. I leaped headlong into the guards, smiting with an excess of fury which I thought, coldly and calculatingly, would deter them more than mocking words. Two fell, not screaming but in the resigned way of the true professional at the moment of truth. The others drew back a space and a hulking great shaven-headed Gon bellowed: "Fetch bows! Bratch, you rasts."

If they were going to start shooting it was time for me to collect Lildra and depart.

I dodged back through the doorway and slammed the heavy oak.

Lildra crouched by the stone wall, dripping wet already and her new blanket sodden, staring along the rampart. More men were running up, presumably from the next tower along—although I had thought that clear. So there was nothing else for it.

The sky burst apart again with an almighty flash and bang; the Castle of Afferatu burned in limpid fire. The noise concussed and the light blinded, and in the ensuing darkness, blindly, I snatched up Princess Lildra, jumped onto the battlemented wall and leaped out into space.

We hurtled down through the air. Faintly and far off a voice shouted. The water hit us shrewdly, but we had twisted in our headlong fall and cleft the water not like two arrows but not like two tumbling carcasses, either. A few powerful strokes, and the surface broke around my ears and I started to swim across the moat with Lildra supported with her head out and in the air. She said nothing and I just hoped nothing was broken. Even then I was concerned for her reactions when the drug of her rescue wore off.

Climbing out on the other bank was a wet and muddy business. Halfway up we slipped and went sprawling into oozing slime. When we staggered up and started to run across the grass we were plastered head to foot with mud. We must have looked a doleful pair. Still Lildra said not a word; her breathing came fast and evenly, and she held herself as though restraining a fury that would undermine the pillars of the world.

So we ran off into the darkness. Thus was Princess Lildra of Hyrklana rescued.

The whole business was just atrociously wet.

Fifteen

Vampires of Sabal

In the days that followed, filled with suns' light and warmth, I began to believe I might feel dry once more. Lildra developed a snuffly little cold that annoyed her, and which made me feel sorry for her, the Savanti nal Aphrasöe having cured me of ailments of that troublesome kind. We joined up with the rebels and their numbers swelled so that soon we were a little army, ragged and ferociously ill-disciplined, but still the beginnings of the force that would topple Queen Fahia.

We cleared the area around the Castle of Afferatu and marched on, gathering strength. The news that Princess Lildra was come to liberate the country spread with the rapidity of sky-zorcas, and we found welcoming crowds of the poor folk everywhere we went, and the more cautious acceptance of the wealthy and lordly of the land. Orlan Mahmud nal Yrmcelt, the queen's chief minister, sent down a general to take command. The rebellion gathered momentum, for everyone awaited the arrival of Princess Lildra. She was the focal point. Without her, I now saw, the rebellion would never begin on any scale likely to succeed.

Orlan's general, a man whose parents had been brutally driven into the Arena because Fahia believed they plotted against her, was a quiet, thoughtful fellow with a bent nose. He called himself Nath the Retributor, although that was not, I judged, his real name. He tried to bring some kind of order to the ragged mob we had with us. I stayed discreetly in the background and kept an eye on Lildra. She, I knew, was the reason I was here, and her welfare was my first priority.

So we progressed northward through the island, our ultimate goal Huringa, the capital city itself. The locals would give up news of troop movements, and we avoided confrontations, garnering our strength. I was content to leave all this to Nath the Retributor. Soon enough our motley collection of rebels would be found by a force of Queen Fahia's soldiers, and then we would have to see just what the rebellion was made of.

During this time I talked a great deal with Lildra, and learned much of her story, for there was pitifully little to tell. She had been born in the kind of genteel captivity Fahia reserved for her sister, Princess Lilah. Lildra's education had been simple and direct, and there was much of which she was completely unaware. I found her one day in a little clearing slashing Charldo's sword about.

She looked at me commandingly.

"You are a great Jikai, I think, a hyr-paktun, although you do not wear the zhantilhead at your throat. I have seen how you handle a thraxter and will have you teach me the art."

"If you desire it—"

"I command it!" She had taken to the adulation heaped on her by the lords and ladies, hostile to Fahia, who now more and more thronged our rebel camp. I did not think this would spoil her. I could see a directness and a brightness of spirit in her—very becoming a young lady who would be queen.

All the same, she joyed in letting me know she was a princess. "I command you to teach me the arts of sword-play, Jak!"

Gravely, I said, "I can't teach you. But it is only you and the spirit that can learn. Also, the arts of killing with the sword are not play."

She didn't like that. It clashed with her romantic notions. She hadn't liked it when I'd remarked, offhandedly, about our leap from the battlements of the Castle of Afferatu, that that was what castle moats were for, for heroes and heroines to jump into. And yet, and yet, with her fair beauty and her lissom figure, her high color and brave spirit, there was a bright aura of romance clinging about Princess Lildra, oh, yes, very much so...

"Well, Jak, the Onker, let us begin and you—"

A loud, raucous and mocking squawk cut rudely across Lildra's words. She took no notice and went on speaking. I knew she could not hear that croaking voice of doom. I looked up. Perched on a tree branch sat a resplendent bird, all gold and scarlet plumage, his head on one side, his beady eye fastened on me. Lildra could not hear or see him, for he was the Gdoinye, the messenger and spy of the Star Lords. I hadn't seen him for a time. He kept observation on me for the Everoinye, and we would insult each other as a matter of protocol—what the devil did he want now?

I ignored him and listened to Lildra, and presently the Gdoinye flew away. The Star Lords kept a watchful eye out on those who merited their attention. So Lildra and I fell to with our swords, and she was a quick learner and I felt confident she would develop—if she wished—into a fine sworder of the cunning and intelligent kind.

News came down fitfully of outside events. Hamal continued on her headstrong way of imperial conquest. The queen's son was grown into a tempestuous youth, determined to have his own way, and it was whispered that King Rogan had no part of his parentage. The Shanks had raided again, down in the southeast, and soldiers had been sent. This accounted for the paucity of opposition we had so far encountered. I did not say this to Lildra. The idea was bruited abroad that the lack of opposition came from men's reluctance to fight against Lildra for Fahia.

Orlan had not told Nath the Retributor who I truly was, and although a quiet, reserved man, he rubbed along well enough with me. For, and I own it with a half-smile, I occupied a special place of privilege, being the man who had rescued the princess. Nath the Retributor was in constant communication with Orlan. We even kept abreast of the fortunes of the four color corners in the Jikhorkdun. I listened avidly as the fortunes of the ruby drang rose and fell. We still had not caught the emerald neemu...

Then a shattering surprise burst about my head.

I just did not believe it. It couldn't be true. Why?

News came down secretly that the Princess Majestrix of Vallia intended to join our rebellion.

By this time I no longer automatically thought of Delia when the Princess Majestrix was mentioned. Delia was now the Empress of Vallia. Lela was the Princess Majestrix—and I hadn't seen her for so many years the pain gnawed mercilessly at me. I'd been flung cruelly back to Earth, and Lela had been sent adventuring for the Sisters of the Rose. That organization of women was secret to men, as it must be, and it was fruitless for any man to seek to uncover its mysteries. What the SoR did in secrecy was done for the good of Vallia and they did much good work for the poor and sick, men and women both. Useless to try to probe, and ultimately futile. As soon try to uncover the mysteries of the Krozairs of Zy. And so my daughter Lela was coming to join the rebellion!

She had been some time in Hyrklana, so Nath the Retributor told me over the campfire one evening with the fat stars pulsing that shimmering Kregan nighttime glow over the camp. Sentries patrolled. We had eaten and drunk, and now we rested for the morrow's labors.

"She has been working in secret against those cramphs of Hamal. One day, Jak, we will have to stamp our heel upon the Hamalese—but it will be a stern task, for they are strong."

"The strong will fall to the shrewd blow."

"You quote San Blarnoi at me. Very well. It is true."

He knew nothing of Spikatur Hunting Sword.

"The Princess Majestrix brings sisterly greetings to our own Princess Lildra. Vallia fights gallantly against Hamal." Nath took a sip of wine, sparingly, as was his custom. "An alliance will be offered, I am sure. When Princess Lildra is queen then we will join with Vallia against Hamal."

"That," I said, "is a development devoutly to be wished." And then somberly I added, "And will it be worth all the dead?"

"Of course, Jak! Of course."

Sometimes I wish I did not have this all-encompassing vision. It knocks the stuffing out of you when you least want that. We had to knock seven kinds of brick dust out of Hamal, and there was no getting over that this damned side of the Ice Floes of Sicce, no, by Vox!

Nath leaned forward and lowered his voice. "There is more, which is not general circulation. I am given to understand that the Princess Majestrix's father will also honor us."

I kept my wine jug steady. The red wine, a medium Mahemj, did not ripple. I lifted the jug and drank and wiped my lips with a mental, By Mother Zinzu the Blessed! I needed that! I looked hard at Nath the Retributor with the look that says you do not believe what you have just heard with your own ears.

"It is true. By Harg! Unlikely, but true. I had it from Orlan Mahmud's messenger personally and only tell you because you are very dear to the princess."

"Oh?" I said, intrigued by this idea. "I wouldn't have thought that."

The Retributor laughed and leaned back and drank, and there was no getting any more out of him that night.

I would like to know how it was that the Emperor of Vallia was going to join the camp he was already in, and how it was he did not know that interesting fact. Yes, by Krun!

When Orlan had received word that Lildra had been rescued by a hulking, scowling, rascally fellow he would have known that was me, and that our plan had worked. Knowing me, as he thought, he probably hadn't given a second thought to my method of departure from his villa. And that despite the key ring and the precautions.

A beautiful warm feeling began in me and continued to grow. The very fact that the Princess Majestrix of Vallia was coming to see Princess Lildra, that Vallia was willing to join hands with the Hyrklese in defending ourselves against Hamal, had a tonic effect on everyone and our ranks grew prodigiously. We were marching on Huringa, a growing tide of eager volunteers. And the name of Vallia meant something, even here, even this far away. So I felt the future glowed with promise.

The very next day as we marched into a town whose inhabitants turned out to cheer us, a contingent of the Hyrklanian army marched in from the other end. There were three regiments of foot and a cavalry regiment of totrixmen. Before an ugly scene developed, the soldiers began to cheer for Princess Lildra. Well! That proved we would win, so said everyone, and much wine flowed and gusts of laughter burst above the mingled camps.

And then, of course, we had news that because the Hyrklanian army was proving unsatisfactory, even disloyal, Queen Fahia was busily at work hiring mercenaries to fight us. A deal of hard talk went on among our people, and when the froth of declamations blew away, it did seem as though we would go on and fight and win. But the news deteriorated even further. More and more mercenaries were pouring into the country, paid for with broad Hyrklanian gold deldys, and we saw we had a fight on our hands.

When we reached the River Llindal we camped just above the water meadows near a copse in which still stood the ruins of a temple to a half-forgotten god. Instead of sending for me when we wished to talk, as was the usual custom, Nath the Retributor sought me out as I dropped sticks onto the fire. By this time I had acquired a fine zorca to ride, and a tent and gear, and a cheerful helpmate in Wango the Mak, a shock-headed fellow who had run off from his master and whom I had taken it on myself to manumit. He was fetching the water. Nath walked up and then, glancing around and seeing we were unobserved, motioned for me to enter my tent. Intrigued, in I went. He followed. At once, the moment we were inside, he started to go into the full incline, that slavish Kregan bow of fulsome proportions, a hateful grovel.

"Stand up, man!" I said, somewhat testily, for of course I could guess what had happened.

"Majister!" said Nath the Retributor.

"Of Vallia, not of Hyrklana. Why do you know now, Nath?"

"I have word from Pallan Orlan Mahmud. The Princess Majestrix will ride in this evening—Orlan felt that you—"

"Considerate of him. And only you know about me?"

"Yes, majister."

"Well, leave it at Jak for the moment. We will see."

"Yes, majister."

By Zair! There we were, back again to the "Yes, majisters" all the time. Confound it!

The meeting during which our chiefs would meet the party who had ridden secretly from Huringa was to take place in the ruined temple. The twin suns slanted into the western sky. The half-forgotten god's name was, I believe, Rhampathey. Wango the Mak finished cooking the meal and I ate hugely and then went off to the River Llindal and, stripping off, plunged in. I did not swim but washed thoroughly. Then I had a Fristle fifi with her cunning scissors clip my hair and trim me up smartly. I took out the scarlet breechclout, neatly washed and pressed, and donned that old favorite, along with my armor and gear. I walked about the camp for a space, talking to no one, meeting no one's eye. When I saw Lildra walking toward me among the tents I turned sharply away and took myself off, pretending not to have seen her. I wandered about. I chewed my lip. I fiddled with my swords and harness. The suns sank... Presently the messenger came for me and, together with Nath the Retributor and others of our chiefs, off I went toward the Temple of Rhampathey.

At my express wish Nath's conduct toward me was no different from usual, and I was just one of the crowd as we went in among the ruins. The stone looked leached. Lichens splotched the pillars and fallen walls, forming ancient faces of mildew and decay. The Maiden with the Many Smiles and She of the Veils were already up, sailing above our heads and casting down their rose and golden radiance. Insects buzzed for a brief space, but the ruins absorbed sound and the place lay dead and silent.

A Chuktar next to me breathed hoarsely through his open mouth. He kept his fist wrapped around his sword hilt. I walked quietly. The place appeared ghostly, uncanny, and no one would have been surprised at ambush or the sudden apparition of skeleton men. All that happened was the approach of a body of people from the other direction, bearing lanterns, unnecessary in the light of the moons.

I stared eagerly toward those people illuminated by the lantern glow. Over there, walking toward me, was Lela!

I did not rush forward. I wanted to savor this moment, so I stayed a little way in rear, moving to the side, staring as the newcomers approached.

And then I saw among those strangers a familiar face.

She had doffed her blue tunic, and her black leathers shone liquidly in the radiance of the moons as though molded to her. Her legs—very long, very lovely legs—stamped along in her tall black boots. Her brown Vallian hair and brown Vallian eyes, the carriage of her, upright, defiant, all gave me a swift and poignant pang of affection and love for my Delia, for this Valona whom I had last met trying to slash me with her claw, while nothing like Delia, yet reminded me of her. She did not remind me of my middle daughter, Dayra, who was called Ros the Claw. But, even as the crowd closed around her, I remembered I had had that feeling I was reminded by her of someone I knew. There had been no time to puzzle out the riddle then, when we'd stormed through the deserted spaces of the Temple of Malab the Kazzin and found Tyfar tied up and then Jaezila, and not much since. All the same, the wearing of black leathers and tall black boots, the swishing about of a rapier, even brown Vallian eyes and hair, do not make two women look the same. Valona, who was not called Valona the Claw, did not resemble in any profound way Delia or Dayra or even Jilian.

We went on in the moon's light and I swallowed and licked my lips.

The idea occurred to me that no man would ever know the secrets of the Sisters of the Rose, nor even how many of them there were, or who wore the steel claw among them. Jilian Sweet Tooth was a good friend to Delia and me and she couldn't tell me so much as a spider's eyelash about the SoR. That Lela had preceded Dayra through Lancival, where these girls learned how with their claws to chop up nasties, seemed eminently logical.

The crowd bunched to pass between craggy buttresses of rotting stone, ancient and stained in the moonshadows, and I was pushed a little to the side. Bushes grew from cracks in the stones and paving flags. The smell of night flowers hung on the air. The two parties hurried forward. Lildra, with Nath in attendance, stepped out ahead.

From the bushes flanking us a movement caught my attention.

Dark forms leaped from their places of concealment. Sharp, acid-bitter faces, white as death, leered from hunched cloaks of shadow. Vampire fangs gleamed. Eyes glared hot and red. And steel blades shimmered death in the moonshadows.

"Sabals!" People screamed and the two bodies, confused, surged and swayed. "Vampires of Sabal!"

I was the nearest. This was a time for the headlong rush into danger, chancing destruction, no time for thought. If Lildra were harmed, I would feel sorrow and the Star Lords would exact vengeance. But if Lela were harmed...!

My sword ripped free and I went into them like a battering ram. Dark forms shrieked about me, fangs struck, swords slashed. I managed to skewer the first and then it was a matter of ducking and dodging and slashing back. Lopping arms presents a small problem when your muscles are powered by a frenzy of fear for your daughter. Calculating the amount of force necessary to put a vampire thing out of action, and not spend overmuch force on that one, ready for the next, is difficult when your head is filled with a breathless panic. Heads rolled.

A lithe form surged into the fight alongside me. A sword struck with precision and economy. The vampire things, fangs glittering, red eyes like demons, screamed and sought to slay us and drink our blood. And we fought back. We fought them for a space and then other people joined in, and a wall of steel barred off the vampire horrors from the princess.

I looked at the girl who had fought at my side and felt the shock overpower me again.

"I thought you were dead, Jak," said Jaezila. She laughed, very splendid in that flowing light, her brown hair severely tied back, her russet leathers plain and workmanlike, her sword a bar of blood in her gloved fist. "Tyfar went back to Hamal and I—well—and what are you doing here?"

"Jaezila!" I said, like a fool. "I am with the rebellion."

"Queen Fahia is like one of her own pet neemus, frantic with fear and rage. So I thought I'd help out—but—" Her face clouded. "We are blade comrades, Jak, you and Ty and I. Yet—yet—"

"I am—glad—to see you, Jaezila. This is not the same silly kind of rebellion Vad Noran attempted. I heard that Tyfar had gone back to Hamal and rejoiced, knowing you and he were safe. But here you are, and very welcome, too."

There was an oddness about this meeting. Yes, I was overjoyed to see Jaezila again, for she was a girl dear to me, as you know. If Prince Tyfar could be along to share in the fun, such as it was, then that would be even more splendid. Then I realized my own stupidity, and chilled. Jaezila was looking at me cautiously. Of course! She thought I worked for Hamal, as did she, and how, then, she would be wondering, could I be a part of a rebellion aimed at seating a princess on the throne who had vowed to join with Vallia against Hamal? This would be tricky.

What was even more tricky was—what was she up to here? There was absolutely no possibility that I would allow harm to come to her if it was discovered she worked for Hamal. She must be attempting to aid the rebellion and unseat Fahia and then turn the coup to the advantage of Hamal. And—would that mean danger for Princess Lildra? I sweated under the night breeze. What a coil!

We walked back to join the two parties, who were now mingled together and all talking away, excited by the sudden attack of the Vampires of Sabal. These things are not your Dracula vampire at all, being creatures who like to guzzle human blood and who hide in out-of-the-way places and who will die by stroke of sword without holy water or a stake through the heart.

For all that, they are vampires, and horrible and mortal foes to humankind.

Valona came running up, waving her claw, which ran red with vampire blood. "Princess! You are safe!" She saw me and said, "Oh!"

"I am glad to see you are safe, princess," said Jaezila.

Staring at Valona, seeing her beauty, I smiled. I, Dray Prescot, smiled with a sudden overpowering gratitude. But, for all that, I said to Jaezila, "So you are a princess! Well, I might have guessed it, and I've been tangling with princesses for a long time now—"

"You—!" said Valona. "But you are the man who said—"

"And you are a princess, too," I said, half-laughing, wishing to tease her. "Jaezila and you are friends? That pleases me."

"We have been through many adventures together, Jak and I," said Jaezila. "He is a blade comrade. I rejoice to see him alive, for I thought he had given his life to save me and—and another. He will give praise to all the gods that Jak lives. She looked at Valona and, I admit it now for I felt it then, I felt a pang—just the smallest, most unworthy feeling—that if you wished to compare the two girls, then Jaezila far outshone Valona. And this was a base and vile thought.

Before any more could be said in this tangle, Nath the Retributor hurried across. With him strode a giant of a man—an apim—with a strong bulldog-like head and massive jaw, a warrior who wore armor and carried four swords. This impressive fighting man was introduced as Hardur Mortiljid, Trylon of Llanikar. I judged him true to his appearance. He bowed formally.

"I am here as escort to the Princess Majestrix of Vallia, bearing a warrant from Klanak the Tresh." Klanak the Tresh was Orlan's cover name, and I felt relief that he had the sense to continue to use it still. We weren't out of the wood yet. The Lahals were made, and then Hardur said to me, "I give you my thanks, horter, for the gallantry of your fight against the Sabals. They are news from the devil, by Harg!"

"The princess is unharmed," I said. I still felt this enormous glow of delight, so I could add, "All the princesses!"

Jaezila laughed. No one else appeared to consider the remark worthy of comment, the fact being that my brand of humor is often considered odd even by the phenomenally peculiar standards of Kregan humor. But Tyfar, Jaezila and I shared our own idiosyncratic laughs together, and the suns were warmer as a consequence. Erndor, the slim Vallian who had tried to spit Tyfar and had then thrown a brick at him, came over. Kaldu, Jaezila's retainer, hovered. Nath the Retributor coughed and cleared his throat. A ring formed with the mingled parties all staring at those in the center, the lantern light falling upon cheekbones and glittering in eyes. I stepped back. The moment approached.

The expectant silence fell oddly into that place of ruins. It trembled invisibly, yet was real, perfectly apparent to everyone. Nath stared at me in puzzlement. I looked back, waiting. And then—of course, onker that I was!—I saw the cause of his embarrassment.

He could not know how things stood between Lela and me. He didn't know that the Star Lords, by hurling me between the stars, had prevented my knowing my own daughter, as Lela's dedication to the SoR prevented her from knowing me. So we all stood about like loons when Nath and the others expected father and daughter to fly into each other's arms.

Valona was quite clearly keyed up. She glowed with excitement, staring about. What it would be—to have two daughters who flourished lethal steel claws!

Hardur Mortiljid slapped one of his swords up and down in the scabbard. He looked down at Nath.

"Well, by Harg, Nath! These Vallians are odd folk!"

Valona glanced up at Hardur.

Nath said, "I will—"

Erndor stepped forward.

"An explanation is owed you, Trylon Hardur, and you, Nath the Retributor, as to you all. If you will allow? We Vallians may be somewhat different from other folk, but in this, the vicissitudes of cruel fate have parted the

Emperor of Vallia and the Princess Majestrix for many seasons. For very many seasons."

The crowd nodded as though perfectly understanding the blows of fate, and the oddness of folk who were not Hyrklese. I looked expectantly at Valona. She stood alertly, waiting... At her side Jaezila stared at Erndor, and then she looked away, searching among the crowd, and coming back again to gaze upon the Vallian. Valona remained bright-eyed and vivid, almost hopping with excitement.

Erndor went on, "So that I do not think one would recognize the other—"

At that revelation, and never mind the blows of fate, the crowd's shocked oohs and aahs were fitting comments on not only the conduct of Vallians, but the way a father had allowed so terrible a degradation of his relationship with his daughter. Even though they did not know of the Everoinye, I felt that censure deeply. I was just about to do something very foolish when Valona began to step forward. Jaezila took her arm and held her, and then my blade comrade said, "So there is no mystery here. Nath the Retributor, if you would kindly do the office of introducing the Emperor of Vallia, the Princess Majestrix will be in your debt." She smiled.

Valona sucked in a breath, and Hardur looked down his nose. The crowd fell silent. I did not move but looked at Valona. Nath was slow.

"Well, Nath the Retributor," said my blade comrade, Jaezila. "The Princess Majestrix is waiting. Is he not here? I would not be surprised. He never seems to be at hand when I need him. Whereabouts is my father skulking now?"

Sixteen

I Stake My Life on the Truth

The world of Kregen went up and down and over and over three times and I was clinging on her for dear life with bleeding fingers to stop being hurled off into a black void of insanity.

Jaezila!

Lela?

And then, the mind does work in strange ways in fraught moments like these, I thought, So Tyfar will be my son-in-law—if all goes as nature intends. Deuced odd!

I felt like a man turning a corner and being blown back by a sea wind gusting past force ten. I struggled to get a breath. Nath the Retributor, all smiles, was saying, "He is here, majestrix, standing here. Now you have explained, of course, of course. These things happen in imperial families."

He was, I am sure, quite unaware of any sarcasm.

"Here is Dray Prescot, Emperor of Vallia! Lahal, majister!"

Jaezila looked at me.

Dayra had looked at me, I recalled with anguish from our first meeting, with loathing and contempt. How would my eldest daughter regard the father who kept on disappearing?

She was beautiful, yes, she was her mother's daughter, regal, commanding, impish—and now a frown dinted in between her eyebrows, and her lips drew down, and her eyes regarded me with a look I just could not fathom.

"Him?" she said. And, then: "Jak the Sturr—my father?" And, then: "He is a blade comrade, Jak, a friend, one who would give his life for me, as I for him, as we have proved. But—the Emperor of Vallia?"

"Jaezila—" I said.

A struggle was going on within her. She had not expected this thunderclap of a revelation. No more had I, by Zair!

But I was over the wonder now. This glorious girl was my daughter Lela. And the magic was—we were blade comrades!

What a splendid contrast to my dismal confrontations with Dayra, who was Ros the Claw!

And of course, Dayra was not evil, only misguided. Now I had an opportunity to talk to Jaezila—Lela—and discover more about Dayra, and find ways for reconciliation. Lela would know about her sister, there was no doubt about that. I confess to a most beautifully euphoric feeling bathing me in wonderful sensations.

Jaezila brought all this down to earth with a thump.

"Whatever my blade comrade has told you, and however much I love him, he is Jak, and not the Emperor of Vallia. I know. I own I am disappointed, for he would have been a good father to me."

"Jaezila," I said. "I mean, Lela—"

"It's not going to do you any good. By Vox! I'll see no harm comes to you. You know that. But the good of Vallia is in this, Jak, and even you cannot jeopardize that."

Just as Princess Lildra stepped forward to have her say, she was pushed aside by Hardur Mortiljid. The giant's face exhibited every indication of bursting. His eyebrows drew down, black with thunder. At his side Nath the Retributor was already drawing his sword. Other men crowded up.

"I stake my life on the Princess Majestrix!" bellowed Hardur. "She has spoken. This man is an impostor. Seize him up!"

Well—I was slow. But I felt as though I'd been hit over the head with a sandbag. They had bonds around my neck and wrists and ankles even as I tried to reason with Jaezila. She looked distraught. I could imagine her anguish.

"Jak!" she called over the hubbub.

The crowd pushed and shoved around us; I was dragged along, shoved up against a stone pillar and the ropes wound round and around pinioning me to the ancient stone. I felt a damned hard edge jabbing me in the back and it was nothing. I couldn't believe all this. Princess Lildra was shouting, but in the uproar her words went unheeded. These people had found a spy in their midst, and mob law was about to run its course.

"Kill him now! Spy!"

"No, make him tell his secrets!"

"Zigging Hamalese rast!"

Jaezila was tall, but Hardur overtopped her as he overtopped most people. Even Jaezila's savage retainer, Kaldu, looked a trifle shrunken as he stepped up to clear a space for his mistress. They were forming a ring around the pillar to which I was bound, and the noise and confusion brought fresh mobs running up from the camp. Lantern light splashed bloodily upon the stones, and the moons tinged the scene with rose and gold. A tiny night breeze blew and the scents of moon blooms filled the air. And I was like to bid good-bye to all this exotic world of Kregen.

Lildra looked flustered and, not so much frightened as overwhelmed. Hardur with his giant stature and giant voice dominated events, and his bellows drowned more rational thought. But I thought. I thought that Jaezila, my blade comrade, worked for Hamal. She might not be my daughter Lela. She disowned me; might not I therefore disown her? We would remain comrades, for the bonds between us were not to be broken lightly—and even this business which was very far from light would not sunder my feelings for her, or hers for me, I was confident. Perhaps, as a spy for Hamal, she had wormed her way in and under the guise of the Princess Majestrix of Vallia, worked a mischief against my country?

I looked toward the knot of chiefs, and they were arguing in their more elegant way, as the mobs were yelling and caterwauling, in their more vehement fashion. They wanted my skin, all of them. No doubt of that, by Vox!

Jaezila was shouting up at Hardur, fierce, like a tigress: "I love that man! If you harm him I will surely kill you!"

"But he is a spy for Hamal! He knows our secrets!"

Lildra screamed, "He is a hyr-paktun and he rescued me and he cannot be the emperor! But—but I do not want him killed, whatever he may have done!"

Nath shouted, "Klanak the Tresh vouches for him—"

"He can be deceived." Hardur boomed out. "I say kill him now, out of hand, as you put your foot upon a filthy rast that infests a dunghill."

I bellowed across, "You'd get a mucky foot, then, Hardur!"

And Jaezila laughed.

By Zair! If she was not my daughter, how I longed for her to be Lela!

Using his height and lungpower, Hardur bartered away at his central point—killing me with all dispatch—in an attempt to convince Princess Lildra. He was a loyal man, if a trifle prone to blustering pigheadedness, and even in his passionate anger he saw he could not just top me in defiance of Lildra's wishes.

The wrangling went on, brute force against sentiment, common sense against sentimentality. If you catch a spy, you have to do what he expects will be done—sometimes. Nath was in a quandary, for he quite liked me and had had word from Orlan; yet my detractors were violent and persuasive. If the argument broke down the middle and it was party against party, we had the outnumbering of them, true. I did not think Hardur Mortiljid was a man to worry over that.

In the uproar and excitement I felt a soft touch on my arm, twisted up around the pillar. I said nothing. A voice whispered. "Make no sign. The Princess Majestrix bids me free you. I still wonder if I should have clawed you before you jumped down the trap."

My bonds fell away at the back and were held up so that while I was free the ropes would not betray me. Barely moving my mouth, I said, "My thanks, Valona. Would you believe I had thought you were my daughter?"

A soft amused snort, and: "You are a splendid paktun, no doubt. But an emperor? Ha! No one has seen me and they will not see me go. Give me four heartbeats to get clear or we will land the Princess Majestrix in trouble. Do you understand?"

"Yes."

Valona had crept from the shadows at the back, unseen. If I betrayed her by leaping free now, Jaezila would also be suspect. Perhaps they would turn on her. Was she Lela? And these were Hyrklese. Perhaps, they would think, this whole affair was a plot on the part of Hamal. It was very likely.

A fleeting succession of shapes passed before the rosily golden face of She of the Veils. For a small moment the moon silhouetted a group of flyers, winging down. Then they winged swiftly on. I looked toward the arguing crowds. Soon the tinder would light and they'd turn ugly. Time to depart. I would go with great regret. I own to a fondness for my own skin; I hungered to talk to Jaezila again, and to satisfy myself she was my daughter, as I was in no doubt I could convince her I was her father, given the time denied us so far. But if I yielded to that almost overpowering temptation, then my fondness for my skin would be set at naught; they'd chop me, for sure.

Valona had placed the severed ends of the bonds in my hands and I held them taut. When I cast them away and leaped from the pillar I would be seen at once. The hue and cry would begin. Maybe I would not depart. Running away was foreign to the nature of the Dray Prescot who had adventured over the face of Kregen, even if it was tending to feature more and more with the Dray Prescot who, in these latter days, shouldered the burdens of empire. By the stinking left nostril of Makki-Grodno! I damned well wouldn't run away! I knew what I'd do, and by Zim-Zair, I'd do it quick!

I threw the ropes away and belted like a hellhound for the arguing group around Jaezila. I could convince her—I would convince her. If she was not my daughter, if she was a Hamalese spy, then we were both done for. I cast aside all doubt. Jaezila was Lela, and both our lives hung on the truth of that.

Instantly I was seen. The hullabaloo started, with yells that the mad paktun was trying to assassinate Lildra, murder the Princess Majestrix, disembowel Hardur and decapitate Nath. I pelted on. Someone hurled a javelin and the stux flew past. On I raced, dodging and ducking, leaping idiots who tried to fling themselves at me. I ran with my hands empty and open, arms up, trying to indicate that, being unarmed, I could not hurt anyone.

Any Krozair of Zy, any Khamorro, would know the lie inherent in that, but it was all I could do.

"Jak!" yelled Jaezila.

"Jak!" screamed Lildra.

"You're running the wrong way!" Jaezila started at me, yelling, and I could see she was choked with laughter. By Krun! What a girl!

Hardur Mortiljid whipped out his sword. Like him, it was big. He rushed. His first swing was designed to part me along the middle and I swerved and hit him on the nose—I had to jump—and hurdled over his falling form. Then I was up to Lildra, who looked distraught, and Jaezila, who looked ready for a fight.

"If you are Lela," I shouted, "as I truly believe, then I have things to tell you that will show you I am—"

"Your back!"

I dodged and the javelin whistled past.

"Don't stand jibber-jabbering, you great fambly! Run for it!"

"I'm not in the habit of running—well, only recently—"

Nath stood back, eyeing me, and his chiefs were suddenly holding back the mobs, bellowing with authority at them. Hardur staggered up with his nose streaming blood black in the moonlight.

"Slay him, you rasts! Strike him down!"

"He is unarmed, Hardur!" roared Nath. "Let the Princess Majestrix hear him out!"

"My thanks, Nath—"

"He may fool her. He will not deceive me!" And Hardur launched himself headlong.

The breathing space I had gained would be gone if Hardur were allowed to overpower them again. I reached up and back and, bending forward, ripped my longsword free. The superb brand gleamed in the light of the moons. I spread my fists on the grip and faced Hardur. He did not check but came on in a gusty rushing charge, yelling a wild whoop, his sword swinging.

"Leave him to me!" bellowed the Mortiljid.

The first blows were delivered with skill and strength, but the Krozair brand deflected them with ease and I leaned to the side and twisted my hands over and so laid the flat against Hardur Mortiljid's head. He fell down.

For an instant a complete silence enveloped the mobs. Into that silence the massed beat of wings brought a rushing note of urgency. Saddle birds landed in flurries of wing-feathers, sending up the dust. Agile men leaped from the saddles. A voice shouted.

"Now what tomfoolery are you up to, father? What's he playing at now, Lela, for the sweet sake of Zair?"

And my lad Jaidur strode forward, very wroth, to confront me.

Seventeen

The Rebellion Falters

We rode hard for Huringa in a jingling, determined cavalcade, with a screen of aerial cavalry winging ahead. We were the Revolution. On our banners glowed the light of coming victory. With us rode Princess Lildra, who would be Queen Lildra. On we rode, confident, bursting with pride, and if we were vainglorious there seemed every reason for that fatuous state.

You cannot have everything in life. Useless to think that wishing will make it so. Everyday reality doesn't work like that. Wish fulfillment does happen, of course—after a deal of damned hard work and luck and the ability to ride with the punches or to come to terms with emotional situations you thought impossible. As for power fantasies, they are for the crippled, and as most of us are crippled in one way or another, ought to be put to a responsible therapeutic use.

Jaezila was Lela.

That was the wonder.

Jaidur, being my raffish, feckless young tearaway of a son, was here in Hyrklana stirring up as much trouble as he could for Hamal. Unable to buy fliers, he had had a hand in the burning of a few of the factories. And he knew somewhat of Spikatur Hunting Sword.

The news he brought from home reassured me. Delia and my comrades had returned to Vallia successfully after the storm that had separated me, and the empress's wishes had sufficed to prevent that hairy swarm of rogues from attempting to devastate Hyrklana and all points south. As for Lela, she had a tale to tell. As we rode toward Huringa through the streaming mingled lights of the Suns of Scorpio, I learned much of my daughter. The odd thing was—and not so odd, when I thought about it—I tended to think of her as Jaezila rather more than as Lela. She had tried to buy airboats in the Dawn Lands of Havilfar, and had not succeeded there. With Prince Tyfar of Hamal as cover, she had tried again here in Hyrklana. As to her true regard for that honorable prince, I asked her, and she told me, and I said, "Then when all this nonsense is over, we will have such a splendid wedding as Hamal and Vallia have never before witnessed."

"That presupposes he will have me."

"Tyfar is no fool."

"Is that an answer?"

"Yes, daughter, it is."

"And love?"

I laughed. Laughing was easy with Jaezila, as it was with Delia, her mother. "If I have never seen love in a man before, I have seen it in Tyfar when he looks at you."

She turned her head away as we rode along, with the rebellion riding along with us. So I went on, "And, talking of love, you have perhaps noticed what is afoot between your brother Jaidur and Princess Lildra?"

"I have."

"And?"

"It pleases me, as I hope it pleases you."

I nodded. Some people in their modern sophistication deny any such force as Mother Nature. They may be right. Here, whatever the force, be it Mother Nature or anything else, the lightnings had struck, the looks had been exchanged, the understandings given and taken. The speed had been breathtaking. Jaidur and Lildra had met and talked, and that was that. It seems I was in for two weddings, when all this nonsense was over.

As a man, I felt lively affection and sympathy. As a father, I felt concern and hope for the future and desire for happiness. And as a cynical old emperor, I looked at the political aspects, and found they could be worse, could be far worse, by Vox!

So we rode toward the capital city and gained a little strength day by day and heard the rumors and came upon the realities. Had those diabolical Shanks attacked in southern Hyrklana when we marched, it would have been our duty to march with the army of Hyrklana and all the mercenaries, and fling the damned Shtarkins back into the sea from whence they came. But they had retired, sailing away in their phenomenally fast ships, and the soldiers turned their attention to the rebellion.

We did not fare well.

On the day after a nasty skirmish when we had to run for it, Hardur Mortiljid breathed heavily, nursing a wounded arm. He said he had forgiven me for clouting him over the head, and I chose to believe him, and saw that I did not turn by back, just in case. Now he flung himself down by the campfire and seized up a stoup.

"We cannot break through," he grumped, and drank, and spat. "They are too strong for us."

Lildra looked unhappy. Whether she objected to his manners or his opinion was beside the point. "But," she said, and her voice faltered, "the rebellion? We must win!"

"What with? We have not enough real soldiers, and the mercenaries are well-paid and ferocious. How do we fight through?"

Lildra looked across at Jaezila. She was frowning.

"The problem is difficult. Fahia is as cunning as a leem."

"We need more men." Nath the Retributor walked across, looking worried. It seemed that all our high hopes had been crushed.

Much of this dismal feeling had been lost on me, wrapped up in the magic of finding my daughter. We spent hours just talking, finding our way to this new relationship, and all the time joyously aware of our friendship that had grown through the times we had spent together and the dangers we had faced. So we had to make an effort to adjust to the grim reality of the rebellion's lack of progress.

A few—not many but enough, damn 'em!—of the lords and ladies who had flocked to Princess Lildra's standards departed. Those who remained looked worried. The suggestion was bruited that we should contact Orlan Mahmud nal Yrmcelt, for messengers had failed to reach us for the past sennight or so, and find out the true situation and what to plan for the future. This was the euphemism for saying, "Whether or not we will continue the rebellion." In the end, I, Jaezila, Jaidur and a small party agreed to venture into Huringa to see Orlan. It would be perilous, and Lildra clung to Jaidur before she would let him go.

I said, "You don't have to come, Jaezila—"

She laughed and that was that. But all the same, I now realized that adventuring with my blade comrade Jaezila was to be even more fraught with anxiety for me. If that is a selfish way of putting it, so be it. I understood rather more of what was entailed than previously. I confess I didn't much care for the idea of my daughter swaggering off into danger swishing her rapier about, magnificent in her leathers and black boots.

But they would, they would, all of them...

And I would be the last person on Kregen to be able to deny them, for they were people as was I, and they did what they wanted to do.

We took the fluttrells and flew into Huringa. The saddle birds with the big ridiculous head vanes are sturdy and willing if not of the highest quality of saddle-flyers of Paz, and soon we circled over the next-but-one villa along from Orlan's. We spied out the land, and seeing no obvious signs of danger, flew in for a landing in a clump of woods in the gardens. Vad Noran's villa had been extensive, with his very own arena; Orlan's was even larger, and without an arena, although he had practice rings, glittering with swept and raked sand under the suns.

The first question of importance anyone asked about Huringa was whether or not the games were on. As we landed we could hear the roar from the Jikhorkdun. The games were, indeed, on.

It had rained earlier but now the skies were clear and the suns burned down as we walked cautiously up to the villa. We had a lord with us who was known to Orlan's servants, and we were assured we could gain an audience without trouble. The place bore the quiet, bored appearance all parts and all peoples of Huringa wore when they were not involved with the games. Our party walked on swiftly under shady trees and along graveled paths to a wicket gate where a dozing Moltingur guard had no time to argue before he was struck down. I said, "Do not slay him, for he may be loyal to Orlan."

Strom Hierayn, the lord who knew Orlan and would get us in, pushed on and we followed. A few slaves moved among the outbuildings and children were playing at kaidurs with wooden swords among the chickens as we passed. Before we attracted attention we were inside the main building. Strom Hierayn, a fattish man with too much paunch and too much jowl and not—quite—enough humility, pressed on down a corridor known to him. The place appeared near deserted. A slave told us that the lord rested in the Fountain Room, and thither Strom Hierayn led us. And, I began to get that uncomfortable old itch up my backbone.

I glanced at Jaezila. She looked at me, and that perfect face drew down into a scowl.

"You feel it too, Jak?"

She continued to call me Jak out of common caution. I nodded. "I do. It smells like Makki-Grodno's left armpit."

Jaidur said, "If that fat Hierayn has played us false... By Zogo the Hyr-whip! I'll have his innards for zorca harness."

One or two others of the party looked concerned, and Hierayn led through an ornate doorway—pale blue and seashell with fern fronds all adangling in marble—into a patio where fountains splashed and the rays of the suns lay muted through crystal. A few slaves moved about carrying towels and basins and a party of girls danced and laughed among the fountains. They saw us. With squeals and shrieks they darted away, and I surmised they had no business there. I saw Jaidur's fist wrap around his sword hilt.

Orlan Mahmud walked out from the shadows of the colonnade into the diffused light among the splashing fountains. He wore a plain blue tunic and he did not wear a sword or dagger. So that, alone, convinced me. He held up his left hand. He was not smiling. Hierayn moved forward quickly, his body wobbling, and called out a greeting. I guessed that fat Strom Hierayn was no part of the plot. But plot there was, by Krun!

"Into cover!" I shouted. "Run!"

Even as I shouted, Orlan threw himself sideways, and he shouted too. A high desperate call. "We are betrayed!"

The javelin that would have destroyed him for his refusal to betray us darted from the colonnade's shadows and barely missed. He was on a knee, stumbling, and then he was half up and staggering. The party with us was fleeing madly away, trying to find shelter. Jaezila, Jaidur and I remained—but only for a moment. Together, the three of us hurtled toward Orlan. Jaidur hoisted him up; Jaezila snapped up her bow and let fly into the colonnade shadows. She is a superb mistress of the bow, deadly with the fletched shaft. I went headlong, with her arrows cutting beside me, slap bang into whatever skulked in the shadows.

Queen Fahia's mercenaries were there, ready to snap us up. In that tricky half-light our blades flickered like quicksilver, erratic, and dreadfully quickly my brand fouled with blood. Jaidur roared into action at my side. Four of the paktuns were down with shafts skewering them, and a fifth, and the fight was too hot and close and Jaezila put her bow away and ripped into the fray with her sword. I truly believe we three would have done the business ourselves. The mercenaries were good, a mix of diff and apim, and we had the beating of them. But others of our party joined in, and Strom Hierayn laid about him with his sword, and after a space we stopped, for there were no foemen left.

Orlan came across. He looked distraught. "Thank Opaz, you are here! But—as you see—I have been betrayed."

"They were waiting for us!" said Jaidur. He spoke accusingly.

Orlan nodded and swallowed; he was sweating. "You were seen flying in. The games may be on, but the queen's paktuns do not sleep because of that."

"We suspected it was too easy," said Jaezila.

"It was that new damned spymaster from Hamal. He ferreted it out. I am finished in Huringa now." Orlan looked at his villa, the fountains, the

287

colonnades, the glowing flowers. He shook his head. "It seems we are all finished."

"There will be more guards." I spoke in a nasty fashion, to brace them up. "And we are not finished yet. You will fly back to the camp, Orlan. With your family and whomever—"

"I have no saddle flyers. They have all been taken."

"Then we must all make room on ours."

"But—"

"Help Pallan Orlan," I said. "And be quick. We must be off and flying before anybody turns up to find out the cause of the disturbance here." And then I said, "Bratch!" in a most unlovely way, and some of them abruptly realized that they were being commanded by an emperor, so they bratched.

When we had it all sorted out, I had the opportunity for enough words with Orlan to have grasped the situation. He was very down. The queen's new mercenaries were her trump card, and we had nothing to pit against them. The army was divided. The people wanted the games in the Jikhork-dun, and excitement, and bread and wine, and whoever could give them those could be queen for all they cared. It was not quite like that, but Orlan's words conveyed those sentiments. The Hyrklese are a tough old lot, having survived on their isolated island for five thousand years or so against all who sought to subject them. The Shanks in their raiding had made of the Hyrklese a hard lot. I nodded when Orlan finished. Jaidur came up and said all was ready for departure.

"Good. Jaidur, you will have to look out for Jaezila—for Lela—"

He snorted derisive amusement. "She can look out for herself, as you well know."

"Good. I will not be flying back with you."

They stared. Then they started protesting. I quieted them.

"We need fighting men. We need a force inside the city to rise and strike when we attack from outside. By Vox! We did it with Vondium, we can do it with Huringa."

"But there is no great force in the city loyal to Lildra!" Orlan protested wearily, almost beaten. "There is no one in the city who will strike a blow for Lildra against Fahia."

"Oh yes there is," I said.

Jaidur perked up. "I will come with you—"

I glared at him. I own I glared in hot and frenzied fury.

"You will not! You will not come with me! You've been an imp of a son, hating me—"

He protested at this, shouting that he'd never hated me, only that his discovery of his parentage had been a shock.

"All right, Vax Neemusbane!" I bellowed at him. "But you've always been disrespectful and sullen and cheeky—and I don't care, for that is your right, now you are a grown man. But in this you will do as you are told, and lump it! You will not come with me!" I was shaking. By Zair! The idea of my lad Jaidur in the Jikhorkdun! "Hasn't your mother told you about the Arena and what goes on there? Don't you know what they did to her with their silver chains and that damned great boloth? Haven't you listened to Balass the Hawk, and Oby, and Naghan the Gnat? Well? They'd start you as a coy, greener than Havil, and you'd not last—"

"I'm as good a swordsman as you, any day!"

"Maybe. But they'd chuck you onto the silver sand with a little dagger to face a strigicaw, or a chavonth. Or maybe a hulking great Chulik in full armor would have a go at you with all his weapons and you with a short spear—"

"I can use a short spear—"

"And you'd have your insides all over the sand; they'd have the iron hook in your ankle and your mother would say what to that, hey? You perverse, ungrateful child!"

He was scarlet. He was bursting. He was a man, a great warrior, a Krozair of Zy, and he worked in secret for Vallia through the Sisters of the Rose, and here he was being talked to as though he were a child. Well, by Zair, and wasn't that what I should have done when I was flung back to Earth instead?

All the same, I added, "You have the right to throw your life away in the Jikhorkdun. You have the right to do as you see fit. I can only advise you and try to guide you, and your honor is your own concern. My view of your honor in this pickle is for you to work for the rebellion and lead on what forces you can against the city as I get the kaidurs to rise inside. I think you would impugn your own honor if you did otherwise. But it is for you to decide. And listen to me, Jaidur, I respect you as my son too much to order you about."

Jaezila said, "Respect!" She did not laugh but her eyes were brilliant on me. And I think she understood even if my own stumbling unhappy words could only convey a tiny fraction of what I felt.

"Well, you've changed your tune," said Jaidur. "First it's 'You must not go,' like a weeping mother as her son goes off to war, and now it's 'You must do as you see fit,' like a Jikaidast mockingly advising an opponent on his next move. Well? You are supposed to be my father, and I your son, and this is Lela my sister, and what do we know of you—"

"Vax Neemusbane.* Jaezila."

"Yes, very well, I grant you—but to skulk outside while you have all the fun in the Jikhorkdun—"

That did it.

---

* Vax Neemusbane (or Neemusjid): Name Vax taken by Jaidur in the Eye of the World. Cognomen from defeat of Athgar the Neemu. A.B.A.

"Fun? I lifted a fist. "In the Arena? Fun!"

"Well..."

"If I catch you so much as sniffing at the Arena, young Jaidur, I'll tan your backside so you won't ride a zorca for a month! What would your mother say? Think of her, for Zair's sake! Kregen is dangerous enough without asking for it."

Now Jaezila did laugh, and stepped forward, and in her own authoritative way said, "You are changing your tune once again, Jak. Jaidur sees which way lies his duty. We will bring all the forces we can against the city when we receive the signal that you are ready to rise. Sooner rather than later."

"Agreed."

"And father, may Opaz through the Invisible Twins guide your sword and strengthen your arm—" Jaezila looked woefully at me. "I don't like this at all, by Vox, not one little bit!"

"Well—" began Jaidur.

I settled it.

"Get flying. Keep up your spirits. When the signal comes, you must be ready, or we will all be chopped."

The woeful look on Jaezila's face, lightened only sporadically by her laughter, depressed me. She was a girl, although of strong mind and iron will, fashioned for sunshine and laughter. When Lela got down, the reasons were hard and cruel. Of course, I felt guilty about causing her unhappiness yet again.

Orlan confirmed that he had been arrested and confined in his own villa in order to trap messengers and visitors. He had not been put to the Question, although, no doubt, that would have followed when enough of the rebels had been captured. Fahia was alternating between confidence and doubt, and no man was safe in her presence. Her pet neemus, black as hell, fed to repletion.

The remberees were said softly and then the fluttrells lifted away. I stared up anxiously. If a Hyrklanian air patrol came sniffing around, or a skein of aerial cavalry investigated, my people up there would be in trouble. But on a day of the games, the games were the thing, and Huringa dozed outside the Arena. So, not without a premonitory shiver, I started off for the Jikhorkdun.

Foolish to run my head into fresh horror? Of course. But what else was there to do? It is easy enough now to think of a dozen different courses of action I might have taken, but of them all, none, I venture to think, would be as swift and efficacious as the course I was now embarked on. Through the level rays of jade and ruby I strode toward the lifting pile of the Jikhorkdun, with the high fortress of the Hakal rising alongside. The beast roars swelled and grew enormous as I approached.

How, I was already wondering, fared the ruby drang?

Eighteen

The Queen's Kaidur

"Not so well, Chaadur," said Cheldur Adria. "Not so well, by Kaidun!"

"Then it is opportune I have come back—"

"More fool you!"

"Mayhap, Cleitar, mayhap. But there is a task set to my hands."

We walked toward the local drinking den. Cleitar Adria, because of his position, could ease me back, saying in explanation that my absence had been caused by illness. There was, in these latter days of the Jikhorkdun, a certain laxness which worked to my advantage. The needleman was rubbish, as we all knew, and a word or two in the right direction settled that. There was no difficulty in getting myself into the Arena. The problems started when I began to lay out the plan of action.

"But you work for the queen, Chaadur!"

I knew this was going to be tricky. Cleitar believed I labored for Queen Fahia, and to this I owed immunity from a deal of unpleasantness. Now I had to persuade him I did not, that I wished him to join with me—more, to lead—a rebellion against the queen. Fahia was generally detested. The coils and twists and turns of intrigue are not particularly difficult to grasp for anyone involved in them; for a bluff cheldur like Cleitar Adria they presented a certain baffling front he failed to penetrate. But he would not admit to ignorance or lack of brainpower. He nodded wisely. He drank and nodded again, and drank more, and listened and I laid it all out.

"So you see, Cleitar, Princess Lildra will be a boon to us all. For a start, you will receive a handsome pension, and a title too, I don't doubt. There will be no need—unless you so desire—to act in the Jikhorkdun ever again." I was on dangerous ground here, for the Jikhorkdun had been Cleitar's life. But his face and absent eye told their own story.

He drank again. He held onto the jug. "I am grown more weary of the Jikhorkdun than I could ever have believed. You see that in me, Chaadur?"

"Yes."

"Never make friends in the Arena. We were never true comrades when you were Drak the Sword. And we were wise. But—" He drank again. "But there was a Khibil lad, Kranlo, brought him up from a coy, very quick with a sword, a good eye—I made a friend of Kranlo, more fool me. He was chosen last sennight by Tipp the Thrax to fight the Queen's Kaidurs."

"I am sorry, Cleitar."

"Aye. Aye. They dragged him out."

His head hit the table and his arms flopped and the wine jug spewed purple Hamish over the floor. I hoisted him up and carted him off to his rooms and dumped him on his bed, and let his slaves care for him. Then I took myself off to the barracks.

Many new faces were apparent, and many faces that might have been new and might not have been, seeing a kaidur takes little notice of the regular passage of arena fodder. Frandu the Franch and Norhan the Flame were pleased to see me, and I more than pleased to see them. I had work for them.

Lights out varied, in these latter days, with the whims of the barracks cheldurs. A one-armed ex-kaidur bucking for cheldur and with a little authority—a nikcheldur—at last suggested we'd better turn the lights out and turn in. The talk of the day's fights went on for a space and then the barracks dropped away into darkness and silence. Not sleeping, I lay and planned what it would be possible to do, and as that was clearly not sufficient, what I would have to do to please the Star Lords and set Lildra on the throne of Hyrklana.

Once I had resurfaced within the structure of the Jikhorkdun there was no possibility of my avoiding notice, and so I had to fight in the days that followed. Hundal the Oivon, our cheldur, as bluff and gruff as ever, got me some interesting combats, which I managed to survive. The name of Chaadur began to be mentioned. And, all the time, we sounded out the feelings of all those we deemed accessible. The mood of the Arena changed. Fahia was no longer the popular young queen; people were more and more seeing her in the light of the aging butcher. For all that, no rebellion could hope to succeed without inside and outside combination of forces. When Lildra's people attacked, we in the Jikhorkdun must rise. And our numbers grew—even though, by reason of our employment, our numbers were cruelly reduced from time to time when Fahia staged a bloodbath.

Any man who is lucky enough to escape from the Arena must be all kinds of idiot voluntarily to return. I kept telling myself that, yes, I was a right onker, a real idiot, but all the same, returning to the Jikhorkdun and rousing all the kaidurs whose personal grudges against those who had put them there would spur them to rebellion had to be clever. Surely? Clever or idiotic, this was the plan, and I was stuck with it. We had a tasty series of tussles with the other colors during a period of high junketings, and the ruby drang inched again up the victory poles. Again, I found myself becoming involved with the fate of the reds and the fortunes of the ruby drang. Then, of course, disaster struck. It could never be unexpected. It was just simply diabolically inconvenient.

I rounded the corner of the barracks, carrying my gear with blood everywhere from some poor devil who hadn't jumped quickly enough, anxious to get into the water and clean all the muck and blood and sweat off, and Kyr Tipp the Thrax limped up. The shriveled, shaven-headed Gon thumped his crooked staff down. It was banded in ivory and silver and glittered. He banged it down, his nutcracker nose and jaw snapping, and lifting it high, beckoned me over. It was a summons that was death to refuse.

I went over and stood looking down on him.

"Chaadur, is it? Yes, Chaadur. You have been mightily honored, mightily honored, by the glass eye and brass sword of Beng Thrax himself."

So, feeling my insides falling away, I said, "Get on with it, man, get on with it. When?"

If we could rise before this one-sided fight...

He snapped his nose and chin, his gimlet eye very nasty.

"You would do well not to talk to me like that—"

"Do you want to tell me, or must I report that you are lax in your duty, Tipp? Well?"

He blinked. In a very menacing tone—very menacing—he said, "I will remember you, Chaadur. Tomorrow. You fight tomorrow."

I cursed. So soon! But that was the way of it. Tipp the Thrax limped off, with a final threatening curse, and I went on to wash up and to receive the commiserations of the kaidurs.

"It's the Ice Floes of Sicce for you, dom!" was the consensus of opinion. This was an estimation of the situation I found myself agreeing with and I detested that argument. Hundal the Oivon wanted to fuss, and Frandu and Norhan wanted to go out and get blind; but I said, "No, fanshos,* no. I am not important in the rebellion. But all the kaidurs, acting together, are."

Had the sounds of fights and arguments not been a common experience floating over the barracks of the kaidurs, someone might have come to investigate. They were all yelling away, belting fists into palms, swearing by all manner of gods and spirits. In the end we decided—I decided—that I must take my chances with the Queen's Kaidurs and the moment of the uprising would be brought forward. The quicker we struck, everyone felt, the more chance we stood. The longer we delayed, the more chances there were that we would be betrayed. As arranged, the message was sent out to our people on the outside.

On the morrow I would go up against an opponent—or opponents—selected from the Queen's Kaidurs. From such encounters few ever walked away, and they were never heard of again. Ever.

When Cleitar Adria found me he looked worried. He kept fiddling with his sword, shoving the thraxter up and down in the scabbard.

"This is a right mess, Chaadur. Couldn't you have ducked out of sight until tomorrow?"

"No chance. I just walked into the damned little Gon. Anyway, if we rise tomorrow as planned, and the message gets through, it will all turn out all right."

---

* Fanshos: "Comrades." "You guys." "Friends."

"You hope."

"There's no chance of my hiding—"

"No. You are now a marked man. You've seen the guards?"

"Aye. They dog my footsteps. Still, I could dispose of them—"

"That would ruin all. We've all laid our lives out on this plan of yours. This plan of ours." For I had insisted that Cleitar and the others join the planning discussions, and, in guiding them, made them feel a part of the conspiracy.

"I'll take my chances with the Queen's Kaidurs." Then, incongruously, I laughed. "I may be able to lift the ruby drang up the victory pole."

A kaidur destined to fight the queen's men did not spend that night in the barracks. The guards marched me off before lights out and quartered me in splendid isolation in a sumptuous room wherein much wine stood around in flagons and amphorae and the food was exotically lavish. I sent the dancing girls packing and, after a good meal and a modicum of wine, got my head down. I was in for a fight on the morrow, and I needed to concentrate on that. If, by any unfortunate chance, I met a champion as good as Prince Mefto the Kazzur, then my days on Kregen were numbered.

No good brooding. I slept.

The day dawned misty, which was a good omen, since I trusted that our rebel army was creeping up on Huringa. I ate a massive breakfast and began the preparation of my gear, for I would be fighting as a churgur, a sword and shield man, against an opponent similarly armed. Tipp the Thrax, very ugly, looked in to tell me I was fighting fourth and last. Three kaidurs from the other colors would be fighting first. Their names were known to me, and we were all halfway or so up the rankings, prime meat for the Queen's Kaidurs to chop. I snarled at Tipp and he scuttled off. As he went he spat out, "You'll sing a lot smaller when I've talked to you again."

I threw a boot at him and went on polishing my sword.

When he turned up next, about an hour before the fight was scheduled to begin, he smirked. He looked different, more pompous, more sure of himself, his shaven head a buttered glisten in the lamplight, for the room was shuttered, although the mist had cleared. With him were ten guards with nets and whips. Just in case...

What he told me gave me a clear understanding of why the Queen's Kaidurs always—or almost always—won out on the silver sand. He joyed in the telling.

"The men in black," he said, "with their tongs and their red-hot pincers and their bone-crushers, their gut-pullers and the rest of their clever inventions in the torture dungeons of the Hakal. If you do not lose, you will die such a death of agony as will make you regret most bitterly you did not lose. And you will make a fight of it before you lose. The queen demands spectacle. She wishes a good fight. You are a fighter, otherwise you would not have been chosen. So fight well. Fight hard. And make sure you lose convincingly." He snickered. "After all, the queen may be in a good mood and choose to spare you."

The men in black sniggered.

I eyed their whips and nets. It was the damned nets that would cause the trouble... Tipp saw my glance and read my intentions in my lowering face.

"Do not try to escape, Chaadur. The men in black are clever with their nets. And there are more outside. You would simply go straight down to the dungeons." He bit a fingernail. "I am told what is done there defies the imagination. Certainly, they do not bury whole bodies, only parts."

I turned my back on him, went on polishing the sword. If that sword went between his ribs now, then down under the Hakal I would go. The rebellion had to succeed, for the sake of Vallia. I'd fight the Queen's Kaidur. But I did not think I would choose to chance fat Queen Fahia's generosity of mood.

Tipp went on to describe in more detail some of the work that went on down in Fahia's torture dungeons, and some of it was stomach-churning, I can tell you. The men in black rattled their nets and flicked their whips. They were men happy in their work—if they were men, that is. I ignored the lot and saw to my gear and, by Vox, I believe if Tipp hadn't had the sense to stop talking and threatening and leave, I'd have lost control and gone headlong into the lot of them. But there was a better way than foolhardiness of that nature...

I could have postured and put on a different face, one which inflicted only a few painful bee stings, and disappeared. But that would have aroused the guards and officials of the Jikhorkdun, and we of the rebellion wanted everything to go on as normal. So I sat and readied my weapons and waited to step out onto the silver sand to face an opponent who had a torture dungeon on his side.

Many a fine arena fighter had chosen to lose and die gracefully rather than face agony beyond belief. Yet I could not allow myself to be blinded by this nauseating trickery to the stark fact that the queen's champions were hyr-kaidurs of very high standing, men who had battled their way to the top. They would expect to win in any case. This intrigue of Tipp's was by way of insurance. And it occurred to me, also, that it was eminently possible that the champions had no knowledge of Tipp and the queen's underhanded dealings to insure the victory. The men chosen were, like myself, from the middle rankings, men the hyr-kaidurs would expect to defeat. Tipp's insurance extended to the one or two among them who had the makings of great champions and who might defeat the queen's man. Selah! What happened would happen, so I went on polishing up the sword and thinking of Delia, and of Jaezila and Jaidur, who ought to be nearing Huringa with our raggedy little army.

Jaezila had told me how she'd unexpectedly met men she knew when she'd tumbled down the trap in the Temple of Malab, and how she had had to be quick to make them see who she truly was, and therefore give them orders that no harm should befall us. That was why Tyfar had been bound and gagged and not slain, and Jaezila, also, out of the subterfuge. I knew Jaezila was a woman of immense resource and guile. And I knew Jaidur to be a right tearaway. With Nath the Retributor and Hardur Mortiljid they must break through quickly once the attack began.

So we were called, and with the trumpets flinging brazen notes over us we marched up into the suns' shine of the Arena.

To catch the atmosphere of the Jikhorkdun! To grasp at the raw essentials of that horrific place! It repels in utter disgust, and, deeply and darkly, it draws on the ancient tides of blood, demanding sacrifice and dedication and adherence to ancient mysteries old before man stood upright. It was not a nice place. For some, it was the only place in all the wide world of Kregen that mattered.

As an earnest of my feelings, I will say that I felt disgruntled that in this, the last fight, I did not step out onto the silver sand from the red corner. My comrades over there rattled their swords along the iron bars, and yelled and screamed insults and encouragement, and I was debarred from them. We men selected to face the queen's champions were herded into a small space to one side of the overhanging mass of the royal box, and from the shadows we looked out upon blinding brilliance. Above us, unseen, sat Fahia and her courtiers, her pet neemus, her slave girls in their pearls and diaphanous gauzes. A square shadow offset to the side from the new balcony lay hard-edged in red and green, twinned shadows across the sand. That podium had not been there when I'd fought as Drak the Sword. I thought I knew why it had been built and stuffed with ranks of archers.

The three other kaidurs sat on the bench and looked glum. A Fristle woman brought the leather bottles of raw red wine, Beng Thrax's Spit, and they drank. The heat stifled in our small slot of shadow. Out on the silver sand men fought and died. Herds of coys were driven out to be slaughtered in picturesque fashion. Animals squealed and slashed, struggled and, killing, died. The business of the day wore on. We were a prime fixture, and the stands and benches, the whole amphitheater, was crowded, a solid mass of sweating faces gleaming in the lights of the suns, waving arms and kerchiefs, the black cavities of open mouths screaming. A wall of sound lifted around the Arena. We sat and waited, and sweated.

The order in which we would step out to fight and lose was: Yellow, green, blue, red. This order had been arrived at by lot.

Of us all, the least glum was the adherent of the sapphire graint. He licked his lips. Wine drops clustered in his beard.

"The blues crown the victory pole," he said. "And don't you forget it."

The men of the diamond zhantil and the emerald neemu looked sullen. The yellow said, "By Nandig's belly! I wish I was home in Ystilbur, on my farm. I swear each vosk would be like a comrade, every chicken a friend."

"What does it matter what color wins?" said the green. "We are dead men." The blue sniffed. "You knew that from the very first day you signed on."

"It makes it no easier to bear."

"Think of the men in black."

"By Harg! I think of nothing else. Suppose my sword slips, and I nick the queen's man, and he dies? What then?"

"Then, my friend, pieces of you will be scattered here and there. You have my condolences."

He merely said that; his mind was on his own problems.

I sat and said nothing.

By the way they talked, they exhibited the hardened toughness of the kaidur. They lived with death, and now they knew they were going to die. Fahia was not often generous. So there was no screaming and breast-beating, no wailing and panicky thrashings about. These men were kaidurs, and they did what kaidurs did, and when their deaths arrived, then their adherence was to the fight and their color, and their deaths were mere codicils to the greater spectacle.

Familiarity with the Arena rarely breeds contempt. No man stepping out onto the silver sand often feels more than the impulses of the moment. The drive of the blood through bodies tensed for combat, the battering of noise from the mobs, the stink of spilled blood and the rank tang of a multitude of animal smells, the feeling of greatness and smallness and of impending doom—all these sensations and emotions flit through a man's concentration upon the single object ahead. He must go out and fight. He must win if he can; but, above all, he must fight.

The first marked for destruction stepped out onto the silver sand. He walked quietly to the designated place where he halted and turned to face the royal box. The high glitter from that place of regal power smote down. We waited in the shadows, unable to see the royal box but all able to see it in our minds' eyes. The yellow lifted his sword, and the first Queen's Kaidur stepped out. The golden trumpets rang. The crowds quieted, ready to be critical. This was no wallowing bloodbath, this was a contest of skills in which the favorite artifice of unequal combat lay not in the weapons but in the men themselves. Sword and shield against sword and shield, with a hyr-kaidur ready to show the crowds his arts in combat against an opponent who was very good, but not quite so good as the queen's man. They liked that, these folk of Huringa.

Sometimes these fights turned into desperate affrays. Then the crowd's enjoyment was great. Our yellow comrade fought well, but he went down, and he did not go down from choice but because he was fairly bested. The green followed, and then it was blue's turn. He looked bloated, this man of the sapphire graint, his face sweating and scarlet with protuberant veins.

Tipp the Thrax was there, well guarded, walking into our place of confinement. It was clear he had been watching us.

"Remember! You lose well, or it is the men in black!" Blue shivered all over. He took a fresh grip on his sword and shield and without a word strode out onto the sand.

"As for you," said Tipp, regarding me with his shriveled look of venom, "remember!"

I shook my sword at him, whereat he stepped back smartly, and his guards closed up. I did not bother to speak to him. Blue was fighting and he was worth the watching. He would, without doubt, have made hyr-kaidur in only a few more fair combats. He fought the queen's man with savage concentration, giving ground and then sidestepping and sweeping in with a clever flank attack. He drew blood. But in the end, he allowed his shield to sag and his thrust to falter, and the Queen's Kaidur chopped him, and blue went down, face first into the bloodied sand.

The trumpets roared, and out I stepped, and the heat of the Suns of Scorpio smote across my shoulders.

The royal box glittered with light.

I looked up, as the others had done. I neglected to give the formal salute, and I did not repeat that obscene sign I had once given Fahia. Instead, I settled myself and waited for my opponent to walk out and go through the formalities before we set to.

Although Kregans do not age much during their better than two hundred years of life, little signs can give you an idea of their age. This fellow looked young. He carried himself well. He must, of necessity, be very good, to be a Queen's Kaidur so young. His face was oval, with bright blue eyes and fair hair, but his nose was pinched and his lips were full and fleshy, glistening red and pouting with self-satisfaction and indulgence. The idea crossed my mind that he looked just like a spoiled brat, but that didn't make sense. His armor and weapons were of superb quality. He flourished his sword about and the thraxter splintered back light. He'd know a whole encyclopedia of tricks of the sworder's art...

As usual at the beginning of each combat, the uproar from the mobs quieted. We circled watchfully. He made a quick rush, feinted and stepped back. I did not move. I saw his face reveal his sudden annoyance that I had not reacted to his move. It was as though I had insulted him.

There was an odd feeling of wrongness about this. The three previous champions had been hyr-kaidurs, men I had seen fight before, hard-bitten and professional. If it made sense at all, this young fellow was an amateur, a dilettante, and you don't get many of those in the Arena, no, by the brass sword and glass eye of Beng Thrax!

Again he feinted and rushed, and again I did not move.

Some of the crowd started to barrack. The raucous shouts came from the greens, the yellows and the blues, partisans who had seen their own men go down in bloody defeat. I circled again, still making no attack, trying to think in the heat and the noise and the stinks.

The smart young fellow came in confidently, and this time he meant it, so his thraxter had to be parried, and he had to be knocked away with the shield. These things were done, and he went staggering back. His face expressed the utmost surprise and savage resentment before he fell smack down on his rear end.

I stood back.

Standing up, he shook himself, set his shield, snouted his sword and came in with a ferocious rush. We tinker-hammered for a space, which is a pretty sight, but useless. Unless you can hack your opponent's shield rim through, this clanging away at shields merely blunts your sword. I gave him a final clout and put enough power into it to smash his shield back into his face. He yelped and skipped away. Over his shield rim his thin nose showed a dribble of blood.

He moved around more cautiously. He looked puzzled. When he came in again he hammered impetuously at my shield and thrust on. His sweating face was inches from my own. He snarled at me.

"Rast! You are supposed to let me win!"

I slid sideways, came back and landed a good welting blow with the flat against his backside. He spun about. His sword and shield went every which way. And the crowd began to laugh.

"Yetch!" he screamed. "Think of the men in black!"

Again I did not answer. The next flurry of action saw his shield failing to deflect a blow. His sword spun up in the air wrenched from his fingers, spinning, glittering end over end to thunk point-first into the sand. It quivered. He panted, staring from the sword to me and back again. I stepped back and bowed and with my own thraxter indicated his.

The crowd howled.

He wrenched the blade from the sand. "You onker! You are meant to let me win!"

"Maybe... It is not supposed to be easy for you, though, is it?"

He possessed a good and varied repertoire of tricks and stratagems and now he settled down to use them in real earnest. Many of the passages I recognized as being developed by hyr-kaidurs of the past, some were the old regulars; he had nothing new. He had been well-trained and his schooling had been thorough, but he lacked the fire, the spirit, the ultimate essence that makes a swordsman.

Breaking my usual habit when fighting, I fell into conversation with him. The incongruity of this did not escape me.

"You've had good teachers, lad. Fine swordmasters—"

"I have, rast!" And he leaped in, hacking and slashing and I foined him off and stood back as he went blundering past.

"All the same," I said, in a conversational voice as he floundered around to face me, "it is a puzzle that you have become a Queen's Kaidur. You don't have the wherewithal for the job."

He shrieked in an access of rage and rushed again, and I twirled his sword out of the way and then—it makes me feel odd to recall—I tripped him with an outstretched foot. It was a mean trick. He tumbled over again and this time he lost his grip on the shield as well as the sword. He lay for a space, winded.

Very gravely, I walked across and picked up his shield and sword. My own shield hung from a single grip on the arm, my own sword was stuck into the sand at my back. With a polite little bow I handed him his weapons. Instantly he was on his feet, the shield swished across and he took a lusty blow at me with his sword, slashing to take my head off. I skipped away.

The crowd booed!

They hadn't liked this display of boorishness. Not when I'd handed him his weapons, and myself without a sword.

This buffoonery went on for a time, and I started to undress him. This was done, I plead on my behalf, out of boredom and to give me something to do while I thought of my best course of action. His straps were slit through. His harness fell. He wore a tasty breechclout in green, so my heart hardened a trifle.

When he was practically mother naked, and still shrieking and sobbing and hurling himself on, telling me what the men in black would do to me, I began to play him a little in earnest. I confess he was run ragged. His face was a scarlet bloom. He gasped for breath. Any number of times he thought he was dead, and at the last minute my blade twitched away. I did give him a haircut though.

The crowd was now silent, with only the occasional long susurration of indrawn breath, or an incongruous laugh at some buffoonery, to indicate aught went forward on the silver sands. He was out of breath now, panting, bursting, and his shield drooped and his sword wavered. Carefully, I chipped away the shield grips, and the shredded thing fell to the ground. Then his sword was upended and went flying through the air, a steel deadliness, spinning up and away to smack hilt-first into the sand.

He faced me, disheveled, sweating, gasping for air, unarmed and shieldless.

With a deliberate step I walked across. I showed him my sword. I was aware that the crossbowmen flanking the royal box were on the move. Out of the corner of my eye I could see them lifting their weapons. If they shafted me, that would not reflect well on the queen. I handed my own sword across to the lad, hilt first, with all the magniloquence of swordsmanship carried to absurd heights.

He did not know, I felt, that even with the sword he wouldn't easily kill a Krozair brother.

The silence in that place of noise was appalling.

I shouted.

"You're supposed to win, lad, if you're a Queen's Krozair. Well, let me help you a little."

The crowd exploded into violent laughter, enormously relishing all this absurdity. And then they fell silent. A single trumpet pealed a golden note. Cautiously keeping the lad in my sight, and taking my sword away, I stared up to the royal box.

The courtiers were bowing and scraping. The neemus were being drawn back on their silver chains and the gauzily clad slave girls huddled away in groups at each side. The fans kept on waving to bring fresher air into the royal box. The color and movement demanded attention from every eye.

Queen Fahia stood up.

She was simply a magnificent blur of color and jewels.

She lifted a hand and the suns struck splintering sparkles from her rings.

The silence was absolute.

"You have made mock of my son, Chaadur the Doomed! Give me one good reason why I should not tell my crossbowmen to loose and pierce you through with fifty bolts."

Her hair piled high with gems lent her a spurious dignity; her white face, painted and powdered, came into focus as I squinted up, seeing her blue eyes and the fair hair and the cosmetics laid on like butter on bread.

"So the lad is your son. He fought as well as he could. It is no discredit to meet a better swordsman in the Jikhordun. As to your question: because you and he have not lost yet and if you gave your bowmen the order to loose you would lose everything."

Her head went back and then slowly forward and she stared at me hard, hard.

"You are impertinent, Chaadur the Doomed!"

"You don't have to worry about that—you should be worrying about your lad, who has lost. What says the queen to that? Is he to live or is he to die? Choose!"

She put a hand to her lips. Even at that distance she could clearly be seen shaking uncontrollably. Then she thrust her hand out, pointing, her forefinger stiff and beringed, glittering on me.

"It is impossible! I know you. Drak the Sword! Drak the Sword!"

Nineteen

In the Dungeons of the High Fortress of the Hakal

There are dungeons and dungeons on Kregen and those beneath the high fortress of the Hakal in Huringa were in a class of their own. They were of a quite exceptional horror. The things done there turned men into drooling imbeciles. An item that confirmed my judgment that Fahia had sadly fallen away lofted to one side, an ornate area with seating and lounging facilities, with tables provided with the best of food and drink, it was quite simply a place of observation where Fahia could sit in her throne and enjoy what went on.

The iron rings stapled into the stone floor were no stronger for her pet neemus than they were for the poor devils out in the dungeon itself. The men in black busied themselves with their apparatus. I crouched in a small iron-barred box. This method of confining criminals and those reserved for judgment was the normal understandable system that insured the poor wight let out of the box would have his muscles so knotted up and be so writhing in pain with the flow of blood that he could be run into the next phase of his ordeal without protest. I knew. Unfortunately.

So it behooved me to attempt a few of the more esoteric Disciplines of the Krozairs. To force blood through constricted passageways was the devil of a job and one which high adepts mastered with difficulty. I did what little I could, using capillaries in the accepted fashions, but I knew my blood was still going to cause me considerable agony—euphemistically termed pins and needles—when I got out of the box. As for the muscles, these offered less of a problem, and by manipulations and tensing and relaxing, I hoped I'd have them limber enough. I did know, and with certainty, that I must leap about in a frenzy of action when they opened the box to lead me off to destruction, and I knew, also, that my body might decide not to obey the dictates of my will. I did not forget the slate slab. So I practiced the Disciplines and glared balefully at that elegant observation area where the lords and ladies in attendance on Fahia ogled with her the sufferings of the unfortunates below.

She had not yet arrived. The men in black moved about in a sullen and yet free way, cracking jokes, sharpening up their implements, oiling their tongs, stoking the braziers. In these pursuits they resembled humankind. When the queen arrived they would assume the stoic, calm, professional aloofness of the true torturer. Strange to attempt to evaluate the processes of another person's mind. What had brought these people to this? Perhaps here, as in some countries, the profession was handed down from father to son. Probably they took pride in their work. As they say on Earth and Kregen, it takes all sorts...

The layout of the torture equipment was of vital importance and the positions and relationship of the various items had to be judged exactly. Chains dangled from the rocky ceiling. At the moment they were free of the skeletons one assumed normally remained there until the chains were required again. A massive pot of oil bubbled and boiled. The metal glistened. The pot was of a size to have fed a cannibal city. Near it a rack with spikes and other strategically placed unpleasantnesses had been cleaned up reasonably well; only a few bloodstains remained. The rack was of a down-to-earth kind, a simple stretcher, but near it a device for turning the victim inside out frowned down far more ominously.

Slaves wearing black breechclouts in place of the more usual gray slave clouts stoked up the fire under the pot of boiling oil, and tended the braziers, occasionally poking the implements in further, or pulling them out to inspect their heat color. The whole place stank. I crouched knotted up in the iron-barred box and cursed fat Queen Fahia and longed for her to put in an appearance so we might begin.

When Fahia at last arrived she put on a regal show with all the trimmings. By that time I was aware that unless I could contrive a breathing space before they ran me up and strapped me into the first piece of their diabolical arsenal of devices, I was done for. Her pet neemus with their round heads and wicked fangs and glittering eyes were handled by experts with the silver chains. Her dancing girls were there—and I could only hope they would shut their eyes. The ranks of the courtiers were thinned, there being only a handful present. Her court wizard was there, a fellow of some discipline or other in which she believed devoutly, I felt sure, with his book of power and his wand and tall hat and his face that showed a too-great love of the wine jug. I glared evilly at the lot of them.

Fahia wore a mountain of clothing. It glittered in that dismal place. She walked over to me, and her walk was a waddle. She had been beautiful once. Never slender, her plumpness had been delightful. Now she was grotesque. Some glandular disaster must have struck, swelling her thighs and buttocks, coarsening her face, thickening her everywhere. The clothes disguised much; they could not conceal the pathetic truth.

"Drak the Sword," she said, and her voice came breathily, her lips red and bloated, "I should have recognized your style earlier."

If there was any one person in all Huringa who knew more about the Jikhordun than Queen Fahia then he was unknown. Looking at her and her grotesque barrel body and ravaged face, the pity in me was perfectly understandable. Her sister, Lilah, I judged, would never have come to this.

That thought made me say, "You did not treat Lilah well, Fahia."

She flinched. Her sway as queen was absolute.

"Yetch! You talk as crudely as ever. Now you will be sorry—"

"I think I am, a little, for you, fat woman."

That was cruel and unkind of me, but, by Zair...!

"Your death will not be easy, Drak the Sword. I remember you claimed to be Dray Prescot, and a multitude of other ridiculous names. We have heard of this Dray Prescot. He is the Emperor of Vallia. So you are forsworn. I do not think the Emperor of Vallia would be found fighting in my Jikhorkdun."

If they didn't let me out soon I'd never be able to move fast enough...

"Think what you will. I bore you no ill will. Now, you have forfeited what friendship I might have—"

"You were never a true friend to me! I thought you so once. But you escaped with that trollop of a slave girl—"

"Let them begin, mother!" The lad who had fought me spoke pettishly, not looking at me. "I want to see him scream and writhe and beg for mercy—for death he will not come by easily—"

"In a moment, Babb. In a moment."

This Babb, the queen's son, wore clothes of a cut that might have made me feel sorry for him. He could hardly be totally blamed for turning out as he had, given the circumstances of his upbringing, which were simple enough to surmise. Perhaps, had he possessed a tithe of the character of Prince Tyfar, he might have stood a chance.

The handful of nobles and the wizard came over to take a closer look at me. The wizard stank. The queen treated him with a marked respect. I had no idea of the sorcerer's powers, but I did not miss the look of loathing bestowed on him by Babb.

The conversation might be unreal in these surroundings, but Fahia was intrigued by the circumstances of my escape. I told her nothing, and insulted her a few more times. My limbs were dead as rotted timbers. The torturers hovered. She could take no more of my rudeness, and with a parting "You will suffer as only Lem knows how, Drak the Sword!" she waddled back to her throne.

The men in black clustered about my box and the locks were snapped open. The iron-barred side fell away.

Instantly, before any of them could reach down to grasp me, I was rolling. Like a bundled-up heap of laundry I rolled over and over across the stone floor. The internal torturers were at work. They inserted a red-hot needle into every joint and muscle, they trailed white-hot streams of agony through my veins. Still I had to keep on rolling. I hit the pot of boiling oil. It tipped. It overturned. Boiling oil foamed out in a broad flood. That was useful. In the abrupt yelling and shrieking, it was not yet enough. On I went, shaking and trembling, feeling as though I were being stretched out on the rack and being turned inside out on that fiendish device, on and toward the braziers. Slaves ran.

A black-clad tormentor jumped in the way, raking down to grab me. I hit him in the knees and he staggered and fell into a brazier. He screamed. Burning coals flew. The next brazier could be hooked over with a foot which felt nothing—there'd be a burn there the size of three deldys—and I had a wooden handle of a red-hot iron in my grip. I swung it about like a sword, and already I was beginning to overcome the cramps and the constrictions and the fresh surge of blood. I felt like a single scarlet bloom of agony, but I was getting back into action. The red-hot iron cleared a space.

The bedlam rang and boomed confusing echoes in the dungeon. Dungeons are called chundrogs on Kregen. Chun means jaws, and my jaws were tightly clenched so that their ache struck through as a welcome relief to the torments tying me up in knots. I caught a torturer an almighty thwack across the face with the red-hot iron and, branded, he shrieked and fell away. Others were running up, but I was getting back to being myself again. It was quick, thanks to the Krozair Disciplines. Without those I would have been a mere mewling bundle of agony writhing on the floor.

Fahia went nowhere these latter days without her guards. Now they clattered down from the observation area. They'd settle my hash too damn quick—if Fahia let them. The chances were she would order them to take me alive, for later attention. I slashed about and ran and dodged, clumsily, looking for the way out.

The boiling oil held up the guards. Fahia was shrieking at them: "Hurry, you rasts! Seize him up! Oh, my heart, my insides!" And then, in a veritable scream: "No! Babb! Do not go down to face him—he is a wild leem, a monster—Babb! Come back here!"

"I'll pull his insides out, mother—"

"He will chew you up and not spit out the pips! Babb! I am your mother and the queen! Do not go down!"

The red-hot iron went sizzling through a torturer's eyeball and I yanked it out and slashed away at another, and sent the pack of them running. I was becoming a little heated. There had to be a way out of this foul place. I saw Fahia, leaning on the shoulders of two of her courtiers. Her face was ghastly. Smoke lifted and the place smelled of oil and stink, and I jumped aside with something like my old agility as crossbowmen loosed.

The bolts whistled past. Everybody was shouting. The guards ran on. I whirled the iron which was cooling and blinked away sweat. Where was the confounded exit?

Up behind the observation area a door opened. It was opened from the other side. That, then, was my way out. I started to run for it, skipping past the edges of the spreading pool of oil. A man appeared in the doorway. He held a small earthenware pot. He threw the pot. It arched in the air, trailing smoke, and landed full among Fahia's guards. It burst. Fire vomited forth.

I looked up.

"Norhan the Flame!"

"Chaadur! Over here!"

Other men ran down into the dungeon from the doorway, kaidurs, men of the silver sand, men running with skilled weapons to destroy the queen's guards and those with her. She was screaming and screaming and nothing, it would seem, would stop her. Babb went down with a stux through his guts. Frandu the Franch cut the wizard's head off. It was a quick and clever blow. The head bounced amid the feet of the slave damsels, and they shrieked and cowered away. It rolled among the black neemus and they devoured it, hissing and chomping. The great golden-bound book of power tumbled in a flutter of dried pages from the wizard's hands. So much for Fahia's hopes of sorcerous aid, stilled and stillborn by a Fristle's sword!

These courtiers in their silks and jewels had mocked and laughed as kaidurs bled and died. They paid gold to their mercenary guards to beat and humiliate the men of the silver sand. The kaidurs did not spare courtiers or guards. As for the neemus, golden-eyed, pricked of ear, they died, every one, struck through by stuxes hurled by experts. The damsels in their gauzes and pearls were not slain, being but poor deluded slaves, chattels just like the fighters of the Jikhorkdun. The dungeon fell to a sudden and eerie silence. I ran up to Frandu, who picked up the golden-bound book and shut it quickly. Smoke hung laced with the smell of charred flesh. The oil bubbled quietly.

Norhan came back with his sack of pots and his wicks and flame equipment and looked at Frandu and then at the dead wizard.

"He's headless!"

"Aye," said Frandu. "From the neck up."

"Well," I said, most unkindly, "it would be wise not to look into his eyes, which the neemus spat out, even though they had no head and the head no body."

Then the babble of reunions took place. The rebellion had begun and the kaidurs were running wild through the city. Ordinary citizens had retired to their houses and shops and barricaded them to await the outcome of the revolution.

"And our people outside?"

"They have begun their attack. We are assisting from within." Hundal the Oivon sweated the good news out. "We came to see what had happened to you. Our fanshos are fighting the mercenaries, and Cleitar Adria leads them on. The rasts are caught between two forces now."

"Then we will go up and help our comrades."

I looked about before we left. The dungeon presented a welcome sight with overturned and smashed torture equipment and dead tormentors in their black clothes lying twisted here and there. I gave thanks to Zair and Opaz and Djan that I had been spared.

Norhan the Flame said, "I thank Sarkalak we got here in time, Chaadur—although you had them worried; you had them worried."

As we went up through the chill stone corridors, Frandu laughed and stroked his whiskers and said, "Oh, we were much too smart for them."

Huringa roared to the skies with the noise of combat. We hurried to join the kaidurs who had attacked the mercenaries from the rear, and I was minded of my thoughts about dropping airborne troops here if we wished to take this city. Instead of warriors flying down astride saddle birds, or jumping from airboats, we had struck with a force already within the city, pent-up, trained, expert with arms and passionate with hatred for their oppressors.

Vollers-sailed up against the brilliance of the sky, and we learned they carried the regiment of Hamalese. Those professional fighting men of Hamal knew when a battle was lost. Let the Hyrklese fight it out among themselves, the swods of the iron legion would have said, by Krun, let them kill themselves off so there are fewer to resist when we return. I wondered if their conduct would have been different if they'd known Vallia had taken a hand in this struggle.

Sandwiched between two forces and yet still fighting bravely, the mercenaries were worn down and hemmed in and, finally, forced to throw down their arms. There was a certain amount of revenge killing, but our chiefs, acting on the most stringent orders from the Princess Lildra, managed to restrain indiscriminate butchery. The paktuns might take service with Lildra, or leave Hyrklana.

The battle was over, our two forces met and the rejoicings began. The celebrations would thunder on for days.

Jaezila and Jaidur were safe, as were most of the chiefs. Nath the Retributor had taken a trifling wound, and Hardur Mortiljid had broken three swords in the fighting. Orlan beamed as his dreams began to be realized, and Princess Lildra was radiant. I asked after Gochert, the one-eyed man of mystery, and was told he had left the city after Vad Noran's failure, fearing he might be taken up as an accomplice. Of course, it had been Jaezila who had betrayed Noran. I could see that now, and the way she had attempted to save Tyfar and me, and would have, but for that damned stupid net. As for Ariane nal Amklana, it was rumored she had flown to Hamal to throw herself at the feet of the Empress Thyllis.

"Much good that will do her," said Jaezila.

"It is not over yet."

"No, it is not," said Jaidur. "But it is a beginning!"

I said, "Where is Queen Fahia?"

Huringa was searched, the high fortress of the Hakal, the villas of her adherents, everywhere. She was not found. Those of her pet neemus not slain in the dungeon, penned in luxury in one of her high palaces, looked sleek and well-fed. Well, it was a thought, and an interesting one. A brooch was found in the pen, a brooch slaves swore was Fahia's. But, for all that, no one in all Kregen ever saw Queen Fahia of Hyrklana again.

Twenty

A Wedding and a Promise

The high fortress of the Hakal in Huringa contained within its grim walls a palace of splendor and magnificence. I stood on a costly carpet of Walfarg weave and I said, "You may be desperately in love and willing to consign the world to oblivion to satisfy your passion, but you are not getting married without your mother present."

"But—"

"And there are no buts about it, Jaidur!"

"Queen Lildra—"

"She has not been crowned yet. But that is beside the point. Your mother didn't even know your sister Velia was married until after she was dead. D'you think I'll let you get married and not have your mother share in the joyous day?"

"Father—"

"Now, Jai, do listen," said Jaezila. "Look, I'll fly back home and tell mother."

"It might," I said, "be more becoming for Jaidur to fly himself and tell his mother he is going to be married."

Jaidur's nostrils pinched in. Jaezila looked at me and laughed. I stared back, no doubt wearing that grim old face of mine that, seemingly, had no power to arouse resentment in Jaezila.

"You said you wouldn't tell your children what to do or order them about, father. Well?"

I breathed hard. We'd won a resounding victory, the rebellion had been a triumph. Queen Fahia was gone no one knew where, and I doubted many cared. Prince Babb was dead. The wizards had fled the country. We were going to see that Lildra was properly crowned and seated on the throne and then we were going to turn our undivided attention on Hamal and mad Empress Thyllis. All this we would do. But here and now, my concern was for Delia. It was unthinkable to me that she should be deprived of the day of her son's wedding. And I'd said so.

About to state what seemed to be an obvious fact, that I was not ordering my lad about but merely pointing out to him what was seemly conduct, I was interrupted.

Lildra stepped forward. Jaidur watched her with the simmering violence of a volcano about to erupt.

"Majister," she said to me in her firm voice, "you are right and yet you are wrong. Jaidur owes love and respect to his mother, but it is we who are to live our lives together. We wish to begin aright, but we cannot allow the past to rule us."

That seemed fair enough, by Vox. But, all the same... Delia's half-brother, Vomanus, who had always seemed to us to be a feckless adventurer, had married in what amounted to secrecy. Valona, who was not Valona the Claw, was Vomanus's daughter. That explained the nagging feeling I'd had that she reminded me of someone I knew. But Delia had been—for her—put out that Vomanus had not told us of his wedding. If her own son Jaidur acted in what was to me a thoughtless fashion, then Delia would be hurt. And I couldn't allow that, if it was possible to prevent that damage.

I said so.

In the end the marriage was postponed for long enough for a fast flier to reach Vallia and return. I could well understand the urgency. The Queen of Hyrklana had to be seen to be firmly seated on the throne, and a powerful husband as king would give the added reassurance. There would be other factions besides ours still in the field. Vad Noran, for one. I wondered how he would view his new sovereign, and if he would take up arms against her. If he did—by Harg!—I'd chop him finer than best mincemeat. At least, that is what I said to Lildra, in reassurance.

Finishing the discussion, there in that sumptuous chamber in the palace of the high fortress of the Hakal, I said, "It is settled. I will fly to Vallia and tell the empress myself. I think she will put aside whatever is afoot to attend your wedding, Jaidur. But if she is absent about business for the Sisters of the Rose—"

"That will be all right." Jaezila spoke firmly. "I will come with you, Jak—father—oh, by Vox! Jak it is going to be."

That pleased me. We made quick preparations for the trip, choosing a voller of speed and comfort. "At least she will not break down, as the Hamalian vollers do," I said. We had still not settled that score with Hamal; now that we had Hyrklana as an ally we had circumvented that problem. The rankle remained.

Among the many urgent tasks to be done in Hyrklana, two very close to my heart would be extraordinarily difficult to deal with. I was a guest in this country. I had no power. All I could do was trust that Jaidur would carry out, not just my wishes, but actions I considered necessary and actions suited to the son of the Emperor of Vallia—even if those actions might not be regarded as expected of a King of Hyrklana. The young devil would find out a little of what being a king meant, then. I thrust aside the contemptible thought, that Jaidur's ascension to the throne, where he would co-reign with Lildra, might transform him into a tyrant. Zair forfend!

Quick and practical, Jaezila organized the flier and we took off for Vallia. I did not much like leaving Hyrklana at this moment, when rival factions might seek to oust Lildra before she was even crowned, but I was determined that Delia should be at her son's wedding. The voller was sleek and fast and superbly equipped, for she had come from Fahia's private flierdrome and was accounted a zorca of the skies. We flew for Vondium.

The reception was tumultuous. I will make no attempt to describe the crowded events of that brief visit. Suffice it to say that before I realized it I was up to my eyebrows in work—as usual. This time I had no intention of being waylaid by affairs of state. My return to Hyrklana was an affair of state. Let my pallans chew on that, by Vox! That a whole retinue of people should elect to accompany Delia, Jaezila and me seemed only natural.

Delia, after a first quick flash of an emotion I could identify and did not mention, was enraptured at the idea of Jaidur being married.

"He's always been a wild young tearaway. Marriage should steady him—although he has been splendid doing what he has for the Sisters of the Rose."

"There are dark debts still outstanding..."

"I hate to think of them, but yes, my heart, there are..."

"It is in my mind that Vallia is entering a great period of prosperity. Our comrades do well everywhere."

"The whole island will be reunited soon. Events move on apace." Then she laughed and I felt the world give its topsy-turvy tug at my heart. "And another thing, Dray Prescot. Lela tells me you informed her you were married to some woman or other called Thylda. Well, husband, what have you to say to that?"

I groaned. "By Zair! You had to find out!"

Then, for a space, we shut out the grim world of Kregen and devoted ourselves to each other, and, later, Delia stretched like a drowsy cat before a fire, purring, and said, "Anyway, Thylda is not such a bad name, after all."

When we went down to the voller, Unmok the Nets limped up, out of the watching throngs. He cradled his middle left stump. He looked happy if a trifle dazed. He had been treated famously.

"So, Jak the Shot, your secret was a secret after all."

"Unmok! You Och rascal—and what are you doing now?"

It turned out he was, as he put it, "Still looking around."

I laughed. He looked surprised that I could laugh like that. I glanced at Delia. "Unmok will astonish us all one day, when he has decided what he will do in life."

Unmok made his peculiar Och grimace. "There is a nice little bangles and beads shop in the Kyro of Drak the Munificent I have seen. But also, I have been offered a part interest in a fancy mazilla silk works. As Ochenshum is my witness, I am not sure—"

"Well, just remember we are still partners."

"Partners! With the Emperor of Vallia?"

"Of course. I may be only a hairy apim, but I do not forget my debts." We talked for a space and then it was time to leave and we moved toward the voller. Unmok yelled the remberees.

Delia smiled. "I find Unmok absolutely charming!"

How gloriously superb she looked! Radiant, glowing, absolutely wonderful, the most fascinating, clever, willful, shrewd, the most absolute woman in two worlds. And she said to me as we walked toward the voller, "I've missed you, my heart. And now Jaidur is off and running. Drak manages things well. I own to no qualms for him. And Dayra—"

"Ros the Claw."

"Aye, Ros the Claw. Those villains she calls friends have been in hiding, lying low. But we have not heard the last of them. And now, you have told me nothing about this Princess Lildra."

"I told you of Princess Lilah, her mother, and the manhounds. Lildra is—rather nice. There is a lot she does not know, owing to her peculiar education and upbringing—"

"She gets on with Lela?"

Jaezila, our daughter Lela, walked ahead of us, swinging along in her russet leathers, her rapier cocked up, her brown hair brilliant in the lights of the suns. I nodded. "Yes. They get along famously."

"And do you think Lildra—?"

I laughed. We observed the fantamyrrh climbing into the airboat. And I laughed. "Silly woflo! She will love you as all men and women love you."

Delia turned to look at the half-ruined palace spread out beneath us and the proud city of Vondium below. She sighed.

"I do hope so, Dray. I really do hope so."

The Lord Farris spared airboats to take the wedding guests, on my assurances that they would be returned and with them a fleet of brand new vollers from the yards of Hyrklana. We took off and the flags fluttered and the trumpets pealed and the breezes blew in our faces. The windrush caught Delia's hair and swirled it back so that the outrageous auburn tints glowed. Her face regarded me with that look of love and passion to which I responded as I always have, as I always will, by Zair. We retired to the cabin for a space and the fleet flew on across the oceans to Hyrklana.

The relief I experienced when we landed at being told that nothing untoward had occurred during my absence revealed much of my own apprehension. Had Lildra been overthrown, had Jaidur been slain, I would not have been surprised and would have blamed myself...

The wedding was lavish.

It went on for ten days of riotous carousing and solemn ceremonies, of much pomp and magnificence and of quiet talk and planning. So many of our friends were there as to make the heart of a warrior kick with expected action.* So Delia's son and my son Jaidur wed his Princess Lildra, and immediately thereafter the pair were enthroned and crowned as King and

---

* Here Prescot gives in loving detail a list of all the wedding guests. It makes brave reading. *A.B.A.*

Queen of Hyrklana. I tried not to regard this as nepotism gone mad, megalomania rife, but it was a near thing, I can tell you.

The dark shadow I feared lay across my mind during all these glittering ceremonies. Hyrklana rejoiced today; tomorrow her people must go up against Hamal. And then, when Hamal had been shown the true path, together, united with all Paz, we would face the menace of the Shanks, the true and fearsome enemies.

And after the Shanks, who knew what other monstrous foes we would face?

My son Drak said to me, "Well, I have seen that rascal Jaidur married off. Now I must fly back to Vallia. We have disquieting news out of the southwest."

My ears pricked up, but all Drak would say was, "We defeated those rasts down there, but I begin to see another reason why you are so set against using mercenaries."

"You'd better tell me—"

"With your leave, I'll be off." A stiff-necked bunch, this family of mine. "It may come to nothing, and you have work here."

"I have. You'll be ready to march against Hamal?"

"The midlands are being cleared by Kov Turko. As soon as we can establish new frontiers and fresh bases, we will be clearer to march. If a job has to be done, it has best be done well."

"Vallia is in good hands with you and the council, Drak. I trust you. If you are having difficulty in the southwest—"

"It is nothing. Rumors only. Our spies are busy."

I sniffed.

He went on, "And Princess Lildra is lovely. Jaidur is a lucky fellow."

"She's a queen now, and Jaidur is a king. Deuced odd."

"Damned odd!"

And we both laughed.

Delia came in and Drak said the remberees. Jaezila would be staying with us. We had an invasion to plan and kingdoms to run. Delia and Jaidur spent a long time together. While that right tearaway I had first met as Vax, Vax Neemusjid, might regard me as a ruffian, he set great store by what Delia said. The world belonged to young people. And, by Zim-Zair, I was young! The Savanti had insured that by their own superhuman powers. I felt young and hot and strong, and Hamal and danger lay ahead. I went galloping out for a gut-jolting ride astride a fine zorca and the blue radiance came stealthily dropping down over me.

The giant form of the Scorpion, limned in blue fire, hovered over me.

With the sound of a mighty rushing wind the crimson radiance of the Star Lords enveloped all the world of Kregen. The thin voice keened.

"Dray Prescot! You are wanted urgently. There is a mission set to your hands—"

I interrupted. I took a whooping breath and started in calling the Ever-oinye all the blackguard names I could put my tongue to. I finished: "And I've a lot to do here that means much to me and Kregen, although not much to you, it seems. Have I not done as you wished, and is not Lildra now Queen of Hyrklana?"

"That is sooth. But you are your usual onkerish self. Listen! Our kregoinye has failed in Hamal. It is urgent that his task be concluded, for there is no time loop available. Why do you think we talk thus to you, when we could hurl you into Hamal without a second thought?"

"Why?"

"Debate that with yourself. The answer is obvious. You will go to Hamal and perform the task we set to your hands and then you may find advantages you had not bargained for."

I felt the amazement. The Star Lords? Talking like this?

The thin voice from the crimson radiance went on: "We have changed our plans, Dray Prescot, from the time when you were first brought to Kregen, all naked and raw. You seem to possess a spark of understanding we thought absent from you. Times are changing."

I gaped. These were the superhuman entities, who had once been men like me and were now aloof, remote, impossibly unknowable?

"Do you grant me a boon?"

I was talking about clothes and weapons, and they knew it.

"No."

"Well then, give me time to make the proper remberees to those I love here."

"That is granted you, Dray Prescot. With the first rays of the twin sons, you will be transmitted to Hamal."

The crimson radiance paled. There had been no interference from the acid green of Ahrinye nor from the warm yellow of Zena Iztar. The Scorpion leered down, and I fancied his bloated figure had a much more friendly appearance. I felt as though I were dreaming. The blue fire returned, the winds blew, and once again I was galloping astride the zorca headlong for Huringa.

Slowing that mad pace, I reflected on my future.

Jaidur, the King of Hyrklana, was now the man who must set in motion at least the most important stages of the coming campaign. He would have assistance. Also, I must entrust to him the promulgations of the two measures I knew he concurred with. Neither would be easy. Both would be diabolically difficult. But we must stamp out slavery in Hyrklana. And we must close the Jikhorkdun.

What two tasks could be more difficult?

Perhaps, just perhaps, what I faced in Hamal would tax the old nerve and sinews a trifle more. I did not know.

All I knew as I rode back to Huringa, the capital of Hyrklana, where King Jaidur and Queen Lildra reigned, was that I must once again say good-bye to Delia. Through the streaming mingled rays of the Suns of Scorpio I rode, the emerald and ruby lights falling about me, and the sweetness of the air intoxicating. This time, I vowed, the parting would not be long. This time I'd do what the Star Lords desired, and then I'd take Hamal to pieces and deal with mad Empress Thyllis as we had dealt with fat Queen Fahia.

And all this, all this, not because the Star Lords had commanded, but so that Delia and I might be together again.

Legions of Antares

Dray Prescot

To survive on the savage and unpredictable world of Kregen Dray Prescot needed to be strong, resourceful, cunning and courageous. Prescot not only survived his headlong adventures on that exotic world orbiting the double star Antares, he has built there a life that has meaning, filled with the love of Delia and the friendship of his blade comrades. Yet his character is far more complex than mere savage survival would require.

Dray Prescot is a man above middle height with brown hair and eyes and a physique of exceptional power, and he moves like a giant hunting cat. He was educated in the harsh environment of Nelson's Navy, and by the Savanti nal Aphrasöe, the well-meaning superhuman but mortal men of the Swinging City who brought Prescot first to Kregen. Although he describes his face as "an ugly old beakhead," other sources state that his face is "noble and fierce." Expert with weapons and a master swordsman, he is aware of his own limitations. That he so often transcends them is a testament to his attitude toward life.

The Everoinye—the Star Lords—have employed Prescot over the years in pursuance of their own schemes for the world and he is now gaining insights into their objectives. Prescot has acquired titles and estates over the seasons of his adventuring. The people of Vallia called him to be their emperor in times of troubles, and now the dawn appears to be breaking for that island empire. The hostile Empire of Hamal, ruled by the Empress Thyllis, is now markedly on the defensive. The Wizard of Loh Phu-Si-Yantong, who cherishes schemes equally as ambitious and insane as those of Thyllis, is now confined to the island of Pandahem. Now, as a fresh set of adventures begins, Prescot knows he must say good-bye to Delia in Hyrklana, an island of which their son Jaidur is the new king. With the dawn as the twin Suns of Scorpio rise, Dray Prescot knows he will be hurled into unknown perils...

One

*Concerns What Followed an Arrangement
with the Star Lords*

You don't argue with the Star Lords. At least, if you make the attempt you'll regret it and that may exclude your chance of living to regret it. All the same, I've hurled some hard words at the Star Lords from time to time, and as for their messenger and spy, the scarlet- and golden-feathered bird of prey, he and I, the Gdoinye and I, have indulged in a few scathing slanging matches.

There can't be a winner from the ranks of mortal men, as I then believed, in any contest with the Star Lords, and I had learned caution.

The spangled stars of Kregen sparkled still in the night sky and the quietness of waiting in those moments before dawn cast an expectant hush over all the rolling world. Delia half-rose in the bed, leaning on an elbow. The sheets slipped down to her waist as she regarded me. Her hair lay in shadow from the bedpost and her face looked upon me woefully.

"When the twin suns rise, my heart," I said.

"I hate the Star Lords!"

"As well hate the storms bursting around your head, or the thunder and lightning. They are not affected by our feelings or what we do. Although," I said, bending to pick up the scarlet breechclout, "although I fancy what we do may have some small effect on the Star Lords. Their man in Hamal has failed and they need me urgently, yet they gave us this night together."

"And I am supposed to love them for that?"

Determination in Delia is a live force. What she knows she knows, what she holds she holds.

"No, you cannot be expected to love the Everoinye. I believe they are beyond love or hate, although once they were mortal human beings like us." I threw down the scarlet breechclout. "I shall not need that."

"I think, my heart—there is light. There... On the window frame..."

The windows of this sumptuous bedchamber high in the fortress of the Hakal in the city of Huringa in Hyrklana were deeply set into the masonry. Rich damask clothed the harsh stone. I looked. A strigicaw embroidered in bright silks shone more clearly than he had before, his snarling muzzle lifted, his ears pricked. Yes, there was light. The red sun and the green sun, Far and Havil, were lifting into the dawn skies over Kregen and it was the time appointed.

Useless to try to stumble out words to say what I felt: Delia saw all that in me as I looked upon her, standing drinking her in, feeling, feeling... She smiled. She made herself smile for me and she stretched out her arms.

I leaped for the bed and clasped her, warm and soft and firm and glorious, glorious. Then, with the feeling of the tormentors in their black hoods at work on me, I released her and stepped back.

All naked, staring forlornly upon Delia, I waited for the Summons of the Scorpion.

"Remberee, Dray, my heart—"

"Remberee, Delia, my love. Remember always, I love you and only you—"

Blue radiance dropped about me, blotting out the world and all I loved, and the bloated shining form of the Scorpion beckoned and whirled me up in the maelstrom of supernatural forces.

As I swirled up in the all-encompassing blueness I realized that, at the least, this time I had not lived with the doomed sense of insecurity, of unsettling expectancy that at any moment, at any damned inconvenient moment, I would be called on by the Star Lords to be flung miles away and dumped down into some barbaric spot on Kregen and hurled headlong into downright unhealthy action. That was like living on one of those half-forgotten islands of the Shrouded Sea, plagued with volcanoes and earthquakes, there one minute and blown up the next, and reappearing somewhere else a few years later.

"Delia!" I bellowed as I went up head over heels. She would not hear me. She would see—what would she have seen? I'd ask her when I got out of this little lot. If I did. If, this time, I managed to scrape through and once more win my way back to my Delia, my Delia of Delphond, my Delia of the Blue Mountains.

The blueness roared about me. I felt the supernal chill. Somewhere in Hamal, the Everoinye had said they needed my help. Well that suited our plans. This time, I vowed, the parting from Delia would not be long. This time I'd do what the Everoinye required in double-quick time, and then I'd take the foul empire of Hamal to pieces and deal with mad Empress Thyllis as we had dealt with fat Queen Fahia. Those were the plans, simple and straightforward. Ha!

Anybody who didn't have a skull as thick as mine would by now have realized that on Kregen, that beautiful and terrible world four hundred light-years from the planet of my birth, nothing was ever simple and straightforward. There was to be a deal of skipping and jumping and skull-bashing before this imbroglio was anywhere near settled.

Naked and weaponless, I landed with a bone-jarring crash. The Star

Lords had really flung me hard, picking me up from Hyrklana, that island realm off the east coast of the southern continent of Havilfar, and slamming me down in Hamal in the northeast of the continent. Gritty rock scratched under my hands and knees. I stood up. My head hit rock. All the famous bells of Beng Kishi clamored in my skull. Damned Everoinye!

Putting out a hand as the blue radiance died, I touched rock. I was in darkness so positively pitchy I could see nothing, nothing except the flakes of light floating in my own eyeballs.

Rock under foot, rock over head. Rock at my sides, and rocky grittiness in front. Turning around cautiously and shuffling like an old gaffer in carpet slippers I tested the air. Only one way lay unblocked. I sniffed. Stale air, flat and dusty and in it a taint of some indefinable odor, gave me no clue to where I was. Slowly, testing every inch, I started to shuffle along this inky warren. The rocky sides of the tunnel narrowed and I started to feel a lively interest, and then—thankfully—they opened and widened so that I walked along with one hand trailing on stone and the other held up into emptiness to protect my head.

The bells of Beng Kishi donged away to silence. I shook my head. It did not fall off, so that was all right.

Slowly, as my eyes adjusted, I began to see tiny spots of radiance festooning the walls. Peering closer, squinting, I made out little clumps of the phosphorescent lichen the Kregans call estilux growing clamped to the rock in crevices and folds. As I stumbled along, the light strengthened, both from the dilation of my pupils and the thickening clumps of estilux. By the time I reached the first carved cavern I could see reasonably well.

Not that there was much to see down here.

"Sink me!" I burst out. "Where's this hell-spawned kregoinye I'm supposed to bale out?"

Although I'd once refused to be called a kregoinye, I was in fact one of those men and women selected by the Everoinye to serve their mysterious purposes on Kregen. Whether I liked it or not.

As though in answer to my rumbled bad temper, a figure rose from a bundle of rocks ahead.

A thin stream trickled along there and he'd been filling a pottery bowl. He saw me. He was not a member of Homo-sapiens, having a beaked bird-like face with fluffy yellow feathers and goggling eyes. He was a Relt, one of those races of diffs on Kregen renowned for their gentleness and when slave more often used as stylors and domestics. The pottery bowl flew up in the air. The Relt let out a frightened squeak and ran stumbling and slipping away across the stream and into the shadows past a rocky outcrop.

I fumed.

The bowl was smashed so there was no use picking it up to return it. And, truth to tell, I suppose, I must have looked a most demonic figure, abruptly appearing all naked and hairy from the shadows. He must have thought me some demon from a Herrelldrin Hell.

Now my face has often been called an ugly old beakhead. In truth, when I look at people at times when I am feeling a little intemperate, I—again— am told that my scowl will stop a dinosaur in its tracks. So I consciously put into use the technique taught me by a master Wizard of Loh, who are a pretty scary bunch of sorcerers, old Deb-Lu-Quienyin, among the most renowned of all Wizards of Loh, and changed my expression. I put on a benign look. No—do not scoff. Dray Prescot, the rascal and ruffian, brawler, Bladesman, Bravo Fighter and much else, including reiver and mercenary, can assume a face that masks all that violent energy. Mind you, a very different face if held for too long exacts punishment, for my face feels as though a million bees have been stinging away happily all night.

So, with a cheerful, friendly expression, I blundered on, shouting: "Hai! Relt! I mean you no harm! Where away are we?"

Only the echo of a squeak floated back.

Still wearing that silly grinning physiognomy, I rounded the outcrop. Fifty paces on, torchlights threw orange streaks from a buttress that soared into shadows.

This looked promising. I did not think the Relt with his soft ways and timid life-style would be the man I was looking for. The Star Lords use tougher material than that. Even so, he might be, for I was becoming more and more aware that the Everoinye's plans for Kregen were far different from those I might once have envisioned.

A rumble began in the ground. The rock all about me shook. Dust drifted down from high overhead and within the dust, chips and shards of razor-edged stone. The noise boomed and buffeted so that, staggering, choking in the dust, I put my hands to my ears. The earthquake roared on, filling the world with haze, rending at my senses, wrenching away at my primeval feelings of solidity with this land I loved. Perhaps only a dozen heartbeats the quake reverberated in that cavern; it seemed like a couple of lifetimes and more.

Dust stung in my nostrils and inflamed my eyes. I squinted, and took my hands away from my ears, and tried to hear and see again. I swallowed. A scrabble, barely heard, down by my right foot, attracted instant attention.

From a rocky crevice newly widened crept a thing like two soup plates jammed together, top and bottom, with a pair of stalked eyes and a long rapierlike proboscis twitching angrily. At the tip of that three-foot-long spiny shaft glittered a drop of poison, green and thick and evil.

This yenalk made a stab at my bare foot.

With a yelp I dodged away.

It trundled after me hungrily, rolling along on a multitude of thin short legs. It moved damned fast. There was only one thing to do, for it would persist in keeping after me until it sank its poisoned proboscis into me, and settled down to eating.

Leaping to the side, I put a foot down on a flat shard of stone. It started to spin around like a loco on a turntable... Without halting the movement I leaped clean over it. On its other side I bent, got my fingers under the lip of its shell and heaved it over onto its back.

It rolled like a dummy figure for a moment. All its legs waved like a forest lashed by a gale. I stared down.

"Rest there a space, yenalk, and if I am minded to come back for you, don't go away."

It rocked slowly to stillness, and its legs writhed helplessly.

Drifting dust still fell in patterns across the torchlights and as I walked up to the buttress I saw that this drifting light-irradiated dust was very beautiful. An odd, irrational thought, perhaps, but for all my uncouthness and barbarity I have, as I think you will understand, an eye for beauty found in places where beauty is not expected to be discovered.

A bunch of people huddled on the hard stones in the light and they were in bad case. Here, I said to myself, is where my labors begin.

The first thing I noticed as I walked among them was their cowed and beaten-down appearance. They were all of races that people on Kregen regard as the delicate and refined ones, the weak and unaggressive diffs. There were Relts and Xaffers, those remote and distant diffs, and Lamnias, shrewd merchants, and others like Lun'elshes* with soft black body hair, and Dunders, squat, thick-hewed, flat-headed men universally employed as carriers. A number of Ennschafften, whom folk normally call Syblians, huddled together, the men bundles of muscles, the women very beautiful, and all with simple naive baby-faces. I stood for a moment staring at this collection of the deprived of Kregen. Even then, Lamnias are not deprived in the sense of worldly goods, for they are wily merchants with the highest reputations.

As I stood thus looking about, a bull voice broke in a roar.

"A damned apim! Well, apim, and what kept you?"

Lying back on a spread cloak of black and yellow lozenges a numim bellowed at me. The lion-man's head was wrapped in a clumsy bandage ripped from the hem of the cloak, and the black and yellow interweavings, like the hide of a sanjit, were stained with blood. In his right fist he gripped a sword whose blade had snapped off a foot from the hilt. He looked to be in the most ferocious of bad tempers. His hide was so dark a brown as to appear black, and his bristling lion mane was a tawny umber. He was not of the golden numims.

"By Numi-Hyrjiv the Golden Splendor! You've been lollygagging around, and here I lie waiting for you! This is not to be born. And have

---

* When a Kregish word contains the letter 'n' followed by an apostrophe, this generally indicates the word 'nik'—small or half—has been elided. A.B.A.

the Everoinye then sunk so low as to send a naked unarmed apim?" His wrathful lion face grimaced then and he put his left hand to the bandage. "My head rings with all the bells of Beng Kishi, and you stand there like a cretin! Jump to it, onker, and fetch me water! I parch!"

About to bark out a choice remark that would cut this supercilious lion-man down to size, I checked myself. I still wore that foolish grinning face. Before I could speak he was ranting on again, acting merely as he usually acted.

"Onker! Why do you stand there? I am Strom Irvil of Pine Mountain. You jump when I speak to you, as any respectable body slave should jump when his master speaks. That fool Zaydo got himself crushed when the roof caved in and I am all alone and—"

"But—" I began.

In Strom Irvil's book that was a serious mistake.

"You never argue with your master, Zaydo! Onker! Nulsh! Get me water or I will stripe you most cruelly."

"My name is not Zaydo—"

"All my body slaves are called Zaydo." He tried to rise, forcing himself up with the broken sword as a crutch. He gasped. He fell back onto the spread cloak. "Water," he said. "Fetch water, Zaydo, and you escape the flogging triangle."

I saw his lion lips were dry and cracked. Without another word I cast about and found a pottery bowl and so went to the stream where I had startled the Relt, and fetched back water for Strom Irvil of Pine Mountain. One Pine Mountain I had heard of lay in Thothangir, in the far south of the continent.

I put the bowl to his lips and he drank, distressedly. I went to lift the bandage to look at his wound, but he knocked my hand away.

"Leave it, Zaydo. I will mend. But the Everoinye will not be pleased if I fail them. You must get us all out of here."

"What happened?"

He glared up at me, the water shining among the cracks of his lips.

"You call me master, Zaydo, and speak with civility and humility, else it is the flogging triangle. I am a great lord, and you are my body slave, sent by the Everoinye. Remember this."

A strom, which is roughly equivalent to an Earthly count, is indeed a title of great nobility in some lands, if of a lesser stature in others. The notion grew in me like a moon-bloom opening to the kiss of the suns' rays after a night of Notor Zan when no moons shine in Kregen's sky. Just why this affair amused me is difficult to say. I knew I would not act the poltroon in Hamal. But looking at this blowhard numim strom as he lay there, gasping, the bloody bandage incongruous on his head, I suppose I half-reasoned out that no good would come of browbeating him now.

322

We had a job to do. If he labored under the delusion I was his body slave Zaydo, what difference would that make? I wanted to finish this thing off, and then get about wrecking Empress Thyllis's crazy ambitions. And, into the bargain, I could do with a good laugh, and this numim appeared to me to be able to furnish mirth aplenty.

So... "Yes, master, no master, very good master, and what has happened here that you are in such poor case and Zaydo is crushed to death?"

He blew his whiskers out and glared up at me.

"You are an onker! The roof fell in, that's what. And when I led these people out through the old mining tunnels, the earthquake brought more down, and so trapped us all again and knocked a damned great hole in my head. Vosk skull!"

"Mayhap, master, a vosk skull, being exceedingly thick, is a good thing to have down here."

"Do you mock me, ingrate?"

"Mock you, master? Why should a humble body slave do that?"

"I labor mightily for the good of the Everoinye. Why they should burden me with an imbecile like you I cannot imagine."

Now this Strom Irvil was only the second kregoinye I had so far met. The first, Pompino, was no doubt either safely at home in Pandahem with his wife, or jaunting about Kregen derring-doing on an errand for the Everoinye. I'd have preferred Pompino here with me now. But as I set about finding a way out for the trapped people, I had to put up with Strom Irvil breathing down my neck.

The truth of our predicament was brought home to me quickly and its brutality made me ponder. We were trapped. We were trapped. These people, representatives of the weaker races of Kregen, had crept here secretly to hold a meeting and listen to the wise words of a wandering preacher. This man, this Pundhri the Serene, sat on a rock higher than the rest, his fist supporting his bearded chin, his face bent down, talking quietly to a group of people gathered about him. His voice came to me as a mellifluous burble whose individual words were lost. He was a diff of that race of ahlnims whose members have for century after century produced mystics and wise men. He looked the part, for his hair, like a Gon's, was chalk white. He did not, like a Gon, shave his head bald and polish it up with butter. His face bore that intent, concentrated look of a man absorbed with the import of what he was saying, determined to make his listeners understand and share his vision. He wore a simple dark-blue tunic, and he held a thick staff, unadorned, although with a stout knob at each end.

Strom Irvil said, "Yes, Zaydo. He is the man the Everoinye wish saved. He is our charge—and me with a damned great hole in my head and a stupid thick-skulled onker of a body slave! It is enough to make a man turn to drink."

"We are trapped—master—but mayhap we can dig a way out. If—"

"We! You mean you will dig a way out, Zaydo! And there are monsters in the tunnels. The old mine workings were abandoned seasons ago. The shrine where the meeting was held has not been used in the memory of living man. But Pundhri the Serene called the meeting there out of the prying eyes of those who would destroy him and his work."

"And what work is that? Master."

He glared and winced. "You see what a miserable band these folk are. Not a fighting man among them..."

"The ahlnims fight, on occasion—"

"Aye! And by thus doing break the tenets of their faith."

I eyed Pundhri's knobbed stick. They call that kind of dual-skull-basher a dwablatter. I surmised that Pundhri had used it often enough before he was dubbed the Serene.

"And you say there are monsters, master?" I almost mocked, beginning to feel the need of opening my shoulders. "I suppose there are flame-spouting risslacas, and giant spiders, and—"

"The giant spiders are as big as two dinner plates and they can snap your leg off like a rotten twig."

That sobered me, I can tell you.

He threw the broken sword at me.

"Get on with it, get on with it, then, Zaydo, you useless lazy hound!"

"Yes, master." I stared about, a trifle vacantly. "Where shall I begin?" After all, if he was the master and I the slave then let him sort out the brainwork.

"Over there where the first tunnel starts, onker!"

The stone chipped away fairly easily at first as I dug the broken blade in and twisted and scraped. A couple of jolly Sybli girls held torches. They had a fair supply of these, being cautious folk. But they would not last forever. There were lanterns, cheap mineral-oil lamps, and these were being saved. Then, after about two arms' lengths, the rock firmed up into mother bedrock. The steel chimed.

I crawled back and stood up, my head and chest covered with rock dust.

"What are you stopping for?" The lion-man roar burst out. "Get on with it."

"No way through here. Master."

"Fool! Then try somewhere else."

"Yes, master." I didn't bother about any more fun and frolic. A careful look around in the uncertain illumination revealed the way the cavern sloped down at one end, with arching rockfalls fanning out from ancient subsidences. One or two of the dark slots looked promising. I marched across to the nearest. I passed near the group listening respectfully to Pundhri the Serene. At the rock face the slot proved too narrow for my shoulders and I turned, intending to go on to the next.

A small ahlnim woman approached, carrying a length of brown cloth. Her hair was pinned neatly at the nape of her neck, as I saw as she bowed her head. Her robe was torn and smeared with dust, and I fancied that was unusual for her. She looked calm and competent and capable of running a household.

"The master offers you this, and all his prayers are for your success."

I took the cloth. "Thank you, hortera," I said, giving her the courtesy title of lady.

She ducked her head and went back to sit comfortably on a flat rock just to the side and rear of Pundhri. I wound the brown cloth about my nakedness and, spitting on my hands, set to work with the broken sword.

At that, I did not fail to complain that the Star Lords habitually sent me off to do their dirty work for them stark naked and weaponless. For this high and mighty Strom Irvil, they supplied clothes and weapons—and a personal body slave!

Some of the Dunders came across and began helping to shift the chips and chunks of rock I flaked off. Squat knots of muscle, short in stubby leg, thick of arm, the Dunders have been blessed—or cursed—by nature or the meddling hand of genetic manipulation with heads as flat across the top as billiard tables. Do not imagine they can be brilliantly intellectual; but they do think, they do suffer from emotions and they are men. Carriers of burdens, the Dunders, and there had been a number of them with us down the Moder before the monsters finished their work forever.

Pausing for a breather, I said to the nearest flat-headed Dunder: "Is the San a healer, dom?"

He shook that strange head. "No, dom, no. I do not think so." Then he added in perfect explanation of his race's outlook: "No one told me he is a healer."

San Pundhri the Serene continued to talk. The title of san, which means master, dominie, sage, was accorded him as by right. He held a magnetic attraction for these poor folk. Not many were slaves, and this, presumably, because slaves of other slave-owners would have been unable to get away to the meeting, and the free folk here could afford few slaves. I went back to rock bashing.

The way opened after considerable effort and a torch, thrust through the first chink to appear onto the rocks tumbled into the tunnel, revealed an empty openness.

"A cavern," I said. "Once we're into that we'll be well away."

The rocky fall was cleared and it was time to try to rouse these people to movement. With a barrage of groans and snorts and burstings of bad temper, Strom Irvil got himself up. He swayed on those dark-furred legs. I gave him an arm for support and he brushed it away, pettishly.

"I can stand, Zaydo, you onker!"

I went across to Pundhri.

"San," I said with due formality. "Will you help to move the people? They are frightened—"

He stared at me and I saw his eyes resting on me with calculation. He grasped his knobbed stick and stood up.

"They have reason to be frightened. You are Zaydo?"

In for a zorca, in for a vove. "Yes, San."

"We have no weapons against the monsters."

I shook rock dust off the broken sword.

He moved off his flat rock. "I will help these people, of course. You need not have asked. But I do not think your broken sword will avail us here."

"It has opened the way. It may yet serve."

He stopped and bent his brows on me. "And you are slave?"

I did not answer but went bashing back to a group of silly Xaffers who wanted to go the wrong way in the confusing torchlit darkness. When we were sorted out and moving through the gap broken in the fall and into the next cavern, I fancied Pundhri might have other things to occupy him besides the character of the slave called Zaydo.

The next cavern echoed hollowly to our voices. The torches, held high, showed the craggy rock at our backs and an empty darkness ahead. Everyone stopped. There was no doubt at all that this place held an eerie atmosphere that worked on the susceptibilities. People spoke in low tones. A subdued apprehension made movements awkward. At any moment horror could burst upon us from the darkness.

"Zaydo!" brayed the lion voice. "Get on, get on! And give me my sword. Slaves do not carry swords."

"There are some countries where slaves carry swords, master."

"If I had my strength I'd knock you flat on your back! Impudent tapo! Insolent yetch!"

Handing the broken sword across, I said: "You will not stripe me, master?"

"I don't see why I should not. My head! You are an ingrate and I am too kind to my slaves. Now get on, and go that way, for I feel a draught there."

There was a draught, a tiny current of air, and so this Strom Irvil wasn't as incapacitated as he wanted to think. Off we went, stumbling and clattering over the uneven floor. The torches lost the rocky wall at our backs, and showed nothing ahead. In darkness, rock underfoot, the torches flaring their orange hair, we staggered on.

Eventually we reached the far wall and squeezed through a crack where air flowed, and came into another cavern, and crossed that. We might spend a dozen lifetimes down there, creeping through the tunnels and struggling across caverns.

"Up!" growled Strom Irvil. "We must go up!"

San Pundhri glanced up, not squinting. Irvil bellowed.

"Zaydo, you useless yetch! Find a way up! By Havil the Green, what a straw scarecrow I'm lumbered with in you, brainless onker!"

I was about to let out a fluent torrent of abuse, when Pundhri cut in quickly.

"You use hard words on your slave, strom. He has done well so far. Can we not—"

"No! Not until we are out of this infernal hellhole."

I walked across to the wall and a Sybli maiden carried a torch, which was near to expiring, and we looked at the fissures within the rock. One or two looked promising. Once we had broken our way back into the mine workings we ought to find it easier going. I reached back for the torch. The Sybli handed it to me, smiling her silly, naïve, endearing Sybli smile, and I eased sideways along the gray stone, the torch picking out veins and spiracles of crystal. Along I went, the torch thrust ahead. The flames flickered, so there was some kind of draught here. The rock pressed against my back. There was barely room before my chest to move my arms. The way tended up.

The ground shook.

The walls moved.

The solid rock groaned as though the very stone labored in agony from unimaginable pressure. Chips of stone flaked off and fell, unheard in that world-shaking rumble. The walls closed together. Arm up holding the torch, arm down levering on, one leg flexed, the other contorted awkwardly, I stopped moving, pinned. Fast fixed within the vise of stone, I could not budge. The jaws of the world snapped on me, closer and closer. I felt my ribcage bending. The torch glared full upon a single glittering drop of green. The drop of poison at the tip of a thin proboscis oozed from the slot beside my head. The yenalk showed as a flat outline, the dust glittering upon his shell. It inched forward along its fissure, aiming at me, aiming that poison-tipped sword straight at my eye.

Two

Strom Irvil Berates Zaydo

The pantheons of Kregen contain many and many an imp and devil, ghastly each in its own fashion. In that moment trapped in the slot, with the world collapsing around me, unable to move, and with a poison-tipped sting hovering before my eye, I fancy I felt more than a few of those devils gibbering and clawing at me.

"By Makki-Grodno's disgusting diseased left eyeball!" I said. I did not move. I dare not move. I could not move. And I, Dray Prescot, was like to have my own personal disgusting diseased left eyeball, and damned quick, at that.

The rumbling subterranean convulsions of the earthquake persisted. The strongest desire to run obsessed me, and I could not move. All around me the stone trembled. I daresay it did not tremble as much as did I.

Sweat rolled off me. I blinked. That single blink might be enough to trigger the yenalk into an attack, into a savage lunged thrust of his sting clear through my eyeball...

He did not move.

I felt the sweat chill on me. The damned thing was as jammed fast as was I!

The world convulsed again and the rock squeezed.

The yenalk squashed. His two soup-plate shells crunched together. His insides squeezed out.

I could not turn my head fully away, and I did not shut my eyes. The disgusting mess slipped and slithered over the face of the wall trapping me. The yenalk was squashed as flat as a bug under a boot heel. Was it my turn next?

The stink in there, highly unpleasant, was no worse than that of some of the slave bagnios I've inhabited from time to time.

Whatever seismological disturbance was going on, whatever planetary gut-rumbling encompassed me, I could not know; its effects I could know and experience. The rock's slipping movement pressed on me. I felt my ribs crunching. My eyes must have been standing out on stalks. I felt all the blood in me clashing and colliding, and I breathed small, and there came one last pressure which pressed the last gasp from me—and the walls folded back. A hand's-breadth, they moved away, shrieking as rock splintered. Dust and debris rained on me. A chunk of sharp-edged stone cracked against my shoulder. And then I was free.

I felt my knees giving way.

The torch shook and orange lights quivered, shadows pirouetted like the encroaching demons of darkness.

By Zair! That had been a narrow one!

A narrow one... No, believe me, I didn't laugh; not just then, anyway.

After that a few more crashings and hangings, with the passageway splitting asunder with a shriek of a banshee, all came as anticlimaxes. I hauled myself around to go back to the others and bumped into Strom Irvil.

His bandage hung all lopsided. He was panting and his lion face was flushed with high blood pressure and consummate anger.

"What are you coming back for, you rascal! Running for it, are you! Get on. The ceiling nearly fell on us out there while you were safe in here."

There was nothing to say. I'd have my laugh later.

Creeping along and following the heaven-sent draught of air, we wormed our way through the passageways and so came out into the ancient mine workings. Here many thick pillars upheld the roof. The lanterns were lit and we pressed on as fast as we could. The people babbled away, scenting escape from these dolorous caverns. Two more earth tremors hit; but they caused us no damage, only alarm that the pillars might collapse and the ceiling fall in. Nothing like that happened and, passing a toppled statue of Havil the Green, smothered in dust and gouged by falling rocks, we began the ascent to the surface.

"I do not think that shrine will ever be used again," observed Pundhri, toiling along near me.

Much as this sage interested me, because the Star Lords wished him preserved, this was not the time or place to prosecute inquiries. So I just said: "There are many shrines on the surface of the world better suited than those stuffed away in dark holes in the ground."

We jostled along, climbing, and Pundhri looked back as Strom Irvil bellowed in his impatient way for me to give him assistance over a patch of splintered rocks. His bandage was unwinding. Putting a hand under his left armpit I hoisted him up. His booted feet scrabbled on rocks. He pitched forward and I held him from falling. The bandage slid down over an ear and eye.

He roared.

"Fool! Onker! Useless ninny! Oh, why am I plagued with rubbish like you? May Numi-Hyrjiv the Golden Splendor look down in mercy upon me. Onker!"

Pundhri started to say, "The slave Zaydo does not merit—"

Strom Irvil thrashed around, trying to shove the black and yellow bandage straight, trying to shrug away from my grip, trying to get his boots onto a flat space in the splinters. "I know what he merits! I know! By all the Devils of the Pines! And I'll give it to him when we're out of this infernal hellhole!"

When I let him go he did not fall down. In truth, I had assisted him, as was patently obvious. I said nothing.

We all wended on, and Irvil breathed his stertorous lion-man snorts, and every now and again he would favor me with a baleful glare. At the time I was quite looking forward to getting out of here myself. I would enjoy being given my just merits from Strom Irvil, as I might return his...

His tawny mane was dark-tipped, his body of a deep brown, quite unlike the golden mane and hide of Rees, who was the Trylon of the Golden Wind, aptly named estates. The wind blew Rees's land away into that deadly golden wind, and I wondered if he was still as rich as he had been, if he still lived, he and Chido, who were boon companions, Bladesmen, rufflers of the Sacred Quarter in Ruathytu, capital of this enemy Empire of Hamal.

My thoughts took a somber turn. When I dealt with mad Empress Thyllis, as I would, and knocked over her foul and insane ambitions to extend the conquests of Hamal far beyond the country's logical limits, would I encounter Rees and Chido? They were touchy on matters of honor. They fought for Hamal. I fought for Vallia, and the two empires were locked in mortal combat. I could never slay Rees or Chido, even though they were supposed to be enemies, because they were comrades, valued friends, a part of the joy of life.

And, even more than Rees and Chido, what of Tyfar? Prince Tyfar of Hamal, who was a blade comrade, and who did not know that I was a Vallian—and because our two countries were at war was his foeman—what of Tyfar? My daughter Jaezila and Tyfar, for all their buffoonery and slanging matches, were deeply in love. I knew that. If Tyfar declared for Thyllis, could I fight him? Could I go up against him with naked steel in my fist? Of course not.

Then I tripped over an outcrop of rock and fell on my nose, and Strom Irvil bellowed out, and I was back in these damned caverns. I sneezed as the dust bit, and stood up, and bashed the dust off, and so stumbled on. If Irvil went up against me fighting for Hamal, I might yet joy in teaching him that Vallians had learned the arts of soldiering.

Then I checked my wandering thoughts. Irvil said he came from Thothangir, right in the south of the continent of Havilfar. He was a kregoinye and worked for the Star Lords. There was no reason why he should fight for Hamal.

Then the confounded giant spiders descended on us.

On glistering lines they dropped from the shadows, bulbous, hairy, many-legged, a nightmare rain of heavy bodies and spindled serrated legs.

"What?" Irvil's lion face charged with passion. "What?"

"Pundhri!" I yelled. The people panicked. They ran screaming every which way, falling staggering into one another, flailing uselessly with weak arms. The moment was ugly and horrific and fraught with greater peril for us than even these monstrous spiders could bring. If Pundhri died... Thothangir at least was on Kregen. I would be banished back to Earth, sent packing through the gulfs between the stars and left to moulder away in a despair far more horrible than that caused by any stupid giant spiders.

Directly ahead and some twenty paces off the jagged round opening of a tunnel offered some protection. People were running for the opening, crying and screaming. Some fell and the bodies of the spiders descended on them, bloating, stingers driving deep, legs folding and closing in.

"Pundhri!" I shouted again. Irvil glared madly at me. Snatching up a chunk of rock I poised and hurled. The missile smashed into the fat body of a spider about to drop onto Pundhri's head. The bloated thing burst. Pundhri moved away, not shouting, his bearded face still calm, still serene. No doubt what happened to him, he believed, happened because it was ordained. That might be so. But the Star Lords thought differently.

"Get him into the tunnel!"

Irvil had the sense to grab at the sage who allowed himself to be led off. Irvil, at that, showed up well, for his bandage at last tumbled off. The wound in his head looked a mess. It was genuine. The blood had caked around the gash and no doubt some of his scalp was pulled off with the bandage. He took no notice now he was in action and there was work to do. He hauled Pundhri off, and his free hand flailed the stump of sword over their heads. The Star Lords do not choose lightly when they select kregoinyes to work for them; this blowhard strom was a fighting man.

Also, he was damned uncivil to his servants.

Spiders swung on their threads, slicing into the rabble. They were, of course, no concern of mine. All the same, there was no question of running off and leaving them. Hurled rocks proved effective, if the aim was good, and ahlnim lads joined in, joyful to expand their chests and knowing they did not break the tenets of their race. I saw a Dunder grab a spider and squash it in his arms, between his arms and chest, before the sting had time to pierce him.

"Well done! Keep them off! Into the tunnel!"

Of course, there might be more spiders, other horrors, in this tunnel...

"Zaydo! Onker!"

Irvil stood in the opening of the tunnel and although he for the moment blocked ingress of anybody else, that did not discommode him. "Catch!"

The flung sword spun end over end toward me.

Pundhri stood close to Irvil and just before they moved back to allow the press to run, crying and wailing, into safety, they watched me. There was no time to lose, no time to playact. The spiders were now crowding in, and rocks were proving useless. The stump sword spun through the air. I took it cleanly by the hilt, slapped it across and then hacked a swinging spider in half. All those motions were merely one continuous flow of action.

Shadows deepened as the lanterns and torches were carried toward the tunnel. A few people were dead and past help; but we dragged more away and so, angrily, we backed up to the tunnel mouth. The broken sword reeked with spider ichor. One or two of the stronger men with me were all for staying and bashing spiders flat with rocks. They were accustomed to being humiliated and maltreated in ordinary life; now they tasted a little of the other side, albeit against hairy giant spiders, and it got into their blood. I had to stop this, stop it cleanly, for it displeased me. Not for these poor folk, not for the spiders, no, not for those reasons...

"The tunnel is clear," shouted Irvil above the din. "Come on, Zaydo, do! Move yourself!"

"Notor," said Pundhri, which is the Hamalese way of addressing a lord. "Notor, the slave fought well with the broken sword."

"Well, and why not? It was my sword, was it not?"

You had to laugh at old Strom Irvil. Everything was perfectly logical to him in his universe.

Shouts rose from the people who had gone ahead along the tunnel, telling us they had broken a way through. Irvil glared at me. "And mind you clean the sword properly, Zaydo. There is one thing I will not abide in my body slaves, dirty habits."

There was nothing to be done for the unfortunate folk who had fallen victim to the spiders. No one could watch the grief of relatives who had survived unmoved; but no good could come from allowing oneself to break down. In one person's death the whole world shares. Also, after the ordeal in the slot when the living rock closed up on me, and the poison-tipped sting aimed for my eye, I was still in overwrought condition.

We all welcomed the sight of daylight. We broke from a shaggily overgrown hole in the side of the mountain, and many a one fell to his knees to give thanks for safe deliverance. I took a long, deep and expansive lungful of the glorious Kregan air. By Vox! What it is to be alive!

The land spread out before us, wide and rolling, yellowish-brown with dust and blued with heat haze. By the position of the suns I saw we faced eastwards. And that brought up my words to that Relt who had received such a shock at the stream. Whereaway were we in Opaz-forsaken Hamal?

Pundhri was blessing the people, and already many of them were hurrying away, skipping and jumping down the slopes. Smoke rose into the air from villages down there. The land looked sparse, but there were herds of cattle, and no doubt chores to be done and absences to be explained.

Pundhri turned to me.

"I give you thanks, Zaydo—"

Strom Irvil blossomed. He shook the bloody bandage at me.

"Thanks to a damned dim-witted slave! You are reputed a wise man, Pundhri the Serene. In this, I think your wits wander. It is to me, Strom Irvil of Pine Mountain, the thanks are due."

Only a few folk were left now, and the ahlnim woman with Pundhri kissed a woman who might have been her twin, and watched her take her children and go down the mountain. I said nothing. Pundhri smiled. The whole cast of his features changed. He looked jolly and mischievous, and as I had thought about his dwablatter and how he must have used that knobby stick before he acquired his name of Serene, so now I thought how he must have laughed and joked before the mysticism took him up.

He looked meaningfully at me. "And is it now you trim the leem's claws, Zaydo the slave?"

The Kregish saying, something like "to cut him down to size," amused me. The leem is an eight-legged devilish hunting animal of incredible ferocity and vicious cunning, and often have I been dubbed both a leem-hunter and a cunning old leem. I thought Pundhri used that particular saying for that reason; seeing in me something foreign to a slave, something of the leem.

"Give me the bandage, strom," I said. "I will do up your head, for you have had a knock."

Now slaves do not usually address lords by their titles. Irvil started to explode, whiskers bristling, and I took the bandage and slapped it on his head so that an end flapped down over his face. His roar abruptly snuffled on bloody cloth.

I sorted him out, and got the bandage neatly tied, and then he started in on me. Pundhri stared with a nicety of expression very exhilarating.

So, knowing what I was doing, I said, "No, san. No, I think not. It amused me at the time, and it amuses me more, now, that Strom Irvil remain as he is. It would be a pity to trim even a single paring from the leem's claws in this."

Irvil bellowed, "I'll have the skin off your back! I'll gastronomate you! You'll be flogged jikaider! So help me—if I had my strength! If my head wasn't broke in two!"

He took a whooping breath and saw his broken sword where I had dropped it on the grass to see about his bandage.

"And you haven't cleaned my sword! Oh, why do I suffer so? What have I done to deserve such an oaf, such an ingrate?"

The woman with Pundhri, whom he called his dear Puhlshi, tugged his sleeve gently. "It is time to go. We should be in Hernsmot already by now."

"Yes, my dear Puhlshi. But we must give our thanks first."

"Hernsmot," I said. "Over by the Mountains of the West."

"A poor place, but there is a meeting there."

"Well, I am for Thothangir as soon as possible." Irvil pushed fretfully at his bandage. "I suppose I shall have to endure you, you useless oaf, Zaydo, until we reach a place where I can hire a flier."

"That will not be easy," Pundhri pointed out. "With the war. The army and the air services—"

"Yes, yes. You Hamalese are in a fine old state with your stupid war."

Puhlshi's ahlnim face turned a dark plum color.

"We detest the war! We speak against it—"

"Ah!" I said, and when they all looked at me in surprise at this intelligent comment, I coughed and looked at the grass. Still and all, that did explain a lot. Perhaps the Star Lords were no longer quite so anxious about Hamal as I had thought? Perhaps my own brave country of Vallia had entered the reckoning? Saying good-bye and calling the remberees, we watched Pundhri and his ahlnim party making their way down the hill. Irvil shook himself, winced, and blamed me for that.

"You are supposed to be a kregoinye," he said. "Although why the Everoinye should choose a stupid apim, and send him to me naked and weaponless, I cannot imagine."

"Do you always arrive where the Everoinye send you with clothes and weapons, master?"

He stared. "If I thought you were serious..."

"Have you been a kregoinye long, master?"

He glowered. "You should address me as master before you speak. You are damned insolent, Zaydo, and this displeases me." He stretched, and, again, he winced. "We will have to find shelter and food. I starve. If you have to carry me on your back—"

"Surely the Everoinye will take care of you?"

"Of course!" He brayed that out. But I saw he was not at all sure. Then he started to shake, and after that he sat down on a boulder on the hillside, and for a space I left him to his own devices.

Presently, he called across: "Zaydo! You are an onker and a hulu. But you fought well down there in the earth's guts. I have been a kregoinye for ten seasons. I was chosen, so they told me, because I am a fighting man with intelligence and a high moral code."

I did not laugh. As though a high moral code would weigh in the scales of the Star Lords!

He went on: "But I was wounded. I think the Everoinye no longer cared for me when I could not do their bidding."

"Yes. But you still live."

"Just, you onker."

A harsh croak floated down from the sky. We both looked up. I, for one, knew what—or who—floated up there on wide pinions, and I guessed Irvil knew, also.

The Gdoinye, the scarlet- and golden-feathered raptor of the Star Lords, circled over us. He turned his bright head and a beady eye surveyed us. I did not, as was my wont, shake my fist at that glorious bird and hurl abuse at him. Instead, I looked to see what Irvil would do. He stood up. He stood up and he stood to attention, smartly, as though on emperor's parade.

"What are your commands, Notor Gdoinye?"

Well, perhaps the only other kregoinye I had known, Pompino, might have spoken thus, and certainly he stood in great awe of this splendid bird; but, all the same, it was extraordinarily difficult for me to keep a straight face and not to burst out with a series of choice epithets to express what I thought of this nurdling great loon of a bird.

Perhaps the Gdoinye saw or sensed those irreverent feelings in me. He winged lower, the suns glisten vanishing from his body and wings as he ruffled his feathers in the draught. Low over our heads he volplaned, swishing down, hurtling over us and then soaring up and up and dwindling to a vanishing dot. As he passed so he let rip one contemptuous squawk.

On this occasion the messenger of the Star Lords had delivered no verbal message. As he was a supernatural creature serving beings with awesome powers, there was no doubt of his opinion of us. Also, there was no doubt his report had gone in. No doubt at all.

Strom Irvil let his body slump. He did not relax, for he looked uneasy. His scowl appeared shifty. "I wanted to complain about the trash they sent me as a body slave, Zaydo, you fambly. But I did not. I do not know why I did not." He picked up his broken sword and hefted it. He was going to throw it to me—at me more likely.

"Get this cleaned up!" His big lion-man bellow broke about my ears, brashly reasserting self-confidence.

A puff of dust lifted about him. Instantly it was apparent that dust was no natural phenomenon. Blue radiance glowed. For the space of two heartbeats the dust flowed and lifted and irradiated by the blue fire formed itself into the semblance of a living lion man. The sapphire statue swirled up in an expanding dissipating cloud.

Strom Irvil no longer stood with me on the mountainside in western Hamal.

Three

A Length of Lumber Instructs Flutsmen

The task was to defeat the Empire of Hamal.

No. No, that was not strictly true. The task was not so much to defeat Hamal as to encourage the people to see the errors in their ways of carrying on. They had to see that instead of trying to conquer and subdue the people around them—and people like Vallians who lived at a considerable distance, by Vox!—they should join with them in a mutual defense against the weird Fishheaded folk who raided all our coasts.

I tasted the wind, looked around the heat-hazed land, remembered a few things, and started off walking.

I headed north.

If it seems ludicrous that a single, unarmed and almost naked man should thus set off to topple a proud empire—well, yes, it may seem passing strange. But it was a task laid on me. Also, and this warmed me as I trudged along, I was not really alone. There were many good friends on Kregen who stood at my side in battle. My country of Vallia would be joined by other nations desirous of ridding themselves of the yoke of Hamal. Together, we would make a mighty flood that would sweep away mad Empress Thyllis.

To return at once to Vallia was a strong and almost overpowering temptation. It had to be resisted.

We in Vallia had suffered devastating invasions and great humiliations from Hamal. Now we planned to gather an army and invade in our turn. But my people at home could deal with all these purely military matters. Much as I wanted to return at once to my capital of Vondium, picking up Delia from Huringa en route, I knew I could be of more use here. Here in Hamal I could work from within, the worm in the bud. Here was the scene of my labors.

So, with joy that I was about the business that obsessed me, and with despair that this duty deprived me of all that I loved, I set off for Paline Valley.

Before that, though, I hankered after going down to the village and seeking Pundhri the Serene. Dressed as I was, in a sober brown loincloth, I could pass easily enough as a free working man. By exercising a little carpentry skill I could pass as a gul, one of the artisans and craftsmen and small shopkeepers of Hamal, rather than as a clum, the festering mass of poor—free but little better than slave.

The village grew clearer as I scrambled down the slope. It looked a dead and alive hole. There would be guls and clums there, possibly; most of them tended to congregate in the towns and cities. One worrying factor was that the military might of Hamal, being strained, was now prepared to accept clums into the army. Along with the mercenaries Hamalian gold could hire, the clums would constitute a new and major threat. They'd take time to train and they'd desert as fast as they could; but the laws of Hamal are as of steel. Once the Hamalian military machine gained control of an individual clum, that once-free man would turn into just another cog in the iron legions of Hamal.

Not a pretty prospect, and yet just one of the hundreds of problems that beset me. There was much to ponder as I walked into the end of the main and only street of the village. Pundhri the Serene was not there. He had taken his little party off at once, riding preysanys, a common form of saddle animal among the less wealthy. I looked at the gaffer who told me this, and shook my head, and went away from that village. I had not cared for their looks.

And this made me even more keenly aware of the strangest part of this whole business.

I was unarmed.

On Kregen, a man does not care to be parted from his arsenal of weapons.

Now I do not wish to impugn the honesty of that village, or the gaffer to whom I had spoken, or his headman. But my surmise is, and I apologize to those unknown Hamalese if I am wrong, my surmise is the gaffer ran off at once to his headman, robe flapping around his ankles, slippers flicking dust, and the headman, fondling his chain of office, nodded sagely and ordered a signal fire lit. It would be a small signal fire. I saw the plume of smoke rise, tall and straight, and I frowned.

Directly ahead a stream crossed my path with a stand of trees from which the village would have been invisible. They were so damned anxious they hadn't even waited until their signal smoke would not be seen by the potential victim.

The smoke rose, thin and unwavering. A one-man signal, that, I guessed.

I splashed across the stream and looked around in the little copse. Finding a length of wood in a forest is not as easy as it sounds. Oh, yes, there is wood aplenty, lumber by the yard. I wanted a stick of a certain thickness, length and shape, and I took perhaps a little longer than circumspection might suggest was advisable. I found the stick. Barehanded, freeing it from its parent involved a deal of grunting and twisting and straining, and I used my teeth to trim up the ends to a rough symmetry. Some three feet long—some meter long, I suppose you latter-day folk would say—it snugged firmly in my fists, spread apart to give leverage. I swung the stick about. It was not a simple cudgel or bludgeon or shillelagh, admirable though they are in the right hands. This length of simple wood held the feel and balance of a Krozair longsword, and with that potent and terrible brand of destruction a man might go up against devils.

So, swinging my pseudo-longsword, I marched off out of the wood and I kept screwing my head around and staring aloft.

They were not long in making their evil appearance.

The piece of wood stopped its circling motions as I loosened up the old muscles. The end where it had ripped away from its parent glistened yellow and clean and sharp, very sharp, a wooden splinter like a fang.

Dots against the brightness of the sky, stringing along in a skein, oh, yes, there they were...

On the exotic and cruel world of Kregen there are many men who make a fat living from the enslavement of other men. There are many varieties of slavers, slavemasters: Aragorn, Katakis, Makansos, and their ilk. From the way these four up there flew they proclaimed themselves flutsmen, reiving mercenaries of the skies. Four would be considered ample to snare up a lone man. They'd flown from their camp, somewhere in a fold of the hills, summoned by the signal smoke. Crossbows would be pouched to their saddles; but they wouldn't want to damage the merchandise and so wouldn't choose to feather me unless they had to.

No doubt my lips ricked back and my ugly old beakhead turned into that devil's visage, destroying the placid look I adopted as a mere common-sense precaution. Well, by Krun! They'd have cause to—good cause!

They spotted me and circled. There seemed no reason to make it easy for them. A few straggly bushes at the side of the path might prove amusing. This land in the rain shadow of the mountains will sprout green crops if watered, as evidenced by the bounteous plenty of the fields around Paline Valley; here beyond the village's stream the land dusted and grew a sparse grass and thorn bush. I did not take up my position in an ordinary bush; rather I hollowed a space beneath a thorn bush. The flutsmen finished circling and dived steeply down.

These four nasty specimens who wanted to sell me off into slavery annoyed me. The feeling swept over me in an uncontrollable burst of animosity. I had to get to Paline Valley and find out if I could move freely in Hamal, and these four flutsmen detained me. Also, I did not want to use the pit under the thorn bush except as a last resort. I marched out into the open and stared up, shading my eyes.

The flutsmen whooped as they dived, high thin shrieks of ferocious intent. This is a familiar and dreadful sight in many parts of Kregen, this headlong attack from the air by flutsmen who care for no one and nothing besides their own greed.

The first two swung down with a net stretched between them. Like a giant scoop the net swished toward me.

The wing tips of the saddle birds swept scurries of dust into the air. Their beaks extended forward and their eyes fastened on me. Fluttrells, they were, powerful if unsubtle saddle birds with that ridiculous aft vane at the back of their heads. The flutsmen leaned in their saddles, pulling the net taut, guiding themselves one each side of me so that the net would snatch me up as though a giant hand from the sky had reached down to return me to the velvet-lined balass box.

Hard yellow fibers formed the net, bristly and tough; even if I'd had a knife it would have been a chancy business to cut a way free before I was swirled up into the sky.

"Hai! Rast!" screeched the left-hand flutsman. His right fist brandished his long polearm, a sword blade mounted on a shaft to give him reaching effect aloft. His comrade hauled the net as the bight sagged, spouting dust and debris of dead grass. The fluttrells inclined outward a fraction. The net lifted from the ground.

Straight forward I dived. Down flat on my nose and with the wooden stick angled above my head. I felt the sliding hiss of the net as it whipped up across the stick, sliding on and away. Instantly I was on my feet, not looking back but at the next pair of devils.

They wouldn't shoot me yet.

If I knew flutsmen they'd be pleasantly surprised. Someone was not to be snapped up meekly. So—there was sport to be had here! They'd have me in the end, so they would think, and enjoy themselves in the doing of it. I would provide a spot of fun for them.

This little encounter was merely a hindrance to my plans. It was quite unimportant. All the same, a fellow could get himself killed in just this kind of insignificant encounter.

As the first pair of fluttrells winged around in a wide careful bank so as not to rupture the net, I caught sight of them. I ignored them. The second pair alighted in flurries of wingbeats and the riders hopped off. They came for me in a rush, swirling their swords. They'd knock a simple country bumpkin over the head with the flat and pop him into the net. Easy.

Two metal swords, the straight cut and thrusters of Havilfar called thraxters, against a length of lumber. Well, the length of lumber was wielded by a Krozair of Zy who understood the Disciplines of the Sword of the Krozairs. The two came on together, which made it more interesting.

They did exactly as I had surmised. Left hand took a welting great swipe at my head, and right hand slashed at my legs. A sideways lean, a little jump, the wood swirling around as my wrists went over and a neat one, two, thunk, thunk. The wood gonged against helmets. They wore brave clumps of feathers in their helmets, and their flying leathers glistened in the red and green radiance all about, and they went over on their backsides. Blood gushed from right hand's nose and mouth. Left hand could not see, for his helmet jammed down over his face. They both lay on the dusty ground and they did not offer to rise. They did not move at all. Terrible is a Krozair longsword, and terrible even when merely a length of wood, in the hands of a Krozair brother.

A giant rustling of feathers through the air warned me. I skipped sideways very smartly, and went flat down again and rolled and the net skittered past flailing dust and dead grasses.

I stood up. Two metal swords lay fallen from nerveless hands. The fluttrells waited twenty or so paces off. The pair with the net circled again. Two polearms, which the flutsmen call ukras, lay in the dust. There were crossbows pouched on the waiting birds. I kept my grip on my length of wood...

Clearly not fully understanding what had befallen their comrades, the pair with the net tired of trying to snare me. They landed and, together, charged.

When the dust settled I was in possession of the complete equipment of four flutsmen, including their mounts.

One of the sky reivers was not quite dead. I bent to him. Blood dribbled from his ears. His eyes were unfocused. I loosened his flying scarf and eased him, finding water in a bottle strapped to a bird's saddle. Moistening his lips gave him a dying spurt of energy.

"Who—who are you?" He croaked the words.

"Rather, dom, who are you? Your band is near?"

"We gather—in the hills."

Whether or not he knew he was dying, I could not say. But he wanted to talk, and he spent his last few moments on Kregen telling me that an army gathered, here in the sparse land by the Mountains of the West. There were mercenaries from all over, and the flutsmen were hired out to join the army as aerial cavalry. He did not know the numbers involved; but he said the army was large—"Many tents, many totrix cavalry and regiments of paktuns—"

"Not all mercenaries are paktuns," I said. "Have they all then won so much renown as to be dubbed paktun and wear the silver mortilhead on its silken ribbons at their throats?"

"You mock me, dom. But there are many hyrpaktuns with them who wear the golden zhantilhead, the pakzhan, at their throats. You will not—I think—mock them."

"I do not mock you. But the trade of mercenary has sadly fallen away in these evil times."

I was not about to tell him I had been a flutsman and mercenary myself; he was dying, and so, discovering he worshipped his god, Geasan the Opulent, with some fervor, I was able to administer the last rites he desired. He was lucky. Many and many a man dies on Kregen without that comfort simply because his god is unknown in the place of his death.

Better to be like me, who acknowledges Zair and Opaz—and Djan!— who need no flummery of that kind, being of the spirit.

After he was dead I left him and his comrades to be buried by the birds of the air.

A disturbing and puzzling fact he had mentioned in his dying ramblings was that this army being gathered here was not for use in the west. There were constant incursions of reivers and other unhealthy fighting creatures from the wild lands to the west, and Hamal's borders here had to be kept tight. So where was this army headed?

When I was ready to fly off, riding one bird and the other three in trail on halters, I looked down. I saluted gravely; not the Jikai, certainly not that! His name had been Olan the Stux. His bird carried in a stuxcal eight of the heavy javelins. They might be useful. If he hadn't been so damned anxious about the merchandise—me—and had shot me or stuxed me, he might still be alive. All passes under the hand of Opaz.

With that sobering thought to remind me of the murkiness of the future, crowded with perils, I took off for Paline Valley.

Four

Of a Spark in the Cells

To carry out nefarious undertakings in Hamal was a mite trickier than in most of the lands of Paz, the grouping of continents and islands on our side of Kregen. The iron-hard laws of the Empire of Hamal saw to that.

Flying due north and resting the fluttrells from time to time, feasting from the food in the saddlebags, I headed for Paline Valley. This place, if any in Hamal, I could consider home. The possession of a cover name that was perfectly genuine had proved of inestimable value. The way of it had been simple and touching, for when the wild men from over the mountains slew the old Lord, Naghan, and his son Hamun, I had fought for them and Naghan, dreadfully wounded, had with his dying breath commended Paline Valley to me. He implored me, he demanded from me, he exulted in his plan to make me his son, and faced with this barrage I had accepted the rank of Amak and the name of Hamun ham Farthytu.

I was Hamun ham Farthytu, Amak of Paline Valley.

Palines, the lusciously delectable berries that grow just about everywhere on Kregen, it seems, were certainly not growing on the parched land beneath. The ground looked like a rhinoceros's hide before his daily dip. Dust devils whirled. Not a sight of humanity, not a single solitary sight, greeted the eyes of the wayfarer on this route. So it was that the importance of the valleys folded into the foothills would be difficult to overestimate. Here cultivation thrived. Paline Valley was, in my biased opinion, the most beautiful and delightful of them all.

Up here, in the far northwest of Hamal, squeezed in between the Mountains of the West and Skull Bay to the north, Paline Valley was remote and cut off from the rest of the empire. All the same, signs of activity grew as I slanted in.

Lest the sight of four fluttrells winging should be mistaken for a prowling flutsman outflyer force, I was circumspect in landing. Palines grew in riotous profusion about me as I jumped off the lead fluttrell and quietened the others down. They had accepted me readily enough. Their beaks gaped and they twisted those silly head vanes about; they were thirsty.

The people who congregated gaped at me. They were slaves.

I felt a furious anger. I felt dismay. As the Amak here I had given my comrade Nulty strict instructions; no slaves were to be handled in the valley. Nulty knew my name was Dray Prescot. He had served the old Amak loyally, and now he served the new. I'd paid a few quick visits here, from time to time; but the last, because of all the unpleasant happenings in Vallia at the Time of Troubles and what followed, had been some time in the past. Even so, I couldn't believe barrel-body, husky, cheerful Nulty would have taken on slaves. Perhaps he was dead? I sincerely hoped not, for he still had a goodly span of his better than two hundred years of life left yet.

The slaves took care of the fluttrells. Clad in flying leathers, yet left loose and open for the heat, and wearing the best of the captured swords strapped to my belt, I walked along toward the gated entrance of the compound. Paline Valley's main village had been burned to the ground in that dread encounter, and Nulty had rebuilt. Now the oval-shaped area with all the houses facing inward so their backs formed a protective wall was of a greater size than it had been, and there were two protected ovals, joined like an hourglass. The shade trees, the well, the people and dogs and calsanys and all the scuttle and bustle of a busy estate brought back the memories.

Two hefty fellows carrying exceedingly knobby sticks walked down and accosted me. Their hairlines and their eyebrows were on nodding acquaintance. They were apim, like me.

"Haiu, dom, and what do you want?"

"No Llahal?" I said, calling their attention to their lack of courtesy in not using the universal form of greeting for a stranger. "And who, dom, are you?"

"You are a Havil-forsaken yetch of a flutsman."

"No. Where is the Crebent?"

Nulty was the Crebent, a kind of bailiff and majordomo and chief troubleshooter rolled into one, and I trusted him.

"There is no Crebent, dom. But there are two of us. You'd best come along quietly, for all you wear a sword. We are used to swords. The Amak will want a word with you."

"The Amak?"

This so much surprised and amused me I allowed myself to be escorted along to the imposing four-story house at the end of the compound. A lot was going on. A few soldiers lounged around the well, laughing and joking. They did not look particularly bright specimens of swods, the ordinary soldiers, and their uniforms were more raggedy than was seemly for representatives of the iron legions of Hamal.

One of my escorts, the one whose nostrils bristled hair, snorted. "Useless onkers."

His companion, who was missing his left ear, spat into the dust. "Line of Supply. They eat us out of house and home. The quicker they go the better."

"But," I said. "Do they not protect you against the wild men from over the mountains?"

Both escorts laughed, showing black snaggly teeth.

"The Amak has the mirvols, beautiful flyers all, and powerful men to fly them. And you speak small when the Amak addresses you."

The mirvol perching towers, indeed, were loaded with splendid flying animals. The two-story house nearby was the barracks for the Amak's personal force. In the old days they had been volunteers from Paline Valley. This new Amak, whoever he was, would have hired mercenaries, I did not doubt.

The house struck cool. Rush mats covered the floor and walls. The light of the twin suns was muted. Water tinkled.

Whoever this fellow was who called himself the Amak, he'd built a splendid house. As I was the Amak, I rather fancied I would enjoy living here.

Although I had removed most of the flaunting marks and feathers and streamers from the flying leathers, the supple clothing was still enough to brand me a flutsman. The four fluttrells also would give this impression. There had seemed no reason not to fly straight to the valley. How I erred in this! After all these seasons, I could still make the most elementary mistake in life on Kregen. The seriousness of this mistake bore in on me only slowly—two stout overseers with cudgels, well, they had not amounted to much. The talk of some resident Amak would be straightened out. But the rank of paktuns who waited for us in the hall and who stuck to me like glue were quite another matter.

"Keep silent. March with us. If you run you will be cut down."

The words slapped out crisp and yet, somehow, flat. The Deldar in command possessed a face much worn away by drink. We marched along the corridor to see that the Amak and the two overseers, their duty done, went back to their work. They could be going up to the paline fields or out onto the dusty grasslands to see that the cattle were herded properly. I confess, I am still enthralled at the sight of vast herds of cattle being handled not by men riding animals on the ground, but flying saddle birds of the air. To see the swift flight, the swerve, and the way the cattle instinctively obey— that is a sight, by Krun!

We marched out under a curved tile roof and the suns blinded down. I blinked. This small open space, after the fashion of an atrium, contained besides the expected fountain and pool and green plants and flowers, the ugly blot of a flogging frame.

Four men, backs bare, were strung up and being flogged.

They were all unconscious. Their heads lolled. The stylor at the side with his slate chalked off the lashes as the Deldars of the Whip struck. I felt that foolish expression on my face tightening and I had to force myself to remain composed. This needed explanation—and perhaps the four men deserved punishment? Although even devoted Nulty would not hand out so vicious a punishment unless the crime was horrendous.

The Deldar commanding the detail marching me along called across. He sounded right jovial.

"Hey, Manchi—save a place for this rast!"

343

The stylor glanced up, his chalk poised. His lips were very red. "They're all the same to me, Deldar Hruntag. Wheel 'em up and I'll jikaider 'em."

The paktuns sniggered and on we marched under the opposite roof and along a corridor where crossbowmen and spearmen stood guard and so to the anteroom of the Amak. Here I was halted and we waited. As Deldar Hruntag said: "You may be a miserable spy for the flutsmen; but the Amak has duties. You wait."

Now, despite all that I had witnessed, and although I could not believe it of Nulty, I was prepared in the deepest recesses of my ugly thoughts to perceive Nulty waiting in judgment. I could not believe it of him; but I was prepared for him to have taken over as Amak.

So that when we wheeled in and I noticed the hall as a place of color and some provincial magnificence, I looked at the man sitting in his chair raised on a dais and felt a profound and grateful sense of relief.

And, immediately thereafter, a profound and alarmed sense of concern for Nulty.

The Amak of Paline Valley looked to be on the younger side of his first half-century, a nervous, intense, dark man, with a leanness to nose and chin and a thinness to lips I found displeasing—and then corrected my prejudiced thoughts. His hair, very dark, lay plastered to his scalp so that he looked like a weasel. He stared at me. He was not at first sight at all a nice kind of person.

"So this is the flutsman spy."

I waited, looking around. I was not bound. I wore my sword. The fellow in his chair, which was done up in gilts and ivories and smothered in a truly magnificent zhantil pelt, a blaze of gold, rested his narrow chin on his fist, which looked all bone, and glowered at me.

I waited no longer.

"I am not a flutsman. Where is Nulty, the Crebent of Paline Valley?"

The command Deldar gave me a backhander across the face. He would have done, except that I moved and he stumbled past. I let him topple on, merely contenting myself with tripping him.

"Answer me, usurper! What have you done with Nulty?"

As you see, I was just as stupid as ever I'd been on Kregen.

All kinds of clever stratagems occurred to me when I woke up in the cells.

The place was dimly lit by a torch mounted just outside the bars. Filthy straw half-covered the stone floor. The walls were bare. Iron chains lay here and there stapled to the walls. No skeletons lay in grotesque bone-yellow contortions within the chains; so I gathered that the Amak killed his prisoners off sharply. A bundle stirred and moaned in the shadows, and another rolled over. A voice spoke from the other side.

"Lie still, Nath. Give your back time to ease."

I knew the voice.

I said, "Nulty!"

The voice whispered. "Is it you—the Amak—is it...?"

A squat form shambled forward to the end of the chain's tether. Torchlight fell across the filthy, bearded, exhausted face of my comrade Nulty, Crebent of Paline Valley.

"When we get out of here, Nulty," I said. "We will let this fellow who calls himself the Amak test these chains."

Nulty sank to his knees. He had been a laughing, barrel-bodied man, constantly in scrapes of which I knew I never learned the quarter. Then I saw his hands. They were knotted into useless lumps, so I knew the cramps that had troubled him had finally destroyed his dexterity.

"Nulty! Brace up. We've been in trouble before—"

"Aye, master. But not like this. And he was my son, my adopted son, and this is his reward for love."

So the story came out when Nulty got over his amazement at my appearance here. It was not clever. Responsible for the whole management of the valley, Nulty had looked around for someone to train up to replace him when he died. Having no family of his own, he had selected a bright and promising lad from a distant cousin's union with a rapscallion of a paktun. The lad was called Hardil the Mak for his black hair. He had promised much and Nulty loved him. Then it all turned sour and Hardil had proclaimed himself Amak, hired his bully boys, ousted Nulty and those faithful to me, and set about making it all legal in the law courts at Ruathytu, the capital.

I said, "I blame myself. Absentee landlords are a sin; but sometimes are unavoidable."

"Not you, notor, not you. Me. I should have descried his character. Bad blood."

"Your hands?"

He was over the first wonderment, now, and so he said matter-of-factly, "Nothing could cure them. They curled up on me and remain curled, useless. It is a judgment."

"Nonsense! We'll find a cure."

I was thinking of the sacred pool of baptism in far Aphrasöe, the Swinging City of the Savanti. A cup of that milky fluid would cure Nulty. That was on my personal agenda for the future.

I said, "I do not have a great deal of time. There are affairs I must manage in Ruathytu."

"Making sure Hardil is ejected as Amak?"

"That, too. The laws are strict. Possession is a great deal; but not all. I am the Amak—as you witnessed, Nulty—and so if this Hardil the Mak is not slain he will stand condemned."

A voice croaked from the straw.

"I believe you to be the real Amak, notor. But Hardil holds the power."

Nulty barked roughly. "Hold still, Nath! You do not know the notor. He will sort this out. I give thanks to all the gods he has returned."

The sinking sensation this kind of faith produced had to be brushed aside. I said, "What support has Hardil apart from his hired paktuns? Can you rely on our people? Tell me the whole situation, Nulty."

Truth to tell, I was anxious to press on to such an extent I was in danger of minimizing the peril here. I just did not want to waste a lot of time. But events forced me to the understanding that I had to take care of these people, who had vowed allegiance to me as their Amak, before I could think of leaving them. This Hardil, following along the road of many a usurper, had instituted a reign of terror to seat himself securely. What was needed to topple him was some way of dealing with his bully boys. His coup had taken place when men of Paline Valley, forming part of an aerial cavalry regiment, had been badly beaten in some sky skirmish. The histories of the wars would not mention that little affray; it had denuded Paline Valley of many stout fighting men.

Again, as is in the nature of these affairs, the survivors were undecided how best to deal with Hardil and divided in their councils. Hardil flogged, maimed and killed. So far he had not killed Nulty, which that tough man attributed to a lingering regard on the part of the usurping Amak for his old foster father. I did not mention that more probably it was a matter of policy. Nulty could do nothing chained in the cells; dead he might become a martyr. That was not certain, but it had its precedents.

"But, master, I could have done something, chained though I am. But my hands, and the ingratitude, and—something died in me."

"We will do it now, Nulty, old friend, and we will do it together."

The bundle of misery on the straw grunted disbelief. So I set myself to kindling the spark here, in the cells. That, it seemed to me, was not only a good place to start, it was the only damned place, by Krun.

The need for speed impelled me to shortcuts. Away in Vallia and in Hyrklana armies were being gathered to invade Hamal. I had to do my part. Perhaps the presence of Train of Supply troops in the valley aided me, for they were sloppy and generally not actively fit men, and their attitudes infected the paktuns hired by Hardil. Slackness spreads insidiously.

The food—awful gunk in pottery bowls—was brought by a bent-over Och crone. The only thing of interest was the spoon. This was wooden. So the first and most simple plan was dashed.

Nulty said, "The guard commander—?"

"Right, Nulty, you old devil. You're coming back to life already."

Had the guard Deldar been up to his job he would never have obliged us. My own instructions to my lads back home covered this kind of unpleasant contingency. He was not foolish enough actually to enter our cell carrying the keys. He glowered down, very bulky, sweating, his leather creaking.

"You cramph," he said, using the insult with relish. "You'd better have something to say. I am not summoned lightly. What do you want?"

I reached over.

"This."

I took his throat between my fists and choked a little, enough to take his mind off going for his sword. He fell down. We got his sword out and the point only broke off when the second staple was free. I threw the chains on the straw and started in on Nulty.

"Hurry, master. One of his men will be along..."

"Don't feel sorry for him, Nulty."

And Nulty laughed. "Oh, no! Not at all."

Nulty's staples came out more easily, for he'd been working on them, the cunning old leem. He could not hold a sword. I looked down on the miserable bundles on the straw, and one of them, the one called Nath, showed the whites of his eyes.

"Free me, notor, please!"

"And you will help against this rast Hardil?"

"Aye!"

He was one arm freed when the guard wandered along to see what had happened to his Deldar. The slackness had, indeed, spread. Had it not, we would not have gained our freedom so easily. The guard collapsed and we had a second sword. This I preserved, for it possessed a point.

When the bundle of misery called Nath stood up, he said, "Give me the guard's dagger, notor."

I handed it across. We had ourselves a recruit.

Five

Concerning Nulty's Sword Arm

We stood in the guardroom and surveyed the five unconscious mercenaries. Nulty's hands prevented him from helping us tie up the guards. Nath and his companion in misery, Lardo—the other two had died on the flogging frames—were not up to taking part in heavy fighting. Refusing to kill the mercenaries in cold blood, I made sure they were bound and gagged securely. Had I wished them slain they'd have died when we burst in here.

"We've made a start," said Nulty, with a considerable return of his husky manner.

"We'll never—" began Lardo. He was a squat, bushy man with a bulbous nose.

"Not if you do not believe it," I said. "We must contact the people loyal to Nulty—"

"Loyal to you, master," interrupted Nulty, a heinous sin in retainers but one in which Nulty had tended to indulge himself freely.

"Loyal to proper management of the valley. From what you tell me, Hardil is a tyrant."

"And unpleasant with it, notor," said Nath.

It seemed to me, what with Nulty's crippled hands and Nath and Lardo walking like crabs with their injured backs, any heavy fighting would devolve on me. Well, and wasn't that what being the Amak was about—in part, at any rate?

Whatever day it was in Kregen's Havilfarian calendar was dying. I was not clear how much time had clasped since I'd been thrown into the cells. We slunk out into the twinned shadows of the compound. A few lights were already going on, and the smells of one of the evening meals wafted in mouth-wateringly. A parcel of guards came along to relieve their comrades, and they had to be knocked on the head and put to sleep. Only two died.

Nulty had found himself a length of rope, and he made Nath and Lardo tie a sword hilt to his wrist and crippled right hand. The blade was reasonably firm, and he it was who cut one of the reliefs down, smiting furiously, unable to judge the exact strength of the blow with the strapped-up sword.

"I did not mean to slay him, master. But his god must have turned his face away from him. The rast."

I did not laugh, for Nulty would not expect that. Grim and horrible though the circumstances were, they were fit subjects for humor, considering what we attempted and the means at our disposal.

All the same, there were men and women loyal to Nulty because he was the Crebent and a just man, and not merely willing to fight for him against Hardil because Hardil was a usurping rast.

"You'll have to keep out of it if we engage in any heavy fighting, Nulty. That contraption strapped to your arm is all very well, but—"

"I'll fight, master. You'll see."

"And," I said as he swung the strapped steel about, gesticulating, "you'll have to be a damned sight more careful with it. You'll have our eyes out or our heads off."

He let rip a snort of amused disgust, compounded of anger at his predicament and delight in the return of hope and the conceit of his friends' heads a-rolling on the straw.

"I'll be careful, master."

348

We had to move with energy and speed. The first house Nulty selected proved to contain a family who would dearly love to string Hardil high and toast his soles. The head of the household, a hard grainy man with a scarred face, spread his hands.

"We are all overjoyed that the true Amak has returned. But we are without weapons, for the Amak—Hardil the Mak—has taken them all away."

This was not the poser it might have seemed. Nath and Lardo unrolled the blanket in which we had wrapped the guards' gear. "Take your pick."

That put a very different complexion on the whole affair.

"There are more where those came from," I said.

From a silly raggle-taggle group trying to topple a lord in power, we slowly grew in strength to a tidy little force. The hired mercenaries would prove the chief problem. Maybe they were slack and not on the top line; for all that they remained men whose trade was killing. I confess I hesitated; it would have been easy for me, now that I was free, to seize a flying beast and simply leave Paline Valley and head for Ruathytu. In a sober assessment of the situation that is probably what I should have done. Life was just bearable for the people here with Hardil in charge. He was vicious and cruel; but his time would pass. Was it only my own self-esteem that made me persevere? Was it a lust for power? All I needed from the valley was a name; Nulty could run the place admirably. Why should men risk their lives just for an Amak who was hardly ever around?

And then one of the people who had taken up a captured sword said, "Notor! We bless the day you return to us, for now we shall be free from a burden on our minds."

Perhaps that was the turning point. A burden on their bodies was expected; but a burden on their minds...?

So we went up against Hardil the Mak and his bought blades and we fought them.

We had to be clever. We had to use all the advantages that people fighting in their own village possess over intruders. Young lads, whooping with joy, flung lassos from rooftops and snared up the mercenaries. Nets dropped from the shadows and entangled fighting men so that they might be stuxed where they struggled. The mercenaries quickly tired of earning their hire, for they were of middling quality only, and they attempted to strike bargains with the people. At that time I was having a merry little ding-dong with a group of the guards who had escorted me into Hardil's imposing house. They were being bested, and starting to fall away, and run, when Nulty ran up, shouting that the mercenaries had surrendered, crying quarter, and would enter the service of the old Amak.

"The new Amak is done for, his power forfeit, his charade at an end," I said, for the benefit of the listening paktuns. "The old Amak has returned to his home."

They got the message.

I left the elders to sort out the details, and accompanied by Nulty and a group of my people with swords in their fists went off to find out about Hardil the Mak. He was discovered cowering in a chest stuffed with silks and sensils, shaking, and yet very ready to damn and blast us all. What he expected at our hands must remain a mystery. Nulty stepped forward to speak to him, and a woman—little more than a slip of a girl with wild brown hair and blank eyes—leaped. The dagger in her fist flamed. She plunged the blade into Hardil's throat, above his tunic and jerkin, dragged it out stained with blood, and so drove it in, again and again, screaming, until she was pulled away. She stood, blood-splashed, quivering, straining to get at Hardil.

He needed no further ministrations on Kregen.

"Lalli," said Nulty in a reproving voice. He knelt at Hardil's side, and I remembered he had adopted the black-haired boy as his son. Nulty bowed his head and we stood respectfully.

Presently, Nulty stood up. The sword strapped to his arm scraped on the floor.

"He was misguided, poor lad, and turned into a monster. But he promised well, at the beginning. I am sad it turned out like this."

Lalli screeched.

"Yes, yes," said Nulty. And, "Help Lalli to her bed, someone. She'll be better when the child is born."

Well, there is no guarantee of that, on Kregen as on Earth.

"It was no plan of mine that Hardil should die," I told Nulty.

"I know you, master, and I know you speak the truth. Mayhap it was better that he did, after all."

Everyone gathered in the main compound under the light of Kregen's first moon, the Maiden with the Many Smiles, and the mercenaries were discharged. They would find employment very quickly and remain tazll for only a short time in Hamal where armies were being formed for projects unknown. I asked after the army of whose structure I remained ignorant, and the soldiers here, who had remained strictly aloof from the fighting, knew nothing beyond their orders, which required them to provide food and provender. An army demands enormous quantities of supplies and mad Empress Thyllis was not choosy about how she obtained the sinews of war.

The Hikdar in command of this supply detachment said to me, "So, notor, you are the real Amak. But it is all one to us. We collect supplies for the army, and you or the other Amak will provide them."

He was a lean man with a tic in his left eye, and a shriveled left arm. I refused to allow myself to think that I was providing supplies for the enemy.

"You will take what your requisitions call for, Hikdar, and not a single sack more."

"Oh, aye, notor. We'll take what the law allows."

And that was a lot, a voracious lot, by Krun.

To Nulty, privily, I said, "We must arrange to depress the figures next season, so that we appear poorer than we are."

"Aye, master. I do not relish growing crops for these leeches to take away."

"Well, every little helps..."

"And we can leave the cattle in the high pastures for a little longer."

"You will risk the wild men—"

"Our young men not in the army can care for the cattle. You will see."

Nulty had striven hard to rebuild the valley and had attracted fresh settlers. Paline Valley was resuming the importance it had once held in the surrounding valleys. Paline was the center one of the Three Valleys— Hammarat, Paline and Thyriodon—and they were all remote and isolated from the current of events in Hamal. Now that I was certain I might travel the empire using my name of Hamun ham Farthytu the urgency to be off obsessed me. Yet much had to be done here for humanity's sake before I could leave.

When I saw Nulty after he had himself cleaned up I gaped. His shock of wild hair was trimmed, his bulbous nose looked respectable, and his walk was not the shambling progression of a hairy graint. Only his twisted hands struck an incongruous note. He wore a neat white tunic cinctured by a plain leather belt—plain but for two plaques of bronze showing, one a chavonth, the other a zorca. He looked spick and span.

"And you will be leaving us soon, master?"

"I must. But Paline Valley can now look forward to a period of prosperity again." I frowned. "You had best show me the treasure young Hardil amassed."

Nulty's face expressed amazement only for two heartbeats; then he sighed and lifted a hand.

"I should have remembered, master, you are as cunning as a leem. Yes, Hardil kept treasure hoarded up for himself."

"It must be returned to its owners—"

"Most of them are dead."

"Then, as the Amak, I will take a tithe. The balance goes to the valley. That is understood?"

"Understood, master."

"Make it so."

The box of tough lenken wood bound in black iron stood under Hardil's bed. Some of Nulty's people dragged the chest out and smashed the locks. They threw the lid back. We all stared in. Treasure... Ah, treasure!

This was the muck men fought and killed for, this was the wonder women schemed for...

There was a fair old quantity of gold and silver, some boxes of gems. Kregans are aware of the magic inherent in a gem if it is cut and faceted, unlike the Ancients of our own world. We hauled the stuff out and Nulty appointed a young stylor to make a reckoning, with elders standing by to oversee. The stylor Manchi was not available. Privately, Nulty told me he thought someone had chopped the stylor's head off and stuffed him into a crack in the mountains. The Whip Deldars, too, suffered a similar fate. Deprecate the bestiality as much as we may, we must also face human nature. So the stylor carefully wrote down an account. I picked up a fine sword. It was a thraxter, but of a fineness that had caused it to be regarded as a treasure rather than a weapon. I hefted it. I bent the blade and it twanged back sweetly.

"Yes, master?" said Nulty.

"Write this among my share," I said.

No one argued.

Perhaps that was as it should be, too. I know I was aware of the amusement that a Hamalian treasure store had yielded a superb sword for an enemy of Hamal. On the blade the etched magical brudstern in its usual open flower shape showed the blade to be of value. Folk tend to whisper rather than proclaim the magic properties inherent in the brudstern. To -me it meant simply the blade had been valued by someone enough to make me accept it as a brand of quality.

Outside, in the sweet air of Kregen, Nulty cocked a fishy eye up at me. "When, notor?"

"I grieve to say it, old friend. But as soon as possible."

"I feared so."

"Then do not fear. You know I repose complete trust in you. You have made of Paline Valley a paradise among the hills. The people love and respect you. I shall be back again to drink a stoup of ale with you and talk over the old days."

"Make it sooner rather than later."

"I will, as Havil is my witness."

A week, I decided, would not be too much of a crime against my people of Vallia. A sennight I would spend with my people of Paline Valley, who were at war with Vallia. As Nulty said, screwing up his eyes against sun-glare as the drums rolled from the watchtowers: "We may be cut off and isolated here, but we try to keep abreast of the news. Pandahem island is all ours now, and parts of Vallia. I have heard little from the south, from the Dawn Lands recently." Then he snorted one of his barking laughs. "I heard precious little, stuck in the cells."

The drum beat brought the people out of the houses. We all stared up.

Wide-winged shapes drifted down among the streaming mingled rays of the Suns of Scorpio. Caught by Nulty's appraisal of Hamal's situation, for if anybody could, he represented grass-roots opinion, I stared at those shapes drifting down. I was surprised. More—I was flabbergasted.

"What—?" I said.

"Aye, master. The new flying ships of the air. Do not ask me why the Air Service uses them, although it is whispered they run short of essential commodities in voller manufacture."

Hamal was never a great seafaring nation; they control airboats, which they call vollers. Together with Hyrklana and other countries of the Dawn Lands—and in Balintol or eastwards, we now believed—they had supplied Paz with vollers, always refusing to sell to old enemies. The secrets of voller manufacture were jealously guarded. We in Vallia had developed flying ships which could rise in the air and grip onto etheric-magnetic lines of force and so sail the skies, tacking and making boards against the wind. It had not seemed Hamal with her sky-spanning fleets of enormous ships would need to descend to mere vessels powered by wind and sails. But, clearly, they had. As the ships of the Train of Supply furled their sails and made bumpy landings, I saw only one true voller, swinging high as tail guard.

Also, I observed that the Hamalese made unhandy sailors.

"They have come to take our produce from us." Nulty was grumpy, bowing under the inevitability of taxation. "Vultures."

"The empire needs supplies, Nulty."

"Oh, yes. We must needs feed and clothe our armies and provender their animals. But we have to defend ourselves against the wild men from the Mountains of the West. And our soldiers are away in the Dawn Lands, or Vallia." He cocked an eye up at me. "They say your namesake there, Dray Prescot, who is the Emperor of Vallia, is a devil spawned from hell and should be stuffed and roasted to a cinder."

"So they say."

Then Nulty surprised me. We walked slowly in the suns light toward the grounded sailing ships of the sky. Nulty said: "Now if the Dray Prescot who is Hamun ham Farthytu could be the Dray Prescot who is Emperor of Vallia, I think he would run things very differently, very differently, by Havil the Green!"

I digested this. If you understand that I felt very small you will not be far from the truth. Difficult to feel ashamed, though, damned difficult, when I was just a simple ordinary sailor man trying to run an empire and chuck out the slavers and the aragorn and the thieving flutsmen and reiving mercenaries, and then trying to join all the lands of Paz into a friendship that was genuine and would last, so that we might together turn our attention to the Opaz-forsaken Shanks who raided us all with fire and blood and misery. Damned difficult.

"Well, Nulty, old friend. I'm just the Amak of Paline Valley here, and have work to do in Ruathytu."

The officers in charge of the supply position were barely polite. I saw they were annoyed at being forced to fly sailing ships of the air, which the Hamalese called famblehoys, instead of queening it through the upper levels aboard vollers. We in Vallia sometimes called our flying sailing ships vorlcas, and as you will see, the two names reflect the respective worth in which the countries held their sky sailers. No doubts at all afflicted me that I must take a very careful look at these aerial vessels. The officers bore down, and although second line troops, the uniforms blazed bullion and lace and flaunted feathers. Nulty pulled a face, and then we were busy trying to keep as much of our produce as we could for ourselves.

Eventually I could leave Nulty and the elders to handle this end of affairs—they'd been doing it and would continue to do it while I was away—and could saunter over to the famblehoys. The aerial ships were large, bulky, deep-keeled, cobbled together and ugly, deuced ugly. The pattern from which they had been copied, it was plain, had come from Vallia.

Good sound timber had been used in their construction, and iron, plenty of iron to act as knees and brackets and generally to hold things together. The masts were solid, somewhat on the short side, and the yards were mere stumps when compared with those gracing galleons or vorlcas of Vallia. This fitted with the Hamalese ideas of seamanship.

Putting on my inane face I puttered around, studying the ships, and drew a number of amused or contemptuous looks from the voswods on the decks, who, being aerial soldiers, would not sully their hands with shipwork or lading. There were precious few soldiers for a convoy of this size, some fifty famblehoys. The produce the fleet could fit into the holds would be enormous. In the name of the Invisible Twins! Where was it going? West against the wild men? Unlikely. South to that mysterious army forming in the sparse land there? Possibly. North—north to Vallia? This, in my frame of mind, seemed the most likely, and raging and cursing at myself, feeling the anxieties crowding on me, I thought how splendid it would be to burn this whole fleet.

By Zair! That would crimp mad Thyllis's ambitions!

But, then—a single supply train of the air, fifty huge ships, well, they would carry a dismayingly small part of all the supplies Hamal had on the move. Still—it would be a start.

The tragedy was, I'd have to burn the supplies, also.

Maybe something might be arranged...

My fondness for Paline Valley was overcoming my sworn duty. Hateful though it would be, and no matter how onerous the task, this must be done.

Barging my way back to see Nulty, I recalled that he had said that Dray Prescot would handle things differently from Dray Prescot. Well, by the Black Chunkrah! now was his chance to see how Dray Prescot, Krozair of Zy, Emperor of Vallia, would handle it!

Six

Of Freedom, Fires and Flyers

"The hospitality of Paline Valley is at your disposal, Jiktar," I said to the officer commanding this Train of Supply. "Wine, food, music, all are yours to command. As to girls, you must pay in blood, if you wish, in that department."

He took my meaning.

All the same, during the festivities in which Nulty raised his eyebrows at the lavishness of ale and wine and dopa I insisted be poured out, a couple of half-drunken voswods attempted young Pansi, who cared for the chickens in the smaller compound. The two were apprehended before much mischief had been done, although Pansi, bleeding from a bruised mouth and her dress ripped, continued to cry out of shock. I said to the Jiktar, a bulky man with a gut and a half, who squinted most dreadfully, "I am not minded to be merciful in this."

"It is an army matter—"

"Not so. I am a noble of Hamal, and you are under my jurisdiction here. There will be a trial."

The laws of Hamal, being tighter than those of the Medes and Persians, lay down observances in all likely situations. I brought the full weight to bear, the full weight carried by a noble, which weight has been used against me enough times, to be sure. A court was set up in the outer room of the Amak's house, a defending counsel was appointed from the supply train's officers, our young bokkerim, that is to say lawyer, Danghandi the Quill, prosecuted, and I presided. I wanted to make it fast.

There was no doubt as to the accuseds' guilt, for they had been seen by dour Honglo the Surly, and Pansi swore through her tears they were the two. Defense pleaded in mitigation that the girl was unharmed. Danghandi made Pansi turn her face to the samphron oil lamps' gleam.

"See the bruise! See the blood!" She had not washed it off. "Harm! Who can say what her ib has suffered?"

I said, "The case is proved. Sentence alone remains."

And there was the rub.

The two voswods looked appalled, frightened, dejected. Damned fools. They deserved all they got. But, all the same, what punishment fitted this crime? The laws of Hamal had it all written out fair and square, and there was nothing I could do but endorse what the book said. The men were led off to be flogged.

Not nice, not nice at all. I bent my head to Nulty.

"This augurs ill."

"Aye, master. The soldiers drink us dry."

I did not say, "So much the better." It was in my mind.

That nasty little business kept the soldiers steadfastly at their drinking instead of roving for other pleasures. So, in Opaz's good time, it worked to my advantage.

I said, "In order to prevent further molestation, make sure a squad of your best young men stay alert and do not drink. They may be needed."

"Yes, master."

"I will retire now. See I am not disturbed on any pretext."

"Yes, master."

A little wind gusted the dust in the light of the torches. I entered the inner rooms and chased out the people who wanted to fuss. We were already manumitting the slaves and arranging for their future welfare as free men and women. I had taken the precaution of finding out Hardil's secret escape hole, and, stripping off the white robe, I wound the scarlet cloth about me and took up a cheap mineral oil lamp. Only a dagger would be needed. I crept out through the secret hole and, running fleetly in the night, reached the far windward end of the ship lines. I looked about.

Each ship slumbered like a stricken behemoth. They might not in truth be stricken yet; very soon they would be. And when that happened I must be safely back in my chambers. The first ship caught at once, the dry wood crackling up in a flare and taking cordage and tarred wood and painted wood and all the gimcrack finery the Hamalians had spared to their despised flying sailers. The flames streamed in the wind. Three ships I fired, one after the other, and then the night watch started in yelling.

Scurries of wind bore the flames down on the next ships in line. That would have to do. The succeeding ships would burn as readily as the first, and the wind would roar the flames on. I hurtled back to the secret hole and ducked in. A hammering on the door indicated Nulty considered the emergency of sufficient importance to wake me despite my instructions. I'd counted on that, knowing Nulty of old.

The scarlet cloth went under the bed. The mineral oil lamp, out but still warm, went with it. I grabbed a simple green wraparound and opened the door. Lights and faces glared in.

"Fire, notor! The ships burn!"

I shouted. I shouted so that they would understand over the hubbub. "If the ships are doomed, then save the cargo! Unload our supplies and see they are safe! Bratch!"

At the command bratch, they bratched, jumping as though I had branded them with words.

Well, our people started in unloading the ships that were still unburned, hurling the bales and boxes out, ferrying the sacks, working like fiends. My orders had been to see the stuff was safe. I had said: Our supplies. See they are safe.

You do not need two good eyes to guide a donkey.

Just how many supplies would be yielded up to the supply officers I could not judge. Precious little, I suspected. And every sack, every bale my folk spirited away was another item to add to the loss suffered by the Hamalian armed forces.

Capital!

Criminal, illegal, horrible—maybe. Gallant conduct in battle—no. But warfare—ah, yes!

If a general is the best tactician and strategist in two worlds and does not understand logistics, he is doomed.

Of the fifty ships the flames spared only five. The neatly mathematical mooring arrangements, inherent in Hamalian military techniques, simply provided the fires with fresh fuel, ship after ship. The five were successfully sailed off before the flames reached them. Afterwards there was a certain amount of difficulty over the supplies removed; but we straightened it all out. I walked down to the heaps of black refuse, shining and cindery, still smoking, smelling of charred hopes. These had once been ships. The memory of the way the fires leaped eagerly up, the crack and sizzle of the flames, the colors and the heat, burned in my brain. The whole episode had not been pleasant, except a blow had been struck against Hamal.

"At least, we won't starve next season," remarked Nulty. And then he kept his own counsel.

In a petty kind of revenge against his bad fortune, the Jiktar of the Supply Train had a shot at requisitioning our saddle flyers. The mirvols on the perching towers were a fine crop that season. I quickly disabused the man of that idea.

"We need the saddle flyers to withstand the raids of the wild men from over the mountains. When the soldiers provide us with protection, then, mayhap, you may take our mirvols."

He tried to bluster and saw, by the laws, he was in the wrong. Oh, he threatened to return with a requisitioning warrant. If he did so, Nulty would know what to do with our mirvols. As though to underline the significance of this incident a patrol of Hamalian army flyers settled with a rush of wings. They had been descried by our lookouts at a distance and authenticated. They flew pale blue and white fluttlanns, smallish birds and a trifle slow, who are willing up to a point and do not eat overmuch. They can barely carry two riders. But they breed phenomenally and are cheap. The patrol leader, a Deldar who would never rise in rank to Hikdar now, walked up to me, saluting with gauntleted hand. He wore a full beard, the lines around his eyes were caked with grime pouching pits of tiredness. His blue uniform was ragged and faded; but his weapons were clean and sharp. The matoc was bellowing at the patrol, some twenty flyers, and keeping them in order while their Deldar sorted out lodgings and food. I gave orders that the Deldar and his men should be treated well.

"And, master, that is all the army can provide the Three Valleys, and Folding Mountain and High-Trail Forks, to give us protection." Nulty spoke as much to the Jiktar of the supply service as to me.

"I suppose they fly from valley to valley on patrol," I said. And, then, in a mean spirit, I added, "I would guess they pray each night that they do not meet wild men on a raid."

Nulty put a hand to his mouth. The Jiktar's brows drew down. But I waved a hand, very much your high and mighty Hamalian lord, acting the part of one of those hateful abusers of authority. "You will be leaving us soon, Jiktar? Good. We have the valley to make flourish again ready for your return. It is not for us to go around collecting food; we have to grow it."

He spluttered.

I went on: "And the hides. Our hides are of the finest. Our people have to grow the animals, and skin the hides, and we tan with birch-bark and emboss a beautiful grain with cunning rollers, and then the hides are bundled ready for you to come and collect—and you burn them all up."

"There is going to be an inquiry, notor." He could hardly get the words out. His face was the color of bruised plum. "A strict inquiry—"

"And very proper, too. Someone was damned lax. As for me, I was asleep at the time. And my people were abed. By themselves." The meaning about the two idiots and Pansi did not escape him. "The laws require me or my Crebent to make full reports of any trials held under our jurisdiction here."

He didn't like that.

As soon as he could he collected his swods and they trooped silently into the five remaining famblehoys. When they took off and spread their canvas into a tidy breeze, we all breathed easier.

The incident had given me hope. And the sight of tough flutswods of the Hamalian army flying brave but inferior little fluttlanns also gave me a lift. Thyllis was really scraping the barrel to continue her wars. And this reminded me that as the man responsible for Vallia I ought to be commanding armies and maneuvering fleets instead of fiddling about burning a few flying sailers. Ruathytu beckoned. I now knew I could move about

Hamal freely using my name of Hamun ham Farthytu. There, in the capital city, I could do more good than here in Paline Valley, and, perhaps, if the gods smiled, more even than commanding those armies and maneuvering those fleets.

A last few duties had to be discharged.

Pansi had to be reassured and I made sure that all we could do was done for her. Lalli, too, had to receive the best attention. Sundry other folk were dealt with according to their desserts. The slaves were integrated. This was not easy, it never is; but Nulty and I showed what we intended and the people who had been slave responded. The valley was not overcrowded yet, and fresh settlers were still welcome. The sennight I had promised myself passed, six busy days, and then I selected a middling quality mirvol from the perching towers.

"But, master!" protested Nulty. "You should take the best."

"No so, old friend. Where I am going he is likely to be stolen as quick as my purse. By the government if nobody else. He will fly me to Ruathytu, never fear."

Amid a dust-blowing threshing of wings the mirvol took off, and the shouts of "Remberee!" shrilled into the morning air. Middling quality this mirvol might have been; he was a superb flying animal, strong and limber, hurling me on through the sky headlong to Ruathytu and perils I could not imagine.

Buckling up the straps of the clerketer tightly I leaned forward along his neck and we pelted into the windrush. A sack of provisions and a sack of coins balanced each other at his sides, for I had taken plenty of food and a share of gold. The fine thraxter snugged in the scabbard. I had a knife at my belt and a crossbow pouched by my knee. That had belonged to an Opaz-forsaken flutsman. The four fluttrells I had left with Nulty, for he had plans for them for the future.

So, whirling across the sky, I flew for Ruathytu, capital city of the empire at war with my own country.

There remained one adventure at least before I reached the brilliant and decadent city at the fork of the rivers, and it began unspectacularly enough as I slanted in to a landing in the square of a small town toward evening. This was Thalansen, two temples, a fortress, a scattering of industry, mostly cattle and mining, huddled houses of brick and enough taverns and inns to make it not worthwhile to count them. The lingering radiance of the twin suns of Antares flooded the town with jade and ruby and cast twinned shadows long and umber. I sent Bluenose, the mirvol, to the perching tower before the inn called The Fluttrell Feather and with my sacks over my shoulder pushed open the door.

Fingers grabbed the sacks and someone hit me over the head with an exceedingly knobby stick.

Seven

Some Artists of Kregen

Had those fingers not grabbed for the sacks first, there was every chance the very knobby stick would have hit me four square. That scrabbling slide of warning gave me time enough to lunge sideways. The confoundedly knobby stick only hit me over the head with sufficient force to drive me headlong into the capacious stomach of a large man and start around half the bells of Beng Kishi clanging in my skull.

The large-stomached man said, "Whoof!"

I fell over him, already starting to pitch onto a shoulder so as to roll and come up snarling. The tap room blurred in a haze and three fierce and deliberate blinks barely cleared the mist in my eyes. Stomach belched and leaned down.

"I'll forgive you the onslaught on my stomach, young man, seeing Black Sadrap hit you." He took a breath. His eyes were large and round and blue, and his cheeks were large and round and red, and his stomach was large and round and being rubbed by a heavy hairy hand. "Best stay still. 'Tis no fight of yours."

The fight was one of your ding-dong knock-down drag-out affairs. There were knobby sticks in evidence, and short straight blatterers, and bludgeons and cudgels of curious expertise. Fists and boots lashed and kicked. But there was not one pointed or edged weapon being used in all the mayhem.

So, feeling my head jumping up and down, I sat back next to the man of the stomach, and we watched the fight, exchanging knowledgeable comments, and oohs and aahs at a particularly clever dirty trick or a spectacular exit from the inn.

The two sacks were still gripped in my left hand, and the man of stomach, who introduced himself with a Llahal as Rollo the Circle, advised me that no one had been attempting to steal them. They had just wanted them out of the way as they knocked me down. And I sat there, and essayed one of my inane smiles, and said nothing. The fight had nothing to do with me. Ergo, I would have nothing to do with it.

The taproom looked to be just another pleasant inn room with a low ceiling, sanded floor, a long bar, and with wooden tables and chairs. A few booths beside the windows had their curtains closed. Against the fall of night the lamps had been brought in, but their mineral oil glow was not yet necessary in the suffusing radiance of Zim and Genodras.

Rollo the Circle told me he was not a fighting man, and kept out of it. He said, "That Black Sadrap will look after our interests for us. We sleep here this night and Horparth Hansh the Perspective must look elsewhere for lodgings."

"I am dry, Rollo the Circle," I said. "A stoup of ale before the meal will set me up nicely."

"Whisht, dom! Careful—"

Two struggling men fell alongside us. Both hit and kicked in an unscientific abandon, very energetically. One had tapped the claret of the other, and he had popped the eye of his assailant. "Which one is yours?"

He looked down over his treble chins thoughtfully. "The one with paint still in his ears. Naghan the Brush. A marvel with red ochre when it comes to sunsets." And Rollo laughed. "And something of a marvel with red, too, when it flows from his nose."

Dodging aside and easing my way to the bar I looked over and as I expected saw a fellow cowering on the floor. I spoke in a conversational tone, pitched just above the din of breaking chairs and grunting fighters. "Two stoups of your best ale, dom."

He glared up at me, half-hiding his face under his green-striped apron. "Are you bereft of your wits! If you think I'm standing up to fetch you ale—"

I regarded him. "Very well. I will fetch the—" I moved sideways and the fellow who tried to bash me with a length of lumber staggered past. I kicked him up the stern to assist him, and finished: "—two stoups of ale."

Out here the ale was kept as wine, in amphorae, and I decided to carry an amphora along so that Rollo and I might sup in comfort without worrying over refills. I judged him a devotee of Beng Dikkane, the patron saint of all the ale drinkers of Paz.

Only three struggling men had to be cleared out of the way back to Rollo. We settled down comfortably under a sturdy table backed against the wall and started in on sharing the amphora. I had taken his cognomen to be an euphemistic reference to his stomach, but as we talked I saw I was mistaken, indeed, that I had misjudged this rotund Rollo the Circle.

"Right hand or left, Zaydo," he said. "And when I'm a trifle merry, both hands at once."

He fished around inside his tunic, which was a bright patchwork of various complementary colors, and produced a stick of chalk. He stared up at the table over our heads, for we half-reclined to fit in. Then—and it was a marvel—he drew a perfect circle on the rough wood. Judging circles is not a profession in which I have taken any degrees; to me the round was perfect.

"It is, it is," said Rollo. He supped ale. "Find the center and stick in a nail and run your string around. Perfect."

"And both hands at once?"

"When I've finished the amphora."

"It is a great gift."

A man fell under our table, his upside down face most comical, his eyes crossed. Rollo pushed him out. He rolled under trampling feet and other bodies crashed down.

"Black Sadrap is taking his time." Rollo cocked an eye and instantly withdrew as a flung tankard clanged against the table edge. "We need our sleep tonight. We are for Ruathytu and must start early."

"You have a commission there?"

"The temple of Werl-am-Nardith by the Hirrume Gate in the old walls. A small edifice and in need of embellishment. Perhaps you know it?"

"Indeed, although I have not patronized it. I've been through the Hirrume Gate and along the Boulevard of Hamando enough times."

Hamando's Boulevard, named after an ancient king of Hamal, led to the Kyro of the Horters. "When the Games are on in the Jikhorkdun and there are races in the merezo," said Rollo, "you get weird sound effects along there." He moved his bulky body to allow a broken chair to smash to further destruction against our table bulwark. "But, of course, we shall be working in the temple inside the old walls."

"In the Sacred Quarter," I said.

He completely mistook my tone. I had some vivid and blustery memories of fights and brawls and general raffish behavior in the Sacred Quarter of Ruathytu, and, for all that the life was essentially decadent and the city an enemy city, there remained an undeniable fascination with that way of life. Strong affinities with my ambivalent attitude to the Arena in the Jikhorkdun, in Huringa and here in Hamal, were only too plain. But Rollo took my attitude to be the awed respect of your ordinary working fellow for the brilliant lords of the Sacred Quarter.

Yet he made no attempt to preen himself on his access to the Sacred Quarter. He did say, "My company are known as first class. We travel where the commissions are, of course; but we have had our share in the Sacred Quarter." He started to tell me of the decorations he'd put up in a sumptuous establishment of the Baths of the Nine, and as the fight bellowed on in smashings and crashings, I gained an insight into the way of life of these traveling artists. He made it sound most attractive.

A knobby stick thumped onto the floor beside our table and a flushed face adorned with a quantity of jet black hair in various positions looked in. "You are safe, master?"

"Perfectly safe, Sadrap. But for the sake of Kaerlan the Merciful, throw Horparth Hansh the Perspective out speedily. I need my meal and bed."

Black Sadrap's bristly face grimaced at me. "Not long now, master." To me he said, "You have a thick skull."

I said, "Do not mention your little mistake again, Sadrap."

"No. Only that I mistook you for Handal the Pigment coming in. He wears just such a silly grin on his face."

Then Black Sadrap went away to bash a few more skulls and earn his hire.

"A useful man," said Rollo. He drank and wiped his mouth. "He is good with his knobby stick."

Now Hamal is a civilized country, and was at this time, but when wars ferment the blood in men's veins and normal values seem pushed aside, all manner of mischiefs break out like diseases. This fight for accommodation at the inn was a simple rambunctious knock-down between rival groups of artists. On the morrow they might nurse sore heads; but that would be the end of it. Or so I judged. So I was unprepared for what followed.

The quietness gradually came back to The Fluttrell Feather and when Rollo and I crawled out Sadrap was helping the company belonging to Horparth Hansh the Perspective out of the door. He used his knobby stick or his boot indifferently for the task.

Rollo stretched. Indeed, his stomach was a glory. We moved away from our table across the windows and past the curtained booths. Here Rollo bent down and picked up a blatterer, the cunning bludgeon. You have to know how to use one of those skull-indenters. They are short, very short, scarce six inches of solid wood past the handgrip. They are sprung here, with leather or a coiled spring, and that gives them their power. But you have to be exceedingly sharp to get in, for you have to get inside, get in close, to deliver the knockout blow.

"That's it, then, fanshos!" called Black Sadrap.

He finished dealing with the fellow he hurled out of the door and swung back. Nath the Brash, the backs of his hands sticky with blood from his nose, bent to a man sprawled on the floor.

"Hup, Hondo, you rascal. Next time—"

The man on the floor unwound. His arm in a split sleeve lifted, drew back, hurled, quicker than Nath the Brush could follow. The blatterer this Hondo threw streaked like a dart for Rollo. Rollo just stood, his mouth agape, gripping the bludgeon he had just picked up.

The blatterer missed him by the thickness of a dying man's last breath.

It slammed into the curtain at our backs, bulging the material in and then rebounding and falling to the floor to roll away under the next curtain. The sound of a glass smashing and a woman's startled cry from the curtained booth was followed immediately by the curtains being swished back. A man's face glared out, enraged, the veins purple on his forehead, his cheeks with their redness almost breaking through the skin. He saw Rollo standing there with the little bludgeon in his hand.

"Rast! We have endured your brawling without complaint. But now you have gone too far."

The woman with him wore a white dress, very décolleté, and sleeveless. Red wine splashed her and the dress from neck to waist. She had that silly vapid kind of face that goes with fluffy fair hair and protuberant blue eyes and thick red lips; but she was just a girl, and some hulking great boor had smashed her wineglass and soaked her dress. She looked most upset.

The man escorting her leaped from the booth. He wore a blue tunic and trousers and around his waist was wound a sash of brown threaded with silver. At his sides on jeweled lockets swung a rapier and main gauche.

In a twinkling he ripped his rapier free and flourished the point under Rollo's three chins.

"You scum have no respect! I shall cut you up and serve you diced to the fluttrells! Cramph, call on your gods of the stews!"

The innocent blatterer fell from Rollo's hand. He took a step back, his stomach quivering, and sweat started up all over his round face.

I said, "Your pardon, horter—"

I got no further in what was intended to be a placating remark. The fellow with the brown and silver sash flicked his blade at my face. He said, "Stand off, rast." The quick flicking strike was intended to cut my cheek. I saw he knew how to use a rapier and main gauche, these weapons having gained a strong foothold in the arsenals of the Hamalese nobility. I moved my head aside.

"This man has done you no wrong," I said, as the rapier switched back. "I will gladly pay for the lady's gown."

The lady sniffed back a sob.

"Cramph! You will pay with your hides! Both of you!"

Black Sadrap started across the floor, knobby stick dangling. He looked worried. He would not tangle with this sword-wielding noble, for Sadrap would be out of his class.

I said, quickly, jerking my head away again from the slice of the rapier: "Stand back, Sadrap. This yetch is no horter." That, I judged, was a suitable insult, for horter, being the name given to a Hamalese gentleman, is highly prized. Also, I called him a yetch, which is not polite at all.

He gobbled in his fury. I wondered if he thought to question why his two—and now three!—quick slashes at my face had failed to strike.

From being just a roughhouse over accommodation, this incident had blown up into what could turn into an ugly and terminal scene. It seemed to me, although this affair was none of my business, that the world of Kregen had need of artists.

As always when I enter a fight I am aware it may be my last. Always, there may be another Prince Mefto the Kazzur to best me, in some if not all of the arts of the sword. I would not fight this stupid red-faced idiot, and I judged from what I had seen of his skill so far he was only of middling proficiency with the rapier and dagger, the Jiktar and the Hikdar. I would not draw my thraxter against him. There was a surer way.

Now he turned his full attention on me, for I wore a sword.

"I shall teach you foul infestations to respect your betters? I am a noble of Hamal, and you—what are you? Lower than rasts that infest dunghills!" This is, of course, no new attitude for the high and mighty of any land, not just Hamal, and not excepting Vallia.

Now, in earnest, he slashed. I stepped aside, moved in—quickly, of course—and with a juicy little hold the Krozairs of Zy teach their students the first or second day of training, took his forearm into the grips. I did not throw him away. I held him, hard enough to make him feel, and to see the pain lines slash quick agony across his gross features. He dropped the rapier. It was a jeweled, expensive weapon out of Zenicce.

"If I do not break your arm, nulsh, it is not out of concern for you." He gobbled at me, the veins of his forehead near bursting. "It is out of concern for the poor damned needleman you will abuse as he tries to patch you up."

He tried to speak, and I jerked, and he writhed like a hooked fish.

"Let me finish, offal of the fish stews in Lowest Ruathytu. You call yourself a noble of Hamal. You disgrace that claim. You are not fit to hold office. Now take the lady and leave this inn." With a last sudden pressure that made him scream out, I let him go. I would not let him annoy me. I dug out three golden deldys. These I handed to the woman as her escort moaned and gripped his aching arm with his other hand.

"Here, my lady. For the dress and with our deepest apologies."

She took the money, dazed and sobbing; but not too dazed to stow the gold away neatly, in one of those secret pockets women have sewn into their dresses. I bent and picked up the rapier. It felt a handy weapon. Extending it, hilt first, I said, "Here, take your rapier and go. Ruathytu can do without the likes of you."

Here I ventured a long bow, at chance, and by the way he reacted to those words, through the ache in his arm, told me I had scored at least an inner. I guessed he was a country nobleman traveling to Ruathytu on business. Then, as he took the rapier, very gingerly, and thought about trying to use it again, I shook my head. "Not unless you wish to die this time."

He managed to splutter out: "Who the devil are you?"

"Who are you?"

As we spoke, I marveled at his fine coarse way of making pappattu and exchanging the Llahals!

"I am a Trylon." There is a way of talking that may be described as grinding out the words. This Trylon ground out what he had to say as though his jaws hurt. "You are no nobleman, I can see that. Be very sure I shall know you again—"

"Next time we meet, Trylon unknown, I hope your manners will have improved, as I trust nothing will occur to give you just cause for offense. Your stupidity was in carrying it too far." I had, all the time, not once felt the need for that old devil Dray Prescot look to flame onto my features, and I was composed, wonderfully composed. "Now, Trylon unknown, you had better go."

He went with bad grace, swishing his rapier as though decapitating flowers along a path through a field. The woman trotted along, trying to hold her dress away from her body, looking distastefully at herself. There was room in all this to feel sorry for her.

Black Sadrap drew a breath. "He will have retainers, slaves, possibly paktuns in his pay. It will not be healthy here."

"I think not, Sadrap. I think he flew here with the woman illicitly, and that was probably a great cause for his foolish actions."

"Not foolish," said Rollo, shaking himself, abruptly returning to life. "Not foolish if you had not been here, Zaydo! He'd have sliced my hide, jikaidered it with his damned sword."

"All the same," I said, casually drifting to the doorway. "I will take a look at the perching towers."

The Trylon was dealing with his saddle flyer himself, so that strengthened my supposition he was here alone with the girl. He flew a zhyan, and the superb white bird flicked his four wings and carried this unnamed Trylon and his lady away and high, flying fast toward the east, toward Ruathytu.

The twin suns, Zim and Genodras, were gone by the time I turned back to the cheery comfort of The Fluttrell Feather.

Eight

In Ruathytu

The first person I bumped into in Ruathytu was Nath Tolfeyr, a Bladesman of exceptional skill, a roisterer and idler, habitué of all the riskiest spots in the Sacred Quarter, and the man who had inducted me into the evil and diabolical cult of Lem the Silver Leem.

He was not wearing a brown sash with silver threads; he was not wearing a single item of brown at all, except his own tanned skin. A silver buckle glittered in the afternoon lights of the suns. He looked at me, all his youthful indolence of manner returning, his long arms and legs most graceful as he strolled across toward the mirvol perching tower in fashionable Screetztyg Kyro. Being a Bladesman and a man of fashion, Nath Tolfeyr would not care to be seen to bustle, even to greet an old drinking friend.

"Now may Havil take it," he observed, halting before me and tipping his hard round Spanish-style hat back. "Hamun! As I live and breathe, Hamun ham Farthytu! Lahal, old fellow." He extended his hand in the Hamalian fashion.

As we shook I felt a passing impression that he did not look overly surprised, and put that down to his languid posing.

"I've just arrived, Nath, and am heartily glad to see a friendly face. You must tell me all the news."

"It's been a long time." He sounded guarded.

I chanced my arm. "Not in the eyes of the Silver Wonder."

"Ah!" he said. He perked up. "So you remember."

I did not want to tell Nath Tolfeyr that if I had my way all the blasphemous temples to Lem the Silver Leem would be burned out, and all the devotees of that cult, who sacrificed babies in their rituals, should be purged in whatever way would best exorcise the evil. Any oblique reference to Silver, to my sorrow and annoyance, might carry undertones of Lem the Silver Abhorrence.

We walked along toward the nearest inn, for they stand cheek by jowl all over most parts of the Sacred Quarter, mingled with private practice rings and dopa dens, and dubious haunts where games never mentioned in polite society are played. The villas of the atrociously wealthy are also to be found in the Sacred Quarter. Paline Valley did not keep up a villa in the capital.

"You have a fine mirvol there, Hamun."

"Bluenose. Aye, very strong and willing."

Most often the different breeds of saddle flyers find their perching places where their masters direct; I had chosen to leave Bluenose in the care of an establishment dealing only in mirvols. I had a good idea the government would snap him up; but there was no way of keeping him out of sight. Not with his appetite.

I asked what I burned to hear.

"What of Rees and Chido? How do they fare?"

For a space as we pushed through the throngs toward the inn, Nath did not answer. We waited as a string of calsanys passed, each animal laden to the ground, it seemed, and then Nath said, "I could do with tea, at the moment. There's the Urn and Spoon, strong henshall tea, if you care for that? Chido does well, very well. He has flowered since his father died and he is the Vad."

"That is good." We entered the tavern next to the inn and looked for a table where we could talk. "Is he here?"

"We expect him any day. He now holds the rank of Chuktar in the army, and has been commanding in the Dawn Lands."

My wonderment at this item of news—burbling chinless Chido ham

367

Thafey now a Vad, which is but one step below a kov, and a high-ranking officer in the army, to boot—changed to pleasure; it could not dissipate my immediate concern over Rees.

"Yes, Hamun. The news of Rees is not good."

"Tell me." We sat down and a curly-headed shishi came to take our order. There were no diffs that I could see in the tea place; everyone was apim like Nath and myself. "Is the trouble very bad?"

"Pretty bad. You know Rees. As proud as anyone you'll ever meet. He refuses all offers of assistance."

"Rees ham Harshur," I said. "Trylon of the Golden Wind. And those damned golden winds have blown his estates away, blown away the topsoil, ruined his agriculture. Is he then so poor?"

"As an archer with one arm."

I made a face. This ancient Kregan saying summed it all up.

Then I said, "But the army? Rees raised a regiment?" Now it was Nath's turn to make a face. "The new laws, Hamun. They are logical and appear just and eminently practical." He watched as the shishi placed the tea things on the table, her arms bare to the elbow rosy and rounded, her movements deft. When she had gone to fetch the pot itself, he went on: "The new laws require substantial levels of wealth to achieve command. Money is the key to everything. Also there is a new spirit abroad, subdued, half-spoken, understood. It makes life difficult for diffs."

"But," I said, shaking my head, "Hamal has no racial prejudice."

"Had none."

Well, I had long since gone through my xenophobic period when I called the array of splendid diffs of Kregen by names like beast-man, and man-beast, and halfling. They were diffs as we belonging to Homo sapiens were apims. Some races of diffs were so different from others that they could not be lumped together for a general judgment. The shishi came back with the tea, and when Nath had poured and we were drinking the first cup of that superb Kregan tea, he said, "They have closed the Jikhorkduns of the Ghat and Thoth. Money and supplies are tight. The army demands continual sacrifice. Hamal does not do well, in these latter days."

I noticed Nath said Hamal and not we. I let that pass. This news was, to the Emperor of Vallia, exhilarating. To the friend and blade comrade of Rees ham Harshur, it was distressing.

"Rees is a numim and therefore..."

Nath nodded and broke in: "He lost his estates, for the wind blew them away, golden and shining. He lost his regiment."

"By Krun! No!"

"Yes. Relatives of his wife took his family in. Now, Rees trains up hordes of clums from the shanty towns. They're taking anyone into the army now. They let him retain a rank of Jiktar, ob-Jiktar."

I placed the teacup down carefully. I did not wish to spill the tea. I glared at Nath Tolfeyr. He would not meet my eyes.

"And this is how Hamal repays her loyal servants! You know when Empress Thyllis overthrew the old emperor, Rees played a great part, was a devoted adherent to her cause?"

"I know."

"It seems to me Hamal has lost the spirit of greatness."

Nath glanced around, casually. He lowered his voice.

"Best not prattle on so, old fellow. At least, not so loudly in a public place."

"Yes, you are right. When do I get to see Rees? Where is he?"

"Over by the mountains of the west, somewhere. I hear they're raising an army. Another army. It will go the same way all the rest went, swallowed up in the Dawn Lands, or Vallia."

This prosaic view of military affairs added nothing to my concerns. Of course armies were being formed. Nath knew as much about them as any idler and gossip, and I still could not say outright to him: "Why is it, Nath Tolfeyr, you are not in the army?"

He could be a spy, a secret agent, working for Thyllis. Why not? She had agents everywhere. That was well known. And Nath Tolfeyr had the habit of turning up unexpectedly.

When we had finished the second cup, I said, "People talk of Prince Tyfar of Hamal. They say he has been on strange travels." Then, cursing my runaway tongue, I said with what I hoped was a casual Sacred Quarter Bladesman's languid poise, "And his father, Prince Nedfar, has been away. Together, I trust."

Nath laughed. "Yes, they've been out of the city. But they are back now and busy with the Air Service." He stared over the rim of his cup. "When you say that people are talking about Prince Tyfar, Hamun, what, precisely, do you have in mind?"

My runaway tongue had led to an interesting avenue, by Krun! Of course I was wrapped up in the fortunes of Tyfar, for he was a blade comrade, a fine companion, and he and my daughter Lela, whom he knew as Jaezila, were deeply in love and unable or unwilling to admit that, one to the other. And Tyfar thought we were Hamalese and labored for Thyllis and his country. Oh, yes, this was a pretty tangle. Tyfar had no idea Jaezila was my daughter, as I had not, by Vox, when we'd adventured and sang and fought our way together across the Dawn Lands. And, now, Nath Tolfeyr looked decidedly warm for a languid wastrel of the Sacred Quarter. Most interesting!

"Oh, the usual, Nath. He is always spoken of as a bookish lad, always with a scroll under his arm and a book to his nose. In these dark days we need fighters."

"I recall he was a studious young prince as a youth. But I understand—I am told, for I do not move in the royal and imperial circles here—that he has some skill with an axe."

"Really?" I said, drinking tea with a fine elegant twirl. "How amusing."

By Krun! But Tyfar had skill with an axe! I'd seen him take two nasty Chuliks apart with two supple sweeps, and then turn to me with an academic quote that fitted the situation marvelously. Oh, yes, I had a very great deal of time for Tyfar, who would, if the gods and this infernally stupid war between our two countries allowed, become my son-in-law. So I passed on in the conversation, asking about Casmas the Deldy and other scamps.

"Casmas?" Nath shoved back in his chair, crumbling a miscil cake between his fingers. "An odd case. He married his widow and became a Rango and lent his money to the empress. But he is—shrunken, in these latter days."

"Casmas? Shrunken? As soon believe that as the Ice Floes of Sicce have gone up in steam!"

He smiled. "I agree. It is true, scatheless."

"There are more unpleasant people to inquire after."

"I notice you did not ask about Strom Rosil Yasi—"

I put my cup down. Strom Rosil, that bastard Kataki, and his equally evil twin brother were raising hell in Vallia. My wits must be wandering. Of course I should have inquired of them, when talking of Rees, against whom they had worked their devil-designs at the instigation of Vad Garnath, one of the biggest evil-doers unhanged. I said, "I trust that crew is all dead?"

"Unfortunately, no. Garnath is with the Air Service. The Rosil twins are in Vallia. Katakis are one race of diffs I am not sorry the new laws bear down on, not sorry at all."

We talked more and I learned how old Nath the Crafty who had always detested diffs had been slain by a Chulik in a brawl, and how much this incident had contributed to the growing distrust of non-apims among the apim ruling classes. Those diffs who were nobles in Hamal, and there were many of them, had become more and more isolated. These were developments I had to ponder, for I had the uneasy conviction—not so much uneasy as panicky, and not so much a conviction as a doubting belief—that in this the Star Lords were interfering. Either them or the Savanti nal Aphrasöe. Times were changing with dramatic speed on Kregen. I felt like the proverbial leaf in a dust storm.

Nath Tolfeyr said he had an afternoon appointment at the Dancing Rostrum, for that riotous if circumspect establishment did better business than ever. People wanted to dance a few burs away and forget their cares. We said the remberees politely, engaging to meet later at a new tavern

Nath had discovered, The Blue Zhyan, in Ohmlad's Alley, off the Street of Thalanns. The pace and bustle of the city engulfed us as we emerged from the Urn and Spoon and went our separate ways. I had learned a great deal, painlessly—well, almost painlessly. There was a very great deal more I must learn to earn my hire as a spy for Vallia and the friends of Vallia against Hamal. The bonus of being able to move about freely in this enemy city as Hamun ham Farthytu had proved itself, and I knew I would have to push that bonus to squeaking point.

The Sacred Quarter of Ruathytu is essentially a higgledy-piggledy collection of narrow streets and tiny alleys and claustrophobic courts ruthlessly slashed through by the wider avenues, after the fashion of Baron Haussmann, which in the strange way of Kregen's architecture, do not always coincide with the new boulevards of the city beyond the old walls to the west. To the north the River Havilthytus flows eastward and joining it from the southwest comes the River Mak. The Sacred Quarter is contained in this triangle. The black waters of the River Mak do not mingle with the ochre waters of the Havilthytus for a considerable distance downstream, and this is one of the remarkable attractions of the place to visitors.

The twin Suns of Scorpio reflected glitteringly from every projection and gable and spire as I sauntered along. People moved everywhere, idling, gaping, with many a hurrying slave slipping quickly through the throngs. And, of course, there were soldiers everywhere, here on leave before departing for any of the fronts mad Empress Thyllis had opened in her senseless wars.

Deeming it a good idea to wander along to The Blue Zhyan and discover what the inn had to offer in the way of accommodation, I reflected on the curious fact that Nath Tolfeyr had not once asked me where I had been or what I'd been up to. He must just have assumed I'd been at Paline Valley, or else serving with the army. The Blue Zhyan, in Ohmlad's Alley, turned out to be a snug little place, angled of roof, with flowers banked around the narrow windows, and with at least two convenient trees for shinnying down and up, if, as I fully intended, I had to go on nefarious expeditions into the city. The landlord rubbed his hands, wine-stained, on his blue-striped apron and frowned and then smiled at sight of the golden deldys that appeared in my hand.

"Of course, Amak. There is a room. We are honored to have you here."

The room was narrow, cramped, and the view looked out onto a shadowed courtyard and a blank wall above the totrix stables where those fractious six-legged saddle animals were kicking up a din anxious to be fed. I looked around, punched the bed, checked the water supply, and nodded.

"Very well, Nodgen the Apron." That was his name, a fat and oily man showing signs of care over continuing supplies wherewith to satisfy his patrons. "I have been traveling and would rest now. See that I am not disturbed."

"No, notor, of course not, notor." He bowed himself out.

I flopped on the bed. If I was going flying through the city tonight I needed to catch up on my sleep. A phantasmal apparition glimmered against the paneled wall opposite the window. The spectral form wavered, and coalesced. I sat up, watchful, cautious. The arch-devil, Phu-Si-Yantong, had spied on me by sending an occult manifestation of himself to descry what I was doing. His kharrna was very great, his capacity to exert supernatural—as we believed—forces that flew in the face of nature. Khe-Hi-Bjanching, who was a Wizard of Loh as well as a friend, had set up defensive barriers against this spying. His arcane arts had been materially assisted and increased by Deb-Lu-Quienyin, who was a Wizard of Loh with a character and a history. He said, himself, that he was not as powerful in the thaumaturgical arts as Phu-Si-Yantong; but I believed Deb-Lu to be equally as powerful, if not more so. He and I had gone through enough adventures together to make me absolutely confident in him, to make me trust implicitly the old Wizard of Loh, who was a comrade and friend.

The wavering form moved as undersea fronds move in the tidal flow. The gaseous outlines thickened. The simple robes, the absence of runes, told me this was Deb-Lu, and then I saw his face, smiling at me in the old way, and I relaxed, and let out a breath.

"You look—perturbed," he said. "I am in lupu and send my projection to talk to you. It is no new thing for you. Why does it affect you so?"

"I'll tell you, Deb-Lu, I'll tell you. I thought it might be that bastard—"

"Hush, majister!" The voice cracked in indisputable command. "Do not speak the name."

I nodded. "Very well."

"Khe-Hi-Bjanching and I have surmounted the problems strewn before us. Our communication is now clear. It was a Daunting Task." I did not mistake his use of Capital Letters, and smiled.

"You are well? How goes it at home?"

"We prosper in most areas; but there is a Blight. Kov Turko has almost succeeded in bringing his kovnate of Falinur into the fold. Soon he will, as you say, hook left against Layco Jhansi. Your son Drak and the Presidio rule Vallia well. I will tell you—"

"The Blight?"

"Ah, yes. It is small at present, and concerns the Southwest."

"Drak said he had a problem down there."

"The man you sent in command of the army to liberate the Southwest has done so. But he raises the standard in his own name, and calls himself the King of Thothclef Vallia."

"The devil he does! I'll have a few strong words to say to Kov Vodun

Alloran, believe me. I'd better come home right away, although this is a damned nuisance, just as I've arrived here."

The apparition raised a hand. I waited for Deb-Lu to speak, speak to me down here in Hamal all the live-long way from Vallia. But he let the hand drop, and for a moment a silence lay between us.

"Well, Deb-Lu? Why should I not go home and sort out this problem? Kov Vodun was the Kov of Kaldi at the hands of the old emperor, Delia's father. I confirmed him in those rights and sent him off with a goodly army. If this is how he behaves we will have to teach him otherwise. Vallia is a united country—well, it will be once we've chucked all the leeches out."

"I think, majister—" When he called me that I knew he was up to mischief. "Prince Drak is handling the affair. I have great affection for Prince Drak, and trust in him. It may be..."

Drak was the sober, grim, intense one of my lads. Yes, yes, I could see what Deb-Lu was saying. I'd left Drak in charge, and I meant to hand over all Vallia and this stupid emperor part of it to him as soon as the country was back in one piece. If I went haring back the moment there was trouble—how would he feel? How would he look in the eyes of those to whom he gave orders? No, it was simple stuff, naïve, really—but Drak could and would handle this.

"Quidang, Deb-Lu! Give Drak my warmest wishes for a speedily concluded successful campaign."

Now it was Deb-Lu-Quienyin's turn to say: "Quidang!" in acknowledgment.

Then he said, "On the other matter. The great devil is active in Pandahem. There have been rebellions, which have been put down with much bloodshed. Some people here think that an invasion of Hamal is premature. We should clear Pandahem first."

"You are sure, Deb-Lu, that that cramph of a Wizard of Loh is not eavesdropping on us?"

"Quite sure. Khe-Hi monitors the conversation."

"Hm. In that case—no, leave it. Let me think on this."

I did not want to say, even like this, that the island of Pandahem between Vallia and Hamal would fall like that fabulous rotten fruit once we invaded Hamal. Go for the bold stroke—that was the way. Allies from the Dawn Lands to the south, allies from Hyrklana in the east, and we from the north, we'd hit Hamal and crush the empire between us. I did not want my Vallian lads tangled up and trapped in Pandahem.

"One thing, majister. The Fifth Army that went with Kov Kaldi to the southwest—the mercenaries declared for him, of course. The Phalanx and many regiments of our army refused and returned to Vondium. The Southwest crawls with mercenaries and flutsmen—but I thought you would like to know the army remained loyal."

"Thank you, Deb-Lu. That is a bright spot."

"Remberee, Jak. My kindest regards to Tyfar when you see him."

"Remberee, Deb-Lu."

The ghostly apparition faded. The paneling showed brown and grained where Deb-Lu-Quienyin, Wizard of Loh, had stood and spoken to me. What he had not said openly was the crux of this situation. The evil Wizard of Loh, Phu-Si-Yantong, was on the move and actively plotting fresh mischief against us. That was sure...

Nine

Blades of Spikatur

By the time the suns had set and the Twins, the two second moons of Kregen eternally revolving one about the other and casting down their fuzzy pink light, rose above the pinnacles and rooftops, Nath Tolfeyr had still not put in an appearance at The Blue Zhyan.

It was in my mind to make a round of some of the more insalubrious nightspots of Ruathytu. Nath would have gone with me, for he enjoyed a good carouse as well as the next fellow. Well, if the Bladesman had not shown up by the time the ob-bur clepsydra drained through, I'd be off without him.

What Deb-Lu-Quienyin had both said and not said remained troubling me. He'd called me Jak, as my daughter Jaezila did, and this comforted me. I'd been using the name Jak a great deal just lately, and this new nonsense of Zaydo afforded me amusement. A lot of people knew me as Jak the this or Jak the that; just now I wanted to be Hamun ham Farthytu. The thought also brought up the problem of Deb-Lu's strange lack of progress in tracing down further details on Spikatur Hunting Sword. We knew in broad outline what had happened, although not why, and we were totally in the dark about what the Spikatur Conspiracy intended. Men had claimed there were no leaders, only local chapters, devoted to hunting. They swore by Sasco, whoever he was. Torture had been applied by Hamalese tormentors in the dungeons of the ghastly fortress of Hanitcha the Harrower on its spit of land extended downriver from the Sacred Quarter, ochre water to the left, black water to the right. Men called that castle of horror the Hanitchik. Before they died, after assassinating Hamalese nobles, the followers of Spikatur Hunting Sword had confessed nothing beyond their deeds.

From this unwholesome fact I had pieced together the notion that the Spikatur Conspiracy was directed against Hamal. We knew they burned voller factories. Anybody who was against Hamal in these parlous times bid fair to be an ally. But these people, whoever and wherever they might be, remained vague and unapproachable.

The very last drop of water splashed in the clepsydra. The water was stained a pleasant apple green color. I turned the clepsydra and picked up my evening cape. This was a natty blue affair with golden cords. If Nath Tolfeyr was not coming, I was going to wait no longer.

The wardrobe I'd taken from Paline Valley contained enough foppish clothes to outfit me as a real dandy, from the hard round stiff-brimmed Spanish-style hat to the blue and gray trousers and polished boots. The cape settled over my left shoulder and I did up the golden clasps. With a rapier and main gauche scabbarded at my sides, I sallied out to partake of the raffish nightlife of Ruathytu's Sacred Quarters. In any other time, this would have been the life by Krun!

Perhaps I should mention that my jacket was stiff with gold braid, and that foolish finery almost concealed the brilliance of the green-dyed material. Well, times change, and we all march on into the future that all too soon becomes the past. Green jackets were all the rage in Hamal. I looked, in fine, your true indolent, high-tempered, mettlesome Bladesman to the life.

Dressing up in fancy clothes is easy enough and does not demand overmuch imagination. Adopting a fresh name also does not demand great cogitation. But a face... Ah, now!

Deb-Lu-Quienyin had taught me the art of so altering my features that I could pass friends unrecognized. The trick was damned painful for faces largely remote from my own arrogant physiognomy; I'd always been able to adopt a foolish sort of face, and had done so in establishing the weak character of Hamun ham Farthytu. So, now, I adopted a face that would be recalled as that of Hamun's, although by subtle touches I removed it from the face that would be remembered as that of Dray Prescot—or Jak or any of the many names I have used on Kregen.

A fat lot of good that did me in the first emergency I encountered.

The idling crowds were out. The taverns and inns were wide open. What was going on in the private rings and arenas of the great ones was not to be dwelled on. I skirted the high brick wall of nobles' villas, for not all the lords rented out small shops fronting the streets. The avenues were brilliantly lit; the streets illuminated passing well, and the alleys pits of darkness and deviltry.

The heady scent of moon blooms hung on the evening air.

Only one attempt was made to rob me as I passed a gloomy alley mouth, and the fellows slunk off when I whipped out the rapier and flourished it at them, meanwhile detailing what portions of their several anatomies would first be sliced up for mincemeat.

Slamming the blade back into the scabbard, I hurried on into the light of cressets bracketed to a high wall where vegetation spilled and moon blooms opened wondrously to She of the Veils, golden and pink, floating high above. I passed a narrow gate above which a lantern dispelled the shadows. The door was open and men laughed and joked inside, their boots loud on the graveled path. A party of gallants out for the night's entertainments, obviously; I wanted no part of that and quickened my pace.

Beyond the end of the wall, where another wall began hiding off the villa of another lord, the alley between looked shadowed and uninviting. I looked hard, hand on hilt, but the little alley between the villas remained silent. I went on.

Up ahead lay a small tree-bowered square where six taverns stood cheek by jowl surrounding the square and the well at its center. Here, during the day, the gossips from this section congregated. This was Veilmon Kyronik, from the name of the graceful, sweet-scented trees. If you wanted a fight after dark, go to Veilmon Kyronik. Someone would always oblige you.

The silly abortive attack on me by those chicken-brained would-be robbers, and the thought that I would have to avoid a fight ahead must have combined to do the trick. People hurried past, and we kept to the left-hand side of the pathway, as was natural, to keep our sword arms free. I barely looked at them, swathed in their clownish fancy-dress and their capes. I moved on and—

A hand clapped me on the shoulder.

"Jak! By Krun! Jak the Sturr, as I live and breathe!"

Emotions of furious anger, thoughts of courses of action, clashed and collided in my skull and through my blood. Instinct almost undid me. My sword was halfway out of the scabbard, I was half-turned, ready to run this brash newcomer through the guts, before I hauled myself up, shivering, as though taken in irons. By the disgusting diseased liver and lights of Makki-Grodno! Here I was, being myself, being Hamun ham Farthytu, and some idiot had recognized me as Jak the Sturr!

I swung about, slamming the rapier back, and there was Lobur the Dagger, beaming away, his merry face alive with laughter, chuckling and shaking his head where the dark curls danced in his long hair. He still wore the silver belt of interlinked leaping chavonths. He was dressed, as was I, in the height of fashion.

"Lobur the Dagger!" I said. And, then, recovering: "Lahal! Well met."

"Lahal, Jak. And well met. I did not think ever to see you again, even though Prince Ty relieved my mind when he recounted his adventures down the Moder. You and he—you had a fine time of it after we got out."

His face clouded.

So, quickly, I said, "There was nothing you could have done, Lobur. We know that. Your duty was to Prince Nedfar and Princess Thefi. You had to see them out safely."

"That is true, Jak the Sturr, and you are a true horter for so saying." He laughed, delighted. "And Prince Ty tells me Sturr was a use name, that you are Jak the Shot."

I brushed that aside. I'd been the Jak the lot, it seemed to me. "And Princess Thefi?"

He smiled and frowned at the same time, a useful trick.

"I am still—and she is—and there is no real hope. And, Kov Thrangulf hovers like a damned black crowbird. Damn him!"

That was a triangle of the classical persuasion, and one I had then, as I say, no inkling of solution or of relevance to me beyond a sympathetic feeling for lovelorn Lobur the Dagger.

"And what are you doing in Ruathytu, Jak?"

Boldly, without hesitation, I said: "I thought to join the Air Service."

"Ah! A very wise ambition. You are a fighting man, that I know from what I've seen with my own eyes and what Prince Ty told me of the Moder. We'll be delighted to enroll you."

"Well—"

"Capital! That's settled. Now, old fellow, I can't delay. Kov Thrangulf, confound him—I'm on the way to his villa now with a message from Prince Ty to Prince Nedfar. I shan't be long, then we can crack a few amphorae and talk of that dark, doomed bloody Moder."

He took my arm and we started back the way I'd come. He rattled on, nothing like dear Chido, of course, but very merry and free and good-hearted. The small group of people I'd heard on the graveled path now appeared on the pathway, still laughing. The lights shone on jewels and gold and lace. The air hung heavy with the scent of night flowers, the sound of laughter rose and singing reached us from the nearest tavern in Veilmon Kyronik. She of the Veils shed her diffuse golden light.

A screech of pure hatred ripped through that leisurely scene.

"Spikatur! Spikatur Hunting Sword! Kill!"

Dark forms leaped from the narrow slot of blackness between the walls. Feral bodies hurtled down on the startled group of Hamalese nobles. Steel glittered like icy fire in the pits of hell.

As one, Lobur and I drew our rapiers and launched ourselves forward. Affrays continually burst into the jollity of the Sacred Quarter and no one paid much heed to a fracas here and there if it was no business of his. As the blades screeched with that horrid scrape of steel on steel and we smashed into the dark-clad forms attacking Prince Nedfar and his party, it was clear this was no ordinary flare-up among Bladesmen. The cries of "Spikatur" told us that. The blood lust smoked into the night air.

"Get that big bastard, Jak!" and: "Your back, Hallam!" and: "By Krun, I'm stuck through the leg like a vosk!"

But, all too soon, the cheerful yells of Bladesmen in combat died away as the party with Nedfar fought for their lives.

We were out matched in numbers; but Lobur proved a fine swordsman, and Prince Nedfar stood like a rock, unmoved, and I did a mite of skipping and leaping. But the killers bore in. Screaming forms staggered from the fight. Men with slashed faces and guts pierced through, men with eyes suddenly blotted out, men who hobbled off to collapse and vomit up their lives, men reeled shrieking away from the knot of combat.

It was nip and tuck, as it so often is; I had a persistent fellow who wanted to drive past me and sink his brand into Prince Nedfar. I caught his blade, twirled, and the sword nicked up into the air. He panted, thick coarse gasping under the bronze mask. The attackers wore nondescript clothes, but each one wore a bronze mask over his face. Their gray floppy-brimmed hats, without feathers or ornamentation, were pulled low.

I grabbed a wight by the neck and jerked him to me.

"I do not want to kill you." The yells resounded about us, the stamp of feet, the slither of steel. I put on a face that bore the mark of Cottmer's Caverns; a devil face with upflung eyebrows and outthrust jaw, and the deep grooves beside the mouth counterpointing that devil-vee above. I bent close. "By Sasco!" I said, with meaning. "You make a mistake to attack Nedfar. He is of value to the foes of Hamal, you onker. Draw your people off. I do not wish to see friends of Spikatur slain."

"You—!" He choked as I eased my grip.

"Get off, fambly. Or you will all be dead."

My face pained me as if I'd been galloped over by a squadron of cataphracts. I couldn't keep that devil mask going much longer.

Someone tried to hit me over the head with his thraxter and I swerved and kicked him, and shook the fellow in my grip. "Call them off! By Sasco! Are you witless!"

"You—strive for Spikatur?"

"Of course! Now—go, or you'll drink steel."

A man pitched into me and coughed bright blood, red in the torchlights. I dodged away and threw the fellow I'd been gripping off. I kicked him up the rump as he staggered.

"Run!" he shrieked. Then he let rip a wild ululating scream that would have frozen the blood in a bullfighter. His companions—who had been taking a severe hammering—checked their onslaughts. "Run, brothers! Flee!"

Lobur's face expressed the utmost fury.

"By Krun! They'll not escape my vengeance!"

He stood hard by Nedfar as he shouted, and I judged Lobur spoke thus not only out of honest anger. The attackers picked themselves up, gathered themselves together, panted. But—they ran. Lobur flourished his rapier after them.

"Come on, Jak—let's crop a few ears."

I did not wish to kill folk who fought against Hamal.

"I'm with you, Lobur!" I hollered. I dissimulated, remembered to put away that devil face and that silly face, and wearing the face of Jak the Shot, I galloped off after Lobur. We lost the hunting party of Spikatur Hunting Sword in a maze of warrens past Veilmon Kyronik. They just vanished. The place was potholed with dopa dens and kaff pits, and an army could hide in there and escape detection. Lobur panted, dashing sweat from his forehead with the back of his right hand which gripped his sword.

"Well, we showed them what Hamalese can do, the rasts."

"Aye," I said. "Did you understand any of it? Who were they?"

"Cramphs who swear on Spikatur. They have caused us much injury. By Krun! I'd like to spit 'em all!"

"A worthy ambition, Lobur. If you can find them."

He didn't like that, and we trailed back to Prince Nedfar.

Nedfar greeted me with warmth, for we had gone together through some of the horrors of the Moder. And I had assisted his son, Prince Tyfar, to escape. He knew about Jak the Shot.

"You are thrice welcome, Horter Jak. Lahal and Lahal."

"Lahal, prince. I am glad to see you are uninjured."

Lobur said, "Jak wishes to join the Air Service—"

"Excellent." Nedfar, a resolute, honest, admirable man, smiled approvingly. "Hamal fights on too many—" Then he checked himself. He shook his head. "Welcome, Horter Jak."

He'd been about to say that Hamal fought on too many fronts and was overextended. That was true. When the invasion broke into their damned homeland they'd have another front, only it would be at their front door.

"I am at your disposal, prince."

Slaves summoned in haste from Kov Thrangulf's villa ran up, and with them the resident needleman. The doctor bent to the wounded. Some of them were bearing their wounds stoically; only a couple screamed and groaned and writhed. This was the ugly face of striving to a good end.

One of the hunters devoted to Spikatur had not been killed. His wounds prevented him from running off. As Lobur approached, no doubt to make some searching and unpleasant inquiries as a preliminary to horror in the dungeons of the Hanitchik, the wounded man drew his dagger and slit his own throat. It was done quickly and efficiently, very bloodily, and most oppressively. The commotion that caused gave me time to get my wind back, metaphorically speaking. I knew Prince Tyfar must have spoken to his father, and to his sister, Princess Thefi, as well as Lobur, about Jak the Shot. At first I'd led them to believe I hailed from Djanduin; later they believed I was Hamalese. I could lay no claims to titles or estates in Hamal, thus Nedfar had called me horter, a plain gentleman. For the moment, this suited me. I had labored long to preserve the integrity of the ham Farthytu name. I would not jeopardize it now.

Lobur delivered Tyfar's message to Prince Nedfar, a simple affair of delay in some voller sheds and that he would meet the party later at The Golden Zhantil. Everyone in Ruathytu had heard of that famous tavern, for it was of the highest possible class, and catered exclusively to a clientele from the upper strata of nobility. During my stay in the Sacred Quarter I had not supposed I'd ever need to go there. Now, it seemed, I was included in this evening party as of right. I found this charming, by Krun!

High up outside the tavern and supported on convoluted iron brackets the massive golden representation of a zhantil lowered down on all who entered. That magnificent eight-legged savage animal glittered in many torchlights. It was reputedly fashioned from solid gold. No one was likely to make the attempt to discover the truth of this story, put about by the owner, Thorndu the Wine, for invariably a crowd of muscle-bulging sword-swinging guards checked on the patrons. If you were not accepted, then you'd go headfirst out onto the cobbles.

The raffish blades of the Quarter used to laugh, and swear by Krun the thing was solid lead with a smear of leaf.

Be that as it may, the interior of The Golden Zhantil was luxurious and sweet-scented and awash with wine and the good things of life. There was no stinting here. Hamal might be at war, and struggling with increasing desperation against the foes she had raised up against her; here decadence breathed lushly, replete with wealth and privilege.

I wondered what Nedfar wanted in a place like this, for he was a man of rectitude, upright and honest, and not much given to the sleazy kind of debauch. When Tyfar turned up, a couple of glasses later, I found out. As for Tyfar—how his eyes popped when he saw me!

The last time we'd seen each other, he'd been haring off with a wounded Jaezila, urged intemperately by me to think of his honor and save our comrade, while I fought off those who sought to slay us. He stood for a moment, the old Tyfar, open, honest, twinkling at me, and then he clapped me on the shoulder, unable to speak.

"I haven't clawed my way back from the Ice Floes of Sicce, prince." I clapped him on the back. I had to remember to speak as though to a prince who did me honor in even acknowledging my existence here in Hamal. "I joy to see you again."

"By Krun, Jak! I hoped, and yet I could not believe—but one should expect miracles where you are concerned, I think."

We two had no truck with mawkishness, valuing a comradeship forged in blood above mere sentimentality.

With the arrival of Tyfar, Prince Nedfar's party, which did not, I was intrigued to notice, include Kov Thrangulf, got down to business. The men they had come to see, high-ranking officers in the Air Service, wanted to finish this business and then devote themselves to the pleasures offered by the tavern.

"There is now no doubt whatsoever, prince," said one of the Air Service Kapts, a Vad Homath. He was a lean man, with a scarred face and bristly hair, much decorated with gold lace. "Our spies confirm the rumors in every detail."

"But you do not know where he has gone?"

Vad Homath stroked a finger down his scarred cheek. "Back to Vallia, I expect, the cramph."

My ears, I felt sure, must have stuck an arm's breadth out of my head. Vallia!

"Well, Homath," said another Kapt impatiently, "that is as may be. But we have to strike at Hyrklana, now, and strike fast, before they are ready to attack us."

"By Barfurd! You have the right of it."

This other Kapt nodded in a truculent way. He was called Kov Naghan, and was a bullet-hard, leather-faced professional fighting man. Astride a saddle-flyer, commanding from the deck of a skyship or ordering the iron legions of Hamal into action, this was the type of man we had to meet and overcome.

But—Vallia! And—a cramph, going back there? I decided to loose a shaft and see what target popped up.

"You speak, notors, of that gretchuk empire of Vallia?" I looked at Nedfar as though seeking his permission to continue. He nodded. "But, Hyrklana? Are they not our allies?"

Tyfar favored me with an odd look.

"Only because we imposed our will, Horter Jak." Kov Naghan spoke with a civility he owed me as a valued associate of Prince Nedfar, who had spoken warmly of our exploits and of my desire to join the Air Service. "But I can tell you, for the news will be general by the morning. Hyrklana has declared against us. The Emperor of Vallia had a hand in that, the Havil-forsaken rast!"

"The Emperor of Vallia!" I said. Then, and I could not stop myself, indulging in this deplorable habit I had of putting as many spokes in as many Hamalian wheels as possible, I said, "That is bad news. I am told this new Emperor of Vallia is a most formidable figure who will destroy the Empress Thyllis if he has the chance."

Now Tyfar did stare at me, hard. I looked back at him, and said, "We fight for Hamal, do we not?"

Nedfar frowned. So I guessed I'd gone too far. Nedfar might be the second cousin of Thyllis; he might detest what she was about; but he was Hamalese and he understood duty and loyalty.

My blade comrade Tyfar saved me. "What Jak is saying makes uncomfortable hearing. But it is true. This is a setback for us. We do fight for Hamal, and we must succeed."

When princes speak, even princes who are a trifle suspect among dour professional fighting men, when there is a prince present who is famous for his integrity and prowess, it behooves lesser mortals to listen—even such high and mighty lesser mortals as these nobles in The Golden Zhantil. They nodded, these generals and nobles, and the consensus of opinion was that we would have to fight that much harder to overcome this setback.

During the more detailed discussions following I had the sense to take myself off and sit at a table by the farthest window. Being too pushy is counterproductive. Presently Tyfar joined me. He was smiling in his frank way, clearly pleased to see me, yet puzzled, too, by my appearance here in Ruathytu. To be absolutely honest, which is a task so difficult of accomplishment as to be virtually impossible, I must admit some notion of what had transpired had been with me from the beginning. From a position within the Hamalian Air Service I would be capitally placed to carry out my work. And, of course, inevitably, that brought up the question of honor. Tyfar and I were true blade comrades. How could I descend to using that friendship to such despicable ends? Easy, my friend, damned easy, when you have the people of an empire to take care of; and hard, abominably hard, when you laugh and talk with your comrade and know you are betraying him. Almost, almost I threw it all in and told Tyfar outright that the girl he knew as Jaezila was the Princess Majestrix of Vallia, and I was her father, and we were at war with Hamal. Almost—but not quite.

We talked over many of the events that had transpired since last we met, and my version was mightily censored, that is obvious. Tyfar had been fully occupied with the Air Service. When Jaezila was mentioned I simply said I looked forward to seeing her again, and did Tyfar know when she would be in Ruathytu. He did not know. Then he said, "You must understand, Jak, I do not fathom that girl at all. One moment I believe she has some friendly feeling for me, and the next, well—" He lifted his glass and put it down without drinking. "I know she detests me and thinks of me as a ninny. I am in despair."

"Then," I said, and I spoke with knowledge from conversations with Jaezila, "you have no need to be. When this stupid war is over, you and Jaezila will—"

"That long, Jak!"

"It may not be all that long, Tyfar. You have difficulty in obtaining vollers, now, more so after Hyrklana declared against us. Your father is a man among men. I think he can see which way the wind is blowing."

"I do not care for the sound of this."

"Agreed. But you have to look facts in the face. You and Jaezila are so dear to me that I—" I stopped. Deliberately I sipped the wine, a good vintage, clear and bright. I could not bear the thought of what had happened to Barty Vessler, who had been stabbed in the back by a rast who would one day pay for that crime, happening to Tyfar. I said heavily, "When you next see Jaezila, then act as your heart prompts you."

He fired up, but delicately I guided the conversation into further talk of the deteriorating military situation. This was what I was in Hamal for. When we invaded I wanted to have as many facts available as possible. The places to strike must be decided without blindfolds; this was crucial. The lives of too many men hung on these decisions for me to make mistakes.

Tyfar shook his head. "These fanatics of Spikatur Hunting Sword burn our voller yards. We guard them well now, and the losses have come down. But that ties up men."

"And the famblehoys?"

He looked surprised. "You are well informed. We try to keep them away from the cities. They are not popular."

"Understandable. And you are recruiting clums into the army—"

"The old days are dead. Now everyone must fight. And the iron legions of Hamal can mould men, make of them soldiers. The army will fight, however poorly the Air Service may do."

So, hating myself and feeling for Tyfar, I said, "But the army loses in Vallia. The iron legions recoil from the army of Vallia. And, we all know of the Battle of Jholaix."

"The Vallians were lucky there and we lost by a fluke. Everyone says so." He gripped his full glass. "The army will fight!"

"Of course. I have heard little news out of Pandahem lately."

"The Hyr Notor commands there, by warrant from the empress. The island remains quiet. But what you say of Vallia is so, Jak, and it rankles. I believe more than one of our armies was broken up there."

The Hyr Notor was the name that maniacal Wizard of Loh, Phu-Si-Yantong, called himself as he pulled the wool over Thyllis's eyes. Both shared the same stupid ambition. Incredible though it may sound, both of them wanted to rule the world—or, more realistically, to control our grouping of islands and continents, the whole gorgeous panoply of lands and peoples called Paz. Nuts, both of them.

Thinking to finish this odd little conversation on a more promising note before Lobur joined us, I said, "I do not believe I have to reiterate to you my admiration for your father. But I must tell you that my obligations in certain quarters are now at an end."

He looked up sharply. He had, along with others, taken the notion which I had fostered that I worked in secret for the Empress Thyllis. That gambit had served. Now I was after bigger fish. I went on, "You do under-stand me, Tyfar?"

"I—think I do. But if anyone else should thus understand what you are most carefully not saying, your head and shoulders would be separated by an air gap, believe you me!"

Ten

Of a Crossbow Bolt

War and Love are intimately bound up in many of the philosophies of Kre-gen as well as giving color and sparkle to the never-ending myth cycles. In the preparations for those two activities a divergence of approach may be discerned. As the sere grasslands flashed past below and the voller swooped headlong for the rickety wooden stockade ahead, I reflected that out of this ship's company and the soldiers she carried, more than ninety-nine in a hundred would far prefer to prepare for Love than War.

The odd less than one in a hundred was, indeed, odd. But these men are found in abundance on Kregen, probably more so than on this Earth. These are the Warlovers. I detest them. But they exist, they are a part of the universe we inhabit, and in times of crisis we understand the reason for their existence.

Vad Homath, his forefinger eternally stroking down his scar, was such a man.

He peered ahead, his narrow face just like any of the famous birds of prey that will have your eyes out like winkles on a pin. An overly ornate helmet covered his bristly hair done in that peculiar style, all smothered in gold lace. That was a new fad in Ruathytu in those days. He was leaving the handling of the airboat to her captain, a Hikdar who kept nervously swallowing, and to the helm-Deldars. Crouched in the bulky main body of the vessel some two hundred and fifty soldiers fidgeted about and coughed, and waited uneasily for the moment of disembarkation.

This was just a practice. The half-regiment of men had gone through basic training, and were now having the final polish applied. Most of them were clums, freemen but the poorest of the poor, at last allowed into the august ranks of the army. I fancied most of them would prefer to be out of it.

"Keep her head up, onker," Vad Homath's words grated.

The Hikdar shrilled in anger at the helm-Deldars, who heaved on their levers and brought the voller's bows up. We were due to skip over the wooden fence, touch down, and see how fast we could disgorge the half-regiment. This was just the kind of exercise I had done a thousand times with my fighting men of Vallia. Here I was in a position to make interesting comparisons. I admit to a fatuous glow at the feeling I was doing my job as a spy—and getting paid for it, too, by the foe!

The windrush over the prow ruffled the flags, those damned purple and golden flags of Thyllis, with the green of Hamal slashed through. I looked down at the soldiers. Their faces under the brims of the helmets looked white. I noticed the way they gripped spears, and crossbows. By the time warlovers like Homath, and the army Jiktar, Landon Thorgur, were finished with them, they'd be drilled, disciplined, regimented, ready to become part of the iron legions of Hamal.

And there lay the problem confronting Vallia and her allies. Insidiously though we might work, cutting here, burning there, in the end we had to face the iron legions. There was no way of avoiding that confrontation.

Men like these had marched west and south and north from Hamal and had conquered everywhere. True, the wild men from the Mountains of the West had checked the advance, and that had been met by a redistribution of forces against more sophisticated enemies. In the Dawn Lands down south Hamal continued her advance. Pandahem lay under her heel, with Phu-Si-Yantong in command and plotting further deviltry. Only in Vallia had a real check met the Hamalese. There we had beaten them fair and square. Rather than be whittled away by the mountain guerilla tactics of the wild men of the west, the Hamalese had turned their attentions south. Only in Vallia had the iron legions been met and worsted, by the radvakkas and by the warriors of Vallia. Thyllis knew that; she'd sent hecatombs of the poor devils who had failed to the horrors of the syatra pit in her throne room, or the jaws of the manhounds in the Hall of Notor Zan. More importantly, in a military sense, those in command of the army, those charged with its continuing performance, would know and, knowing, prepare countermeasures.

As Vad Homath ostentatiously lifted his left hand in the air I knew what I was doing had a direct bearing on the struggles to come. He shook the ruffles at his wrist free. Then, with an equally meaningful gesture, he placed his right middle finger over his pulse. We all knew that he would time us to the last heartbeat.

A glance ahead showed the wooden fence skipping beneath us. The Hikdar shouted, the helm-Deldars thrust their levers hard over, and the voller plunged for the ground.

She hit heavily. The whole fabric of the airboat shook and she groaned, for she was an ancient craft, in Hamalian terms good only for training, although in Vallia we'd have had her through force of circumstance in the front fighting line. Dust spouted up from the hard ground. The Deldars were bellowing as Deldars always do bellow. The wooden flaps covering the openings along the sides crashed down and the men started to run out over these ramps. You could taste the sweat and fear. The Deldars did not actually brandish whips; but the impression was there, hard and vivid, like desert sunshine. The noise of bronze- and iron-studded sandals clattered into the hot air. The uproar battered on. I was supposed to be observing what went on and learning. I did think that a bunch of smart girls with bows could have made a sorry mess of these iron legionaries as they debouched from the voller.

All around us the flat horizon of Central Hamal showed specks of trees, dust and grit, mountains lifting to the north and a river meandering along vegetation-choked banks to the south. The swods panted and stamped down the ramps and ran out onto the parched ground. They formed up smartly enough, for that was a parade-ground evolution. But one or two tripped quitting the airboat, and others piled up, and, all in all and quite without the black-faced fury of Vad Homath to warn us, we knew the evolution had been a disaster.

That didn't bother me. Callous, of course, but gleeful, by Vox!

One Deldar simply picked up a poor wight all entangled with his own crossbow and fairly hurled him head-first down the ramp. The swearing flowered to the burning sky. He catapulted full into his buddies and they collapsed down the ramp in an arm and leg wriggling mess. This was an active-service exercise, a practice disembarkation under threat of opposition, and the crossbowmen were landing with loaded weapons. Some idiot couldn't have latched his safety properly. A crossbow twanged from the middle of the confusion. The bolt went an arm's length from Vad Homath's head.

He didn't move or flinch. Give him that. He looked down on that particular ramp, and the heap of struggling men, and at the Deldars, and abruptly it was not funny any more. I knew—everyone knew—heads would roll for this foul-up. On Kregen, in Hamal, the expression "heads would roll" was not idle, oh, no, very far from idle.

Out of that squirming heap of uniformed humanity, a voice burst, high, hard, rapturous: "Spikatur! Hai, Spikatur!"

So the crossbow bolt had not been an accident. The only mistake here had been that the quarrel had missed...

"Down there!" ordered Homath. He did not scream or rage; he cracked out his orders as though in the midst of battle. Well, for his life, it had been a battle. "Arrest all those men. You—" he spoke to me directly. "Down there. Do not let any of them escape. On your head."

Jumping down onto the ground I joined the Deldars and other officers rounding up the tangled group of soldiers. We sorted them out. They stood in a line, quivering, shaking, the sweat starting out in sheening rivulets all over their faces. If no one knew who had shouted, they were all for the question, no doubt of that whatsoever. I felt sorry for them, that was a normal human response. But I felt angry, too. Was this the way I wanted to fight Hamal?

Vad Homath called off the exercise at once. As a Kapt, a most high-ranking general, he had chosen in his capacity as overlord of the Nineteenth Army, his immediate responsibility, and member of the army council, to check out the progress being made by the new units. Prince Nedfar had asked him to take me along to gain experience. Homath's rage was contained within himself. Like an icy chip caught between ice floes, he froze the marrow in the bones of his subordinates.

The upshot of the affair came when the suspects, lined up in the virulent blaze of the suns, awaited interrogation. One man leaped out. His face was a mere mask of contorted hatred as he tried to get at Vad Homath. The crossbowmen of the guard shot him to pieces. He died. Useless to rage at the guard. Homath didn't even bother to check them. They had their orders. The immutable laws of Hamal laid down procedures. Their job was to protect the Kapt, and this they did. Any thought of sparing the man's life for questioning must remain subordinate to that.

One thing you could say, these fellows of Spikatur Hunting Sword were not afraid to die for their beliefs.

The man's name was Nath the Tumbs. His dead face showed the freckles like peeling paint.

"Take him away," said Homath, and turned back to the voller.

The thought occurred to me that I might put this incident to advantage. I marched up beside Homath and said, "With respect, notor, it might be advantageous to us to find out more of this man."

His finger stroked his scar. He stared at me. He nodded his head. "Very well." It was all nicely done, calculated to impress. It did impress. This man was no fool, and he was an enemy of my country. I saluted and wheeled off pronto.

The security officers in his suite would make their own inquiries, no doubt of that. I fancied my line of inquiry would differ from theirs.

There was no chance of donning the gear of a simple swod in the ranks and joining in as an equal. Nearly all these fellows were clums and I learned that Nath the Tumbs had been a taciturn man, not a clum, who kept himself to himself. Nothing of any note was known of him. He came from a small village away in the south of Hamal, or, at least, he said he did. One bearded swod, sweating, fidgeting with his stux, the spear-haft sheening, told me that Nath the Tumbs had been a fine swordsman. The summoning bugle call for the next meal rang out. The bearded swod saluted.

"I must go, horter. And we will not eat any looshas pudding this day, bad cess to Nath the Tumbs for that."

Looshas pudding is one of the favorite desserts of the soldiers in the ranks. Then this swod added, "Although Nath the Tumbs had no real liking for the looshas. He swore he knew a place in Ruathytu where they served the best celene flan in all the world."

On Kregen rainbows are, by reason of the two suns, somewhat spectacular affairs. A common name for rainbow is celene, and celene pie or celene flan is made from a mixture of fruits and honey and, while rather sweet to my taste, is a delicacy. I nodded, half-listening, as the bearded swod, who was called Lon the Surdu, saluted again and wheeled off for the meal. As he went he said over his shoulder: "Oh, and, your pardon, horter. Once when he was more merry than he expected, for Hambo Hambohan sold him his ration, he boasted he was of the Mitdel'hur persuasion. But he denied it afterward."

Lon the Surdu trailed his spear and fairly ran to fall into line for the meal. Everyone was on edge after the assassination attempt, and the officers would be merciless over any infringement. The religion of Mitdel'hur, insignificant in adherents, was little known to me. At the time I had a vague idea they stripped off in their temples and ritually bathed each other, and then shared a communal meal. If there was harm in the sect, it was hidden from me. This might be a start to unravel Nath the Tumbs's background and find a lead to Spikatur Hunting Sword.

In any event, my dilemma about reporting in this item of information was unnecessary; the officers charged with investigating the affair had also found it out.

"Mitdel'hur?" said Vad Homath. "A petty religion." He looked at the group of staff officers surrounding him as they prepared for their meal, in somewhat grander style than the soldiers. "Follow it up, follow it up. But it will be a waste of time."

For a man who had just survived a murderous attempt on his life, Homath appeared composed. He was your true professional fighting man. That, in many a view, should have inclined him even more against assassins and caused him to react with a display of anger. Instead, he went meticulously through the faults he had observed in what had been performed of the exercise. Eventually he handed over to Jiktar Landon Thorgur, and, his forefinger stroking down his scar, gave orders for the return journey.

We were a subdued party on the way back to Ruathytu.

The close brushing of the wings of death made us all realize afresh that the steel-headed crossbow bolt can take the life of the greatest of men as easily as the least.

Eleven

Lobur the Dagger Fidgets

"Our spies in Vallia," said Kov Naghan, "report massive preparations. An enormous buildup is taking place in that devilish land. And therefore it is necessary for us to reinforce Pandahem."

Vad Homath, stroking his scar, said, "I agree—if it is Pandahem."

They sat at their ease at a table in the window corner of the Golden Zhantil, these two Kapts with other high-ranking officers and pallans, and with Prince Nedfar. I closed my eyes, leaning against the wall at a discreet distance. Prince Tyfar was signaling for a fresh round of drinks, and I listened as best I could to what this informal war-council discussed. It was not satisfactory and only Zair knew how different from what I anticipated and hoped—but... But! Spies in Vallia! Damned Hamalese spies sniffing out our secrets!

The situation amused me, despite the seriousness. Here was I, growing righteous over damned spies in my own country, and calmly doing my best to spy on the enemy. And, at least for the moment, my best was nowhere near good enough.

Kov Naghan pulled at his jaw, growling, unhappy. "We must hit Hyrklana to knock those rasts off-balance, and we must put more men into Pandahem. Troops, troops, always it is more troops."

Nedfar spoke pleasantly enough; there was no mistaking the steel underlying his words. "The army has taken many clums into the ranks, strong, simpleminded men who do not think overmuch and therefore may be considered to make good soldiers." Now I knew Nedfar had pondered this question of the imaginations of soldiers, and so saw he spoke indirectly. But the people at the table were not reassured by his tone.

"No army commander ever has enough men, prince," said a shriveled little man, doubled up as the result of an old wound imperfectly healed. He was the Pallan of Metals. "If I produce a reserve of swords or spears, the Kapt go out and find men to use them." And he laughed, a choked dry cackle.

"If, prince," said Kov Naghan, bullet-hard, unswerving, "we face war on two—no, three—fronts again, we shall have need of every man and voller and saddle flyer Hamal can produce, hire or steal."

"True."

"Pandahem or Hyrklana?" said Vad Homath.

At that point Tyfar called and I joined him at the table being prepared by the servants. Lobur drifted over and with him a few of the other aides to the great chiefs. I had been appointed aide to Prince Tyfar, which was useful, and which gave enormous amusement to Tyfar, who jested with me, his blade comrade. As I sat down I reflected that although eavesdropping on the chiefs as they talked was small beer, in this case I had been pointed toward a new and potentially fruitful path. As we drank and our conversation drowned out anything else, I leaned over and as though concerned, said, "If the Vallians attack us in Pandahem, that could be nasty."

"They don't stand a chance!" The bulky body and sweating face of Famdi ham Horstu, aide to Kov Naghan, gave importance to what he said. He banged his fist on the table and the bottles and glasses jumped. "We'll reinforce Pandahem and chase the damned Vallians all the way home, by Krun!"

The consensus, expressed in a growl that rippled around the table, agreed with this summation. Tyfar looked grave.

"And Hyrklana?"

"Them, too!" yelped the company.

So, all in all, I felt pleased. This was just what we wanted. We wanted the Hamalese to pour men and materials into Pandahem, so that when we bypassed them and hit Hamal, they'd be left high and dry. By the time they were recalled we'd hope to have a hot reception awaiting them. By Vox! We'd run rings around these confounded Hamalese!

Since the return from the exercise in which Homath had nearly been sent down to the Ice Floes of Sicce, I'd been in communication with Deb-Lu-Quienyin half a dozen times, keeping him informed of progress and learning what went forward in Vallia. Assured that my work here was important enough to keep me away from home, and the projects there of expanding and then consolidating our frontiers went ahead, I breathed a little easier. The trouble in the Southwest of Vallia was being handled by Drak, and I left him strictly to handle the affair himself. If he was going to be emperor—and the sooner the better, by Zair!—then this was a damned good way of learning. Delia had gone back to Vondium on business for the Sisters of the Rose, and Jaezila, declining to accompany her mother, had declared she had work still to do in Hamal.

I own my heart sank at that. I didn't want my daughter swanning around in enemy Hamal. Of course, there was nothing I could do to stop her, for she was her own woman. I just trusted in her own prowess and skill and courage, made a few private invocations, and promised myself I'd try to persuade her to leave off the spying and go back home. As for the situation between her and Tyfar, that was hideously complicated. All I could do there, I fancied, was to urge our war preparations along, invade Hamal, knock seven kinds of brick dust out of the damned place, and then make a good and just peace. Then Tyfar and Jaezila could settle their own affairs.

Before that devoutly wished-for end could be reached, before our invasion could succeed, we had to weaken Hamal's capacity to wage war.

And, as you will notice, in all these cogitations, I would not face the scene to come when Tyfar discovered the truth of Jaezila and me.

He was laughing now, open and frank, joying in life, cracking jokes. Lobur the Dagger played up to the prince, and the other aides joined in. Lobur was being twitted about his hopeless passion for the Princess Thefi, Tyfar's sister, and yet Tyfar did not tease him. Tyfar knew that situation well. Kov Thrangulf, sober, industrious, was the raven in the picture, and yet Tyfar and I both felt that Thrangulf had been seriously misjudged by those who mocked him. Yes, he was stuffy, but that is no hanging crime.

Tyfar leaned across.

"You had no joy of those naked prancers, the folk of the Mitdel'hur persuasion, Jak?"

"None. They swore they'd never heard of Nath the Tumbs. I believe them. They seem a harmless lot."

"Vad Homath is still alive, for which we give thanks. He has probably pushed the incident out of his head. He has grave responsibilities." Tyfar looked straightly at me. "Where would you commit our forces, Jak—Hyrklana or Pandahem?"

"I am thankful I do not have to make the decision. But Pandahem is rich, and we gain much there. To lose the island now would be harmful. We have already lost the vollers from Hyrklana, so—"

"So, you would reinforce Pandahem against the Vallians?"

"That would seem judicious."

"And then those Hyrklese could fly in to attack."

"Hamal has enough troops, surely, to—"

Tyfar closed his eyes. Then, again looking at me, unblinkingly, he said, "Yes, we have the troops. But our Air Service—we are in trouble there, Jak, you know."

I didn't know. I was willing to learn.

"Surely, prince," interrupted Famdi ham Horstu, his face florid in the lamplight, "surely this is only temporary."

"And," pointed out Tyfar in his mild voice, "in that temporary period we may be invaded."

"The army will deal with any invasion."

"Of course. We have perfect faith in the army. But it makes life a little easier on the ground during a battle if you control the air."

There was a general nodding of agreement. The point was so obvious I knew Tyfar aimed at a different mark.

Lobur sat sideways on his chair, looking about the elegant room. He fidgeted. He could not keep still. Something of moment bothered Lobur the Dagger, that was clear. In the small pause that ensued after Prince Tyfar's unnecessary yet important comment, I heard the chiefs at the next table talking of the Empress Thyllis's war room. Some of the generals wanted to go across to the palace of Hammabi el Lamma reared on its island in the River Havilthytus to check on the maps adorning the walls of the war room.

Then Famdi ham Horstu banged his fist again, and the glasses and bottles jumped, and he said, "By Krun! If we cannot make enough silver boxes and are short of vollers, then the aerial cavalry will have to cover the army. I do not like it—"

"None of us likes it," said Tyfar. "Famblehoys will have to fill the gap."

"Famblehoys!" Disgust dripped. "They are useless!"

Thinking it time to put my oar in, I said, "They have been used with success by our enemies."

Tyfar nodded. "Jak is right. If the Vallians, who cannot even build their own vollers, can use flying sailing ships, then surely we can, also?"

Lobur twisted back, fidgeting with the dagger slung at his waist. "The damned Vallians are a seafaring folk. We are not. They understand sails and how to use the wind."

"Then, while there is a shortage of silver boxes to power our vollers, we must also learn to use the wind."

They looked sullen and rebellious at that; but Tyfar was right, and I warmed to him. He was willing to go on and face the future, using whatever means came to his hand. He would not uselessly repine over what was not possible.

Lobur had spoken damned sharply to the prince. Tyfar took no notice, continuing to talk and laugh with the others; Lobur sat sideways on his chair and fidgeted and looked black. In one of those little pauses that break up any general conversation the chiefs from the next table, talking with growing heat, made themselves heard.

Van Homath was saying: "...any time we like. I'll prove my point in the moorn vew—"

"Let us go, then, and we'll see." Nedfar rose. They quite clearly were going to the moorn vew, the war room in Thyllis's unholy palace. I perked up... But my hopes were premature, for the chiefs agreed that they had no need of us aides and we could carouse the night away if we wished. There was the other watch to come on duty who would take over during the night. I slumped back in my chair. And Lobur, when I turned to speak to him, had gone.

His florid face a sheen of sweat, Famdi ham Horstu looked furious. "As Malahak is my witness! Lobur is a strange fellow!"

Tyfar smiled. "As San Blarnoi says, understanding a man is like peeling an onion, the task is tortuous and tearful."

We all laughed, for the aphorisms of San Blarnoi can usually turn up an opposite quote, and Lobur had been acting deuced oddly, no doubt about it. With the rest of their duty thus cancelled, the bloods among the gathered aides decided to go out on the town. Tyfar raised his eyebrow at me. I nodded, and making our farewells, we went off together.

"And Lobur?" I said. "Something ails him, for sure."

"It is my sister, of course."

"Of course."

For him, Tyfar spoke a little fretfully. "Lobur is a good companion, bright and quick and eager to please. There is no reason why he could not make his way in the world, and secure Thefi in a marriage that would be agreeable to my father. As it is—"

Feeling a traitor, I said, "Lobur is eager to please."

"Ah!"

We walked along in silence for a space among the throngs out to enjoy themselves, their faces animated in the torchlights becketed to walls and archways. The air smelled sweet, even here in the Sacred Quarter, and the scent of moon blooms drenched down, refreshing and nostalgic.

Then Tyfar said, "I refuse to listen to anything said against Lobur, as you know. Thefi is in love with him, I think."

"You think?"

He lifted a hand, the gesture a helpless appeal. "I am not sure. Kov Thrangulf is everywhere laughed at as a stick in the mud, a bore. He has no ham in his name, true, but he held onto the kovnate. I think he is more worthy than folk are willing to give him credit for."

Very quickly I decided this moil was not for me. I liked Princess Thefi well enough, and she was Tyfar's sister. Lobur, despite the dealings I had had with him, remained an unknown quantity. I did not believe the triangle of passion and hatred here could affect my work for Vallia. Well, in that I was wrong, as you shall hear.

So, in that honest if misguided conception, I could say, "There is every indication that this evil war will hot up, and when it does Lobur will be in the thick of it. A man's fortunes may change overnight."

Tyfar glanced back, and I knew he was not checking if the four guards assigned us were following on discreetly, as feeling the annoyance that a man could not take a stroll in the Sacred Quarter without guards. A straightforward Bladesman's ruffling fight, all swirling capes and shouts of "Ha!" and "Hai!" and much leaping and twirling, well, that was one thing. And the ever-present possibility of a hired stikitche going in to earn his hire and assassinate you was another. But this new business of Spikatur Hunting Sword, where men didn't give a damn if they died or not just so they could skewer you—well, that did call for four hulking guards to dog the prince's footsteps.

He swung back and gave that fighting man's hitch to his belt where his axe snugged ready to hand. We'd never satisfactorily settled between us how soon Tyfar could dispose of a rapier and main-gauche Bladesman with his axe, and we'd mocked each other, saying the rapier would snick past a clumsy axe swing and an axe would lop a head before the onker realized and so forth, and so forth. Now Tyfar took his hat off and bashed it against his thigh, and punched it, and put it back on his head.

"We are for the Twentieth Army and the mountains," he said.

I stopped walking. I stared at him where a torchlight threw orange smears like butter down his cheeks and set skull-shadows under the hatbrim.

"The Twentieth? The mountains of the west? You said nothing—"

"No. Security. I suppose I should be pleased. After all, I am young and have been given an army."

I glared at my comrade. I spoke as the Ice Floes of Sicce must grate and grind together as they suck down the ibs of the departed. "I give you my congratulations, prince, on your new command."

"Jak!" He flung up one hand, appealing, his face distorted in that orange and black grotesquerie.

"You are my comrade, Tyfar, and dear to me. But, by Krun, you don't expect me to follow you to the Twentieth, do you? Molder away out in the West?"

"I take over from Kapt Thorhan, who fell from his bird. I know the army guards the western frontier against the wild men, I know we should be facing the other three points of the compass, I know the men will be dispirited and sullen—"

"They'll be mutinous, a rabble—"

"—but my father commands it." He was appealing to me, to understand and, perhaps, to forgive. "You are a fighting man with your way to make in the world, just like Lobur. I shall not hold you. Havil knows, I would escape this posting if I could; but I am given an army as a trial. If I fail, if I refuse..."

"It will lead on, Tyfar, to greater commands. Of course."

I couldn't go blindly back to the western mountains and sit in strongholds and fly patrols against the wild men! I had so many hooks baited the fish would be snapping at my ankles. And Tyfar, as a prince, still had to work his way up the hierarchy of command. The Hamalese are not stupid—or not more so than most peoples—when it comes to handing out responsible posts.

"You will write to me—?"

"If you leave an address."

"Your letters will reach me at Hammansax."

I nodded.

He went on, "The wild men have caused disturbances among the vo'drins."

I knew about the volgendrins, marvelous flying islands where the

Hamalese grew an abundance of pashams, honey-melon-sized fruits which, although they might smell like old socks and taste like the sweepings of a totrix stable, were processed to form a component in voller production. And facts clicked into place. Production of the silver boxes which powered vollers in the air was down. The wild men were "creating disturbances."

Slowly and with meaning, I said, "It could be this posting is vitally important. You won't be sitting on your hands out there."

Tyfar drew a breath. "Then you'll come?"

"No."

"I do understand. I shall miss you." We walked on past the brilliantly lit entrance to a lord's villa and into the shadows beyond where small shops flickered their lesser lights. "What will you do? The Air Service needs support."

To be honest, I was not absolutely sure of what would be best as my next step. I had a certain project to accomplish here in Ruathytu before I hared off down south into the Dawn Lands to help coordinate their attacks on Hamal. I anticipated objections to our plans down there.

"As your aide I have been granted the honorary rank of ob-Jiktar. I appreciate that. Will it open doors?"

"Ah!" Ahead of us now past the shoulders of folk pushing into and out of the shops a tavern's sign proclaimed The Bolt and Quarrel and we made for a quick wet. "The rank may be honorary but I shall have a few words in the right ears. You wish to command a voller with a little more weight than that a Hikdar pulls?"

"Yes."

"Then consider it done. Who knows? You may even fly out to visit me as I moulder away in those damned mountainous forts."

I quelled my sigh of relief. I thoroughly detested bamboozling my friend and comrade like this. I wanted command of a Hamalese flier for reasons that would make Tyfar's hair stand on end.

"Jak, one thing—you'll probably have to find your own crew. We are stretched for quality voswods and, another thing, it may be possible that instead of a voller they'll assign you to a famblehoy."

I made a face. "If that is to be, I'll accept. But a voller—"

"I'll do what I can."

Thoughts of my days on Earth when as a first lieutenant of a seventy-four I had hungered for my own command mocked me. How relatively easy it was to obtain your heart's desire when you had Influence!

The Bolt and Quarrel was packed with army officers, and the diffs among them, paktuns, kept themselves to themselves along one side. This new and unpleasant hostility to diffs in Hamal showed least among fighting men. A warrior recognizes another warrior, no matter if he has scales, or a tail, or three or four arms. We managed to acquire a couple of glasses and then went outside to the patio, under the torchlights which drowned the moon-radiance of She of the Veils. If there was a tension between us, it would pass.

At the far end of the patio a troupe of jugglers and fire-eaters and magicians went through their repertoire of tricks, and the roars of delight and wonder as a man swallowed a flaming brand or a pyramid of muscle-bound fellows stood on one another's heads drove us farther away. Our talk although offhand remained of vital importance to us both. At length Tyfar could not keep back the thought that stood foremost in his mind. He put his glass down. "You are going away again, Jak. And Jaezila? By Havil! How I miss her!"

I said, with a fervor that was absolutely genuine: "So do I!"

Despite the uproar with the jugglers, or perhaps because of that, and with the tavern crowded with fighting men, there was in the air, strong and unmistakable, the feeling of departure. Soldiers shouting out good-bye, and the people waving and calling as the armies left—yes, this feeling is one dreadfully familiar. That feeling itched everyone here this night, even though the departures lay for the morrow. With what lay between Tyfar and me we did not make a night of it, but took ourselves back. Two days later Tyfar was gone.

He had been as good as his word. I had been made up to dwa-Jiktar and given a voller to command. If I could not find a crew within a month of the Maiden with the Many Smiles, the voller would be taken away and given to someone who could.

The Hamalese officers commiserated with me, being helpful and encouraging, saying things like, "You'll never find a crew these days," and, "Let the nobles take the commands, they can always find crews."

My problem was quite the opposite from what these Hamalese imagined.

On the question of crewing my new voller, once I made known in certain quarters I needed men, I would be inundated by offers, and infamously injure the good feelings of magnificent fighting men by having to choose elsewhere. And, by Zair! How was I to make the choices? How was I to select a mere fifty or sixty fellows from the thousands who would fight to be with me?

Twelve

Mathdi

As the voller bore on steadily southward I wrote names on a sheet of paper. The first sheet filled up rapidly, and I took another from the rack. A glance through the forward windows—they were more than scuttles—showed me the empty sky and the high clouds all suffused with the glory of Zim and Genodras shining refulgently. The second sheet filled. At the fourth sheet I sat back, in despair, knowing the task was impossible.

The voller the Hamalese Air Service had assigned me flew well and confidence could be reposed in her that she would not arbitrarily break down as the airboats the Hamalese used to sell abroad would invariably do. She was called Mathdi. I was alone. The reason for the flight I had given was firstly to test out Mathdi and get the feel of her, and secondly to recruit a crew of volmen and the fighting component of voswods. Having said that, I could say nothing about the age and state of the craft, for Mathdi was old and if not decrepit then weak at the knees.

In the current fraught state of voller production in Hamal everything that could fly had been pressed into service. In the normal course of events Mathdi would have been broken up and her silver boxes freshened up to give them a longer lease of life before they turned black and useless, and a new ship built around them. There was no time for that now. She was a beamy craft of two decks, with fighting towers and balconies and her design had long since been superseded by new models. She carried the venerable air of fragile antiquity about her, and I loved her.

All the same, to find her crew... Every name I had written down had been winnowed from a much longer list in my head. I needed men who could carry off a deception and who would not instantly bellow out at the sight of a Hamalese and go charging down to blatter the poor fellow. Many of those names you know—and plenty you have not so far been introduced to—and every one a ferocious fighting man, a warrior, a soldier, a man who knew his trade and, more importantly, knew why he fought.

Mathdi would sink under the weight of the men who would clamor to follow me into battle.

Not, I confess, a comfortable thought. I am not one of your charismatic killers. At least, I devoutly hope not. I do have that special form of charisma the Kregans call the yrium, and this may curse or bless indifferently. Men will follow me. With that responsibility on my shoulders I had to lead well, so that as few as possible suffered. Not easy. Not easy at all, by Zodjuin of the Silver Stux!

And, too, although I would disagree with the judgment, some people might say that reluctance to send men off to their deaths caused me to joy so much in adventuring off by myself or with a chosen band of comrades. The reasons for that were quite obvious, and quite removed from considerations of empire.

Unable to come to any sensible decision over the lists I threw the paper onto the chart desk and took myself off on another tour of inspection. The controls were locked to a steady level flight. Up on the topmost lookout tower where on Earth the crow's nest would have perched, I stared around the wide horizons. By Zair! What a world is Kregen!

Ahead hills stretched in folds of blue and gray threaded by sillver watercourses. Dense clumps of trees strewed the flanks of the hills with darker greens and browns. The sky lifted, sheer, crystalline, suffused with the radiance of the Suns of Scorpio. I looked down. Mathdi looked, as all ships look small from the masthead, a cunningly wrought toy. Her bulwarks were solid lenk, the oak of Kregen, and her fighting towers were armored in iron and bronze. As for her teeth—the ballistae snouted along her sides, ranked deck by deck, and catapults lifted in cleared areas. She might be old and creaky; she was a beautiful craft, and I overlooked the severe dint in her larboard flank where, in the long ago, some idiot had rammed her.

Her main color scheme tended to blue, with gray and white adornments. There was precious little gilt left, and the gingerbread work was mostly gone. The eyes in her bows, one larboard, the other starboard, had been freshly painted. No need to wonder that the sea and air-faring folk of Kregen adorn their ships with eyes, still, as we did—and do, by Zair!—here on Earth to let the ship see where she's going. Mathdi was clearly Hamalian in origin and to avoid as much unpleasantness as possible where I was going I'd prepared a few flags ahead of time. The flagstaffs were all bare. With a sigh I climbed down to the deck and went into the armored conning tower just forward of amidships to make sure the lock on the controls was still in place. I'd had experience, on Earth, of old ships where one sailed in the constant expectation of the bottom falling out. The conning tower with its racks of crossbows and stuxes, its air of spartan efficiency, did not depress me. From here a captain would conn his ship in action, if he did not, like me, feel more at home out on the open deck.

Soon Mathdi would resound to the noise of her crew. And still I could not choose from all those splendid fighting men. A thought occurred to me. Of course! I could not simply take away men from their regiments, their ships, their aerial cavalry squadrons—of course not. I would say, firmly, that their duty demanded they continue the struggle there, and not go haring off with me. Well—it might work.

"By the revolting pestilential carcass of Makki Grodno exhumed!" I said. "Sink me! I'll line 'em all up on paper and toss an arrow for each one. That's what I'll do, by Vox!"

Let chance decide among peers.

Just to give myself an edge, I could push the crew of Mathdi up to a hundred. She'd take that number without bending in half or having bits fall off.

So, alone in the ship, on we pressed, Mathdi and I, on to what of peril the Dawn Lands would afford us.

No difficulty presented itself in choosing a course to take us clear of any continuing fighting. With such a large area and so long a frontier, inevitably the gaps between actions, sieges and routs were immense. A sharp lookout had to be kept to spot the aerial patrols the contending forces would maintain between their major areas. With the River Os, He of the Commendable Countenance, left far to the north, Mathdi and I flew on over the Dawn Lands of Havilfar.

From staring overside I brought my gaze back to look forward along that sweet curve of Mathdi's decks. Deb-Lu-Quienyin stood just beside the third starboard varter, a pale shimmer of ghost-shine about his robed figure. I climbed down and walked toward this apparition.

"Jak! You'll have to go to Ingleslad—that's the capital of Layerdrin—right away."

"I know it's the capital, Deb-Lu—and what's the trouble this time—?"

I stopped speaking, for I was speaking to myself. The solid wood and iron of the varter showed through the Wizard of Loh, and as he vanished so the ballista exuded a breath of cold. Well, now. Deb-Lu was in the devil of a hurry. So, obediently, I went back to the conning tower and directed Mathdi on course for Ingleslad. Layerdrin was just one of the small countries of the Dawn Lands, long since overrun by the iron legions of Hamal. The distance was on the order of five hundred or so miles, and I'd make it in six hours or so. Locking the controls again I went off for a bite to eat.

The necessity of keeping up my cover as a dwa-Jiktar in the Hamalian Air Service, commanding a voller, made me wonder how long I could stretch this flight before reporting back. Truth to tell, the thought that I would not have to decide on the names in those confounded lists today cheered me up, coward that I am. As soon as I'd found out what Deb-Lu's mysterious words meant, I'd have to high tail it for Ruathytu and the Air Service berths at Urnmayern where I was based.

The people of Layerdrin had lived under the Hamalese yoke for some time now and were thoroughly cowed. The chances of a revolt originating there seemed remote. Yet as I slanted in through a gap in the Mountains of Yallom fringing the eastern boundaries of the country, with a wide basin ahead threaded by rivers and patterned with agriculture, I saw the old and dreadful signs of combat ahead.

Swarms of flyers winged high above the city. Flames shot up and smoke rolled away downwind. The flyers were mostly fluttrells and, for a moment of horrid doubt, I thought they were flutsmen. Then, as I swung in nearer, I saw the picture and realized the truth, a truth so overwhelming I hammered a fist onto the lenken coaming before me and swore.

"By the putrescent putrid eyeballs of Makki Grodno! The idiots!"

But it was true. Here in this cleft between the mountains the first invasion of Hamal had begun.

Down there, and swinging high in the sky, the armies of our allies from the central and southern nations of the Dawn Lands fought the Hamalese garrison, seeking to batter their way through. This should have taken place when the armies from Hyrklana and Vallia invaded, so as to provide a pincer movement that prevented the Hamalese from reinforcing any one front. A combined offensive had every chance of succeeding. But these hotheads had struck ahead of time. They could be crushed, and the Hamalese turn, fresh from victory, to deal with the invasions from north and east.

And, as I flew in toward the flames and action, I could guess who was running some, at least, of the show down there.

Through the windrush the noise bloomed ahead, hideous and clangorous with combat. A flight of fluttrells winged over toward me. And that brought me—belatedly—to my senses.

If our allies down there were idiots, then I was an onker of onkers, a get onker, by Krun! Here was I, flying in with an empty voller marked as Hamalian—either way I was on the receiving end. Instantly I fled for the conning tower and bashing the controls free, sent Mathdi over in a wind-splitting swerve away from those inquisitive flutswods. By their streaming banners I knew they were from Arachosia, allies from the windy city in the mountains far to the south, here to bash in the heads of Hamalese. They wouldn't hesitate. Mathdi dived for the crags below.

In a straight flight a voller would outpace a bird; but I needed to get down below and bash a few heads myself—friends' heads, to knock some sense into them. What would my pallans of Vallia say to this debacle? What would Jaidur say, new King of Hyrklana and awaiting the signal? Had I been a wizard or magician with the power of invisibility or teleportation I'd have been in better case and would have thrown off those ferocious fellows from Arachosia. As it was, I had to twist and turn among the crags and gradually pull ahead, outdistancing the pursuit, and throwing myself miles off course.

By the time I'd lost them the decision had to be made.

If I hung around I'd be late reporting back. Under the strict laws of Hamal, which extended even more stringently into the armed forces, there would be an appropriate paragraph and sub-section dealing with my offense. Well, then, to hell with Hamalian rules and regulations. I had to see my friends here.

The decision was made and acted on and Mathdi hurtled back, keeping low, fairly skipping over the mountains and sliding down into the narrow valleys. We came around in a wide circle and headed north again. Selecting a likely-looking clump of trees below and landing the voller was easy enough; then I had to inch her in gingerly under the trees. There was still plenty of daylight left. The leaves rustled overhead and as Mathdi settled the sounds of the forest dwellers reached me. That was heartening.

Moving out of the trees I finished clasping up the short red cape. That had been stowed very secretly, for obvious reasons, and I just hoped it would be enough to stop some overzealous swod loosing into me at first sight. The path ahead led to an encampment of many tents and cooking fires and totrix lines. Not many zorcas, though. I strode on briskly, cursing this waste of time, and knowing that to land a Hamalian voller into the little lot ahead would be like leaping into the jaws of a shark. Even my flags would not have sufficed, I judged, for it was my guess the Air Service people here would know every airboat they owned. Any stranger would be an enemy.

The camp was deserted of fighting men, properly so, as they were all besieging the city of Ingleslad. A few servants moved about and meals were being prepared. The most likely-looking mount was a freymul, the poor man's zorca, and I simply unhitched him from the post outside a tent, mounted up and galloped off. An angry shout floated after me. I did not look back.

Despite that first appalled glance when the sky had seemed filled with aerial combat, the truth was that for a siege of this scale there were precious few flyers and even fewer fliers. I was not molested from the air as I rode on toward the lines. A steady trickle of wounded passed going back to the camp. The position of the commander was easy to ascertain and I guided the freymul toward the cluster of tents well out of catapult range. Beyond them the town burned and the dark frantic figures of soldiers were silhouetted against the blaze. Whatever the outcome, the city of Ingleslad was doomed.

Sentries stopped me and I was polite to them, inquiring the name of the commander, dismounting with the crackle of the flames in our ears and the yells of men thin and screeching from the walls.

"Dav Olmes, Vad of Bilsley commands here."

"Oh," I said. Then, "I might have known."

"Have a care, dom, how you speak of the Vad."

"I shall, I shall. Pray, tell Vad Dav Olmes that I am here and I would have a word or three with him. Tell him my name is Jak. Mention the king korf to him, and Kazz Jikaida. I think he will see me."

The sentries, hard men in mail with spears and crossbows, stared at me. I glared at them and, Zair forgive me, that old devilish Dray Prescot look must have flashed into my face, for they turned away, shuffling, and their Deldar mumbled about at once, notor, at once. So I waited, and then instead of being conducted up the little stony path to the tent with the flags I saw a figure burst from the tent and come hurtling down on me. A great mop of fair hair blew, a round, pugnacious, cheerful face, the embrace of muscular arms, and I was being greeted as Dav Olmes greets people—overpoweringly.

"Jak! Jak you crafty leem! Here! You are welcome, for we need all the swordsmen we can lay hands on! Tell me—"

"Tsleetha-tsleethi," I said, which is to say, softly, softly. "I am overjoyed to see you, Dav. But what in the name of a Herrelldrin Hell are you doing? Who gave the orders for this attack, who ordered the invasion begun?"

He stepped back. He looked at me with a quick flush rising, his face expressing bewilderment at my tone. I had to get the protocol over, and fast, for Dav Olmes was a vad, and used to command, and a stouthearted fellow, and he knew me as just a wandering adventurer with whom he had shared some fraught moments.

"The council—" he began. "By Spag the Junc! They told—"

"I am glad to see they gave you a command, Dav. I did not know you were here. Tell me, when do you anticipate taking the city?"

At this fresh line he brightened up. "Havandua the Green Wonder has smiled. Yes, the city burns, which is a damned pity. But we'll be in before nightfall. And then—"

"And you and your army are not alone?"

"Of course not." Being Dav Olmes he was already looking around for a stoup of ale, and a servant hurried up with a tray loaded with best quality goblets and best quality ale. We drank, and Dav said, "Konec commands against Felsheim, and—"

I interrupted. If Vad Dav Olmes grew prickly over a mere paktun—even a hyr-paktun—treating him so cavalierly I might be in for a ticklish moment or two. But Dav was a good-natured fellow and shrewd with it, so that he listened, for all his happy bellowings. I said, "So the general invasion has begun. The nations of the Dawn Lands have risen against Hamal. So be it. You are premature—"

"I know! But we could not wait for signals from parts so distant as Vallia and Hyrklana and Pandahem! Jak, we waited and the men grew restless, so we marched." He gestured with his goblet. "And we are damned short of air, too."

"The Hamalese are short, also."

"Bad cess to 'em, by Spag the Junc!"

We talked on, and I inquired after old friends, Fropo and Bevon the Brukaj and others. Some were dead. Well, that is a fact of life on Kregen, as anywhere else. The shortage of vollers was worrying, and the armies assembled for the invasion would mostly march on their feet all the livelong way to Ruathytu. The legions were on the move, the standards leading on.

"Bevon," I said. "I would like to have seen him; but I cannot tarry."

"He'll be through the walls before the suns go down. You were always a mysterious fellow, Jak, damned mysterious. Will you tell me—?"

"Yes—but not now. I am merely a part of all this." This was true. "When the King of Hyrklana starts, he will sort out the Hamalese. I pray you are not overwhelmed first."

"We understood the risks when the council ordered us to march."

"I am keeping my temper, Dav, in a wonderful way." I kept my face impassive, for I felt like bursting out with a really wild impassioned denunciation of the council of the Dawn Lands. "The risk to your forces you accept. All very good. But if you imperil the invasion plan, what of the risk to the other lives involved? Hyrklana? Vallia?"

"We have heard there is a new king in Hyrklana. As for Vallia, well, their emperor, this Dray Prescot, we hear is so wild and savage a leem he could chew a harness of armor and spit out the rivets."

"He would," I said. "And who could blame him?"

After a pause, Dav said, "Will you stay with me and help?"

"I would like to. But I have a duty that presses on me."

"And you will not tell me what that is?"

"As I have said, I will. Later." I eyed him. He was a stout fighter, we had fought in Kazz-Jikaida, which is a bloody game on Kregen. "If I asked for Bevon the Brukaj, you could not spare him?"

He looked taken aback. "Well, Jak—"

"Very well, Dav. I understand. Then spare me six lusty fellows, and let Deldar Jorg the Fist command them."

"I am not overly endowed with men; but six." He laughed, that roaring laugh of Dav Olmes that echoes and fills the world wherever he happens to be. "Deldar Jorg and five of the best, then. But take care of 'em, Jak, take care."

"I will." It was a promise. "And I give you thanks."

At that point a Hikdar in the supply train came clattering up awkwardly riding a calsany, swearing and shaking his fists. He was the owner of the freymul I had borrowed. Well, in sorting him out and smoothing his ruffled feathers, for he was a Rapa, the tension was broken. There was a deal of jollity as I started back with my six men, and Deldar Jorg, giving me that wolfish smile, had expressed himself of the opinion that if I was involved he was in for some fun and games.

"You are right, Jorg. And the quicker we set about them the better."

So back to Mathdi I went with the first six of her crew. I anticipated a somewhat lively time as I explained just what was afoot. A somewhat lively time...

Thirteen

Signs

The lively time began with: "Among the damned Hamalese! I'd as lief slit their throats as look at 'em!" and ended with, "It's so cunning a scheme I'll be a better Hamalese than any of 'em, as Havandua the Green Wonder bears witness!"

I sighed. Deldar Jorg the Fist and his five men clustered about me, straining their harness, their faces inflamed, breathing hard. "Havandua is not of Hamal."

"No, dom, no, that is right. I'll allow you that."

"So it will be Havil, or Krun—Dernun?"

The word dernun came out inquiringly and not insultingly, but it was hard enough, in its demand for their understanding, to make them snap up.

"Understood," said Jorg, and he winked, a fine raffish leering wink that made me turn away so that they should not see the foolish smile I could not contain. We sped for Ruathytu and the six swods rid themselves of insignia that would mark them as enemies of Hamal. Each man knew his business. I had the nucleus of a crew. That proved the straw to which I clung as the obnoxious ord-Jiktar Morthnin chewed me out. As an ord-Jiktar, eight steps up the Jiktar ladder of promotions, he stood six above me, a dwa-Jiktar. I listened to what he had to say, watching his face twitch with his own passionate anger, realizing that he was in a position which he, himself, did not think he could handle. You have to feel sorry for men in that situation, of course...

"You will be severely reprimanded, Jiktar, most severely. I shall see to it myself—"

"I have the beginnings of a crew, Jiktar Morthnin. If you wish to make any more of this, then run me up before the Chuktar. He'll chew you out for wasting his time. I have a full month of the Maiden with the Many Smiles. Only then will you have anything to say to me—now let me get on with seeing to my command."

His face approached in color a plum left too long in the light of the suns. He gobbled.

I marched off, giving him no time to spit out the retort he was frenziedly attempting to put into words.

Not pretty. He was a Hamalese, so that made it a little more bearable for me...

At the time, I must emphasize, at the time only. We had to get together with the people of Hamal to resist the damned Shanks raiding from over the curve of the world. But, first things first.

The premature invasion of Hamal from the south created a whole new slew of problems, for the Hamalese no less than for the allies. The tempo of life increased and the feeling of being at the heart of world affairs broadened. Ruathytu became even more a city of contrasts, as the seriousness of the situation was brought home by the open comings and goings with the wind of fleets of famblehoys. The swift vollers plied their routes through the skies, and the famblehoys bumbled along as best they could. I took more than a few moments of amusement from the unhandiness of the Hamalese sky sailors.

Many of the fresh troops were bundled off down south and the officers of the garrisons left and the training barracks were of the opinion that many of the regiments being sent to the front were not yet ready. I listened. During these days I learned a great deal. The Empress Thyllis kept herself closeted more and more, not seeing her pallans, going with her favorites to any of the secluded and secret villas she kept up in various parts of the country. The streets of Ruathytu resounded to the tramp of marching men as units were called in to be dispatched south.

All the same, as I went about collecting a crew, I heard what Vad Homath had to say. He was bashing his Nineteenth Army into shape with a frenzy that reflected the urgency he, at least, saw in the situation.

"I am going to Hyrklana and take them apart, the cramphs, even if the whole Dawn Lands rise against us."

Someone in the crowded tavern where we talked and argued and drank was foolhardy enough to say, "Is that wise?"

Homath's scar flamed. "Wise! Onker! They invade from the south to weaken us here and in the east." He looked savage. "As for the north, the Hyr Notor will have to handle that. He has powers ordinary men know nothing of, by Krun!"

He was talking of the great devil, Phu-Si-Yantong, and he was right, uncomfortably right. Our own Wizards of Loh would have to meet and front the deviltry of Phu-Si-Yantong.

"Where do you intend to hit the Hyrklese, notor?" I spoke casually, lifting a goblet. "Neck, belly or groin?"

He was filled with his own anger at what was going on and the stupidity of others, and so was a little off guard. He knew what he was going to do. "I shall go for the belly. A straight drop on Huringa. That will settle the whole issue in a day."

"Excellent, notor," I said, and sat back, and drank.

The incautious fellow—he was an under-pallan at the treasury or something similar, I believe—piped up again. "There are other armies involved, Homath. Their Kapts will—"

Homath left off stroking his scar. He bristled. "I have been given the mangy Nineteenth but I remain in command of the force! Don't forget that. Kapts Hindimun and Naghan and Lart will obey my orders or their armies will be commanded by fresh faces. Believe me."

The foolhardy under-pallan drew a breath, and sat back, and took refuge in his wine. Homath, hard professional as he was, had clearly been severely shaken by what the Hamalese considered the treacherous attack from the Dawn Lands. Useless to rage, myself, thinking of the marvelous opportunity we had missed. Had Hyrklana and Vallia struck, and then the allies from the Dawn Lands... But we had to work with the tools fates placed in our hands.

"I shall clear the whole of Hyrklana in three months. I shall return with all the vollers they have. It will be up to the armies of the south to hold these yetches from the Dawn Lands." Homath drank, fiercely, and banged his glass down. "Maintain the aim, that is what we must do and pin our hopes on Havil and the soundness of our military doctrine."

The others gathered around the Kapt in the tavern agreed in their various styles. They were confident, and had every right to be, for the soundness of the Hamalian military thinking had been proved time and again on battlefields and in sieges where their organization, skill and courage had crowned their standards with victory.

I stood up to make my excuses, for I intended to leave early on the morrow. "My felicitations for success in Hyrklana," I said, which was, considering all things, sneaky enough.

Homath was talking to a Chulik Chuktar and he half turned to acknowledge my departure. He had no need to, of course. I saluted and threw a few respectful remberees to others in the company I had come to know. Now an interesting reversal, almost a revulsion, of feeling had possessed the people of Ruathytu when news came in of the invasion. Diffs were now, suddenly, welcomed again. My own view was that the apim nobles of Hamal had been growing restive at the increasing number of diff nobles; certainly the fighting men considered diff or apim or whatever only from the prowess, the skill and courage that a racial stock would confer. Whatever the reasons, diffs now moved about much more freely and were once more a splendid part of the magnificent spectacle of Kregan life.

The Chulik Chuktar was saying, "Prisoners confirm that this evil cult of Spikatur Hunting Sword is behind the invasion."

Homath grunted. Pausing, I waited a moment, standing at the end of the table and with the back of the incautious under-pallan off my starboard wing, listening.

"You were unable to get any more, Chuktar Rarbonatch? No, these fellows of Spikatur chop themselves. I know."

"By Likshu the Treacherous, notor! You are right. But we confirmed they have no leaders."

"Or will not admit to them."

The Chulik polished up his starboard tusk, the one with the ruby inset beneath the gold band. "Our security Jiktar believed it, notor. Although it is difficult to understand."

Chuliks are trained from birth to handle weapons and serve as mercenaries, and know little of humanity; but they do understand chains of command. That warriors would fight without due heed of officers to command them puzzled the Chulik.

He pulled a piece of paper from his wallet and passed it across to Homath, who looked, made a disgusted sound and threw the paper onto the table. It showed in simple black-ink lines the outline of a sword piercing a heart.

"These signs appear everywhere, notor," said Chuktar Rarbonatch. "Painted on doors, chalked on walls. We remove them; but they reappear."

"Remove the sign-writers!" shouted Chuktar Thrend, and the company indicated they shared that opinion. It was time for me to leave. As I left the tavern the sign above the door creaked. The wooden slat was painted in vivid colors, greens and blues and yellows, showing a leem being shot by crossbow bolts. I had thought that Spikatur Hunting Sword would turn out to be a grand conspiracy directed against Hamal and of material assistance to our plans. Well, I was half right and half wrong. By Zair, yes!

The secret adherents of Spikatur might want to get at the Hamalese; but they had, by prodding the allies from the Dawn Lands into a premature attack, materially hampered our plans.

And then, as I went back to the barracks in a not-too-happy frame of mind, there on a wall the chalked sign of the sword piercing the heart gave me heart, reminding me that we did not struggle against this puissant Empire of Hamal alone.

I decided the early start was going to be considerably earlier than anyone expected. Rousing out my lads I told Jorg to get Mathdi ready for a long flight. Then I went to see Chuktar Fydur ham Thorfrann, not giving a damn for poor old ord-Jiktar Morthnin and protocol. Chuktar Thorfrann at least knew his job, being a choleric, stout, astute sky-commander, having charge of a wing of twelve vollers. He was bucking for promotion to command one of the awe-inspiring Hamalian skyships. He woke up rubbing his eyes and cursing me.

"I am leaving for a longish flight, Chuk—and I don't want that idiot Morthnin doing himself an injury worrying about me. If we can recruit diffs again, then I can fill my crew."

"Why do I put up with you, Jak the Insufferable! By Havil the Green! All right! Go and get your crew. But if you're not back here on time—"

"I shall be, Chuk."

It was all both a laugh and petty at the same time. I was tempted to wing off at once, take Mathdi to join forces with my friends, and so join in with the invasion. But I could serve much more important ends by remaining within the Air Service of Hamal. And, also, in my treatment of Morthnin and my toadying to ham Thorfrann, I writhed in remembered indignation and resentment at other days, when I had suffered from puffed-up nincompoops with Influence. Thorfrann allowed me a long leash because of my friendship with Prince Tyfar and Prince Nedfar. I remember, I made myself a promise to make amends to poor old ord-Jiktar Morthnin, if I could.

"You think you know where you can pick up crewmen, Jak?"

"I'm hopeful." I sounded cautious.

"Well, if you can find a few extra—the Wing needs men to fill out the crews. We're in for the big one, if I'm not mistaken."

"You mean—we'll go south?"

He laughed, purple, apoplectic, spluttering. "No, Jak, you fambly! Not those pathetic fools from the Dawn Lands."

"Hyrklana, then? But Kapt Homath said nothing—"

Again that taint of Influence. That I, a mere dwa-Jiktar, could talk and even drink on easy terms with a vad and a Kapt must have annoyed Chuktar ham Thorfrann. But he just wheezed again, and said: "Vallia!" and laughed, and threw me out.

Of only one thing could I be reasonably sure—about that. I did not think Hamal could possibly put another onslaught onto Vallia, my homeland, together with all the problems she had from south and east and in Pandahem. If I was wrong... No, confound it! By the Black Chunkrah! I said to myself. Maintain the aim, that was what Homath had said, quoting sage military doctrine, and that was what I would do. If ham Thorfrann had reason to believe Vallia was a target, he must be talking about the Hamalese reinforcements for Pandahem. He had to be.

Jorg had Mathdi ready and we took off at once.

I'd appointed Jorg the Fist as ship-Deldar, which post just about equates with the responsible position of boatswain on Earth. If the ship fell to pieces, Jorg would be the one to make inquiries of...

We set off eastwards. I fancied my lad Jaidur, who was King of Hyrklana, would be vastly interested in what Kapt Homath had had to say in The Bolted Leem tavern. Vastly.

Fourteen

"Zair does will it!"

Jaidur was now king in Hyrklana, with Lildra, the queen, radiant at his side. It was therefore very necessary to be circumspect, cautious, civil— even ceremonious—in tackling that young tearaway. And, of course, even the youngest of right tearaways grows up in time. Jaidur, my youngest lad, had unmistakably grown in stature and in wisdom. For all that he was still as sharp and cutting as ever as Mathdi alighted with the swarm of patrolling flyers surrounding her.

We landed sweetly enough on a platform of the High Hakal, the fortress and palaces of Huringa. Flags flew and trumpets pealed, and there was a plethora of gold and gems ablaze in the light of the suns.

The Lahals rang out. Jaidur and Lildra waited for me. I was conscious that I had left this place borne by the magical powers of the Star Lords, leaving Delia, leaving all that I loved. Now, in returning by mere mortal airboat, I was not in any real sense completing a circle.

There was no time to waste. I did not intend to shilly-shally here with protocol and tiresome formalities. I told Jaidur what lay in store for Huringa, capital of Hyrklana, and added: "Your invasion of Hamal is still vital. Even more so; but—"

"But can you expect me to leave Huringa unprotected?"

"No. But I have forewarned you. You know this Kapt Homath is bringing four armies against you. Therefore you deal with them with your Home Forces. Jaidur—you must invade Hamal. The plan calls for it."

"The plan—well, I was not king in Hyrklana when that plan was forged."

Lildra, smiling, placatory, knowing how much Jaidur had had to put up with an absentee father in the past, and, too, I feel sure, remembering how it had rained when I'd taken her out of the Castle of Afferatu, intervened.

"Hyrklana has been almost untouched by the wars. There are many brave fighting men, Jaidur. You know that."

"I know it." His brows made a bar above his nose. "My scouts reported a swarm of those devilish ships of the Shanks sailing north. They keep well away from the coast. But it could be they seek to lull us. Should they reverse course and strike Hyrklana... do I need to spell it out, father?"

"Shanks. There were many of them?"

"More than any man can remember having seen in one fleet before."

"Then that is all the more reason for the invasion plan. We have to make Hamal and all the countries of Paz understand they must stand together against these confounded Shanks."

"That is surely a dream—"

"No!"

Lildra, with a laugh more nervous than any of us liked, said: "Cannot we talk to the Empress Thyllis? Surely diplomacy will make her understand?"

"She's a she-leem," said Jaidur.

"I would try diplomacy," I said, somewhat heavily. "But you tend to be stabbed in the back after you make treaties and arrangements. I know. I think Hamal will listen more readily to sensible proposals when an allied army is camped in Ruathytu." I tried to clear my frown away, and could not. "But I do not like it, by Vox. I would to Zair there was no need for wars!"

"Well, father, there is and we are in one, whether we like it or not." Jaidur motioned the hovering servants with their silver trays of refreshments to approach. "You will eat and drink? For I see you are, as ever, anxious to be gone."

"I am going to Vallia. I shall convey your love and respect to your mother—if she's in Valka or Vondium. Now, Jaidur—Vax Neemusbane— will you send that army to invade?"

He nodded. I'd known him as Vax before he knew I was his father. "Yes. Rely on me. If I cannot lead the army myself, I shall send the best men I have."

"Thank Zair! And I need twenty-five men from you for my ship. Men who can carry off a deception—I know their names."

He laughed. "Norhan the Flame and Frandu the Franch, I suppose—"

"If they are available and willing. I suppose no one has run across that numim, Mazdo the Splandu? No?" as they shook their heads. "Well, I have the feeling he will turn up again."

"You are welcome to them, a pair of know-it-all rogues."

"Then the next time we meet will be in Ruathytu."

He looked grave, the laughter lines flown. "If Zair wills it."

I glared at him. I felt young and impetuous and to hell with gravity and long faces, despite all the difficulties and dangers ahead. The dip in the magical Pool of Baptism in far Aphrasöe had kept me young, physically certainly and, I trusted sincerely and with fervor, mentally as well. So I spoke with an energy that made Lildra glance up quickly.

"Zair does will it, Jaidur! And, in truth, so do Havil and Havandua and Djan and any other godhead you can imagine, save those few bloody-minded warrior gods among whom Djan is not numbered. The people of Paz may believe in and worship any number of different deities; they are all united against whatever Fish-headed demons rule the Leem-loving Shanks who raid us all indifferently."

"I believe you, father. By Vox! You are touchy—"

Almost, almost, I said, "You'd be touchy if you had my problems." But I did not and stilled my tongue.

During the alfresco lunch we discussed in more detail just how the Hamalian onslaught on Huringa might best be met, and I flatter myself I was extraordinarily tactful in giving Jaidur advice. Anyway, he was a Krozair of Zy which, although the Krozairs are doughty fighters, does not automatically turn a Krozair Brother into a strategist. It does give a fellow more than an inkling of military matters. The Krozairs, martial and mystic, an order to which I am devoted, for all their disciplines and skills do not concern themselves overmuch with the problems of aerial warfare.

"And it is in the air lies the key!" said Lildra.

"Yes." Jaidur swallowed his mouthful. "Did the news come in yet of the raids on the voller production centers?"

I shook my head. "I've received no intelligence. But the raids must have done some good, for production of the silver boxes is causing the damned Hamalese severe headaches."

"And their flying sailers, these famblehoys. They really are inferior to our vorlcas?"

"Only in the sail plan and in the handling. If you have the opportunity of capturing any, do so, by all means. Vallian shipmasters can soon make respectable sailers out of them."

"H'm," he said, and took another huge bite, and chewed, and Lildra, looking brilliant, drank her parclear off. I sat back and pondered how it was the Good Lord delivered to us children of so diverse a nature. Still, that conundrum makes two worlds go round, surely...

The twenty-five men I asked for arrived, carrying their possessions in bundles tied to sticks, ready for anything.

I eyed Norhan the Flame sternly. His shock hair had been cut and trimmed, so that he looked most odd to me, who was used to seeing him fighting in the Arena with his hair mass about him. But he still possessed that knowing twist to his lips and that remarkably evil fishy eye. Next to him, Frandu the Franch exhibited all the symptoms of intense pleasure open to a Fristle, and so I guessed they'd been arguing as usual.

"Norhan," I said, "you will be very careful with any pots of combustibles you happen to have about your person."

"They will find useful employment on the decks of Hamalians."

The fact that these stout fighting men must act the part of Hamalese was spelled out for them. Frandu riffled his whiskers. "We're too smart for them! By Numi-Hyrjiv the Golden Splendor, we'll run rings around them!"

So, with an augmented crew and the remberees ringing high, we took off for Valka and Vallia.

At this time a certain number of locations on Kregen were, for all that the planet remained marvelous and evocative wherever I happened to be, of special importance. Strombor, Djanduin, Valka. And, yes, it would be totally dishonest to exclude Paline Valley from this number. Strombor, the city enclave of Zenicce, of which I was lord, was located on the west coast of the continent of Segesthes and was for all practical purposes out of the conflict centered on Hamal. Djanduin, peopled by ferocious four-armed Djangs and clever gerbil-faced two-armed Djangs, lay in the far southwest of Havilfar and would most certainly be embroiled in the war. I am King of Djanduin. But—Valka. Ah, Valka! That beautiful island off the east coast of Vallia means so very much—the people there Fetched me to be their strom, and Delia and I had made a wonderfully happy home in the high fortress of Esser Rarioch overlooking Valkanium and the bay.

To Valkanium and Esser Rarioch I flew in Mathdi.

The journey time was occupied in beginning the organization of the increased crew nucleus and of drawing up a provisional watch list. The man I wanted for ship-Hikdar, equivalent to the First Lieutenant, Bonnu Varander ti Valkor, might not be available. Here lay one of the ever-present problems of selecting men for command; you give them a job and they do it well and you have to weigh up the advantages of shifting them around against the disadvantages. Anyway, Bonnu could handle a voller with superb efficiency and a panache I think peculiar to Valkans. But then, I am prejudiced.

Most of the men—many of whom you have met in my narrative—with whom I had fought and worked earlier were now fully occupied. Certainly, if Drak could spare a few I'd take members of the emperor's guards, and agonize over the choices.

Valka swam up out of the shimmering sea in a haze of blue and a rising tide of happy nostalgia. Useless to repeat ecstatic descriptions of the island. Superb, simply superb, Valka, and my home of Esser Rarioch the jewel in the crown.

Because dear old creaky Mathdi was so clearly Hamalian in origin I ran up the flags Jaidur had given me. The Hamalese, in the days when they built and sold vollers, usually manufactured those for themselves to different designs from those for export. Mathdi was aggressively Hamalian. The brave flutter of red and yellow and red and white flags from her staffs should at least cause the Valkan patrols to think again before shooting us to pieces.

However, it was a Deldar I knew, astride his flutduin, the powerful bird docile to his commands, lethal to foes, who landed on Mathdi's deck and leaped off his saddle-flyer. He was beaming from ear to ear, bearded, girded with weapons, muscled, alert, a fighter who would never cry quarter—in short, your typical Valkan.

"Strom!" he bellowed. "Lahal and Lahal!"

"Lahal, Virko, you great rascal. It is good to see you." His patrol flew circles about us, watchfully, as per standing orders. "Come and drink a stoup. And tell me all the news."

"Quidang, strom!"

I believe even those fighting rogues I had brought from Hyrklana and the Dawn Lands took notice of Deldar Virko the Chunkrah, impressed despite themselves.

The news was almost uniformly good. That made a pleasant change, by Vox! But I interrupted Deldar Virko to say, "Now hear me, Virko. You called me strom, which—"

I stopped speaking at sight of his powerful face which crumpled as though in anticipation of unjustified punishment.

I cursed myself. My Valkans called me strom instead of majister because to them I was their strom first, and the emperor a long place after. This was acceptable, more—it gave me a fine warm feeling. But this was not the cause of my words. I started over.

"You did right to call me strom, Virko." He brightened and tugged his beard, listening hard. "In fact, you have given me an idea. I do not want these fellows with me—fine fighting lads—to know I am the Emperor of Vallia."

Virko nodded sagely. I went on, "If it is to be strom, it cannot be Strom of Valka, for folk know he is Emperor of Vallia also. There is that pretty little island with the wild gregarians, you know it, Virko—Thydun—I fancy I'll have to be called Strom Jak of Thydun for a bit."

"Quidang!" rapped Virko. "The word will be passed."

He was bursting with the importance he attached to this mild example of skullduggery and was as excited by it as though winging down into a fight. Anyway, Thydun was a simple enough name, and fitted well enough. He went on with the news and as I listened I realized that it might be better if instead of going to Vondium, capital of Vallia, as I had planned, I sent for the people I wanted. That would keep the operation within bounds, tidy. Also, I would get back to Hamal considerably faster.

Turko had just about reclaimed his kovnate, both the Blue and Black Hills of Central Western Vallia were cleared, and the lines between us and the recalcitrants to the north had stabilized. Now, as you know, that last was not to my liking. But in the present circumstances when we needed to bring every fighting man against Hamal, firm frontiers, even if temporary, were far better than fighting campaigns up there. Virko flew off to pass my immediate orders by word of mouth, and I settled down to write orders that would summon the folk I needed, to redistribute some of the forces and—and set the Host of Vallia in motion.

Only one man stood in my mind to lead the Vallians.

To Seg I wrote, in part: "As the allies from the Dawn Lands have moved ahead of time you must move decisively and fast. Get the forces in motion and keep either Deb-Lu-Quienyin or Khe-Hi-Bjanching at your side always to contact me. As soon as I can discover the deployment plans of the Hamalese, the Wizards of Loh will inform you." I went on into more detail, but I knew that Seg Segutorio, who traditionally commanded the vaward of the armies of Vallia, would not fail.

Seg Segutorio, Master Bowman of Loh, from Erthyrdrin—the finest comrade any man could ever find on two worlds, by Zair!

To my own bitter disappointment in order to maintain the cover name of Strom Jak na Thydun, I did not land at Esser Rarioch in Valkanium. We bypassed Valka and touched down on Thydun, a pretty little island, as I had said, filled with suns shine and ripening fruit and simple folk whose villages were models of tidiness and charm. Here we watered and Deldar Virko, appointed into the temporary capacity as chief of merkers, kept me informed. Merkers, aerial messengers, usually fly fluttcleppers or volclep-pers; but Virko handled his duties well. Fast airboats trafficked between Valkanium and Thydun, and I waited and kicked my heels, and presently Mathdi began to fill up with the bronzed keen faces and tough bodies of the men I needed.

Each one was now given a double task of deception. He was to call me Strom Jak, and he was to act the part of a Hamalese.

By Krun! I can tell you these doughty fighters joyed in these games of skullduggery!

In any event, I crammed a hundred and ten souls into Mathdi. Plans for their employment filled an idle hour with dark schemes. I will not detail their names. Each one was accounted a kampeon, a veteran of the army or Air Service, and many were hyr-paktuns returned to their homeland to fight for Vallia. As soon as we were all aboard, Mathdi lifted up and away from Thydun, and we dropped the blue haze of Valka astern of us. We flew on over the sea, heading south, heading for Hamal and our foes and for perils and adventures that would, if the light of Opaz shone upon us, bring us the victory.

Fifteen

Of the Power of Hamal

The conceit of our enterprise filled the swods with unholy glee. Or, given the feelings we had of a great crusade, perhaps it would be correct to say holy joy. We were bringing a Hamalian Air Service vessel to join with the Hamalese, and she was stuffed with Vallians and Hyrklese and men from the Dawn Lands, foes of Hamal! As I say, the conceit charmed us all.

414

We maintained a strict discipline from the very start, doing everything by the Hamalian book, which Chuktar Fydur ham Thorfrann, our wing commander, had made sure I thoroughly understood. There were hitches, of course. Much laughter boomed and rang about Mathdi as some wight forgot he was no longer a Vallian and started cursing away and bellowing "By Vox!" until he was reminded that "By Krun!" was now de rigueur. There were surprisingly few fights between the contingents, and protocol was quickly settled as the watch list was promulgated and men knew the jobs they were expected to fill.

Among the intelligence I had received had come news that Drak was about to relinquish command of the forces arrayed against the rebels in the southwest and return to Vondium. The insurrection down there looked to be quashed. If he intended to lead the Vallian armies in the coming invasion, I would have to think very carefully. In all probability, although not liking the solution, I would instigate two separate invasion columns, giving one to Seg and one to Drak. That way, at least, we'd make the Hamalese split their forces yet again.

Vast distances across Kregen may be covered in a voller, and, conversely, if you are down on your own two feet those distances stretch to enormous proportions. It was mighty comforting to know I had a voller which would not almost inevitably break down.

We gave the island of Pandahem a wide berth. The lord of the countries there groaning under his evil dictatorship was Phu-Si-Yantong, and I knew he would not sit tamely and do nothing while the invasion struck at Hamal. We had to be quick, damned quick!

The ship-Hikdar, Bonnu, came up to me and said, "I'd like to paint over that damage in the larboard beam, maji—strom. It detracts from the look of the ship."

I beamed on Bonnu ti Valkor. If an observer might recently have decided I'd been far more interested in my new voller Mathdi than in the invasion, he could be forgiven. He'd have been wrong, but understandably so. I fancy Bonnu was more concerned about Mathdi than about anything else. Well, and so he should be, as any first lieutenant should, until the action began.

I shook my head. "Leave the dint there, Bonnu. It makes the ship look older and more fragile than she is. Camouflage."

He didn't like the idea.

"I'm used to running a taut ship—"

"Of course. That's why I asked for you."

He stared. "Asked, maji—strom? You have merely to give the orders and men obey."

"It's not," I said with something of a grunt, "always like that."

The ramshackle empire the people of Vallia had asked me to save for them was now much more healthy. But, all the same, I still didn't take kindly to despotic overlordship, having suffered from nastiness of that kind for much of my life. Had the Lord Farris, commanding the Vallian Air Service, told me Bonnu was tied up, I'd have accepted that, and gone for Hikdar Vinko the Shrewd. He was running the second largest skyship we possessed. The largest was run by Hikdar Naghan Erdmor, and I did not wish to deprive him of that task. So I said, "You have to compromise when you run an empire, unlike running a ship, Bonnu."

"Yes, strom."

"Although," I added, "arranging watches and selecting men and deciding on tasks is not simply a matter of giving orders, is it now?"

"We-ell—"

And we both smiled as Mathdi bore on through the level air.

"You must keep on at the men in their deception as Hamalese, Bonnu. We cannot risk a slip-up jeopardizing the enterprise."

"Many of them have been mercenaries, as you know, strom. And the Hamalese are accustomed to strangers serving them. Even renegade Vallians, may Opaz frown upon their misdeeds."

This was perfectly true. There were men from many nations and races serving with the Hamalian forces, and strange oaths and customs were accepted.

As it turned out, the crew of Mathdi integrated easily enough with the crews of the other eleven vollers in Thorfrann's wing. I'd warned them about the obnoxious ord-Jiktar Morthnin, and our lads were wary of that one. Chuktar ham Thorfrann greeted me with open surprise at the crew and the mettle of them, and with news that was not only unwelcome, news that was a bombshell of disaster for my plans.

"I don't believe it, Chuk!" I said. I know I must have looked wild.

"It is true, Jak, and there is nothing we can do about it."

"But we have to fight the invasion! Those cramphs from the Dawn Lands are marching on Ruathytu! We can't go flying off to the west and leave the action!"

"Our orders are just that. We have to reinforce the air arm tangling with the wild men over on the Mountains of the West and those are our orders and must be obeyed."

I fumed. What a debacle! I'd already refused to go to the west with Tyfar, and had got out of that through friendship. Now I was under orders to go. If I refused I'd be deprived of command and Mathdi would be given to another captain. And with her, her crew... Her very special crew...

The voller yards at Urnmayern, just outside the city to the north, resounded to the noise of vessels being given last-minute attention and with the preparations for early departure. Provisions were being loaded, and ammunition was trundling up the ramps into the fliers. We'd water last, and then we'd be off.

"Look, Jak." Chuktar ham Thorfrann's apoplectic face betrayed resignation. "You're in an odd position. You are a Jiktar commanding a single voller, an unusual situation. Yet look at the wing I command. Mathdi is old and creaky; yet she is as good as most of the wing. The truth is, we are tantamount to a second-line formation. We are what the Air Service can scrape up to send against the wild men and the raids on the voller plants. You have to accept that. We'd be massacred if we went up against the vollers of Hyrklana."

"Mathdi would give an account—" I started to bluster.

He shook his head, that acceptance of his position forced on him and to be obeyed according to the laws of Hamal. "Oh, you'd fight. And you have found yourself a hell of a crew. Just how you'd have done that I don't know. But do not delude yourself."

"Hamal has to throw everything against the invasions—"

"Everything except an army and its air to stem the stab in the back. Our task is vital. If the wild men are allowed to break in—do you know the geography out there? Where the volgendrins are?"

"A little—"

"It's a big country. If the raiders can stop production of the contents of the silver boxes—" He eyed me. Hamal kept information strictly secret on the details of production of the silver boxes. They were crucial, which was why we'd sent off raids against the centers. We'd done a great deal, and Hamal's voller fleets were reduced as a consequence. And now I was to fly off to try to stop my own people! Ludicrous? Not really, funny, yes. Damned inconvenient, of a certainty.

"Well," went on Thorfrann. "Best not to know too much about the silver boxes. We use them to power our fliers, and that is all we need know. Our task is to safeguard their production."

The dilemma facing me was a moral as well as a strategic one. Political considerations weighed, too. Where would I best serve the interests of Vallia and the alliance?

In my frustrated impatience it appeared to me some malignant fate insisted on dragging me away from the invasions over to the Mountains of the West. The decision not to take command of any individual column advancing into Hamal had been arrived at some time ago, my decision being to keep a free hand. The idea had been to keep a watching brief on the progress of the different armies. Stuck out over in the far west would allow me little freedom of movement. So, I fumed.

As a result I spoke a trifle warmly. "You told me we were due for the big one, against Vallia—"

He brisked up, prickling. "Not so! I happened to mention the name Vallia." He wheezed around in his fiery way and then, because he was a true horter, he shouted: "Yes, yes, Jak the Insufferable! I thought we were going to teach those cramphs of Vallese a lesson. But I am disappointed. Our wing has been detached from the expedition; Chuk ham Gorthnil is going instead."

At that point it was vitally necessary for me to keep a civil tongue and to make my face conceal the volcanic spate of rage that shook me. I put my left hand on my sword hilt and gripped so that it hurt. Somehow, from some small stock of common sense I possess, I managed to say, "A great pity, a great pity. We could have done a deal of mischief against the Vallese. When does the expedition leave?"

"The same time as we leave for the west. Now clear out, Jak. I have work to do—I'm not just a voller captain with nothing to do—that ship-Hikdar you have is a smart one."

"A smart one," I repeated like a lunatic parrot. Somehow I saluted and took myself off. This news was devastating—our onslaught on Hamal was akin to poking a hornet's nest with a stick. Thyllis's empire might be fighting on more than one front, they might be forced to send squadrons and armies east and south, and find men for the west—now they had the strength to dispatch an expedition north. I tell you, at that moment as I walked out into the clamor of the voller berths, I felt a chill sweat start at this fresh realization of the horrible power of Hamal.

The vital need now was to discover the composition of the forces flying against Vallia, their point of onslaught and their plans. When we flew west, they would be flying north.

The hornet's nest was buzzing with furious energy and venom.

The Hamalian high command knew exactly what it was doing. These days what the planners had contrived would be called a preemptive strike. They'd hit Hyrklana and Vallia, force them back on the defensive, make them think twice before committing forces to the invasion in support of the allies from the south.

I made the round of the taverns and inns of the Sacred Quarter. The Bolted Leem, the Thraxter and Voller, the Ruby Prychan and the Diamond Lily drew blanks. I needed to talk to Prince Nedfar and his entourage. He would know. If he was in the Golden Zhantil, I believe I'd have forced my way in. As it was, I ran him to ground in the Bolt and Quarrel. He was sitting with his friends, drinking and laughing, and everyone was in high good spirits, so that I guessed they were all due to fly off very very soon.

I made myself smile.

If any unpleasantness had to be employed, I was perfectly clear in my mind that nothing short of absolute necessity could make me lift a hand against Nedfar. And was not an attack on Vallia an example of the absolute necessity? I trusted that Opaz in his infinite wisdom of the Invisible Twins would spare me that.

Because Nedfar had chosen a tavern he had heretofore not often patronized—I am sure this had something to do with the recently altered attitudes to diffs—others beside myself had difficulty in tracking him down. I guessed he wanted a little of privacy and yet would not forgo the company of good friends. As I entered and began to steer a course between packed tables, a man pushed past, urgently, shoving me out of the way. Because I was playing a part I allowed myself to be shoved.

"Immediate message for the prince!" he snapped at me as he bustled past by way of explanation and apology.

He got Nedfar's instant attention.

Just as I came up to the table, Nedfar's eager, eagle look changed. All the sparkle went out of him. He looked drained.

"Tonight?"

"Three burs ago, my prince. Heads will roll—but the mischief is done—"

The messenger wore drab clothes, with the air of a stylor and clerk about him. He was frightened, too.

Nedfar stood up.

"My friends. You must excuse me." Then he could not contain himself or the bad news. "I have just heard that my daughter, the Princess Thefi, has absconded with my aide, Lobur the Dagger."

Instantly the prince's friends started up from their chairs to express their concern and a babble of voices filled the tavern with noise. I stood back. The messenger bowed and withdrew, happy to escape. Nedfar looked haggard. He loved his daughter and was fond of his aide, but an alliance between the two had not, I surmised, occurred to him. Perhaps Tyfar and I had seen more than most—without any special aptitude on our parts. Kov Thrangulf, who was serving with a regiment of personal zorcamen in command of a division down in the Dawn Lands, had been the man chosen to wed Princess Thefi. No doubt Nedfar would send for him. As for Lobur the Dagger—he had cut adrift from friends, home and family, casting himself and Thefi into the treacherous currents of fate. I could only wish Thefi well. It was not my business.

My business was discovering all I could of the projected attack on my own homeland.

Quite useless to attempt to speak with Nedfar now. His every thought was of his daughter. I stepped back, out of the way, watching. One of the pallans at the table, speaking heatedly to the man at his side, was the Pallan of the Hammabi el Lamma, the man in charge of arrangements at the palace on its artificial island. He and Nedfar must have become acquainted in the course of Nedfar's visits to his cousin the empress.

Surrounded by his friends and with the ever-vigilant guards in attendance, Prince Nedfar left the Bolt and Quarrel. As he went the jugglers were performing on the patio, and a small booth with gaudy decorations was playing one of those silly, sly country farces the Kregans do so well, all oversized noses and stuffed pants and bludgeons and falling about. The musical accompaniment battled against the surrounding noise.

If Prince Nedfar's thoughts seethed with concern for Thefi, my thoughts boiled with apprehension for Vallia.

Now while it is not universally true to say, as so many do, that if anything in a military operation can go wrong it will, there is so much truth in the saying as to make it vital of cognizance in any planning. The multiple invasions of Hamal had been projected with just this probability in mind. If one went wrong, others would succeed. The Dawn Lands and their infernal lack of patience to strike back at the despoilers of their lands had made a nonsense of most of our planning. But some could be saved, if we could stave off the preemptive strikes against Hyrklana and Vallia.

There lay no doubt whatsoever in my mind now as to what must be done. Back at the Urnmayern voller berths I roused out a few of my rascals. They lined up on the tween decks of Mathdi, and sentries were posted. I looked at them, these cheerful cutthroats. I stared particularly at Norhan the Flame.

"I've a job for you, Norhan. And the rest of you will be advised to listen to Norhan."

They listened to me and then they listened to Norhan, and by the time the Twins rose into the night sky over Ruathytu we were prowling through the back alleys, a gang of desperadoes, and woe betide anyone who stood in our path.

They split into teams, and my last words to them as they went off were: "And if questioned you are merely disaffected volswods. You have nothing to do with Vallia. Dernun?"

"Quidang!"

So we went off about our nefarious tasks.

A night breeze blew the scents of moon blooms, and clouds scuttered across the faces of the moons. Torchlights waved their golden glow from the corners of walls. At this late hour few sounds broke the stillness of the city; but occasionally a hubbub broke distantly from the Sacred Quarter. Over there the Bladesmen still able to live it up were trying to carry on the hell-for-leather traditions in such marked contrast to the rest of the country. The clouds layered thick shadows. The voller berths were closely guarded as a result of previous attempts on the part of fanatics of Spikatur Hunting Sword and spies and saboteurs. We crept on, muffled in cloaks, to all appearances a drunken party returning home clutching our pots and jugs to us. We staggered.

Chuktar Naghan ham Gorthnil's wing of vollers, which had been selected to replace ours in the attack on Vallia, lay berthed at the Hlunub Yards. The walls reared tall and stark and anti-aerial precautions, although in our view slack, still presented problems to any onslaught from the sky. We threw ropes with grapnels and swarmed up onto the walls. Only two sentries were encountered during this phase of the proceedings, and both went to sleep peacefully enough.

In the shifting light of the moons the yards lay spread out before us. Gorthnil's vollers, all twelve of them, lay ranked and neat, according to regulations. And, in truth, they were of superior quality to Thorfrann's.

Norhan said in a slurred whisper, "They'll do nicely."

"And make it fast, O Man of the Flame!"

Like shadowy demons cloaked in a mummer's play, the saboteurs disappeared between the ranked vessels. Saboteurs, yes; but this was an act of war, distasteful though it might be. When the first tongues of flame rose, I cursed, for they broke through a hatch in the nearest ship. That voller must have been loaded with combustible stores. Before anyone could realize, she was a torch, spouting to the sky.

"Run!" I bellowed down. Now it was a race, a race between our returning lads and the guards tumbling out of the guardroom.

All the eerie darkness of the opening moves was gone. No longer were we a band of secret saboteurs; now we were a handful of fighting men. The little group with me, increasing in size as each team rejoined, drew their swords and prepared to battle on against the onrushing Hamalese guards to give our men a chance of escape.

The whole business was nip and tuck. But for that voller crammed with materials that took the flame and roared into the night sky the plan would have been perfect. Now we had to scrabble to redeem what we could. This we did in swords.

No doubt believing us to be adherents of Spikatur and therefore unwilling to be taken alive, the guards simply bored straight in to slay us all. The fight blossomed along the wall as men cursed and shouted and struggled along the narrow walkway. Dark figures pitched out into thin air, screaming. The Twins suddenly poured down their refulgent pinkish light and the battle along the wall was revealed in rose-lit clarity. We fought. Steel clashed against steel. More and more guards climbed the narrow stone steps to get at us. I glanced back over the outer edge of the wall.

"Start going down!" I shouted to the men at my side. They wanted to protest; I was rude to them, and one by one they dropped down the ropes. The last party who had fired the farthest ship now appeared, panting, and were incontinently dispatched over the wall. Soon only Norhan and I were left.

"Over with you, Norhan."

"But—"

"Go now, fambly—and—"

But he read my mind and hurled his last pot of combustibles into the mass of guards who stepped over the bodies of their comrades. In a smothering roar of flames they stumbled back. Norhan slid down his rope and, after a quick look around, I went down after him. I may say I went down smartish. Very.

We had the luck with us. By the time other guards opened the massive gates onto the Yards and ran out we had taken to our heels. All the Hamalese swods saw were disappearing shadows.

We carried our wounded with us. Two men—two good men—died of their wounds and we buried them with due honor, if secretly; but none of us had been left at the voller yards. We had put in our own preemptive strike. The men settled down as though nothing had happened. When the news of the night's attacks came in, we were all as astounded and enraged as any other good Hamalese.

Disgust dripped from Chuktar Fydur ham Thorfrann. His apoplectic face in its ripeness betrayed scorn for Chuktar Gorthnil, delight in a rival's discomfiture and desperate anger over a serious blow at the Hamalian Air Service. He stood in the little courtyard of the barrack block as I came out and he rocked back on his heels, fuming. "You've heard, Jak?"

"Aye." Then I thought of what seemed to be a clever idea. "We fought off the cramphs who tried to set your wing alight, Chuk. Praise Havil we were alert."

That furious color darkened even more. "What!"

I nodded, very serious, very dedicated. "Yes. Trouble is, they ran off and we couldn't catch them. Is it serious?"

"Serious? Are you a fambly, Jak? Of course it's serious—although, now maybe we will be sent to Vallia."

And, believe it or not, that eventuality had not occurred to me, not found a single lodgment in my thick old vosk-skull.

Sixteen

Fracas Under the Moons

The pace of life changed in Ruathytu when the invasions began and yet the impression I gained was at variance with what I—or any Vallian—would have expected of a capital city during these parlous times. The contrast between Ruathytu and Vondium when we had been besieged was most marked. Yet this was a perfectly natural and proper occurrence, for nations on Kregen no less than races react in different ways. Vallians had reacted with the joyfulness of a man coming through a painful illness and facing imminent death; death held no terrors and the task was to beat back death in the shape of the enemy and regain health and strength. That the Vallians had done that gave warning that, as a nation, they might be wrong-headed over many issues, but they possessed the spirit without which a nation is a mere collection of peoples.

In their very different way the Hamalese reacted with a stoic adherence to their purposes. It was openly acknowledged that the aggrandizement of Hamal into a continent and island-spanning empire was the dream of the Empress Thyllis and must therefore be upheld; privately more and more doubts were current. The pace quickened, yes; but fewer and fewer folk cared to lead on at the head of the columns. Those ardent spirits who did yearn to lead on found a ready acceptance within the mass of the people, for the prospects of empire brightened cupidity, and so much wealth had already stuffed the coffers that any cessation of the flow of booty could only be contemplated with horror. It remained to be seen in the contest of arms if that horror could be banished in the horrors of approaching conflict.

"When are we going to burn a few more vollers?" demanded Norhan the Flame.

"They'll never catch us," said Frandu the Franch, "for we can outsmart them with ease."

"When I say so," I said. "And your stations are filthy and you'd best get your lads on cleaning up. Hikdar Bonnu is not a man to cross in the matter of dirt and polish, believe me."

From which it was clearly evident that we had not yet left for the west or Vallia. Thorfrann told me he now believed the high command were keeping his wing in reserve. "Just in case any of those damned invaders gets too close to Ruathytu."

Being of the military, we had access to more information than civilians; but that information was sparse and unreliable. That forces had landed in Hamal everyone knew. What they were up to was obscure. The most worrying problem I now had was the lack of communication from Deb-Lu-Quienyin. Why hadn't the Wizard of Loh contacted me?

There was little more I could tell him of the plans and dispositions of the Hamalese. Everyone in Ruathytu knew the high command had devised a plan that would utterly destroy the allies. Unable to decide in my own mind if such a plan existed or was merely a sop to public opinion, I hesitated. During this period Kov Thrangulf, bluff and unhappy and conscious of his own defects, arrived in the capital. But there was no word of Lobur the Dagger or Princess Thefi. Nedfar withdrew into his shell. Once, I'd saved Lobur from falling off a roof. At the time, I'd been wearing a gray mask, and told him my name was Drax; I fancied Nedfar and Thrangulf would far prefer me to have let Lobur fall to his death, had they known of that little incident. As for Tyfar, I thought I knew him well enough to know he would not wish for Lobur's death. Tyfar was not released from command of the Twentieth Army and was battling against incursions of the wild men.

One evening I summoned ship-Hikdar Bonnu and said, "I shall be going out tonight, Bonnu. If anyone asks for me say I am sick in the guts and am not to be disturbed."

"Alone?"

"Aye, alone."

"But—"

"Alone."

He killed his frown of displeasure. He was just like all the folk of Vallia and Valka; each one considered him or herself entirely responsible for my welfare. It was warming; it had in the past proved hampering. Now I would disregard it.

To Thorfrann I said: "Chuk. I have a pain in the guts—"

He laughed. "That'll teach you to drink cheap wine, Jak! Go on, sleep it off."

So, with these precautions tidily attended to, I put on a smart uniform, all bullion and silver lace, with plenty of greenery and feathery decorations, girded up a rapier and main gauche and went off to break into the castle of Hammabi el Lamma. I had done this before, pretending to be a messenger, and this time the ploy carried me past the first guardroom. Thereafter the scheme went wrong, for although the empress was absent the place was more tightly gripped in security than ever before. Well, to cut a period of cut and thrusting short I had to evacuate smartly and came roaring out onto the jetty by the Havilthytus with a pack of rascals trying to cut me down. There was a wild scene of flickering blades and twinkling steel before I got away. Of only one thing was I thankful; all during this stupid fracas I'd managed to hang onto a face that was not my own.

By Zair, though! It was frustrating. In there, in the palace, in the map room, hung the information I needed. Somehow, I had to look at the maps and learn what plots the Hamalese were hatching to discomfit our invasions.

The next morning Thorfrann told me I looked the worse for wear, and he laughed and went purple, and I gave him a smile that would have melted iron.

When I went along to Mathdi for morning rounds Bonnu reported that a messenger had arrived. He spoke quietly, and his eyebrows shot up and down, so I knew the messenger was no Hamalese. I was right. He turned out to be Nath Winharman, one of Seg's young aides, flown in by a circuitous route from home. My people had hidden his fluttrell away. He looked tired, disheveled and yet full of fight.

"Majister—" he began.

"Shastum, Nath," says I, and then, in a lighter tone: "In Hamal Jik will do. Your news?"

"Prince Drak leaves the southwest uneasily, maji—Jik. This King of Kaldi has gone back to his mountains again." We went down to the cramped stateroom and I made Winharman sit down and take refreshment. His news was not all bad; but it was not all good. Of the many items he recited, the most important was that the Wizards of Loh were again in contention. Phu-Si-Yantong had brought great powers to bear. I sat there, feeling sick, seeing all our plans being brought to nothing. Deb-Lu struggled to overcome the enormous kharrna of Yantong, and he would do so, I was absolutely confident, in time. But time was now a commodity of which we were in short supply.

"Kov Seg is arranging a messenger system, but the journey is wearisome, and the seas—"

"I know. Seg will manage." Clearly, Seg, in command of one of the Vallian columns pushing south into Hamal, was in contact back via ships and flyers with Vallia. It was a chancy business, flying out over the sea on a saddle bird and finding a ship at her designated spot. Damned chancy. While it was important that Nath Winharman should return as soon as possible with my messages, he had to have rest. Bonnu saw to that and I settled down to write.

What I could tell Seg and Drak and my chiefs was all useful material; what I could not tell them was vital. Here I was, at the heart of our enemy's war preparations, and I could learn nothing of his plans. As a spy I might as well pack up shop and take up arms and fight at the head of our army. So I was not in a particularly agreeable mood as, the day's routine over and Nath Winharman, fed and rested and his bird cared for, took off for the first stage of his night flight, I walked down into the Sacred Quarter. It was in my mind to seek out Kov Naghan and apply for a transfer. In my eyes I was accomplishing nothing.

The truth was, and is clearly apparent, that I was in a down mood. And, in the nature of these things, chance popped up like a Jack-in-the-box. Cronies told me Kov Naghan had gone to The Rokveil's Ank. This select tavern had experienced its share of rowdy nights; but in general was quieter than most. The moment I pushed in through the low doorway and looked around the taproom I saw Prince Nedfar in close converse with Kov Thrangulf, who looked as hard and jumpy and put-upon as ever. Everyone wore casual evening clothes, loose and comfortable, and everyone wore weapons. Nedfar saw me.

"Jak! You have news?"

I shook my head. The news he wanted, hungered for, was news of his daughter Thefi. "I have heard nothing, prince."

"No one has seen or heard of them since they disappeared."

Now I have mentioned my high regard for Nedfar and yet I know I have given no proofs of great substance to support your belief in my view, as I did with Tyfar, for our adventures together with Jaezila had bound us together as comrades. Now Nedfar in these dark days bore up with a strength of character that, while not disdaining grief, held it at arm's length while his country battled against invaders. He sank back into the old blackwood chair, shaking his head, and repeating, "No one has seen or heard of them."

Thrangulf made some commonplace observation. Kov Naghan was not in the taproom, so with a polite circumlocution I asked for his whereabouts.

"Hammabi el Lamma," said Nedfar. He spoke wearily. "We spend too much of our time there these days. I feel guilty about snatching a few hours off." He glanced up. "You have business with Kov Naghan?"

"Only to seek a transfer—"

The folk who had told me Naghan would be at The Rokveil's Ank had been casually definite; if he had gone back to the palace maybe Something Was Up...

"A transfer, Jak?" Nedfar moved his glass about on the table by its base. His hands were finely shaped. "You are tired of the Air Service?"

"No. Suffocated, perhaps."

"I see." He spoke purposefully, yet the old snap and ring of command lacked the urgent energy of yesterday. "Lobur—my aide has left me, Jak. I am allowed a replacement. Would you serve as an aide?"

No hesitation at all as I said, "Wholeheartedly, prince. It is an honor—"

He smiled, interrupted and spoke shrewdly, "You left the service of my son."

"Only because he was posted away from action, prince."

"Yes, that rings true. We went through much suffering and terror down the Moder, Jak. I do not forget those times."

So, like a beautiful ripe fruit plopping into my hands, the chance at Thyllis's map room was given to me—free.

Mind you, by Zair! If I make this sound an easy decision, it was not all that easy. Moral dilemmas, they are the stuff of life, it seems, and we chart our course from rock to rock and hope to escape disasters as we blunder along. My lads crewing Mathdi must be thought of. I couldn't have that hairy crew of cutthroats rampaging around Ruathytu—or could I? Why not? The glow grew in me as I went off to arrange matters. Why not, indeed! What a riotous shambles they would make before they were all caught and tortured to death.

That could not be allowed. The dreaded Laws of Hamal would specify the exact nature of their crimes and the appropriate punishments, down to the number of turns of the rack and thumbscrews, the twists of the ank-chun, and the length of time they would be allowed to linger in torment before they were executed. No, no. That would not do. My lads in Mathdi were far too valuable for that condign fate.

Chuktar Thorfrann heaved up a sigh when I told him I was leaving, and he wished me well. If he experienced envy, he concealed it in his explosive apoplectic way. I packed my gear. The latest intelligence from the various fronts was of a steady advance of the different columns. A few battles had been fought; but no major engagements had taken place, and everyone lived in Ruathytu with the thrilling conviction that the high command had events well in hand and were waiting their time to strike.

Again I weighed the advisability of my leaving the capital and joining one of our invading armies, and again I was forced to the conclusion that my sphere of greatest advantage lay just here, where I was, and where, by Vox, I would be as soon as I gained free entry into the palace. Once into the Hammabi el Lamma as an accredited aide to Prince Nedfar, I'd be into the map room, whether allowed or not.

We held a full muster of the crew of Mathdi. Bonnu held them in their ranks as I appeared. I wore a plain gray tunic and trousers, tucked into low-cut boots. But, around my waist and looped over my left shoulder, I wore a flaunting scarlet sash.

What I had to say was short and, if you like, brutal.

Boiled down, it went thus, "You may do what you will to the cramphs of Hamalese, but you will fly this ship to Kov Seg's army, and you will not lose a man here, and you will arrive sober and in good order. Dernun?"

The shout of "Quidang!" shook the old ship. They understood me, right enough. My private feelings were that this was a tame ending to their adventure; but I could not risk their lives heedlessly, and Mathdi, old and creaky maybe, would be a capital addition to Seg's aerial forces. On that, they dismissed and I went off to the barracks to collect my gear.

The gold I'd brought from Paline Valley was holding out well, although Bluenose had been swept up by the Hamalese for their mirvol scouting forces. That thought reminded me that Nath Tolfeyr had been absent from the capital, and again I wondered if that mysterious man operated for the empress. Somehow, even then, I doubted that. Their characters would not have been compatible enough, for Thyllis was an overbearing personality so used to command as to be incapable of understanding opposition to her wishes, and Nath Tolfeyr always trod an independent path. That I had been able to keep my real if secret identity of Hamun ham Farthytu, Amak of Paline Valley, in the background without recourse to use pleased me mightily. So, as dwa-Jiktar Jak the Shot, I stepped out onto the next part of the course I had chosen.

My fingers had just gripped the handle of one of my lenken chests when a figure stepped out of the rear quarters. He wore a cloak and a muffling scarf, and he held a crossbow, fully spanned. The steel quarrel head glittered. It was aimed at my heart.

"Jak!" The voice rasped hoarsely. "Jak, I am in the most desperate straits. For the sake of the friendship I bear you, you must help me!"

The scarf fell away. The gaunt, haggard, desperate features of Lobur the Dagger stared out.

"You've got to help me! Or we are both dead men!"

Seventeen

Into the Hammabi el Lamma

The leather-wrapped rope handle contracted as my fingers gripped. The chest, although lenken, was not large and was moderately filled with clothing. Lobur's crossbow quivered. He didn't know it, but I rather fancied I could have the chest swinging in a short arc before me to take the impact of the bolt. With his weapon discharged, Lobur's famous dagger wouldn't stop me from taking his neck between my fists and asking him a few pointed questions.

Deliberately, moving slowly, I released the handle. I straightened up. I stared at Lobur. He licked his lips.

"I mean it, Jak! You must help me, or—"

"Where is Princess Thefi?"

"She is safe now—"

"Now?"

He flinched at my tone. "She's been ill—but she is all right now. Jak! Listen—we have to get out of Ruathytu—"

He didn't like my expression. I moved my hand, carefully. "You'd better tell me all about it, Lobur. I've a bottle somewhere here, it's a middling Stuvan; but it will serve." I went across to the wall cupboard and took down the straw-wrapped bottle. The crossbow swung to cover me.

"Jak! Are you listening? We can't get hold of a voller or a flyer, there are guards everywhere. Prince Nedfar has his people beating up the whole—"

"So you can't get out of Ruathytu and you want me to do it for you. Here." I handed across a goblet filled to the brim. "How do you expect me to do it, then? A magic zorca?"

He looked at the wine and licked his lips again. His face was fuzzed with beard, drawn and dirty. The crossbow trembled.

"Do you want the wine or not?"

He crumbled. He put the crossbow down and reached for the wine. There was no hesitation on my part as he took the goblet.

"My thanks, Jak. I have no one else to turn to."

"You know how Nedfar has taken this?"

"He will agree in the end. His high and mighty honor has been besmirched, that's what riles him. If he were like an ordinary man instead of a stuck-up prince it would be easy. As for that buffoon Thrangulf, I'll stick him if he crosses me."

This Lobur before me now was a very different fellow from the Lobur I'd known before. I kicked the chest to the side.

"We are going to Thefi now, Lobur. You'd better pray she is in good health and spirits. D'you forget Tyfar?"

"No." He finished his wine at a gulp. "I do not forget Tyfar!"

Outside the quarters in the courtyard a little Och slave with only three arms who pushed a broom all day caused Lobur to jump and dodge into the shadows. I called the Och, and I put on the strong haughtily casual voice of your habitual hateful slave-handler.

"Slave! Go at once to Hikdar Bonnu in Mathdi and tell him Jiktar Jak orders him to wait. He will receive a message. Is that clear?" I tossed a copper ob into the air.

"Clear, master." The Och spluttered out the words. He dropped his broom and caught the copper coin skillfully. He ran across the dusty courtyard.

I said to Lobur, "You can come out now, Dagger—the little three-armed Och slave has gone." Well, I was not feeling too happy about Lobur the Dagger. "We cannot delay. You do not know what those fellows of mine will get up too if I'm not around."

"Then, for the sake of Havil, let us hurry!"

He didn't know the half of it about hurrying, by Krun! Just as I had things organized; myself with ingress into the map room and my lads in Mathdi to cut up rough and perform a little mayhem and then join Seg, this idiot Lobur brought his passionate elopement into the picture. As they say, Men sow for Zair to reap.

Through the fuzz I noticed how long and lean Lobur's chin looked, and the way the line of his lips twisted down and then up as he spoke. He looked both haunted and hunted.

My first concern now must be for the safety and welfare of Thefi. It wasn't Lobur's fault he'd fallen in love with a girl whose hand, however willing she might be, he could win only by the most prodigious of efforts. As Tyfar had said in his gentle way, Lobur did not appear to be making any efforts. Once I was satisfied about Thefi, I could think about Lobur and the pair of them. If this is a priggish holier-than-thou attitude, then so be it. It was the way it was going to be, at least, for me.

We found Thefi huddled on a pallet in a miserable garret with a holed roof and splintered floors, high in a warren off Fish Fin Street, leading down to the Havilthytus. The place possessed its own aroma. I do not care for fish. Thefi looked better than I'd feared. She started up as we entered, drawing a shawl about her. Her hair was combed, her face was clean, and the draggly old dress she wore was stitched and decent.

"Jak! But—but—" Then, almost accusingly: "Lobur! You shouldn't have brought Jak into this. We could all be—"

"Hush, Thefi! Jak is a friend. You remember the Moder? He will find us a voller, you'll see."

I said, "Princess. You are well?"

"Yes, yes. But we must get away—"

Did this answer my unvoiced queries? Was Thefi heart and soul in this business? Some reticence about her could be easily explained by the circumstances and her natural fears. All the same, I fancied I detected a hesitation here.

They explained that they were paying an extortionate amount to the rogue who owned the tenement, that Thefi had been unable to bring much cash, and that she had in the rush of their elopement dropped the bag containing her jewels. Someone had had a find, then. I passed across the bag I had with me, which contained enough to satisfy the landlord for a pair of sennights.

"By Krun! He is charging you—but you had best stay here until I can arrange for your departure."

"If Prince Nedfar gets wind of where we are—"

"He will not from me, Lobur." Then I looked directly at Thefi. "And you, princess?"

She understood well enough what I was asking. She leaned her head back, and brushed a strand of hair from her forehead.

"I did not think it would—would be like this."

There was nothing else I could get from her, short of asking outright and thus precipitating a nasty scene with Lobur. I promised to return with news, again assured them of my best will, and told them not to take any foolish chances. My warnings were unnecessary; but they served to emphasize the plight Thefi found herself in.

Then, just as I was leaving, Lobur said, "You are captain of a voller. If we can reach Pandahem I have a good friend there. He will do anything for us. You will be rewarded."

"Pandahem, is it, Lobur? Well, I'm not in this for reward."

"No. No, of course not, Jak. I should have realized."

During this short and uneasy conversation Lobur stood by the door on the alert. This grasping landlord would spy on them if he could. They had told him they were Nath and Natema hiding from Nath's outraged wife. Once the fellow understood she was Princess Thefi, daughter of Prince

Nedfar, he'd be off to collect his reward like a bolt from an arbalest. They took care.

Joining with this subterfuge, I pulled my scarf up around my face, and calling, "Remberee, Nath, Natema," I blundered down the rickety stairs and out onto Fish Fin Street. The scarf—it was a green flamanch with yellow borders—served double duty here, for it also filtered out some of the odors.

When I trotted out my orders in the stateroom of Mathdi, Bonnu screwed up his face. His head went up.

"As they say—to hear is to obey. But, in this—!"

"I know, Bonnu. The lads are spoiling for a fight. But they'll get all the fighting they want when they serve with Kov Seg. Mark my words!"

As just about all the Quoffas and krahniks, as superior draught animals, were pulling government equipment, I had to employ a lopsided mytzer whose low-slung body shuffled along on nine instead of his ration of ten legs all moving in unison. He hauled a two-wheeled cart on which my gear was piled. His driver was a Relt, whose beaked miserable face showed patches of missing feathers where his master had taken a crop to him with too heavy a hand. We presented an odd spectacle, I daresay, a strapping dwa-Jiktar of the Hamalian Air Service marching at the rear of a bouncy little cart hauled by a poor tradesman's mytzer. For all that, these animals give excellent service and have splendid pulling power. We trundled along the busy streets of Ruathytu en route for Prince Nedfar's villa where I was to be quartered as his newest aide.

Reposing confidence in ship-Hikdar Bonnu, and knowing that for the moment there was nothing I could do about the Lobur-Thefi situation, I could let those events for the moment hang fire—an expression not found on Kregen yet, thank Zair. I could concentrate on getting into the map room of the palace.

This was an odd experience.

Rather naturally, I was not Nedfar's only aide. As a prince with a mind of his own, who had shown that he did not always see eye to eye with the empress, he yet wielded immense powers. His uprightness and strength of character endeared him to many Hamalese, and brought contumely on his head from the more fanatical of Thyllis's adherents. There were four of us in the skiff as we were rowed across the Havilthytus toward the artificial island. The palace reared, stark and somber and yet spired and turreted, a masterpiece of Kregan architecture, giving off an aura of splendor and pomp, and of chill horror.

The other two aides were nobles both, Strom Nath and Trylon Handur, youngish men with their careers to make, wealthy, resplendent with health and fancy uniforms, adept with weapons, and alike—almost—as two peas in a pod. But they were not buffoons, and they knew their duties. Nedfar would not have bothered with them had they not been competent.

I was dressed up in a fine ornate uniform of blue with green trimmings and with much gold lace and feathers. The thing itched abominably. But it would serve as a passport. The skiff touched the green-slimed gray stones and we let Nedfar jump out first. Always, I had to quell that instinctive movement to be first to leave a boat, last to enter. The sentries stiffened into bronze and iron statues and we went through the iron-bound gates and so entered Hammabi el Lamma.

Everything breathed opulence. The passageways would have taken three zorca chariots abreast. The ceilings were high enough for voller aerobatics. Marble and gold and dudinter smothered the walls. Curtains and drapes hung in artful folds, and the tapestries must have been worth millions. The fusty smell of a vast hive of people could not take away the impression of grandeur. We marched along like ants. Guards, sentries, paktuns, officers of all the armed services, stylors and slaves passed and repassed amid a continuous murmur of thousands of voices. I kept tag of the way we went by counting the enormous jars of Pandahem ware that stood, smothered in flowers, at every corner and angle. Truly, the place was a labyrinth of wealth.

We passed a party of women all beautifully dressed and who were neat and competent and feminine in the way Kregan ladies are. Nedfar stopped for a few words with their grand dame, who smiled and was gracious, her hair done up with pearls, her dress a blue and silver marvel. When he rejoined us, Nedfar said:

"Kovneva Dorena, a most powerful lady, charming and understanding. They are here as a delegation to offer their jewels in Hamal's dark days."

I perked up at mention of dark days for Hamal. Like most folk, I was in the dark as to the true situation, and the darker it was for Hamal the brighter for the allies. All the same, I vowed that all this nonsense of dark and bright would be swept away once the war was over. We had, as a united Paz, to face the dreaded Shanks.

More guards saluted and we passed through corridor after corridor. Far below lay the dungeons and the cells where once I had languished. As for the Hall of Notor Zan, we did not go near that somber place. Thyllis's throne room with its horrible syatra pit lay in a different wing as we climbed the last flight of marble stairs to the military planning wing. I felt a tremble along my limbs. The famous moorn vew, the map room, lay only a few paces ahead. After all this, would there be nothing of value to my friends on those jealously guarded maps?

And then we three aides halted in an anteroom and Nedfar said, "Amuse yourselves for a bur or two." He strode off, upright, purposeful, his desperate concern for his daughter thrust aside in his concern for his country.

I just stared. I had to close my mouth.

I turned to Trylon Handur, who walked across to a side table for the wine. "Trylon—do we not accompany the prince?"

Handur looked over his shoulder. He was casual. "No. He has gone to the map room. We are not allowed in there."

Somehow or other I was still standing there, my face politely blank, still the perfect aide. Somehow or other I was not rushing madly after Nedfar, and shouldering past, and hurtling into the room where the secrets of our enemy's dispositions were revealed. Perhaps they were, perhaps they were not. But I was still standing there, starting to look around for the wine, still dwa-Jiktar Jak the Shot. How it was done escapes me.

Strom Nath followed me. "I wish this unfortunate business over the prince's daughter had not occurred just now." I roused myself and we reached for wineglasses together. "The prince is the chief hope of Hamal. That gretchuk empire of Vallia is very strong—"

"But we are stronger, Nath," said Trylon Handur.

"Oh, yes. But there is Hyrklana and the Dawn Lands, too—"

Double doors at the side of the room opened as the Chulik guards drew the valves aside and a messenger ran in. He ran. He was splashed with mud and had wisps of grass in his hair, so we surmised he'd come a cropper. His blue uniform, that of the messenger corps of the Air Service, was ripped. He said to Trylon Handur, "An urgent signal, Trylon—" He handed across an oilskin-sealed packet.

Randur took it, put his glass down, ran across to the smaller door in the corner where two Chuliks opened it as he arrived. He vanished inside. The messenger fell into a chair.

Strom Nath handed him wine and he tossed it off in a gulp.

Presently, the messenger said, "It will be no secret soon. Kapt Hlandli ham Therdun has been beaten. His army is in ruins and streaming back from Hallandlad."

Now this was news! Ruathytu lies some one thousand miles south of the north coast, and Hallandlad is fair and square halfway between. The army was Seg's, that had won the victory. He was forced to march most of the way, for we had nowhere near enough aerial transport. He would leapfrog what regiments he could, of course; but the danger of that was being caught by detachments. The messenger went on speaking, and from what he did not say I gathered Seg had made use of the natural capacity in military matters of his opposing general, this Kapt Hlandli ham Therdun. He'd sucked ham Therdun into the belief Seg was overextended, the Hamalese had attacked, screeching their war cry of "Hanitch! Hanitch!" and Seg had dumped the bulk of his army on them from a great height. I gloated.

Trylon Handur came out of that small door and handed Strom Nath a message packet. "For Kapt Naghan. He is to move at once."

Now here was the dilemma. I now knew that Naghan was to take his army, held in reserve in Ruathytu, north to attack Seg. But there was no way I could warn him of this. What the hell had happened to Deb-Lu-Quienyin?

I shuddered to believe the obvious. That devil Phu-Si-Yantong had used his enormous powers and forced Deb-Lu onto the defensive, unable to use his own kharrna to communicate with me.

Handur shook his head in admiration. "The prince is a marvel! This disastrous news, and he checks the maps—which we are not allowed to see—writes, and gives his orders. With his worries about his daughter, he knows exactly the right plan to smash these damned Vallian invaders."

I said, "He is indeed a marvel. All the same, this is not the great plan that will save Hamal altogether."

"Oh, no. But that exists. Everyone knows that."

If I couldn't get into that map room soon I fancied I'd burst!

Six tall windows each side of the double doors let in light. I strolled across—seething!—and looked out. A landing platform here had been built high against the wall, with the sky above and a nasty drop below. On the platform were ranked a number of courier vollers. To one side and neatly segregated stood perching towers for mirvols and scratching bars for fluttcleppers and volcleppers. The vollers were all just about the same, small two-place jobs with a van-like rear. They were all-over green in color and along their sides and sterns painted in yellow-gold was the word courier.

I rubbed my chin. Now one of those vollers would serve Lobur and Thefi a treat. Also, one would get me through to Seg or Drak later in the game. A landing platform to be borne in mind, then...

The guards out there were mostly apims; but there were Chuliks and Khibils and a couple of Rapas. There were no Pachaks I could see. Inside this anteroom the guards stood woodenly at their doors, opening them when necessary, and by the time I'd dealt with them all, reinforcements would come pelting in in overwhelming numbers.

The door in the fourth wall opened and a crowd of aides to other members of the high command jostled through. They'd been eating heavily and drinking well, for we with Nedfar were late arrivals. The uproar of laughter and conversation filled the anteroom. No doubt some of the high command would be members of the Nine Faceless Ones of Hamal who directed many affairs and particularly appointed nobles to the production of vollers. The news of the disastrous Battle of Hallandlad sobered the boisterous aides. For my part, I knew that the colors of my regiments in the battle would bear the honor embroidered in gold thread. Sink me else!

Shortly thereafter a deal of coming and going ensued as fresh orders were written and sent off. Ruathytu would be like a beehive tonight. This was to the good. If men were drawn off to the north they could not reinforce the armies facing the invasions from east and south.

When an aide was required from the group waiting a man would come out of that small door and bellow his name. This man presented a singular appearance, for he was blind. He wore a silly over-ornate uniform and a velvet cap with a feather; but his legs were chained so that he could just walk and not run. He carried a yellow stick with a bronze head, with which he felt along the walls and floor, although long custom in this occupation had given him a sure sense of direction.

"Trylon Handur!" he shouted in a parade-ground bellow. He must have been an old warrior, blinded in action, and now peculiarly suited for this work. Handur started up and ran through the door.

No doubt because of the seriousness of the news and the tenseness of the atmosphere in the anteroom, so far not one of the aides had strolled over to inspect the new aide. Among a certain type of noble—no less in Vallia than Hamal—the desire to bully and humiliate inferiors and new acquaintances is an old and nauseating phenomenon. I was in no mood to be temperate; but I did keep myself to myself, over by the windows.

When Handur reappeared he carried the oilskin packet that was the hallmark of the messengers' trade. I had to take it to the Chuktar of the artillery park over in the soldiers' quarter, north of the river. "Take a messenger voller," said Handur. "And be quick. The packet cannot be entrusted to anyone else."

I nodded and taking the packet went out through the double doors. The Jiktar on duty pointed out a voller and pilot I might use. The green-painted craft with the yellow-gold lettering looked flimsy; but she was fast with rakish lines. Her pilot settled at the controls and we were off.

He was a cheerful sort who invariably began any sentence with a little laugh. His fair hair blew about. He said his one desire was for the war to finish, as he had no enmity for Vallia, having been there and liking the place. He told me he was called Bonzo, although that was not his name. One day, I surmised, when he scraped up enough courage to disdain the job in which he found himself, he would make his mark upon the world. In this I was right.

The packet was duly delivered to the Chuktar, who brooded over his stores of varters and catapults and nasty darts and stones, and we flew back. The wind blustered and the Courier craft sped between the clouds. Ruathytu presented the spectacle of huge areas of darkness, and avenues and streets of light in other quarters. The Sacred Quarter spouted to the night sky.

I said a cheerful Remberee to Bonzo the Courier and went into the anteroom. Handur had gone off, I was told, and so I hitched up my sword and marched up to the small door. The Chuliks made no offer to open it.

"Open the door," I said, in that cutting way. "Message for Prince Nedfar."

I waited for what seemed a damned long time; then the left-hand Chulik, who wore a golden thread braided into his dangling pigtail, opened the door. He did not speak. I looked inside, along a corridor, and marched in as to the manner born.

The corridor was short, no more than half a dozen paces, carpeted in dark blue, with paler blue walls and ceiling. The only two pieces of furniture were a chair and a table. On the table stood a jug and a glass of water, a loaf of bread and a heel of cheese, together with a pottery dish of palines. Painted outlines on the table circumscribed the areas to be occupied by these refreshments. I noticed there was no butter. Some of the provinces of Hamal supply troops who will have nothing of butter or preserves or relishes. They furnish good quality fighting men, though. In the chair sat the blind man. As I entered he began to rise, for his hearing was sharp. As I closed the door after me he stood up very quickly, and called: "Do not shut the door, notor. Give me your message." And he held out his free hand.

I looked at him, seeing the seamed weather-beaten features of an old kampeon, and I sighed. I walked on, very softly, and his stick switched up. The stick barred the passage. "Notor?"

Some things a man does in life he will not dwell on. I was as gentle as I could be, and arranged the old warrior in his chair comfortably, his stick propped at his side. What a world it was, when the Emperor of Vallia was reduced to dealing with old blind men!

His name was Nath the Bullet, for he had been a zan-Deldar of slingers.

The door beyond his slouched shoulder pushed open on oiled hinges. A small square room, carpeted and walled in green and blue checks, revealed three more doors. The one on my left was open to show a spartan bedroom. That on my right opened as I entered and a portly snuffly man emerged blowing his nose. That was the lavatory. He wore fussy robes, girded with golden links, and his jowly snuffly face had no time to express astonishment before he went to sleep. I was not as gentle with him as with Nath the Bullet.

The door ahead opened with a bang and a voice called: "Come on, Larghos! The fate of Hamal is being decided and you sit—"

The speaker was sumptuously dressed in blue and yellow and gold and he was a hard case, blue-jowled, heavy of eyebrow, scornful of lip.

"By Krun!" he exclaimed, seeing me.

I crossed that little square room like a leem. He collapsed. But other voices lifted beyond the open door. I looked in. Impressions jostled. People standing around a huge table, many lights, tall curtained windows, a square black opening in the far wall, the blackness as of a night of Notor Zan. I saw Nedfar look up from the table which, in the single glance I gave it, I saw was a superbly crafted model of Hamal, sculptured and painted in miniature perfection. Clumps and columns of color on this map table represented the armies marching and countermarching. The maps on the walls paled by comparison.

Two men rushed me. They drew their swords and they did not wait for Nedfar's abrupt cry. "Hold! He is my aide—"

"Then he is a dead man!" shouted one of these fellows, and he lunged. Like many of the newer nobility he carried the rapier and main gauche, having discarded the traditional weapon of Havilfar, the thraxter. His face showed the clear determination to skewer me. I drew, put the point through his shoulder, and then whipped my own left-hand dagger before the eyes of his comrade.

"A message!" I bellowed.

Nedfar started for the door. Other men and women crowded up. The man I had pinked fell down, screaming, gripping the hole in his shoulder. Then the other one slashed at me, and I ducked, and I had to stick him in the thigh. He staggered back, yelping.

"Jak! Jak—what are you about?"

In a rush a twinkle of swords broke like a massive comber breaking into foam on a pebbly beach. I skipped and jumped and I bellowed out as though mortally afraid.

"I meant no harm! I have a message— Stop fighting, notors!"

But whatever Nedfar might have thought, the others were in no doubt. They did not bother to call for the guards. The doors between muffled all sounds. And no guards, no aides, no one was allowed into the map room. They tried to get past me to the door and run out to raise the alarm. I had to stop them and began to use the hilt, thunking them into peaceful sleep. Even the women fought like she cats, and with the fate of empires at stake, women had to be treated as equals with men, which is what they would have asked for. Nedfar stood back, shaking his head. He drew his rapier; but he held it point down.

When he and I stood alone, he said: "I knew you were a swordsman, Jak, a Bladesman. Now I wonder what you are."

"I am your friend and admirer, prince. That is the truth, as Havil—as Djan—is my witness."

He smiled. Yes, he was a gentleman. "Not Havil? You are not Hamalese, as you pretended?"

"No, prince. But I am not your enemy."

"Spikatur Hunting Sword?"

"No. I am not sure I approve of their methods."

"And you are here to...?"

"Is it not obvious?" I gestured to the map table.

"I see. Then it is my duty to stop you."

"I know it is. And it is my duty to look. What can we do about it, prince?"

"You call yourself Jak the Shot. Will you add to that?"

"No."

"Then we must fight."

"I think not. I have promised—first myself, and then Tyfar, although he does not know of my promise or the need for it—that I would never raise hand against you." Deliberately, I lowered the point of my rapier. All the time I moved closer to the table. "You are, I think, one of the Faceless Nine, one of the Nine Faceless Ones?"

He started. "You should not even know of their existence!"

"That I do proves a point. Also, Nedfar, I would willingly see Thyllis cast down to the Ice Floes of Sicce and you as the Emperor of Hamal. This, I think, is what I am about at the moment."

"You talk—"

"Best you should understand the implications. We are friends, and I intend us to remain so. For the sake of Tyfar as much as anything else."

"You talk wildly, about things you should not know, about treason. Thyllis is my cousin—"

"Second cousin."

"Second cousin. I will not be a traitor."

"I would not expect you to be. After we have defeated her you will be the choice. There is no other with your—"

"The king, the emperor—"

"You, Nedfar, and you alone, will be the Emperor of Hamal. Now, to business. I intend to look at that map table. I will not fight you. So—"

"And I will prevent you, and will fight you."

Close enough now to the table, I fancied... Close enough to act...

As I leaped, I said—and it was pure bravura, stupid—"I will not fight. But I will do—this!"

The single clean blow stretched Nedfar upon the floor. I looked down on him, and then bent and picked up my main gauche. The knuckles of my left hand did not even tingle, so nicely judged was the blow.

Then I turned to the map table and the secrets of the high command of Hamal.

Eighteen

I Am Peremptory With Princess Thefi

The high command of Hamal had no secret master plan to defeat the invasions. The story was a cleverly concocted propaganda exercise. I gripped the edge of the map table and stared wolfishly at the sculptured contours, the greenery denoting vegetation, the winding of rivers and the clumping of mountains that formed a miniature model of Hamal. Scattered across the land lay markers of various colors. These were representative of the armies and air fleets that marched and flew. These were the secrets.

The Hamalese had disposed their forces according to sound military doctrines, operating on interior lines, dispersing to march, concentrating to fight, keeping on the move so as not to exhaust the country.

It was all laid out. Broad arrows made from wood blocks and positioned before each army indicated its line of march. In front of the invasion columns more than one set of arrows indicated by their different sizes the probable direction. The tallest wood block arrows showed the route the Hamalese planners calculated the columns would move, the smallest the least likely. A few moments of study convinced me the Hamalese had covered just about all eventualities. Their response moves were all worked out. I looked and committed the plans to memory.

A hoarse snuffle from the floor where the high command sprawled brought my attention to one of the men, a rotund, big-bodied man with a simple taste in clothes. He snuffled again and rolled over. His face was doughy, multi-chinned, yet unmistakably the face of a man who gave orders. I bent to him to put him to sleep again. At his throat he wore a small version of the pakzhan, indicating he was a hyr-paktun. No doubt that was where he'd picked up his expertise. As I straightened up my eye was caught by the favor he had pinned to the shoulder of his tunic. It was of black and green feathers, and was pinned by the golden representation of a grascent. The grascent is one of the more interesting varieties of Kregan dinosaur. I stared. Feathers of black and green and a golden grascent—I had seen this badge before.

The arch wizard, Phu-Si-Yantong employed men as his tools, and some had worn a badge like this.

Studying the table, walking around the room checking on elaborations of details on the wall maps, I had to face the simple fact that Phu-si-Yantong's insane ambition to rule all of Paz—all of Kregen for all I knew, he was mad enough even for that—must cause him to keep a watch on the most powerful of the rulers whom he must bend to his will. This doughy-faced fellow took orders from Yantong and betrayed Thyllis.

That Yantong kept up a corps of spies seemed a common sense enough conjecture. He was able to go into that weird trance state of lupu and spy out incidents at vast distances; but that kharrna could be interfered with. Thyllis had once kept her own secret personal Wizard of Loh. I rather fancied from what little I knew of Yantong's character that he would never tolerate another Wizard of Loh in his own affairs.

The wall maps took my attention then for the last one showed in neatly inked outline and color what the Hamalese high command planned as their defenses of Ruathytu—always assuming any of the invasion columns managed to reach the place.

The plan was elegant and simple as good plans usually are. The ground forces would be dealt with according to their strengths, so that over the last miles of the advance they would be resisted where weak, allowed a relatively easy progress where strong. The Hamalian Air Service would keep most of its strength disengaged and away from the capital. The Hamalese had no fear of other aerial forces. When the last attack went in, with aerial support or not, the Hamalian Air Service would pounce. They would catch the attack columns in that vulnerable moment when they advanced to the assault. The picture formed in my head—clear skies with Vallian and Hyrklanian and Dawn Lands various aerial forces pressing on above the troops below, everything going well, shouting and uproar, and on, on— and then the enormous Hamalian skyships dropping down and the swift vollers and the clouds of fluttrells and mirvols—yes, that picture formed, and it was a picture of darkness and death for all our hopes.

High morale, determination, and knowing the moment to strike—these were the Hamalese secret weapons.

Prince Nedfar stirred. I had struck with as little force as possible, less than I should have done to do the job properly. A line from a poem by Covell of the Golden Tongue, one of the preeminent poets of Vondium, crossed my mind. He was a lively, intelligent and sensitive man who abhorred violence. Useless to attempt to render the poetry into terrestrial tongues, the Kregish is unique and beautiful. He sings: "To see no hope in romance and love in human relationships is death; loneliness is the true unhappiness."

Zair knew, I'd been lonely in my time. Among all the splendid friends fortune had favored me with on Kregen, this man, this noble of an enemy country, this Nedfar, numbered; it was time for me to leave crazy Empress Thyllis's map room and be about my proper business.

I gave a last swift look around, then crossed to dough-face and ripped away the black and green feathered golden grascent. I stuffed it into my pocket. Nedfar groaned. I gave him a polite salute and left the moorn vew, closing the door on the square room after me and closing also the door from that room onto the corridor. Nath the Bullet slumbered. I made sure he was still comfortable as I went by, and propped his stick to give him extra support.

Then, bracing back my shoulders, head up, face wearing a scornful aide's rendition of a man with an important mission, I marched out into the anteroom.

As far as I was concerned I might not have bothered. The place looked exactly the same, if a little noisier. Across at the double doors the Chulik guards had no compunction about letting me out. The terrace presented a blotched look from scattered lanterns and lamps, orange lozenges, yellow ovals, white rectangles of light. The landing platform held a number of courier vollers and messenger flyers; but protocol must be observed. I felt the old itch up my back. That roomful of sleeping beauties would be found soon—must be found. They knew who I was. I was dwa-Jiktar Jak the Shot, of the Hamalian Air Service, captain of Mathdi. I heaved up a sigh as the Jiktar approached, already signaling for the next voller inline.

"Trouble, Jik?" said this Jiktar, short, stout, breathless, officious.

"Aye, Jik. Herrelldrin never has a Hell deep enough. Oh, well, life is life. Is this my voller?"

"Ready and waiting, Jik!" called a cheerful voice. But before the words were spoken there was this little apologetic almost internal laugh. Bonzo's cheerful face stared up at me, his fair hair about to take off from his head.

There was nothing else for it. If Bonzo got in the way, Bonzo would go to sleep. Bratch!

We shot away in his usual style of piloting. "Where to, Jik?"

"The Urnmayern voller berths."

He cocked a blue eye at me. I knew what he was thinking. Aides did not have the free run of courier vollers to take them back to quarters. Hamal's laws were strict on the point. And that is a redundant remark; Hamal's damned laws were strict on every point. On that short flight I learned that Bonzo was a gambling man; what he did not know about zorca or sleeth racing odds would scarcely have weighed down a copper ob. I told him gambling was a mug's game, and asking him to wait as I went off to Mathdi, reflected that the gambles I habitually took were far more foolish.

Hikdar Bonnu was raring to go, and when I told him where he'd be off, almost before the words were out of my mouth. The little three-armed Och with his broom had stirred up more problems.

"I know, Bonnu, I know. Order, counter-order, disorder. But things have come up. You know the Caves of Kov Mak about twenty dwaburs north?" He nodded. These caves, so called because of their exceeding lack of light, tunneled miles into the hillsides and had been used since the first flint-handlers. "Wait for me there. Keep Mathdi out of sight. If you have to fight to maintain concealment, make sure you win and do not let news of your presence spread." Those were fierce orders, indeed! "I shall join you as soon as possible, certainly within a day."

"Quidang," he said. "But skulking in caves—"

"I know, I know. There will be more fighting for you all before this little lot is seen off. Now—move!"

He went off to roust out Mathdi's crew and I returned to the green-painted voller. The yellow-gold COURIER on the sides glittered in the lantern lights. Bonzo laughed and we took off.

"Where now, Jik?"

Sink me! I said to myself. That was a heavy question!

Taking Bonzo's Courier voller was vitally necessary; taking Bonzo was not. There was no hesitation in my mind. I would not harm him; he was too artless for that. "Fly to the Havilthytus by the Camdenorm quay."

His first reaction was, "That's a fishy destination," and the laugh preceded and succeeded his words. Then: "I'm only allowed to carry you about on official business, Jik."

"This is."

He did not quibble; no doubt he was grumbling away to himself about puffed-up aides doing their shopping for a fish supper on his time. We whirled over the rooftops. Ruathytu was now awake and bubbling as the troops ordered to move north roused out. Kapt Naghan was not a commanding general who tolerated slackness. The broad stretch of river was flecked with the lights of boats, and the pile of the Hammabi el Lamma and, downstream, the Temple of Havil the Green and the Castle of Hanitcha the Harrower threw their own ribbons of colored light upon the waters. We slanted in for the fish quays and Bonzo made for the Camdenorm.

A few stalls were still open but the majority were wrapped in shadows. I alighted and told Bonzo to wait. Fish Fin Street lay less than ten murs away. As I climbed the stairs and knocked on the door I wondered if Bonzo would wait; discipline was ingrained in Hamal yet even he must sense something more than a little odd in the night's doings. If he did not wait, I would have to adopt a different plan. Lobur and Thefi crept out, their faces drawn, and we moved rapidly back along the shadowed side of the street to the Camdenorm quay. Bonzo waited. A torch light glittered across the yellow-gold COURIER.

I said to him: "There are two passengers for the van section in the rear of your voller, Bonzo."

He looked up at me, opened his mouth, did not laugh as he said: "And?"

"And what?"

"And what do I say to my Jiktar, Jik?"

"You are doing the right thing. You have no need to worry."

Lobur walked in front of Thefi, both huddled in cloaks, and I unlatched the doors to the vanlike rear of the courier voller.

Just as they were entering, Lobur started to speak, and I said, "Shastum!" which is one way of saying "Silence!" and Bonzo got out of the pilot's seat and came around the back. He gave that little swallowing laugh, a cough to precede a statement.

"I am a courier now, Jik. But I have eyes, and have been well-schooled, if prematurely cut off, as my father was a businessman who traveled the world. I do not think—"

"Good!" I said.

"What—?"

"Good. It is good that you do not think."

"But, Jik—I do. And what I think—"

I walked around to the pilot's seat and jumped in. Bonzo let out a yell. We took off even as he ran up and made a frantic grab at his Courier voller. I looked down and through the windrush I yelled, "Remberee, Bonzo! I'll try to give your voller back."

Over my shoulder I could hear Thefi laughing.

Hamal's laws ensure that the Hamalese number everything. I had been a number in the Heavenly Mines. A brass plate gave the number of this voller as Jay Kay Pe 448 with an appended V to indicate she was of recent construction. The wind blustered past and we lifted and three inquisitive patrols, one after the other, nosed up and saw the little green airboat with the big yellow-gold courier and simply flew away. Our credentials were impeccable.

Now Lobur laughed, also.

"Pandahem, Jak!" he called over my shoulder. "My thanks!"

My uneasiness persisted. I could not make up my mind about Lobur. Tyfar had appeared to approve of his sister's attachment to the Dagger, and I fancied Tyfar would accept what had happened if it was what his sister wished. As for Nedfar, I felt the worst of scoundrels and rogues, for his love for his daughter had not encompassed the idea of her going off in this way. And Thefi herself? Here was the source of my greatest concern. Was she merely caught up in the romance of this affair, liking Lobur and being carried along by his vehemence? Would she bitterly regret her impulsive acquiescence? I did not know. Useless to say it was no business of mine. By Zair! It was business of mine, now, because I had been brought into it no less than for my love for the participants. If only my daughter Jaezila was here! She'd know what was right like a shot.

A bur and a half later—for courier vollers by the nature of their business must be fleet craft—we reached the Caves of Kov Mak. As I began to descend, Lobur, who was in fine spirits, called, "You go down!"

"Aye."

Because things had worked out so well I was almost bound to be at the rendezvous before Mathdi. This was all to the good. We touched down and the airboat rocked to stillness. We all got out.

"Why, Jak?" said Thefi.

I found a smile for her. Her face tilted up and by the light of the Moons of Kregen she looked lovely, by Zair. If there was hesitation on that face, was not that understandable?

"I leave you here, princess. You may fly to Pandahem at will."

Lobur's laugh rang out. He was in fine fettle, brimming with good spirits. "You are a marvel, Jak, a real marvel."

"I want to have a word with the princess in private." I did not wait for him either to acquiesce or argue; I took Thefi by the elbow and moved away into the darkness. Surprised, she allowed herself to be drawn along. She was totally unused to such behavior.

"Listen, Thefi—"

"You—you are peremptory, Jak!"

"And if you say I am presumptuous, I shall say I presume on my affection for Tyfar and my regard for your father. Listen, Thefi. Do you really wish to go with Lobur?"

Now it was out, flat and bald and ugly, and I heard the stupidity of it even as I spoke. What else could she say but the answer she gave? But she spoke well, give her that.

"But for my friendship for you, Jak, I should be displeased. Lobur and I—we thank you for what you have done for us. You will be rewarded, and I say that in no demeaning way. Somehow I shall make sure of that. But, anything else—you run friendship perilously close to animosity—"

"Because you are a princess? Or because you are not sure?"

In the light of the Moons her face darkened as the blood rose to her skin. "No more, Jak. I command you."

No more was right. By Vox! What a ninny I was even to dream she would deign to confide in me. I was just a plug-ugly adventurer, a hyr-paktun, a man who had rendered service to her father and brother. Beside Lobur the Dagger I was a nothing in her eyes. So, with a grimace that might have been a smile, I said: "You are right, princess. But when I tell Tyfar I shall tell him you went away happily. This is true, because you say so."

"It is!"

Then Lobur came up and it was time for them to go. They had a fair old way to go; but the time would pass quickly for them.

So the courier voller lifted off and vanished amid moon glow and star glitter. I shook my head and stared at the jagged line of hills where the Caves of Kov Mak tunneled for miles, and I turned around, and Mathdi, showing lights, descended an ulm away.

A voller landing just here right now had to be Mathdi. I walked across and as I neared I let rip a bellow or three to let them know I was coming. If I had done right, if I had done wrong, I did not know. What I did know was that the escapades of lovers would no longer play any part in my plans for empire.

Stern business and hard fighting lay under my hand, and I would wish they did not. Rather, I reflected as, observing the fantamyrrh, I climbed aboard Mathdi, rather the adventures of star-crossed lovers than the bloody adventures of battle.

Nineteen

A Grand Tour Weaves the Net

Over the succeeding days a very great deal of work was done. Organization and reorganization followed on our experiences. We regrouped. Now this word is often used euphemistically to cover the collecting together of shattered forces after a battle and getting the men in the right frame of mind to fight again; our regrouping was carried out with other ends in view. I made a kind of grand tour of the invading forces, beginning with Seg's in the north. He was his usual magnificent self, filled with zeal, a comrade I would trust with my life, a man among men.

"And, my old dom," he said, his wild blue eyes afire with what he saw of the future, for the folk of Erthyrdrin are fey. "Your plan will work. In the knowledge of Erthyr the Bow, I see it!"

"And you will bear the brunt of it, Seg."

"Rightly so. By the Veiled Froyvil, Dray! Of course! I'll have the most troops, so—"

"You'll have precious little air."

He sniffed. We sat outside his tent with a wide panorama spread before us and the noise of the host in our ears. The Suns of Scorpio shone and I joyed in the company of Seg Segutorio, and I pushed aside the hateful darkness that might blight his happiness. He glanced up to where a skein of flutduins from Valka flew strongly out on patrol. He jerked his chin up.

"Oh, aye," I said. "But the skyships of Hamal shrug off saddle flyers as a calsany shrugs off flies."

"Maybe, maybe."

We spent a glorious two days together, and bemoaned the absence of Inch and Turko and the others, and then I was off again, to see Drak. By this time Mathdi had been repainted in a decent russet and ochre color scheme and much of her Hamalian nature had been obscured. She flew the red and yellow flags of Vallia and the red and white of Valka, and the blue and yellow of Zamra, and, also, the orange and gray of Djanduin. When I saw Drak he wanted to know why Seg was to have the glory.

"Glory! Glory? Have you learned nothing?"

He was stubborn. Well, he would be. He was intense, serious, and I believed dedicated to Vallia and capable of being a truly great emperor. I was abrupt with him.

"When you take over as emperor, my lad, then you may order as you see fit. But the people saw fit to Fetch me to be their emperor, and I am telling you that Seg will take the risks—"

"You perhaps think to shield me, because I am your son—"

"Because you are the future Emperor of Vallia, ninny! And the quicker we can sort everything out the quicker you can take over. And I will not hear anything about your refusing the job. By Zair! I've had enough of it!"

"I believe you—but—"

"I'm off to Vallia to see your mother, if she's not off adventuring. Have you any messages?"

"My deepest regards to Queen Lushfymi—"

He saw my expression and he quelled the fury that flowered into his face. He spoke with precision.

"I hold the queen in great esteem. Her country of Lome will be freed one day, and then—"

"If you suggest you'll go off and be King of Lome I'll—I'll—I'll—"

"Yes?" Now he was amused.

"You're getting as bad as your brother Jaidur! At least he has acquired some sense now he's King of Hyrklana."

"I do not design to be King of Lome." He smiled and the day warmed up. "And give my—regards—to Silda."

"I will." Silda was Seg's daughter, and Delia and I would dearly wish to see Drak have the sense to marry her instead of scheming Queen Lush of Lome. So, with the ice melting a little, I called the remberees and Mathdi was off for Vallia.

As I had feared, Delia was not in Vondium, and no one knew where she was. Rather, the Sisters of the Rose knew, but they would never tell a mere man. So I had Mathdi seen to again and replaced some of her ballistae with the superior Vallian gros-varter, and then we were off, flying hard, to see Jaidur. During that short period in Vondium I had attended to a deal of detail and got through a pile of work, the effects of some of which will no doubt surface later in this narrative...

Amid all the political wheeling and dealing I'd gone through in Vondium, and the minimal social occasions, the major concern was the problem of the Wizards of Loh. As to social occasions, minimal but of a nature I could not and would not cut: How refuse to attend a ceremony honoring Vallia's dead, and bestowing medals on the wounded survivors? How to avoid spending a precious two hours opening a new school complex where the children sang and danced and behaved with amazing decorum, quite unlike their real selves which were harum-scarum to a delightful degree? An emperor's life is not all giving orders, pigging at banquets, having people's heads off and fighting battles.

Deb-Lu told me, "Phu-Si-Yantong is exercising his powers again in exemplary fashion. Khe-Hi and I resist; but it takes effort." He looked tired, his turban awry, his red hair straggling. As for Khe-Hi, that young wizard looked murderous with frustration. "We believe we can overcome Yantong if it comes to the final struggle in the occult. I do apologize, Jak—majis—I do apologize for failing to make contact. But I must warn you that even that communication could be broken—"

"You mean Yantong would know, would listen in?"

"Suspect, at the least." Deb-Lu abruptly reverted to old habit, and Spoke In Capitals. "I have Managed to Keep an Observation upon You, and in Lupu Watched. Your Messages were Taken In."

"At least, that is something. But I fancy the attack on Vallia will not now take place. The Hamalese are pressed back."

"They lure you on, and seek to destroy you by a trap."

I told Deb-Lu, and finished, "We're just going to have to make our trap snap harder than theirs. It's all we can do."

Khe-Hi handed me a small bronze brooch. "A signomant, majis. It will help our communications." I pinned on the brooch, pleased.

Jaidur and Lildra were pleased to see me. I wasn't too happy about Lildra accompanying her new husband on campaign; but that little word "new" explained it all. They were confident and when I expounded the plan agreed to go along with it. Although Jaidur in his reckless way, said, "We will cut them up, and finish them, by Vox!" and Lildra held his arm, smiling, I had to squash any feelings of unease. After all, Seg was shouldering the major burden of battle.

"As soon as we reach the best point, I'll have the troops marching," promised Jaidur.

"Good. Remember—timing is important, so leave plenty of time for emergencies."

"I will."

He told me he had formed a bodyguard after the style of the Emperor's Sword Watch and the Emperor's Yellow Jackets. Well, that was his privilege. Those two corps had been formed by others for my protection, as I had formed the Empress's Devoted Life Guard and intended to form a second body of a similar nature. I explained it to Jaidur. "They say it is better to have more than a single bodyguard, Jaidur. You split the command. Then you don't have palace revolutions. That is the theory."

"But your ESW is with Drak, and the EYJ are with Seg."

"True." I did not exactly laugh as let my lad see my amusement. "If they want to be revolting, they can be—after we've dealt with Hamal. Anyway, the first regiments only are there. The second regiments are occupied elsewhere."

We talked for a space, for my life had denied a great deal of my family's company, and then Jaidur said, "It is a great sadness that Thelda died. But Seg is well over the death of his wife now. And—" Here Jaidur made an expressive gesture. "Aunt Thelda always fussed so."

I turned the conversation as soon as I could. I did know that the moment Hamal was turned into an ally against the Shanks, I would speak to Seg about Thelda. I am a coward in these matters; I know that.

Before I left for the south I cautioned Jaidur. "Seg has the most troops and the post of greatest danger. But you will be severely attacked, and will be thin on the ground. Don't take any foolish chances. Run if you have to."

"Run!"

"Aye, Vax Neemusjid. Run!"

His glare was a marvel of compressed ferocity. Lildra put a hand on his arm. "I learned a very great deal when I ran in the rain from the Castle of Afferatu, my love. Listen to your father. He speaks sense."

So we left it at that, and Mathdi took off for the south.

"By Spag the Junc!" quoth Dav Olmes when we touched down, and I explained to him. "It might work—no, it will work!"

"I do not want to be too long away from Ruathytu, for I have unfinished business there. But you folk from the Dawn Lands have so many different columns—"

"We have, and wisely so, since many of the countries do not get along. But I will have the word spread. The King of Hambascett marches a full two days apart from the King of Ezionn—back home they'd be at each other's throats at the least excuse. But I'll see to all that."

"You fellows from the Dawn Lands—united you could walk all over Hamal."

"Maybe. But we are as we are. A patchwork quilt of honor and enmity and friendship. A Rapa of Sinopa would as lief slit the gizzard of a Rapa of Sokotro as any old Fristle. I tell you, Jak, it's a balancing act even to get 'em all to march."

"Any news of Kov Konec?"

"His illness persists; but he is gaining strength. I do not think he will join the army in time for the last battle."

I didn't bother to ask if there was news of Prince Mefto the Kazzur. Dav's forces were in good heart, and he did have a fair quantity of air, which was heartening. His king had entrusted a sizeable force to him, and Dav had grown easily to fill the position. I nodded to a party of Mionches shambling along over the brow of the hill. They did not look happy. Their helmets, high-horned, were pushed back on straps over their shoulders, and their round shields and pairs of spears dangled and slanted any old how. At their head they carried a banner; but this was cased.

Dav shook his head. "I know, Jak. But I can only do what any sensible commander does. Everyone knows Chuliks will not serve in any army containing Mionches. Perhaps it is because a Mionch has tusks twice as long as those of a Chulik."

"Perhaps. Although I fancy there is more to it than that."

Whatever the reason, mercenary Mionches would not be tolerated by Chuliks, and as the fighting ratio was something of the order of six to one, any sensible commander would do what Dav was forced to do. All the same, you could not help feeling a stab of sympathy for the Mionches.

Although Dav would contact other columns marching up to the northwards, we in Mathdi made sure we visited the kings and kapts commanding the armies that might be—quite by accident—left out. By representing myself as a pallan at large from the Emperor of Vallia and the King of Hyrklana, I managed to obtain overall consent to our joint plans. Mind you, it would be folly to imagine everything would go smoothly. Always there would be the odd joker who disagreed, had a better plan, was feeling out of sorts, any excuse just so he or she could carry on doing what they wanted to do. I did my best to weld the disparate forces together, seeing more and more the task of the Dawn Lands armies as grapplers of the Hamalese as the Vallians and Hyrklese delivered the knock-out blows. Our greatest concern was that the enemy would concentrate overwhelming strength against one of our columns; and to thwart this an arrangement of patrols and scouts kept well ahead to apprise us of any forward movement. Then the aerial forces would bring reinforcements and succor as fast as they could fly. So far we had not experienced any disasters.

During this time as I flew from army to army it was my fortune to witness only two battles, and these mere delaying skirmishes on the part of the Hamalese. They held us up, when we landed in rear they would detour and run. Then, a few sennights later, they'd set up another block. Their plans were being carried out.

Soon—but not all that soon, by Krun!—it was time for me to go Djanduin.

The little signomant in the form of a bronze brooch given me by Khe-Hi contained nine gems of different colors and values arranged in a circle. Weird though it was, I knew that the two Wizards of Loh could go into their trance state of lupu and witness events through these gems. The value of this brooch was immense, because usually Wizards of Loh concealed their signomants in massive bronzen plates so as to make movement difficult. Yet the task was difficult and fraught with peril, for if Yantong caught a sniff of our Wizards of Loh at work, his own kharrna would lash out with diabolical viciousness. What might happen then I did not care to dwell on.

Perhaps when I reached Djanduin and flew to the capital, Djanguraj, and touched down in the court of the Stux of Zodjuin in the palace there, our Wizards of Loh might have freer access.

The folk of Windy Djanguraj welcomed us as only Djangs can.

The immensely ferocious four-armed Dwadjangs and the shrewd two-armed Obdjangs with their pert gerbil-faces might be no rivals in the twin fields of war and diplomacy; they are well-matched when it comes to entertaining guests and comrades. For a moment I allowed the tensions and worries to slip away. If I felt any guilt I looked at that question squarely and decided that the campaign was running smoothly, I was not indispensable, and I needed to spend time with my people of Djanduin.

Kytun Kholin Dom did his usual trick. His upper left arm enfolded me, his lower left thumped me on the back, his upper right hand gripped my own right hand and his lower right fist tattooed against my ribs. I gripped and hammered back with my half of his equipment. By Djan! It was good to be back in Djanduin!

Ortyg Fellin Coper, his whiskers dancing, forced himself into the melee to greet me, and his wife Sinkie threw herself on me. Oh, yes, this was coming home with a vengeance.

We went through the outrageous extravaganza of Djang celebrations, with processions and bonfires and torchlights and enormous mountains of food and rushing rivers of wine. The people yelled themselves hoarse. I went everywhere and saw everyone and felt great comfort in the prosperity of the country. The local enemy, the Gorgrens, would not be a threat again for some time. They would come back, in the end, for they are a malignant lot and pose problems of unity.

"And so we march against Hamal, Dray?"

"Aye."

"You speak with a heavy heart," said O. Fellin Coper. He brushed his whiskers, his face concerned, alert, one of the controlling minds of the country, my co-regent with Kytun.

"I think of the price we will pay—for megalomania."

K. Kholin Dom swelled his massive ribcage, and his magnificent simpleness revealed itself as he said, "We do not often venture from Djanduin, but we have certain news of what these Hamalese are up to. They will not stop by themselves. The only sure way of stopping them is to stop them ourselves." He picked up a flagon and held it. "No, Ortyg, no, you are right. The king has a heavy heart, as do we all for the fine fighting men who will die. But if this sacrifice is not made, far worse will follow." Then he let rip a yell which brought all the faces along the tables up to stare at us. "By Zodjuin of the Silver Stux! Here is to Notor Prescot, King of Djanduin, and hell and damnation to all our foes!"

I lowered my eyelids as the deafening roar of approbation broke in the banqueting hall. With Djangs at a fellow's back, what is there to fear from mortal men on Kregen?

Enough, by Zair, as you shall hear...

Through the following days we discussed plans. Rather, we elaborated and refined The Plan. For, in Djan's own truth, there was but the one ploy open to us, and chancy though it might be and dangerous, it offered a rapid end to bloodshed. And when it comes to a gamble in war, there is no one like a Djang to snatch up the challenge with a fearsome shout of laughter. The regiments were inspected and the fliers and flyers of the Air

Services. The four-armed Djangs are among the most impressive of fighting men on Kregen, their prowess immeasurable among their peer; and for all that they are little known outside the southwest corner of Havilfar, for they keep themselves to themselves. They are not the brightest of strategists. Point them in the right direction and start them going, and very little will stop them. It is the gerbil-faced Obdjangs who are the brains of the country, and the two races love each other and work together splendidly.

I might add that my crew of rascally fighting men in Mathdi were most polite during their stay in Djanduin, and Bonnu kept them well in hand.

During all my adventures over Kregen I had always, as you know, taken every opportunity to write to the places on that terrible and beautiful world of special interest to me, and Kytun and Ortyg were up to date with news. As a consequence of that they had been in communication with Valka, where many Djangs trained up Valkans to fly flutduins, and had employed Valkans—and Vallians—in work more suited to apims. This was how they knew of affairs in Hamal. Reports came in during that time bringing the latest information on the progress of the invasions, of the incursions of the wild men over the Mountains of the West. In many of these reports the name of Prince Tyfar was prominent.

I said to Ortyg and Kytun, "Listen, my friends. This Prince Tyfar. He is a great man. He is no enemy, for he shares our dream of uniting all Paz." I stretched the truth here a little, but it was true, even if not yet spelled out. "We will never raise hand against him or his father, Prince Nedfar."

"Then if he brings his army against us?"

I frowned. "I do not know for a surety. But I do not think he will desert his post. The wild men are a pest."

They nodded. And I knew what they were thinking. If anybody— anybody—tried to fight me or them, the Djangs would be ruthless in protecting me and themselves. Selah!

Then, as though continuing a thought begun in his head, Ortyg said, "This Empire of Hamal is a rich country, enormously wealthy. We can live off the land if we have to. But—our vollers remain unreliable, as ever."

"At least they are vollers," I said. "The Vallians are using enormous fleets of sailers of the skies. Their vorlcas must use the winds. And there have been some fair old battles along the lines of communication. Yes, we live off Hamal. We'd never be able to invade at all if we could not."

This point seemed the appropriate one for me to apprise them of my intentions.

"Mathdi will be going back to Kov Seg and Prince Drak and King Jaidur and then around to Dav Olmes and that oddball collection of Dawn Lands armies." The word was not oddball, being a Kregish word, but that fits. They are a rum bunch in the Dawn Lands, by Krun. "Then she'll be coming back to you for the assault."

"And you, Dray?"

"I'm going to deprive you of a single-place flier. I am for Ruathytu."

"Burn the place down," grunted Kytun.

"But leave the treasury," said Ortyg.

That was my Djangs, to the life.

At that point in the preparations there were three separate plans in operation, each resting on the shoulders of the one preceding. Maybe it was a pretty notion that the simple plan of the Hamalese high command should be used to confound itself; if we failed all Hamal would gloat in our discomfiture. As for us, well, a lot of us would be dead.

They'd heard down in Djanduin of Pundhri the Serene, the philosopher I had rescued at the behest of the Star Lords. They approved of his work and teachings, for neither Dwadjang nor Obdjang was apim, and I realized that perhaps I had underestimated not only Pundhri's importance but the acumen of the Everoinye. Here was a focal point for the future, a strong motivation for the realization of the dreams I had for all of Paz.

There were tremendous scenes as I boarded the little single-place voller. I observed the fantamyrrh in the sight of the people and their noise shook the stones of the palace. The ruby and jade lights of the Suns of Scorpio in their streaming mingled radiance bathed the sea of faces uplifted to the landing platform. I looked down and lifted my arm in salute. They were yelling in unison now, chanting it out.

"Notor Prescot, King of Djanduin! Jikai!" Then, as the voller lifted: "Remberee, Notor Prescot! Remberee!"

"Remberee!" I bellowed down, and turned my face away up to the sky. What it is to have folk like the Djangs as friends!

A damned sight better than having them as foes, believe me.

Everything was drawing together beautifully. Always, something goes wrong with the best of plans, naturally, given the contrary nature of the fates or chance or skill that rule our lives; but short of a major catastrophe we had set up the situation so as to gain the most advantage from any eventuality. The flier soared up and away from Djanduin, heading north and east, and on course for Hamal not by the most direct route but by the safest. My reading of the situation was that it would be criminal of me to take a chance now when I flew a voller that might break down at any moment. So the dwaburs to Hamal were eaten up and the expectations rose in me headily.

What a vision! To encompass the downfall of Empress Thyllis and to make of Hamal an ally in the greater struggles ahead! Slung over my back I wore hidden under my cloak a Krozair longsword, one of those I now attempted to have stored in places where I had friends and where I might turn up in need. Djanguraj now had an armory of Krozair longswords—rather, swords made in Djanduin by Wil of the Bellows, after the pattern of

Krozair longswords. Believe me when I say that I, a Brother of the Krozairs of Zy, took thankful comfort from the feel of that superb brand snugged close to my body. A tug, a twist, a cunning draw—and the blade would flame free in a heartbeat.

As I hurtled on over the face of Kregen under the Suns of Scorpio, I felt convinced the Krozair brand would play a part in the dangers ahead. By Zair! I tremble to think that, had I known—had I but known!—the nature of the horror that lurked waiting for me in Ruathytu, I would have turned the voller in the air and flown away, anywhere away from the capital city of Hamal.

Twenty

The Empress Thyllis of Hamal

Far-reaching changes had taken place in Ruathytu during my absence, for I had been away some time as the invading armies approached the capital. For one thing, Pundhri the Serene was in the city and preaching, for the exposition of his philosophy approached the preacher's art and fire. For another, only the great Arena remained in use; slaves had become too valuable to slaughter by the carload as in the old days. The number of fighting men had increased significantly, both mercenaries and swods of the iron legions. Also, aerial strength was marked by its absence. Here were clear signs of the high command's plan in operation. Seg would have to face the final onslaught and face many more adversaries than we had calculated.

The odd and annoying outcome of the Star Lords' instructions to rescue Pundhri worked to our disadvantage, however meritorious the end in view. Now that diffs were no longer regarded with contumely, the ranks of Hamal's fighting formations were filling with them. Pundhri took much of that credit, together with a general revulsion of feeling against racism. I approved; but it was making life difficult for the allies, by Krun.

Not caring to frequent the haunts where I was known as Jak, I spent a few days as Hamun ham Farthytu, and realized afresh how easy it would be to sink into the ways of life of the Sacred Quarter. I saw and kept out of the way of that stupid boorish Trylon with whom I'd had a run in at The Fluttrell Feather in Thalansen. Inquiries elicited the information that he was Horgil Hunderd, Trylon of Deep Valley, still enormously wealthy, a womanizer, an upstart, and here to present the three regiments of paktuns he had raised to the empress.

One of the more disturbing sights abroad—at least to me—was the numbers of Katakis everywhere employed. Katakis are a nasty race of diffs, low-browed, fierce and savage of aspect, armed with long whiplike tails to which they strap six niches of bladed steel. Their main joy in life, it is said, is inflicting pain, they are sworn at as jibrfarils, and their main occupation is slaving. They were here to chain up the remnants of the armies invading Hamal after the Hamalese had won.

A few theaters remained open and I saw a performance of The Queen's Secret, an anonymous play written only three hundred seasons or so ago. It is in my opinion overvalued; but it was better than the populist blood-thumpers dished up everywhere to drum up morale. I spent one evening in The Chuktar Hofardu, an inn named for a long-dead Hamalese kampeon, where I learned a deal of the grass-roots opinions of the swods and something of their morale, and where we finished up the night singing the old songs. Odd, singing songs with swods again in Ruathytu. We went through "When the Fluttrell Flirts His Wing" and "Chuktar's Orders" and "The Chulik's Bent Tusk." We rollicked out "Sogandar the Upright and the Sylvie" and we all had No Idea At All, at all, No idea at all, and the laughter threatened the rafters. Damned odd, when very soon I'd be leading warriors to fight and slay these warriors who sang with me.

I steered clear of The Scented Sylvie and other like places. Ruathytu was bubbling nicely, and news of the various invasion columns was that they continued their advance, living off the land and fighting off attacks on their communications. Not long now...

The temple of Werl-am-Nardith by the Hirrume Gate had been beautifully embellished within, and as I passed by on a morning of high cloud with the suns of Antares striking glints of ruby and jade from every cornice and dome, Black Sadrap hailed me.

We shook hands and then Rollo the Circle waddled over. He was, if anything, even larger of stomach.

"I am pleased to see you, Zaydo! We're all finished here and what do you think of our news?"

I managed a smile, for I was pleased to see Rollo and his band of wandering artists. I didn't know his news; but when he told me I was dutifully impressed.

"The Empress of all Hamal has commanded us! We are to decorate some of her glorious chambers! I tell you, Zaydo, this will be the making of us."

"My congratulations." I did not add that he might be very lucky to be paid. Thyllis would have the work done and spend the money on her mercenaries and fob Rollo off with a title. She had been distributing patents of nobility lavishly in these latter days. Well, perhaps Rollo knew that, and calculated that to be a greater advantage. We talked in the suns light and then we went for a wet and I had to keep up the Zaydo role, and, in fine, I got myself a job assisting in mixing paint and carrying ladders and scaffolding and generally being useful.

I seized the opportunity.

By Vox! This was capital!

Now the Krozair longsword I wore hidden under my cloak had been built with quillons just wide enough to afford proper protection to the hands. We had built a few examples with quillons which folded forward along the blade, and by the press of a stud would spring out into place. Wil of the Bellows pursed up his lips at these, and wiped his hands on his leather apron, saying "Well, I would not like to trust those if a particularly powerful blow is struck full against them, by Zodjuin of the Sword, no!"

So I had this example. But it was clearly not going to be easy for me to scuttle up and down ladders carrying pots of paint with a great bar of steel over my back.

The artists were assigned quarters in some moldering sheds in a little-used court to the east of the Hammabi el Lamma, near the point of the artificial island. There was the usual fuss from the sentries in allowing us ingress; but after a sennight we became a part of the furnishings, and could come and go with our aprons all the colors of the rainbow, and paint in our hair and daubing our faces. I made sure my face was wonderfully streaked with color. Carrying a ladder or a length of plank enabled a fellow to wander past the sentries with a familiar: "Lahal, dom!" and some comment on the progress of the factions in the Jikhorkdun. Majordomos showed us the chambers to be decorated, a complex in a side corridor from the throne room which Thyllis was bringing back into use.

There was every reason to refuse to allow myself to become excited. Yes, I was in Thyllis's palace. I was near her infernal throne room with the manhounds snarling on the steps, and her diabolical syatra pit. A deal more useful would have been to be near the map room...

Among all the paraphernalia of the artists' equipment there were ample hiding places for the longsword and I got into the habit of keeping it handy wrapped in a length of paint-stained sacking. Among the medley of paints and pots and ladders and boxes it passed unnoticed. The reasons for this are easy to discern—the reasons for my wanting the Krozair brand handy...

The combination of arms into which the allies against Hamal had entered creaked along with many hitches and holdups. But the plans did progress and, thanks be to Zair, there were no major disasters. The day of the Seeking after Truth, as they say in the Risslaca Hork in Balintol, drew nearer with every suns rise. At the time I fancied that what next occurred was purest coincidence; very soon thereafter I was disabused of that paltry notion.

The high command's plans appeared to be working, for they had checked a number of our weaker columns and only Seg's army pressed on. We kept abreast of the news, and I was aware of the mounting tension. Damned uneasy it all was, too, knowing that Seg gambled with the deaths of thousands of good men, and with his own death, also. His army had been reinforced and was stronger than the Hamalese knew, and our aerial forces were massed ready to hit the enemy as they pounced. When Seg halted to give battle short of Ruathytu, the expressions of surprise amongst the Hamalese amused me. Good old Seg!

At this stage of this macabre dance of death Kytun and Seg would be in constant communication. Unless I heard to the contrary then, the day on which Rollo the Circle planned to paint the ceiling of Thyllis's Chamber of the Chemzite Graints would be the day when that ceiling might collapse in tiles and plaster.

On that evening which ought to be the last evening of the old order in Hamal, Thyllis held a levee in her throne room for the forces who would march out. They would hit Seg with almost everything they had, and yet they would still leave forces inside the city, for the high command were not novices at war. I cleaned myself up, put on a neat dark blue tunic over the old scarlet breechclout, gray trousers and ankle boots of soft leather proved comfortable, and the silver-gray fur edging of the green cape was suitably foppish. That cape was cut both high and low and concealed the longsword. I buckled up rapier and dagger and, not wearing a hat, sallied forth wearing a quite different face I calculated I could hold for some time without too much discomfort. Joining the army officers and commanders of the paktuns, and looking grim and stern and remote, I went with them along to the throne room. It was easy enough, and I felt reassured that it was not too easy, for I dodged the sentries carrying out their checks by the simple expedient of temporarily assuming the face of a fellow in the crowd to the rear. I do not know if he got in or if they threw him out; certainly there was no fuss.

And so I entered Empress Thyllis's throne room.

The most awesome single impression of that room was that you did not notice its height or length or width or the lavish decorations. Every eye was instantly drawn to the throne fashioned from its colossal block of multi-faceted crystal. Brightly colored rugs lay scattered across the dais below the throne and over the steps where the scantily clad golden-chained slave girls, the Chail Sheom, simpered and shuddered. For the manhounds were there, the jiklos, lolling their red tongues, their teeth sharp and jagged—the Manhounds of Antares, apims cruelly contorted by genetic science to run on all fours and to be more vicious than a hunting cat of the jungle. The chains that held them were of solid iron. To one side the golden railings encircled the marble slab with its chains and rollers.

And so to Thyllis herself.

She had changed. The face was as white and sharp as ever; but her jaw line had thickened and even in the blaze of light coruscating about her and reflecting from the solid mass of gems that smothered her, her body lacked the old slenderness of waist. Her green eyes slanted cruelly upon her courtiers and the officers gathered here in the evening levee prepared to march out on the morrow for the defense of her city.

Her lips were as red as ever, and fuller, more sensuous, and still she caught up one corner in her sharp white teeth.

The Womoxes at her back waved their faerling fans and their horns were gilded and polished, and their size proved they were still picked from the finest specimens Thyllis could come by.

I admit, I was caught up in watching this woman. Evil? Thyllis, was she a wicked woman? Well, she was if you call throwing people down into her syatra pit, or letting her manhounds loose to munch on them in the Hall of Notor Zan wicked. But, some folk would claim these are some of the mere tiresome duties of being an empress. She was a creature of her time and circumstances. In her the Scorpion had stung the Frog, and, willy-nilly, her life had followed with the inevitability of high tragedy. I had been drawn here almost against my own inclination to see her for the last time before I joined Kytun. It seemed to me only fit and proper that the Emperor of Vallia should look upon the Empress of Hamal before the final confrontation.

Despite the size of the throne room the closeness of the atmosphere made us clammy, the smell breathed in redolent with scents and sweat and fear. The noise of the crowd hung muted in shuffling of feet, the clink of swords, the jangle of golden ornaments. When a manhound yawned revealing a red cavern hedged in fangs the women jumped and the men looked unhappy, reflexively grasping their sword hilts. And, over the whole barbaric scene the presence of Thyllis brooded.

Yet she was being gracious. She was aware that these soldiers would march out to fight for her. That they obeyed her because of fear or for reward was for the moment pushed aside. But not far aside; as though to reinforce that chill grip of fear she inspired, a screaming wretch was dragged in. It was given out that he was a Chuktar, condemned for attempting to betray his empress for gold. The gathered mob began that dreadful chant.

"Syatra! Syatra! Syatra!"

Yet the sound did not ring and vibrate in the room as it once had done, it did not beat against the gilded rafters or echo in the groined vaultings. A man near me kept his mouth firmly closed, and a woman put a lace kerchief to her face. Half a dozen other poor wretches were dragged in, all accused of one crime or another. An iron hoop containing many of the best-quality torches of Kregen lowered over the round marble slab. Their light splashed weirdly down over the scene.

The shouts came mostly from the mercenaries. "Syatra! Syatra!" Guards pulled and whipped the condemned men forward. An old Xaffer shuffled up and removed a section of the gilded railings and the pulleys and rollers lifted and trundled the marble slab aside. A hole as black as the cloak of Notor Zan revealed itself in the floor, a blackness that gradually lightened to a leprous greenish-whiteness. Everyone craned to see.

Shrieking and struggling the doomed men were dragged on and hurled down into the pit. The round opening in the roof was not cleared for the rays of the suns to shine through for Zim and Genodras had sunk below the horizon, unwilling to shine upon this horror.

"By Havil! I do not like this!" said a horter at my side.

"Those poor men," said his wife. "But the empress knows what she is doing."

There was a perceptible delay before the man said, "Of course, my dear, of course she does."

In my time I had been called rough and tough and ruthless; I decided I could stomach no more of this. It had been a mistake to take a last look at Thyllis. She was doomed, if the allies could ordain fate, and I felt a great uplift of the spirit. And, in that moment, the coincidence that was no matter of chance brought high-ringing peals from golden trumpets, and the buzz of talk and comment in the room stilled instantly.

Into the cleared space before the crystal throne stepped a group of Katakis. Richly clad they were, and yet bearing with them the darkness of their vile profession. And, at their head, his arrogant whiptail upflung so the torchlight splintered against the curved blade—Rosil na Morcray, the Chuktar Strom!

He had wrought my friends and me much harm, and had helped to ravage Vallia. He was here because we had defeated him in our homeland. And as I stared hotly at him, I heard a tinkling tingling as of a multitude of tiny bells—so I knew. I knew!

Sixteen Womoxes, horns all gilded, and clad in black tabards girt with green lizard skins, bore the palanquin. The cloth of gold curtains were half drawn so that the dark shape of the occupant showed against the red-gold gleam, all liquid eye-watering, of the cushions within. The tiny golden bells tingled with their eerie, spine-chilling tinklings. Following the palanquin came the retinue of Relt stylors and chained Chail Sheom, of guards and slaves. They forced a note of obtrusive displayed power within Thyllis's throne room. She sat up straight on her crystal throne, and her manhounds yawned and closed their eyes, and she put a hand to the mass of gems clustered above her heart.

"What means—" she began.

The voice whispered. It held that curious double-echo, soft and breathy, as though echoing in a cave of vampire bats, yet it carried clearly throughout the vaults of the throne room.

"Empress Thyllis, you are a foolish woman."

The assembled courtiers and soldiers were too astounded to gasp. Fans waved, swords were grasped, faces turned white, but no one uttered a sound, gripped by what went forward here.

I, Dray Prescot, I swallowed down, and I felt the pain in my left hand as I gripped the rapier hilt.

This palanquin with its ornate embellishments, these Womoxes, this retinue, this power and wealth flaunted in the face of the Empress of Hamal—one man, one man only would dare. One man who was more than a man, one being who was a Wizard of Loh—

Phu-Si-Yantong.

He was here, within the same room, here with his people and his Katakis, here under my hand. And I stood, and felt the blackness boiling in me and the bile rising to my throat.

Phu-Si-Yantong, the architect of misery, the creator of chaos, the purveyor of pain and the maniac who sought the dominance of all Paz, here, here before me.

Now people whispered: "The Hyr Notor!"

The ghastly whispering voice spoke again. "You are foolish, empress, on two counts, and the lesser is your loss of Ruathytu."

Thyllis looked a glittering image, frozen, as she said, "Ruathytu? Lost?"

"You will send the flower of your army out to fight the Vallians on the morrow. Fool! They suck you in. A great army carried in an armada of vollers will descend on your city tomorrow."

"You lie!"

"You do not, empress, speak to a Wizard of Loh in those terms. The Emperor of Vallia has tricked you. As he tricked you before when you thought he was Bagor ti Hemlad, as he tricked you when he escaped after your coronation as empress. He is the King of Djanduin. Had you forgotten? His army of Djangs will destroy your city on the morrow if it was left to you."

"It cannot be? Our scouts—the plans—" Thyllis looked around her, panting, shattered. Then she drew herself together. "If what you say is true, Hyr Notor, then we will meet and defeat the Djangs. But you said there were two—"

"Two counts that make you a fool. Aye. But I do not think you will live to learn the second."

The Empress of Hamal flashed her slanting green eyes. She exerted all her scorn. "You—" she began to speak.

The eerie breathy voice said, "Strom Rosil!"

Rosil, the Kataki Strom, stepped forward and lifted the crossbow. He loosed. It was very quick. The bolt struck Thyllis near the center of her body, through her breast, over her heart. It jutted there, hard and black and ugly. And Thyllis uttered no sound. She sat upright, a burnished statue, glittering, resplendent and dead.

Again that whispering voice cut through the room.

"I am the Emperor of Hamal. Woe to anyone who forgets this or who opposes me."

The crowds surged as the tides surge through between barren rocks. Women were shrieking, and men, too were screaming and some ran out of the throne room, and Katakis appeared, many Katakis, with bladed tails. Phu-Si-Yantong had prepared well.

In the uproar I stood like a loon. It was difficult to grasp that mad Empress Thyllis was truly dead. Still she sat, upheld by her carapace of gems, and her white face looked as it had looked in life, with her slanting green eyes bearing down in malicious cruelty upon her suppliants.

Phu-Si-Yantong spoke again, and I listened in a daze. In the groups of people in the retinue, fleetingly glimpsed, there looked to be a man remarkably like Lobur the Dagger. But it could not be him. He was safely away with Thefi in Pandahem...

"The second mistake this foolish woman made," said Yantong, "the second reason she is no longer fit to be your empress, I will tell you." The Katakis now bunched before every doorway. Strom Rosil handed his crossbow to a lackey who set about respanning and loading it. Rosil looked about, his low-drawn brow, his flaring nostrils and gape-jawed mouth, and his wide-spaced eyes, cold and unfeeling, made the people flinch back.

"I will tell you. She did not know that the Emperor of Vallia watched and listened to her petty plans. She did not know that the arch-devil, Dray Prescot, is here in this room, now!"

There was uproar at this as everyone looked around, panicky, searching their neighbors' faces to find the devil himself.

In the bedlam as people shouted and men were seized on suspicion and the Katakis began to force their way in a line and push the people into protesting straggling groups, the chains and the rollers of the cover to the syatra pit were abandoned. Down there in a corpse-light grew a monstrous plant, with rib-crushing tentacles and spiny growths like Venus flytraps that would crunch a man in and suck from him all his juices. Horror grew and writhed in that dank pit. And horror gripped the Hamalese in the throne room.

The Katakis were not gentle. Strom Rosil snatched back his crossbow. The cloth of gold curtains framing the palanquin shook as Phu-Si-Yantong laughed at his own cleverness.

And I was trapped.

Looking about for the quickest way out, I saw the number of Katakis, and saw, also, that Chuliks were entering the chamber in support. Yantong had brought a private army of great strength, strength sufficient, certainly, to seal off the throne room and this wing of the palace, and powerful enough in sheer numbers, let alone quality, to take me up like a fly in treacle.

And, of course, that bastard of a Wizard of Loh knew exactly where I was standing.

A thin white hand, so pale and wan as to appear green, beckoned between the cloth of gold curtains. The Kataki Strom bent. The pale hand lifted and pointed. The forefinger pointed directly at me.

Rosil laughed, his coarse bellow without humor of any sort, a raw sound of triumph. He lifted the crossbow.

I took off, running, pushing people out of the way, haring like a maniac for the marble slab. The crossbow bolt flicked past my bent head. At full speed I leaped the golden railings. I snatched a torch from the hoop. Without hesitation, headlong, I dived into the pit of the syatra.

Twenty-one

Phu-Si-Yantong

Torchlight blazed orange down the slimed walls of the pit, and reflected like a sunset of Earth from the stagnant water pools at the bottom. The suffocating heat and dampness wrapped around my falling body. Steam gushed coiling. Head over heels, spinning arms and legs, I fell. I hit.

The torch went flame first into the water and was instantly extinguished.

The breath was knocked out of me and it was vitally necessary to blink away the phantasmal afterimages of the torchlight, to see in the ghastly corpse-light, to see the syatra, to see and dodge.

The first tentacle wriggled across a mud patch as I staggered up, treading through the hot water upon a thick crust of bones, human bones. Piles of skulls formed lodgments, thighbones terraces, vertebrae, scattered pavings. Steam lifted in curling vapors like beckoning skeletal fingers of mist, matches for the yellowing bones beneath the water. Glaring around, trying to see, dashing the sweat and condensation from my face, I drew the rapier and then, even faster than I'd drawn, thrust it back into the scabbard. The first tentacle writhed long and evil from the steam.

The cloud of steam moved and my eyes grew more used to the greenish light. The whole place stank like a—like—well, in brief, like a syatra pit. I moved back from that first seeking tendril. There had to be a way out of here. Logic said so. There was running water, hot and steaming. That came in and went out. If it came or went through an opening smaller than was I—the tentacle struck.

A rift in the steam, my own movement, the vegetable sense stirred into blind insensate action... The tentacle lapped about my ankle. I unlimbered the longsword and cut the tentacle away, it writhed and contorted and withdrew. The heat bore down like a steam chest. This wall at my back was solid. The shaft was circular and I edged around, knowing I would have to meet the syatra at some point, and hoping I'd reach an opening before that unwanted meeting.

Syatras are unpleasant plants. Corpse-white, equipped with powerful tentacles that seize on prey and stuff it into the coffin-sized spiny traps ranged around the plant, they do very well in Chemish jungles. In more moderate climates they usually grow where there is a supply of warm water from a hot spring. No one had mentioned to me the existence of hot springs below the Hammabi el Lamma.

In daylight with the suns shining through the opening the syatra would reach up the shaft to the light. It could scoop a fellow off the lip of the marble slab. Now it had digested the victims recently flung to it and that would make not the slightest difference to its appetite, by Krun. More tentacles appeared out of the coiling vapor and the impression of a vast body, moving, flickered in green and white and black, rising and lifting and towering up...

The thing broke through the vapor above me. It lowered down, and a multitude of tentacles dangling before it writhed into more purposeful action. At the foot of the main stem were ranged the coffin-sized traps, spined and barbed, grinning with their vegetable grins. Venus Flytraps writ enormous, they waited to snap shut and pierce with spines and suck with relish upon human flesh and blood.

The Krozair brand did not flame in that dolorous greenish whitish half-light.

But the longsword bit through lashing tentacles, bit and cut and sent severed ends plopping into the steamy water. In a few moments a dozen tentacles drew back, coiling around each other like crazed beanplants. In that moment I saw water boiling up in a spout and had time just to leap back and fling myself to the side.

A trap the size of a double-bed foamed out of the water, borne at the end of a short thick stalk. It looked like a fly swatter doubled up for luck, and I the fly intended to be squashed. In a vegetable fury the trap opened and closed, insensately seeking its prey. I circled around, stepping cautiously, got to one side and with a single blow severed the hinge. The trap hung slackly. And a damned tentacle slapped around my neck, all slimy and stinky and horrible, and I had to slice blindly with the longsword to lop it off and so rip it away. Not nice, not nice at all, this fighting a syatra in a repellent pit of stenches.

Eventually by the slow drift of water I found the opening. By this time a great deal of syatra had been cut away and floated or sank, I didn't care which. Downstream did not appeal to me. The opening was large enough to take me—just. The thought occurred that inspections had to be carried out from time to time, and some poor devils of slaves would have to crawl through here. With a last slash at the syatra, which deprived it of six foot of tendril, I ducked down and started to splash along upstream. The corpse-green light persisted, tiny flecks of it in the walls giving just about enough light to prevent Notor Zan from flinging his cloak over all.

The water grew hotter as I went along. Perhaps I'd been stupid to choose the upstream—if I got boiled I would know I had been stupid. But at about the time the water grew too hot to be comfortably tolerable, I came to the first overhead grating and without any hesitation gripped the iron rungs and hauled myself up. No doubt ahead lay a hot spring or a huge furnace room with slaves heating the water for the syatra. Either way, this grating looked more promising.

After a heave and a grunt, the grating slid sideways. I pulled myself out. A quick look showed me a room filled with buckets and brooms and cleaning equipment. I crawled into a corner. I sat propped against the wall. I just sat. If I make this confrontation with the syatra a mere routine affair, that was the way I wanted to regard it at the time. The truth was it was a horrid heart-thumping brush with a squashy kind of death.

The problem and the truth here were the same. I could not sit huddled into a corner like Little Jack Horner when my Djangs flew down into battle very soon now and would be met by foemen whom I had thought would be away fighting Seg. All the cleverness—of both sides—had been brought to nothing by Phu-Si-Yantong. He had cut through everything and imposed his own solutions.

Whenever anyone of my people marches out to battle I worry.

I always have and I always will.

I was fretting about ferocious four-armed Djangs getting into a fight. Yes, I know it is laughable. But I could not stop this concern for my soldiers then, and I do not now, nor do I ever see why I should not be concerned.

Warnings would have to given, Seg would have to be brought on to the city with great rapidity, and I had to get out of here to start all this rolling.

The best way not to be so concerned over the welfare of soldiers is not to have wars.

The scales of the balance are either up or down or level. Unless you smash the scales you cannot have both scales up or both scales down. Life is like that, too...

Getting out was not overly difficult and there was the necessity of skull-bashing only twice. Smartening myself up after the steambath effect of the syatra pit I found a way out through the various corridors back to the Chamber of the Chemzite Graints. Rollo was spending the night before he began prowling around and cocking his head up at the ceiling and preparing himself for what he did in life. I must prepare myself for what I did.

Rollo looked at me as I went past. He did not say anything as I picked up my old clothes with the paint stains and put them on loosely over the blue tunic. I went out carrying a pot of paint and a small ladder, and Rollo the Circle stared up at the ceiling like a man drugged. So, because it was necessary to save an artist from the risks of himself, I dug out Black Sadrap and told him there was likely to be trouble on the morrow and it would be for the best if he took Rollo and the members of the artists company to a place of safety away from the palace. He was a hard-headed fellow and he agreed, and I did not give him time to ask me where I'd come by the information. I took off—literally took off—by jumping over the wall of our hovels into the river.

I found a small and uninquisitive inn and spent the rest of the night resting, if not truly sleeping. Uninquisitive the inn might be; avaricious most certainly. I had to deal with two lean and rascally intrusions after my portable property—and not at the same time, either. By morning and the glorious rising of Zim and Genodras, I was feeling much better in a contrary kind of way, and up and about and wolfing an enormous breakfast of vosk rashers and loloo's eggs and Kregan bread done in the bols fashion and finishing off with unlimited supplies of tea and palines. Thus fortified for battle I went out for the Great Temple of Havil the Green intending to climb the highest possible pinnacle and by gestures attract the Djangs. As I rounded the corner into the Kyro of the Vadvars I saw Khe-Hi-Bjanching walk up to me.

He looked very real. He was eager and dressed in plain gray clothes and a hat of the kind they call a havchun was clamped around his head quite concealing every last vestige of red hair. His apparition held with clarity.

"By the Seven Arcades, majis!" he said. "I am overjoyed to see you—"

"You look damned real, Khe-Hi," I said to the lupal projection. "Damned real. Tell me the news!"

The corner of the street and kyro held a convenient nook under a balcony and were anyone to glance at us we would look just like any couple of chaps having a chat early in the morning. My clothes were somewhat wrinkled, it is true, and the fur was more mildewy than I liked, and I could swear the trousers had shrunk; but we'd pass, we'd pass. One thing was certain; no one would guess only one man stood there.

Thinking this I heard Khe-Hi say that the armies had begun their advance. I felt relief. At least, something was going right. "And I am pleased I found you so easily. Deb-Lu guided me, I am happy to say."

"I am going to join in the mayhem," I said. "So will bid you good day. By Krun!" I said, reaching out a hand. "You do look real!"

I put my hand on Khe-Hi's arm expecting it to pass through as through vapor, and I hit his arm, and felt the flesh and bone.

"Oh, no!" I gripped on. "You're real!"

"Of course I'm real!" Khe-Hi was most hurt. "I mean, majis, I am real. It's just that I am here that surprised you."

"Now what in the name of a Herrelldrin Hell am I going to do with you, Khe-Hi?"

We solved that problem by both going up to the highest pinnacle of the Great Temple we could reach. There was no trouble. Among the sightseers were a number of soldiers; but they did not stay long. Ruathytu was under arms. Yet in the nature of cunning stratagem little evidence showed. And, the Hamalese did not know on which precise day we would strike. So when the first waves came in there was a breathing space before the reaction and Khe-Hi and I could be picked up. Kytun did the picking, as one would expect, flying a smallish waspish voller.

The Battle for a City is a somber, blood-chilling business. It is also riotous, uproarious, exciting and frightening. Much depends on the characteristics of the combatants. My Djangs are a blood-curdling lot, to be sure.

"This is the moment, Dray!" called Kytun as he stood with wide-braced legs astern of his pilot who raced the waspish craft between the Temple and the Hanitchik.

"Aye," I said, looking up to where the Djang aerial armada swooped on the city. Hamalese airboats and saddle flyers rose to do combat and the sky filled with scurrying battle. "Thyllis is dead—shot by a villain unhanged—and Phu-Si-Yantong claims to be emperor now."

"Then he's next!" roared Kytun, face aflame as he watched his fellows hurtling into the attack.

Vollers cruised in low to slip the ground forces past the Hamalese defense. Regiment after regiment of Djangs leaped out and raced to take up positions. One thing was sure, they knew how to do that evolution in a way to make the swods who had exercised with Vad Homath look the coys they were. Hordes of flutduins with black beaks pointed, and wide yellow wings bearing them purposefully on, flew to tangle with the fluttrells and mirvols of Hamal. My Djangs were superb. After the first clash between the aerial cavalry we had no further problems with Hamalese saddle flyers.

The odd idiot might come flying over, screeching and waving his crossbow; but he usually didn't get back.

Make no mistake. The Hamalese fought and they used all the expertise and cunning and sheer professionalism of the iron legions. But they had very many mercenaries in the ranks now. The old iron legions, those men who had marched and conquered, were either far away or dead. I do not think of all the clashes that took place as the city was cleared, that the Hamalese won one.

When Seg's army arrived the end was certain. Acting on my strictest instructions fire was not used as a weapon against the city. We burned the skyships. The small agile fliers piloted by Djangs who were masters of their craft would fly up and over a monstrous Hamalian skyship. All her serried rows of varters would shoot, and sometimes the Djang would be shot out of the sky, sometimes he would get through to drop his pots of combustibles. We had more small nippy vollers than there were of enormous skyships.

So, working smoothly together, the forces from Djanduin and from Vallia together with those of Hyrklana and the Dawn Lands entered into Ruathytu, capital city of Hamal, and took it with all its buildings and walls and treasure.

Quite a day, from the first day to the last, for we had given the Hamalese no chance of creating a siege situation. One of the last pockets of resistance was by the Arena. Strong parties had already secured the palace and the Hanitchik and the Temple and now we rather fancied the Jikhorkdun.

A burning skyship had fallen across the north-south boulevard called the Arrow of Hork and black drifts of smoke fouled the air and visibility. Now I have deliberately refrained from detailing the regiments and the people involved in what came inevitably to be called the Taking of Ruathytu. Suffice it—they were there! Now Nath Karidge who was always the Light Cavalryman par excellence, said, "By the Spurs of Lasal the Vakka!" which is your light cavalryman's oath to the life and nothing mild about it. "Let us go straight into them with a yell!"

The Chuktar commanding a brigade of nikvoves reined up beside Nath Karidge, and resplendent they both looked, cavalrymen, used to getting on with the job. This Chuktar Nalgre was a Heavy Cavalryman and everything about him told you that, so I suppose you could say he was a strong cavalryman as he said, "By Rorvreng the Vakka! You lights would bounce. Let us heavies go in!"

"Tsleetha-tsleethi," I told them. "This is an infantry party."

No need to ask or guess which infantry were here and raring to go in. Apart from a few unfortunate wights in the second regiments, they were all here. They dismounted and formed up, turning from cavalry into infantry as their feet hit the ground. Reconnaissance of the Arena, which was an enormous place, revealed forces dug in and ready to contest every last stone, every patch of sand. I turned to face the two regiments, ready and waiting, 1ESW and 1EYJ, and I decided I would not throw them away in a stupidity like this. There was no need to take the confounded Jikhorkdun.

"Let 'em rot in there!" I called, making a joke of it, turning their minds away from the expected fight. And then, up there, bursting through the black shroud of smoke over the Arrow of Hork, a voller pitched end over end. She was surrounded by flutduins, and the superb birds were ridden by Djangs and Valkans. The voller crashed out of sight into the Arena. One of the flutduins planed away and glided in to land nearby. Jiktar Eriden ti Vulheim saluted and said, "The voller tried to escape, strom. There is something odd about her, for she was stuffed with damned Katakis and yet they tried to run."

So I knew.

"You have done well, Jik Eriden. The swods are going in and your flyers will give them cover."

"Quidang!"

So, with a heavy heart, I gave the orders my lads expected, curtailing their puzzlement over my remarks about not fighting for the Jikhorkdun. In there, trapped with his vicious Katakis, Phu-Si-Yantong stood at bay.

The mercenaries who fought were mostly Chuliks and Khibils, with a scattering of others like Brokelsh and blegs and a large number of numims who outnumbered the Fristles, which is unusual. Most of the other mercenaries had fled, prepared to change sides. There was a single group of Pachaks, about a dozen, and they fought until the end, their nikobi not to be dishonored.

We fought our way into the Jikhorkdun with the black smoke acidic and raw in our mouths and nostrils. The fight raged under the seating, through the tunnels, past the caged areas and so out onto the silver sand. No time now for thoughts of the Arena in Huringa in Hyrklana. We fought Katakis in the Jikhorkdun of Ruathytu, and they were driven on through fear of their Hyr Notor, Phu-Si-Yantong.

My lads of the Sword Watch and the Yellow Jackets got stuck in in splendid style. The Katakis, joined by others of their evil kind, withstood the first attacks. Tails swished and the bladed steel glittered. The suns were nearly gone and I wanted this business finished before they sank.

That was easier said than done. Darkness leached the light from the scene. When a city is taken, no matter how many orders are given, something is going to burn. Flames licked up from the houses and villas. The stars began to glitter down erratically between the smoke clouds. And still the Katakis fought to protect their lord.

No doubt the Wizard of Loh saw his people could not win. He had had every faith in Katakis as immensely powerful fighters; now that they were beaten he had no more time for them. Battling with half a dozen whip-tails over the sand was not the kind of duty an emperor should concern himself with. I knew that. But when my lads went roaring into battle I couldn't lag in the rear. And I'd been picked on by six whip-tails out to finish me. The scrimmage was a pore-opening skip and jump and three of the bladed tails lay on the sand before the EYJ came in from the left and the ESW came in from the right, and a howling bunch of maniacal Djangs catapulted through in the center. So I could be hauled off by Khe-Hi who looked flustered and agitated and, if it were possible, walking along six inches in the air.

"Well, Khe-Hi?"

"Deb-Lu and I—we face a battle now such as you would not comprehend—look!"

And he turned and stared up at the empress's box overlooking the silver sand. The palanquin stood there, the cloth of gold curtains drawn back. A few torches threw liquid gleams on the gold and the purple, and drove clustering shadows about the form of Phu-Si-Yantong. He was indistinct. A hint of movement, of blackness with purple-gold, the glitter of gems. An arm lifted and something flashed.

At my side Khe-Hi drew in a ragged, gasping breath. He stiffened. His arms did not raise from his side as though he was about to go into lupu, rather he became inflated, taller, drawn up by a force he called down to him—fanciful notions? I do not know. I only know that between the two Wizards of Loh grew a circle of shimmering light in thin air, high between them, twisting and hurling off sparks, brighter and brighter, glittering. The disc of light moved back and forth as each sorcerer strove to overcome the other. This eerie manifestation of power is called the Quern of Gramarye. I had seen one destroy a bazaar. I stood back.

Sweat poured from Khe-Hi's face. His eyes glared and his teeth were gritted. He exerted his powers to keep Yantong at bay, forcing all his knowledge and art into the struggle. His teeth grated together, nerve-shudderingly, and then he managed to pry his jaws apart and to gasp a few words. "Deb-Lu! Deb-Lu-Quienyin! Deb-Lu!"

And Khe-Hi-Bjanching, borne down by the colossal supernatural power of Phu-Si-Yantong, fell. I caught him in my arms. His face was slack; but still his eyes glared and still the radiant disc of light spun and coruscated in thin air as the opposing thaumaturgical forces met and clashed. I held Khe-Hi gently and I did not interpose my head between his eyes and the Quern of Gramarye. A new look appeared on his face, a fresh resolution and a disc of light spun more rapidly and the light increased ten fold and bathed all the Arena in light. So I knew Deb-Lu had joined his comrade and together they sought to stem the onslaught. And then, again, the disc of light brightened, and Khe-Hi husked out: "He has another Wizard of Loh!" and they struggled on, occult powers pitted one against the other, seeking for the advantage, supernatural strengths revealed through the coruscations of light bursting from the Quern of Gramarye.

The unearthly light illuminated the gray stones, caught in the cornices, silhouetted the dark standards. It splashed like fire across those serried rows and ranks of empty seats. But no spectacle like this had been witnessed in the Arena, the silver sand did not shake to the stamp of iron-studded boots and shiver with the blood dropping upon it, it lay bathed in a light flaming from realms and dominions far removed from everyday.

This was the battle to decide our fates.

Wizards of Loh, locked in mortal combat, in the fight to the death.

Among the terrible scenes going on all about as a great city fell to her enemies, none could be more terrible than this sorcerous struggle.

The end came with unexpected suddenness and violence. Deb-Lu had often expressed his deepest respect for the powers of Yantong, and Khe-Hi would bite his lip if they were mentioned. Yantong had received sorcerous help from another Wizard of Loh and this more clearly than anything else indicated his own frame of mind. No more the tinkling tingling bells. No more the cloth of gold. No more the beautiful half-naked slave girls girt in silver and pearls. No more the snap of a finger to gain instant obedience.

Quick, sudden and deadly.

The Quern of Gramarye swelled, bloated, grew and smashed straight across the Arena. It crashed into the empress's box and blew everything there away. It roared on as an insensate fiery whirlwind. It carved an enormous cavern through the Jikhorkdun and walls and ceilings fell and smashed into the black gaps of its passing.

And as for Phu-Si-Yantong, no doubt he was a smeared black atom among all the wreckage.

Thus fell Ruathytu of Hamal, the great city.

Thus died Phu-Si-Yantong, Wizard of Loh.

Now we must spit on our hands and take a hitch in our belts and trusting in the pantheons of the gods and beneficent spirits begin to reconstruct the land against the greater perils ahead.

Allies of Antares

Dray Prescot

To those unfamiliar with the Saga of Dray Prescot, all that it is necessary to know is that he has been summoned to Kregen, an exotic world orbiting the double star Antares, to carry out the mysterious purposes of the Star Lords. To survive the perils that confront him on that beautiful and terrible world he must be resourceful and courageous, strong and devious. There is no denying he presents an enigmatic figure. There are more profound depths to his character than are called for by mere savage survival.

Educated in the harsh environment of Nelson's navy and by the Savanti nal Aphrasöe of Kregen, he is a man above middle height, with brown hair and eyes, the quiet movements of a hunting big cat and a physique of exceptional power.

Taking on the job of Emperor of Vallia, with the Empress Delia by his side, Prescot is determined to press on with his schemes to unite in friendship all the peoples of their half of Kregen in the union of Paz. Vallia and her allies, Djanduin, Hyrklana and some of the realms of the Dawn Lands, have defeated the puissant Empire of Hamal; but Hamal is not laid in ruins. From over the curve of the world dark and more terrible dangers sail down to destroy the bright civilization of Paz. Together with Delia, his family and his comrades, Prescot sees this as a time to make a fresh start. This is the opportunity to forge new alliances against all perils under the Suns of Scorpio.

One

Ructions in the Peace Conference

During the second week of the Peace Conference only forty-nine duels were fought, so the delegates realized they were making real progress.

The main sessions took place in a long-disused assembly chamber of the palace of Ruathytu and here day by day the benches filled with vociferous people all determined to have their say about the horrible fate to be meted out to defeated Hamal. The people divided by nation and race, and each faction felt convinced its own solution was not only the perfect one, but the one to be adopted by everyone else.

This led to differences of opinion.

"A gold deldy per person," shouted a king from the Dawn Lands. In the overheated atmosphere, with the drapes drawn away from the long windows and still the air stifling, his face looked a bronze mask of sweat. He shook his fist. "Nothing less—"

"Less?" A king from a neighboring realm of the Dawn Lands sneered, white lace kerchief to face, not bothering to rise to speak. "Less? Make it two gold deldys."

"Aye!" called a high-ranking noble, gold-bedecked. "Hamal has the gold. Hamal can pay!" Then, no doubt feeling that although no king he must maintain his dignity, he bellowed: "And make it three gold deldys!"

Stylors wrote busily at long tables positioned near the center of the open space between the ranked seating. They covered reams of paper with what was said, proposals and counterproposals. They recorded very few agreements.

Other delegates joined in the raising of the indemnity, and shouts of "four!" and "five" and "seven" brought the blood flushing to forehead and cheeks, brought a sparkle to eyes, brought feathers ruffling dangerously and fur sparking with static. The punishment rose until there was scarcely gold in all of Paz, let alone merely the empire of Hamal, to pay what would be demanded. Then someone raised the question of saddle flyers being taken in compensation, demanding their fair share of zhyans in preference to lesser birds. This caused fresh outbreaks of acrimony. Another delegate banged his sword on the floor and demanded full restitution plus damages for all the airboats his country had lost.

"Take all the fliers that Hamal has!" he cried. "And—"

"You would fly your own airboats home and claim they were lost!" challenged a puffy-faced king with hair noticeable by its absence, for it had been torn off by a wild animal seasons ago. "The Peace Conference demands a full accounting from you—"

"Aye! And from you, King Nodgen the Bald! We have sure proof you flew undamaged vollers back to your black-hearted kingdom and—"

The ensuing sword-flourishing and blade-whickering was dealt with by the marshals. On this day that task fell by rotation to four-armed Djangs, who had no trouble separating the combatants and escorting them back to their seats. Djangs, aside from being among the most superb fighting men of Kregen, are less in awe of kings and nobles not of Djanduin.

"You are not allowed to fight in the Peace Conference." The Djang Hikdar in command of the marshal detail carried off his duties with that Djang blend of competent military expertise and wild warrior fanaticism. He made sure the rival kings were both sitting in their seats before he marched his men off. No blood was spilled on that occasion over that particular quarrel in the chamber; blood flowed in the duel that followed. Outside.

All in all, the Peace Conference to decide what to do with Hamal presented a sorry spectacle.

From Vallia, Drak, the Prince Majister, and Kov Seg Segutorio made eloquent appeals for progress. King Jaidur of Hyrklana expressed his contempt for the delegates. His queen, Lildra, hushed him in her queenly way; but the feeling was abroad that the Peace Conference was doomed.

Young King Rogpe of Mandua announced that he did not feel secure enough on his throne to waste time in Hamal. He had only turned up after the battles, his armies being commanded by Kov Konec and Vad Dav Olmes, because his succession to his father had been challenged and the law had, tardily, upheld his claim. If everyone began to go home, Hamal was likely to be plundered without check in revenge for her own sins of the past.

The Kingdom of Djanduin was represented by O. Fellin Coper. As an Obdjang—equipped by nature with a cheerful pert gerbil-like face and only two arms and a keenly incisive brain—he was no fighting man. At his side sat K. Kholin Dom. As a Dwadjang—equipped by nature with a ferocious assemblage of fighting equipment and a brain completely at sea in the arcana of Higher Command—he was a warrior who upheld O. Fellin Coper's decisions. The aerial assault delivered on the Hamalian capital city of Ruathytu had decided the issue and won the battle. That assault had been a Djanduin affair. The forces commanded by Seg Segutorio had joined in the final assault.

Now that mere mortal kings and princes and kovs sought to put together a Peace Treaty, the actual course of the fighting was conveniently pushed aside. Everyone demanded an equal say. That proved perfectly acceptable, provided common sense prevailed. As the Prince Majister of Vallia said: "Common sense seems to have fled! By Vox! Are we all a pack of ninnies unable to agree on anything?"

Some of the delegates from the Dawn Lands left off arguing and quarreling among themselves long enough to shout answers. Then, they went back to slanging one another.

Seg said, "I suggest we take into consideration the views of those members of the conference—"

Jaidur interrupted. "We take no notice, Uncle Seg! We tell these idiots from the Dawn Lands what we decide!"

Drak—serious, intense, dedicated—leaned forward, frowning. "The Dawn Lands contributed greatly to the success. And to ignore them because we are united and thus stronger is illegal."

Seg sat back, saying nothing. His blue eyes revealed nothing of his thoughts, and his reckless face was composed.

"Illegal!" Jaidur laughed. He was still a right tearaway despite having come to the throne of Hyrklana, a rich island off the east coast of Havilfar, and with the realm its queen, Lildra. His mother, Delia of Vallia, had great hopes that he would reform and become a dutiful king. Now he roared his enjoyment of the jest. "Illegal, brother! What we decide will settle the fate of Hamal for many seasons to come. We must decide in our favor. If these fools from the Dawn Lands—"

"Gently, Jaidur, gently," said Seg.

King Jaidur sat back in his chair. He put a hand to his lips and Lildra put her hand down on his shoulder. Jaidur leaned back, closing his eyes, and he touched Lildra's hand. He drew reassurance and strength from the contact. Just so had his father gained reassurance and strength from Jaidur's mother.

"The problem is the Dawn Lands will not choose a spokesman. They are individuals, and are contrary for the sake of contrariness and drive everyone else into frenzy by their quarrels."

"True, prince," said Seg.

"We have complete agreement," said Ortyg Fellin Coper, brushing his whiskers, being brisk, "between Djanduin, Vallia and Hyrklana. That combination is, indeed, very powerful."

"Powerful!" shouted across that king from the Dawn Lands who had begun the escalation of the gold indemnity. "But we in the Dawn Lands can put more troops into the field, more vollers, more saddle flyers. Woe to anyone who forgets that."

Jaidur burst out: "More! Of course! And woe to you for forgetting it as Hamal destroyed you piecemeal!"

Seg moved with the speed of a Bowman of Loh. He stopped in front of Jaidur, half-bending as though talking, and he motioned to Lildra. It was nicely done. The fatuous king was left talking to Kov Seg's backside, Lildra was smiling at him, and Jaidur was being masked—and, no doubt, having a severe and nostalgic telling-off from his Uncle Seg. Had a duel been fought Jaidur would certainly have won, being a Krozair of Zy; but the deplorable publicity would have done Hyrklana and Vallia no good. Kytun Kholin Dom, clever enough in matters of this nature, rolled over to the Dawn Lands king and, taking him in comradely fashion by the elbow, lifted him away, saying something like: "And I can show you a Jholaix we dug out of the wine cellars you've never dreamed existed."

The Peace Conference survived these bruises; but no one was prepared to say how long such damage could go on.

In all these arguments and statements of opinion and position, no one bothered to think what the Hamalese might say. They had been beaten. Ergo, they must pay up and do as they were told and thank all their gods they were still alive. Yet to claim that no one bothered to think of the Hamalese is to avoid the real issue. Everyone shied away from the central point, the overriding question, the problem that put all the others—including the details of compensation and punishment—into the shade.

All the delegates to the Peace Conference were only too acutely aware that they must think of the Hamalese. And they kept fobbing off that dominant issue.

Who was to rule Hamal now that the old Empress, Empress Thyllis, was dead and buried?

"Dismember the damned place," was a commonly voiced solution.

"Split it up into kovnates and vadvarates and Stromnates and do not allow a single kingdom. Divide and rule." This was a solution favored of many. The rulers from the Dawn Lands would feel far more comfortable if north of the River Os lay, instead of a single huge nation, a whole series of little ones in reflection of themselves.

It was left to Drak to point out: "And have continual warfare between the little countries—as you do all the time?"

By Vox! You win a battle and take a city and have a peace conference—and you start to find out where the problems really are!

Seg said, "Little is beautiful, and big is beautiful. Big is unwieldy and little is plain suicidal. We have to find a median way."

Because the invasion from Vallia had sidestepped the island of Pandahem and gone straight into Hamal, the future held problems there, also. As Drak said, "Now the nations of Pandahem have the dread of the devilish Wizard of Loh, Phu-Si-Yantong, removed, they will rapidly throw out the Hamalese occupation forces. I am sure they will want a say in what is decided for Hamal."

One of the Dawn Lands rulers—King Nafun of Hambascett, who had begun the auction in increasing gold deldys—snorted his disgust. He reared up in his seat, glaring about, the sweat now appearing to be melting from a wax death mask. "Pandahem? Pandahem? Have they sent troops? Have they aided us? No! They have no right to sit at the table that decides the fate of Hamal. We who fought, we—"

His neighbor-king, wily King Harmburr of Ezionn, bellowed out at that. "Fought? Fought? I saw no troops of Hambascett the Treacherous when I fought the Hamalese mercenaries—"

"And I saw not a swod of Decadent Ezionn when I routed the Hamalese heavy cavalry—"

"By the Veiled Froyvil!" said Seg. He let rip a sigh that was more like a stentor blowing to gain passage for a swifter than a lovesick swain languishing for his lady. "Cannot you two either leave each other alone, fight it out, or just shut up?"

Now a kov does not ordinarily talk to two kings in quite those terms.

Drak sat forward anxiously, and Jaidur looked with swift concern over at Seg. Both Drak and Jaidur—with their brother Zeg—had known and loved Seg Segutorio from the moment they had been aware of his existence.

King Harmburr of Ezionn and King Nafun of Hambascett turned to look at Seg. He continued to sit. He had prevented a confrontation with Jaidur, only to precipitate a worse one on his own head.

Drak said, "We have done enough for the day. Let us depart and reconvene on the morrow when—"

"Softly, Prince of Vallia!" quoth Nafun. He wiped his face with a sodden kerchief. "I have been insulted—"

"You!" snapped King Harmburr. He was a waspish little fellow. "You! The lout insulted me—"

Seg stood up. He moved lazily. He smiled. "I shall not fight either of you, or your hired champions. You two are stupid cretins, and what is more, you know it. Aye!" He drowned out their protestations. "I can see ahead. I can see perhaps things that would not please you. You both know we must deal with Hamal fairly, or there will never be peace. So think. Act like kings. Even if it is difficult to act like men."

"The kov speaks with the words of the gods," said Drak. He knew when to bring religion into it. Cunning, resourceful, ruthless, Drak, Prince Majister of Vallia, and yet upright, honest, loyal, a man of the highest principles. Sometimes those high principles made life for lesser mortals damned uncomfortable. Jaidur, his brother, was of altogether more volatile a nature. As for Zeg, the middle brother, who was now King Zeg of Zandikar miles and miles away in the inner sea, the Eye of the World, I'd not heard from him for just not long enough to make me worried. Pretty soon, when this Hamal nonsense was cleared up, I was due a trip to the Eye of the World...

The two kings were in nowise chastened. But other delegates were growing tired of this incessant wrangling. Even rulers of countries of the Dawn Lands traditionally opposed to one another cooled in face of the problems ahead. Various candidates for various sections of Hamal were touted. We all agreed that those nations of the Dawn Lands with frontiers on the River Os, the southern boundary of Hamal, had a prior right in the decisions affecting the parcels of land across their borders. This seemed fair to the delegates.

Even that caused disagreement. A number of the nations right in the north of the Dawn Lands immediately to the south of the River Os, He of the Commendable Countenance, had been in subjection to Hamal for so long they had not contributed anything to the armies of the alliance. In fact, some of them had actually had their own men in the ranks of the Hamalian army. These difficulties had to be discussed and agreements reached.

What at first glance seemed fair, on closer inspection turned ugly with imponderables.

Many of the delegates supported rival claimants. No one was aware of any legitimate issue of the Empress Thyllis and her nonentity of a husband. He had disappeared long ago. A number of relations existed: distant cousins aplenty, and a group of men and women claiming the emperor as their uncle. After Thyllis had been shot to death by a crossbow bolt, loosed by Rosil, the Kataki Strom, Phu-Si-Yantong had proclaimed himself as Emperor of Hamal. Now what seemed to many of the delegates a ludicrous legal situation arose. Did this brief occupation of the throne acquire legality, and, if so, how did it affect the claims of Thyllis's husband's cousins and nephews?

Intriguing.

Nothing would stop the lawyers from inflicting day-long speeches upon the subject with all the happy hunting ground of the inflexible Laws of Hamal in which to play—short of nipping the problem in the bud. Drak, Prince Majister of Vallia, did just that.

"No legitimacy accrues to the Wizard of Loh, Phu-Si-Yantong, now dead—thanks be to Opaz!—or any of his assigns or heirs through this illegal usurpation of the throne." Drak looked around the chamber meaningfully. There was so much gold and silver displayed, so many gems, that the delegates could blind with radiance the unwary eye. "We have enough problems sorting out who is to take over in Hamal without saddling ourselves with more."

"Agreed!" The shouts were unanimous. On one subject, then, the famous Conquerors of Hamal could agree...

In the tiny hush of reaction to the outburst, young King Rogpe of Mandua stood up. He drew his sumptuous robes about him in the instinctive gathering of resources gesture of one about to plunge into unpleasant argument; almost immediately he loosened the fur-trimmed velvet, for Hamal was warmer than Mandua. "There is a matter I must have settled before I return." He held up a hand as some delegates started to protest.

Young and uncertain, Rogpe might be; in what he had to say he was in deadly earnest and therefore articulate and convincing.

"Here me! I speak of the case of those countries who actively allied themselves with Hamal! Most notably that of Shanodrin!"

"Slay 'em all!" and, "Burn their towns around their ears!" The suggestions on what should be done with collaborators bubbled up merrily and uglily.

"Prince Mefto A'Shanofero, known as Mefto the Kazzur! He stands indicted before this assembly! He and his accomplices must be brought to trial."

No one there in that glittering chamber was unaware that Mefto the Kazzur had sought through his alliance with the Hamalese to dominate much of the Dawn Lands. The Kingdom of Mandua had suffered. Now Rogpe put a hand to his quiff of fair hair. He smiled, a nervous smile yet one which revealed his feelings of triumph at delayed revenge accomplished.

Puffy faced, impatient, King Nodgen the Bald leaped to his feet. He shook a fist at Rogpe.

"Yes, yes, my young fighting king, yes! We will deal with the traitor Mefto the Kazzur. But we have more zhantils to saddle here. There is no doubt that if Hamal is to be kept under proper control the empire must be given a Hamalese to rule. That man is King Telmont—"

Nodgen the Bald's words were lost in a chorus of catcalls and fiercely amused expostulations and accusations.

"King Telmont is not related in any way to Thyllis—"

"He cowers in his kingdom in the far Black Hills—"

"He is spineless!"

The knowledge of family relationships and intricate blood ties and links and alliances through marriage were meat and drink to the rulers in the Dawn Lands. Such knowledge was of vital consequence. By understanding why one king did this and one queen did the opposite through the promptings of family loyalties enabled a tricky course of diplomacy to be set. The delegates had to keep themselves informed of the intrigues that fomented all the time. It was a matter of survival, along with always remembering names, for by forgetting a name one might lose a kingdom.

The rival king who had accused Nodgen the Bald of flying his airboats back home and then claiming compensation for their loss rose to shout with great scorn: "We know why you champion this King Telmont, Nodgen the Bald! How much gold has he paid you? What promises has he made?"

The marshal Djangs eased forward, wary.

"I spit on your robe, King Nalgre the Defaced! I deny your accusations, I hurl them back into your teeth—"

Fresh fuel was heaped on the fire of enmity; the duel that would follow later might enlarge catastrophically to include two entire countries, at each other's throats—as usual. These local wars had been contained in the mutual onslaught on Hamal. Now, with the sad inevitability of human nature, they would burst out again, raw and red and bloody.

The damping down of that squabble—a damping down only, for to extinguish it would take longer and demand harsher means—was left to Drak. By the grimness of his demeanor he left no one in any doubt of his anger and contempt. He tried to bring the Peace Conference back to considerations of what lay immediately to hand. "We each have a rapier to sharpen, and so accommodations must be made. If the delegates from the Dawn Lands insist on fighting among themselves, we deplore that but accept it as a burden of history. The future of Hamal must be assured. Let no one forget that all of us face a greater menace from the Shanks who raid us from over the oceans."

"Aye," said Jaidur. This was a matter touching him and his new kingdom nearly. "And I suspect the damned Shanks will soon stop raiding and attempt permanent settlements—"

Fresh uproar at this statement could not conceal the wave of dread that swept over the chamber. All men of this grouping of continents and islands called Paz who lived near a coastline were dreadfully aware of the menace of the Shanks. Fish heads, they called them, Leem Lovers, any scurrilous name a man could put his tongue to, all revealing the horror their name conjured up.

As though the mere mention of the Shanks put a pause to the precedent proceedings, a fresh session opened with a concerted attack on the delegates from Vallia, Hyrklana and Djanduin.

Nodgen the Bald, irked at the dismissal of his claims for King Telmont, pointed a forefinger at Drak. He swept that indicting digit around to encompass Seg, Jaidur, Kytun and O. Fellin Coper. The unmistakable result of the gesture was to isolate these men and to range the other delegates against them.

"You sit there fulminating against us. You sit there pompously pontificating. Yet who are you? You are not of Havilfar North and Central—"

Kytun bellowed: "We are of Havilfar South West!"

Jaidur said, "We are of Hyrklana off Havilfar East!"

Drak and Seg remained silent, very sensibly.

"Look at you!" Nodgen waggled that forefinger. "All of you, lackeys. Aye, lackeys!"

Kytun's four arms windmilled and Ortyg, with a squeak of alarm, tugged at his comrade's military cape. "Let him chatter, Kytun!"

"Lackeys!" roared K. Kholin Dom, fearsome, ferocious, a warrior four-armed Dwadjang. "Explain yourself—king!"

"That is not difficult!" shouted another delegate.

"No! Lackeys—all of you—lackeys of one man!"

"Let me blatter 'em!" pleaded Kytun, his face a black sunburst.

"Hold still, Kytun, do!" Ortyg's gerbil-face expressed concern for Kytun, nothing for the shouted accusations.

Nodgen the Bald bellowed: "One man commands you, the father of the King of Hyrklana; the King of Djanduin; the Emperor of Vallia. One man—and where is he? Why is he not here to talk to us—does he think himself so far above us—?"

The picture wavered.

As though heated air rose before the scene in the assembly chamber the whole glittering assemblage shivered and undulated.

"Your pardon," said Deb-Lu-Quienyin. "I must admit I allowed my concentration to lapse."

The Wizard of Loh's eyes encompassed the world. I stared into those eyes and looked through the sorcerous power of Deb-Lu into the Peace Conference. People in there were shouting and waving fists although, I was thankful to observe, no one was foolish enough to draw a sword.

"It is all right, Deb-Lu," I said. "I must be tiring you. And what they say is right, in one way. I do not wish to go down and sit among them for these dreary proceedings."

"Very practical."

"And if that is being high and mighty—so be it."

"Shall I go on?"

"It is hardly worth it. They will decide nothing. But Drak tries hard. No, I need a wet and—"

The picture I saw through the Wizard of Loh's eyes came into focus. We sat comfortably in a small aerie high in the Mirvol Keep of the palace of Ruathytu, the Hammabi el Lamma. Whoever had lived here before, probably a Chuktar of saddle birds, had done himself well. There was ample provision of wine and fine fare. The picture steadied and the resplendent assembly came back into focus. Deb-Lu-Quienyin had arranged a signomant, a device which eased his powers of observation at a distance, and its placing discreetly in the chamber allowed us excellent vision all around, if in a little foreshortened a fashion.

The wet I promised myself had to wait for the double doors at the far end of the assembly chamber crashed open. The Djangs on duty there recovered swiftly and their stuxes thrust steel heads at the man who burst in. They halted their instinctive reaction at once, for the man was clearly a merker, a messenger who had flown hard. His leathers were glazed with dust.

He held up a hand and shouted so that all could hear.

"Lahal, notors! King Telmont has gathered a great army and marches on us. He vows vengeance. He has sworn to retake the city of Ruathytu and to place the crown of empire upon his head. And his chief promise is this: he will seize by the heels and utterly destroy the man called Dray Prescot."

Deb-Lu let out a cry and the picture I saw through his eyes vanished instantly. I blinked.

"Jak!" said Deb-Lu. "This is serious—"

"What?" I said. "Not you, too? You did not think, like those delegates down there, that by one battle and the taking of their capital the whole puissant Empire of Hamal would be conquered?"

Two

We Fly For the Mountains of the West

"But we must find him! From what you say of him he is the only one. It is certain this King Telmont is a buffoon."

"Drak is right," said Jaidur. "We must find him—and damn quickly."

The Peace Conference had closed the session for the day and those delegates who had been so scathingly denounced by King Nodgen the Bald gathered with Deb-Lu and me in one of the apartments given over to our use in the Hammabi el Lamma.

"I can vouch for him," said Deb-Lu. He still wore his turban, and it was still lopsided; but for all that he looked what he was—a Wizard of Loh and among the most feared and respected of sorcerers of all Kregen. "Yes. Prince Nedfar is all your father has said."

"And," said Jaezila with a force that for all its passion did scarce justice to the tumult within her, as I could see and, seeing, feel for her, "if we do not quickly tell Tyfar the truth, I, for one, will not answer for the consequences."

"That settles it," I said. We were all supposed to be relaxing after a hard day, and we were all tensed up and unhappy and aware of the pressures. The idiot King Telmont had scraped an army together and was marching on Ruathytu. The delegates from the Dawn Lands squabbled among themselves. And everyone wanted the business finished quickly so they might go home to the problems that awaited them there. "We must find Nedfar. He is the man who will be emperor. Just how we convince the others is another problem."

"We will convince them, Dray," said Kytun, using all four arms to express his feelings and to feed himself.

"Not by edge of sword."

"Of course not!" said Ortyg. His shrewd face expressed pained surprise at my suggestion. "We will discuss this—"

"I'll discuss it," promised Kytun.

"And Tyfar?" Jaezila was really worried. She and Tyfar were at one and the same time madly in love and forever at loggerheads, a most intriguing situation.

"I'll fly out, Jaezila," I said.

Drak looked cross. "I do wish, Father, you wouldn't call Lela Jaezila all the time. She is my sister, and your daughter, and she calls you Jak and you call her Jaezila. Most unsettling."

"We were blade comrades, Drak. I know Jaezila as Jaezila more than I do as Lela. Anyway, Tyfar must be told."

Jaidur swallowed his drink and said, "And where was this Prince Nedfar during the Taking of Ruathytu?"

I said, "I do not know. But I give thanks to Opaz and to Djan that he was not here. I do not like to contemplate what would have happened had we met in battle."

Kytun's fierce Djang face contained an amazingly placid look as he said, "I am glad we did not meet in the fight."

There was no mistaking his meaning. My Djangs would allow no harm to come to their king. I did not make the mistake of assuming I could overrule their loyalty by my desire to promote a new emperor in Hamal, for all my admiration of the emperor-elect and my affection for his son.

"Well, then, Jak," Jaezila stood up, tall and graceful and superb in her hunting leathers and in no mood to stand any nonsense from her father. "If you're flying out with me, let's get started."

"Lela!" exclaimed Drak, outraged.

"We can't shilly-shally around. Tyfar is stuck out there by the Mountains of the West and being attacked by those confounded wild men, I expect, and getting all kinds of garbled messages about what's happened to Ruathytu. What do you think he's imagining, feeling? By Vox! Have you no heart!"

Not one of those fighting men who swore allegiance to me even thought of saying that, well, Prince Tyfar was a Hamalese, after all. They had fought the Hamalese; now they understood my dreams and desires for the future.

I stood up. I put the wine glass down.

"Wenda!"*

So, when we'd sorted out who was going and who staying to attend the

---

* Wenda! Let's go! A.B.A.

483

tiresome Peace Conference, we all went up to the most convenient landing platform where a selection of captured Hamalian airboats rested.

Drak could not be released from his lynch-pin position in the conference. Lildra was reluctant to let Jaidur go as they were comparatively recent newly weds, and this appeared to be just. Ortyg was not too keen on Kytun going, preferring him rather to stay to keep an eye on the unruly elements here.

Seg said, "I'm going, my old dom, and joy in it."

I admit I felt a leap of my spirits as Seg spoke. What it was to go off adventuring with a blade comrade, a true friend, the greatest bowman in all Loh!

Drak looked stern. He could have stood for a portrait of an elder judging a tribe, a statesman adjudicating on empires—well, he was all those things, of course; but he so looked the part. "I do not like the idea of you going haring off all over the place, Father. It is—it is undignified."

"I've never, save in one instance, bothered about dignity."

"But you are the Emperor of Vallia! Emperors do not go off flying—"

"This one does. Oh, and don't forget to mention when Kytun and Ortyg are here, the King of Djanduin. Anyway, Drak, you will have to shoulder the burden of being Emperor of Vallia soon."

This, as you will readily perceive, was one of my very good reasons for leaving Drak. He had to be made to understand I meant it when I said he was to take over. He was perfectly capable. It was only his damned rectitude and sense of what was fitting that made him declare he would never become emperor while his mother, Delia, and I lived.

"You know my thoughts on that—" he began.

"Enough! Let us take off—"

Drak went doggedly on. "And we are supposed to be concerning ourselves about this Prince Nedfar you have selected to be the Emperor of Hamal. Where is he? He is who—"

"Listen, Drak! It is my guess Nedfar has flown to the Mountains of the West. He's visiting his son, Tyfar. That's what I think. If we hang about he will be rushing back here and no doubt become embroiled with some stupid idiot from the Dawn Lands, or this King Telmont, or anything untoward—" I finished speaking somewhat more lamely than I'd begun. I could hear myself talking, and that is always fatal to ordered thought.

Over our heads a few clouds scattered pink and golden light from their edges, radiant whorls of darkness, as they obscured the face of the Maiden with the Many Smiles. The stars clustered thickly, fat and bright and twinkling merrily, and a tiny night breeze blew the scents of moon blooms festooning the walls of the landing platform. I breathed in deeply. The air of Kregen is sweet, sweet...

Everything had been prepared. Now that the decision had been made I was anxious to be off, for I well knew what would happen if word of this got around to my people. There would be an instant outcry. To tell the truth, I found it uncanny how well my decision to fly off was being taken. If my lads of the Emperor's Sword Watch, or the Emperor's Yellow Jackets, got wind of an adventure in the offing—well! And Delia's warriors of the Empress's Devoted Life Guard—they'd want to come, too. And, I saw, if we didn't get off sharpish, nothing was going to stop Kytun from leaping aboard the flier and joining us.

Drak looked up at us three lining along the rail of the airboat. He gave us a smile. Suddenly, I wondered if he was pleased to see me go, to get me out of his hair. Well, if that was the case—and I doubted it—then it would be mutual only in the sense that what I was going to do where we were going was all a part and parcel of what had to be done for Hamal and Vallia.

Deft-Fingered Minch stared up at us, his bearded face as crusty and concerned as ever, for he was a kampeon I counted as a comrade, and I have no doubt at all that he was running over in his mind the preparations he had made for us. We had given him little time; but Minch was not called Deft-Fingered for nothing. I had no doubts that the airboat had been stocked, and fully stocked, with all that we would need.

Seg suddenly leaned even farther over the rail and shouted down to a fiery-haired fellow with wide shoulders clad in sober russet who looked up in just such a way as Minch.

"Lije!" shouted Seg. "Did you put in that knobbly stave I have in pickle?"

"Aye, I did that. And you shouldn't be flying off alone without me—"

"By Vox!" said Drak, as though struck by a shaft from Erthyr the Bow himself. "That is right! What am I doing allowing you and Lela to fly off—"

"By the Veiled Froyvil!" sang out Seg. "Your mother and father, and Thelda and me, walked all through the hostile territories of Turismond together—"

"And Jak and Tyfar and I have gone adventuring, Drak," called Jaezila who was Lela to her brother. "So stop worrying."

I shot a hard look at Seg. He had the grace to brace his shoulders back and tilt his head, but he knew he had roused a storm that might delay us. "Get her up, Seg!"

"Aye, my old dom. Let's get away from all these nannies."

As the remberees were shouted and our voller lifted up into the night sky, I looked closely at Drak. Already he was swinging away, cape flaring, to bellow at his people standing further back on the landing platform.

"Make it fast," I said to Seg at the controls. "Drak will send half the army after us."

"More likely your Sword Watch," said Jaezila.

"If that rapscallion bunch get half a chance to go off aroving you won't see their tails for dust. And," I said, feeling the injustice of it all, remembering Delia's father and his complaints about the way his pallans and guards cramped his fun, "and they'll stop us enjoying ourselves."

The flier sped swiftly into the moonshot darkness, speeding above Ruathytu, heading due west.

ESW and EYJ had been formed to protect the emperor. They did this with such devotion that a wall of bodies stood between me and danger. Only by an impassioned call for their loyalty to Drak, who was doing the fighting, and to Seg, who led the major portion of Vallia's forces, had I managed to keep my guards off my neck. Delia had given Nath Karidge permission to take three quarters of the Empress's Devoted Life Guard off to the war against Hamal. Nath wouldn't hang about if he could follow me, well knowing he'd see action. Into the equation I must add the crew of Mathdi, the voller used to such good effect in the days leading up to the Taking of Ruathytu.

So we slammed the speed lever over to the stop and we hurtled beneath the Moons of Kregen, for now there were four shining between the clouds, the Maiden with the Many Smiles, the Twins, and She of the Veils.

In an attempt to shake off these forebodings—which were selfish and ungrateful, to be sure—and lighten our mood, I said to Seg, "Why bring a bowstave you have in pickle, Seg? Surely it is better to keep it in a vat?"

"So some bowyers claim. You know I've been used to pickling 'em on the move." Here Seg glanced sideways at Jaezila, her face flushed in the rose and golden light of the moons. "And this is a very special stave. I want to keep an eye on it."

"Oh?"

"It is not yerthyr wood. I've learned a very great deal since I left Erthyrdrin, believe me. For one thing, the rose-colored feathers from the zim korf of Valka are as good as the blue feathers of the king korf of my own mountains."

"As good as?"

Seg laughed. "Well, my old dom, you can't really expect me to admit they are better!"

"And the other thing?"

"Why, that the wood of the lisehn tree of Vallia is as good as yerthyr wood—"

"As good as?"

And Jaezila laughed.

Seg composed himself, for we all knew we'd tease him over these arcane points of archery and bow-building. "This brave young prince of yours, Lela—you say he is a bowman?"

"Yes, Seg, but—"

"For a Hamalese," I said, and ducked away in mock reaction as Jaezila struck out in mock buffet. "He is an axeman, Seg, superb. Not like Inch, though. But Jaezila can best him with a bow."

"She can best just about anyone," said Seg. "I know. I trained her."

"Then, Seg," I said, speaking comfortably. "Tyfar owes you his life, for Jaezila—Lela—feathered a thing all fangs and jaws in a swamp. It would have chomped Tyfar's head for dinner; but Jaezila's shot was precisely through one red-slitted eye."

Jaezila looked at me over a shoulder, all round and firm under her russets. "Aye, Jak! And in the next heartbeat you sworded the monster's mate that would have had me for its dinner."

"I remember. You asked me if Tyfar was my son—"

"I did. And you were my father all the time! Opaz plays strange tricks on us, to be sure."

Seg laughed, turning back to the controls. "And if all I hear and see is true then this Prince Tyfar will be your son Dray, after all."

"If he has any sense," I said in more of a growl than I intended.

The airboat bore on marvelously, for to Seg flying a voller without constant fear that she'd break down at any minute was liberating. We rummaged in the wicker hampers provided by Minch and Lije and munched and talked and ate and talked and drank and talked. Seg expressed himself as of the opinion, by the Veiled Froyvil, that it would be capital if Inch was with us.

"But I knew he had a stern task up in those Black Mountains of his. He has done very well to clear out the mercenaries and slavers. With Korf Aighos to the south clearing out the Blue Mountains, and Turko to the east managing to make something of Falinur—" Here Seg paused, and Jaezila started to say something and, behind Seg's back, I cautioned her to silence.

Presently, Seg went on speaking. "Turko will make those Falinurese understand what is required of them. But, had I to do it all over again—"

"You did the right thing, Seg. Turko will be harder than I could wish for; but we must work with what we have. In Hamal, for instance, do you think we can stamp out slavery even when Prince Nedfar is emperor?"

This was a stumper of a question, and we ate in silence for a time. Slavery at the moment was an intractable problem. One day, in the light of Opaz, one day, we'd be free of the blight.

Jaezila said, "And as well as our friends what of our foes?"

Well, there was enough of them about, by Krun!

We flew this leg of our course a few degrees south of west and, to the south of us and about halfway to the River Os, rose the Black Hills. From this range of heights flowed the River Mak, to empty into the Havilthytus at Ruathytu. King Telmont, then, must be marching along from the kingdom, a part of the Empire of Hamal, which gave him his name. Jaezila mentioned our foes; there was a man down there, a vad from Middle Nalem to the west of the Black Hills, who would as lief put me in an oubliette as kill me out of hand. This fellow, Garnath ham Hestan, Vad of Middle Nalem, had been associated with two other scoundrels, the Kataki Strom and Phu-Si-Yantong. Well, Yantong was dead, blown away by the Quern of Gramarye. Now, I suspected, Vad Garnath had transferred his evil allegiance to King Telmont.

Jaezila lowered her goblet and the wine shone on her lips.

"Jak—would you think it weak of me if I said I wished Shara was here?"

"Not in the least," I said at once. "I always feel more at ease when Melow the Supple goes with your mother, and Kardo with Drak."

Melow the Supple and her twins were safely out of Faol. They were Manhounds, horrific beings genetically structured to run on all fours and to rip and rend and destroy, more fearsome than hunting cats. Yet they were as essentially apim as I was. Chance had given Melow the opportunity to win free of her malign masters, and now she, and Kardo and Shara, were our friends. And the truth was that with a Manhound at your side you could wish for very few better comrades in a fight.

The voller proved a swift craft and we took turns to sleep, and before dawn threw ruby and jade sparks onto the lesser heights we closed with the Mountains of the West.

Not as lofty or awe-inspiring a range as the Stratemsk, but the Western Mountains of Hamal present a solemn and splendid spectacle. Probably not every hidden valley has been trodden by the foot of man. There are secrets in those interleaved folds of crag and scarp still. We aimed our flight for Hammansax where Tyfar had said he could be reached.

Color throbbed in the early morning. The air held a tang. Seg knuckled his eyes and stared all around and stretched, elbows back, spine arched, chest expanded, all the physique of a master bowman eloquent of his strength and skill, I clapped him on the back.

"Hai! Seg! A day for deeds!"

"Since our dip in that magical pool I feel like a youngster. May Opaz witness that it is good to be alive!"

Jaezila called from the side, turning to face us, still half leaning over. "There is a stream down there. I'm for a swim."

So, down we went in that dawn light and stripped off and plunged in, our daggers belted around our waists. Had there been any of the wonderful gallery of nasty creatures of Kregen swimming around hungry for breakfast he, she or it would have had short shrift from us three.

Dripping wet, we shouted and laughed and threw handfuls of water about and generally acted in a way that might have made Drak dub us undignified. I had a shrewd idea he'd join in...

By the time we'd dried off and cooked up some breakfast and stuffed ourselves to repletion with vosk rashers and loloo's eggs and masses of tea and palines, we felt in remarkable spirits.

Hammansax lay over the next ridge, far enough from the main mass of the mountain chain to afford it warning when the wild men attacked. As I told Seg, "It's not a question of if the wild men attack. It's always when."

Seg looked up, squinting against the morning light.

"Like now?"

We whirled.

They were there, flying in long skeins, sharp and dark against the brightness. The wings of their saddlebirds beating up and down, up and down, and the wink and glitter of weapons and armor, the flare of feathered decorations driving home with force their power and contempt for opposition. Not one of the civilized races, these moorkrim, these wild men.

"They haven't seen us." Jaezila threw her cape onto our little fire and the few last wisps of smoke died. "That was a nice cape. I particularly liked the zhantil-motif edging."

Still staring into the sky at those distant malefic figures, I said, "You can pick out the edging and stitch it back onto a new cape."

"They're flying away," said Seg.

"Aye."

"They've been up to mischief, then, if they're like any reivers I've known."

"Aye."

Jaezila bent for the cape and bashed it on the ground. Seg and I turned our heads to watch her, and I felt the quick spurt of love for her as she banged the cape on the dusty ground. The wild men up there, so like flutsmen and yet not civilized to any degree that would enable easy parleys to be held, undulating on beating wings, flew away, far away to the west.

"So we'd better go and see."

"If—" said Jaezila, holding the burned rag between her fists. "If Tyfar is—"

"Let us go and see."

Like any sensible Kregan in unfamiliar territory with a voller to consider, we'd concealed the airboat in the trees. The wild-men had not spotted her. We scuffed the fire out and Jaezila marched off to the voller. She let the cape fall to the ground. It was of a russet color, with a high velvet collar and those golden zhantils entwined and leaping as edging. Seg started after Jaezila.

I picked up the burned cape. I rolled it up. I shoved it under my arm. I started for the airboat. Jaezila was damned upset and I didn't like that.

She took the controls and sent the little craft up in a violent surge. We swung over the trees and pelted for the ridge. The gray rock and the trees whipped away below and we looked over the ridge into the valley folded between the mountain arms.

Fire, smoke, destruction…

Hammansax burned.

"Tyfar—"

"He'll be all right, Jaezila. You know how resourceful he is."

"That's the trouble. He's likely to go rushing out and get himself killed."

We did not speak much as the voller shot down toward burning Hammansax.

The town had been a small prosperous frontier post—the sax in the name indicated that—and the raiders had failed to destroy the character of the place. Walls still stood, a few roofs remained unfallen. But smoke choked everywhere and people ran and yelled among the flames. They had come out of hiding after the wildmen flew off and now strove to save their town from further destruction.

In a flierdrome to one side, the wreck of a green-painted Courier voller lay twisted grotesquely, the flames little blue devils amid the smoke along her frame. Beyond her the flierdrome was empty.

"No one here when the wildmen struck," said Seg.

"Perhaps Tyfar wasn't here." Jaezila hurled the airboat down into the principal square. Only two sides burned, the other two containing stalls remained intact. People looked up and shouted as we landed on the beaten earth of the square.

We soon discovered the story. Prince Tyfar had not been in Hammansax for a time. The stink of raw ashes, hot and shiny, got up our nostrils. Whirls of black cinders swept into the air from the burning houses. The people were dazed. This was a disaster which, although always a possibility in their imaginations, had really arrived and with it—horror. No matter these folk lived on the frontier and expected trouble; when that trouble came it was always fresh and terrible and so much greater than the anticipation could prepare. Yet we could not stop and help.

"We have sent off messengers," one of the chief men of the town told us. "The army will follow the moorkrim and try to get our people back; but the wildmen will fly far, far." He wiped black soot around his eyes, which were red and inflamed. "May Havil rot their wings."

Despite all the ridiculous toughness I am supposed to have, be and represent, despite all the aloof power and authority vested in me, despite all this flummery, I felt the keen dagger of guilt. This was my fault. By invading Hamal we had drawn off vitally needed men to guard these frontier posts against the wildmen. Oh, yes, the burdens hanging on the shoulders of men and women foolish enough to rule empires crush their victims unless resisted with other weapons than simple brute force.

If you cannot make an omelette without breaking eggs, then one innocent person will save a city of guilty people.

We did what we could to help the people, but that was little enough, Zair help us.

They were aware that their empire had been defeated in a battle in the capital city. But that was a long way away. Cultivation and husbandry and constant vigilance against the wild-men from over the mountains was the reality, was the here and now.

They'd go on living this way, living their lives, and whoever ruled in Ruathytu would demand taxes and would send not enough forces to help in defense. We had done little for Hammansax. Prince Tyfar, we were told by the landlord of what had been The Jolly Vodrin—now a pile of rubble and burned timbers—had taken what the Empress Thyllis had left him of his army to a high pass in the mountains called the Jaws of Laca.

"How do you know that for certain?" demanded Jaezila.

She looked splendid, fierce and radiant and burning with anger and anxiety.

The landlord, half of whose hair had burned away, wiped blistered hands gently on an ointment rag. He was Hamdal the Measure.

Seg said, very gently, "He will know, Lela."

What Seg did not say, what I did not say, was that Jaezila would also know why a landlord of an inn popular with the soldiers would be aware of their orders. This is a fact of military life in certain quarters. Cautious generals must legislate against it by counter-cunning.

"Where is the Lacachun?" asked Jaezila.

Hamdal the Measure held up one blistered hand, pointing to the southwest. "Between the two tallest peaks within view from that peak, the Ivory Cone. You can't miss it."

I said, "How many men did Prince Tyfar take?"

Hamdal made a face, and winced. "Two regiments? I do not know. Perhaps more. A lord came asking these questions just before the wildmen attacked—"

"Another lord?"

"Aye, notor. Another great lord. He sought Prince Tyfar with great urgency—just as you do."

Seg looked across at me, questioning.

"Thank you, Hamdal the Measure," I said. "We must leave you. But help will reach you soon—"

"Aye," said the landlord. "Aye—too late, as usual."

We went back to our flier.

"Another lord—" said Seg.

"Prince Nedfar," said Jaezila. "It must have been."

"Yes." The coaming of the voller struck warm under my hands. "Probably." The twin suns burned down. "Possibly. Let us hope that it was Prince Nedfar."

Three

Concerning Shooting Wagers

From the Ivory Cone the two distant peaks looked very much like the jaws of a dinosaur, head upturned, gaping at the sky. That was why they were called the Lacachun.

"If they've crunched down on Ty—" Jaezila gripped the rail and her voice was unsteady. I did not touch her.

"You know Tyfar."

"As I said—I do!"

The Ivory Cone passed away to the side, sleek and pointed and shining white, with long gray falls between the snow slopes. We all wore thick flying furs. Our faces glowed, nipped by the chill. On we drove and we looked keenly ahead, ready to sight whatever of peril lay before us.

This airboat—she had no name, only in the Hamalian way a number—carried us over the snow sheets and down past the saddle. We corkscrewed between sheer rock faces. A fear that we were entering a massif took hold of us and had to be resisted. We sped along over gulfs and soared up over slopes of scree and so whirled out again into space. We three were old campaigners. Not one of us even considered rising into the higher levels and simply flying over the top.

We wished to arrive unseen and unheralded.

The wildmen who had trapped the voller below were not so careful. These were their mountains and here they ruled.

The situation was laid out for us as we hovered in the rock of a striated rock cliff. A ledge protruded from the crumbled rock face, perhaps halfway up from the stream below, a mere silver thread. The lip high above threw shadows over us. The wildmen circled and shot at the stranded airboat on the ledge. Others had alighted and crept up between boulders tumbled on the ledge. They approached from each end, yet they hesitated, and we saw shafts lifting from the airboat and the stones about her.

"It is just a matter of time," said Seg. He reached for the longbow that was never absent for long from his side.

Jaezila had the controls.

"Can you—?" Seg started to say, and then stopped. Jaezila deftly brought the voller in among the shadows close to the cliff. She eased her along. Like a ghost we slithered with our starboard flank against the rock striations. Ahead and below, the ledge and the voller there and the swirling forms of the wildmen stood out in suns shine.

I picked up a longbow. Seg nodded. "A good choice, Dray. That stave I built when I was Kov in Falinur."

"You never stop making bows, Seg; how you keep track of 'em all is the mystery."

But, of course, that was no mystery...

"Each bow is different," said Seg, selecting the first arrow from the quiver strapped to the voller's rail. "Each one has character. You know that."

"Yes. And there are no bows in all Kregen to match the ones built by Seg Segutorio."

"That," said Jaezila, bringing the airboat to a halt in midair and relinquishing the controls, "is true."

"How many d'you make 'em, Dray?"

There were eight moorkrim flying like the crazy savages they were in the air space before the ledge, rising and falling, swinging in to loose and diving or zooming away.

"The young braves of the tribe," I said. "You know the kind of pecking order they're likely to have and the necessity of gaining credit among their peer group. The more mature warriors will be on the ledge, under cover."

"Yes. I make seven saddle flyers this side—"

"And ten on the other end," said Jaezila. She took up her longbow. Like the others, this was a Lohvian longbow built by Seg. If you have to have a hobby on Kregen it is useful if it is connected with survival.

"Twenty-five," said Seg. "We've shafted more than that before breakfast."

"Maybe so, Seg. And each time we do it, it could be the last. So, my old dom, watch it!"

He laughed, throwing back his head. His black hair waved wildly and his fey blue eyes looked now with the steady regard of the bowman—wild and impulsive and shrewd and practical are the folk of Erthyrdrin, and Seg showed all that blend now as he fitted nock to string.

"Father!" Jaezila looked at me, the arrow in her fingers as long and lethal as those held by Seg and me. I felt surprise that she thus called me.

"Lela?"

"You told me, I seem to remember, when I was little, that you and Uncle Seg used to wager when you shot."

Again Seg laughed, lifting the bow. His russet tunic hid what was going on among the muscles of his back and arms, but they would have made a sculptor weep for joy.

"So we did, Lela, my love, so we did! What is it to be, then, a gold talen a hit?"

Macabre, gruesome, unfeeling? Wagering on killing other people? Of course. Once we began to shoot, the wildmen would not bother about anything as decadently sophisticated as gambling on how they slew us. They would simply whoop in with the one blood-red desire to chew us up and hurl the refuse into the gulf. That is the way of wildmen.

Perhaps, if you thought about it, that was more savagely honest? All

I knew was that I was on Kregen, my comrade and my daughter were about to face deadly peril, and a man I admired was about to die unless we stopped his killers.

We shot.

Three of the eight pirouetting in midair before the ledge were shafted, and then three more. The remaining two swung away, the wings of their tyryvols beating madly and Seg and Jaezila saw to them as I switched my aim.

The targets among the boulders proved more tricky, and I know two of my shafts missed. Return shots started to come up; but we were a small and protected target in the voller among the clustered shadows.

We three worked together sweetly in the shooting.

When the wildmen at the far end of the ledge broke from their boulders and, leaping astride their saddle flyers, shot up into the air and headed for us, Seg and Jaezila went methodically to work on them while I remained winkling out the fellows in the rocks this end.

A crossbow bolt punched clean up through the skin of the voller.

Seg said, "That looks nasty."

"They capture crossbows from time to time. They can't make 'em, can't even do repairs. When they break they throw them away. They tart them up with feathers and skins and hair. But they can shoot well with them."

Seg loosed and flipped a fresh arrow into place and loosed again, all in a smooth twinkling motion, before he spoke.

"That's one crossbow fellow who won't shoot again."

And Jaezila laughed. "Two shafts, Uncle Seg, for one crossbow man?"

"I'll pay you the gold talen, Lela, don't fret."

The ten flyers were whittled down to four before they reached the voller. Seg shot and took out a moorkrim with his hair black and greasy braided into a fantastic halo. Jaezila's shot merely transfixed the wildman's arm; that wouldn't stop the savage from advancing.

"Swords!"

As the three wildmen flung their tyryvols at the airboat in a welter of thrashing wings, we drew our blades. That churning of the air, a favorite trick of men who fight astride saddle flyers, prevented accurate shooting. The three hit the deck and came for us. Their stink preceded them.

When fighting on foot wildmen employ shields, usually of wicker and skins, and spears or swords if they can come by them, for they find the metallurgy of swords a little above their capacities. These three screeched war cries. They snatched their shields up and into place. One had a sword, a Hamalian army thraxter, and he pressed on boldly. The one Jaezila had wounded didn't seem to know he had been hit. The arrow transfixed his arm and with a petty gesture he broke it off, fore and aft, and then slapped his shield back across again.

You had to admire the fortitude of the wildmen, if nothing else.

Not caring to waste time, for the fellows below kept up their pressure on the stranded voller, I whipped out the Krozair longsword and cocked it between spread fists.

"Let me have 'em," I shouted at Seg and Jaezila. "You see off those fellows in the rocks."

Giving my comrade and my daughter no time to argue I pushed past to the front, faced the small deck space where the wildmen ran on as only warriors at home in the air can run, and met the first onslaught.

A Krozair longsword does not take a deal of notice of a wicker shield. The first man sank to the deck with a cleft skull.

The next two, rushing up together on bandy legs bent like springs, leaped for me. The Krozair brand switched left and as I rolled my wrists flailed back right. Two swift and unmerciful blows, and the two moorkrim toppled aside. Both fell, slipped and, shrieking, pitched over into space. I put my foot against the first one, whose blood and brains oozed out, and pushed him over the side.

The smell of the wildmen, which comes as much from themselves as from the muck they smear on their greased and braided hair, hung about the voller. It would persist.

Seg bellowed, "They are rushing the airboat!"

"Down!" Jaezila sprang for the controls. She slammed the levers hard over and our flier pitched down as though the bottom of the world had fallen out.

She brought us in with superb piloting. We flashed over the boulders. Seg leaned over, very thoughtfully, and sent two flashing shafts into billets as we passed. It is my unalterable opinion that there is no greater bowman in all Kregen than Seg Segutorio.

We landed slap bang in the middle of the rest of them as they rushed the flier. The ensuing dust up was interesting, for Seg and Jaezila can handle blade as well as bow.

The tyryvols fluttered their wings but could not rise as the wildmen had tethered them with rocks for the final foot charge. Our blades glittered and fouled with blood. We fought fiercely for a space and then there were no more moorkrim to fight.

Seg had a small nick along his right wrist, a nothing, and Jaezila a score along her side. I frowned.

"Damned careless of you, my girl. Let me look."

"It's nothing, Jak!"

It was nothing, really, but we dug out the first aid which consisted of a gel in a bandage, and slapped it on. Seg looked up from the crashed flier. He shouted.

"You won't believe what's here!"

We went across the rocks. The aftermath of a fight is often a strange time, when noises ring in your ears, and the air seems irradiated with color, and the world moves under your feet.

Seg was right.

There were dead men sprawled here and there, curled up in nooks and crannies, huddled behind the rocks that had punched through the voller's skin in the crash. She was done for. One of the silver boxes had broken and—it being the paol box—the cayferm it contained had wafted away to be lost in the air. A shivering man crouched behind a box which had saved him, for its stout wooden side was feathered with arrows like a pincushion. He held the windlass of a crossbow.

"Look," said Seg.

Prince Nedfar lay half on his side, his hands outstretched gripping the crossbow. It was clear what had been going on. The man behind the box was a Relt, a gentle specimen of a race of diffs who are not warriors, and he had been spanning the crossbow for Nedfar. Nedfar's face showed greasy and strained, dirty with grimed sweat. His eyes were sunken.

Among the dead men a few living men rose to greet us.

They were retainers, the Relt stylor, the cooks and valets, a groom, and I felt the pang at what must have happened. I bent to Nedfar. His sunken eyes looked like plums, bruised against bruised flesh.

"Prince!"

He opened his eyes.

In his right shoulder the butt end of a quarrel stood up. It looked obscene. Judging by the amount of wooden flight showing, its steel head was buried deeply into Nedfar's shoulder. He saw me. He recognized me. He spoke one word.

"Traitor!"

Four

Of a Walk in the Mist

"Now, now, prince. That's all over." I tried to take the crossbow from his hands. "You're safe now. We have to make you comfortable—"

"Jak the Shot—traitor! You betrayed Hamal!"

"He's off his head," said Seg. "And I can see he is a fine-looking man, just as you said. A real prince."

"Yes. We've got to take care of him."

What had happened was clear enough. The fighting men with Nedfar had fought. They had been killed. They must have held off the wildmen for a goodly long time. The end was in sight when we turned up. I judged that the twenty-five we had dealt with had been left to finish the thing from a larger war-band.

"Hamal—" Nedfar looked in a bad way. His face was of that color of the lead in old sewers. "You betrayed our plans to our enemies, Jak—"

Jaezila brought water and moistened his lips. He saw her.

"Jaezila—what—the man Jak the Shot—do not, do not—"

"Prince!" Jaezila spoke in a voice like diamond. "Where is Tyfar?"

"Tyfar? My son Tyfar?"

"Yes, yes! Is he still in the Pass of Lacachun?"

"Oh, yes. He is still there—"

Nedfar's mind was not wandering; but he was very tired and his wound gave him a distancing from reality. No doubt past and present clashed in his brain. He sounded very weak.

"We must take Nedfar to a doctor." I tried to sound matter of fact. "We could take the bolt out of his shoulder; but the pain might do for him, brave though he is. A needleman is absolutely vital."

"You're right. And we'll have to go in our airboat."

Again Jaezila bent to Nedfar.

"Tyfar." She spoke with compressed urgency. "Your son Tyfar. Is all well with him?"

The prince's voice rasped weakly. His head rolled.

"All is—is not well—with Tyfar."

We bent closer, intent, concentrating on the halting words.

"They trapped him—the message was—was a trick. A trap. I flew for help—help—Tyfar! They will slay him and all his men—"

Nedfar tried to lift himself, fighting back the pain. He glared up at Jaezila; she bent over him, her soft brown hair a glory about her face. On that face an expression of loving care was replaced by horror and then by a savage determination. The whole story was there, on Jaezila's face, to be read.

"He will be killed." She jumped up, swinging about and the suns light caught in her hair and across her russets and she looked glorious, glorious. "No time, no time—"

She was out of the wreck of the voller in the rocks, leaping to the nearest tethered flyer. The tyryvol's black and ochre scales glistened in the light. She gave him a clip alongside those ugly jaws and freed the tether. All in a fluid line of motion she leaped for the saddle, clamping those long slender legs in hard, giving the flying beast a licking flick with a loose rein, sending him bolting up, legs trailing, tail splattering dust and rock chips, flung him high and hard into the blaze of suns light.

"Jaezila!"

She did not bother to answer but strapped up the clerketer and stretched out to reduce headwinds. The tyryvol opened his wings and beat and beat again and soared up and up.

"Jaezila!"

Seg said, "We'll have to go after her, my old dom."

"Aye," I said. "I will. But you will have to take Nedfar back to the needleman—"

"Me!"

We looked at the prince, who slumped back, looking dreadful. His eyes closed.

"Yes, you, Seg. Don't you see?"

"No, Dray, I do not! You're the one who wants to make this Nedfar fellow the Emperor of Hamal."

"I do. But I can't let Jaezila fly off—"

"No more can I! By the Veiled Froyvil! You know you're the one to handle those idiots at the Peace Conference—"

"Drak can do that! So can you, come to that. There's no time to waste—"

"There's no time, agreed! You—"

"Nedfar is to be the Emperor of Hamal, that's all arranged—"

"I don't give a rast's hind parts for the Emperor of Hamal! But I give a very great deal for Lela! Don't you understand! She's the Princess Majestrix of Vallia, flying off alone into these confounded mountains with packs of wildmen out ahunting! I'm not going the other way—"

"This is—"

"Listen to me, Dray Prescot! You're the Emperor of Vallia and my old dom and your place is with the Peace Conference sorting out these idiot Hamalese and setting up this Nedfar fellow as their new emperor! By Vox! Why can't I ever knock any sense into that vosk skull of a head of yours!"

"Just because Jaezila is my daughter!"

There was no question of my giving orders to Seg. We did not operate on that level. He was right. I knew he was right. But Nedfar had to be taken to a doctor and I had to go after my daughter. The decision was made, irrational and selfish, maybe, but made.

I bellowed back as I vaulted out of the wreckage, "I'll be back soon! Get Nedfar to a doctor!"

As I laid hands on the nearest tyryvol, Seg yelled something I will not repeat. But I knew he would care for Nedfar. I'd trust Seg Segutorio to the ends of both Earth and Kregen.

There existed no doubt in our minds that one of us had to go with Nedfar. Unable to care for himself and a prince of Hamal, he would be at the mercy of any of the many folk who might see profit in his hide. His retainers left alive were not fighting men, and they had been unnerved— shattered—by the viciousness of the wildmen's onslaught and the carnage and blood all about them. Not everyone on Kregen is a bold brave roistering warrior, or a hunting-leather-clad girl ready with whip and rapier.

The tyryvol smashed his wings down under my intemperate handling and we rocketed into the air. Grabbing at the leather straps of the clerketer, I glanced down. Seg stood there, hands on hips, head upflung, glaring up. As he dwindled away I could visualize the expression on that face of his and although I did not laugh I felt the affection bubbling up.

Good old Seg Segutorio!

That forkful of dungy straw he'd bunged in my face when first we met away there in the Eye of the World had paid dividends in the best comrade a man could ever hope for.

As we lifted away the tyryvol showed his disinclination to rise too high past the ledge. Ahead the world was blotted out in a swirl of mist, dank and gray, writhing down from the higher peaks and spreading out in the cleft between the precipices. I let the flying beast hurtle on at the level he chose, only making sure he was aimed in the right direction and going as fast as he could.

They are splendid flyers, tyryvols, adapted to the tricky cross-currents hereabouts. Of all the wonderful array of saddle flyers of Havilfar, the flutduin of Djanduin stands supreme, in my estimation. I think the snow-white zhyans are truly regal among flyers, but overpriced and tricky as to temper. We flew on and followed the windings of the cleft in the mountains. The silence, apart from the rush of air and the beat of wings, fell strangely after the bedlam of only moments ago.

If Nedfar died, then my plans for Hamal would be thrown out of joint. This buffoon King Telmont was quite unsuitable to be emperor. And if, as I darkly suspected, Vad Garnath had thrown in his lot with Telmont, that was another and even more sinister mark against the king from the Black Hills.

I suppose we could have ignored Nedfar's pain and pushed the crossbow bolt through his shoulder. Drawing it out would have been tricky; but we could have done it. We had a few simple medicaments. But the chance of the prince's death would have been too great; in our own reckless argumentative way, Seg and I had done what had to be done, albeit with suppressed feelings. We'd taken a shaft from old Larghos the So, cutting it off level with his skin and then putting a rod against it and giving it one hell of a thwack with the flat of a sword. Larghos had yelled blue bloody murder. But Nedfar?—Larghos had survived. I wondered if Nedfar would have weathered that kind of treatment. As the tyryvol carried me on strongly I found I was working out just how many seasons ago it was that Seg and I had fought at old Larghos the So's side.

Too many...

He was probably dead now. When a mercenary earns the coveted title of paktun and wears the silver pakmort at his throat he stands a better chance of survival than an ordinary mercenary. He stands an even better chance when he becomes a hyr-paktun and wears the golden pakzhan.

The mist lowered down and tendrils swept away in long cobwebby strands. The tyryvol's wings lathered the mist. He was a fine strong beast, and his scales were polished up. The saddle was relatively crude, being made of wicker and leather and very little padding. It was practical, and from it the ukra, the long polearm of the flyer, could be wielded to deadly effect. The peaks around us seemed to stab like ukras, like the toonons of the flyers of Turismond; seemed to thrust jagged barbs to stop our onward passage. The mist forced us lower and lower.

I'd often pondered a scheme to bring some of the impressive coal black impiters over from the Stratemsk in Turismond. They were hardy flyers and would do well in any new environment of Vallia or Havilfar. And you don't need barbs in an aerial polearm...

I cursed. I realized what I was doing. My thoughts were maundering on like this because I could not face the truth.

My daughter Jaezila had gone flying off to find Tyfar, alone, hurtling into danger. And I was flailing along after her and this pestiferous mist shut down and prevented me from finding the way.

By Zair! If the mist clamped in... That I might be dashed to death on the rocks seemed to me then a mere trifle, a passing side effect of the greater tragedy. I had to get to the Pass of Lacachun!

Tyfar was trapped. Nedfar had mumbled something about a message being a trick. So Tyfar had gone to the rendezvous with a couple of regiments or so and had been trapped. If Jaezila flew into that scene... I used the loose strap on the tyryvol and he responded, beating strongly and churning the air. It was cold and dank and miserable; I scarcely noticed. The furs lay back in our voller. I barely missed them. All the chill deadliness of the Ice Floes of Sicce would not have worried me then. I flew after my daughter, and I refused to think of the time in the Eye of the World when I had flown after Velia, my daughter...

Zair would not allow that to happen again. He could not...

To left and right the craggy mountainsides lifted up to vanish into the clouds. Ahead the mist hung like congealed cobwebs. Below lay a boulder-choked stream, a mere ligament of silver wire. As we flew on and the jaws of the mountains closed, the river spouted closer and closer. Ahead of us now the pass lifted with the stream tumbling down in fronds of spouting silver and the mist crushing down from above. Most birds and flying animals will balk at flying through clouds, although some—the flutduin par excellence—can manage that tricky evolution. The wise men say the flutduins have an extra sense in their souls. Whatever the truth of that, the tyryvol flew lower and lower above the stream spouting amid boulders in the pass and would not fly higher into the mist.

Eventually the mist and cloud touched the ground ahead.

The way was barred.

No use hitting the flying animal. He craned his neck around, hissing. Each scale carried a drop of moisture. The leather was dark with water. I jumped off and, gripping the reins in a fist like a knobbly tree bole, I started walking, leading the flying beast along. He strutted, lashing his tail, most unhappy.

Boulders sprang away under my feet. Sharp edges of rock snapped at my ankles. I almost fell and dragged on the leading rein to support my weight.

The animal balked, rearing, flailing his wings.

"Come on, tyry! You can do it!"

A ferocious haul on the lead pulled him on. He saw there was nothing else for it. Wings folded, tail tucked, head outstretched, he followed me into the mist.

Dampness clung everywhere. The chill bit to the quick. At least, the stink of the wildmen eased from the saddle and accoutrements. It was necessary to keep on hauling on the lead, pulling the beast along. His clawed feet clicked and clacked among the stones. He maintained a nasty hissing sound, which indicated not vicious anger but rather a sort of misery. No time to feel sorry for him. Somewhere ahead in the Pass of the Jaws of Laca Jaezila might be facing dangers that would appall a paktun...

The whole world of Kregen consisted merely of a silvery gray whirl. Nothing existed except the stones under my feet and the leather leading rein in my fist. Sounds thinned. The clatter of the tyryvol at my back sounded as if it came from the other end of Kregen. The mist got into my body. I felt as though I floated. Yet upward lay the way. Upward over rounded boulders which rolled treacherously, and sharp-fanged slabs of rock that gashed at ankles and legs.

My state may be imagined when I say it took me a long time to realize what this mixture of rock and boulders meant...

A rushing sibilant sound gradually intruded on my dulled senses. In these dolorous conditions I half expected the Star Lords to appear with their blue radiance and their Giant Scorpion and snatch me up and away. But the roaring welter of sound growing louder as I stumbled on came from the stream. Here it must be leaping off some higher crag to the side and splashing onto the rocks. In a few moments drops of solid water flew out of the mist, stinging like hail.

I stopped, turning my head. The tyryvol, a mere shapeless blot of shadow at my back, hunkered down. The waterfall was wearing away the cliff, and every now and again a cascade of sharp rocks would fall. Hauling on the rein I started off, edging a little to my left, away from the fall.

The mist looked to be in agitated movement over to the right; the boulders slicked with wet. I stumbled and half fell, gripping the rein. The tyryvol let out a tremendous squawk and dived over me, wings out and flapping, and giving me a welt with his tail. I sprawled forward under the flying beast. He went on, and I could still see him, and he dragged me after him, bursting out of the mist and soaring out over nothingness.

Spinning like a spider at the end of a thread, I dangled beneath the flyer; all below me, thousands of feet down, spread out a vast rock-enclosed valley. Helplessly, I swung along under the flyer, who thrashed his wings in an ecstasy of flight after the prison of the mist.

The leather rein cut into my hand.

Gyrating like a bobbin, I saw the mountains circling me, spinning around and around. The stream spouted off the cliff and hissed down to hit at the side of the path where the tyryvol had dived into space. Mist pressed down above, shading everything into tones of gray and slate and purple. Across the valley the opposite cleft shot into view and out again as I spun. Up there lay the Pass of the Jaws of Laca.

My weight at the end of the rein dragged the animal's head down. He kept trying to lift himself and wagged his head from side to side. I swung. Freed from the goading manthing who rode his back, the tyryvol wanted to free himself from the weight dragging his head down.

He began to claw and bite at the rein, twisting his head to seize the leather between his fangs, grasping it with his talons to steady it and wrench at it. The leather was good and strong and would last; but not for very long. Below me lay a drop into the Ice Floes of Sicce, for sure.

Hand over hand, I started to climb up the leading rein.

It was a race and the dratted flying beast knew it.

Sweat poured off my face. My muscles knotted. I hauled up disdaining to use my feet, for there was no time. It was a case of heave up, grab, heave up. The wind whistled about my ears. The tyryvol's wings beat remorselessly, up and down, and his tail flicked about nastily.

The opposite side of the valley swam nearer.

His teeth were yellow and wicked. He tore at the rein. His head was dragged down with each upward lunge I managed. I jerked the leather, and then gasped; that might snap the stuff clean through. Up I went, and click click went his teeth. Oh, yes, a fine old to-do, sweaty and alarming and windy.

It was a damned long way down, by Krun!

He nearly had my hand off when I reached up for the last purchase. Snatching my hand away, I glared up at the beast. His eye glared back, malefic and wrought up. Clearly, he was saying, "If you can't fly me properly then drop off!"

Gripping the leather with both hands I swung back. On the return swing, face uppermost, I forced the swing on. Like a phantom bursting from the pits of horror and disappearing, a flyer whipped past. The impression was all of flailing wings and rippling feathers, of a sharp beak and bright eye, and of a wildman skirling and screeching and prodding with his polearm.

The leather cut into my hand as I spun. The newcomer volplaned up, turning, revealing himself to be a small fluttlann, all white and pale blue. His rider shook his pole-mounted blade at me. His teeth showed. He was laughing at my predicament! He kicked in and the fluttlann pirouetted and dived on extended wings. Not fast, fluttlanns, not one of the more prized saddle birds of Havilfar; but they are pressed into service when nothing better can be had. It was perfectly clear this wildman saw himself gaining a powerful tyryvol. All he had to do was fly in and slash the leather leading rein away, the idiot who had fallen off his saddle would drop into the gulf, and the tyryvol would change ownership.

My tyryvol lifted his head. I swung about underneath. The fluttlann straightened, turned into a horizontal bar with a double blob at the center. The sharp steel blade of the ukra did not glitter in that mist-shrouded light, but it looked highly lethal and unpleasant.

No time now to go through the contortions of fighting a way past the tyryvol's fangs up onto the saddle. By the time all that had been done the wildman would have finished it with a single blow.

Gripping onto the rein with my feet, catching a loop and drawing that over and down one foot to stand on it with the other, gave me a crazy kind of anchorage. My left hand held the leading rein. My right hauled out the Krozair brand. I nearly went head over heels into nothingness; but the blade whipped free. The fluttlann swerved at the last moment and the ukra slashed, wide and horizontal and deadly.

The Krozair brand met that sweep. Steel chingled against steel. The shock made the tyryvol's head bob up and down like a water duck. Gyrating like an insect caught in a spider's web, I got a breath, took a fresh grip on the handle of the sword, glared about the sky for the wildman.

He spun up, circled, turned and then hurtled down again.

This time, set, I angled the blow. The Krozair steel simply sliced clean through the stout wooden shaft of his ukra. The steel head spun away below.

He screeched—wild, incoherent mouthings. I shook the sword at him.

"If you want to finish it, come in! Otherwise—clear off."

He circled. No doubt he was waiting for me to put the sword away so as to climb up. It occurred to me to consider the way Seg would handle this situation.

Seg could have done it easily, I know.

It was more difficult for me.

The wildman circled, around and around. The little fluttlann was willing. The tyryvol ploughed on, heading for the opposite side of the valley. That was my direction, also. There lay the Pass of Lacachun.

The wildman wouldn't be going away. He'd wait. He had me. If I didn't tire and fall off, he could sweep in any time he liked. His patience would be rewarded.

Savage and barbaric tribesmen are noted for impetuous anger and headlong attacks; also they do not take kindly to fools. Often they are less noted for patience, although patience is one of the basic necessities of survival in barbaric communities. Yet this very readiness to wait blinded the wildman to a simple answer to the problem. It was simple only if he trusted his own skill, and I judged him a young man, an unfledged would-be warrior who sought to gain a great coup by the capture of this tyryvol. So as I put the longsword away and reached around on my back, the wildman drew his leather-wrapped bowcase.

His gorytus was decorated in only the most rudimentary fashion: a line of beads and a handful of feathers. As he gained in stature the gorytus would become smothered in applied marks of his prowess. But if I got my shot in first his gorytus would remain undecorated forever.

Now here was where Seg would have come into his own.

I held the leather leading rein in my left hand and into that hand, parallel with the rein, I transferred the bow. An arrow drew from the quiver with that initial little resistance to show it was firmly affixed and would not fall out when I stood on my head—an occurrence of routine nature, I assure you, in aerial combat.

The wildman had drawn his bow from his gorytus by this time. He eyed me, quite aware what I was up to. I saw his teeth again. We fitted shafts within the space of the same heartbeat. He nudged his fluttlann and I felt the choke of bile in my throat as he flew a little way to the side. I was dangling uselessly and swinging in the opposite direction.

I contorted my body like a chiff-shush dancer out of Balintol, all liquid wrigglings and writhings. The tyryvol poked his head down and I sagged in the air. I looked up.

"Hold still, tyry, you ungrateful beast! That wildman will beat you, for sure."

The leather coiled the other way...

The wildman shot a tiniest fraction of time before I did.

His arrow buzzed off somewhere. My shaft took him in the thigh. That was not my point of aim. Seg would not have missed.

The moorkrim let out a shriek of rage and reached for another shaft. He had not faced a Lohvian longbow before. His own flat bow, while a fine weapon for aerial combat, did not draw with the same long power as a Lohvian longbow. He had no idea that the steel-headed arrow, piercing through his thigh, pierced on into the body of his fluttlann.

The saddlebird faltered in the air.

His pale blue and white wings flurried, beat with a panicky stroke, another, slowed the rhythm, drew out to a wide-planing glide angle. The wildman shook his bow at me. His mouth was an oblong blot of shrieked anger.

I felt for the fluttlann. Like the freymul which is called the poor man's zorca because it lacks much of the superbness of the zorca, the fluttlann is regarded as a second-class saddle flyer. The strange and, if you care to delve, pathetic item to note about the freymul on land and the fluttlann in the sky is that, both being regarded a little slightingly, both are better than reports say, and both are willing and courageous and will serve to the utmost of their strength. This fluttlann tried to keep up; but his wound was sore and deep. Slowly, he gave up the unequal struggle and planed away, spiraling, looking for a good place to alight. With him he carried one moorkrim who was wilder than most wildmen in those dying moments of conflict.

My tyryvol tried to bite off my left hand.

I stuck the bowstave up, in a reflexive gesture, and knocked his head away.

My problems were not over yet, by Krun!

A quick grab saved me from falling. The bow went back over my shoulder. The tyryvol turned his head sideways and surveyed me with an eye that was not so much beady as downright voraciously calculating.

I started to swing, holding on with both hands, freeing my legs, swinging myself up and down like a pendulum. It was bend, pull, stretch, bend, pull, stretch. The animal's head went with me like an upside down yo-yo. Like a pendulum I swung horizontally, along the line of his body, and I got my feet into the base of his neck where it joined his scaly body. I'd have liked to have landed him one in the guts; but I couldn't reach that far.

He gave a choked up kind of squawk.

"That'll show you you won't shake me off, tyry!"

Down I swung and up and then down and around again, swinging like a monkey after a coconut. In the wind rush and bluster the sound of a ripping, tearing, death-bringing parting of the leather rein told me this was my last chance.

On that swing, just as the rein finally parted, I got my leg hooked around the tyryvol's neck. I hung from one crooked knee. His scales cut into me. His head drove down and tucked in and his fangs, all yellow and serrated and sharp, slashed at my dangling head. His talons raked up from the rear to scrape me off and hurl me away.

I swung.

Sideways on my bent knee I hauled myself up. A flailing hand scraped on his scales, caught and gripped. With a frenzied cracking of muscles I heaved up. His talons gored my side and I swore at him.

His clashing fangs missed me by a whisker. His head shot up and he twisted around to get at me on the other side. I straddled the thick part of his neck. I held on. I held on!

I took three huge draughts of air.

The valley below swam dizzily.

By the disgusting diseased liver and lights of Makki Grodno! This was no time to test out Sir Isaac's theories...

I sat up, clipped the tyryvol alongside his head, told him that his fun and games were over. He would come under control all right. Mind you, he'd be frisky for some time. He'd quite enjoyed it all.

The sweat lay on me thickly, clammy, chill and damned unpleasant.

After that it was headlong for the Pass of Lacachun.

By Zair! I don't relish going through that kind of nightmare too often, believe you me.

Five

Trapped in the Pass of Lacachun

The landlord of The Jolly Vodrin, Hamdal the Measure, had told us Prince Tyfar had taken two regiments. The reason for the statement now seemed clear as I circled briefly between the peaks, glaring down onto the Pass of Lacachun. The men down there were of two kinds: crossbowmen and spearmen. Hamdal had seen that and reported. Just how many there had been to start with I did not know; I did know and with dreadful certainty that there were not many left now.

These soldiers were trapped. They huddled in what cover they could find on a projecting floor of rock standing proud of the south side of the pass. To either side the sheer faces of the lower cliffs lifted to the peaks above. Yes, rather like jaws, those peaks. And the tidbit in their gullet was being gobbled up by the clouds of skirling wildmen.

Against the north face I flew in shadow. The sounds of the yelling down there drifted up attenuated. The floor of rock jutting out into the pass, smothered with fallen boulders, provided the best—the only—place for defense.

The wovenwork shields of the wildmen were no proof against the crossbow bolts of the defenders. Salix plants of various varieties grew in the upland soils, and, stripped, provided light strong canes for weaving. Many moorkrim carried hide-and-skin shields, some fastened around wickerwork foundations. The Hamalian shields of the spearmen down there would keep out an arrow cast from a flat bow if the angle was not perfectly at right angles. All the same, the wildmen had bottled up this little force and were going about their business of exterminating it completely.

Nothing was going to stop me from bursting through them and landing among the survivors. Down there Jaezila stood in the cover of a rock and, even as I watched, she shot her longbow and took out a wildman who attempted to get his shot in first. He went over sideways, flailing, with the long rose-fletched arrow through him.

At Jaezila's side, Tyfar stood, his head bandaged, giving orders to his men.

A nasty situation...

Down I went, hurtling with the tyryvol now thoroughly of the opinion that this manthing on his back was no longer to be trifled with. Most of the wildmen had landed and taken cover the better to shoot up at the ledge of rock; but enough remained flying to make me punch through them with a rush and a whoop.

Even then, with me hollering like a dervish and crashing through in a thrashing of wings, a couple of the swods below loosed their crossbows. Both bolts hissed past. I yelled.

"I'm on your side, you pack of famblys!"

And then the wildmen took it on themselves to show their nastiness, and they shot my tyryvol under me.

I felt his body bunch and jerk with the bite of the arrows. He uttered a shrill squawk and then a dolorous descending moan. His wings trembled. He fell. We pitched down for the last ten or fifteen feet and I was only saved from a broken neck by his collapsing body. I leaped off, feeling immense sadness for him. After his little escapade over the valley with me dangling like a bobbin, we had come to an understanding. His bright eyes glazed over. His slim head on its slender neck shuddered and drooped laxly, and he was dead.

For a moment—a stupid, defenseless moment—I stood looking down on him.

"Jak! Get your fool head down!"

"All right, Tyfar, all right."

I stomped across to his rock. Two arrows broke against the face as I dodged into cover.

"Jak!" said Jaezila. "Prince Nedfar—?"

"He'll be all right. Seg went back with him to find a needleman."

"And you two came after me." Tyfar put his hands on his hips and glared at us. Trim, defiant, eager, a true comrade, he shook his head. He looked as though he could go ten rounds with a dinosaur, bandaged head and all.

He winced when he shook his head.

"We came after you, Ty, because we didn't think you could be trusted out alone." Jaezila spoke sweetly.

He looked at her. "You mean you couldn't keep away from my funeral."

"Now, Ty—"

He gestured with a blood-splashed hand. "Well, look! We're boxed in here. I told Jaezila she was a ninny to fly in alone. Now you do the same."

He was right, of course. And we were not about to go into maudlin scenes of swearing eternal comradeship as we were chopped. For a start, neither Jaezila nor I intended to be chopped, and Tyfar wouldn't, either, once we jollied him out of his mood.

"What happened?"

"He fouled it up," said Jaezila, with her haughtiness of manner most pronounced.

"Well?"

Tyfar looked chastened. "I had a message to come here to catch a damned bandi—"

"We heard something of that. The message was a trap."

"Yes. I've been hitting the moorkrim hard lately and this is their way of getting rid of me."

"And all you brought was two regiments?"

He looked furious. "We're thin on the ground and just about nonexistent in the air. I'm supposed to command the Twentieth Army, and they stripped most of my troops. Tell me, Jak, for the sweet sake of Havil, what really happened in Ruathytu? We heard garbled reports of a battle—"

"First of all, what was your father doing here?"

"He wanted to see me. What about I've no idea. He heard where I'd gone and followed. He descried the situation and tried to go for help. It seems that wildmen brought him down. And then you—"

"Seg will bring up help. There is no doubt whatsoever of that."

"I don't know who Seg is—"

"A friend. A good friend."

"Now tell me about the battle—"

I frowned. How to tell a young keen general commanding troops that his country had been defeated not only in a battle but in the war? That his foemen lorded it in his capital city? I swallowed. I tried.

His face lengthened. He half turned away. He put a hand on the rock behind which we sheltered.

"You mean to say we lost?"

"Yes."

For only a heartbeat I doubted him; then he proved once again that he was Prince Tyfar.

"Well, we lost this one. But we won't lose the next—"

"I knew you would say that, Tyfar. I have to try to make you see that the Vallians and Hyrklese, particularly, desire friendship with Hamal."

"A fine way they have of showing it." He was suffering now as the enormity of what had befallen his country sank in. "You mean they just took Ruathytu? Just like that?"

"It was not easy. It was a bonny fight. But the Djangs settled the issue."

He listened as the story of the Taking of Ruathytu unfolded. He stood very still. I watched his hands. Slowly they constricted into fists, knobby and hard, the fists of a fighting man as, spread on a page, they were the shapely hands of a scholar. A man of parts, Prince Tyfar.

"We three have been through some rousing adventures," he said, stirring himself. "The Empress Thyllis made a pact with the Hyr Notor, who was a Wizard of Loh. I remember our times, Jak, with Deb-Lu-Quienyin. I could have wished he had been there, at the Battle of Ruathytu, to help us."

I could not look at him, at my comrade. Deb-Lu had been there. Without his sorcerous powers we might well have lost. In the end it had been Deb-Lu, aided by Khe-Hi-Bjanching, who had defeated Phu-Si-Yantong, the Wizard of Loh whom Tyfar knew as the Hyr Notor. Tyfar would have to know one day. How would he react when he recalled our conversation?

That was merely a smaller component of the greater puzzle. And now Tyfar, all unknowing, heaped fresh fuel on the blaze that would explode when the time came.

"So the Djangs took a hand? I know little of them but, Jak, you once said you were from Djanduin, that you had estates there."

"I did and I have."

He cocked an eye at me.

"The Hamalese were beaten by a combination of people who had grown tired of Thyllis's mad dreams of empire, and they were aided by the Djangs—"

"That is easy enough to understand." Tyfar sounded bitter. "If Vallia entered the fight against us, then that arch devil, Dray Prescot, is Emperor of Vallia and King of Djanduin. His evil influence brought about our ruin."

"Ty—" said Jaezila.

She looked most unhappy. She stretched out a hand toward this young Prince of Hamal, and a shower of insects burst from a pot flung over the rocks. The pot smashed to bits on the stone and the buzzing, winging, stinging insects swarmed out. Instantly we were hard at work swatting and dancing and banging. Arrows flew in.

"Keep your eyes front!" bellowed Tyfar at the swods as he flailed away at the clouds of maddening stingers. "We'll take the insects off you! Look to your front!"

The Deldars took up his orders and the swods stuck grimly to their posts, clutching crossbow and spear, and when the attack came screeching in it was met by disciplined men under orders. We stepped up to fight, and we met and rebuffed the onslaught. When the wildmen retreated, leaving their dead, we slumped back, exhausted.

"They won't repeat that trick in a hurry. It must have taken them a long time to collect the insects. How many pots did they throw in?"

"Twenty, at least."

'They'll try something else soon.'

A number of openings into the cliff where the ledge joined led into a series of caves. A stream ran through to fall away into a sink hole. Into this sanctuary the wounded were carried. Tyfar had brought a doctor with this little force; but he had been wounded. Now he lay on a cloak and told other less wounded men what to do to alleviate suffering.

Tyfar explained that he'd brought four vollers, small craft, and all four had been burned by the wildmen. The men had fought their way through to this outcrop and made of it a fortress. The moorkrim clearly considered the affray and its successful outcome for them to be merely a matter of time. "We started with two regiments, crossbows and spears, and they were weak, anyway. Now we're down to what amounts to little over one reasonably strong regiment, five hundred or so men. We take the roll call; but it is depressing."

I learned what had happened to the rest of Tyfar's Twentieth Army. The bulk was spread along his sector of the frontier, with strong contingents removed and sent east. I pondered this. I did not think any elements of the Twentieth had been in action against us in Ruathytu. I pursed up my lips, and then, casually, I said, "D'you know anything about King Telmont, Tyfar? What sort of fellow he is?"

"Telmont?" Tyfar turned back at the entrance of the caves with a final encouraging word to a spearman with a shaft through his shoulder. "Not much. He was called Telmont the Hot and Cold until he hanged and burned enough people to stop the name being bandied about. But it is true. He can't make up his mind on anything, except hanging and burning."

"Any chance that, now that Empress Thyllis is dead, the people would shout for Telmont as emperor?"

Tyfar swiveled to stare at me. His eyes opened.

"It is a thought—one that had not occurred to me. But—well, he is a king of some means. He could buy support." Tyfar frowned and then laughed. "No, no, Jak. He'd never make up his mind to reach for the crown. He'd have to have someone to kick him up the backside."

Thinking of Vad Garnath, and the Kataki Strom, I said, "Perhaps he has. He is supposed to be marching on Ruathytu."

Then Tyfar said something that stopped me in my tracks.

"He is! To throw out this devilish alliance! Then I must hurry and join him and drive back the Vallians and their despicable allies!"

"Oh, Ty!" exclaimed Jaezila.

She looked fierce.

"Now what's the matter? I mean, of course, when we get out of this pickle we're in."

510

We went back to the rocks, and there was a jaunty bounce to Tyfar's step. Now he had an aim in life. I refused to despair. Tyfar now believed our friend Seg would bring relief. Then Tyfar would collect what men he could and rush off to join King Telmont. That made sense to a loyal Hamalese. Sweet sense.

"Listen, Tyfar. I heard no good spoken of Telmont—"

"Of course not! He's a fool. But if he is raising the standard of resistance to Vallia—"

"Your father has a greater claim to the crown and throne of Hamal. Think of that."

"You have spoken of this before—"

"Aye! Even when Thyllis sat on the throne. Now that she is dead I speak openly. I want to see you father, Nedfar, Emperor of Hamal."

Tyfar put a hand to his bandage. "Yes, but—" He walked on. "We have no real support. Thyllis saw to that. She maneuvered father away from the center of power. He was included in the high command only because he is an astute soldier. No, Jak. No one would stand with father—"

I took a breath. I said, "Suppose the alliance stood for him? Suppose Djanduin and Hyrklana and Vallia all said Prince Nedfar, Emperor of Hamal, Jikai! What then?"

He controlled his contemptuous anger. "You mean treat with our enemies? Supplicate them, be beholden to them? Fawn on them as slaves fawn on their master who brings the slopbowl of porridge?"

"One thing, Tyfar, you'd have to get straight." His honest anger nettled me. "If it is to work you'd have to get rid of slavery. I can tell you that is one thing the Vallians and Djangs won't tolerate."

His cheeks were pinched in and white. "I detest slavery, too, yet it is a necessity for ordered life—"

"We won't go into that now. I know your point of view. I respect you too much to think you a hypocrite. But leave that for now. Think about your father as emperor, with friends at his side—"

"Friends!"

"Aye, Ty, you ninny! Friends!" Jaezila was as wrought up as the man she loved and who loved her—although they fenced one with the other, afraid, it seemed, to acknowledge their own emotions.

"I don't understand this." Perplexity made Tyfar calm. "What authority do you have to make this suggestion?"

Not now. Not the right time...

"It is a serious proposal I heard about. You and your father were not available, and so could not be approached. But you will be. The Vallians are in deadly earnest about this. They don't want continual war with Hamal. There are the damned Leem-loving Shanks—"

"I know,. But here come the wildmen and they are our first concern..."

511

So we took up our weapons and went smashing into action again, slashing and thrusting and driving the moorkrim back over the lip of the ledge. They went flying over, their skins and furs and feathers a panoply of savage warriors, our steel in their hearts. We fought them. But we lost men and our numbers were thinned and we knew we would never last too many assaults of that ferocious nature.

Tyfar panted. "The devils! By Krun! If only we had a voller!"

The medicaments were holding out and we patched up our wounds. We drank thirstily from the stream. The water was ice cold. As for food, that was in good supply and we could eat heartily, in the grim understanding that we were likely to be killed before we starved to death.

Jaezila finished putting a gel-impregnated bandage on Barkindrar the Bullet's leg. He was a hairy Brokelsh, a faithful retainer to Tyfar, a comrade with whom we had gone through perils. Nath the Shaft, a bowman from Ruathytu, tut-tutted and said: "You stick your leg out when you sling, Barkindrar, and you expect to get a shaft in it."

"It's just a hole. Had it been a slingshot it'd have busted my leg—"

"All right, you two," said Jaezila. "Save your temper for the wildmen."

"Yes, my lady," they said together. They put great store by Jaezila, did these two, Barkindrar and Nath, Bullet and Shaft.

Intrigued by Tyfar's passionate yearning for a voller, I asked him what one voller would do, since he had lost four.

"Do? Jak! Why, man, get Jaezila to safety, of course!"

A pandemonium of yells and screams at our backs coincided with the next onslaught. Wildmen roared onto the platform and as we fought them others dropped like monkeys from the caves in the cliff, howled down upon our backs, trapped us in jaws of death.

Six

Seg and Kytun Are Not Repentant

Like big fat flies dropping off a carcass the wildmen plummeted out of the holes in the cliff. They howled down upon our astonished soldiers. The wildmen in front and now these suddenly appearing demons in the rear...

"Steady!" Tyfar stood up, not so much fearless as indifferent to anything but holding his men. "Face front! You—face rear—" he bellowed in a voice that astonished me. He sorted the men out even as the two sides sought to close upon us and crush us in the jaws of death.

As for me—the Krozair brand leaped like a live spirit. The wildmen, hairy and shaggy and nasty, bore in with skirling bravery, scorning cuts and bruises, only dropping when some serious portion of their anatomy was chopped away, only dying when not enough remained of that anatomy to sustain life. Dust puffed under stamping feet. Sweat shone briefly, and the dust covered the sweat and caked men's faces and arms. That peculiar haze of dust and sweat hovered above the battle as brings back the memories to an old fighting man.

Jaezila swirled splendidly, her sword wreaking devastation upon the hairy skin-clad host. Diplomatically I left Tyfar and Jaezila to work out a modus vivendi between themselves. Contenting myself with keeping my own skin unpunctured I could watch out for them and knock the odd persistent fellow away and still let them fight on, back to back, defiant and splendid. And, by Vox! The fight was warm, exceedingly warm. We were overmatched in numbers. The very animal vitality of the moorkrim astonished by its ability to sustain damage and to leap from rock to crag to boulder, swinging sword or thrusting with polearm all along the way. It was like fighting a collection of Springheeled Jacks.

In the midst of the fight, Jaezila and Tyfar kept on at each other. Back to back for much of the time, they each made lurid guesses as to the activity of the other: "Have you untangled your feet yet, Ty?" and: "I should have worn a thicker backplate with you there, Zila," and so nonsensically forth. Tyfar's axe, dull and fouled with blood, cut mercilessly down with massive sweeps. No one was getting past him to sink a blade into Jaezila's undefended back.

For a moment or two it became vitally necessary for me to leap and skip about as a dozen or so scuttling horrors plopped down from a cliff-edge hole. They came for me as a target. These were the caving experts of the moorkrim, often called moorakrim, swarthy of skin, bent of back, grimed with the marks of soil. Their fingers were long, bony and taloned, and their hands formed scoops. Like all the wildmen, they were bandy. Without doubt once the Hamalese had been killed these two sorts of moorkrim would fight among themselves for the spoil.

They hurled javelins at me, they threw stones, and the stones were more dangerous than the javelins.

Great displeasure is taken by a Krozair of Zy if he is forced to beat away flung stones with his Krozair longsword. Beating away arrows and javelins is one thing; driving off a stone over mid-off is quite another. I felt the chunks of stone cracking against the steel.

"You mangy pack of powkies!" I yelled, and started off for them, howling all manner of abuse and swirling the sword, as much to scare them as to bash away their stones. They hesitated. One or two hopped about from one bandy leg to another.

"Schtump!" I bellowed and ran faster, and caught the two nearest fellows, the two bravest or more foolhardy, I dare say, and swept them into four. I shook the Krozair brand at the others and charged at them, thinking among all the scarlet flashes of annoyance how my Krozair brothers would frown at this wanton display of vanity.

But the wildmen scuttled back on their bandy legs and with swinging skins about their shoulders disappeared into a hole in the cliff. To let them go was no decision. I started back to Tyfar and Jaezila and saw one of the commanding officers of the regiments fall. The Jiktar simply fell straight down. His helmet was dented by a thrown rock—a very large rock.

Up on a ledge over our heads a group of the moorakrim worked busily at what was—what had to be—a catapult.

I stared up. The suns were slipping down the sky and the light lay full on the cliff face. The wildmen up there did have a catapult, a small affair with a squat beam and a narrow twisted sinew spring. But it could throw.

The arm came over and the clang distinctly preceded the arrival of the stone. That one missed.

Then a wildman tried to spit me and I parried and riposted and looked up at the ledge and that catapult.

"Cover me, Deldar!" I said to the neatly groomed officer—he had a spot of dirt on his cheek and his right shoulder arm-piece was cut through—who staggered back with half a dozen of his men. They recoiled from an advancing line of wildmen, moving now with purpose as they sought to clear the platform.

There was no time for question and answer. I stuck the longsword through my belt, not in the scabbard, and shoved it back out of the way. The Lohvian longbow came off my shoulder sweetly to hand. The arrow nocked as it seemed of its own accord. Brace, push, pull, bend—shooting in a longbow demands skill and skill I had been taught by Seg. The first rose-fletched shaft skewered the wildman about to place the next stone. He fell back, the shaft through him, and before he hit the ledge his comrade started to fall beside him, feathered through the chest. His arm struck the release latch and the arm, missileless, slapped forward. The whole catapult jumped and a crack of an exceedingly rich and juicy sound floated down.

"Bad cess to you," I said, loosing again and taking a wildman in the rump who was trying to take cover.

The very neat Deldar had formed his handful of men in a line among the boulders and we were separated by a short open space from Tyfar and Jaezila. I shot again. Tyfar and Jaezila fought on, and I switched my aim and was able to take out a couple of moorkrim and so assist my comrades. I reached for another arrow and—lo!—the quiver was empty. So much for hotheaded intemperate rushings after people; Seg would be scathing with me for so glaring a dereliction of the archer code.

Dealing with the wildmen who lined out after us was not as difficult as I'd expected, for the neat Deldar was neat in swordsmanship and neat in his handling of his men. When we straightened up after that small affray within the larger, we were down two men and the wildmen, those still alive, drew back.

I said to Deldar, "Your name, Deldar?"

"Fresk Thyfurnin, notor."

"If all the swods fought like your men, I'd be easier."

"I think, notor," said this Deldar Fresk Thyfurnin, "that this is our last fight."

"I'll not have that kind of talk—" I started to bluster. Thyfurnin simply pointed along the cleft of the Pass of Lacachun.

They flew up and they seemed to fill the air between the two rock faces. The cliffs echoed to the rustle of their wings. The mist drifted past, very high, shredded now for some time to allow the radiance of the twin suns to burn through. Below the mist they flew on, hundreds and hundreds, it seemed, drawn to the pickings to be found at Laca's Jaws.

"Well, now. Deldar Fresk. I still do not think you right. We will have to pull back to the caves and defend ourselves there."

"Of course, notor. And guard our backs against the moorkrim creeping along their holes in the cliffs. Our wounded were lucky to have escaped them. But we will fight."

Tyfar and Jaezila dispatched the last of their opponents and walked across the open ground toward our group. Everyone looked depressed. The darkness in the air shadowed from that enormous flying host was enough to make a laughing hyena weep. We gathered together before the entrances to the caves.

"We've won this fight." Tyfar sounded as though he would burst a blood vessel. "No one thought we could win; but we did. We beat 'em. And now we have this whole new force to reckon with."

"How many men do we have?"

Deldar Fresk, it turned out, was the senior surviving officer. All the Hikdars, each commanding a pastang, and the two Jiktars had been slain. The roll was a lamentable affair.

The host in the sky flew nearer.

In defeating the flying wildmen and the cave wildmen we had lost over two hundred men. We had, counting lightly wounded, some two hundred and twenty remaining.

The noise of beating wings filled the air now, close and closer. The volume of sound caught and re-echoed from cliff to cliff bore down oppressively, making the nerves twitch. We took a fresh grip on our weapons and positioned ourselves among the boulders and the cave mouths. In that small breathing space I took the opportunity to fetch what arrows I could find embedded in moorkrim corpses. I managed to bring in ten.

So a moorkrim bow and a few full quivers had to be brought back. Each arrow was a life. The flying host began to descend and the leading elements planed in for the platform. They could see the dead people lying everywhere.

Deldar Fresk served in the crossbow regiment.

Tyfar called across, "As soon as they are in range."

"Quidang, prince," said Fresk, and set himself.

Now this Deldar Fresk was a fine fellow and the swods were of value. But there was no shadow of a doubt in my mind, no shadow of doubt whatsoever, that what I was going to do would be done, and would be the right thing to do. I anticipated no opposition from Tyfar. The moment I laid my hands on a tyryvol—or any other quality saddle-flyer—I'd have him or her and get Jaezila away. Tyfar would help. We'd get Jaezila out of this debacle alive if it was the last thing we did.

The leading tyryvols alighted on the platform and Fresk opened up on them, the crossbows clanging and hissing in rotation. Of the two hundred and twenty swods some ninety were crossbowmen. Shooting in the harshly disciplined Hamalian way, they carried out considerable execution. Return shafts came in, outranged by the crossbows but brought into range by the advance of the shooters between the rocks. Such was the weight of the enemy's dustrectium* and the numbers of his swordsmen that this snapshooting party would not last very long. The force on the ground built up and positioned itself nastily and neatly and started the advance.

We watched the vulpine forms of the wildmen slipping between the rocks, skulking forward, jumping across open spaces and affording no chance for a shot. They edged forward.

"I—" began Tyfar.

"Not so, Tyfar." I put a hand on his shoulder. We stood just within the overhang of the cave so that descending arrows could not strike us. Jaezila stood at the side, her face calm, brooding, perhaps. We all had a deal to brood over, by Zair! "In this the task falls to my hand."

"You do not know what—" Then he stopped speaking. He closed his mouth, opened it deliberately, said: "I am an onker! All this time we have been comrades, and still I try to make stupid suggestions that you and I do not think alike. Of course. Except, Jak, except—the task falls to me."

"You are the general of the Twentieth Army, and this handful of men is your total command here and now. If you make a run for it and they see you—and, believe me, they'll see you!—what will they think of Kapt Tyfar, Prince of Hamal? Hey?"

"You are my blade comrade, Jak, and you have a damned sneaky underhand downright illegal way with you!"

"See that wildman just alighting?" I nodded toward a splendid-looking

---

* *dustrectium:* firepower.

saddlebird and a splendid-looking rider. Among the others fluttering down to be hidden in the rocks, this man stood out.

Tyfar said, "Just grab the first one—"

"Oh, come now, Ty! While we have a choice, let us exercise it. That is the flyer we will have."

"The wildman is a leader, a Jedgar, and he'll have a canny bunch of his fellows with him."

Jedgar is simply a corruption of the word Jiktar, and generally denotes barbarian or irregular captain, and what Tyfar said about this moorkrim Jedgar was perfectly correct. In my frame of mind, with Jaezila in such dire danger, I rather fancied going as near to the top as I could contrive.

"His canny bunch will be no crazier than we are."

"That is true."

"So that is settled."

"You have the besting of me," Tyfar grumped, "in this argument. But I fancy I shall rank Deldars again, and soon, and then we shall see."

The moorkrim rose from their places of concealment. Screeching their battle cries they hurtled on. Difficult to kill, yes. Not as difficult as reptilian schrepims, with their phenomenal speed and insensate capacity to stay alive and battling when they should be dead, having been cut up into pieces. The eyes of schrepims contain the pigment rhodopsin which confers good night vision and which also glows in reflected light. As Kregans say: "To see the eyes of schrepims glowing at night is to look on the watchfires of hell." As the wildmen raced in I took a silly and, although stupid, real comfort from the thought that I was glad they were not schrepims. This is paradox of a low-volume capacity, of course; but it serves to illustrate the frame of mind I was in. Jaezila had to be flown away to safety. Besides that—nothing else mattered.

Tyfar agreed with me. Honor meant nothing to either of us if honor meant Jaezila would be killed.

We'd both cut and run, escorting her to safety, and leave those brave swods to fight on to the end.

Contemptuous on our part? Yes. I do not deny it.

I remembered Velia.

It was what I would have done, without doubt.

There was no need.

Glorious!

Men shouted and pointed. Among the flying clouds of wildmen swirls became visible. As though a broom clashed along sweeping up autumn leaves, so some force brisked along the pass driving the tyryvols and their moorkrim riders before it.

The mist darkened as the twin suns struck more sharply upon its upper surface, and the level rays of jade and ruby pierced through below to shine along the pass. In that strange almost undersea radiance, a hollow luminescence, powerful winged shapes bustled through the whirling tyryvols. Black beaks slashed left and right, and frightened flyers fluttered away from wicked polished talons.

The massed feathering of yellow wings heralded the storming onslaught of ferocious four-armed fighters. Impetuous, unstoppable, superb, my Djangs roared onto the platform and chopped the wildmen up fine and served them up frittered. The fight exploded in a frenetic movement of blades and was still. Kytun rolled over toward me, shaking drops from his sword, his dagger being wiped with an oily rag—already!—and his remaining hand lifted in cheerful salute.

Up there over Kytun's head the roiling mass of wildmen pressed back and we could see the aerial conflict clearly.

If you cared for aerial evolutions it was extraordinarily clever. The maneuvering and pirouetting were of a high standard; but everyone watching saw instantly that the flutduins, whether flown by Djangs or apims of Valka, had the mastery of the wildmen no matter what saddle flyer they flew.

I frowned and, staring up, called to Kytun: "Is that all of you?"

"All of us—"

I yelled then, loudly, at him and bounded out onto the platform, hurdling boulders, reaching him as he thought to indulge in our back-slapping, arm-gripping, gut-punching rhapsody of delight in meeting. Instead, I said in his ear: "Call me Jak or I'll three-arm you! No king! Is that clear, Kytun?"

"But, Dray—you are the—"

"Jak and no king!"

"Very well—"

"Is that all of you, up there and here?"

"That's all, Dra—Jak. And I am fortunate my party found you. We split up and split up, and in the end I imagined looking for you all on my own."

"Where's Seg?"

Kytun laughed in that huge Djang way and looked about. At that moment a moorkrim fell from the sky to splat on the rocks. My eye was caught by the movement and as Kytun said, "There he is," I saw the rose-fletched arrow, a clothyard shaft, through the wildman. Moments later Seg landed and leaped off his flutduin and hurried over. He said: "Jak!"

"All right, Seg," said Kytun. "I forgot."

Seg sighed. "Djangs," he said.

"And not many of you." Looking up and around, it seemed to me there were barely three or four hundred in this relief force, Djang and Valkan combined.

Tyfar and Jaezila came over. The introductions went well and when this pappattu was finished it was a general "Lahal!" and the remark from Jaez-ila: "It looks as though you've just brought in more fellows to be trapped with us."

Again that massive Djang laugh scorched up echoes from the cliffs. "Not likely, by Zodjuin of the Silver Stux! Look, up there. The wildmen have had a bellyful. They fly."

It was true. Not only did they fly, they fled.

"Remarkable." Tyfar had not cleaned or put down his axe; it cocked up in his fists, ready for action. He looked at Kytun, a magnificent, fearsome, four-armed fighting man, and he looked at Seg, lithe and limber, broad with an archer's build, and he saw the way they greeted me. His open face bore the shadow of a frown. I felt for Tyfar. My heart—to use one Kregan expression—turned over for him.

Jaezila felt more. She was pale, very pale. Her head was held up, erect, and her eyes were brilliant. She was a woman who had made her own way on a harsh and hostile world; she may have been my daughter, she was her own woman now.

Slowly, Tyfar said, "I am beholden to you, Kov Kytun, and you, Kov Seg, and your people, for my life and the lives of my people. But, if I mistake it not, you are no friends to Hamal."

"Of course they're friends, Ty!"

"They are your friends, Jaezila."

"Oh!"

But it was not a moment for lightness.

Tyfar went on: "Djangs overthrew my city of Ruathytu. Valkans are from Vallia, and they joined in the fight. And here we are, a Djang kov and a Valkan kov and—" He turned to look at me. "And you, Jak?"

I could say nothing.

Tyfar turned and looked at Jaezila.

"And you, friends with these enemies, Jaezila?"

Seg said, "The Empress Thyllis asked for trouble, bought trouble, stored up trouble ahead of time. Now she has paid. And, by the Veiled Froy-vil, she's only paid a tithe of the mischief she caused." He lifted a hand, and he was not smiling. "No, Prince Tyfar, wait and hear me. You talk about Hamal as 'your country' and we respect you for that. But you must know the stench and offense Hamal has become because of mad Empress Thyllis."

"And that maniac Phu-Si-Yantong," chipped in Kytun.

One thing was sure, they weren't repentant about beating the Hamalese and taking their capital city, and they weren't about to become remorseful now because a defeated prince chose to feel sad.

"And you, Djang and Valkan, sack my capital—"

"No, prince. No sack."

"I would like to believe that. But soldiers tend to go berserk if they have to fight to take a city—"

"True. Damage was caused, mostly by the Wizard of Loh. The Djangs," said Kytun, "keep the peace and ensure order in Hamal these days."

"The truth is, Ty, Hamal is much better off without Thyllis. You know what you have to do to secure the throne for your father—"

"Zila! How can I—in honor? With enemy help?"

I put my teeth together and clamped my jaws. I refused to speak. You can drive, as they say, and never make.

Seg was in full command of all the details, all the plans, all the emotions of what we hoped for.

"Hamal used to be an enemy to the lands surrounding her and also other countries over the seas. That is no longer so. The alliance embraces Hamal. Safeguards—"

"Conditions and terms of servitude?"

Tyfar's contempt cut like a quality blade.

The suns' rays lay long and level through the pass. More Djangs and Valkans alighted and began to tend the wounded Hamalese. Fires were lit from the provision commissariat birds' loads together with what of brush and gorse grew sparsely in crevices. Water heated. Food was prepared. The group around Prince Tyfar was left alone, and the talk and wrangling went on. After all, Jaezila was in a privileged position here in Tyfar's eyes—as, I suppose, was I, had I cared to exercise that option—and Tyfar was a prince talking with two kovs. So it was easy for me to ease back and observe.

"Do you believe I want the best for you, Ty? The best personally, I mean?"

"How can you ask such a question?"

Jaezila bit her lip.

"I know, I know. We spar and fence. Something makes me treat you badly, and laugh." She looked away, and back at Tyfar. "But you respond, now. You never used to."

"Maybe I have learned—"

"Precisely! But you have not learned enough! We all want the best for you, for your father, and for Hamal. Yet you will not listen to us!"

"So you do ally yourself with—"

"Ally? Of course if you were going to say our enemies—"

"Our late enemies, it seems."

"Or do you want to see King Telmont on the throne?"

Tyfar put a hand to his bandaged head. Over by the lines the lads staked out for the flutduins, a commotion arose, to be settled quickly. You cannot expect Djangs to be plaster saints. The suns slid away beyond the hills. A breeze got up and blew along the pass. After the exertions of the day it would be nice to eat a gargantuan meal, to drink some good wine and to sing some of the old songs of Kregen. Then a profound sleep and a few pleasant dreams. The morrow would dawn and bring fresh problems, but, by Vox, we'd be fit to tackle 'em!

One of the Jiktars from Valka walked up, Erdil Avnar, talking to one of his Hikdars. They were lithe and agile men who had joined the Valkan aerial cavalry early. They wore equipment and uniforms of the particular splendor Valka brings to this kind of martial show, bullion, flounders, lace, pelisses, frogging—a parade of the tailor's art no less than that of the military designer's. They saw me and Erdil Avnar bellowed out: "Lahal, strom, lahal!"

"Lahal, Erdil. Lahal, Edin," to the Hikdar. "How was it aloft?"

"These wildmen fight like cornered leem."

"Aye. But you bested them."

"Of course they bested them," said Jaezila from over my shoulder. "And now we are trying to make that victory worth something even more than simple victory."

Erdil and Edin straightened up into a rigidity like unto the pine forests of the petrified mountains. Their chests swelled, creaking their equipment. As one, they slapped up full salutes, and bellowed: "Quidang, majestrix!"

Now quidang means an agreement and acquiescence in orders rather like the terrestrial navy style of "aye aye, sir!" Tyfar looked hard at the Jiktar and the Hikdar, and then with a puzzled expression at Jaezila. For majestrix is the way empresses and queens are addressed, and the eldest princesses, the princess majestrix of her country. Tyfar was not called majister, not even Nedfar his father, although it was sometimes known in a strictly irregular way. So Tyfar frowned.

And I thought to myself—as though ice had started to melt in my head, for thought and I had been damned distant relations of late—I thought that perhaps if Tyfar knew what there was to know, it would help to crystallize the problem and force him to make up his mind.

Rather naturally, I expected him to see the advantages of what was offered in time—although I was prepared for his final refusal—and to join with us in persuading his father.

"Erdil, Edin," said Jaezila. "You are very welcome. You must tell me more of the fight."

"Right willingly, majestrix," barked out Erdil, straight and rigid and straining his equipment.

"Majestrix?" said Tyfar.

"You misheard, prince," said Seg, stepping up and putting a shoulder between Tyfar and the two Valkan flyers. "The Valkans compared the wildmen to masichieri. Your head—"

"I'm not an imbecile, Kov Seg. Think that at your peril."

My daughter Lela, called Jaezila, looked at me. I stared back at her, and I raised my eyebrows. That was a giant grimace, in those conditions, meaning much. Jaezila nodded, hard.

She put a hand on Seg's arm. He turned at once, head bent and face intent, completely attentive.

"It is time Prince Tyfar of Hamal learned, Uncle Seg. Would you do us the honor of making the pappattu?"

"Pappattu?" said Tyfar. "Between us? We were introduced, as I recall, after our first meeting in that hayloft when you held an arrow nocked on us." He pointed off to the side of the cave where in firelight Barkindrar the Bullet and Nath the Shaft stood up to watch, sensing some crisis by the way we held ourselves. "When you cared for Barkindrar in the hayloft in Blue Vosk Street."

I said, "When the beastie tried to chomp you in the swamp, you both reacted, and we were using names. I recall it perfectly. No pappattu has been made between you."

Both Jaezila and Tyfar looked surprised. They began to cast back in their minds to see if I was right, and, more or less, so I was.

"Then this flummery cloaks a deeper design—"

"Of course, Ty. Now, Seg, you know who Prince Tyfar of Hamal is. Go on."

Seg cleared his throat. Kytun moved up a trifle closer and he casually freed one of his swords. Seg spoke: "Prince Tyfar of Hamal, you have the honor of being in the presence of and of being introduced to Lela, Princess Majestrix of Vallia."

Seven

Of the Wounds of Prince Tyfar of Hamal

Well, and wasn't it right and proper, perfectly fitting, that Seg Segutorio should make the introduction? Should close one episode and open up a whole bushelful of new?

Seg stepped back, and he was smiling as only he can, the kind of smile that reaches right down into a fellow and curls his toes.

Tyfar closed his mouth. It had been open only just long enough to have trapped half a dozen flies, had any been foolish enough to enter.

"Lela. Princess Majestrix of Vallia."

Tyfar did not lose the color from his face. He stood up straight, watchful, like a deer pausing on the edge of a water hole. His head was lifted, and slightly inclined. He remained perfectly still.

522

"Ty?"

Apprehension—that showed in Jaezila.

We stood there among the mountains, on a dusty ledge blood-soaked and cumbered with corpses, and the sounds of men moaning and the crackle of the fires mingled with the snorting of the saddle flyers and the rustle of their wings. How to overemphasize the shock of this revelation to Tyfar? Warily, he looked at Jaezila, and warily I looked at him. In one way I could expect any wild reaction, and in another I guessed what his reaction would be. I could still be wrong...

"I loved you, Jaezila, and you worked against me, betrayed me—"

"Not you, prince," said Seg sharply. "Against that maniac Thyllis."

Tyfar barely heard Seg. His gaze fastened on Jaezila. She stared back, and after that first tremor, she did not flinch.

"I've called you a ninny, Ty, and it isn't true. How do you think I felt? Do you imagine I liked acting this part with a man—with the man—?"

"Why didn't you tell me?"

Kytun slapped that everready sword back into the scabbard with the hand that happened to be grasping it at the time, and gestured irritably with two others. "Act your age, prince!"

"A spy—" Tyfar drew a breath. "Sucking our secrets—"

Seg broke in, as annoyed as Kytun.

"We've offered to support your father's just claim to the throne. We've all heard excellent reports of you. We want to be your friends. You've got to accept the realities, prince; you have to accept the needle."

If this was the right way or the wrong way, I did not know. Seg and Kytun were in no doubt. Jaezila was in agony, and so was Tyfar, and all because a silly woman who was Empress of Hamal had been obsessed with ambitions and conquest.

I said, "That Jaezila is the Princess Majestrix of Vallia has no bearing on our friendship. We have said we are blade comrades. Well, then, let us prove it."

"You are right, of course." Tyfar spoke in a musing way that would, for anyone who did not know him, cause intense astonishment that he was not roaring and swearing away and dragging out his sword and threatening all kinds of dire retributions and hurling recriminations about like hailstones. "It was a shock. My opinion of Vallia has not been high."

I could feel keenly for Tyfar. A shock, he said. By Zair! What he must be feeling now! And yet his face remained calm and composed, a trifle too pale, and that bandage beginning to leak an ugly red stain.

Jaezila cried out. "Ty! Your head!" She swung on Jiktar Erdil Avnar, who had proved the catalyst in the revelation. "Erdil, run for the needleman— the prince bleeds!"

"Quidang, majestrix—"

"It's only a scratch, Zila," protested Ty.

I let out a breath. A big, a mighty big, hurdle had been leaped in those few words.

The dam broke on that, and a babble of words flowed out, everyone talking at once, and then stopping, and starting up again. Tyfar sat down on the ground, thump, suddenly. Jaezila bent above him, her face drawn with concern. The doctor with Kytun was a Djang, and he swung his four arms into action at once, putting a fresh bandage around Tyfar's head and sticking a few acupuncture needles artfully into him to take away the pain. Tyfar fretted under this fussing.

"I'm all right. And you—Zila—you're a damned Vallian, and a spy, and a princess—no. No. The Princess Majestrix—"

"I couldn't have told you before, Ty. Could I? You see that?"

"Of course." He looked up at me. "And you, Jak?"

"I did not know until very recently. It was a shock to me, too."

"And you didn't—"

"There was just one chance of telling you, Tyfar, and it passed away because I considered that this matter lay between you and Jaezila."

"I suppose we should call you Lela now, Zila."

"No. I like Jaezila."

I heard what I had just spoken. The words rang in my head. I had as good as said this was no concern of mine. Well, Zair knows, I've dropped myself into plenty of scrapes on Kregen in affairs that were no concern of mine. But, in this...

I stood back a little. I looked down on Tyfar who had been made comfortable on the ground with a cloak, and on Jaezila who sat at his side, holding his hand. No doubt assailed me that they would reach their own understanding. Tyfar was probably more hurt and weaker than he realized. But my own words thundered at me, and the implications drew blackness into my face. This business really was between these two. Their lives were involved, not mine, their futures together were at stake, not mine. But it was my business, too.

Tyfar saw my face. At the sudden frown Jaezila twisted to look up at me.

I said, "Prince Tyfar, we must set the record straight, seeing we have been through much together, and have an empire to heal and a deadly foe across the seas to fight."

"Jak?" He was puzzled. "Now what—?"

I stared down at him, aware of the firelight against the rocks, of the evening breeze, of the silence now that the needlemen had tended the wounded and eased their pains.

"Prince Tyfar, Jaezila is my daughter."

He laughed.

Tyfar laughed. His head fell back against the bunched folds of the cloak. The bandage stood out in a streak of yellow against the blue.

"Your daughter? Does that devil Prescot, the Emperor of Vallia know? Is that why you two venture off—?"

He sat up. He sat up as though bitten clean through.

He glared at me, and the blood rushed and collided in his face, and his eyes caught the firelight and glared in red madness.

I nodded.

"Yes, Tyfar. That is the way of it. Jaezila is my daughter in all honor. So that makes me—"

He shook his head and did not wince.

"You needn't say it." He sounded drugged.

"So that I can and will have your father, Prince Nedfar, crowned Emperor of Hamal."

"Is that all you can think of, Father?"

"No. But it is a good thought to hold onto now."

"Dray Prescot." Tyfar savored the words, the name, rolling it around his mouth like a gob of rotten fruit. He spat it out. "The great devil, Dray Prescot. By Krun! You've had a good laugh at my—"

"Tyfar! Do not think that! By Vox, lad, never think that!"

"Oh, no Ty! Surely you can see father would never laugh at you like that! For the sweet sake of Opaz! We are blade comrades!"

Tyfar fell back on the cloak. His face remained flushed and his eyes looked feverish. Sweat shone on his forehead under the bandage. Jaezila sponged the sweat away gently.

Seg rolled over. He put his hands on his hips, looking down on Tyfar. He said, "Prince, I can tell you this. Dray Prescot may be a cunning old leem hunter but he is a man who knows friends and what friendship means. If you are fortunate enough to count yourself a comrade of Dray Prescot, then you are fortunate above most men. And I know."

I repeat this, you will readily perceive, to illustrate the arguments various folk used to ease the torment Tyfar was experiencing. I think chiefly he felt used, diminished in his own eyes. But I believed in him. Jaezila was no fool. She knew Tyfar better than did I, and she was not deceived in him, I felt sure.

This scene had been painful for us all. Now it had to finish. In the ensuing hours, on and off, Tyfar would talk of the times we'd had together, and see them in a new light. "All the time I was working for Hamal, you were working for Vallia."

"For Vallia." Jaezila's face, caught in reflected fire glow, looked impassioned. "That is the point, Ty! Had you seen some of the terrible things the mercenaries and slavers did in Vallia, at the command of that horrible woman—and who weeps now that she is dead?—had you seen that..."

"War—"

"Not the kind of war the new Vallia fights. No. If those dreadful things had happened to your Hamal, wouldn't you fight?"

He looked weak, his face wan, the yellow bandage unhealthy against his skin. "I did fight—"

"The position is," said Seg. "Thyllis has been got rid of with the minimum of damage and trouble. Hamal is virtually unharmed. Your father can take over a running empire. Back in Vallia we still face the troubles your country has brought us."

At times desultory with exhaustion, at others impassioned, the talk went on through the night. No one slept very much. Too much lay at stake here. These hours witnessed events of the most momentous significance. We all felt that. The very night air seemed imbued with intimations of the future.

At one point Tyfar sat up, looking wild. "I feel so dirty!"

"That is a natural reaction, understandable. The name of spy is universally condemned. But if a spy acts in honor—"

"As we have done, Tyfar," I put in, speaking hard.

Jaezila nodded vehemently. "And you had better rest. I don't like that hole in your head."

And Tyfar said, "Which one?"

Barkindrar the Bullet and Nath the Shaft, who had been with us through many perils, looked numbed when they were told. They were flabbergasted. I watched them narrowly, believing they would take their lead from their prince; but ready in case they decided that their duty to their country called on them to attempt to slay the Emperor and Princess Majestrix of Vallia.

"Jak?" said Barkindrar in his uncouth Brokelsh way. "You're an emperor?"

"Of Vallia?" Nath the Shaft's brown fingers curled around his bowstave. It was not a great Lohvian longbow; but he was a remarkable shot with the compound reflex weapon.

"When I am in Vallia. Here I am Jak the Shot, your comrade, and comrade to Prince Tyfar. You must help him grapple with this. After all, we went through the Moder together, and that underground horror was far worse."

Tyfar, whom I had thought asleep, rolled over and half sat up. "I wonder?"

That worried me.

"I must bathe myself," he said in a slurred voice. "I must take the Baths of the Nine."

Nath and Barkindrar looked concerned. "There are no facilities—"

"Here, prince?"

"Fetch the needleman!" cried Jaezila.

When the Djang doctor arrived and examined Tyfar he pursed up his lips.

"It is not promising, king, not promising at all. The prince will develop a fever and needs better attention than we can give him here."

"Like father like son," said Seg. "I left Nedfar with the best needleman in Hammansax. We'll have to get this fiery young zhantil to him as well."

"Yes."

"Except that I left the voller with him to take Nedfar on. Hammansax itself was in a bad way, as you know."

"We'll have to mount up, strap Tyfar on, and fly as fast as we can. If any bird can do it, a flutduin can."

"The flight—" The needleman spread his hands. All four of them. "I cannot answer for—"

"We understand, Khotan," said Jaezila.

Khotan the Needle nodded, not very happy at the prospects.

Barkindrar and Nath turned away, out of the firelight.

Some of the wounded were too badly hurt to move, and men and attention must be left with them until we could get a flier back. Jaezila looked across the fire at me, her cheeks shining and lined with shadow so that, for a moment, I shivered. I shook myself roughly. By Vox! Tyfar had had a shock; he'd get over it, get over the mental wounding as surely as he would the physical. All the same, one had to be prepared for him to break out as a high-tempered prince, strong on honor, had every right to do. This mess was nowhere near over yet. If Tyfar took himself off into a voluntary exile to brood over his betrayal, as he would see these unfortunate circumstances, and then resolved to join King Telmont to strike against his country's victors—who could blame him? In my view he would be wrong; but I was prejudiced.

As the twin Suns of Scorpio rose between the mountain peaks bringing with them a new day of puzzles and emotions, I was thinking that, by Zair! what it would be to be just a semi-brainless adventurer wandering the face of Kregen with a ready sword, instead of a semi-brainless emperor attempting to guide the destinies of a world. Shouts of mingled anger and mirth lifted and I turned to see a group of swods manhandling somebody out of a cave entrance, somebody who struck me instantly as strange, weird, eerie.

Eight

Pale Vampire Worms

Over by the flutduin lines Tyfar was being assisted into the saddle by his own people. The Djang owners of the saddlebirds stood back. Jaezila hovered, anxious, with Seg and Kytun beside her. We all sensed that at this moment Tyfar wished to have his own people about him. This mood would pass. I had to believe that.

The group of yelling men dragged their captive down toward us. My first reaction remained, reinforced the nearer he came. A shock of wild hair, brown and gray, sticking out like a porcupine's quills, a raggedy collection of skins and leaves, scrawny arms and legs, those bandy legs of the wildmen, and a face like a squashed rat's convinced me this fellow was bad news to anyone. He was gagged tightly with a strip of leather so that his face was drawn back into a stretched grin.

"A Havil-forsaken moorkrim sorcerer!"

"Cut off his head—now!"

"Burn him!"

The uproar continued as the swods roughhoused their prisoner across the rocks to their Deldar. Deldar Fresk Thyfurnin looked grave. Like us all he was exhausted from the aftereffects of the fighting and the lack of sleep. He said to me, "They were lucky to catch the Arditchoith. Nasty customers, as dangerous as a wounded leem."

One of the sub-officers, a matoc, reported in that the wildman sorcerer, the Arditchoith, had been snapped up by a party as he tumbled from a rocky ledge in the cave. Both sides had been surprised and shocked. But here was the sorcerer, wild as all hell, safely gagged and bound.

"Make sure the gag is tight, matoc."

"Quidang, by Kuerden the Merciless!"

The uproar attracted Seg and Kytun and they walked across from the flutduin lines. Presently we would have to take off with Tyfar and pray he survived his ordeal.

Seg was just saying, "They'll never get any information out of him if they rough him up like that," in a judicious way when the sorcerer—by some sleight of thaumaturgy, no doubt—broke momentarily free. Those few moments were enough. His bandy legs twinkling, he broke through the startled swods, leaped for a boulder, balanced, leaped for the far side, and tumbled clean into the all-embracing arms of a party of Djangs come to see what the excitement was all about. They held him, and he would not escape them.

"By Zodjuin of the Silver Stux!" rapped Kytun. "This fellow is a man! Let's find out more about him."

The Djangs grasped the wildman and he was run up to stand defiantly before Kytun. Now Kytun is a majestically impressive figure, broad, bulky, regal of mien, and his four arms are so evidently capable of dealing out punishment and destruction that he inspires universal respect. Also, as I know, those same four muscular arms and deadly hands can be infinitely tender in caring for those he loves, and in looking after the flowers that so delight him in his garden back home in his paradise island of Uttar Djombey.

An imposing, dominating, intimidating figure, then, Kytun Kholin Dom. The wildman sorcerer, the Arditchoith, stared furiously up through his shock of disarranged hair with a look of malignant hatred. His whole posture, the jumping of the muscles in his face above the gag, spoke eloquently of vivid resentment and animosity and nothing of fear or trembling.

"Spying on us, were you?" quoth Kytun. "Well, we'll soon find out if there are any more of you. Take off his gag. There are questions he must be asked."

Sinewy Djang fingers stripped away the leather gag.

A frenzied chorus of shrieks battered into the air.

"Don't take off the gag!"

"Stop! Stop!"

"Keep him tongueless!"

It was too late.

The horrified shouts of the Hamalese soldiers changed to shrieks of consternation and fear.

The wildman sorcerer spoke.

What he said he spat out in no language I knew, although the language genetically coded pill I'd taken years ago enabled me to grasp at the essence of what he was saying.

Rather—at what he was calling up.

In a screeched invective-laden invocation he called upon the Pale Vampire Worms. His stutter of words seemed to swell and crackle among the rocks. The soldiers yelled and fought to climb aboard the nearest tyryvol or flutduin. A coldness dropped upon the platform in the canyon and clouds passed before the faces of the suns.

From a myriad cracks grazing the surface of the platform elongated white forms emerged. They writhed. Sinewy, puffed, bloated with pale slime shining, they oozed from the dank recesses of nightmare to swarm onto the ledge and descend upon the panic-stricken people.

A crack at my feet disgorged a plump white worm—I'd not noticed any crack there before—and as I stumbled back the thing lifted into the air. White, corrugated like a concertina, slime-running, the Pale Vampire Worm looked upon me with two round crimson eyes protruding prominently. Real power, then, he had, this wildman wizard.

The sword was in my fist and the blade went around in a horizontal slash before I knew what was happening.

The worm fell in two severed halves, and the tail end shriveled into a pale wormcast and the head spun about, the two bulging eyes red as freshly spilled blood, and began to grow a new tail.

The air filled with the horrors, and those of us left on the ledge slashed and leaped and flailed away—and many a man fell with a worm fastened to his throat, kicking and struggling as the Pale Vampire Worm turned the color of blood.

Kytun slashed with four djangirs and the frighteningly efficient short sword of Djanduin in his capable grip kept the horrors at bay. But they oozed from the clefts in the rock and swarmed upon us. Our blades ran with ichor and tails fell to shrivel; but the heads pirouetted and grew afresh and came on again.

Deldar Fresk tripped one of his men, running in blind panic. The man tumbled over and Fresk grabbed his crossbow. For a Deldar of Hamalian crossbowmen to span and load was a matter of training and drill and superb expertise. Even as I cut and hacked with sword and main gauche I saw Fresk aim the crossbow and loose.

The bolt struck the wildman sorcerer in the head.

His head exploded.

Instantly, every Pale Vampire Worm vanished.

There was no craze of cracks fretting the surface of the platform.

Kytun used his lower left hand's forefinger to wipe away a scrap of brain from his cheek.

"Djan!"

"You!" said Seg. "Take his gag off... Let's ask him some questions...

It became extraordinarily urgent for me to step up and speak in a bright voice which, with a sigh I confess, came out like a rough-edged file. But they listened.

"Forget the damned sorcerer and the Pale Vampire Worms. Where is Tyfar? And Jaezila?"

Seg and Kytun were my comrades and had recently been introduced to Tyfar, a fellow comrade. The simmer of the volcano heralding a verbal slanging match over the Pale Vampire Worms and the cause of their appearance was instantly forgotten. Down by the flutduin lines, as where the tyryvols had been tethered by their late owners, the confusion ebbed as men realized the worms no longer existed. Few birds were left. Men sprawled on the ground, drained of blood, and they remained and did not rise up returned to full health. Wherever the damned worms had gone they'd taken the blood with them.

There was no sign of Tyfar or his people, and Jaezila was missing also. I just hoped she was sticking like glue to Tyfar, caring for him and gaining protection from his people's swordarms. I swung on Deldar Fresk.

"Well done, Deldar! We owe our lives to you."

"I have heard of these Havil-forsaken moorkrim wizards. I do not wish to meet another."

"Unless," said Seg with a look at Kytun, "unless he's well and truly gagged."

"I'll have the leather gag and thongs ready, I promise, by all the Warrior Gods of Djanduin!"

And—we all laughed.

Khotan the Needle had vanished and I sincerely trusted he was in attendance on Tyfar. I could guess that Barkindrar and Nath the Shaft, faithful to their creed and duty—not so rare a habit of mind on Kregen as it has become on Earth—had bundled their prince and Jaezila and the needleman aboard saddlebirds and thwacked them into the air. I'd been skipping and jumping and slashing at Pale Vampire Worms at the time.

Fresk said, "We shall be all right here, notor."

I looked at him.

He nodded to the flutduins remaining. "Clearly, you will fly back to Ruathytu."

"Yes," I said. I roused myself. This burden of imposition on men who were men like myself was a part of the punishment I endured for the presumption of allowing myself to be made an emperor. But I refused to become lost in self-pity. There was another side to being an emperor. I had no authority in the Hamalian army, but...

"I shall see to it, Deldar Fresk, that you are made up to Jiktar. I have noticed you."

He did not flush or stammer. He looked me in the eye and I wondered if he wanted to spit in my eye.

Then he said, "Thank you, notor."

That was all.

Well, by Krun! And what else did I expect?

So, because we were lords and masters and of the high ones of Kregen, we took the flutduins and the tyryvols and flew away. We left Deldar Fresk and the men without mounts to await subsequent rescue. I did not look back. By Zair! Only overpoweringly important issues would cause me to fly off and leave brave men in a plight like that.

And, the truth was, without question, that the problems I faced were overpoweringly important. As we flew up into the radiances of Zim and Genodras, it was the overpowering part of that thought that was the most daunting.

Nine

I Mention the Emperor of Pandahem

The Freak Merchants and the magicians and the conjurers had returned to their usual haunts in Ruathytu. Under the strict laws of Hamal they found life harder than in most of the exotic cities of Kregen; but in the eternal strength of their kind they survived.

In the brawling sprawling smoking open-air souk the man next to the fellow whose trick was pouring boiling water over various parts of his anatomy without apparent effect caught up his ungainly reptiles and hung them about him, tails curling and fangs clashing. Copper obs rattled in the earthenware bowls. The noise and stink and confusion racketed to the bright sky where the twin suns shone down serenely. The uproar was truly prodigious.

Strings of laden calsanys trotted past. Slaves scurried about their business, for master or mistress, down-drooping of mien, sunk in the busy apathy of slavery. The riders who spurred through the throngs were cursed at and spat after; but they forced a way through. The dust lifted, thick and choking. The smells could have been sculpted by chisels.

"He's down here somewhere," said Seg, avoiding a brass bowl on the end of a chain at the end of a pole at the end of a procession of brass-bowl-bearing slaves.

"Somewhere."

"Well, by the sign of The Crushed Toad."

"That infamous place," said Hamdi the Yenakker, a very great rogue but tall and upright and carrying himself with a swagger, a Hamalese who had sworn eternal fidelity to Vallia as the new power, "that sink of iniquity is there." He pointed. The place was tumbledown and smothered in creeping vines; but a soldier would see the thickness of the walls and the placement of slit windows high in the angles. "But there is no sign of your man."

"Your man, Hamdi," said Seg, moving out of the way of a cowled woman with a bosom and a basket.

"I merely repeat what I was told. He can tell you what you wish to know about Spikatur Hunting Sword."

"And," I said, "I have the bag of gold he asks for and I'd sooner he took charge of it. I've had a dozen fingers clutching at it already."

We all wore nondescript clothes of the swathing kind concealing most of our weaponry. In here they'd take your favorite jeweled dagger off you at one end and sell it back to you at the other. The Souk of Opportunity, this place was called, and no one was in any doubt whose opportunity it was.

Opportunity was another name for Hamdi the Yenakker. There is little that needs to be said about him. There are Vicars of Bray on Kregen, but his wholehearted embracing of Vallia and all things Vallian after the taking of Ruathytu was most certainly not an unalloyed advantage. Oh, yes, Hamdi had his connections, and we were to find great use for him. But his attitude, which unkind men might dub fawning on Vallia, was like to offend others, others like Prince Nedfar and Prince Tyfar. Happily they were both recovered of their wounds and day by day as the Peace Conference broke up around our ears and King Telmont marched nearer, we worked on Nedfar to accept our proposals. It was not an easy time.

Nothing much to be said about Hamdi the Yenakker, and, yet, surely, there was this to be said for him—he was one embodiment of our desire for Hamal and Vallia to work together for the future of the whole of Paz against the Shanks. So, as shrewd Ortyg Fellin Coper pointed out: "The realization of honest plans does not always bring the expected result."

We pushed our way toward The Crushed Toad. This Souk of Opportunity had grown up over the seasons in a section of one of the two Wayfarer's Drinniks, and the wide dusty space was now more congested than usual. The reasons were simple. Hamal's commerce normally went by air but since the wars and our virtual destruction of Hamal's air arm, the various forms of land transport returned to favor of necessity. This Urn-Clef Wayfarer's Drinnik northwest of the city just outside the Walls of the Suns, with the sky-spanning arches of the aqueduct carrying water down to the Arena slanting across the eastern section, sent off caravans to the northern parts of Hamal. The River Havilthytus serviced the west. Lacking the impressive canal system of Vallia, Hamal's land communications were superior, for ownership of an airboat remained still a pricey business.

Inside The Crushed Toad Hamdi led us to a small upper room which we entered with fists wrapped around sword hilts. Only one man sat at table, his shirt open to the waist revealing a forest of blackish hairs, his double chins partially obscured by an ale jug. Liquid dribbled down the creases in his skin. He slapped the jug down and bellowed.

"Lahal, Hamdi, you rogue! Where is the gold?"

Hamdi caught my eye and nodded, very stiff.

"This is Nath the Dwa. His twin, Nath the Ob,* did not survive the Empress Thyllis's invitation to an outing in her Arena."

"The bosks stuck him clear through the guts," said this Nath the Dwa. "I own I was glad to learn that bitch Thyllis was dead, although the manner of her death escapes me."

"She was blown away by sorcery," I said. The lesten-hide bag of gold thumped down on the table. "Here is the gold. Now tell us of Spika—"

"Hush, man! Hamdi—you were followed? Check the stairs."

---

* *Dwa:* two. *Ob:* one.

Seg looked out of the door, went to the landing, came back. "All clear. We were not followed."

Nath the Dwa took another draught. A heel of bread and a chunk of cheese lay dying on a wooden platter. There was no flick-flick plant in the room; there were a dozen or so flies.

"I joined Spikatur, for I was angry and wanted my revenge. By Sasco! I wanted to split the throats of as many nobles as I could! But it went wrong—"

We did not sit down as Nath the Dwa talked on. He did not explain why it went wrong or why he had been expelled. But he told us details in return for gold, details that will become apparent as my narrative continues. "And they're flooding into Hamal, now. You must watch out for a fellow thin as a stick, ferret-faced, with one eye, and the other covered with a patch of emeralds and diamonds, crusted thick together."

"Gochert," I said.

He looked surprised. "You know him?"

"No. I have seen him."

"He is a master swordsman. He spitted Henorlo the Blade clean as a whistle. As a Bladesman he has few equals."

"Well," spluttered Hamdi, "I'm not going to cross swords with him!"

I said, "Are there really no leaders of the Spikatur Hunting Sword conspiracy?"

Nath the Dwa swilled ale and swallowed. "Not in the way you or I would understand leaders. But there are those who tell others their thoughts and desires, and these others do them with a gusto." No names had passed from us to Nath and we both wanted it that way, so there was no bandying about of polite forms of address. "Gochert is one such."

"The adherents of Spikatur believed in fighting Hamal and they assassinated Hamalese nobles. They gave their lives willingly. Why should they continue now that Hamal is defeated?"

Nath the Dwa wiped his lips. "And King Telmont?"

"His army will disappear—" began Seg.

"His army," pointed out Nath the Dwa, "is a fresh army containing many mercenaries. They are out for loot. They will fight you. Anyway—" he made a dismissive gesture "—the rasts from the Dawn Lands return home. Soon there will be only the detachments from Vallia, Hyrklana and Djanduin to stop Telmont. His strength will grow as yours shrinks. He will sweep you away."

"We're not here to discuss high strategy. Is there anything else you can tell us for the gold you have been paid?"

"Yes. A great lady has lately arrived in Ruathytu. She travels in secrecy. She is veiled—"

"From Loh?" said Seg.

"Who knows?" Nath the Dwa reached for a refill from the wooden ale bottle. "She keeps her own counsel on that." He poured with a gurgle. He did not offer us refreshment. "She is come, it is said, in Spikatur's name to wreak vengeance on her foes. She is seen by few."

"Her name?"

The jug paused on its way to his lips.

"Name? I have heard her called Helvia the Proud."

"But that is not her name?"

He drank and laughed. "Probably not."

"And where may we find this Helvia the Proud?"

The jug described a circle in the air.

"As to that, a man from the high council of Hamal who asked questions was fished out of the River Mak. At least, some of him was."

"We heard. So that is what befell him."

"He was not a very good spy."

A knock sounded on the door, a very timid knock. Nath the Dwa slapped down his jug and looked pleased. "That will be Filli with the so-lunch. And I am sharp set." He raised his voice. "Come in Filli."

A silver-gray-furred Fristle fifi entered, nervous, head bent, bearing a cloth-covered tray. She wore a blue bow tastefully adorning her tail, and her Hamalese clothes were of the short and skimpy kind. She placed the tray on the table and without looking at us went out. Nath the Dwa whisked the cloth away and delicious aromas lifted into the room. He wrinkled up his nose, closing his eyes.

"There is nothing more here," said Seg.

"No. You are right."

The tray contained thin slices of vosk and golden-yellow momolams, all in a rich gravy. At the side a green salad fairly sparkled with dewy freshness. For sweet an earthenware dish supported a pie, a glorious, crusty, honey-gold pie. A mixture of scents rose, fruits of many kinds blending into a heady mouth-watering delectation.

"Celene pie," said Nath. "How I dote on it. But first, the vosk and momolams. I shall spend your gold well, horters, very well, and grow myself a belly to astound the world."

Seg laughed and we went out, closing the door on Nath, who was already hard at work. "He sounds like Inch and his squish pie," said Seg. "Although celene pie is too rich for me." Celene, a common name for rainbow, describes in this case a pie or flan made from a mixture of fruits and honey. I led the way down the stairs and back into the Souk of Opportunity, mulling over what we had learned. One thing was sure, we had not heard the last of Spikatur Hunting Sword.

The noise and heat and dust smote us as we left The Crushed Toad. A train of Quoffas, enormous patient hearth-rug animals, shambled along drawing carts loaded with freight that would demand a dozen lesser animals to draw. A caravan was forming up, and the guards curveted about astride a typical Kregan collection of riding animals, brandishing their weapons and screeching and kicking dust. The scene might be barbaric and intimidating to a sober citizen from a civilized terrestrial town, but these guards were only having fun and kicking up a shindig before departure to impress their employers. In times of trouble the bandits swarm up out of their rat holes, and caravans must be guarded.

Even in Hamal, strict as to laws...

We walked across to where we had left our animals.

"The more I hear about this Spikatur thing," said Seg, "the more I am puzzled. I thought they sought to bring Hamal down to her knees. Well, haven't we done that?"

"Except for what mischief Telmont may get up to. I wish Nedfar would make up his mind. Once he decides to be emperor I'm sure people who want a peaceful life will rally to him."

"They'll have to fight before they get their peace."

"Aye."

"And if the Spikatur people turn against him?"

"That is something I wish we did not have to consider. But we do. They have already tried to kill him, and I can only hope that now that the situation is changed, their attitude will change as well." We passed an awning-shaded stall where brass pots glittered, spilling out into the suns light. One of those on a journey was useful. "I think that both Tyfar and Nedfar feel that in accepting our help they are in some way disgraced. It may be that the Spikatur conspiracy to destroy Hamalese nobles weighs on their minds."

"Not on Tyfar's! He is a right gallant young prince."

"Oh, he is. A good comrade. And that reminds me, Seg. The island of Pandahem. We have to settle that yet. How would you like to be a king in Pandahem?"

He gaped at me. Then he threw back his head and laughed.

"I was Kov of Falinur and look at the mess I made of that—"

"No! That I won't have. You did the right things—"

"And they failed. Turko will handle them more harshly, and that is probably what they want. As for me—a king? Anyway, the kingdoms in Pandahem are all spoken for."

"Precisely. We shall descend on the island and clear out all the slavers and mercenaries and the rulers will breathe easier again. It is in my mind that they could do with having an emperor to guide them, keep them from each other's throats. Somebody who is above their feuding. How does Seg Segutorio, Emperor of Pandahem, ring in your ears?"

He did not hesitate. "Like a passing bell on the way to the Ice Floes of Sicce." He stopped and stared at me. "Dray! What are you thinking of?"

"It's all right, Seg. I'm not crazy and I haven't allowed megalomania to overtake me. Just that I think it would be useful all around. Anyway, it would give you something to do."

"I'm busily rebuilding the Kroveres of Iztar."

"That is more important than being an emperor, I grant you. But think about it, for my sake."

We walked on through the crowds and found our riding animals and mounted up, giving a silver sinver to the slave who had held them for us. They were hirvels, for we did not wish to attract attention. The silver might have done that, all things considered. Then we trotted slowly off back to the palace.

Ten

The scorpion and The Scorpion

In the following period as the Peace Conference fell apart and the delegations from the Dawn Lands returned home and King Telmont gathered his strength and advanced and reports came in of a buildup in the adherents of Spikatur Hunting Sword, Prince Nedfar deliberated.

"For the sweet sake of Opaz, prince! And for the equally sweet sake of the poorest family trying to scrape a living in the fish stews! Make up your mind!"

Nedfar looked steadily back at me. "You are the Emperor of Vallia, Jak, and I have not recovered from the shock of that yet. I called you traitor. No wonder you studied in the map room. But—"

"Look, Nedfar. We're talking about your country. So I fooled you. I have had to do many things in my life... You have never—I do not guess but am certain—never been slave."

"Of course not."

"I have. It is not nice. If this is your sticking point, I well understand that manumission will not come overnight."

"Slaves like to be slaves."

We talked and walked about, gesturing irritably, in a splendid room of the palace, the Hammabi el Lamma, on its artificial island in the River Havilthytus. Strong bodies of Djangs and Vallians guarded the palace. Nedfar had to be brought to the point, he had to accept the needle, and, as I said, "It's not as though you have to come to the fluttrell's vane, either." Which is to say that this was not just making the best of a bad business.

"Hamal needs you. By the disgusting diseased liver and lights of Makki Grodno! I need you!"

"Ah! It is for Vallia—"

"Spare me," I said, and stalked off to the side table where the flagons and bottles were ranked like a phalanx.

"The Emperor of Vallia," he said, and shook his head. "And you were slave down the Moder."

"And other foul places. Look, Nedfar. You know how it is between your son Tyfar and my daughter Jaezila—"

"You mean, do you not, majister, Lela, the Princess Majestrix of Vallia?"

"I so do. But Jaezila has a sound to it that pleases us. And you do understand that Jaezila outweighs in my mind all this fancy talk of empires?"

He pursed up his lips. "I wonder—"

I did not roar out about whether he doubted my word and similar hot-tempered and rational retorts. I looked at him.

Now he was a great Prince of Hamal, well used to power and unthinkingly accepting instant obedience. He lowered his eyelids and turned his head away, and a stain flooded into his cheeks.

"By Havil! You are the devil men say you are."

Often, to that remark, I had replied in the cheap way: "Believe it!" Now I took up a goblet, a thing of gold and rubies, and filled it with a fine Jholaix and carried it across.

"Drink, Nedfar. You will have to run Hamal with your own wits and resources, your own skills and statecraft. Do not misjudge the situation. We of Vallia will not be looking over your shoulder all the time, there will be no taint and no disgrace in this." I finished that up most bitterly. "We in Vallia have our hands full repairing the mischief you lot from Hamal have caused us."

He took that splendid goblet and held it, his fingers lapped around the gems. The red of the rubies glowed. He lifted his head and stared at me, a hard, calculating, shrewd assessment. Then: "I would not be beholden to an enemy for a throne."

"Agreed. Am I your enemy? Have I ever been—truly?"

It was a nice point.

We talked on, this way and that, and he did agree that I had never borne him any ill will—even when I'd been slave. Then he said, "I have heard the stories of how you became Emperor of Vallia. You did this entirely on your own, for all your friends and cronies, for some unexplained reason, deserted you."

"Wrong on two counts, prince. My friends did not desert me. And no man or woman becomes emperor or empress without help."

"But you were a lone man—a strange figure—the stories are legion concerning Dray Prescot."

538

"And how many are true?"

"You know."

"I know that if Hamal and Vallia do not stand together and show this example to the rest of Paz, the damned thieving, raping, burning Shanks will ruin us all."

On that point, after hours of discussion, the decision pivoted. Nedfar was an honest man whose honor had got out of hand when he was faced with the realities of the situation. I convinced him at last that there was no dishonor in accepting the throne, and the bargain was struck. As we shook hands the bell hung by the door tinkled, and so I shouted and the doors opened and they all crowded in.

Well! The hullabaloo was expected and soothing for what it portended. Tyfar solemnly shook his father's hand. Jaezila kissed him. Kytun boomed and Ortyg squeaked. All of us were overjoyed—and I own my pleasure came from relief that the thing was done and seen to be done. I was even cynical enough to wonder if being an emperor would change Nedfar for the worse. And then I relented and allowed the pleasure to creep in. After all, emperors are not made every day—even on Kregen.

With all the experience of his short time as King of Hyrklana lighting up his face, Jaidur said, "Now we must get the whole of Hamal to support you, Nedfar. I would say that a treaty of friendship now exists between your country and mine."

"My hand on it!" exclaimed Nedfar.

Jaezila held Tyfar's arm. Kytun's hands were nowhere near his sword hilts. Ortyg brushed his whiskers. As I say, we were all very pleased with ourselves...

Every one of our loyal friends wanted to come up and congratulate Nedfar, and a sort of mini-reception was held. I heard Tyfar say to Jaezila, "I look forward to meeting your sister Dayra, Zila. You must miss her."

"I do." Jaezila put a hand to her hair. "Yes, to be honest, I do. She was always a little minx. And she's done some things that are too terrible even to think about, let alone tell a prince of Hamal." Jaezila laughed, and turned and saw me looking at her. The smile faltered through the laugh.

"I dearly wish to see Dayra again," I said. "I love her, as you know, and if you should happen to see her, Jaezila, be sure you tell her that. I do not think she understands." I looked over across the heads of the happily chattering throng. "Jaidur took long enough, Zair knows."

"I will tell Dayra, father," said Jaezila, and she was suddenly deadly serious. "She runs with bad company and there is a reckoning overdue for them. I will tell her."

The fear that clutched me then was that the overdue reckoning for the villains who had bedazzled Dayra would fall upon her also. She was a headlong, vivacious girl, known as Ros the Claw, and I found it well-nigh insupportable that her enmity for me so distressed her mother, Delia.

Nedfar still held the golden goblet studded with rubies. I believe he felt the same as did I, that this goblet formed a covenant between us, the act of drinking a sacrament to and for the future of our two countries.

The news spread and the gathering turned into a party and the party atmosphere permeated the palace and extended into the city so that Ruathytu exploded to the stars. Prince Nedfar was well-liked, and now that he was emperor people could look forward to getting back to normal after the war. Things would change, of course; but life could go on and folk could breathe a little easier. Hamalese nobles crowded in to swear their allegiance. I moved a little way apart—I confess I was looking for a piece of squish pie—and I saw a reddish brown scorpion peering at me over the lip of a chased silver bowl packed with palines.

I stood stock still.

His body-segments glistened. His stinger lifted, hard and black. He stared at me. I guessed no one else in the lofty chamber could see this scorpion but me.

His feelers and his stinger waved. They moved commandingly. Still gripping my goblet of best Jholaix, I walked slowly to the nearest door and went out into the corridor and turned along past two Valkan sentries, who managed to hide their smiles and who saluted with stiff and ridiculous punctilio. The scorpion appeared ahead, along the corridor, and with a quiet word to the sentries, I followed him. The carpet muffled my footsteps. The air was close and hot and spiced with scents. The scorpion led me into a small room where two slave girls, stark naked, lay asleep on a truckle bed locked in each other's arms. They were Sylvies. I took my gaze away from them, saw the domestic cleaning gear in the room, looked at the scorpion, wondering who had money to waste in buying seductive Sylvies to use as palace maids.

Blue radiance dropped about me.

The little reddish-brown scorpion vanished. In his place and glowing with the blue radiance of unimaginable distance, swelling and bloating over me, the immense form of The Scorpion told me I was summoned to the presence of the Star Lords. Huge, that phantom Scorpion, encompassing a crushing bulk far larger than could possibly be confined in this small room. The coldness swept over me.

The naked girls dwindled away. The room spun. I was falling and spinning, wrapped in the coldness of ice.

Winds tore at me, buffeting, roaring. Spinning end over end and still clutching the goblet, I whirled away into the vasty deeps of darkness.

Eleven

The Star Lords—Allies?

The cold lingered and clung chill, and then went away and I could breathe again.

Insubstantial tremors, gossamer strokings, thistledown brushings confused my senses; I stood on grass soft underfoot and strode granite floorings, and cavorted through blustery winds high in the air. Gasping with a shudder I made no attempt to suppress, I opened my eyes.

Silver-gray veils shot through with rainbow colors like butterflies' wings hung before me. Each hung alternately from right and left, curving gracefully to the center. Reaching out a hand I saw the insubstantial material lift away like a curtain before I touched it, rising to reveal a curtain beyond hanging from the opposite corner. As I advanced, each curtain lifted up and away to the side in turn, on and on. Do not ask why I did not look about me. The lifting veils ahead, innumerable veils, mesmerized me.

As though advancing along a corridor filled with veil after veil, I walked on, and beneath my feet the floor pulsed and banked like morning mist.

As if unraveling a tangled ball, I continued.

The beckoning veils drew away silently. The first chamber opened out ahead and on either side, walled in crimson light, floored with crimson tiles and roofed with crimson radiance. I walked on. Vague forms drifted at the edges of vision, to coalesce and glide apart again like phantom underwater fronds undulating in unfelt currents. The veils closed about like the wings of moths, soft and furred. So I went on.

The next chamber breathed a subdued greenness composed of spring grass and jungle fronds, damp and dewy, and the moss underfoot darkened with each footprint and faded as I passed along.

The third chamber after innumerable opening veils proved as I expected it to be.

All of yellow, golden amber yellows, bright brilliant yellows, light and sunshine and airiness, and that chamber passed and I went on following the opening way ahead.

In a myriad glittering lights like the eyes of dragonflies I stepped past the ultimate veil and put that curtain away and stood forth in massive silence into a chamber robed in ebon.

Here I stopped.

I looked about.

On the right hand wall of blackness three pictures were arranged in a horizontal row. They were oval in shape, thickly framed in silver, and each showed a painting of a world set against darkness, a world I recognized as

Kregen, with the continents and islands of Paz clearly visible between bands and streaks of whiteness. I looked at the three pictures, and away to the other side of the chamber where the lights pirouetted. Perhaps a shape moved there; perhaps there was only a flicker of light upon shadow in my own eyes.

I opened my mouth.

"Everoinye! Star Lords!"

For three heartbeats the echo of my voice rang in the chamber.

Then—

"Dray Prescot, onker of onkers, prince of onkers."

"Yes," I shouted. "I am stupid, an onker, and I own it. And you—what are you?"

The rustling voice expanded within my head as well as around me in the warmed and scented air.

"We are the Everoinye."

I cocked my head to the side in a silly instinctive gesture. Was there the faintest ghost-echo of humor in the voice, a tiny trace of mirth, like the last bubble in a forgotten glass of champagne? The Star Lords?

"You, Dray Prescot, are much changed. You were the blow-hard, the rough, tough warrior who swore and cursed and reviled us even when you faced what you imagined to be death or worse than death, even when you were slave. Now you are an emperor who makes emperors and kings, and you speak softly, owning to your state of onkerishness. Have you anything to say?"

The latter-day change in the character I ascribed to the Star Lords amazed me. They had treated me in the past not so much with contempt as with indifference. I carried out their missions for them or I was banished back to Earth. That, clearly, was a situation that had suffered change.

The black wall opposite the three pictures of Kregen was no wall as I looked broodingly in that direction, wondering what to say to the Everoinye that would convince them I was, indeed, the sober, sensible emperor and not the roaring tearaway I had been, still was, and no doubt would continue to be... That wall was an emptiness, a void, a gulf. At least, I thought it was, for it seemed, as I looked, to extend beyond the confines of infinity, if such a thought be possible, and the flickering motes of light danced and danced like fireflies in the evening.

"Say, Star Lords? Only that I have work to do on Kregen and you interfere with that work, as you have—" I stopped.

"As we have always done?"

"If you say it."

The hollow voice sharpened and struck with a return of an ancient vigor. "Do not attempt to dissemble. We are privy to what you desire."

"Then you must know what lies before me."

"The continuation of our plans for Paz."

I sucked in a breath.

And then, in that fog of bewilderment, I suddenly realized I still held the goblet of wine. It lay in my grip, hard and polished and real. I lifted the goblet, and drank, and emptied it, and so looked about—most ostentatiously—for a table whereon to place the precious thing.

Like a speeded-up growth, a mushroom-shaped table sprouted from the ebon floor.

So close it was, so quick, it nearly caught me betwixt wind and water. I looked up.

"And, had it done so, Everoinye—would you have laughed?"

The voice ghosted in on a sigh I heard with an amazing clarity.

"We were once mortal men like you, Dray Prescot. We have not forgotten how to laugh, but there is no occasion for that these days. You say you have work to do. We must warn you—"

I opened my mouth; my fists were gripped on the goblet, I opened my black-fanged winespout and I almost bellowed in the old intemperate Dray Prescot way. And then I closed my mouth and clamped my teeth, and waited.

"—warn you that your work has just begun."

I waited.

"The Shanks."

"They have many unpleasant names and that seems a popular one. I do not care for the results of their operations. Their hobbies are not to my taste. My people fight them. And you?"

If I expected the transformation of the Star Lords to encompass their rising to that bait, I was mistaken.

"You will fight them, Dray Prescot, for that is what we wish."

A sudden, anguished, intolerable horror prostrated me. Was I to be hurled all naked and unarmed among the Shanks, the fish-heads, the Leem-Lovers? No, by Zair, that I couldn't bear...

The all-pervading voice of the Everoinye encased me in words like spider-silk.

"We are old, Dray Prescot, old beyond anything even you with a thousand years of life could comprehend. There are objectives we must accomplish in due time. You have proved of value to us. We do not deny this. It is strange—as you would say, passing strange—that this should be so, for you are a harum-scarum miscreant, a rogue with delusions of grandeur, an emperor with charisma who can bring a whole world to do your bidding. And we understand the causes of your present meekness and level-headed tolerance. We approve and are not deceived."

If this was a trap, I was not going to fall into it.

I said, "And what help can you give me?" I spoke with more harshness than I'd intended.

"We may not send you back to your planet of birth."

Again, was there that dying champagne bubble of mirth?

"And positive help?"

"That, Dray Prescot, you must wait to find out."

Then, understanding they would not elaborate on this point, I passed on to something I dearly wished to know.

"Tell me, Everoinye, why did you seed Kregen with so many wonderfully different races and animals?"

"You do not know that we did so, and, had we done so, it would not be for you to know the answer."

"So you're fobbing me off again? By Krun! I thought—"

The whispering voice was now—it had to be!—tinged with genuine mirth. "You are forgetful, emperor?"

I put the goblet on the table. It looked forlorn, perched there alone. I drew a breath. Before I could speak, the insufferable whisper said, "We had a hand in what was done on Kregen, as did Others of whom we will not speak."

"You will not give me reasons, if you will not own up to your meddling. I fancy the Savanti may have some answers—"

"They know nothing. They objected at the time because of what the Curshin did. But the Savanti understood only some of the results; they have no knowledge of the reasons or the causes."

"All the same—"

"Enough, Dray Prescot! We do not wish to send you back to your Earth."

That, as you know, by Zair! was enough to scare me witless.

The Savanti, superhuman but mortal men and women, in their Swinging City of Aphrasöe, had first brought me to Kregen in order to work for them as a Savapim and help bring civilization to the world. I had failed their tests, now I was beginning to understand, because of the inherent rebellious recklessness of my nature that abhorred unjust authority. The Star Lords in their inscrutable purposes had taken me up and employed me and thus served my own ends in returning me to Kregen where all that I really wanted in two worlds awaited me. Delia! My Delia of Delphond, my Delia of the Blue Mountains! All this flummery was for her, and only her, and I wondered if these disembodied ghost voices, these vast brains, really understood that.

"You know I will not willingly return to Earth. Your determination to have your own way does go against the grain, for you are not gods..." I paused for only a moment, holding myself steady, wondering if they would blast me on the spot for what they would take as blasphemy. I went on: "You say you are old. You have plans for Kregen. Why me? Why—"

"You are not the first."

"I suspected that."

"Kregen is vastly different now from what it was. Our times run perilously short and there is much to do. You will do what you can against the Shanks. Perhaps that is all we can ask of you."

To say I was astounded upon amazement upon stupefaction is to phrase my feelings very slightly. I swallowed.

"Oh, we'll have a go at the Shanks. Nobody likes them."

"Precisely."

I ruminated. "What does that mean?"

"Precisely what it says. Now, Dray Prescot, lest you presume because we have told you a few small matters, be warned! The days ahead are filled with peril. Tread carefully. For all your intemperate hotheadedness, which you affect so cleverly, you may fall to the blade, to the arrow."

"And?"

Well, insult them how you might, you wouldn't startle a Star Lord easily this side of the Ice Floes of Sicce.

"And hew to your path."

"Is that all?"

"It is all and enough, for it contains all."

I rubbed the back of my neck and it was my turn to be startled. I looked down quickly. I still wore the comfortable lounging clothes I was wearing when talking to Nedfar. Odd. In encounters with the Star Lords material things like clothes and wine goblets tended to escape attention.

"Tell me," I said, squinting at the confusing dragonfly lights, "what of your rebellious young Star Lord who challenged you. What of Ahrinye?"

"He is on a task beyond your comprehension and it is no concern of yours."

"Et cetera," I said, and I own the rebellious ugliness sounded threatening in my voice.

The reaction was rapid.

"Enough, Dray Prescot, who is called Emperor of Emperors! Beware the wrath of the Everoinye! Begone!"

It was quick, damned quick, I'll say that for them, the invisible, black-humored pack of leems.

I was standing in the small room staring down at the entwined Sylvies, naked limbs glistening with unguents, hair glossy about flushed faces. They looked up at me, newly awoken, and before they could scream I'd slammed the door open and stalked out, clutching my robes about me, furious past anger so that I wanted to roar with laughter, and did not, because I hewed to a new path and would not be deflected.

My entrance following the scorpion into their room had awoken the Sylvies. When I returned to the party no one even remarked on my absence, everything was as it had been before, and the clepsydra could have dropped barely a score of splashes to mark the passage of time.

One fact I knew and kept in the forefront of my thick vosk skull of a head. The Star Lords possessed power, real power, terrible power. It was fortunate for us all that their wishes and mine coincided.

Twelve

What I Learned in The Leather Bottle

"You do intend to go to my father's coronation, then, Jak?" Tyfar spoke with such mirth, the young devil, I was minded to play dumb and plead prior engagements. "After all, you are by way of being an expert."

The main and overridingly important thing to notice here was that Tyfar and I could joke about a horrible experience through which I had gone when Hamal and Vallia had been enemies.

That she-leem Thyllis during the pomp and circumstance of her coronation had had me, naked and filthy and hairy, dragged around Ruathytu at the tail of a calsany.

That Tyfar could rest assured that he might make this nature of joke without offense heartened me. He now fully accepted that what we said we said in good faith. Only his own prickly sense of honor had stood in the way of immediate acceptance.

"Do you, Tyfar, have any particular calsany in mind?"

"I have my eye on a particularly fine animal. And we all know what calsanys do when they are upset or excited." Then a sudden seriousness brought his mockery to a close as he said, "Although, by Havil! I certainly would not, nor would my father, sink so low as to drag a defeated foeman around the streets like that. I saw it, and never knew who you were. It was something that, even then, revolted me."

Then we were joined by Hamalese nobles and Djang nobles and the conversation expanded. Now all our thoughts were set upon the coronation of Nedfar so that all the people of Hamal might have a lawful emperor, and the expected confrontation with the enormous raiding fleet of Shanks. This fleet was being watched and shadowed, and all men trembled lest it turn in their direction. The brutal fact was, the Shank fleet would turn in someone's direction—without fail.

As for the rest of that evening, it remains a mystery to me. My mind filled with speculations on that remarkable encounter with the Star Lords. By Vox, but they'd changed in the time I'd known them!

On and off, thinking about the changed situation in the ensuing days,

I fancied that the key words, the clue, lay in the words of the Everoinye: "We are growing old…" I had some thousand years of life stretching ahead of me thanks to the baptism in the sacred pool of the River Zelph in far Aphrasöe, and I had no idea of what length of time the Star Lords would count as making them old. Millions upon millions of years had been my feeling. Perhaps that was mere superstitious impressionism? Maybe the Everoinye grew old and dropped dead at far more frequent intervals.

The idea did not give me the same glow as it would have done a few seasons ago.

Here and now I had to assume the Everoinye would leave me to get on with the job. The ready acceptance of Prince Nedfar as Emperor of Hamal was no closeted palace coup, for the rejoicing extended in genuine feeling throughout the city and into the provinces as the news spread. Tyfar saw about making sure of the army, and many a fine fellow you have met in my narrative rolled up to swear allegiance, and many and many more I knew well and have not mentioned, also. The Air Service wanted to know when they could expect some vollers.

This exposed the whole vexed question of the position of the realms of the Dawn Lands. Most of those monarchs who had so bitterly quarreled had gone home, expecting dissension to rend Hamal for seasons to come. And there was always King Telmont. Our spies reported he had taken a wide swing around to the south. He and his army—which grew from disaffected mercenaries—were watched. So the few airboats left were handed over to the new Hamalian Air Service.

Many people have called me an uncouth fighting man, and that never worries me. It now occurred to me that it would be tactful if I left Ruathytu for a space, to give the new emperor room to swing his scepter. We intended to begin as we meant to go along, and Ortyg fretted over the accounts due in Djanduin and Jaidur itched to return with Lildra to Hyrklana and Kytun wanted to put into practice some new ideas for the army he'd picked up. So we agreed. We'd leave Hamal to the Hamalese for a space, and all return for the coronation. As for the detachments of our armies and their commanders—they would remain.

Tyfar said, "Only true comrades could do this, Jak."

"Aye."

"My father tells me he even feels shame for doubting you. I—"

"You are a young rip, who has a stern task before him. As for the emperor; he and I understand each other. Now I'm off to have a quiet look at King Telmont and his army. If Rosil is there, well, he will be a bonus, and Vad Garnath, the rast."

"Take care, Jak—"

"And you."

He continued to call me Jak at my express wish. Soon enough he'd be able to accept my name without a tremble. Everything is not sweetness and light in the blink of an eyelid.

Jaezila said she would stay with Tyfar. Saying the remberees to them I checked my impatient query: "When will you two knock some sense into each other's heads and get married, or whatever relationship you desire, instead of pussyfooting around each other like a manhound and a wersting?"

As we said the remberees, Jaezila kissed me. "And, Jak, Father, you might run into Mother. You never know."

As I fired up and demanded to know what she meant, she put a finger to her lips, laughing. "You know, Father, you mustn't know! It is Sisters of the Rose. Sufficient?"

"No. But no more than I expect." The Sisters of the Rose, that secret organization of women, was secret. No man was privy to its secrets, for that would have negated the art and craft of female autonomy. It was all sub-rosa, and with that feeble twin-world-language idiocy in my head, I took off.

There had been the usual to-do over getting away alone, but I'd managed it. Seg refused to be hurt. As he said, "I have the Kroveres of Iztar to see to. They will have a lot to do in Vallia now."

"And in Hamal and the rest of Paz, Seg."

"Of course."

So I flew south ready to act the spy again and see what this King Telmont and his associates were made of.

As I sped southwards in a fast two-place flier I wondered if I would meet those two unhanged rogues, Rosil, the Kataki Strom, and Vad Garnath. I'd spoken to Nedfar about rewards. Deldar Fresk, who had not lost another man there in the Pass of Lacachun, was made up to Jiktar. I particularly wanted to make sure Rees and Chido were safe. They were very dear to me, Bladesmen of my ruffling days in Ruathytu's Sacred Quarter and good companions. Chido, I was told, had returned to his estates of Eurys in the east, where he was the Vad. Rees, whose estates had blown away on the Golden Wind from which he took his name, had been badly treated by Thyllis. There were many people in the same position. It was not difficult to arrange with Nedfar to reinstate them, and reward them, and I'd put Rees's name prominently on the list. As to his whereabouts, no one seemed to know.

Rees had suffered most cruelly from the Kataki Strom and Van Garnath, his eldest son, Reesnik, being slain by their hired assassins. We'd spent some rousing times together, and I had brought his daughter, Saffi, the golden lion-maid, out of a hideous bondage. But Rees and Chido knew me as Hamun ham Farthytu, the Amak of Paline Valley. That was a name I owned to in honor and intended to keep inviolate. I'd have to do some fancy footwork when we all met up, by Krun!

The dwaburs sped past below. Hamal is a rich country and Nedfar would make of it a fine and wonderful place. All we had to do was deal with Telmont and his hired army, and then close our ranks against the Leem-Lovers from over the curve of the world.

Simple plans are very often but not always the best. All I intended to do was turn up at Telmont's current army camp as a simple paktun, a mercenary at the moment tazll and therefore willing to take employment. I'd have a good look around and nose into what did not concern me and then, having sized up things that spies could not tell from outside vantage points, return to work out ways of dealing with what I had discovered. It seemed a not unuseful idea to drop down into a town first and ask around before committing myself to the army. Anyway, I wanted to hide the voller first.

Take it all nice and easy... No sweat... Just fly down and stow the airboat and then wander into town... All free and easy... Ask around, casual like, all smiles... Easy...

Ha!

This was Kregan and I was Dray Prescot, and that combination is, I have to point out, volatile.

Stowing the voller was simple enough at the back of a stand of timber. Walking around the curve of the hill along the dusty yellow road into town was simple, too.

They grabbed me as I started off across the square toward the nearest tavern. Now, my reputation holds different values in different pans of Kregen, and had these folk known who I was they would no doubt—without a damned doubt at all, by Vox!—have used edged and pointed weapons. As it was they tried to lay me out with cudgels.

Townsfolk, they looked, rosy of cheek, shocked of hair, wearing simple country town clothes. But their bludgeons whistled about my ears like billy-oh.

"Hold on!" I bellowed, weaving and dodging. "Hold on, for the sweet sake of Kaerlan the Merciful! I mean you no harm."

They meant me harm, though.

I dragged out my thraxter and used the straight cut and thrust to parry blows, to thwunk a few tousled heads, to trip up folk who insisted on trying to brain me. The townsfolk were all hurrying up, screaming abuse, women hurling rotten gregarians and children flinging all kinds of unmentionables. The mob bludgeoned and pelted and shrieked and I soon turned into a dungy fruit-juicy lumpen scarecrow.

"By Krun!" I said. "I'm not standing for this!"

So, there and then, without more ado, I ran. I ran off. I ran away from an indignant mob of townsfolk with their brooms and cudgels and rotten fruit. Run! I ran, I can tell you!

They chucked refuse after me and a stinking bamber hit me behind the ear, and squelched all glistery brown down my neck, stinking to the heavens. I ran faster than they did, and reached the voller and took off. They stood under the craft and shrieked imprecations up at me, shaking their fists and their clumsy rabble weapons. They were not shouting the remberees. And, by Krun, I hadn't stopped to observe the fantamyrrh as I boarded the voller.

Whirling away and up over the trees I turned to glance back. They were still there, jumping up and down and waving their weapons and no doubt bellowing fit to wake the dead. By the disgusting leprous left nostril of Makki Grodno! Now what had that all been about?

Moving this time with much greater circumspection at the next town along and mingling in unobtrusive clothes with folk entering the narrow streets in a religious procession, for the little towns in this section were unwalled, I discovered the answer to the riddle.

And, to an old campaigner, an old paktun, that answer was perfectly obvious and deucedly uncomfortable to a fighting man. I had laughed like a loon leaving that first town, for the ludicrous situation appealed to me; now I did not laugh.

The explanation, simple and ugly, was merely that the townsfolk had been plundered rotten by the mercenaries of King Telmont's army. Simple, direct, and, as I say, ugly.

My clothes, fighting man's gear, and my weapons, marked me for a paktun. These townsfolk, brave enough to remain in their little towns, would deal most unkindly with a lone soldier.

The religious procession wended along to an adobe temple erected to the greater glory of the goddess Dafnisha the Ample, a goddess much favored in these parts, having a deal to do with the births of healthy twins. The chanting and the shuffle of feet died. I hitched up the old blanket coat that, ragged and dingy, draped my left shoulder, leaving a not-too-clean blue shirt displaying a fringe of shaggy ruffles, and went over to the nearest tavern, The Leather Bottle. It is always the nearest tavern a fellow enters when he is thirsty—almost. I didn't want to share a place with the devotees of the plump and fertile goddess Dafnisha the Ample when they boiled out after their service with their tongues hanging out.

The Leather Bottle was like many another small tavern in this section of Hamal—quiet, dusty, provided with one good supply of ale and wine and the rest indifferent stuff. Three frugally produced copper obs started me off, enough to quench my thirst, and a few more brought an earthenware platter so that I stuffed chunks of bread and slivers of cheese into my mouth as I drank, chewing with distended cheeks, and thus conveyed the impression I wished to create. I had, also, given a little twist to my face, as Deb-Lu-Quienyin had taught, so that I seemed your typical laboring fellow on the lookout.

Soon I was in conversation. The suns warmed the room and a flick-flick plant stirred to life now and again.

"King Telmont?" The speaker, a fellow with a wooden leg and a cast in his left eye, spat. He was a good shot. "We hid what we thought we could keep and sent all the women out into the hills. That stinking yetch's men took what we left—"

"Ah, but Nath," spoke up his companion, a lean-faced man with the marks of the cobbler upon him. "We worked it well, did we not? Just enough left in the town to be taken, and not so little that the soldiers became suspicious there was more."

"Aye, Mildo, we fooled the cramph." Three eyes turned in my direction, the fourth inspecting the opposite wall.

I held up a hand, busily chewing an onion, raw and rich and juicy, and spraying among the odor bits and pieces as I spoke. "Now then, doms— I'm just a traveling man." I always enjoyed handing out this one, for it was in its own way perfectly true. "D'you want a ditch dug? A fence repaired— although that's pretty technical—the wood chopped? I ran ten dwaburs without stopping when Telmont's army showed up."

No doubt about it, ragged, not-too-clean, leering, uncouth, I looked my part.

Nath the Peg sniffed and I shuffled out five more copper obs onto the sturm wood table. "You'll join me, doms?"

"Aye, dom, we'll join you."

Their thoughts were transparent. I was probably not a spy for Telmont's quartermasters come to check up on the paucity of supplies from this lit- tle town of Homis Creek. But if I were they had me in their clutches and would find me out.

The delicate Och maiden brought the fresh ale with the grace of a being of Creation blessed with six limbs. As she turned to go, I said, "May Ochenshum bless you."

She favored me with a startled look over her shoulder, and fled, and I wondered if it was my words that had surprised her or the bits of onion that sprayed against her shoulders.

Mildo the Last supped and wiped his lips. "We don't take kindly to mercenaries around here and we fooled Telmont. But he'll have this new Emperor Nedfar where he wants him. Aye, that is certain sure."

The cavortings of kings and emperors affected places like Homis Creek only in indirect ways—matters of billeting soldiers and taxes—which were direct enough when they bit.

"How so?" I said, around a fresh onion that crunched beautifully, rich and juicy.

"Why, the emperor's daughter, of course, and her fancy man."

So surprising, these words, that I couldn't stop myself from blurting out along with sprays of onion: "The princess Thefi and Lobur the Dagger?"

"You've heard about them, then? Oh, aye, they're with the army all right.

And now he's got them, old Hot and Cold Telmont will make Emperor Nedfar dance to his tune, you mark my words."

Thirteen

Princess Thefi and Lobur the Dagger

There is a venerable saying on Kregen, attributed to various sources, among whom scholars squabble most fiercely over the competing claims of Nalgre ti Liancesmot, a long-dead playwright, and San Blarnoi, a possibly mythical figure or consortium of wise men of the past, which runs: "When you look too long upon the face of a leem you may grow a leem's tail."

As I stowed the flier in a patch of woods and started out to walk into King Telmont's camp, I recalled this saying, and its meaning. Typically Kregan is that modifier, "May." If you take that ferocious eight-legged hunting beast, the leem, as a symbol for terror and horrific evil, then Kregans do not say if you fight against monsters or devils you will turn into a monster or a devil. You may possibly not grow a leem's tail.

Never think for an instant that I was unaware that because of the deeds I had been called on to perform on Kregen I might grow to be like those against whom I struggled. There are two orders of fighting men, and I believe if you have listened to my words through my story you will understand the kind of fighting man I am, whether or not fate played a part in that. If you do not see that, then I have been spending my breath to no avail.

So, as I walked between the outlying totrix lines with those fractious six-legged saddle animals tugging at the ropes, I pondered how I would react when face-to-face with Vad Garnath and his evil associate, the Kataki Strom.

Bone-headed heroes of many of the stirring tales of Kregen would simply barge in swinging. I'd been like that, once upon a time. I still was, Zair forgive me, but I had learned—not much, a little, enough to make me look first; and that, by Vox, makes the doing of the deed a thousand times harder and more dangerous.

"Hey, dom!" called the bristle-haired Brokelsh Deldar. "You tazll?"

"Aye, dom."

"Then join my pastang, we have a vacancy since that onker Norlgo drank himself into the well. You look handy."

"What happened to Norlgo?"

"Why, he drank himself into the well."

I stopped. The path had been churned up by military boots, some of the ranked tents were decrepit, most were in that middle stage of life when repairs were constant, and only a half-dozen were new. Flags fluttered. Men moved about over the endless fatigues inseparable from an army encampment.

"How so?"

"I told you, dom. Norlgo thought he would drink a score of flagons, and he could only manage sixteen and then he fell down the well and cracked his head open."

"Oh, I see. Let me look around first, Deldar, as to which pastang I join."

"As you wish. It's all the same to me. But you'll find none as open-handed as our Jiktar, who spreads gold every pay day with a lavish hand."

"I thank you for your information." Walking down, casual, not hurrying, it seemed clear to me that recruits were welcomed here. Oh, yes, I was clearly a paktun, well-armed, lithe and limber and wearing the silver pakmort at my throat and with a dangling array of trophy rings in the pakai at my shoulder. Counting tents, counting heads, counting animals—counting damn well everything and totting it all up in my head—I walked on.

Camps vary considerably from race to race and army to army, but where you have a commander he will usually inhabit a tent larger and more luxurious than the general mob. King Telmont's marquee lofted, striped blue and green, bright with banners, set snugly by the small grove of trees sheltering the well down which, no doubt, sixteen-flagon Norlgo tumbled. I marched up to the guards bold as Krasny work.

"Aye, dom," said the Deldar on duty. He was apim, like me. "We can always take a paktun of the right mettle. You look likely."

"Easy, Deldar. I'm still looking."

He squinted in the radiance of the suns, and showed a snaggle of teeth. "The King's Ironfists offer to take you. You will not do better than that."

This was, given the nature of this army, probably true.

I really had no wish to waste time going through the business of hiring out as a mercenary; but I had to gain entrance into the kingly enclosures. I just wanted this business to be a quick in and out and away clean, with Lobur and Thefi in tow.

As I have remarked, the problems of retaining a semblance of humanity on a factory production line, of beating the rush hour into the office, or getting to milk the cows, of doing all the humdrum tasks demanded of us here on this Earth are far more pressing than setting off to rescue a princess and her lover from a wicked enemy on a distant world. Paying the bills hits us more shrewdly than swinging a sword at a monster. All the same, I was on Kregen, and on Kregen rescuing princesses and swinging swords are part of normal life.

That is, part of normal life for some folk on Kregen, not all; for folk who take up the adventuring career, who seek their fortunes on that exotic and bizarre world of peril and beauty, for—in short—poor doomed damned souls like me.

"Make up your mind, dom."

"I will—" I said, and then a fancy dandy tricked-out little Hikdar appeared. Now it is possible in some armies of Kregen for a young man with the right connections and qualities to enter on a military career as a Hikdar without going through the tedious business of rising through the ranks as a Deldar. Most Deldars are bluff and rough and bellow—well, to be honest, just about all Deldars bellow.

This Hikdar with the gold bullion and flounders minced over, almost tangled in his own sword, looking agitated.

"Brassud, Deldar!" he called out in a throttled squeak. Brassud is not quite the same as "Attention!" being more of an adjuration to brace up; but it achieved results. "The king is coming!"

That was enough.

Hot and Cold Telmont was on his rounds. To retain some semblance of loyalty among their troops kings have to go out and about from time to time, like politicians kissing babies. Telmont and his retinue trotted into sight.

A gilded bunch, a blaze of gold and jewelry, of plumes and feathers and cloaks. Their zorcas were fine-spirited animals. Among the group riding in attendance on the king came the Princess Thefi and Lobur the Dagger.

Well, now!

This, I had not expected.

If Telmont held Thefi as a threat to her father, as a surety that Nedfar would do as Telmont wanted, then it was to be expected she would be held in durance vile. As it was, here she came, trotting along on a splendid gray zorca, laughing and joking with Lobur, who looked just the rapscallion he was. His smile was brilliant. He leaned across to Thefi and she responded, laughing, and they trotted on in the lights of the suns, and I gaped up at them.

They saw me.

"Jak!"

Well, it was reunion time. I had last seen these two as they escaped in a green-painted Courier voller, eloping and in love. As the swods of the guards stood, stiff as icicles, and the Hikdar aped their pose if not their manner, old Hot and Cold Telmont rode on at the head of his retinue. All I noticed of him was the litter of jewels on his armor and the flowing green cloak, the way he sat lumpily in his saddle, and the face like a half-empty sack of flour rescued from a burning mill.

Thefi and Lobur reined in, and while Lobur sat his saddle, puzzled and half smiling, Thefi impulsively dismounted and then stood, abruptly embarrassed, gripping her zorca's saddle bow.

"Jak!"

"Lahal, princess," I said, and I spoke gravely. "Lahal, Lobur."

Lobur did not answer. He turned an ugly face on the Hikdar. "All right, fambly! Get on about your own business."

"Quidang, notor!" babbled the youngster, pink-tinged, and in turn rounding on the Deldar. The Deldar's blunt face expressed no emotion at the kicking order of the world as he bellowed his guard back to duty.

The Dagger looked much as I had last seen him. His dark hair cut long and curled, his nose rather shorter than longer, his casual free air, all reminded me of his past impression—except that I could find no trace of that old forthright candor in his eyes. His dagger swung at his belt. He wore bright clothes, with only a few gems. As for Thefi—well, she looked decidedly the same, beautiful and willful, and also markedly different. She had chosen to elope with Lobur and I had assisted them both. I had thought she might regret her actions when high-flown emotions drove rational thought from her head. In my guise as a gruff old warrior paktun I would not again commit the gaffe of questioning her on so tender a point.

I said, "I am surprised to see you here. I thought you were flying to Pandahem."

Still fixed in that stiff pose by her zorca, Thefi said, "We did, Jak, we did. Then when the Hyr Notor came to Ruathytu—"

"The Hyr Notor!"

She flinched back at my tone, my expression. There was no time to curse myself.

"Why, yes. He received us very kindly in Pandahem. Then in Ruathytu—" She faltered.

Lobur swung an elegant leg over his zorca and jumped down. "You are distressing the princess, Jak. You know what happened in the city? What happened to the Hyr Notor?"

I knew all right. The Hyr Notor was—had been—the Wizard of Loh Phu-Si-Yantong, and even now I did not know if he had been all evil, or if there had been a spot of goodness in him as I hoped. He had been blown away by the Quern of Gramarye fashioned in sorcery by Deb-Lu-Quienyin and Khe-Hi-Bjanching, good comrades both. Quite obviously he had planned to use Thefi in schemes against her father, just as Vad Garnath and King Telmont were now doing.

"I heard," I said.

"We have to resist those devils of Vallia and Hyrklana and drive them back." Lobur's fist fastened onto his dagger handle. His name was Lobur ham Hufadet, from an ancient and honorable family of Trefimlad. But he did not own a fortune. Tyfar had offered the opinion that if Lobur wished to marry his sister then he must do a great deed in the world. Was this the great deed?

As though my thoughts were transparent to her, Thefi said, "And Tyfar? You have seen him? He is well?"

"He is well. Yes, I have seen him. He grieves for you, Thefi, unknowing of your fate."

Then Lobur surprised me, in an area in which I should not have been surprised.

"You call the princess princess, Jak. Have you forgotten?"

I shook my head, a universal gesture among apims. "No. And Prince Nedfar—"

"How is he, Jak?" Thefi let go of the zorca and took a step forward. "We heard such terrible stories—Ruathytu is in flames, and the horrible Vallians have Father chained up and put a crown of mockery upon his head—"

Well, that was to be expected. This belief just made life more difficult for me.

"The prince is well. There is no crown of mockery."

"I do not quite—?"

The zorca hooves clickety-clicking along faded on the warm air, and the shouts of soldiers drifted in, the clink and clatter of weapons training mingling incongruously with the domestic sounds of buckets and plates, knives and forks. One of the important and impressive mealtimes of Kregen was due, and the army drew in deep breaths of appreciative expectation. That warm Kregan air swarmed with mouth-watering scents. It was roast ordel and yellow-juiced shollos and thick gravy and it smelled heavenly.

Trust old Hot and Cold to ride out on rounds when the men were being well fed.

"Why are you here with Telmont, princess?"

She looked startled and then puzzled. The smoothness of her forehead suddenly showed shadowed lines. "But we—"

"We have to fight our enemies, Jak, and that is why you have joined us." Lobur spoke with an edginess that made me think he had his mind on other schemes.

"Fight our enemies, yes. But we have to establish just who our enemies are—"

"Jak!" Thefi burst out. "We know that!"

"I am not so sure. You do not know the half of it."

Lobur's dagger clicked as he loosened it. "You'd better explain what you mean."

"I shall. But I would prefer to talk more privately."

By the suppurating scabies of Makki Grodno! Here I'd expected to have to carve my way through a wall of living flesh and wade through drenchings of blood to free these two, and that would have been the easy part, by

Krun. They were here of their own free will, anxious to help King Telmont, and in no need of rescue. It was enough to make a person turn to drink, or temperance, given your previous inclination.

Walking along between them as they led their zorcas quietly along we skirted past the voller lines. A little wind blew the serried flags. Telmont was short of vollers, and they were well guarded. Among them I noticed a courier flier, painted green, with the big yellow-gold word COURIER blazoned on her sides. She was number Jay Kay Pe 448 Ve and had been piloted by cheerful young Bonzo before Lobur and Thefi brought her away out of Ruathytu. I'd seen to it that Bonzo was all right and with that little swallowing laugh he'd said he was going to do what he wanted to do, and I'd told him that the war was not over yet. He flew Courier vollers for a time yet, did Bonzo. Any thoughts that I might once again steal that flier away vanished as I appreciated the strength of the guard details.

"Now then, Jak," said Thefi as we walked on into an open space where we would not be overheard, "I gather you want to tell us something we do not know." She shivered. "I feel it will be evil..."

"Not so, princess. Rather, good news. Splendid news."

After a few sentences in which I tried to explain the new situation, Thefi burst out furiously. "I don't believe my father or my brother would believe what the Vallians say! It can't be true! We have to fight them—"

"No, princess, we do not have to fight them. We have to fight the Shanks, and I could wish we did not have to do even that."

"I grant you we must fight the Shanks when they raid," said Lobur. "But, as for the rest of this fabrication, why, it makes me think strangely. You have always been a mysterious fellow, first hailing from Djanduin, then Hamal, and now where?" He looked at me, his brows drawn down, and his fist on his dagger handle. "Vallia, perhaps?"

I took a breath—

A party of guards marched briskly along, their spears all sloped exactly, their helmets shining, for they were of the King's Ironfists. No difficult calculation told me I could fight my way through them and probably seize a voller, chained down or not. I might even manage that with Thefi draped around my neck and shrieking blue murder that she was being abducted. Even, perhaps, with Lobur and his damned dagger to contend with.

Yes, I might have done all those things in the typical bone-headed way of your barbarian hero—but that would alienate Thefi. That seemed clear. She would struggle and scream and in the ensuing excitement some stray arrow or stux might kill her instead of me. That was a chance I would not take.

The truth of her father's position as I saw it was not the truth as she saw it.

I said, "Your father, Prince Nedfar, is now the Emperor of Hamal and in alliance with Vallia, Hyrklana, Djanduin and other forward-looking countries."

Lobur looked disgusted.

Thefi blanched.

"You have been deceived, Jak! You must have been. My father would never join hands with Vallia. Tyfar has told me. He and father would never do it."

"But they have—"

"No! Never! Treat that great devil Dray Prescot as a human being? It is unthinkable."

"But he is a human being, princess."

"I wonder!" Her head was up, her chin in the air, and her eyes held a look of haughty imperiousness—and, also, of doubt?

"You know what happened to the Hyr Notor, Jak?" Lobur hauled his zorca along to keep up, for the beast wanted to have a quiet crop at the sparse grass. "Down the Moder we met Ariane nal Amklana, of Hyrklana. She came to the Empress Thyllis for help, we saw her again, and she was with the Hyr Notor when he died."

"I did not know that."

"It was some devilish trick of Dray Prescot's that did that mischief. Now we must resist with all our willpower."

"We must resist the Shanks, the leem-lovers." I spoke firmly, and Lobur jumped, and looked mean.

"You—"

"There is no time left for me to explain it all again. Hamal and Vallia are now in alliance. Did you know, Thefi, that Prince Tyfar and the Princess Majestrix of Vallia are—"

"No!"

Her cry broke forth as an anguished wail. "No, no. That cannot be so!"

In these matters of the convoluted affairs of state and the heart there is no need to spell it all out for a princess. Thefi understood at once, and was horrified, shattered, degraded in her own eyes.

And I'd had enough.

"You misunderstood me, princess. This is no state-arranged marriage. Tyfar and the Princess Majestrix love each other dearly—although they somehow manage to skirt around the subject. It was thought you would help in this."

She put a hand on my arm and looked up into my face.

"Jak, you bring such strange news. And Tyfar... Why, he and this horrible Vallian princess have never met. How could they love each other so soon?" She shook her head, and her hair gleamed. "We must resist the Vallians. King Telmont says so—"

"Old Hot end Cold? Surely you mean Vad Garnath?"

"Maybe." She looked away, "I do not like him. But, Jak—you are strange—and Tyfar and father—it is all—"

"It is all very simple," cut in Lobur. "If we are not to lose everything, we fight the damned Vallians and their allies."

"You, Lobur, were Nedfar's aide-de-camp. Would you obey him if he told you?"

All the forthright candor fled from Lobur's eyes.

"Treachery—?"

As I say, I'd had enough.

"I must leave you to think this over. I repeat, Hamal no longer stands in enmity with Vallia. We have great enemies, greater foes even after the Shanks have been dealt with. Now I must see to my animals and eat and bathe. I shall see you when the suns have gone."

Before they had time to remonstrate, I turned away and marched off. I was fuming. But, then, how else had I expected them to react?

Fourteen

Chained Like a Leem

The eating and the bathing were accomplished easily enough on payment of a suitable sum; the nonexistent animals no doubt took care of themselves. My voller waited in her clump of trees. I spent the rest of the day moving about and discovering all I could. Telmont had a formidable little army, not over-large but of high quality, and he even had under command a number of regiments of the old Hamalian army, all of whom believed they were acting in the best interests of Hamal. It was those regiments who had allied with Vallia that were the renegades and treacherous werstings.

Try as I might, I could find no other solution to this pretty problem than simply taking Thefi to see her father and letting her see the truth for herself. As for Lobur, he might not wish to face Prince Nedfar, now the Emperor of Hamal. I would not drag the Dagger along by the scruff of the neck, but he ought to be given the chance of making up his own mind about coming with us.

That was it, then.

There were four regiments of swarthmen in whom I took an interest, for the swarth, a dinosaur-like saddle animal of great power and lumbering strength, was often regarded as a mere appendage to the cavalry arm or as the battle-winning strike force, depending on the viewpoint of the riders. These fellows in their harsh scaled armor and blazoned blue and gold looked useful. Also, Telmont had a fine corps of crossbowmen. His churgurs, the solid heavy sword and shield men looked to me to be somewhat thin on the ground. But this army would prove a tough nut to crack.

So I wandered about, spying away in the best cloak and dagger fashion, until the suns set and the first of the night's moons rose. She of the Veils shone refulgently down, all rose and gold, and I took heart. Although claiming to have no favorites among the seven moons of Kregen, I rather fancy I take to She of the Veils just a trifle more than the others...

This was not unimportant, as you shall hear.

By the time the Maiden with the Many Smiles rose over the horizon, I wanted this frustrating business with Lobur and Thefi over and done with.

They had been given a tent of some magnificence by King Telmont, and rather to my surprise I discovered that Lobur was no gilded appendage to the king's retinue, having taken command of a totrix regiment which he strove to improve and turn into the best in the army. With gold and rose moonlight dropping over the lines of tents and animals, I nodded to the sentries at the tent flap and went inside. The information that would have been startling to anyone here, that Jak the Shot was in reality Dray Prescot, had not reached the camp and Nedfar had kept that business on the quiet side. Very few were privy to that item of hot gossip. I wondered, as I watched Thefi approach in the lamplight over the carpets, whether I should tell her.

She looked pale. Her eyes were brilliant.

"Jak! I have been thinking over what you said. It is terrible, terrible—"

"Agreed, princess. Everyone is heartily sick of wars and fighting. But we must brace ourselves. We have to face the Shanks, for they will destroy us if we do not."

"I did not mean that. Everyone knows that. I mean about my brother and that awful princess of Vallia."

I just couldn't help myself. "Oh," I said. "So you've met her then."

"What? No, of course not."

"Then, princess, how do you know she is awful?"

Stupid and petty vindictivenesses like that can be quickly and firmly put down. She stared at me. "She is Vallian, isn't she?" That, of course in her eyes, was explanation enough. I, clever Dray Prescot, was quickly and firmly put down.

"Where's Lobur, princess?"

"Seeing to his regiment. And I have made my mind up. I will not—I cannot—return to Ruathytu. My father would be—would be unkind to Lobur. And I could not bear that."

I studied her. She breathed passion and fire and all the delightful and worthwhile things of dreams, and I could not ask her again to think a second time and, perhaps, to betray her lover. As always, my thoughts of Delia gave me what I hoped was a better understanding in delicate affairs. How would Delia react in these circumstances? That is a touchstone that never fails me.

"Very well—but Telmont bears your father no good will."

"Oh, Jak! Telmont is fighting for Hamal. Once we throw off the yoke of oppression—"

"Vallia does not—"

She half-turned away and her frown pained me. We still stood. She had offered no seat, no refreshments.

"We are taking a big swing down into the south and east, to gather more men. Just north of He of the Commendable Countenance, Telmont has good friends."

The river marking the southern boundary of Hamal, the River Os, divided before it reached the sea on the east coast and the two arms enclosed the independent country of Ifilion. Much of the river and deltas were called the Land of Shining Mud. You could scrape up thousands of levies there, who might fight if they were chained and stapled to the ground. There were other troops to be had. Chido's estates were in that part of Hamal. And, so Thefi said, some of the realms south of the river in the northern sections of the Dawn Lands still would fight for Hamal, since they had been in thrall for so long. I thought of our abject performances in the Peace Conference. This was one result of shilly-shallying when we should have been making decisions and implementing them.

Lobur walked in with a swing and a swagger, shouting that he could only stop for a stoup of ale—no wine for him tonight on guard duty—before he saw me. He halted, his helmet swinging by its straps from his fist, and his face congested. He wore a smartly ornate uniform, but he was a fighting man.

"Lahal, Lobur."

"You are not welcome, Jak. It pains me to say that, after all you have done for us. But—"

I interrupted and made a last attempt to persuade them to see that Telmont might protest his honest intentions but that Vad Garnath pulled the strings. "Between them, and Rosil, the Kataki Strom, they will try to destroy your father, princess. It was Rosil who shot Thyllis."

But they would not listen, and Lobur, flinging an impatient glance at the clepsydra, said he had to be off or those lazy good-for-nothings would be snoring instead of standing watch. He left, with a warning look at Thefi which I ignored. He did not say the remberees.

"Princess—"

"No, Jak. My father is held by the Vallians and we must fight them to free him. My mind is made up."

Seeing I had failed, I hitched up my sword belt—which is a useful if redundant preliminary to action—and started to walk quietly toward Thefi. I picked her up and bundled her under my arm and walked out of there.

Ha!

The only real bit of luck I had was that Vad Garnath and Strom Rosil were not in the camp—oh, and that the guards didn't knock my brains out there and then. They flung iron nets over me in the evilly efficient way Kataki slavers have, and iron nets will hold a leem. I fell to the ground, tangled up, cursing away, struggling to draw a sword and break free. The nets enfolded me. Katakis with their tails swishing bladed steel hauled me out. Nasty are Katakis, a race of diffs with habits that set them apart from the normal run of humanity. Low-browed, dark, snaggle-toothed, and with those sinuous whip tails to which they strap six inches of bladed steel, Katakis are man-managers. Thefi screamed and I cursed and rolled over, and a Kataki hit me on the head and the night of Notor Zan enfolded me in darkness.

I woke up, chained and stapled to the ground like some poor devil of a levy swept up into an army for which he had no desire whatsoever to fight.

The stars sparkled above, the Maiden with the Many Smiles performed her serene pink smile, the night breeze rustled the bushes, and I struggled and was chained like a wild beast.

Two guards stood watch over me.

One said, "You're awake, then?"

His companion said, "When the king sees you, you'll—"

The first one laughed. "You mean Vad Garnath, don't you, Thafnal? King Telmont is—" He stopped, and looked swiftly about.

"Aye, Ortyg. Best watch your mouth."

All the notorious Bells of Beng Kishi rang and collided in my skull. I licked my lips and swallowed. I could move about half an inch. The chains were thick and strong and of iron.

The fancy dandy little Hikdar trotted up, managing not to trip over his own sword. He put on a big frown, bending his brows down, and I guessed he had caught this guard duty and was not too pleased about it, no doubt having other and more pleasant occupations planned for the night. The two swods looked across as he appeared in the moons light and stood at attention—casually.

"No trouble?" squeaked the little fellow.

"No trouble, Hik."

"Good, good."

I'd given no trouble because I'd been enveloped in the black folds of Notor Zan's cloak. I strained at the chains and could not break them or budge the stakes to which they were stapled. The Hikdar jumped.

"Watch him! There are express orders from Jiktar Nairn. He is to wait judgment from the king himself."

"Very good, Hik."

With a careful flick at his sword to clear it away from his legs, he trotted off.

"Who's he?" I said, in my conversational voice. I didn't give a damn who he was; I wanted to get the conversation flowing easily.

"Hikdar Naghan ham Halahan, and you mind your mouth."

"D'you have a mouth-wet around here?"

The one called Thafnal hoicked forward a bottle. His face was scarred and dark, seamed with seasons of campaigning. "Open your black-fanged winespout, dom, and I'll pour you a draught."

I did as he bid and took in a sloshing mouthful of cheap wine. It was refreshing, tangy though it might be.

"My thanks, dom."

As the stars and moons wheeled across the sky I crouched there, chained like a wild animal, and cogitated. My thoughts were as cloudy as the sky, where dark masses erratically obscured the moons, and then blew free in wispy streamers until the following clouds cast their shadows upon the land.

Just a little of this famous cogitation convinced me that out of a hundred chances, ninety-nine would say that Lobur the Dagger had betrayed me. He was frightened that I would convince Thefi to return, and Lobur would not face her father. This saddened me. It showed how little he understood the depth of her feelings for him.

Also, the unwelcome thought occurred to me that Lobur knew more than he said—certainly not that I was who I was, for in that case my head would be rolling away over the ground—but was probably aware of the true situation in Ruathytu through his contact with Garnath. He had not told Thefi. I felt my faith in Lobur slipping away depressingly.

If I hadn't saved him from falling off a rooftop in Jikaida City—and he did not know that Drax, Gray Mask, was me—he wouldn't be alive now and a whole train of incidents that had followed would not have taken place.

In the confusing lights of the moons Hikdar Naghan ham Halahan came mincing back. He looked different, and was trying to strut along with all the pomp his position demanded, and making a strange hash of it. He'd be more dangerous to his own men in a fight, I was thinking, as he wheeled up toward the two guards, Thafnal and Ortyg, who barely took enough notice of him save to come to their sloppy attention. They were so long in the tooth as extended-service swods they could get away with murder among the forest of Hamalian regulations.

"A prowler in the zorca lines," squeaked ham Halahan, his voice higher and yet struggling to sound hoarse. "Get off there at once. I'll stand guard here. Bratch!"

That hard word of command made them move. Thafnal said: "He won't get away, Hik—"

Ham Halahan pointed, his helmet casting deep shadows over his face, his cloak wrapped about his uniform. The two swods picked up their spears and marched off, whistling. They knew to a nicety how far to go in baiting jumped-up young officers.

The Hikdar watched them go. He was trembling. They disappeared beyond the corner of the nearest tent toward the zorca lines as clouds threw down shadows.

"Jak! We must be quick!"

In a single heartbeat I stopped my stupid "Wha—?" and instead said, "I thank you, princess. The chains are of iron."

"I have the key. I stole it from Lobur. Here..."

She bent over me and I sensed her perfume. The uniform showed under the cloak, impressive, far too impressive to be that of a Hikdar, however important he thought himself, and it fitted ill. One of Lobur's, of course. The key clinked. The lock made a sound like a wersting savaged by a leem. The chains fell away. I rubbed my wrists, my ankles, but the shackles had not been tight enough to restrict circulation.

"Why?"

She would not look at me. Strands of hair wisped free of the harsh helmet brim.

"You were a good friend to us. I couldn't see you—"

"Is that all?"

Now she looked at me as I stood up, her eyes dark and pained, and I felt for her pain.

"No. Lobur—he was talking to Garnath—"

"That great devil is here?"

"They said—I overheard and I couldn't believe—and yet I still love Lobur—"

"What did they say?" I looked about, and I know my face was as savage as faces may ever become. "We must move away from here." We moved off into the shadows and I held her arm.

"Garnath and my Lobur—what you said is true, Jak. And Lobur knew all the time. He knew! My father is the emperor and they plan to destroy him and use me... Use me to..."

She trembled under my touch.

"It isn't pretty, Thefi. Will you stay with Lobur?"

"I want to... But how can I? I do not know what to do!"

She wore a sword, a straight cut and thruster used all over Havilfar. The thraxter looked to be a quality blade as I drew it from the scabbard, quickly, before she could move.

"Jak! You will not kill me?"

564

"Hold still, princess. No—run for the nearest voller if you wish to escape. I will follow."

She turned her head to look where I stared and saw the advancing forms of soldiers, weapons bared.

"Oh, Jak! They will surely kill you—"

"And you too, and still make your father dance to Garnath's tune. Now, run—run for the nearest voller. And, my girl, run fast!"

Then I swung about and switched up the sword, ready to take on the yelling guards who ran in with weapons brandished.

Fifteen

Hometruths

Thefi had saved me from almost certain death, and now in order to save her I had to face another round with almost certain death. Well, that is life on Kregen. The guards ran on yelling. One or two screeched the chilling Hamalese war cry "Hanitch! Hanitch!"—a sound that has risen in triumph over very many battlefields.

My blade slithered across the first guard's sword, turned, thrust, retrieved—all, it seemed, of its own volition. He staggered back, arms upflung, and already the dark blood spouted.

Three more came on, hard, panting, and I foined around and cut and pierced them, and danced away, risking a quick glance over one shoulder. Thefi had reached the voller lines and—by Krun, she was the daughter of her father and sister to her brother!—she pointed imperiously at me and as the guard obediently ran past to join the fray, she took off her helmet and hit him over the head with it. He collapsed in a smother of cloak and his dinted helmet fell off and as Thefi bent with a glitter of steel in her fist I swiveled back to my own fight.

There were a lot of them, and they ran in from different sides, so I back-tracked, taking them as they came. Some were what an unfeeling Kapt once called "blade-fodder," some were your ordinary seasoned fighting men more at home in the line with their regiments. Some, three or four, were superior bladesmen. These consumed time. And, of course, I was never unaware that at any disastrous moment I would front up to a man—or woman—who was a better sworder than I was.

If that happened—and it had happened and could occur at any moment—it would be highly inconvenient.

A burly fellow with a tuft of green feathers in his helmet proved clever, working in combination with his oppo, a slighter man with a wizened face. These two held me up and others were running up, hullabalooing. I just avoided a clever cut at my thigh which changed trajectory with a cunning roll of the wrist and aimed to degut me, blades chingled and rang, I riposted against the little fellow and let my body go with the turn, avoiding the big fellow's degutting stroke. They bored in again and two more started to circle around to my left side.

I yelled.

"By Krun! Behind you, rasts!"

And, with the yell, I leaped.

Cheap, melodramatic trick? Yes. But the big fellow flung a startled look back so that I could ignore him for the instant it took me to engage with wizened-face, circle his blade and punch him through, and then slice down across the throat of the big fellow as he pivoted back. I jumped clear. They fell. The other two hung back. But there were more. I ran. I hared off toward the vollers and saw Thefi at the controls of the green-painted courier voller we had liberated from Ruathytu and in which she and Lobur had traveled to Pandahem and back here.

"Here, Jak! Run!"

Without wasting any more breath I sprinted for the green flier and leaped aboard, tumbling in any old way. As it was, an arrow sprouted from the wooden coaming. I frowned as I untangled myself and then fell against Thefi as she swept the voller into the air. She could not rise at a steep angle, as we would have wished, for the vollers had been staked out in the lee of a gaggle of half-stunted trees. These were small enough, and yet large enough to be an obstacle. We went hurtling along in a wild swinging curve and then straightening to plunge up at the end of the trees.

We never made it.

I was just saying, "Well done, Thefi!"

A mustard-colored voller started up at right angles to our course, coming in from the left-hand side. It hesitated, and then plunged on and Thefi, quite unable to hold the courier flier back or drive her up in time, screamed.

We went slap bang wallop into the side of the maxi-mustard flier and I had a glimpse of Kregen cartwheeling upside down. The courier voller splintered all forrard, turning end over end, slewing away as the maxi-mustard airboat collapsed sideways.

Thefi and I fell out in a wild tangle onto the grass.

No time to feel winded or take notice of the bruising pain in my left shin or the thwack behind my left ear. Time only to snatch Thefi up, hurl her on stumbling across the muddy grass toward the next flier. She was the penultimate one in the tethered line. Thefi's hair streamed loose, her helmet, its work done, long abandoned. We fled for the voller.

The stupid pilot of the mustardy voller, who had pulled out right in front of Thefi, hung upside down from the coaming, blood streaming from his nostrils. Served the fool right.

"I'll do the chains," I bellowed. "Up with you!"

She did not argue.

The first staple came free with a single heave. The second proved more stubborn, the cunning voller attendants having burred the staple end and cross-pinned it. I ducked out from under the airboat and called up.

"Is there a crowbar, Thefi?"

I looked back. The pursuers, well outdistanced by our brief flight, would soon be up with us, howling like a pack of hunting werstings. The pilot of the voller who had caused the accident, as I now saw, was a woman, not a man. She'd been no heroine trying to halt us, but some incompetent pilot who imagined a voller took up less than half the airspace required. The crowbar appeared over the side and Thefi said, "I'm all ready to go."

"In half a leem's spring."

The crowbar snugged between chain and staple, I leaned back, forces took the strain, balanced, gave. The staple wrenched clear and the chain fell to the mud.

Thefi yelled.

"Guards!"

She did not scream; but the urgency of her tone made me turn sharply enough to crack my head on the voller's keel. I was suffering far too many of these cracks on the head just lately. Half-crouched, I stopped moving. Two boots, black and muddy, showed beneath the keelson. They were positioned in just such a way as would tell the trained eye of a sword fighter that the owner of the boots stood braced and poised, weapon lifted ready to strike down at anyone crawling out from under the flier.

I hefted the crowbar.

The bar of iron cracked against an ankle bone with a most unpleasant sound and the pair of boots hopped madly into the air. In an instant I was out from under the airboat and bringing the crowbar around again in a blow that stretched the guard senseless. His helmet fell off. Others of his comrades were running up, for Telmont had taken the sensible precaution of placing a strong guard on his vollers. The woman who had crashed into us had been attended to and sent off, and the guards must have gone back for a quiet wet until our commotion brought them running back.

Using the crowbar after the fashion of an Aleyexim's trakir, a hefty sliver of iron sharpened at both ends and hurled by the warlike Aleyexim in battle to deadly effect, I managed to knock over the first of the yelling guards. Thefi stared over the coaming, her face apprehensive and yet betraying no real concern.

"Hurry, Jak!"

Without answering—and remarkably heartened by Thefi's obvious confidence—I leaped aboard. She slammed the control levers over to the stops and we shot away.

Looking down as we passed over the last voller, I felt a pungent regret. She was not an enormous skyship, but she was an airboat of good size, of three decks and many fighting tops and walkways, and my regret really did me no credit. Gunpowder had not yet been invented on Kregen—if the Star Lords so willed it might never be invented—and that was most probably a good thing. But right there and then, the idea of toppling a keg of best gunpowder with a short fuse down onto that ship appealed to me with some force.

"Well done, Thefi. Turn a little right and dive below the tree line. I don't think they'll expect us to do that."

She flung me a puzzled glance.

"Wouldn't it be best to make for Ruathytu at once? This is a fast voller."

"If you so order, princess, that we shall do. But I have my own voller parked down there and—"

"Of course!" Her color was up, rosy in the radiance of the moons between clouds. "I see! And you will send me off to Ruathytu in this voller and lead them off on a false scent in yours, no doubt fighting them for the daring of it!"

This was not sarcasm, not irony; it was the hurt of a girl being placed in a situation she detested.

"The thought had crossed my mind—"

"Well, uncross it then, Jak! We fly together."

"Very well. I just hope Garnath or one of his bully boys misses my voller. She was only loaned to me."

Thefi laughed, her head up, her throat exposed.

"My father will buy you a dozen airboats." Then she sobered, quickly—so quickly that I knew she remembered her own troubles with Lobur, black and depressing, and her laughter sounded hateful and mocking in her own ears.

To make any of the superficial and routine comforting remarks would be redundant and clumsy. She had just discovered that Lobur the Dagger was not the man she thought he was. That order of discovery, entailing that degree of hurt, is not survived with the aid of a few kind words.

All the same...

"Your father, and Tyfar, too, may want to condemn Lobur too harshly, for they love you and have been—"

"Worried?"

"More than that, Thefi, more than that."

My voice sounded hard, even in my own head.

"And if they do—they do..."

"But at least we can see Lobur's reasons, why he did what he did. I can understand him, I think. He had no chance with you unless he performed some bold stroke, a Jikai—"

"And this is a Jikai! Betrayal!"

"When a man loves a woman concepts like that blur and lose their meaning."

She turned her eyes to look at me, over the bridge we had built between us out of our situation. She half-nodded.

"You speak as though—as though you—"

"I know."

Well, my Delia would confirm what I said. No doubt of that at all.

We flew on, and talked desultorily, and soon it was clear that Thefi's thoughts stopped her from speaking altogether. Wondering if I was doing the right thing or making matters worse, I felt I didn't want Thefi to brood too much alone with her thoughts. If this negated my previous feelings on the matter, well, that was my privilege.

"There is a woman," I said. "Whose father—well, she was a girl, then—whose father ordered my head chopped off, at once. I swore at him, I remember, most heatedly. But afterward we fell into a sort of relationship we could both endure. He wasn't such a bad old buffer, and he always wanted to get into the fighting, although his people prevented him." I was talking to myself as well, now. This was a point that rankled still. "When he was killed I had gone—well, never mind that. He was slain by a damned traitor who makes Lobur a miracle of upright rectitude by comparison— I think—and I returned too late. So you see, Thefi, it all works out in the end."

She lifted her head to stare at me, for the weight of her feelings dragged down her head so that her hair fell forward over her eyes.

"You are telling me things that pain you. I know. But, if you can, Jak, tell me. If this woman's father ordered your head cut off and you are here—the order was not carried out."

"I'm not broken from the ib, Thefi, I'm no ghost. I was saved by the best comrade a man can have."

"And the woman?"

"You'll meet her. You'll get on, the pair of you."

"Oh, yes? We'll see."

Below us the land fled past and careful scrutiny of the sky rearward showed no betraying flickers of motion beneath the stars. The moons shone no reflections from pursuing vollers.

Thefi said, "We keep abreast of all the foreign news, in Hamal, all the scandals and gossip." Then, right out of the blue, she said, "We heard the story that the old Emperor of Vallia ordered that awful Dray Prescot's head cut off, and he escaped and forced the Princess Majestrix to marry him. It was a great scandal. That was before Thyllis dragged him around Ruathytu tied to the tail of a calsany, of course. A pity he escaped, for then we would not be in such terrible trouble now. Your story, Jak, reminds me of that scandal." She arched her brows. "Perhaps you just made that up to make me feel less—"

"No. Did you see Thyllis's coronation?"

"No. But I heard about how Dray Prescot was dragged past. He was all dirt and hairs, anyway."

"Yes."

The Maiden with the Many Smiles shone forth and iced the voller in pink. The wind of our passage blew past. I pulled my lip, ruminating, staring at Thefi. Well, by Zair! And why not now?

I said, "I did not make up the story, Thefi. I think of you as a friend, and you know Tyfar and I are comrades."

"I know. We owe you so much—"

"No, no—or, perhaps, more than you think."

Now that was a damned stupid thing to say...!

"Look, Thefi. We'll work something out with Lobur. I do know about these affairs. I bear him no ill will. Do you believe that?"

She did not reply at once. Then, "Yes, I believe you."

"Good. Then I can tell you that when Thyllis dragged me around Ruathytu tied to the tail of a calsany it was damned uncomfortable. And my daughter Lela, the Princess Majestrix, is deeply in love with Tyfar, as he with her, and it's our job to do all we can to make them—"

She put a hand to her mouth. She let go of the controls. Her face looked like a lily, pale and glimmering above a tomb.

"You—you are joking, Jak? Jak?"

"No joke, princess, except a joke on my fate. And not Jak, although I have grown used to the name. I am Dray Prescot—the awful, horrible, great devil, in person."

She did not faint.

She might well have, seeing that she had been stuffed full of the most terrible stories of the hateful Emperor of Vallia. She swayed. I did not move. Her eyes regarded me over her hand which spread and dug so that her fingers and thumb bit deeply into the sides of her mouth.

So, with intent and not particularly caring for the way I had to say it, I said: "Now you will understand that when I say Hamal and Vallia are friends, and comrades in arms against the Shanks and our other enemies, you will see I speak the truth."

She took her hand away. She breathed in. "I see you believe it."

"I believe it because it is true." Then I brisked it all up and spoke smartly. "Now go and rest in the cabin. I will call you when Ruathytu is in sight."

She did as she was bid.

If I say that as I stood at the controls I did not stand with my back square onto the door of the aft cabin, but rather a little to one side, you may feel contempt. I share that contempt; but, also, I am an old paktun and I would prefer to stay alive rather than be killed through an oversight. Thefi, like most princesses who survived on Kregen, would be quick with a dagger.

She did sleep. A quiet look into the aft cabin proved reassuring, for she lay on the bunk bed, sprawled out and breathing slowly and evenly and not scrunched up into a fetal ball, hard and agonized. Some provisions had been stowed in the flier and a search brought to light smoked vosk rashers and loloo's eggs, with a plentiful supply of the ubiquitous palines. So we could eat when Thefi awoke. She joined me and as we ate she said little, eating enough again to reassure me. She combed her hair and washed her face and dealt with the necessities of life in a way that, princess-like though it might be, revealed she was also a girl in a situation that ought to frighten her into screaming hysteria.

She said, "Why am I not frightened, majister, emperor, Dray Prescot, great devil?"

"Call me Jak."

"Oh?"

"A lot of people do until they are easier in their minds. As to being frightened of me, if you were I would feel insulted."

"I would have killed you and joyed in the doing of it—"

"That's a lot of the trouble, Thefi. Lies make us do things we would not ordinarily dream even of contemplating."

She was not yet over the shock of this, to her, astounding revelation. After all, she was not accustomed to emperors who went off adventuring around the world and whose tastes did not run to gold and flunkies and having people's heads off.

When Ruathytu came into sight she sighed.

"After I have seen Father and Tyfar I am going to wallow through every single one of the rooms in the Baths of the Nine!"

"Every single one?"

She lowered her eyelids. "Well, not in the zanvew."*

Patrols of vollers and saddle flyers whirled up to inspect us and we waved and were escorted down. I recognized some of the flutswods astride their fluttrells, and no doubt my battleship-face was familiar to them also. We touched down on the high landing platform of the Hammabi el Lamma and Thefi was instantly swept away in a bustle of women as Prince Nedfar and Tyfar advanced, beaming, welcoming, all smiles.

"And Lobur?" they asked after the Lahals.

I told them.

"There is no sense in pursuing this matter further at the moment." Nedfar

---

* *Zan:* ten. *Vew:* room.

looked every inch the emperor he was. "What you say of Telmont's sweep into the southeast concerns us more."

We walked through into private chambers where refreshments were served. Tyfar and his father were concerned about Telmont and his army, yet they ached to hare off—leaving me—to see Thefi. They thanked me, not effusively, but with a quiet sincerity that warmed, as I said, "It was Thefi who saved me."

Jaezila looked ravishing. I refused to worry over the future relationship between her and Thefi. I saw the way she and Tyfar looked at each other, the way they avoided entering too closely into the body-space of the other, the comical and yet frustrating way they circled each other like fighting men seeking an opening. I hoped Thefi, seeing the truth, would help. She might be the catalyst that would precipitate the actions everyone who knew them longed for and despaired of contriving.

Sixteen

Affray at the Baths of the Nine

Seg said, "Well, my old dom, I'm for the Baths of the Nine. You coming?"

The Peace Conference had died the death. Most of the delegations from the Dawn Lands had gone home to carry on their intrigues and wars among themselves. Ortyg and Kytun had returned to Djanduin, and Jaidur and Lildra to Hyrklana. The city prepared for Nedfar's coronation as emperor and we fighting men readied a fresh army to lead against Telmont. There was time to indulge a few burs in the Baths of the Nine.

"You're on, Seg."

"Which establishment? I have taken to patronizing The Sensil Paradise. It is perhaps a little larger than I'd prefer, but the exercise floor is splendid."

"Well, I suppose you can't have it both ways."

There were many establishments in Ruathytu called The Paradise, qualified by gushing descriptives, and the Sensil was, indeed, a fine place, not too far from the Old Walls in the Sacred Quarter. We could take a couple of flyers from the palace and be there in no time at all.

Tyfar breezed into the small room where we spent a deal of time arguing over the maps and eating and drinking and generally trying to keep out of the way. Instantly he declared himself ready to join us in the Sensil.

"After all, when your father is an emperor, there are a devil of a lot of time-consuming nothings to do."

"Yes, Tyfar, and when you're emperor there are a damn sight more, by Krun."

He gave me a hard stare, and I said as though a part of the foregoing: "Not that you'll be emperor—at least of Hamal—for very many seasons yet."

Seg laughed and changed the subject. Successions are tricky problems, as I knew. Drak would return from Vallia for Nedfar's coronation, and I wanted him to take over being Emperor of Vallia so that I could have a free hand. I did not think Nedfar would early relinquish his throne and crown to Tyfar.

In the end Nedfar joined us with a gaggle of people from his suite, including Kov Thrangulf. That plain man was most subdued. After Thefi had eloped with Lobur, Thrangulf had shriveled into himself. Nedfar's plans for Thrangulf and Thefi to wed, thrown into disarray, might now never be realized. Yet I, along with one or two others—not, sadly, including Tyfar—saw far more in Kov Thrangulf than met the eye.

So quite a crowd of us flew off to The Sensil Paradise.

Taking the Baths of the Nine is more than merely having a good wash. It is a social occasion. The place was thronged with people. No one wore any clothes, of course. When you take a bath you do not customarily wear clothes, although the folk of Wihtess solemnly wear what they call sponge-garments when they take a bath, for they have some funny ideas about the naked human body. The halls were lofty with radiance, wide with marble floors, heated and kind. The folk filled the various chambers and rooms with chatter and vivaciousness, their skins and furs and scales of striking variety. Among the apims with rosy skins, and brown and black and golden-yellow skins, the blue and green teguments of Hem-vilar and Olinmurs added a pleasing color contrast. Very few people paid much attention to color or texture of the body-covering of the folk with whom they bathed or swam or played games.

As we walked through into the heated air and the laughter and horse-play, Seg, very quietly, said to me, "These Hamalese have got over the war very quickly."

"Aye. I'm pleased."

He caught a ball hurled by one of a group of girls whose strengths over-mastered her skill, and threw it back.

"They caused enough suffering, and, by the Veiled Froyvil, look at 'em! You'd think they won!"

This comment did not discompose me, for I was well aware Seg shared my views—in fact he had had a part in shaping mine—on our coming confrontation with the Shanks and he was merely feeling the disgruntlement of the fighting man. Seg, like myself, was no bloodthirsty warmonger. It was just that his honest sense of wages due for sins committed was outraged by the sight of Hamalese enjoying themselves, like this, now, when perhaps a more studious demeanor would be more appropriate. Then the ball flew through the air toward us again, and we realized that these jolly girls were not unskillful—far from it—but wished us to join in their game.

So we did.

The scented and heated air resounded to the shouts and laughter bouncing off the high walls and roof, and the splashes of divers and swimmers, the click and clack of gamesters in their corners. Everyone worked up a splendid sweat to be washed sweetly off in the pools.

Tall bronze doors with engraved scenes of flower gardens in their panels separated by borders of intertwined flowers gave access to the next chamber. We heard before we saw. The yells of laughter and enjoyment changed to yells of fear and screams of panic. We looked. The high doors opened. Armed and armored men pushed through, slashing with swords to clear a path. Ahead of them, speedily glimpsed through the panicking horde of naked bodies, ran a youth brandishing a sword. He saw us, he saw Nedfar and Tyfar, and he pointed the sword.

He wore a bronze mask, and his helmet bore a tuft of feathers, brown and silver.

The men following him wore over their armor short blue capes adorned with badges. I recognized the badge, for the schturval showed in outline a picture of a sword piercing a heart. This schturval was the badge of the adherents of Spikatur Hunting Sword.

How, I wondered, with a sinking feeling of despair and a scalding feeling of anger, did that fit in with the ominous brown and silver feathers?

Everywhere naked men and women, boys and girls, were screaming and running, stumbling and falling. Like a stone dropped into a pool, the group of hard dark armored men created retreating ripples around them. The youth at their head ran eagerly on, fleeting over the marble toward Nedfar and Tyfar...

"You must get away, Father!" yelled Tyfar. He grabbed the emperor's arm and started to drag him to the side. I knew well enough that Tyfar, himself, would not run. Nedfar struggled.

"I will not deign to flee from miserable assassins..."

"We are naked and unarmed!"

Seg ignored the emperor and his son. He glanced at me, and I nodded, and so we moved a little ahead. How damned strange it was to be in this situation, one of the classic idiots'—only delights detested and dreaded by Kregans! On Kregen you never go anywhere—if you are a fighting sort of person—without your sword, or bow, spear or axe. But, taking the Baths of the Nine, you expect the proprietors of the establishment to provide guards who check everyone entering for weapons. An assassin must have problems concealing a deadly weapon on his naked body. No doubt the hired guards of The Sensil Paradise were sprawled in their own blood, puddled on the floor of their guardroom.

"Now if Turko were here," said Seg casually, flexing his muscles.

"He is a great Khamorro who can kill an armed warrior with his bare hands. He has taught you a few tricks, Seg, I know. But you'd better let me take the first fellow and his weapon."

The running youth was almost on us now, isolated as we were on the marble floor, the roof high above us, the suns light streaming mingled jade and ruby all about us. Tyfar joined us.

"Ty!" I said very quickly. I usually never called him Ty. "Let me."

"Nedfar is my father—"

The youth with his armor and sword and brown and silver feathers that were the colors of the evil cult of Lem the Silver Leem halted and stared at us. His mask glittered.

"Stand aside, unless you wish to die. The emperor is doomed for destruction."

Tyfar started to shout, "No, cramph. It is you—!"

I leaped.

The young fellow was not expecting a naked and unarmed man to leap on him, clad in armor as he was and wielding a sword... He'd probably never been slave, and when you are slave you become accustomed to nakedness. Mind you, as I took his throat in my grip, I reflected that a bight of slave's chains might have come in handy to throttle him with. I choked him and took his sword away and threw it back. I wondered who would grab it first, Tyfar or Seg.

A single punch laid the young lad low. He was a boy and not a girl; his armor shape would not have accommodated a real girl, only, as Zolta might have said, "Those poor creatures who have not been blessed with the bounty of Zim." As I straightened up, Seg's fruity bellow reached me.

"Stux!"

I dropped lower and the flung spear whistled past above my head. No time to grab it—but as I glared with a malevolent fury toward the assassins the next stux hurtled in. I leaned to the side, took the stux from the air, reversed it, poised ready to hurl it back. Then I changed that plan, satisfying though it was, and tossed the throwing weapon back. With its small cross-quillons beneath the head the pig-sticker would make a handy weapon for a man who otherwise must rely on bare hands.

Seg had grabbed the sword, so Tyfar took the stux.

We did not wait for the other assassins to close in. We went hurtling down into them. And Tyfar screeched, "Hanitch! Hanitch!" I pushed any thoughts of displeasure out of my mind, dodged the sweep of a sword, kicked the fellow in the guts with a tingle all the way from toes to pelvis, grabbed another man's arm, pulled him, stuck two fingers up his nostrils, threw him away, seized the chap at his side who tried to stick me with his rapier. The rapier changed hands. It is a trick.

He staggered back, his hands clasped to his face, and the blood was shared between the rapier blade and his eye.

"Spikatur!" The yells of anger lifted as the rest charged on. "Spikatur Hunting Sword!"

More naked men crowded up to range alongside us and a flung stux punched through the chest of a young Nath Hindolf. He coughed and clutched the ugly shaft transfixing him, and staggered back. I felt the anger.

"Keep out of the way until we have weapons!" I yelled. I felt mad clear through. What a waste!

Kov Thrangulf, his belly thinned over the past months, muscled up, breathing in a snorting rasp.

"I'll take a weapon, aye, and break it over their heads, by Krun!"

I had to flick a spear away with the rapier and then we were at hand strokes with the rest of the assassins of Spikatur.

It was a right old ding-dong, to use a soldier's descriptive.

Seg's sword flashed and glittered, and then fouled with blood. Tyfar might not have been wielding an axe, but his stux went in and out like a trip-hammer, and each time he did not miss his target. Thrangulf snatched up a sword from the limp hand of a dead man and waded in, shouting blood-curdling promises. And, as he did so, so Princess Thefi and a gaggle of naked girls ran yelling from the side room pursued by more armed and armored stikitches. Although, to be fair, we did not call the assassins of Spikatur Hunting Sword stikitches in the same way we dubbed the professional assassins of Kregen as stikitches. The girls ran and we naked men tried to stay close around and so afford some protection.

Jaezila appeared, and she wielded a sword and so I knew she'd dealt with at least one of these ugly customers. As she plunged into the fight at our side, Tyfar went berserk.

"Ty!" shouted Jaezila. She plunged after Tyfar as he tore through the assassins before him.

Just how anyone might expect unarmed and naked men to hold armed and armored stikitches, let alone defeat them, passed understanding. All I had hoped to do was create enough time to enable our friends to escape. And, now, here they were, all yelling and hurling themselves into the fray!

Well, we fought. Some of us were killed. Just how many opponents we had, just how many adherents of Spikatur had broken in, we did not know. We fought them. It was not pretty. Although, in the aftermath, it must have been amusing, not to say ludicrous. As you may imagine.

Tyfar and Jaezila appeared as flashing limbs and flashing blades. Desperate with fear for my daughter, I went headlong into the bunch fronting her and Tyfar, and we sliced and lopped and hacked, occasionally as the opportunity offered time, thrusting.

This was all a desperate chancy business and entirely hateful to me. Jaezila and Tyfar, risking their necks like wild young bloods in a savage challenge of dare and counter-dare! Seg stood with me and we sliced and slashed and took cuts and felt the sting and the blood, and still we battled on.

The people who had fled screaming from the exercise hall flooded back, shrieking and moaning, tearing their hair. We heard their frenzied yells.

"The doors are locked! We cannot get out! We cannot escape!"

The interruption drew a small space about Seg and me, and in the instant I leaped for the glistening form of Jaezila—glistening with the blood of others—Seg bellowed: "The rasts have worked this sweetly, Erthyr rot 'em!"

"Aye! We have to finish this."

Jaezila insisted on plunging on. Tyfar flung a quick look at me as I hauled on his arm, risking an instinctive blow.

"No, Jak, no! If Jaezila goes on—so do I!"

My rapier flicked up and swept a stux away. I bellowed.

"You young idiot! Get Jaezila to have sense!"

"She is too much like her father!"

By the Black Chunkrah! I pushed Tyfar aside and ran on, and the two black-clad men who tried to cut Jaezila down stared in shocked surprise first at the floor and then at the ceiling as they collapsed. I'd used the hilt, one-two and bang. Now I raced to stand before Jaezila.

Before I could speak, she said, most crossly, "Get out of the way, Father, do!"

"If you get yourself killed—"

We paused in our family conversation then as assassins strove to break past and get at Nedfar. Seg and Tyfar ran up. Tyfar had salvaged an axe. Now his true stature as a fighting man revealed itself in the short economical strokes of the axe, the way he parried and swept on, the trick he had of whirling and then, in a seeming check, sweeping on to slice a neck or a thigh. He was good, was Tyfar, very good with an axe.

The fight swirled about the great hall, and blood swirled in mocking echo in the water of the bathing pool.

Through the armor-clad ranks fronting us, and who would in the end overwhelm us with weight, I glimpsed a thin, a painfully thin, man whose eye socket glittered with gems. He was urging his men on, although not himself running to the fore.

"Gochert!"

"So that's the fellow," said Seg. "I'll mark him."

His sword blurred and drove into the eye socket of the bulky man whose massive armor failed to save him from Seg's precise thrust. As he fell Seg stepped away and got his blade into a most painful spot through the next man's armor. But blood showed streaked across Seg's arms and chest, and the blood was his own. That blood was precious to me.

The brown and yellow feathers bristled around a Rapa's beak as he hurled his stux at Seg. I leaped, took the spear from midair with my left hand. I reversed it and hurled it back—but not at the Rapa. He squeaked and ducked away. The stux flew for Gochert. It missed. No time to curse. Time only to cross blades with the next assassin and try to stay alive.

"We're done for, my old dom," Seg panted. "But we've had a good—" Here he parried, riposted, withdrew and the fellow who had tried to stick him—a hairy Brokelsh—dropped with only one good eye, "—time. I've no regrets. Not even Thelda, now."

"We're not done for yet, Seg!" I spoke sharply. Seg, from Erthyrdrin, possessed a fey capacity to seek the future only to fill himself with information no one needs. His wild and yet practical nature was in violent contrast. "We have to hold the rasts. Just hold 'em!"

"Oh, aye. We'll do that."

Then we were pressed back in a confused tangle of blades. Only a few arrows arched, and in that press the assassins would as likely slay their own. Not, from what we knew of Spikatur, that that would deter them. The most obvious explanation for the lack of bows and shafts was the simple difficulty of smuggling them in. As we fought and were forced back and saw good men go down I reflected that I'd smuggled a Lohvian longbow and shafts into places more difficult than The Sensil Paradise. My opinion of the adherents of Spikatur Hunting Sword, which had vacillated up and down, now fell even more. They were going against what I felt to be the best interests of all the people now, and they couldn't even do this job properly.

Tyfar and Jaezila, with Thrangulf and young Hando and the others, pressed back around Nedfar. He was most annoyed. We could all see that even with these assassins' lack of skill, we could not last forever.

The next fellow to tangle with me—he was a Moltingur whose horny shoulder carapace needed to be only lightly armored, and whose faceted eyes and tunnel mouth with its rows of needlelike teeth bore down to devour me—suddenly lifted himself up, tall. His eyes crossed. He looked suddenly perplexed. As he fell I saw the dint in the metal of his helmet flap over his temple. In all that uproar of clanging blades and screams and shouts and the stamp of feet, I heard the rattle of the leaden bullet across the marble.

The man before Tyfar took an arrow through his neck, above the corselet rim.

Then a shower of arrows arched and we saw the rows of men along the balconies shooting down, and slinging bullets. But I knew who had slung and loosed first. Barkindrar the Bullet and Nath the Shaft, for sure.

Jaezila's personal retainer, Kaldu, simply leaped from the balcony rail full into the armored ranks of the assassins of Spikatur.

"Kaldu!"

"Into them!" I bellowed and we all rushed forward, screeching like rampant devils. Which we were.

After that, all the people of Spikatur Hunting Sword wished to do was escape. We chased them to the doors, which now lay unlocked. We did not catch Gochert. He, no doubt, the moment he had seen the plan go wrong, had been the one to unlock the doors and the first to flee.

Panting, blood-splashed, elated, we stood on the steps brandishing our swords, and the good folk of Ruathytu gaped up at this crowd of madmen who paraded naked in the open before the steps of The Sensil Paradise. The air kissed our heated skins. The fellows couldn't stop talking. All I was thankful for was that Jaezila and Seg and Tyfar were safe.

Needlemen were summoned to tend the wounded, and then we went back to wash off all the muck and blood. At least, we were already in the perfect place to do that.

Seventeen

Delia Commands the Dance

Deb-Lu-Quienyin hurried into the little room we habitually used and, pushing his turban straight, said, "I have to inform you that the empress is coming."

I saw that he teased me, and that he shared my joy. Nedfar had no empress—or empress-to-be—since his wife had died he had not, as he put it, had the heart to marry again. So, since empresses do not flock in great numbers, even on Kregen, I could let a great fatuous smile spread all across my ugly old beakhead.

"Delia!"

"Aye, Jak, the Empress Delia, may all the gods and spirits have her in their keeping."

"When?"

He spread his hands. The mystical powers of Wizards of Loh were very great, very great indeed, and yet I fancy there are gaps and inconsistencies in what they can and cannot do in these fringes of the occult. "She speeds toward Ruathytu. There is wind and freshness and a tumult of sea far below."

"Well, I just hope she's all right—"

"Jak! Majister! I should rebuke you for a Lack of Trust." When Deb-Lu spoke in Capital Letters in these latter days he often did so out of amusement and self-mockery. He was now, in my estimation, just about the most powerful Wizard of Loh there was, certainly in Hamal and most probably in all Havilfar and Vallia combined.

When Seg heard the news he fired up and we started making plans for enjoying ourselves in the short interval between Nedfar's coronation and our departure to deal with King Telmont.

The strong parties of guards who had, perforce, to go everywhere with the notables irked us; but slackness on our part and a relaxation of watchfulness had resulted in the ugly affray at The Sensil Paradise. We could not afford to have Nedfar killed, in a cold political way, and in the warm concerns of friendship.

Coronations, tiresome though they are in reality, are generally regarded as occasions of the utmost importance.

If I say that Nedfar's coronation as Emperor of Hamal proved a splendid affair, filled with pomp and circumstance, impressive and magnificent with its civilized fashions superimposed on but not obliterating the savage Kregan customs underlying all ritual I should have to qualify that judgment. And, too, if I say that in all these grand ceremonies I remember mainly the presence of Delia and the holiday we spent together between the coronation and the battles, I think you will not misunderstand me. My Delia! She grew more beautiful, more lovely, more damned mischievous, every season, so it seemed to me. Her work for the Sisters of the Rose, that mysterious organization of women devoted to good works, the alleviation of suffering, the sword and the whip, kept her apart from me for long periods. Just as, to my sadness, the Star Lords threw me off about Kregen to labor for them. So Delia and I snatched what happiness we could when we could.

Drak came with his mother, leaving affairs in Vallia in capable hands, and we stood for Nedfar at his coronation, and were warmed by the plaudits of the multitude.

"At least the people seem to like their new emperor," said Drak, as we relaxed after the second day of the ceremonies.

"So they should," said Seg. "For a Hamalese he is a fine man, a fine man." He cocked his shrewd blue eye at me. "And I'll admit, just maybe, we may have misjudged the Hamalese in the past." Then he laughed, his reckless mocking laugh. "Crossbows and all!"

"You are incorrigible," said Delia, and we who knew her smiled at the way she thus mocked what the conventionally minded would take as a daring and clever remark. Subtle, is Delia, Empress of Vallia—as I know, by Zair!

During all the junketing we had to discuss the forthcoming campaign against Vad Garnath and King Telmont, and the processions and parades gave us an opportunity to take a look at the forces we might be able to muster. Many of the men had gone home, of course, as that is a sensible course of action when you lose a war. The old regiments were in disarray, many disappeared, many shrunken, many broken up. The Air Service was a parody of its once powerful force. I spent time with Nedfar telling him how we had liberated Vallia.

"And so it is true, Jak, that you employed no mercenaries? We heard the stories at the time, when our armies, commanded by the Hyr Notor, invaded and sought to subdue you, and we could scarcely credit them."

"Don't harp on all that, Nedfar. I know you set your face against Thyllis's crazy ambitions and had no part in the invasion of Vallia. You displease me by referring to what we want forgotten, and the blame you seek to take on yourself."

He smiled.

"We first met when I was a prince and you a slave, I think? And now— well, times change, times change. And the stories about Vallia throwing out the mercenaries are true."

"Yes. But you don't have the same luxury. You will have to employ what forces we of Vallia and Hyrklana have, what Djanduin can bring, and minimize their importance. For Hamal to rise again as a great power of integrity in the world it seems to me you have to do what we in Vallia did. You have to sort out your affairs yourself." I stared at him, willing him to understand. "I could have brought a great army of my Djangs to Vallia, and taken the rebels and misguided ensorcelled wights to pieces. But then, what would Vallians have said?"

"They would not have been overjoyed—"

"No. The same here. You must show the world that it was a Hamalian army that fought and beat the damned rebels of Vad Garnath and his puppet, Telmont."

"I see that. But the Hamalese army—"

"It can and will be done, Nedfar. There will be Vallian support, discreetly as may be, but there. Just in case."

"Now," I said, and I own my voice took a brisker, harsher note I detested, "I must talk about a matter far more important than battles and armies and wars."

"Oh?"

"Aye! Your son Tyfar and my daughter Jaezila—that is, Lela. Cannot you make them see sense?"

He relaxed, reaching out for the wine which stood upon a table whose legs were formed after the fashion of zhantils. A tall blue drape curtained each segment of the windows, the samphron oil lamps were lit, the study was snug and secure; Nedfar liked some of the things I could take pleasure in.

"Sense? I see what everyone sees. But Tyfar is—well, he is a son to a father. I see your fine son Drak—does he bow and scrape when you whistle?"

"Too damned right he does not!"

"So how can I—"

A knock on the door—discreet but unmistakably the knock of the sentry's spear—heralded Delia. She looked radiant, dressed in sheerest white, her brown hair highlighted by its own gorgeous auburn tints, devoid of jewelry. She wore those two small brooches, one beside the other, and a narrow jeweled belt from which swung a long Vallian dagger. Her smiles filled the room with more sunshine mustered by Zim and Genodras together.

Nedfar rose at once.

"Lahal, majestrix."

"Lahal, majister—although, to be sure, you are halfway between prince and majister this night, I suppose."

"True. And I would not be a half-emperor this night if Jak here had not—"

Delia looked at me and then at Nedfar. I knew what she was thinking.

"Nedfar," I said. "My name is Dray."

He nodded, a slow thoughtful nod. "Yes. But I am told that few people are allowed the intimacy of calling you Dray, at least, to your face."

"That is true. Although, for some reason, it is not that they are not allowed as, that—well—they—"

"They shrivel with their effrontery when they look at you, dear heart!" And Delia curled up, laughing.

Honestly, I really wished Nedfar were not there; and then, to compound the mischief, other people joined us. The conversation centered on what to do about this silly situation of lack of communication between Tyfar and Jaezila. I tended to call Lela Jaezila all the time now, except in formal use. Seg and Drak had their heads together, drinking and arguing, and I knew they'd come up with nothing. Thefi was there, flushed and pretty, and soon the crowd moved to the adjoining chamber, which was larger and had comfortable seats and tables loaded with bottles. More people came in. This is the Kregan way, of course. Kregen is a world of joiners, it seems. The noise rose, and, wherever you listened, everyone was arguing away about the best methods of lifting the shades from the eyes of Tyfar and Jaezila and of organizing them and, in general, of seeing to it that their love had a happy ending.

The noise, although loud, formed itself around those two names, so often repeated—Jaezila and Tyfar.

The door opened and Prince Tyfar of Hamal and the Princess Majestrix of Vallia entered.

Silence.

Like fish frozen for centuries in the ice of the polar seas, the good folk who only heartbeats ago had been happily chattering away remained still and silent. The experience was edifying. And yet there was good-heartedness in it, and all the more reason for the flush of guilt to strike the people dumb, for every person there wished only well for these star-crossed lovers.

Delia said to me, "Dray! You will dance?"

As a question it would have brought a regiment of the toughest swods on Kregen to instant obedience.

"I will dance, Delia."

So, solemnly, to the strains of a discreet orchestra—a little band, really, of only twenty instruments—we danced and very quickly—thankfully quickly, by Zair!—the room filled with dancers. Tyfar and Jaezila danced. And I wondered if they had any real inkling of that silence when they entered, the silence that Delia's imperious command had filled with the music for the dance.

Anybody might have called for the dance to cover that blank moment of general embarrassment. Oh, yes. But few, damn few if any, by Vox, could have done it with the charm and skill and downright cunning of my Delia!

These social occasions gave us the opportunity to talk and assess the fighting men and women who would battle for the future of Hamal. And, as I saw it, for Paz, our half of Kregen.

Many of the men who would march out with us you have met in my narrative, and many more who have not been introduced, men I had come to know and respect and assess. Nath Karidge, who commanded Delia's personal bodyguard, the Empress's Devoted Life Guard, the EDLG, was now up-ranked to a zan-Chuktar, a rank of great height. He was a fine Beau-Sabreur, your light cavalryman, from his boots to his plume. Being a zorca man, he did not favor spurs. Deep in conversation with Mileon Ristemer, he became aware of the shadow at his shoulder, and looked up and saw me. Instantly his raffish smile broke out, to-be followed by that drawing of himself up to attention.

"Easy, Nath. Your regiment is a credit to you. But I wanted to talk to Mileon here."

"Of course, majister. I will—"

"You will stay and give us the benefit of your advice."

He smiled and looked pleased. In the perfumed air of the chamber where the dancers gyrated and the orchestra scraped and blew away in melodious style, where feathers and fans fluttered and the naked arms of ladies wrapped about their partners' necks or waists as the lines of dancers closed and parted, more than one knot of grim fighting men spoke of the prospects of the morrow.

"Your plan to use the thomplods, Mileon. I have some experience with turiloths who are monstrous great beasts and can knock down a gate as quick as you like."

Mileon Ristemer nodded, absorbed at once. He was a paktun, son to old Nomile Ristemer, a banker of Vondium, who had come home to fight for his country. A stout, chunky man, he wore the silver mortilhead at his throat and was now a Jiktar commanding the newly formed fourth regiment of the Emperor's Yellow Jackets, the 4EYJ. He was due for promotion to ob-Chuktar any day now, continuing in command of the regiment. He had ideas, had Mileon Ristemer, on using gigantic beasts crowned with howdahs stuffed with fighting men to act as a species of land-born battleship in the midst of the fray.

"Turiloths?" he said. "The boloth of Turismond. Yes."

"We were besieged in Zandikar and we shot the damned turiloths with varters as they came in."

"Oh, yes, majister, I grant you that. But my thomplods will be in the battle line. It will be difficult to wheel up handy varters or catapults to shoot them there."

"Well, you will have your chance. You have arranged it all with Unmok the Nets?"

Now he laughed and Nath bellowed his enjoyment.

"Aye, majister. He is a little Och I have great respect for. He was talking about going into the wine-making business, but he agreed to contact his sources and supply thomplods. They are not easy to find, being unwieldy brutes at the best of times."

"So why not use boloths, or dermiflons, or—well, Kregen is stuffed with wonderful animals." Here I paused and frowned.

"And the idea of using them in men's battles does not please me."

It was left to Nath Karidge to say, "Agreed, majister. But if we ride zorcas into battle—and there is no animal on all of Kregen to equal a zorca—then anything else must follow."

This argument was fallacious, but it was convincing, for all that. We didn't like it; we liked less the thought of what might happen—what would happen—if we failed to use all our efforts to secure ourselves against our foes.

So, in the ending of that small conversation, one of many of a like nature, it was agreed the thomplods with their armored howdahs, their saxnikcals, or, sometimes, calsaxes, should be started off early toward the southeast. 4EYJ would go along. I forbore to inquire from Mileon, who was filled with enthusiasm, just what the swods of his Guard regiment had to say about acting as nursemaids to a bunch of plodding haystacks. The advantage gained by using thomplods was that they could upset many breeds of saddle animal. Once the thomplods got near enough to the enemy cavalry we trusted they would run off, banished from the battle.

"I have had many barrels of the mixture made up, majister. Our thomplods will have no smell to disturb our cavalry on the march."

Nath said, "And don't forget the water to wash off the mixture, Mileon, just before we start. And—" here he looked fierce "—and if your monsters panic our own cavalry I'll not answer for your fate."

"Well, your zorca regiment will be safe."

"So will Telmont's zorca cavalry."

"So that means," I said, "you have a fine target, Nath."

Because this was Kregen, where customs differ country by country and race by race, it was perfectly proper and natural for the dancing to stop and the singing to begin, which is a civilized occurrence in general favor.

We sang the old songs, and new ones composed in honor of Nedfar and also, I was pleased to note, the alliances that were so new and were to be tested in battle. In the days of Thyllis the Hamalese had tended to the mournful kind of song, at least to the ears of a Vallian. Now we sang songs of greater cheer, and old favorites like "When the Havilthytus Runs Red" were not to be heard. Which was a Good Thing. We sang "When the Fluttrell Flirts His Wing" and "Nine Times She Chose a Ring." We did not, I may say, in this company sing "Sogandar the Upright and the Sylvie" or "The Maid with the Single Veil."

We Vallians gave them "The Swifter with the Kink," which was perhaps not as politic as might have been desired, since Hamal had no seagoing navy to talk of, and Vallia's galleons were the finest—barring those of the Shanks—afloat, so that we could afford to sing a song poking fun at a swifter, a fast, not very seaworthy Kregan galleass. The evening had grown into an Occasion. We all faced daunting perils in the future and so seized the fleeting opportunity to enjoy ourselves while we could. Delia leaned across to me as we stood by a linen-covered table where the bottles shone and goblets and glasses were filled and refilled. When Delia wishes to show a little style in our self-mocking way, she uses a fan. Now she flicked the fan open to conceal the lower half of her face. Her eyes sparked up explosions in me. Those brown eyes in which I can drown forever... I put down my glass.

Chamberlains appeared and I gave them a look, saying, "We are leaving. No fuss, for the sake of Havil the Green." They retired, bowing, understanding, perhaps; perhaps understanding only that the ways of the high ones of Vallia were vastly different from those they were used to in Hamal.

So Delia and I left the shindig and I had no feelings of being an old fogey traipsing off to bed before the fun had finished. We had battles and campaigns to fight and then would be the time to sing and dance, hoping we would live through the conflicts. Someone started singing "She Kissed the Mortilhead," which tells of a princess who ran away from her palace for love of a paktun. Delia smiled as we left. "That, I think," she said, "will be Seg."

This evening the guard detail on the suite of apartments given over to our use in the Hammabi el Lamma, the Alshyss Tower, was from 1ESW. They had flown in with Drak. Of the juruk I knew every jurukker, every guardsman in the Guard was a comrade. We were jocular, jurukkers and Delia and I. I went in and closed the door. I shut the door and bolted it. Swords in hand, Delia and I went around the rooms. We were on Kregen and in a magnificent palace, and so this was a sensible precaution.

Then we could shut out the whole damned world altogether.

Eighteen

Mutiny

Mud.

The Land of Shining Mud was—muddy.

Seg picked off splotches of dried mud from his uniform and made a face.

"He's heading for the higher ground away to the west. I've kept the scouts after him. But he still outnumbers us, and—"

"Our fellows will be here in time, Seg."

"Oh, aye." Seg looked around the camp, which appeared to be slipping beneath the mud, and his orderly—Yando the Limp—brought him up a stoup of ale which Seg knocked back in a swallow. "Oh, aye," he said, wiping his mouth. "But if we slip up and Garnath catches us before we're ready—we're for the Ice Floes of Sicce, my old dom."

"We've run rings around him so far."

"H'umph! Well, that's only because you're—" He stopped, blew his nose, made a face and then hauled his longbow forward to look critically at it. "Damn weather."

Nedfar walked across from a campfire, holding a leg of a chicken and gnawing into the meat. "Does the rast still run, kov?"

"Aye, majister. We have him bluffed. He still thinks we outnumber him."

"I wish our forces would arrive." Nedfar swallowed. "We can't go on deceiving Garnath forever. I remember him as a slippery customer, and he has this Havil-forsaken rast the Kataki Strom to advise him, also."

I said, "I wonder what King Telmont is doing in all this?"

"Playing with his women, most likely. He is a cipher."

"He's after your crown," said Seg.

The days passed as what became known as the Campaign of Mud progressed. We had rushed forces into the southeast only to discover that Telmont's recruiting drive had proved phenomenally successful. He had imported thousands of mercenaries. He had drummed up levies—who would probably run away the moment the first shafts rose—and although weak in the air, as were we, now possessed a hardened core to his army and a froth of units of dubious value. The hardened core was large and comfortable.

Deb-Lu had advised me that he felt sure Garnath and Strom Rosil the Kataki had laid their hands on Phu-si-Yantong's treasure and were using it to hire their clouds of paktuns.

We just had to keep the enemy in play until our army came up.

I heard that Telmont had with him two Air Service Kapts I knew, hard professional warriors who commanded armies, Vad Homath and Kov Naghan. Wounded, they were now recovered. They would prove formidable adversaries, and I could wish they had forgone what they considered their loyalty to their country and given that loyalty and their expertise to Nedfar, who was now their emperor and unacknowledged by both of them.

"He has a great crowd of Katakis with him," said Seg, bending and poking up the fire. "And those damned Jibr-farils have organized themselves into regiments. Not much like Whiptails."

"The Katakis have stepped forward into the world of late," said Nedfar. "As slavers they have—" He looked at me, and said, "Had their uses. But no one likes a Whiptail."

"He has swarth cavalry—"

"Mileon's thomplods should stink them off."

"If Erthyr wills it," said Seg, quite calmly.

Nedfar said, "I do not wish to sound petty or resentful but I find it exceedingly strange that of our few forces here the bulk are Vallians, with Hyrklese and Djangs, and my Hamalese conspicuous by their absence."

"Oh, come on, Nedfar! Your lads are getting here just as fast as they can!"

"Well, the quicker the better."

"We're running rings around Garnath and we'll continue to do so." I made no bones about my views. "I will not throw good men away. We attack when we are sure of beating him. Not before."

So the days passed in the campaign; we marched long hours, camping and marching again, drawing a baffling web about Garnath. There were cavalry confrontations and contests, and occasionally the flyers clashed. The days stretched. The configuration of the country here in the southeast corner of Hamal was of importance to our maneuvers. Everything has a name, of course, but I will not weary you with too detailed a description. The River Os, He of the Commendable Countenance, ran eastward into the sea, dividing into two branches to enclose Ifilion. If there was magic in Ifilion, as was rumored, maybe that was the cause of their independence. To the south of the river, the Dawn Lands stretched and the countries on the line of the river were mostly cowed by memories of the iron legions of Hamal. To the north of Ifilion the land lifted enough so that good grasslands blew under the suns. Every time I thought of that land I thought of Chido, who was the Vad of Eurys there. He knew me only as Hamun ham Farthytu, the Amak of Paline Valley, and he and Rees represented a great deal of comradeship to me in dark days, and formed a void in my present life when I had not seen them again. Well, I would. That I promised myself.

One thing was certain: Vad Garnath would raise no troops in Eurys, for Garnath was a deadly enemy to Rees, Trylon of the Golden Wind, and thence to Chido and to me.

In what I made appear casual conversation I'd discovered that Chido, who had risen to the rank of Chuktar and command out in the west of Hamal, was known to Tyfar, who spoke well of him. "Although Chido ham Thafey retired from the army after—after our defeat. He secluded himself on his estates in Eurys."

"I knew his father, the old vad," said Nedfar. "An upright man. I could hope that the new Vad Chido will join me."

Because we were near Eurys, Chido's name cropping up was a natural occurrence; we all felt he would have to declare his allegiance soon. I could feel for him, as for so many others. The choice was agonizingly difficult.

By maneuvering and marching and counter marching we held off Garnath's two major attempts to launch attacks. We trended more to the east, to draw him away from the higher ground in the west. Tyfar looked concerned as we stood in a mud paddy watching the troops march past.

"If we get our backs to He of the Commendable Countenance and our flank to the sea, Jak—and—"

"Garnath will decide he has us trapped, yes."

"And?"

"Oh, Dray's got it all worked out, Tyfar," said Seg.

"I hope it is worked out. We draw Garnath on, as we have been doing, never allowing him to hit us. Every day our army marches closer. When it is in a position to strike, we stop and Garnath lunges, and—"

"And we catch him between two horns!"

"Well, we hope so. It will take cunning deployment."

"We'll be the anvil, and the army with those thumping great thomplods will be the sledgehammer."

"That is the theory. Had we attempted to draw him further to the west, he would never have followed. He must know an army marches. So we must dazzle him at the end, when we strike."

"Dazzle him? We'll blind the cramph!"

And then I nearly had a mutiny on my hands—a mutiny, moreover, in the crack regiment, the First Regiment of the Emperor's Sword Watch. The lads of 1ESW really threatened to cut up rough. Many of them have been introduced into my narrative and, sadly, many had died. New faces replaced the old. Now there was a spot of bother in Vallia—what that spot of bother was will become apparent later on in my narrative—and Drak had to return. I had told 1ESW that they should serve and guard Drak, as the future emperor. Now they threatened mutiny, saying, in effect, "We are your Juruk and we formed ourselves to guard you, much though we love your son Drak."

I remonstrated with them, drawn up in their ranks outside the tent lines.

They said, "There is a battle coming on. D'you think we will go tamely back and leave you?"

Drak cut that knot by saying he would leave 1ESW. Then he said, "And, father, I shall have to have a bodyguard, I suppose, like Jaidur and most kings and emperors. Yes?"

"Yes. Go and form one and choose good men. I own I shall be glad to have 1ESW back. There is no other unit quite like them."

"I know!"

Then I gave him the same advice I'd given his brother Jaidur when he'd married Lildra and become King of Hyrklana. "Do not form just one bodyguard. Have at least two and do not appoint a single Captain of the Guard. You are the personal commander over all the units of your Juruk."

"I will do as you say."

As we stood to wave the remberees, I said to Drak, sternly, "And accustom yourself to the idea of being the Emperor of Vallia."

His protests I would not listen to. He flew off. And his face was as black as the cloak of Notor Zan.

By Zair! If I was to go off adventuring over Kregen I wanted the weight of Vallia, at the least, off my mind. I had the shrewd suspicion that I would not be able thus easily to shuffle off being the King of Djanduin. Kytun and Ortyg, I felt sure, would make me see the error of my ways. As for being the Lord of Strombor—well, I was, and would remain so for as long as Zair and Opaz willed. Gloag saw to things for me in Strombor. And—my wild clansmen of Segesthes! Their loyalty could be severed only by death.

Nath Karidge wheeled up, saluting, saying, "Scouts report that Garnath is following us up with forced marches. Two in the last three days."

"Ha!" I said as we turned away from watching Drak's voller vanish into the clouds. "So he's had word from his scouts that our army approaches his rear! Good! Now we'll play the rast!"

Nath said, "The Kataki Strom has had experience fighting us. We beat him in Vallia. He will know of the Phalanx."

"He'll know. But will Garnath listen?"

"I'd have thought all Hamalese would know what a Vallian Phalanx has done to their iron legions."

"Only in the right circumstances. I look forward to seeing Nath Nazabhan—Nath na Kochwold, of course—and his brumbytes in the phalanxes."

"They march well. The war ruined the Air Services, more's the pity—"

"Not so, Nath, not so. For, don't forget, Hamal had the most powerful Air Service of Havilfar. No, we're better off marching on our own feet."

"Better yet riding a zorca."

"I won't argue that."

They were gathering, gathering here in this corner of Hamal, the choicest fighting men of Vallia. And the Djangs were here, as well as not inconsiderable contingents from Hyrklana. Only token forces marched with us from the Dawn Lands. That wild patchwork quilt of a land demanded great labor for the future. And, in all this, we had to make it seem the Hamalese rid themselves of the mercenaries who fought under the banner of a king who sought to make himself emperor, aided by as miserable a bunch of cutthroat tapos as ever remained unhanged.

Our little force maintained good order and discipline, and we had only two cases which ended with the culprits hanged. There were atrocity stories to be gathered from the huddled villages in the mud, stories of what King Telmont's army had done as they marched through. I thought of Homis Creek, and shook my head, and we did what we could to assist those in trouble.

On the maps the forces drew together as we marched the pins across the colored outlines. Gradually the place where a suitable confrontation might take place became clearer, narrowing down to a relatively mud-free area slightly higher than the rest of the country. It was near the coast, with Eurys to the north, and the river gratifyingly far enough away. Our provisions held out well, and logistics worked wonders. Also, two things operated to assist us here: the army coming down from the north and west carried plentiful supplies, and our flying services brought in fresh food and provender.

There was a well near the place we selected as the site for the battle, known as Plasto's Well. Some of the men began to talk in terms of the great victory we would win at the Battle of Plasto's Well.

Just how decisions reached in conference that should have been secret had circulated among the troops presented a problem I refused to worry about; this little force of picked men were to be trusted to fight and to know when to keep silent. Or so I believed, and by this time any new-comer spy would have stuck out like a neemu among a pack of werstings.

Among the forces arrayed against us was, I discovered, Horgil Hunderd, Trylon of Deep Valley, who, having lost his first three regiments of paktuns had raised three more. We promised ourselves that that unpleasant character would lose the new three.

Toward the end of that month of the Maiden with the Many Smiles we were plagued with thunderstorms. The rain fell down solidly. The very mud itself danced.

In this filthy weather we were reluctant to send the Djang aerial cavalry off on patrol. Our small force of vollers, many of them converted civil craft, performed well. The Suns of Scorpio remained veiled in heavy cloud. And it was wet.

Also, the flying sailing ships, Hamalian famblehoys and Vallian vorlcas alike, were grounded.

For a time we had to pull in our belts. When the weather cleared and the suns shone and the land steamed, the first reports indicated that Garnath had proved a clever and capable commander. During the worst of the weather he had marched his army around us to reach northward, away from the river, and so slip out from between the jaws of our two forces.

"The rast is a cramph and a kleesh," said Seg. "But you have to admire that little maneuver."

"We will still have him, Seg. If you look at the map—here—you will see how Chido's estates extend like a funnel into these low hills. And the sea is there. Garnath will be heavily slowed down if he crosses into Chido's land."

Seg looked at me. He had never met Chido. "You talk as though—as though you know this Vad of Eurys."

I had to ignore the offered opening and so went on to talk of our plans and the way we would turn Garnath's own cunning and expertise to our own advantage. We followed up and a few supplies came in. Feeding an army and bringing up enough provender for the animals are the keys to success in campaigns. The land over which Garnath marched lay stripped and barren, desolate, after he had passed. We found piles of bones, mostly vosk together with the notorious vosk skulls, for the folk hereabouts produced a variety of vosk which provided succulent sweet meat of first-class quality. As the swods said, it was all the damn mud.

Very few people did not like crisp vosk rashers, or a prime side of vosk cooked in the Kregan way. Our own rations were on the frugal side and included vast amounts of mergem, that all-purpose nourishment, and capital though mergem is and invaluable to a quartermaster supplying an army on campaign, mergem is still mergem, and prime vosk is a world apart. We had plentiful supplies of palines, though, so that kept the swods happy.

The promised Battle of Plasto's Well would now not take place.

We maneuvered and marched and, one day when the earth showed more green growing things than sheets of shining mud, we gathered for an O group around Nedfar's tent. Our Kapts and Chuktars attended. Infantry, cavalry, artillery and air, we stood in all manner of gorgeous uniforms—mostly tattered now and many faded and bedraggled—and listened as Nedfar expounded the final plan. For, on the morrow, we had Garnath. On the morrow, in that finger of Chido's land between the hills, we would crunch Garnath and his army between our two forces. It was now inevitable and, I guessed, in the enemy camp they would see the inevitableness of it, and gird themselves for the fray.

"Tomorrow we shall smash Vad Garnath and his puppet, King Telmont," said Nedfar. "Through the guidance afforded us from Havil and Opaz, and also our Vallian and Djang and Hyrklese allies, Hamal will on the morrow once more lift up her head in pride. For we shall eradicate the blot upon our honor."

There was more.

It all boiled down to the simple and gratifying fact; on the morrow Garnath would get his come-uppance.

On the morrow, then, our army marched out toward battle. Trapped in the finger of land, Garnath drew his forces up ready to face us, and drew up more to face to his rear where our other army, arrived and rested, deployed. This was going to be a day remembered in the annals of Hamal, and sung and storied until the Ice Floes of Sicce melted.

In our Earth's Renaissance period when a mercenary army was trapped like Garnath's army, they often would not bother to fight. The outcome was certain. The chiefs would gather and talk terms. It was civilized. Maybe. Maybe nations in arms and the citizen levy, in changing all that, changed man's outlook on war for the good, despite the horrors it brought in train.

Once again the Kapts and the Chuktars gathered around Nedfar for a few final words before we took up our positions with our forces. For battle, the uniforms that had been carefully preserved were brought out and donned, so that the fighting men blazed with gold, bullion and lace, sparkled with silver, and the colors patterned the field with fire. Very splendid they all looked. As for myself, I had elected to wear the brave old scarlet, with a sensible amount of armor, and I'd hung the essential armory of a Kregan warrior about me. No man relishes the idea of having his sword snap in the heat of battle—and not another instantly ready to hand. Our forces stood forth arrayed beneath their banners.*

---

* Here Prescot lovingly details all the regiments of the armies, with their commanders and insignia and strengths and equipments. Vollers, saddle-flyers, cavalry and artillery are listed. Many men feature in the muster rolls. They make fascinating reading. *A.B.A.*

592

A voller flew in fast and low and she was not one of ours. I was not concerned that any last-minute attempt at assassination could succeed. Long before the voller reached shooting distance she was surrounded by flutduins bearing Djangs of exceeding toughness and escorted to earth. Very shortly thereafter the guards brought the occupants of the airboat in for our inspection.

The sweet scent of blossoms drifted in the air, most refreshing after the eternal stink of mud. The sky smiled with air and suns shine. And we stood in a glittering group of power and magnificence, with our army ranked ready for battle.

The guards marched up in two ranks, spears all slanted, and wheeled out flanking the newcomers. These two stood, staring at us and then at Nedfar, conspicuous in the center. These two stood hardly, firmly, not showing defiance but proudly as men in their own right, and, too, quite clearly men in the devil of a hurry. Some measure of their quality must be gained in that they had persuaded the guard to let them in and to see the emperor in these finals moments before we attacked.

"I recognize you as Prince Nedfar, now the emperor," said Rees, his glorious golden lion-man's face intense with his purpose. "We give you the Lahal. There is a matter of the utmost importance—"

"Gently," said Nedfar. "You presume—"

"There's no time to be gentle," said Chido, dear chinless Chido, now clad as a soldier, looking hardened and mature. But he still could not pronounce his R's and they all came out as W's. "The Twylon Wees and I must tell you—"

"You are the Vad of Eurys," said Tyfar. "You have come to fight at our side? To swear allegiance to the emperor?"

"Listen, you fambly!" bellowed Rees in his old numim roar.

"The Shanks! There's a whole damn army of the rasts landed on the coast and murdering and pillaging their way inland. This is no raid! They've invaded. And they're here to stay—unless we stop them right now!"

Nineteen

"We must all wally wound!"

Down in the fingerlike valley the dark masses of Garnath's troops sparkled with light as the suns struck sword and spear, reflected back from helmet and cuirass. In only a few murs the aerial cavalry would clash. Soon the rolling columns of our forces would deploy into line and go rushing down on Garnath and sweep him away to destruction.

Nedfar's face resembled a face carved from marble to stand mute for ever above a silent tomb.

"Shanks!" bellowed Rees. He looked just the same, hot, quick, enormously vital, a man among men, and a good comrade. Maybe his misfortunes had not weighed him down as much as I had feared. The idea that Rees and Chido would not recognize Hamun ham Farthytu was one I could not entertain seriously. Even after all this lapse of time. So I looked like Dray Prescot, with all the foolishness of Hamun's face fled, and my own craggy old beakhead serving me in the office of a face.

Nedfar glanced at me, for I had—with an instinct I had failed to quell—drawn back a fraction. The instinct was not one of flight, I believe, as one of reluctance to jeopardize the character of Hamun. And, also, to let the world see that the Emperor of Hamal and not of Vallia commanded here.

"Dray?"

"There is only one thing we can do." As I spoke I was aware of the eyes of Rees and Chido. Lion-man's eyes, and apim eyes, they sized me up. Yes, the thoughts behind those eyes seemed to be saying, yes, you may be the Emperor of Vallia; but we have spent a large part of our lives fighting your friends. Why should we trust you now?

I spoke. I used the didactic, proclaiming style, forceful, rather pompously foolish to me.

"As for Vallia, we will fight Shanks whenever and wherever they may be found."

"Aye!" roared my officers, clustered to the side of the Hamalese.

"And for Djanduin, likewise, I pledge ourselves."

Now the Djangs bellowed.

"And I speak for Hyrklana," shouted Hardur Mortiljid, Trylon of Llanikar. That massive man in full armor and with his arsenal of weapons towered impressively. "We slay Shanks!"

Now the Hyrklese raised their cheer.

Every eye fastened on Nedfar.

Every eye but mine.

I looked at Tyfar.

The choice here was between advantage and honor, between the life and the death of the spirit. The alternatives were clear cut and unambiguous. Tyfar stood poised, as though ready to spring into instant action. I thought I knew him, from the moment down the Moder he had used his intelligence to work out the riddle and his courage to pull the chain that might kill him. I thought Jaezila would not choose amiss.

One of Nedfar's pallans, a man of the utmost honesty, a man who had exhibited extreme loyalty in difficult times, Strom Nevius, leaned forward toward Nedfar. Nevius had a nervous tic about his face, and a bad skin; but he was a man valued in our camp.

"Majister, to do as these people ask is to let King Telmont slip away. Who knows if another chance like this will occur again? And the Shanks can be dealt with later."

Rees heard.

"They are many. They came in a vast fleet. Once they are established you may never dislodge them. And they eat the heart out of Vad Chido's lands!"

Tyfar came to life.

"We must send word to King Telmont. He will direct his army to march with us against our common enemy."

"Garnath will never let him!" shouted someone from the other side of Nedfar.

"We are all Hamalese!" shouted someone else.

"Let us march on our own account!"

"The Shanks will overpower us!"

"Will you take the message?" said Nedfar, and the hullabaloo died as the emperor spoke. "Trylon Rees, will you take our imperial message to Vad Garnath? Tell him we march to fight the Shanks and invite him to march at our side."

Chido let out a yell.

"That is not possible—"

"Wait, wait, Chido," rumbled Rees. His golden whiskers blazed.

Tyfar said, "What is the problem? We are all committed here to our commands."

"I understand that." Rees stared at us, at our glittering popinjay show. His armor was plain and workmanlike. "You are far too committed to leave your commands."

It was perfectly clear that these people here did not know the situation between Garnath and Rees. Garnath had sent assassins and they had slain Rees's eldest son. The two men must have kept apart in the intervening years. The famous laws of Hamal, knowing nothing of Garnath's actions, would unhesitatingly condemn Rees if he took the law into his own hands. And he was not a man for assassins.

I said, "This fellow Garnath does not know me. I shall go down and tell him where his duty lies. Aye, and old Hot and Cold, too."

Tyfar said, "Jak! He'll have you killed—"

"You cannot go, Dray," said Nedfar. "I forbid it."

Seg laughed.

"Let the Emperor of Vallia go, if he wills!" shouted up Rees. "Let the Vallians do some good in the world for a change."

"We must all wally wound!" That was Chido, spluttering as of old, and yet hard now, bitter with what the years had done to his country and to Rees. Obviously, Chido had taken Rees in and cared for him after the debacle. We three had been comrades. Rather, these two and Hamun had been comrades.

"I'm going, anyway," I said.

With that I broke away from the splendid group around Nedfar and stalked across to my zorca, old Snuffle-nose, a beautiful gray, whom I had not intended to ride in the battle. Generals on white horses, despite the superstitions regarding generals on black horses, tend to get shot at.

Tyfar started, "Jak!" Then, knowing me, he swung on his father and the assembled Kapts. "Get the army started! We march for the coast. Vad Chido! You will guide us."

"Right willingly, prince," sang out Chido.

He and Rees stared after me, for I turned back to see if the folk back there had made up their minds. They had, for messengers sped off to the various banners to carry the new orders. I swung up on Snuffle-nose and shook the reins.

I felt absolutely no surprise to see Seg riding up. There was no need for him to say anything. We rode out before the army, to the edge of the hill, in silence.

Then Seg said, "Your Sword Watch and your Yellow Jackets will follow. You know that."

"When you are Emperor of Pandahem, Seg, you'll have your own damn worries about bodyguards. I can't wait for the day."

"By the Veiled Froyvil, my old dom! I haven't made up my mind yet!"

"I'm not forcing you. I just happen to know it's a job you can do."

With the accompaniment of the clip-clop of the zorca's hooves, the creak of leather and jingle of harness, we rode slowly down the hill, talking about anything save the business we were engaged in.

"You've really got it in for me, haven't you? Trying to make me an emperor."

"Ever since the day I took a forkful of dungy straw."

"Ha!"

It would be absolutely superfluous to point out that as we rode down we were each perfectly prepared to give our lives for the other...

"They're moving about down there, Dray."

"Like the proverbial ant's nest stirred by a stick."

The masses of infantry looked like blocks of multicolored glitter. Cavalry rode out along the wings. The artillery, mainly varters with a few catapults, were lined up ready to swathe in a sleeting discharge of stones and bolts. As archery and ballistae do not fire, but loose or shoot, one cannot really speak of firepower in reference to a Kregan army. The Kregish word is dustrectium. Their dustrectium down there was formidable. We rode on.

596

Every now and then Seg turned in the saddle to glance back. Presently he grunted, and dropped back into the saddle, looking ahead.

"ESW is moving."

"Then EYJ will be with them."

"Aye. Their rivalry is a bracing experience."

"And just what is that rast Garnath thinking, watching two lone riders come trotting down? We have no flag of truce."

"He's cunning enough to hear what we have to say."

"As to that, Seg, you are right. He knows he is trapped. He'll listen to us."

Seg looked back. "ESW and EYJ are following us, and are picking up speed. I must say they look a frightening bunch."

No need for me to look back. I could imagine what the regiments of my guard looked like, a dark solid mass of zorcamen with a froth of steel, proud with banners, riding knee to knee, or riding knee tucked behind knee in the nik-vove regiments.

Seg said, "Garnath's army will think we're attacking them. For sure."

"You're right, Seg." I patted Snuffle-nose's neck. His spiral single horn cut the air as he nodded. "That could be inconvenient."

"Inconvenient! It could get us both killed."

"You're right, Seg. Well, you'll just have to ride back and stop them. Explain the situation. You carry the weight of authority, and you can quote what I'll do to the lads if they don't obey orders."

Seg's furious bellow made me laugh out loud.

"You cunning, deceiving devil! You planned this! That's why you didn't send word for the Sword Watch and the Yellow Jackets to stand fast!"

"It crossed my mind."

Seg was fuming. "And EDLG are in it, now. You can't expect a fellow like Nath Karidge not to ride after his emperor, can you?"

"Well—my old dom—you ride back and stop 'em."

"Dray, Dray! If we get out of this I'll—"

I nudged Snuffle-nose into a canter. As we went off down the hill I bellowed back at Seg. "I'll see you as soon as Garnath and Telmont move toward the coast. We have Shanks to deal with."

Seg's answer was partially muffled in the stamp of zorca hooves. But words like cunning and devious and ungrateful figured prominently. But he saw that if we didn't stop the Guard, the enemy would shoot first and not bother to ask questions.

The moment two squadrons of zorcamen rode out from the enemy ranks I knew Seg had stopped the Guard. No doubt the air was a livid blue above the ranks of my lads. The oncoming zorcamen rode with weapons ready. They closed up about me and I shouted: "King Telmont and Vad Garnath! I must speak with them—now!"

A fellow with the insignia of a Jiktar started to bellow his authority, and

I cut him to the quick with a few words. I finished: "There is no time to waste, dom. Shanks. D'you understand? Shanks!"

The dread name worked like a passport and I was surrounded and we rode rapidly for the slight eminence on the valley floor where Garnath had set up his headquarters.

King Telmont was just as I had seen him last, a figure to be stared at in all its imposing majesty and then forgotten as the eminence grise, this Garnath, imposed his will. He was much as I remembered him, and I forced all that old unhappy history out of my head. If the Shanks established a foothold in Havilfar they would spread out and subdue everyone. This was all too clear.

Garnath ham Hestan, Vad of Middle Nalem, ought to have answered for his crimes seasons ago; that he had not I had to attribute to the protection afforded him by Phu-si-Yantong's sorcerous powers. Well, that particular Wizard of Loh was now dead. It remained to be seen how long Garnath would remain alive.

The odd thing was—difficult though it had been for me to keep silence with Rees and Chido, instead of doing as I longed to do and roar up to them, bellowing greetings, to keep silence before this yetch Garnath was even more difficult. I wanted to let him know who I was, and tell him a few home truths.

That I'd be fighting for my life in the instant thereafter would have been merely a normal occurrence.

Instead, I stared at him with all the powerful look that emperors can bring to bear.

He wore a gilded armor that ill became him. His short military cape was of green and blue; but he wore a sash of brown and silver, the colors of Lem the Silver Leem, that foul cult that many decent men were pledged to exterminate. His thick face shone with sweat trapped in the creases. His dark combed hair glittered with brilliants. His fingers were not as white, perhaps, as once they had been; but now every finger wore a jeweled ring. He looked at once bloated, ridiculous and obscene.

I said, "Shanks. We must march—"

He cut me off. His face congested.

"Yetch! You speak with propriety to me! Who are you?"

"You may call me Jak the Nose."

He might imagine this referred to my own beak of a nose; in fact it was an oblique reference to the Bladesman's duel we had fought, when Garnath had drugged me and I'd managed to summon the Disciplines of the Krozairs of Zy to my aid, and so claim first blood, and force his yetch to grovel on his nose. That, of course, was before I'd encountered Mefto the Kazzur...

"Then, Jak the Nose, you stand in peril of your life."

"As do you of yours. You know you are trapped. Your army is doomed. The Emperor of Hamal offers you the chance of fighting for your country against Shanks—"

"I am the Emperor of Hamal!" said Telmont, starting forward.

"I crave your silence for a moment, king." Garnath spoke without looking at Telmont, his gaze fastened on me. He spoke almost unthinkingly, like one accustomed to rote words that achieve a desired end.

"Yes, but Shanks—"

"Majister!"

Telmont turned away, brilliant of color, smothered in jewels and feathers and fur trimmings, blinding of aspect in the lights of the suns. I quelled an instinctive feeling of pity for him. Time allowed thought for only one aim.

"We must move against the Shanks, all of us, your army, my—the emperor's—army." I stared hard at Garnath, knowing he would never remember Hamun ham Farthytu in connection with this unpleasant Jak the Nose. "You must know what the Shanks will do."

Telmont huffed up to speak again, but Garnath waved a hand, and Telmont subsided.

"Why should I throw away what we have fought for? Your army is quitting the field. Look!"

A single glance back up the hillside showed the blocks of color thinning and elongating as the regiments formed columns and marched away over the brow of the hill.

"Aye! They march to fight the Leem-Lovers! Will you?"

"Hamal lies in my grasp now. In King Telmont's grasp who is, or will soon be, emperor."

Among the gilded retinue surrounding the chiefs on this slight eminence of the valley floor stood many Katakis. Ranked in the background, waiting, the lines of the King's Ironfists showed the dull gleam of iron and the wink of steel. They would prove first-class opponents. And, looking about, one hand holding Snuffle-nose's reins, I saw no sign of Strom Rosil, the Kataki Strom. No doubt he was with a part of the army, his skills as a soldier being used to the full, for he had been promoted from Chuktar to Kapt, and now was no longer the Chuktar Strom but the Kapt Strom. The damned Kataki Strom, rast of a Whiptail, was the better description.

Despicable of character and unpleasant of personality though Vad Garnath was acknowledged to be, it still seemed to me impossible for a Hamalese not to answer the call to defend his country against the raiding Shtarkins, the Shants or Shanks. Even though Garnath professed in secret the cult of Lem the Silver Leem, still I could not see him refusing to answer his call.

"Will you give the order to march, vad? Now!"

"The Shanks have drawn both your armies off and given me the chance to strike. How can I refuse what the gods proffer?"

"You are a dead man—"

He preened, the sweat thick in the creases on his face.

"I have been reported dead more than once. And the reports have been believed. But here I am, and ready to march—on Ruathytu!"

I said, "I do not think even your Whiptails would obey that order now."

A harsh-faced Chulik, whose yellow-ribboned pigtail was wound around his shaven head ready for him to don his helmet, spoke up. His tusks, which indented the corners of his thin lips, were banded in gold and silver, and studded with gems. He said, "With your permission to speak, Vad Garnath. My men will fight Shanks."

They'd been raided, had these mercenary Chuliks, in their own homelands. Shanks didn't share the usual awe of Chuliks.

There were no Pachaks I could see among those surrounding Garnath and Telmont. A group of Khibil officers, foxy faces alert, indicated their willingness to fight Shanks. A Rapa Chuktar riffled his feathers, and his beaked face betrayed a vulturine appetite for blood as he promised to rip out the tripes of any Shanks that came the way of his regiments.

Garnath's conquested face swung from man to man, and his jaw stuck out in a fashion I saw with wonder was more petulant than grim. The situation was slipping away from him, and he could not grasp that.

A ferret-faced, gimlet-eyed Lliptoh wearing mesh armor and many feathers put one hand to a sword hilt. "As they say in the Risslaca Hork in Balintol, where I come from: 'This is the day of the Seeking After Truth.' I am a hyr-paktun and I wear the pakzhan and I will march against the Shanks, for they are enemies to every man."

This expressed the feelings of the officers gathered here. Looking about, I fancied they might be relieved that they did not have to fight in a battle they were bound to lose; any combat with Shanks was far worse than fighting against fellow men as the Shanks were vindictive slaughterers. These fellows were stepping out of the frying pan into the fire, and knew it—and as I saw with joy—welcomed it.

Garnath's fury began to shake him with frightening passion.

He shared the view of the generality of people that all paktuns were merely hirelings, paid to kill, devoid of feelings. That they were not was being revealed to him now.

King Telmont stepped forward again. He wet his lips. He was a man obsessed with rank and position and the baubles and symbols that went with the trappings of power. He was the diametric opposite of an eminence grise.

"You say your name is Jak the Nose. Yet you are clearly a person of position, of rank."

Garnath looked about and white showed in his eyes.

"I am skilled in war and I know what is happening. This is a trap! Nedfar's army pretends to march off, to lure us on. It is a trick—"

"You are a fool, Garnath," I said, and I own much of my feelings for this man rasped in my voice. "There would be no need for tricks and traps if Nedfar wished to crush you. As he will, as he will. Your army was doomed. Your men know it, but they have been hired to fight, and so would have fought enough to earn their money, before throwing down their arms. We march to fight the Shanks. There lies a battlefield where men may stand forth to a sterner test."

He frothed and leaped for me.

I backhanded him away.

Telmont looked agitated and the Chuktar of the Ironfists stepped up, flushed, bulky, aggressive and completely at sea now.

"King Telmont. You are a man of honor. Start your army toward the coast. Together we will smash the Shanks back into the sea." My words battered at his indecision.

He wouldn't change in a flash, as they say. He was still old Hot and Cold. But he could see what his assembled officers thought. So, I thought to add a little spice. As I mounted up on Snufflenose, I looked around the gathered warriors.

"If any paktun wishes to leave his hire in honor, there is a place for him in the emperor's army that marches to fight the Leem-Lovers."

With that, I cantered off.

Mind you, I would not have been surprised had a crossbow bolt buried itself between my shoulder blades.

Twenty

We Fight for Paz

There was no doubt whatsoever in anyone's mind that this was the most important battle we had ever fought.

There would be other even more important battles in the future if we won this day. If we lost—well, there would be no more of anything quite apart from battles.

From the strength of the Shanks ranged before us the inescapable conclusion had to be drawn that they had at last made the move we had for so long anticipated and dreaded. Their sporadic raiding had turned into a full-scale invasion.

Tyfar pulled his nose as we sat our zorcas, looking out over the host. "Why pick on Hamal? Why now?"

"I would have thought," said Nedfar, "that Hyrklana would be easier for them."

Seg glanced across at me and then said, "It is believed that the Shanks are in communication with—persons—in our lands; where, we do not know. They have been told that Hamal was in turmoil and easy pickings. Hyrklana now has a strong king and is ready once again. The Leem-Lovers would not have known that Hamal now has a strong emperor."

Nedfar's face did not change; but Seg's words came out as he said them, unaffected, making the point, and I saw that Nedfar was pleased.

From the ranks of fighting men a steady hum rose. Everything was going forward quietly and easily. There was time for the imposition of strict silence, although, to be sure, many of Kregen's fighting men do not expect to remain in a disciplined silence during the preliminaries to battle. From a slight eminence where a ruined temple showed splintered walls and fallen columns, the view was breathtaking. Between the sea, a steely bar flecked with light, and the ruins, revealed two armies. The Shanks had offered battle and we had accepted, marching up in good order, and now we and the Fish-heads glared at one another across a sandy waste fringed by the sea and gorse-clad slopes.

We were seriously short of cavalry. This is inevitable as wars progress, the toll of saddle animals—whether of the land or flying variety—cannot easily be made up within the normal spans of birth and growth. Animals had been imported, and we had a number of formations of superb quality. Many were the crack cavalry regiments, however, mounted on beasts of indifferent quality, and presenting in many cases spectacles so cruelly ludicrous I will forbear to mention them.

This was one very good reason why Mileon Ristemer's thundering great thomplods were entertained as serious war weapons. We'd armored the huge perambulating haystacks as well as we could against darts and stones. Their castles towered, stuffed with archers, and fleet-footed light infantry ran alongside, ready to guide and assist and to drive off any enemy two-handed swordsmen or axemen who tried to chop the thomplods' twelve legs off.

Vad Garnath, who was here and who had exerted much of his old authority to reassert his position, proved most scathing about our famous thomplods. His relationship with King Telmont had undergone a change. Telmont was no longer so much in the background; but he had the sense to leave the handling of his army to Garnath. No one of his officers mentioned the scene in which Garnath had bowed to the will of his mercenaries; but some surprise was evinced by those hardened professionals, as by his Hamalian regiments, that Jak the Nose was other than he had claimed.

Garnath, swelling up again now that he felt himself back in command, said: "Those stupid beasts will frighten my cavalry with their stink! Keep them away!"

Mileon, quietly, said: "The thomplods are doused down with a mixture that cuts their offensive smell. When we attack, the ointment will be washed off. It will be the damned Shanks' cavalry that will panic."

Well, I said, but to myself, we all devoutly hope so.

Being an emperor, as I have remarked, is often a wearisome burden; but there are compensations. One was that I could gallop about freely, with a small troop of 1ESW at my back, to poke my nose into any and everything that went forward. I asked after Lobur the Dagger and Telmont's people informed me that Lobur had disappeared after that fraught night. I thought I knew the Dagger enough to know he would turn up again in his own good time. Rees commanded a brigade of totrix cavalry. He did not know it; but that was my doing, a word in Tyfar's ear had performed the trick. Chido, who was a Chuktar, having no saddle flyers, opted to ride with Rees this day. Because we were on his land he had brought with him a contingent of his own people. These were not soldiers; they were, if such a thing be possible, a willing levy. That they were anxious to kick the Shanks out was an advantage, but not everyone on Kregen is a fighter and I hoped Chido could keep them out of mischief.

Back along our trail lay piles of chains and stakes. I'd told Nedfar, firmly, that I could not fight in any army where poor devils of levies were chained up and stapled to the ground. He'd agreed. If our masses of spear- and shield-armed levies ran off, they would do what everyone expected them to do, and so morale would, instead of being depressed, rise with a fresh resolve. That was the theory.

We outnumbered the Shanks by something like three to two. I would have preferred to have been twice as strong. The Shanks were ferocious fighters and we would be facing the sternest struggle yet.

Nath Karidge listened when I spoke to him. He was kitted out in full fighting fig, and looked magnificent. "I have to say to you, Nath, that you will—" I saw his face.

He nodded. "I know, majister. And you know I know. But the regiment will fight. We are too short of cavalry for anything else."

"Choose your best squadron. I know I ask a hard task of you, but—" Again I stopped. This time he looked highly devious.

"The Princess Majestrix has told me that she will ride with the empress today."

I came quiveringly alert. "I don't like the sound of that!" I was highly suspicious. "The pair of—Look, Nath, if they start pushing forward and get their necks—well—"

"I know, majister. It will be the best squadron."

"I'd like to chain 'em down for this kind of thing like poor damned levies. Only, being women, they would take exception to that in a quite different fashion. The Sisters of the Rose! Be thankful your Cissy doesn't belong."

He smiled. "Cissy is a member of the Sisters of Opaz Munificent—I think that's the name. Secretive, these ladies."

"Agreed. I wish you well, Nath. May Opaz go with you."

"May the Light of the Invisible Twins shine upon you."

So, feeling that ticklish itch where Delia and danger are concerned, I rode on. I'd speak to her most firmly before the battle, and she would do exactly as she wanted to do afterward.

Another itch bothered me. I could give the greetings and the good wishes to my comrades, and feel free with them before the possibility of death claimed us all. But Rees and Chido? I just could not go into battle without talking to them. So, foolishly, of course, if you consider I was supposed to be an emperor and about to command an army in a crucial battle, I went off to the line of chiefs' tents and told Naghan ti Lodkwara, who happened by rotation to command the duty squadron, to hold fast. Korero the Shield would ride at my back. Cleitar the Smith would carry my standard, and Ortyg the Tresh the flag of Vallia. Volodu the Lungs would be the trumpeter. Targon the Tapster, Uthnior Chavonthjid and many another famed kampeon was there, ready to ride into the worst Herrelldrin Hell at my back.

When I left the tent no one saw me and I exited under a sodsheet at the rear. On my face the foolish smiling features of Hamun ham Farthytu were plastered in that special way I had of screwing them up ready for action. Rees and Chido would know me, for sure.

Borrowing the zorca belonging to Deft-Fingered Minch, the bearded, crusty kampeon who ran my field quarters, I cantered off into the suns shine. Knowing where every unit was stationed was something I had to know—largely because I'd argued like stink in council with the other notables over the placing of the various formations—and so I soon found myself riding up to the knot of officers at the head of Rees's brigade of totrix cavalry. To their side Chido's men stood in raggedy lines.

Well, Rees looked magnificent, and Chido looked—well, this martial figure was dear chinless Chido; but how he had changed!

They saw me.

Now, we had not seen each other for a very long time. I had spotted these two in the Eye of the World, and they had not known I was there. So, now, jaws dropped, eyes bulged, greetings fairly frothed. By Krun! But it was good!

They wanted to know everything. I spun them a yarn and said I was committed to another part of the battle line; but, afterwards! We agreed to a rendezvous at one of our favorite taverns of the Sacred Quarter in

Ruathytu. We wished one another well. This moment before impending battle was worth a very great deal to me.

Rees's daughter, the golden lion-maid Saffi, thrived, and was still not married but was dogged by a string of suitors a dwabur long. And his son, Roban, was now a powerful paktun, driven overseas through his father's misfortunes.

"But he's coming back, Hamun! He's never forgotten that you once gave him a left-hand dagger."

"That was the day he became a man."

Chido broke in, for that was the day Rees's eldest son, Reesnik, had been murdered.

Chido was married, with two sets of twins, and I was overjoyed for him and we promised great reunions. Then I wished them well, consigning them to the care of Opaz and Krun, and turned away. Despite the risks, despite the dereliction of an emperor's duty, that had been necessary and worthwhile.

And, anyway, I only just got back in time, for Deft-Fingered Minch's personal zorca was being pressed into service with one of our cavalry regiments.

Back again in the brave old scarlet, my weapons slung about me, I stepped out of the front of the tent. If only all the disguises and stratagems I had played on Kregen worked as well!

The name of Garnath had cropped up, to be dismissed. Chido's glance had warned me. But Rees, like a sleeping volcano, had not forgotten. How could any father?

Trumpets pealed. Flags flew. It was necessary for me to ride along the ranks of my men, as the other chiefs displayed themselves before their contingents. Religious ceremonies of many kinds were solemnly performed, and men committed themselves to the protection and mercy of their own deities and spirits.

The time approached.

These spiritual inquiries of the multitude of Kregan deities followed the more material inquiries of the Todalpheme, the wise men who monitored the movements of heavenly bodies and the surge and sweep of the tides. The Tides of Kregen can be fierce and savage beyond understanding—as you know. We had established from the Akhram that we need have no fear of a sudden surprise tide sweeping us away; the water was in balance between the attractions of moons and suns and we could expect a rise of a couple of feet only. Where we intended to fight lay smooth and level and here the tides could sweep in for twenty miles at speeds that would outrun a galloping zorca.

Delia said to me as I patted Snufflenose's muzzle, "You will not ride him today, will you, Dray?"

"I thought—"

"Ride Blastyoureyes."

Blastyoureyes was a nik-vove, a shining chestnut, with eight powerful legs and a body to match in weight and speed. He would carry me until he dropped dead. "Very well. And you?"

She laughed. "I ride with Nath Karidge—"

"I see. Then, my heart, mind you keep out of—" I stopped. I breathed in. Then I said, "Take care."

"There is too much in the world to let it go for a foolishness."

She wore armor, mesh and plate cunningly matched, and a scarlet military cape, and she carried weapons. Weapons, I mean, of edged and pointed steel. She would ride Yzovult, a splendid chestnut, of the same glorious coloring as Blastyoureyes.

But, in the whole wide world of Kregen and the no less extraordinary world of Earth, there was not a single solitary soul who could match my Delia.

So, simply, we kissed, and she jingled off to ride alongside Chuktar Nath at the head of the elite squadron of the EDLG and I swung my nik-vove and headed off for headquarters. I had words for Nedfar and Tyfar, and for Garnath, too, if he would listen.

As I jumped off Blastyoureyes and handed him over to orderlies of the staff lines I did not know, Seg walked across. His face looked black. "Well, my old dom, and they've gone and done it. Rather, they have gone and not done it."

His fey blue eyes held danger signals. He scowled.

"They have given the vaward to young Tyfar."

Seg Segutorio, in battles in which I commanded, habitually took the vaward. He would take over total command if necessary—had done so, at Kochwold—and he was a man who knew how to sweep a front clean.

"I do not command, Seg, but—and listen!—I am glad."

"Glad for your Tyfar, I suppose."

"If you get maudlin moody you'll be no use! No, glad because it leaves you free to handle all the Vallian forces. Unless you would prefer to handle the Djangs? It is up to you; but I will not command the two together, for the plans call for—"

"I know! Yes, yes! Well, if it is all the same to you, I shall be honored to command the Vallians. By the Veiled Froyvil, my old dom, honor it truly is."

"Good."

"Mind you, the thought of your four-armed Djangs raging into battle tempts a fellow, tempts him direly..."

"You've chosen to command the Vallians, and it's too late. I'll take the Djangs. And we'll see who is first to their Great Standard."

606

"What, that floating fish thing? Sooner burn the thing."

"It means as much to them as the flag of Vallia to us—"

"Not as much, I'll wager, as your personal standard, Old Superb!"

The scarlet flag, the yellow cross on the scarlet field, my battle flag that fighting men call Old Superb! Well, Cleitar the Standard carried that this day.

That thought made me say, "I'd like to keep the duty squadron of 1ESW if you don't mind."

Now Seg is a fey, wild and reckless fellow; he is also shrewd and practical, not to say cunning. Handing him command of the Vallians meant, since I used the Guard as a division of the army, handing command of that elite unit over, also. So now he said, "Trade me one of your best Djangs for every man you keep out of 1ESW, and you're on."

"Ingrate!"

"Credulous!"

"Quidang, then, Seg. One for one of the best for the best."

Trumpets battered golden notes into the bright sky, for the suns had not stopped still while we maneuvered and mustered under our banners and talked and shouted, swore and prayed, and tried to ignore the fears within us. Flutduin patrols came fleeting back to our part of the line, as mirvols and fluttrells to the Hamalese. The Hyrklese fought with us this day.

"They move! They move!"

So we were off.

A very tame beginning, I was thinking, as Seg wheeled away, not in his usual fashion to the vaward, but to command all the chivalry and pride of Vallia.

My Djangs set up a racket when I cantered up. If sheer noise could win battles, we'd won all-four-hands-each down.

Anticipating this outcome, I wore a flaunting great scarf of orange and gray, the colors of Djanduin, and a Jiktar chosen by lot for the highest honor carried the sacred banner of Djanduin. Looking at the glowing orange and gray and the embroidery and gold bullion, tassels and thread alike glittering, I became aware of Ortyg the Tresh with the Vallian Union flag. I looked away. I couldn't summon the hardness of heart to send him away after Seg—and there were enough Vallian flags waving over the ranks of the army, the files of the Phalanx.

So, in response to the shouts, we, too, moved forward.

The sight uplifted the emotions. Every person of Paz—except for those few misguided traitors we now believed to exist—detested, hated and feared the Shanks. But, these Fishheads were brave, clever and resourceful men who swarmed up out of their own homelands, locations unknown to us, driven by impulses not too far different from those animating any nomadic clansman, any glory-seeking warrior. Anathema to us; Shanks,

Fish-heads, were men still. Pundhri the Serene had preached on this subject, taking as his text the commandments of life developed by a long-dead Pachak. These unwanted thoughts of a rational world where men did not fight and slay other men intruded upon the stern resolve so vital to survival this day.

"We must harden the heart and make strong the sinews," I said, quoting, to N. Strathyn Danmer, an old friend who, as a gerbil-faced two-armed Obdjang, was a cunning, resourceful and immensely devious army commander. He could handle the Djang forces here with as much ease as a drill Deldar flung an audo of swods about the parade ground. Also, he could sense the point d'appui and was wise in the way of reserves.

He said, sitting his zorca upright and alert: "You ride again with Djangs now, majister."

I inclined my head. It was a rebuke I deserved. In a good cause there is no more ferocious or skilled fighter than a Djang, and they go through Katakis by the dozen. Perhaps my Clansmen—but no—idle thoughts...

Garnath's schemes to chain up masses of levies to soak up the first waves of the attack having been rejected, our plans called for these crowds of spear and shield men to draw the Fish-heads into a counterattack that would strike into the confusion. Here the thomplods would have to earn their keep.

"I am going to have an impossible task to hold them back, by Zodjuin of the Silver Stux!" said N. Strathyn Danmer. "Any plan that calls for Djangs to hang back is—"

"The emperor Nedfar commands, Nath, not I. But if we incline gently toward the sea, we will be in a better position."

"Agreed. At least, that will keep them on the move and not sitting fretting."

Danmer cracked out his orders to two of our messengers and they went off lickety-split. From our position on the extreme left of the line we could see the dun masses of the enemy moving forward, crowned with the sparkle of steel. Further along to our right stood the Vallians, with the few contingents from the Dawn Lands, and then the Hyrklese formed a connecting link with the mass of Hamalese who held the right center and flank. Positioned just to the rear of the levies and rising like haystacks over fields of stubble, the thomplods looked impressive and menacing to us. How they would appear to the Shanks remained to be seen.

The air having been cleared, the armies could get down to the main struggle.*

---

* Here Prescot gives the compositions of the armies, muster by muster, roll by roll. It is noticeable that many of the names he lists (many of which I have omitted) are no longer mentioned in his narrative after the battle. They do appear in the casualty lists. Evidently, the battle was far worse than he cares to tell us.

Although this stretch of the coast in Chido's Eurys bore the name of The Level Race, the battle came to be known by another name, which I will tell you anon. It is not my intention to give a full blow-by-blow account. Other currents were at work here to which this great and important battle formed a backdrop. A craggy and bloody backdrop, to be sure; but these currents of emotion flowing past in the foreground were in their own way no less violent.

Soon the Shanks advanced and the armies clashed and our levies duly ran away.

We could hear above the clangor that shrill and sickening hissing from the Fish-heads as they rushed wildly on. There were all manner of different species or kinds, animated armored figures with fish heads crowned with scales in brilliant colors and designs. As with the feathers of a Rapa, it was difficult to tell if the majority of the scales were natural or decoration.

Now it is quite impossible for a man sitting his saddle to see every part of what occurs on a battlefield and much of what follows was told me by eyewitnesses. The onrushing Shanks, victorious over our poor levies, should have run full tilt into the stink of the thomplods. Their cavalry should have panicked. At that moment, Tyfar with the mass of our vaward, would have nutcracker crunched them in both flanks. Then we Djangs would circle inwards, with the Hamalese right, and with the Vallians as the hinge, close in and destroy utterly...

Something will always go wrong, and you just hope it will not be a big or important thing.

The odd thing was, our plan, simple though it was, would have worked splendidly, for nothing attributable to us went wrong.

The Shanks tipped the balance in the center.

The smell of thomplods is not really detectable by humans; its effect is disastrous upon many animals. Now a fresh smell rose over the mingled odors of leather and sweat and fear and blood. A rich, full-bodied, kitchen kind of smell, a burning and roasting, a crisping sort of smell that brought the saliva to the mouth. Fires were visible through the ranks ahead.

A thomplod in the van which had been forging on like an animated battering ram, his archers loosing again and again and his twelve feet squashing Fish-heads with juicy crunches, stopped. His haystack hide appeared to bristle. He let rip a snorting shriek and backed off, started to turn around, stepping on our own kreutzin, for the light infantry did well with the thomplod protection duty they had been handed. He screamed again, turned around and barged straight back—berserk.

Between the two armies the ground crackled into life and flame. Spots of fire, racing from the Shanks toward us, spots of fire that ran on twinkling legs.

Someone yelled, so I was told: "The cruel bastards!"

The Fish-heads, these Leem-Lovers, had taken a great herd of vosks—those stupid, ungainly, rasher-providing animals—and smeared them with tar and combustibles and set them alight and launched them, squealing, at our thomplods.

Disgusting.

The vosks ran dementedly. Their hides crisped. The hair frizzled. The smell was like an army kitchen the day vosk rashers are on. The squeaks and squeals scratched irritatingly above the expected clangor of spear and shield, the scream of dying men.

The stink of burnt vosk outdid the stink of spilled blood.

By ones and twos, and then fives and sixes as the burning vosks reached them, the thomplods lumbered about and ran.

Our totrix cavalry instantly turned tail and fled.

Many of the regiments we had mounted on other kinds of saddle animals ran.

The zorcas remained unaffected—at least by the smell—and I own to a short but intensely painful moment of apprehension as the Djangs astride their joats from Djanduin held their mounts and reimposed control. The joats quieted. At this moment Tyfar led the vaward forward to what should have been a crunching charge and instead turned into a desperate, scrambling melee.

Lucky it was for Vallia and her allies that we had the benefit of Filbarrka's lancers and archers, for these zorcamen pirouetted and lanced in, mace crunching from the rear ranks, and darted out. The sleeths most of the Shanks rode were no match for zorcas. Green ichor stank on the air, mingling with the raw smell of the red blood of Paz and the stench of the burning vosks.

Thomplods burst back through the lines, and those regiments who were too slow to open ranks and let the beasts through suffered the consequences of slack drill. Seg handled the Vallians magnificently. They opened out and the thomplods careered through and Seg's archers shot the poor devils of vosks to a merciful end. Then the Vallians closed up, and set themselves, and advanced.

Kapt Danmer twisted his Obdjang moustache—the left one, for his right hand held a sword and he, like me, had but the pair of hands. "I cannot hold them any more, majister. We must charge."

"By all means, Natch. And may Djan ride with you."

So, the trumpets pealed and the Djangs let out their joats and those splendid riding animals, the best juts in Havilfar, roared out in a dark and glittering tide.

Perfectly confident that the left wing was now secure and the center about to be closed, I flung a harsh word of command at my squadron of 1ESW. "Hold! You follow me, not the Djangs." And I swung Blastyoureyes and nudged him into his eight-legged flowing motion, heading to the right, heading to where our lines sagged and bulged and where the Leem-Lovers were about to break through in triumph.

For a considerable distance to our rear the sands were covered by fleeing men. Most were the unfortunate levies, but a few bodies held a loose cohesion that told they had once been regiments of fighting men, now huddling together for safety in adversity. We rode on, shouldering aside fugitives. By Krun! The more I looked the more it seemed the whole army was turning tail.

But Nedfar held the center and right. From the eminence crowned by its ruins he could see the course of the battle better than could I, and it was at this time that, observing his left and center were about to be secure, he flung in everything he had on his right. Also, it was at this time, in the small cleared space between Nedfar and the onrushing Shanks, that his massed archers wreaked such horrible confusion upon the enemy. And every Shank that fell was worth two of our men—except for some, of course...

The Hamalese regulars fought like demons. No doubt they smarted with the hurt to their professional pride their defeat at the Battle of Ruathytu caused them. And the paktuns fought as only hard men who fight for a living know how. By the time I reached the knoll and rode up to the ruins, Nedfar—impressive, pointing, dominating his surroundings—had the situation contained. It was not quite under control; but even as I reined in at his side and stared out and down onto the battlefield, my Djangs hit the flank of the forces attempting to halt the Vallians. In a very short time there were no Shanks in that portion of the field—no living Shanks.

"Dray!" said Nedfar. He looked exalted. "I see your people have done all and more than is required. It is all in the hands of us Hamalese now."

"I have no doubts whatsoever."

There were few men left in his retinue. The death toll among messengers and gallopers was high. My squadron of 1ESW waited quietly but inwardly fuming in the hollow behind the rise. As I said to Korero: "If the lads wanted a fight then bodyguarding an emperor in a battle like this is no place to find it."

To which Korero, in his cutting way, had replied nothing.

Over to the right where Vad Garnath struggled to hold a line and prevent the Shanks from overlapping us and striking inwards at the rear of our center—which was exactly what the Djangs were now doing to the Shanks—the Hamalese had a grim conflict on their hands. As we stared a shout of joy broke from the group around Nedfar. Up from the rear, kicking sand, racing with their six-legged ungainly gait, came the totrix cavalry, rallied and raging to rejoin the fight.

Rees and Chido would be at the head of that headlong onward rally, furious they had been cut out of the battle and determined to show us all their true mettle. Nedfar gave fresh urgent orders and more of his aides galloped off. Now it did seem as though we people of Paz could successfully resist the Shanks. And, through it all, I was aware of the detachment, of the way in which I rode about so grandly directing operations and had not even drawn a sword from its scabbard. This was a far cry from the sweat and muck and blood of the heat of battle.

The passions that burned in the forefront of the battle backdrop, also, passed me by and left me with just the same manner of detachment. In the event, in the two events, I own I was glad I was passed by. In this wise...

"I shall ride to join Garnath's wing," I shouted at Nedfar, and in no time at all Blastyoureyes was carrying me thundering off to the right with my little group of 1ESW hard on my heels. We hit at the same time as the returning totrix cavalry, smashing into a screeching horde of Shanks who thought they had won. A single squadron, superb though they were, could make little difference and the bulk of the work was done by the totrix cavalry, with those elements who, having recoiled, reformed to press on again. The swarth cavalry lumbered up afterward at their slower gait and they tipped the scales. For a few moments we were in a real battle, with men yelling and animals rearing, with the lethal sweep of steel and the sudden spurt of blood. Then the Shanks were no longer facing us, and the totrixmen let out bright yells of triumph. I saw Rees. His golden lion face lowered down upon a pile of corpses, tumbled any old how in a welter of red and green.

I felt my heart kick. Chido...!

I cantered over, with the nik-vove avoiding the heaps of slain. Rees looked up. Still his face bore no readable expression.

"You are all right, Chuktar?" My voice was rough-edged.

"Perfectly, thank you."

"You looked as though you have lost someone dear to you."

I know I felt what I could not express, a great proud emperor sitting a magnificent charger among the slaughter, talking to Rees like a stranger. Chido, I wanted to scream out, Chido...

"Yes, majister, I have lost someone. Someone, I own, I now see to have been dear to me. But not, I fancy, in the way you may imagine." He looked down and touched a headless corpse with his boot. The corpse rolled away, slithering.

There, a trident's tines through both eyes and the third smashing the bridge of his nose, lay Vad Garnath.

Rees looked up. "This—person—was known to me."

"Well, he is dead now. You can forget him."

A trumpet pealed, high and carrying brilliant overtones, a series of notes piercing the sky. I looked away. I had work to do. I would see Rees and Chido in the Sacred Quarter.

I rode away. Only when I was returning to the headquarters was the realization borne in on me that I had spoken deucedly oddly to Rees. Any normal reaction would have been one of sorrow for a friend lost. Who would know, here, of the deadly enmity between Rees and Garnath? Well, that would be explained away, for emperors often do not operate under normal rules—and that is not always a good thing, either.

Figures fought beneath the old ruined temple on the rise.

Thinking that, I was glad Rees had not had to slay Garnath in the end, and that that evil man had met his death from a Shank trident—how appropriate! a worshipper of Lem the Silver Leem slaughtered by the Leem-Lovers!—I saw the scene ahead more clearly.

Nedfar fought for his life, surrounded by swordsmen.

I dug my heels into Blastyoureyes and sent him galloping madly ahead. We thundered up the rise, his eight legs pumping in wonderful unison, and I flung myself off, blade in hand, to roar into the fight. My lads followed and in only moments the swordsmen were dispatched. Nedfar held his arm from which the blood flowed. He, like Rees, looked down on a pile of corpses.

"Nedfar! You are unharmed?"

"Just a scratch, Dray. I'd have been dead—Spikatur, they are from Spikatur Hunting Sword."

"So I see."

"I'd have been killed for sure—but for him."

Nedfar pointed to Lobur the Dagger who sprawled across two dead men. The sword in his fist was snapped off. I advanced, beginning to kneel down, when Lobur sat up, dazed, looking past me up to Nedfar.

"Prince—I mean emperor—I wronged you, I know. But—"

"Keep quiet, Lobur, you great fambly," I said. "You have a hole in your chest we could drive a damned thomplod through."

"Jak?" He frowned, dizzied by his wound. "What are you doing here?" He gazed about. "I betrayed you to Garnath, and—"

"Garnath is dead. And you have been an idiot, a get onker; but you must rest now." I heard the voices, light, excited, tumultuous with events, and I said, "And here is Thefi to see you."

As I turned she paused on the slope of the rise, staring at her father, and then at Lobur. She screamed and rushed forward to fling herself on him.

"Easy, Thefi, easy. He's only punctured. Let him breathe."

Thefi bent over Lobur and her hair fell loose and shrouded her face as she kissed him. "Oh, Lobur!"

The other ladies walked forward, content to let Thefi have her moment. In the background Nath Karidge and the EDLG stood in their ranks—and they were bloodied and the bright uniforms were slashed and torn, and their ranks were thinned. I looked at Delia as she walked forward with a swing at the side of Jaezila, and I own I felt the faintness of relief.

"Dray!"

I pulled myself together. Time enough for the stories afterward. I could not allow detachment. Delia was safe! That mattered.

"You promised you wouldn't get into the fight—"

Jaezila said, "When Ty went in—well, I wasn't going to sit around doing nothing. And mother came too."

"Between us all it looks as though we've won," I said. "All of us, all peoples of Paz. We've come a long way together this day. This fight, the Battle of the Flaming Vosks, will be remembered as a beginning. And as an end."

After that there ensued a great deal of talking and excitement and rushing about clearing up and seeing to the wounded and burying the dead. The fish smell would persist for days. The reaction made us all tremble. Seg was safe, thank all the gods of Kregen. And Tyfar trotted in, his equipment just about ripped to shreds, wearing an enormous smile and waving a Shank trident.

Delia took my arm.

"A great deal has happened, dearest, and I know you will say there is a great deal more left to do."

"As there is. You are leading up to something. So?"

"You want to lay down the burden of empire and let Drak take over. I agree. Oh, and, Dray Prescot, if you think I shall allow anyone to call me the Dowager Empress—!"

I laughed. "Of course not. We're young!"

"We are young. Also, can you guess what old Hot and Cold has in his baggage train?"

"Apart from scantily clad young ladies, you mean?"

"We-ell, they could figure... And I shall be less than scantily clad, believe me."

So I guessed. But I let Delia tell me.

"King Telmont has a full outfit, all in tents and marquees, with huge boilers and furnaces and pipes and things. He has the whole works, a complete mobile Baths of the Nine."

"Lead on," I said. "What are we waiting for?"

A Glossary to the Spikatur Cycle

Compiled by Els Withers

References to the four books of the cycle are given as:

BOA: Beasts of Antares
ROA: Rebel of Antares
LOA: Legions of Antares
AOA: Allies of Antares

NB: Previous glossaries covering items not included here can be found in Volume 5: Prince of Scorpio, Volume 7: Arena of Antares, Volume 11: Armada of Antares, Volume 14: Krozair of Kregen, Volume 18: Golden Scorpio, and Volume 22: A Victory for Kregen.

A

Afferatu, Castle of: where Queen Fahia imprisoned her niece Lildra, later rescued by Prescot. ROA

ahlnim: a race of diffs which produces many mystics and wise men.

Allakar, Chamber of: an audience chamber in the imperial palace in Vondium.

Alloran, Kov Vodun of Kaldi: Sent by Prescot to liberate southwest Vallia, but became a traitor. BOA

Almuensis, Cult of: a cult of sorcerers of considerable powers.

Ambath, Homan ham: the ambassador from Hamal to Hyrklana appointed by Empress Thyllis. ROA

angerim: a race of diffs with much hair and large ears; very untidy in their living habits.

Arachosia: a windy city of the mountains of far southern Havilfar.

Arclay, Genal: the Vad of the province of Valhotra in Vallia. BOA

Arclay, Tom: the son of Genal Arclay, in the Vallian Air Service. BOA

Arclay, Travok: the son of Genal Arclay, in the Vallian Air Service. Was killed in a flying accident. BOA

Arditchoith: a moorkrim sorcerer. AOA

Arrian nal Amklana: the husband of Princess Lilah of Hyrklana and the father of Queen Lildra; was slain by the agents of Lildra's predecessor Fahia.

Babb: the son of Queen Fahia of Hyrklana. ROA

Balkash: the stromnate province of Dray Segutorio.

Battle of the Flaming Vosks: in which the allied forces of Paz repelled the first exploratory invasion by the Shanks. AOA

Blastyoureyes: a nikvove ridden by Prescot at the Battle of Incendiary Vosks. AOA

The Blue Zhyan: a tavern in Ruathytu. LOA

The Bolt and Quarrel: a tavern in Ruathytu. LOA

Bolan the Tumbs: a cadet in the Vallian Air Service. BOA

Bonzo: a Hamalese courier-pilot. LOA

cadade: captain of the guard.

celene: rainbow.

celene pie: made from a mixture of fruits and honey.

Chaadur the Iarvin: an alias used by Prescot in Huringa. BOA

Chandror: an island south of Gremivoh.

Charldo: one of the jailers of Princess Lildra. ROA

cheldur: a trainer in the Jikhorkdun.

Chobishaw: a nation of southwest Segesthes.

"Chuktar's Orders": a drinking song.

"Chulik's Bent Tusk, The": a drinking song.

chun: jaws.

churmod: a hunting beast with a hide of uniform slate-blue, eight legs, and slit-eyes of lambent crimson. It has a reputation for sadism and viciousness.

Corandian: a red wine of low alcohol content.

Covell of the Golden Tongue: a prominent poet of Vondium.

The Crushed Toad: an extremely low-class tavern in Ruathytu. AOA

Dafnisha the Ample: a goddess having to do with the births of healthy twins.

Dorndorf: the captain of Opazfaril. BOA

Doxology of San Destinakon: a cult of powerful sorcerers.

Dunder: a race of diffs with heads as flat across as the top of a table; they are often employed as porters.

dwablatter: a type of staff with knobs at both ends.

E

Edin: a Hikdar in the Vallian aerial cavalry. AOA

EDLG: the Empress's Devoted Life Guard; the personal bodyguard of the Empress of Vallia.

Erndor: a Vallian agent working with Valona in Hyrklana. ROA

Ezionn: a country of the Dawn lands in southern Havilfar.

F

The Faerling's Feathers: a tavern in Huringa. ROA

famblehoy: the name given by the Hamalese to the type of voller without the power of propulsion by sub-etheric force.

Famphreon, Kov Nath: the son of Natyzha Famphreon, Kovneva of Falkerdrin.

Fanahal: the chief port of Hyrklana South.

Fantor, San: a sage of Vallia; charged by Prescot with the task of designing the flying belt. BOA

Filbarrka: the king of a country in Persinia.

Fish Fin Street: a street in Ruathytu, near the Havilthytus.

Floria: one of Delia's handmaids.

fluttlann: a smallish saddle bird, blue and white; willing up to a point and does not eat overmuch. Breeds phenomenally and is cheap.

The Fluttrell Feather: a tavern in Thalansen. LOA

flying belt: a safety device for fliers whose design was commissioned by Prescot after the death of Travok Arclay; has lifting power sufficient for one person.

Fordan: a slave of Vad Noran; protected Tilly while she was a slave of Vad Noran. BOA

Forest of the Departed: located in Hyrklana near Huringa; so named because of the many graves located therein.

Frandu the Franch: a kaidur and comrade of Prescot in the revolution against Queen Fahia. ROA

Fransha: a lady of Vallia, the daughter of the Lord of Mavindeul; kidnapped by the Racters and rescued by Prescot. BOA

Froshak the Shine: the partner of Prescot and Unmok in the beast-catching business; rather taciturn and skilled with a sailor's knife. Killed by a churmod. BOA, ROA

G

Gaji's bowels, by: a Hyrklanian oath.

Gochert: a ferret-faced figure who wears a jeweled patch over his left eye; one of the leaders of Spikatur Hunting Sword. BOA

The Golden Zhantil: a tavern in Ruathytu of the highest possible class. LOA

Gorthnil, Naghan ham: a Chuktar in the Vallian Air Service. LOA

Goss, Fridil: Ortyg Voinderam's rival for the hand of Lady Fransha. BOA

Gremivoh: an island off the coast of Vallia.

gretchuk: vile.

H

Hamando's Boulevard: a street in Ruathytu.

Hambascett: one of the countries of the Dawn Lands.

Hamdal the Measure: the landlord of the Jolly Vo'drin in Hammansax. AOA

Hamdi the Yenakker: a Hamalese who aided in the occupation of Vallia. AOA

Hammansax: a town in western Hamal, a prosperous frontier post.

Handur, Trylon: one of Nedfar's aides as Prince. BOA

Hansh, Horparth: known as the Perspective; a rival artist to Rollo the Circle. LOA

Happy Calsany, Kyro of the: a square in Huringa.

Hardil the Mak: the usurper of Prescot's position as Amak of Paline Valley; deposed by Prescot and killed by a local woman. LOA

Harg, by: a Hyrklanian oath.

Harmburr: the king of Ezionn. AOA

Helvia the Proud: a lady of high rank in Spikatur Hunting Sword. AOA

Hernsmot: a village in Hamal near the Mountains of the West.

Hirrume Gate: in Ruathytu

Hlunub Yards: voller yards in Ruathytu.

Hofardu, Chuktar: a long-dead Hamalese kampeon.

Hofnar: a stromnate province in the Black Hills of Hamal.

Homath, Vad: a Kapt in the Hamalian Air Service. LOA

hork: bow.

Hot and Cold: a nickname for King Telmont.

Hue the Grasshopper: a stablehand working for Vad Noran. ROA

hulfoo: a sort of Hyrklanian goose.

Hundal the Oivon: a cheldur who trained Prescot during his last sojourn in the Jikhorkdun of Huringa. ROA

Hunderd, Horgil: the Trylon of Deep Valley in Hamal. LOA

Hyr Notor; the name used by Phu-Si-Yantong at the court of Hamal.

I

ig: green.

Ilurndil: an animal about six feet long, with a hide thick enough to make roof tiles out of, and a pair of horns superposed between piggy eyes.

Infinon of the Crossroads: a village in Vallia.

Ingadot: a town in Hyrklana.

Ingeslad: the capital of Layerdrin.

Irvil: the Strom of Pine Mountain in Thothangir; a kregoinye whom Prescot saved in Hamal. LOA

Ivory Cone: a peak in the Mountains of the West in Hamal.

J

Jaezila: an alias used by Prescot's daughter Lela in Havilfar. ROA

Jak the Shot: name given to Prescot by the crew of Pearl of Klanadun. BOA

Jaws of Laca: see Lacachun.

Jedgar: a barbarian or irregular captain.

jibrfaril: an epithet applied to Katakis.

The Jolly Vo'drin: a tavern in Hammansax. AOA

Jorg the Fist: the ship-Deldar of Mathdi. LOA

K

Kalei: a spearman in the Fifteenth Regiment. BOA

Karidge, Nath: the Chuktar of the Empress's Devoted Life Guard. BOA

Khovala: a vadvarate province in Vallia.

Klactoil: a strange race of diffs, parchment-colored, only about three feet tall, with a thick ridged array of spines down the backbone, a walloping tail, and a fishy look to the face; rumored to be the product of miscegenation of Shanks and some doomed race now extinct.

Klanak: a mythical hero of Hyrklana.

Klanak the Tresh: an alias used by Orlan Mahmud na Yrmcelt in the rebellion against Queen Fahia. ROA

kontos: spear.

Kov Mak, Caves of: located about twenty dwaburs north of Ruathytu.

L

Lacachun: a high pass in the Mountains of the West in Hamal.

Lasal the Vakka, by: a cavalryman's oath.

Layerdrin: one of the small countries of the Dawn Lands.

Leaping Fishes, River of: the river on whose banks Huringa is located.

Lildra: the daughter of Princess Lilah of Hyrklana and Arrian nal Amklana. Was rescued by Prescot from the Castle of Afferatu where she was imprisoned by her aunt Fahia. Became Queen of Hyrklana upon the overthrow of Fahia. The wife of Prescot's son Jaidur. ROA

lisehn: a Vallian species of tree whose wood is excellent for bowstaves.

Llindal River: in Hyrklana.

Lliptoh: a race of diffs with ferret faces and gimlet eyes.

Lun'elsh: a race of diffs with black body hair.

M

Macsadu the Kroks: as illegitimate son of Layco Jhansi. BOA

Maglo the Ears: a dishonest beast-catcher in competition with Unmok the Nets. BOA

Mahmud, Orlan na Yrmcelt: the Chief Pallan under Queen Fahia of Hyrklana; one of the leaders of the rebellion against her. ROA

mak: black.

Malab the Kazzin: a religious figure, also known as Malab the Wounded or Malab the Fount. Believers seek mercy and wisdom, luck and health in the blood that pours from his wounded head.

Mandua: one of the countries of the Dawn Lands.

Mathdi: a voller in the Hamalian Air Service commanded by Prescot. BOA

maztik: a junior noncommissioned officer.

Mevek, Chuktar: an ally of Prescot against Layco Jhansi. BOA

Mev-ira-Halviren: a pagan idol.

"Milkmaid's Pail, The": a drinking song.

Mionch: a race of diffs with tusks twice as long as those of a Chulik.

Mitdel'hur: a religion of few adherents in Havilfar.

moorakrim: caving experts of the moorkrim.

moorkrim: wild men living west of Hamal.

moorn: war.

Morthnin: a Jiktar in the Hamalian Air Service. LOA

Mortiljid, Hardur: the Trylon of the province of Llanikar in Vallia; escort to Princess Lela in Hyrklana. ROA

Mother Dikkana: the mother of Beng Dikkane.

N

Nafun, King: the king of Hambascett. AOA

Naghan the Barrel: see Raerdu, Naghan.

Naghan the Brush: an artist in the troop of Rollo the Circle. LOA

Naghan na Hanak, Kov: the owner of a voller yard in Huringa. ROA

Nalgre ti Liancesmot: a long-dead playwright.

Na-Pla, Natema: the daughter of Planath Pe-Na. BOA

Nath the Bows; the captain of Pearl of Klanadun. BOA

Nath na Kochwold: the name given by Prescot to Nath Nazabhan. BOA

Nath the Retributor: name used by a general in the rebellion against Queen Fahia. ROA

Nath, Strom: one of Nedfar's aides as prince. LOA

Nevius, Strom: one of Emperor Nedfar's pallans. AOA

nikumshal: 'half-shadow'; the Kregan term for a shadow from a single light source.

Nodgen the Bald: the king of one of the countries of the Dawn Lands. AOA

Noran, Vad: a Hyrklanian who plotted against Queen Fahia. BOA, ROA

Norhan the Flame: a comrade of Prescot in the rebellion against Queen Fahia. ROA

O

Ohmlad's Alley: a street in Ruathytu.

Olinmur: a race of diffs with blue skins.

oraneflut: a bird with browny-white feathers.

Orndalt, Nalgre: the manager of a Hyrklanian voller factory. BOA

Orvendel: an imperial province of Vallia, south of Vennar.

P

Pafnut, King: the king of Chobishaw. BOA

Pale Vampire Worm: a supernatural type of worm called forth by an Arditchoith.

Parlin, Avec: a lawyer who served Unmok the Nets. BOA

Pearl of Klanadun: ship employed by Unmok the Nets to transport beasts.

Pershaw: a nation in Persinia.

Pettarsmot: a town in the province of Malpettar in Tomboram.

Pondar the Iumfrey: a Khibil mercenary in the hire of Unmok the Nets. BOA

Puhlshi: Pundhri the Serene's female companion. LOA

Pundhri the Serene: a philosopher saved by Prescot in Hamal. LOA

Q

The Queen's Head: an inn in Huringa. BOA

Queen's Kaidurs: an elite group of gladiators fighting in the arena of Hyrklana.

The Queen's Secret: an anonymous play written about 300 years ago.

Quern of Gramarye: a radiant disc of sorcerous power which appears in battles between wizards.

R

Raerdu, Naghan: Prescot's personal spymaster. BOA

Randalar: a mercenary in the hire of Unmok the Nets. BOA

Randalsh, Noive: an assistant Pallan working on the island of Chandror. BOA

Ristemer, Mileon: the son of Nomile Ristemer. BOA

Ristemer, Nomile: an elite banker of Vondium. BOA

Rodan: a Jiktar in 2ESW. BOA

Rogpe: the king of Mandua in the Dawn lands. AOA

The Rokveil's Ank: a tavern in Ruathytu. LOA

Rollo the Circle: the leader of a troop of artists whom Prescot met on his way to Ruathytu. LOA

ron: red.

Rorvreng the Vakka, by: a cavalryman's oath.

Rosala: one of Delia's handmaids.

S

Sabal: see Vampires of Sabal.

Sadrap, Black: a member of Rollo the Circle's band of artists. LOA

Saradush: a subrace of the schrepims.

Sasco, by: an oath used by the adherents of Spikatur.

schrepim: a race of diffs with lizard-like features; very intelligent, swift-moving, and skilled with weapons.

Screetztyg Kyro: a square in Ruathytu.

Segutorio, Silda: the daughter of Seg Segutorio and Thelda.

The Sensil Paradise: a bathing establishment in Ruathytu. AOA

Shanks: fish-headed reivers who sail or fly from the hemisphere of Kregen opposite Paz. From coastal raids on the nations of Paz they have progressed to a massive invasion.

"She Kissed the Mortilhead": a song which tells of a princess who ran away from her palace for love of a paktun.

Shining Mud, Land of: the name given to much of the delta of the River Os in Havilfar.

SHS: an abbreviation for Spikatur Hunting Sword.

The Sign of the Headless Zorcaman: an inn in Vondium where Prescot met Chuktar Mevek. BOA

The Silver Fluttrell: an inn in Huringa. ROA

Sinopa: one of the countries of the Dawn lands.

Sissy: one of Delia's fellow slaves under Nyleen Gillois; sold into slavery by her parents. 28

Sisters of Opaz Munificent: a sorority of Vallia.

Sjames: the favorite nikvove of Zenobya. BOA

Slacamen: a nickname for schrepims.

Sleeths, Avenue of: a street in Huringa.

Snowdrop: an urvivel ridden by Prescot in Hyrklana. ROA

Sokotro: one of the countries of the Dawn lands.

Soparan: a subrace of the schrepims.

Souk of Trifles: a market in Huringa.

Spag the Junc, by: an oath used in the Dawn Lands.

Spikatur Hunting Sword: a secret organization initially devoted to the overthrow of the Empress Thyllis and her corrupt government.

Spurs of Lasal the Vakka, by the: a light cavalryman's oath.

Strandar, Naghan: chief Pallan and a senator in the Presidio of Vallia.

T

Tardalvoh: a variety of wine.

Telmont, King: nicknamed King Hot and Cold; sought to take the imperial throne of Hamal after the death of Empress Thyllis. AOA

Thalanns, Street of: located in Ruathytu.

Thalansen: a town in western Hamal.

Therfenen, San: a sage working for Prescot as the Emperor of Vallia. BOA

thomplod: a remarkable animal resembling a haystack, with six feet on each side; it exudes a smell which upsets many saddle animals.

Thorfrann, Fydur ham: a Chuktar in the Hamalian Air Service. LOA

Thorndu the Wine: the owner of the Golden Zhantil in Ruathytu. LOA

Thyfurnin, Fresk: a Deldar in the Hamalian army who fought with Prescot and Tyfar at the Lacachun Pass. AOA

tikshvu: Kregan equivalent to the word missy, used with a threatening implication toward a girl who, powerless, yet insists on rebelling.

Tipp the Thrax: a Queen's cheldur in the Arena of Huringa. ROA

tresh: flag.

Trompipluns, Gate of the: a gate in the outer walls of Huringa.

U

umshal: shadow.

Unmok the Nets: a Hyrklese working in the business of catching beasts for the Arena of Huringa; became a partner and good friend of Prescot. BOA, ROA

V

Vadvars, Kyro of the: a square in Ruathytu.

Vallian Freedom Army: the name of the army of Vallia formed by Prescot.

Valona: the daughter of Vomanus and Saenci the Locks; worked as an agent of Vallia in Hyrklana. ROA

Vampire of Sabal: an animal, not supernatural, which likes to hide in out-of-the-way places and guzzle human blood.

Vanderini the Dagger: one of Chuktar Mevek's men.

Vandrop, Ian: a Vallian paktun. BOA

Vantile, Nazab: an imperial Justicar serving Prescot. BOA

Varander, Bonnu ti Valkor: the ship-Hikdar of Mathdi. LOA

Veilmon Kyronik: a small, tree-bowered square in Ruathytu.

The Vengeance of Kov Rheinglaf: a play from the third book of The Vicissitudes of Panadian the Ibreiver.

vew: room.

Vinnur's Garden: a coveted section of land between Falinur and Vindelka.

Voinderam, Antar: the Vad of the province of Khovala. BOA

Voinderam, Ortyg: the son of Antar Voinderam. BOA

vorlca: the name given by the Vallians to a skyship not capable of movement by gripping the lines of sub-etheric force.

W

Westmin, Nogan: a pallan and member of the Presidio of Vallia. BOA

"When the Havilthytus Runs Red": a rather depressing Hamalian song.

"When you look too long upon the face of a leem you may grow a leem's tail": an aphorism variously attributed to San Blarnoi or Nalgre ti Liancesmot, warning of the dangers inherent in struggling against evil.

Whetti Orbium: the manifestation of Opaz responsible for the weather.

Winharman, Nath: a young aide to Seg Segutorio. LOA

woflovol: a small batlike animal.

Y

Yallom, Mountains of: mountains located in southern Havilfar.

Yando the Limp: a groom, formerly a soldier but wounded at the Battle of Kochwold. BOA

yenalk: a cave-dwelling animal with a body like two soup plates jammed together, many thin short legs, stalked eyes, and a long poisonous rapierlike proboscis.

Z

Zaydo: a name given to Prescot by Strom Irvil of Pine Mountain. LOA

Zenobya: Queen of the nation of Pershaw in Persinia. BOA

Milton Keynes UK
Ingram Content Group UK Ltd.
UKHW010733230823
427308UK00001B/67